Carmen Reid is the author of the bestselling novels *Three In A Bed, Did The Earth Move?*, *How Was It For You?* and *Up All Night*. Her new novel is *The Personal Shopper*. After working as a journalist in London she moved to Glasgow, Scotland where she looks after one husband, two children, a puppy, three goldfish and writes almost all the rest of the time.

You can drop her a line at www.carmenreid.com

Also by Carmen Reid

DID THE EARTH MOVE?
HOW WAS IT FOR YOU?
UP ALL NIGHT
THE PERSONAL SHOPPER

and published by Corgi Books

Three
In A Bed

Carmen Reid

CORGI BOOKS

TRANSWORLD PUBLISHERS
61-63 Uxbridge Road, London W5 5SA
a division of The Random House Group Ltd
www.rbooks.co.uk

THREE IN A BED
A CORGI BOOK : 9780552155816

First publication in Great Britain
Corgi edition published 2002
Corgi edition reissued 2007

Addresses for Random House Group Ltd companies outside
the UK can be found at: www.randomhouse.co.uk
The Random House Group Ltd Reg. No. 954009.

The Random House Group Limited makes every effort to
ensure that the papers used in its books are made from trees
that have been legally sourced from well-managed and
credibly certified forests. Our paper procurement policy can
be found on www.randomhouse.co.uk

Mixed Sources
Product group from well-managed
forests and other controlled sources
www.fsc.org Cert no. TT-COC-2139
© 1996 Forest Stewardship Council

Typeset in 11/12pt Palatino by
Phoenix Typesetting, Burley-in-Wharfedale, West Yorkshire.
Printed in the UK by CPI Cox & Wyman, Reading, RG1 8EX.

2 4 6 8 10 9 7 5 3 1

For Thomas and my sisters,
Natasha and Sonya

Acknowledgements

Thank you, Thomas Quinn, for total support in the decision to quit the day job, have babies and write novels. You are a brave and lovely man and I couldn't have done any of it without you.

Thank you also to my fantastic agents at the Darley Anderson Literary Agency. This book would never have happened without Darley's encouragement and inspired advice, and Carrie Neilson's absolute faith in it. I can't thank you enough and know I'm in very good hands.

I'm very grateful to everyone involved at Transworld for being so enthusiastic about Bella, especially Diana Beaumont.

I owe a huge debt to my friends and family who have been so helpful in all sorts of ways. Thank you to everyone who read drafts, took photos, looked after Sam, or simply made me believe it would work out.

Much love to the people I leaned on when the going got tough: my parents, my sisters Tash and Son, Scott and Dorothy Luke, Mairi Mallon, Glyn Pugh, Lucy Rock and Jo Sewell.

And finally, a big kiss for my little son, Sam – a daily inspiration.

Chapter One

It was 6.29 a.m. The digital alarm clock beside the bed was about to go off. Just as it started up with its nasty little beeping, the bedside phone began to ring too.

Bella leaned over to click off the alarm and answer the phone.

'Hello?'

She heard a distant 'Hello!' far from the other end of a crackling line, followed by singing.

'Happy birthday to you, happy birthday to you . . .'

'*Don!*' she shouted and heard it echo back at her.

'Hello Bella, wake up, I love you, I want phone sex now.'

'I love you too,' she said laughing.

'What? It's a terrible line.'

'I love you too!' she shouted. 'When are you allowed to come home?'

'Ah ha . . . well I'm phoning you from Grozny airport. By the time you get back from work, I'll be there.'

'Yeah?! I can't believe it! That's bloody brilliant!'

'My job here is done,' he said in mock superhero voice. 'Seriously, it's been a nightmare and it's getting dangerous now, so they're pulling me out. Plus I told them it was your birthday and I had to get home, or else a fate worse than a rebel gunman awaited.'

'Are you OK?' she asked.

'I'm very tired, it's been three weeks from hell. Oh bugger, hon, I have to go now, I'll see you tonight and I am so looking forward to it.'

'Me too. Take care.'

'Missing you already,' he joked, then the line went dead.

She was smiling hard, was going to be smiling all day long, she thought, as she got out of bed and started on Operation Bella. The difference between Bella and other women whose looks were somewhere between moderate to good on the scale was that she tried harder. In fact, 'tries hard' was a description that had peppered her report cards since she was tiny.

At the very start of her career, she'd spent a long summer on assignment in New York and it was there that she had found her spiritual sisters, the immaculate New York women who jogged, gym-ed, power manicured and treated sex as just another way to business network. Her eyes had been opened and she always joked that she'd checked all her insecurities in at JFK airport and never bothered to check them out again. This wasn't exactly true, the insecurities were still there, she'd just learned to hide them well.

She pulled on her running clothes and trainers now, because Monday to Friday, she jogged for twenty-five minutes every morning with NO EXCEPTIONS. She loathed almost every second, but it was the only way to shake off any remaining booze from the night before, stay on the slim side of curvaceous and guarantee that she got some exercise crammed into her day.

After the run, she showered, shaved, dried off and moisturized. Then, with her hair wrapped up in a big white towel, she stood in front of the bathroom mirror.

She stared hard at her face. Twenty-eight years old today. Pulling a smile, she looked at the tiny crinkles radiating out from her eyes and the very first hint of bagginess on her eyelids. It was obviously all downhill from here.

She sponged a generous squeeze of foundation from collarbone to hairline and loaded up a powder brush to dredge over her face. She thanked God every morning for make-up. Then she shook her hair out of the towel and blasted it dry, before bundling it up into the loose chignon which she thought made her look older and more serious for work.

Back in the bedroom, she pulled open her underwear drawer and rifled through it. Don was coming home! He'd been away so long, he'd find her a turn-on in greying pants and a jogging bra, but hell he deserved a treat. She took out her newest pink and black underwired lace bra and matching G-strings, then opened the wardrobe. She slipped into a crisp shirt and hold-up stockings then buttoned on a black suit with tightly fitted jacket and a narrow skirt which fell to the knee.

She checked herself over in the long bedroom

mirror and approved. Of course, since New York, nothing about Bella's workwear was left to chance. She'd taken the hair and make-up lessons, been colour-consulted and image madeover. Her perfectly appropriate outfit, about to be perfectly accessorized, was supposed to scream 'woman headed for the top'.

She fished about in her jewellery drawer for small chic earrings and the tiny platinum pendant Don had given her, fiddled to put them on then grabbed high-heeled leather pumps from the shoe rack and hurried into the kitchen.

Two oranges were blitzed in the small electric squeezer. She put the glass of juice and a pot of yoghurt onto the tiny marble-topped table in the kitchen, then went to the front door of the flat to bring in the newspapers. She sat down and studied the *Financial Times* carefully as she had breakfast, then flicked through Don's tabloid until she found his latest report, and read every word.

At 7.45 it was time to go, so she collected raincoat, briefcase, laptop and keys and headed out to work. As her left hand pushed shut the heavy wooden and glass front door of the mansion block, her eyes fell on the thin platinum band, sparkling with tiny diamonds on her fourth finger, and she couldn't help smiling. God! Marriage was still such a novelty.

Just one birthday ago, she'd woken up in yet another unfamiliar 'loft-style' bedroom, with make-up caked deep into her pores and the roots of a truly monumental hangover taking hold in her skull. Her nostrils had burned suspiciously and she'd

12

been repulsed to see a fleshy, snoring equities trader, whose name she couldn't recall, fast asleep beside her.

She had retrieved her underwear, pulled on a dress stiff with sweat from the night before, picked up her bag and shoes and crept out of the flat. Three heart-attack-inducing espressos later in an Italian café on the corner, she'd come to the realization that it was time to put as much effort into her personal life as she'd put into her career. And about a month after that, all psyched up to stay away from men and sex and one night stands until she'd got her head together, she'd bumped smack bang straight into The One. After a thirteen-week romance, the longest she'd had for years, they got hitched. Fear of commitment, ha!

She had crossed that line, made the jump, taken the plunge. Well, actually, Don had seen straight through the tough City-girl-shagger defence to the person underneath, the one who hadn't dared to fall in love since Big Romance Number One had gone all horribly wrong. Don had taken her hand and convinced her this was the real thing. He'd urged her to make the leap with him and when he'd slid the slim ring onto her finger, she'd felt a surprising solemnity. She'd felt terrified of it too. But there was so much love just radiating out of him, she had committed, signed on the line, sealed the deal.

She turned away from the front door into the lukewarm May sunshine. In the distance she could hear the gentle roar of traffic: anther day in the capital was already under way. She unlocked the door of her low, cream-coloured classic

Mercedes 280/SL soft-top, threw her coat and bags onto the passenger seat and climbed in, smudging her right calf with oil on the door frame.

'*Damn*,' she said out loud, then leaned over to the tiny glove compartment and popped the button, causing half a dozen packets of black hold-ups to slide out onto the floor. She held her leg out of the car door, whipped off the smudged stocking, rolled on a new one then, tossing the spoiled one into the back, she fired up the engine and set off for the office.

At 8.25 a.m., juggling coat, briefcase and laptop with the packet of twenty Marlboro Lights and large bottle of Evian from the shop round the corner, Bella arrived at Prentice and Partners, one of the City's smallest, but sharpest, firms of management consultants.

'Morning, Kitty,' she said as she walked in.

'Hi, Bella.' Kitty looked up from her desk in the large reception area.

'Is Susan in?'

'Of course.'

'Girls first. Are the boys in to play today?'

'Yup, Hector's due in any time and –' Kitty checked her screen – 'Chris will be in for the afternoon meeting but he might be earlier.'

'OK. I'll just go through my diary and put the coffee on then I'll be ready for you,' Bella said with a smile.

She went into her little office and settled in, hanging up her coat and filling the coffee machine before she took out her laptop, checked through her e-mails and clicked open her schedule.

14

MAY 8

Tuesday

* Happy Birthday – just in case you've forgotten. Old Bag.

* Put in follow-up call to Petersham's office to answer/reassure on queries/nerves/cold feet.

* Prepare for meet with Merris.

* BOLLOCK Hector.

* Chris and Susan meet 2 pm – Petersham's and Merris details.

* Get pregnant?

What???! She re-read that last bit. God, why had she put that in there? It was on her mind, but that didn't mean it had to be in her diary. She hit delete. It was off the screen, but not out of her head. She knew she wanted a baby: really, really wanted one. Something that had begun as a vague interest several months ago had now grown into a fully-fledged desire. It was weird.

Why did she want one so much? She'd tried to analyse her reasons endlessly: maybe because her own parents had made such a mess of things and she wanted to do better, maybe because she worried a lot about what the future held for her and Don without kids. He was thirteen years older than her and she couldn't help imagining herself growing ancient, all alone with deranged, incontinent cats for company instead of children and grandchildren.

Bella also worried that it might take a very long time to have a baby. Her own mother had given birth to her at 29, then spent eight years enduring miscarriage after miscarriage before finally giving up hope of a second child. She remembered the little cradle and the boxes of baby clothes, all carefully labelled, in the upstairs loft room and how sometimes as a small girl she would find her mother up there, weeping furiously.

But Bella's biggest problem right now was that when she married Don seven months ago, he didn't want children – said he was too old, too independent, too set in his ways – and she'd agreed 'no kids' with him. But now she knew she hadn't meant it, hadn't really thought it through.

The idea was beginning to form in her mind that if a pregnancy were to happen 'accidentally', Don would of course be shocked, but she was sure he would come round to it. Anyway, her mother's experience had left Bella with the belief that conception was a million miles away from actually having a baby. So, would it be so bad to get pregnant and see what happened?

There was a knock on the door and Bella was interrupted from her thoughts by Kitty.

Bella poured them both coffee and, as usual, teased Kitty about her latest office outfit, in between briefing her for the day.

Kitty, small, spiky red-haired and generously curved, was crammed into silver hipster trousers, a tiny purple T-shirt and a silver padded waistcoat. Platform-soled trainers with flashing lights completed the look.

'When is the mother ship due to land?' Bella asked with raised eyebrows.

Kitty looked at her blankly.

'You do not speak the language of earthlings?' Bella added.

'Shut up, Bella.' A grin split Kitty's face. 'Just because you like looking like an airline hostess, you twentieth-century throwback.' She ignored Bella's exaggerated gasps of horror and added: 'Silver is so *now*.'

'But are you dressed for success, Kitty? I think not,' Bella answered.

'You are such a corporate clone! Power dressing does not equal power,' Kitty snapped back. 'Where are you headed Bella? Straight for the glass ceiling.'

'Oh God,' Bella groaned. 'It is way too early for a radical feminist rant, *please*.' She cracked open her pack of cigarettes and lit up, closing her eyes with pleasure for the first drag of the day.

As it headed towards 9 a.m., Bella shooed Kitty out of her office and started on her calls. She was in a gap between two big contracts and restless to drum up new business. After she'd made the first call, the phone on her desk buzzed.

'Hello. Bella Browning,' She answered.

'Bella, it's Kitty, I've got a very angry caller for you. Do you want me to say you're busy?'

'No, they'll just ring back. I might as well face the music. Who is it?'

'Tom Proctor at AMP.'

'OK, give me just thirty secs then put him through.'

She closed her eyes and took a deep breath,

willing herself to stay calm as she slowly put her finger over the flashing extension button to connect him.

'Hello Tom, how are you?' she said.

'Don't call me Tom, you bitch,' he shot back at her. 'You know perfectly well how I am. I'm fucking sacked. Sacked after seventeen years of working my arse off for this company only to have you come in here for eight weeks and pull the entire thing apart.'

This was the worst part of her job, the part that racked her with guilt. Tom was 53 with three kids in full-time education and a very expensive lifestyle to maintain. He did not have a great track record and was going to find it hard to get another job as good as the one she'd had him fired from.

'Have you any idea how much damage you've done here?' he raged. 'My colleagues, men with families and young children to look after, are packing their things into bin liners and leaving in tears.'

She swallowed hard, really not wanting to hear this.

'Just who do you think you are?' he screamed down the phone. 'I'll tell you – you're some cocky little graduate with a bollocks business degree whose only idea of cost-efficiency is sacking people and you probably only got your ludicrously over-paid position by sucking every cock in the city.'

Christ, that was way too much.

She answered coolly: 'Mr Proctor, I have a starred first in Economics from the London School of Economics, where I was top of my MA year. I spent four years working for the biggest consultants in the country before I joined Prentice and Partners. And Susan Prentice is a woman, so I certainly didn't need to suck her cock.'

Undeterred, he shouted back: 'We didn't fucking well need you lot of bloodsuckers in here. You've destroyed us. I'm going to make sure you never get another contract in the City again, you smug cunt.'

She couldn't believe she was hearing this. She stood up at her desk and her voice began to rise: 'If you were even half as good at your job as I am at mine, AMP would never have needed to call consultants in. Without my help that firm would have gone to the wall in two years max and everyone would have been laid off without the kind of generous redundancy payout you've received.'

Just for good measure she added: 'How dare you phone up to insult me? You kept telling me one day you'd move to the country and restore antique furniture, so why don't you sod off and do it?'

Damn, she instantly regretted that, but *cunt*! Cunt? How dare he?

At that moment, she glanced over to the door and saw Chris grinning at her and giving her the thumbs up. That was all she needed, Susan's number two listening in on this. Quickly she added: 'Mr Proctor, I'm very busy, you'll have to excuse me. Thank you for your call.'

She heard an astonished gasp, but put the phone down before he could say anything else.

'Phew, you tell them Bella,' Chris grinned at her. 'Just sod off to the country and restore antique furniture. I must remember that the next time someone calls me a cocksucker.'

19

'Chris, you heartless shit,' she said, relieved he was treating this lightly. 'I'm really embarrassed you heard that. Are you going to fire me now?' She asked with a little arch of her eyebrows.

'No,' he paused for effect, 'but I may have to get very firm with you, Ms Browning.' Then he added: 'Just try not to make too many enemies for life. Anyway, how was your weekend?'

'Good,' she replied. 'Don wasn't around so I did girlie things, you know, drank ten pints of lager, did three lines of coke, shagged a complete stranger in the toilets.'

He gave her an intrigued look.

'I'm joking, Chris.' Then the penny dropped. 'Oh!! You actually did that. Well you're a lucky boy, but at your age you have to think of your health, you know.'

'I'm only 34!'

'Mmm, but you have the added stress of being a senior partner,' she teased.

'A job you would probably kill me to get. Which is why I never send you out for sandwiches.'

'I'd never go!'

'Bella –' he reached for the door handle. 'It's been a pleasure as always, but we have lots of work to put together before this afternoon's meeting. Merris, Petersham, any queries, I'm next door, watching you through my spyhole.'

'See you later,' she said and he was gone, leaving her with a slightly too flirtatious smile on her face.

There was another knock on the door.

'Come in.' She knew it was Hector. Hector, the fresh out of university new boy who seemed never to tire of telling them about his heroic Highland pedigree. And that was just one of his many annoying qualities.

'You wanted to see me?' He poked a tousled head round the door.

'Yes,' she said.

He came in, looking arrogantly crumpled, as usual. He still bought into that boho tweedy suit, pashmina, I'm not going to conform or try too hard kind of look. He was a very brilliant guy: why else would he be working here? But he really was going to have to get it together.

He sat down on the chair opposite her desk.

'So, what is this piece of crap?' She tossed a thick, spiral-bound report onto the desk.

'Ah, I was wondering if a few inaccuracies might have crept in.'

'A few inaccuracies!!' She picked the report up again. 'Let me just open it at random . . . 32 per cent of £586,000? That is . . .' she barely paused, '£187,520. Yet unbelievably, you've got £28,500 down here. Totally, utterly out of the ball park.'

'Well, I suppose I'm not a mathematical genius like you, Bella,' he had the nerve to reply.

'What does that have to do with it? Why don't you buy yourself a sodding calculator?' she snapped. 'In fact go and buy a proper sodding suit while you're at it. It's about time you sharpened up.'

He looked up at her rather surprised, but she continued: 'You've been here for four months now and you don't seem to have learned anything. This report is about a major company, you were working out their profits, their losses, their expenses. Your mistakes could have cost hundreds of thousands of pounds, could have cost people their jobs. This is not a game, Hector, this is not a theoretical problem you discuss in a tutorial. Christ. It's all very well having potential if you're 10. There comes a time when you have to prove it.'

There was a long pause.

Hector wondered why Bella was holding the report right in front of her face and shaking slightly.

'Are you OK?' he asked.

He was surprised to hear a snort of laughter emerge from behind the pages.

'Oh God,' she put the report down on the table. 'You really deserve a strip torn off you, but I can't do this with a straight face.'

'Er . . . I'm sorry. Do you want me to do it again?' he asked.

'No, I've already sorted it. Will you just try and concentrate hard on the next thing you get from me?'

'Yeah, sorry.'

When Bella was on her own in her office again, she laughed at herself. 'Potential is all very well if you're 10' – she suspected she'd read that on a bill-board somewhere.

She lit up another cigarette, took a deep drag and massaged her temples. This was turning into one hell of a day.

There was another knock and Kitty came in with an enormous bouquet of flowers.

'You thought we'd all forgotten, didn't you?'

'Forgotten what?' Bella asked.

'Your birthday, you idiot.'

'Oh God . . . thanks.' She went over to take the flowers, reading the note signed by all four of them.

'Thanks,' she said again, looking round her room and wondering where to put them.

'There's a vase at reception, shall I keep them out there till the end of play?' Kitty asked.

'Yeah, you're a star, Kitty. I bet everyone else would have forgotten.'

Nine hours later, after hundreds of calls, calculations and a gruelling meeting with Chris and Susan, Bella was finally tapping in her last memo and tidying her desk for the day. It was 7.15 p.m. when Chris appeared at the door to ask if she was coming for a drink over the road.

She declined because, at last, it was time to get home to Don. The traffic was infuriatingly slow all the way back across town, so she redid her make-up, sprayed on perfume and flipped through her CDs before giving up in disgust and enduring the radio. She couldn't wait to see Don again. Three whole weeks: it was the longest they'd ever been apart.

When she finally made it back to the block she swung open the front door, ran to the lift and impatiently jabbed on the button over and over again until the doors pinged open.

In the flat everything was still and for a heart-crushing moment she thought Don hadn't been able to make it back. Then she saw his bag and his battered oilskin coat in the hall. Quietly she walked through to the bedroom. The curtains were closed and Don was lying in bed fast asleep.

She was so happy to see him she felt her stomach flip. She moved closer to take a long look at him. His face was brown against the white pillow, but tired and drawn. His thick steely-grey hair was rumpled and still wet from the shower he must have taken. His glasses were on the bedside table and he looked deliciously clean and freshly shaven.

She was sure he was naked under the duvet and she couldn't help herself, she longed to feel his body against hers. She put down her bags and coat, took off her shoes and undressed, then slid into the bed beside him, curling her naked body up against her husband's warm, naked back. Wrapping her arms round him, she put her nose to the nape of his neck, breathing in the smell of the sandalwood soap she'd been using too because she missed him so much: 'Hello Don,' she whispered.

He stirred a little and answered with a 'hmm' so she moved closer. She ran her hands down his warm, fuzzy chest and stomach until she reached his sleeping cock.

A longer, throatier 'mmmm' came from him now as she held his cock in her hands.

'Hello,' she said. 'Aren't you going to wake up and say hi?'

'Oh yes,' he answered, surfacing from sleep now. He rolled round to face her and kissed her on the lips.

Then he smiled, creasing the skin round his eyes and looking at her with so much love and longing she felt a lump in her throat.

'Hon, I'm so glad to be back, you have no idea,' he said in a voice still thick with sleep.

'I've missed you too.' She kissed him back, winding her legs round his, pulling him so close their pubic hair brushed together and she could feel

24

his cock stir against her as he moved his hands down from her waist to her buttocks.

'I still can't believe I'm married to you . . .' he said, in between small hungry kisses, 'and you're naked!'

He kissed her properly now, squeezing her into him and parting her lips with his tongue. She tasted his hot, minty mouth.

As he pulled her up against his hard erection, she wound her fingers into his hair and placed teasing kisses on his neck and round his ear.

'I have missed you so much,' she whispered.

'I've missed you too, especially your breasts,' he said with a smile, gently stroking and licking at her nipples and the soft white skin around them.

They felt and touched and kissed and licked until she rolled over and pulled him on top of her. Watching her face, he pushed inside and slowly moved in and out all the way along the length of his penis.

'You tease,' she murmured, holding her hands on his hips and moving him faster until they were gasping together in a fast and frantic fuck.

When they fell apart, they were slightly sweaty and breathing heavily.

'God you're good,' she said with a smile. 'I still can't believe you're my husband. I mean husbands are meant to wear slippers and wash the car, not give a girl multiple orgasms.'

'All in a day's work!' he answered.

'Hey!' she sat up, loving the fact that he couldn't take his eyes off her breasts. 'You better not have forgotten it's my birthday today.'

'I phoned you first thing, remember.'

'Yeah, you phoned, but where is my large, expensive present?'

25

'Bella, I've just come back from a war zone, there wasn't much to buy . . . give me a chance.'

She didn't know what to say. Maybe she was being unfair. What could Chechen Duty Free have had to offer?

'But . . .' he leaned over to fish about under the bed, 'I did get you this.' He handed her a big, khaki green furry hat with earflaps. 'Genuine Russian Army issue,' he said with a mischievous smile.

'Oh! Thanks.' She tried to look appreciative, then added, 'My first ever birthday present from you. Next year, remind me to get a different husband.'

'And –' he reached under the bed – 'I can't tell you how hard I had to barter on the black market to get this.' He turned round and presented her with a glossy pink box tied with ribbon.

'Happy birthday.'

She untied the ribbon and lifted the lid. Inside was an extravagant set of lilac and black silk underwear. A lace-trimmed bra and G-string, a camisole top and French knickers. She picked the bra up and looked at the label – correct size. She was impressed. Black market ha, ha.

'Is this a present for me or for you?' she asked, but before he could answer, said: 'Thank you very much. You're very sweet,' and kissed him on the mouth.

'Oh good, I'm glad you like them, because I *really* like them. Now stay there,' he said, getting out of bed and putting his dressing gown on.

'I'm opening the wine, ordering Chinese, and I'm going to try and persuade you to spend the whole evening in bed with me.'

'Well, OK then, since I now have the outfit for it,' she said, lifting the camisole out of the box.

They ate the food in bed and made each other laugh, Bella talking about work and Don telling war stories.

'God, I do wonder if I'm getting a bit old for it, though,' he said, serious for a moment.

'Will you stop it?' she told him. 'You are not old, you're 41, you're very fit,' she leaned over, letting her dressing gown fall open and kissing him on the forehead.

'In many ways, you're like a man half your age,' she teased.

He pulled her across so she was sitting in his lap. 'Thank you for your vote of confidence darling,' he kissed her on the mouth.

'Yeuuck, black bean sauce.' She screwed up her face in mock horror.

'I'm going to kiss you somewhere else then.' He dropped her down onto her back and began to kiss her breasts and her stomach. Then he moved down to her pubic hair and blew on it gently. She drew one foot up, bending her knee.

He pressed his tongue onto her small nub of clitoris, listening to her sharp intakes of breath, then rolled her hard nipples between his fingers and thumbs. She said in a soft voice: 'Mmmm. This is what every girl needs on her birthday. It's much nicer than cake *and* less fattening.'

He pulled himself up over her and she moved her legs apart so he could enter.

She tensed every muscle for his thrusts and he felt her coming underneath him, clinging to his body to soak up the pleasure of his every move.

He took much longer and finally came as she was screwing up her eyes and whispering to him: 'I can't do this much longer . . . I can't . . .'

She kept him on top of her, feeling his penis slowly fall out of the spermy wetness between her legs and a huge sense of satisfaction welled up inside her as she thought about how she would not be taking her pill tonight, because she wanted to get pregnant.

Chapter Two

Flicking through her e-mails in the office, she was trying hard to think about the contract they were making a final pitch for next week, but her mind was wandering.

She couldn't believe three months had gone by and she still wasn't pregnant. Each period had been a surprisingly crushing disappointment.

Oh well, they'd just have to have more sex. Hardly an awful prospect.

'Bella? Bella, hello!' Kitty was at the door, in pink dungarees with a fluffy white cat apliquéed on the front pocket.

'Yes?' Bella stared at the cat.

'Susan's ready, you can go in now. Chris will be along in a minute.'

'Thanks, hon . . . but what's with the cat?' Bella asked as she gathered up her papers and headed for Susan's office.

'Post-postmodern,' Kitty replied.

Surprise, surprise, Susan was on the phone. She waved Bella in and pointed to a chair.

Bella's one-time mentor and now her boss was in

her forties, a rapier-thin, control freaky workaholic. She had scarily huge hair and only ever dressed in very expensive beige. She was married to an equally successful man. No kids.

Susan had been one of the stars at Laurence and Co., the fuck-off, major league consultancy firm Bella had joined after university. But Susan had left to set up on her own after a row with one of the MDs. There had been an almighty fuss, she was taken to court for breach of contract, they'd tried to drag her through the dirt, but it had all just made scary Sue even more determined to succeed. She'd finally agreed to let Bella join her a year later.

No matter how early Bella arrived at the office, Susan was there first and she always stayed late. Her only look was 100 per cent perfect and because she was constantly on her mobile, it was clipped to her waistband with a dainty headset which ran from her pearl-studded ear to her beige-brown mouth. This allowed her to tap into her tiny, shiny, titanium-cased laptop without a break in conversations.

'Hello, Bella,' she said as she finally ended the call, but didn't take the headset off.

'I was just speaking to Anne, you remember from the job last year? She's just had a baby so I'm supposed to be all thrilled and excited for her. Good grief, I'm so glad you're not planning to sprog. That's why I hired you, really. I needed another woman, a good one. But I didn't want someone who was going to go off and do the whole baby thing on me.'

Barely pausing for breath, she added: 'No matter what working mothers tell you, no good career

30

woman is ever the same afterwards. They just haven't got their whole mind on the job once they have children. In fact,' she paused to give a little sarcastic smile, 'They haven't got their whole mind.'

Bella forced herself to return the smile, but suspected it had come out like a Cherie Blair grimace. She remembered exactly when she'd told Susan she didn't want children. It was when she'd first approached – make that pestered – her for a job. Obviously it had never entered Susan's head that now Bella was married, she might have changed her mind. It amazed Bella that Susan was often guilty of the most appalling sexist crap no male boss would dare to utter unless hidden in a pall of cigar smoke in the safe confines of a gentleman's club.

Luckily she was saved from having to make any sort of answer by Chris coming in. The meeting kicked off.

It was a little short of 5 p.m. when they finished, but there wasn't much else to do, so Susan sent them away early.

Bella headed for the car. The traffic looked grim but the sun was shining and she was going to drive with the roof down wearing her new sunglasses, so suddenly it didn't seem too bad a prospect. She was in a long queue at a roundabout, when she gave Don a call on the mobile.

'Hello, hon, it's me.'

'Hi Bella – do I hear traffic in the background? God, you're not out of the office, are you?'

'Yes, out early for good behaviour.'

'I'm in town,' he said. 'Job's nearly over, but I won't have to go back to the newsroom now, so d'you want to meet up? We could go out for dinner round here somewhere.'

'Uh-oh, you've forgotten about the drinks party!'

'Errrrr . . .'

'Drinkies, darling,' she trilled in a silly voice, then added, 'At eight-ish with Mel, Jasper, Lucy and somebody's client. I can't remember who's paying for this one.'

'Ahh,' said Don, not at all disappointed. It was always fun going out to play with the City boys and girls.

'I'm going home to get dressed up. Are you coming back as well? Or d'you want to meet there?'

'I'll meet you there,' he said.

She gave him the details and they said their good-byes.

When Bella and the gang had all worked at Laurence and Co. together, they had been an incredibly close little group. They had seemed so exactly the same: young, precociously clever, ambitious, impatient to get ahead. They had worked hard and played harder in an inseparable band with their own private jokes, code words, pet hates and games. Even when they had all moved on to different companies, the intimacy had remained for a long time.

But over the past few months, Bella had noticed that she no longer really felt part of it – a difference she could only put down to marriage. She didn't want to be out socializing all night, every night. She wanted to go home to Don. She was starting to find the gossip dull, all the 'who's sleeping with who tonight/last night/tomorrow night' and the 'who's been hired, who's been fired' and how much their bonus was worth.

Even worse, Bella knew her little gang had picked this up and now thought of her as a slightly honorary member. She kind of wanted to be out of it, but was still hurt that they had sidelined her, closed ranks without her. It also really pissed her off that they didn't get Don at all, couldn't fathom what she was doing with a man who wasn't interested in *money*.

It did not take Bella long to get ready. She showered again and picked out a tried and tested outfit. Her get-dressed philosophy was simple – work the good stuff. She liked her face, her breasts and her hair and her legs from the knee down, so she never wore trousers except at the weekend and she always did heels and cleavage of some sort. Her long, dark hair was either piled up in a big chic bundle or let glossy-mane loose.

She walked into the smart little function room shortly after 8 p.m. and could see Don perched on a stool by the side of the bar already but, before she could get over to him, she was leapt on by Mel.

'Daaahling' – kiss, kiss – 'how are you? Looking foxy.'

Mel looked pretty slinky herself in a tight crimson number.

'Now come over here, Lucy wants you to meet the mob she's working with at the moment and Jaz is around somewhere.'

Bella managed a wave at Don before she was bombarded with a flurry of introductions. She set her face to interested smile and prepared to handshake. Network, network ... that's what it was all about.

Almost an hour had passed before she finally made it over to see Don.

'Hello.' She put her arms round his waist and kissed him on the mouth, tasting whisky.

'Hi Bella, you look lovely,' he said.

'Well you know, it's my version of "Speak softly and carry a big stick".'

'What is?' he laughed.

'Speak like a financial whiz but wear a see-through dress,' she answered.

'Killer combination,' he agreed.

'Irresistible,' she said and lit a cigarette.

'D'you want to stay much longer?' he asked.

'A bit longer. I'll go speak to Jasper and his new buddies, then we'll make a move. You're not too bored, are you?'

'Nooo,' he answered, 'I'm chatting to everyone who drifts past.'

'D'you want to come and speak to Jasper?'

'OK, if you like.'

He stood up and followed his wife through the throng, watching the glances she was attracting, dressed in her tight black satin skirt topped with a dark green chiffon blouse which looked demure, but on closer inspection turned out to be entirely transparent with the merest wisp of bra underneath.

It pleased him to think how surprised the fleshy faces in pinstriped three-pieces would look when she left with him – the oldest and scruffiest man there, in a badly creased suit and scuffed suede boots.

Finally they got out of the place and crammed

34

into her tiny little car to race back home, Don marvelling at the fact that she could actually drive in those heels and that she'd restricted herself to two glasses of champagne – he hoped.

As soon as they were back at the flat, Bella pushed him playfully up against the front door for a long, probing homecoming kiss. She felt him relax as she leaned into him. Slowly Don ran his hands down from her shoulders to her hips, pulling her in close to him.

As they kissed, he felt for the zip at the back of her skirt and tugged it down so the satin slid into a heap at her feet. He moved his hands down, registering his appreciation that beyond the stocking tops, there was no underwear.

'Oh God, I want to fuck you,' he whispered into her ear.

'Well . . . OK then,' she said, putting her hand in his trousers.

Later in bed, she lay curled up beside him and felt a flicker of guilt. Would he really forgive her if she got pregnant? She could reel off a list of reasons why he was not exactly a great Dad candidate: he was the chief reporter with a tabloid newspaper, so he worked really long hours, was away a lot, and liked a good drink with the lads. Even worse, he was in his forties, his own dad had left when he was just a small boy *and* he didn't want kids.

Christ. She leaned over to get a cigarette out of her handbag.

He'd told her before they were married he didn't want to spend his fifties dealing with a teenager and his retirement paying for a student. And yet . . . somehow she was convinced she could change his mind because she knew he was a good man and he loved her.

'Don't smoke in bed,' Don groaned.

'Don, please . . . I need a cigarette.' She sat up now, so he could see her breasts bounce lightly against her chest, and put the cigarette between her lips. She clicked the lighter and took a deep drag, causing the end to glow and crackle.

'OK, I'm going for a shower.' He got up, leaving her in the bed in a pale cloud.

Bella didn't care; a warm plume of smoke was hitting the back of her throat and nicotine was surging into her veins. She lay back against the pillows and daydreamed about the gorgeous little baby they were going to have.

Chapter Three

Bella let her hair down and brushed it through. She checked herself over in her small handbag compact and decided to apply the full-on red lipstick.

How many times do we go out to celebrate winning a £500,000 contract? she thought to herself, smiling smugly. The Danson's job was finally in the bag and it was due to her. She had met the company director socially and she had reeled him in.

She was buzzing with excitement, too much nicotine and the small vat of coffee she'd consumed. The test she'd done this morning confirmed it was something else too – she was about to ovulate and by the law of the jungle, she should be hunting down a mate.

The word put David Attenborough into her head . . . *And here we have the Bella. She is 28 and she has to mate this season or her chance could be over. She will be cast out of the herd and the bull will reproduce with younger, more fertile females.*

God, listen to me, she checked herself. I'm still years away from my prime. Isn't it scientifically proven not to kick in till 36?

She knew she was looking good today in a smart but more than slightly sexy black, very tailored suit (which had cost about three times more than she'd ever intended to spend. Ooops). Her red silk shirt was casually unbuttoned to reveal a diamond slung onto a short chain and just a hint of cappuccino-coloured lace if she leaned over.

She checked the time: 5.30 p.m., surely it wouldn't be unreasonable for everyone to down tools and start the celebrations now? She e-mailed Chris.

Can we go yet? you lovely sweet man. I've got bugger all else to do and I'm gasping for a nice cool glass of wine.

Hello Bella – OK fine, so long as you're still wearing that very hot suit you had on earlier.

Of course I'm still wearing it. I don't often prance around my office naked getting changed.

Shame.

When the alarm clock went off the next morning, she woke with a pounding head and a disgusting taste at the back of her nose and throat.

'Oh God,' she groaned. The worst thing was, it was Friday today so she would still have to go for a jog and back into work to face the music.

How could four professional people have made such a mess of a night out with the boss? Of course they had all drunk far too much. Susan had kept them waiting at the restaurant's bar for three hours. And it wasn't just drink.

She didn't know if it was Hector or Chris who had brought the coke in to spice up the celebrations, but Bella and Kitty had been passed a wrap and had sneaked off to the loos for a dose. Bottles and bottles of champagne, and cocaine as well. Bella cringed when she remembered what they were doing when Susan finally arrived – holding a farmyard noises competition.

Somehow, with intense concentration, everyone had managed to sit at a table, order food and attempt to eat it. But Hector and Kit kept taking turns at getting up to go to the loo, sniffing heavily when they came back.

Then they went off together and didn't come back at all. Bella and Chris had been left at the table with Susan and she remembered trying to keep the sinking conversation afloat, painfully aware of the fact that she could hardly control her lips.

Finally Susan had slammed her platinum Amex down on the table, paid the bill and left in obvious fury. And that was when the real trouble had begun.

There was a newly opened bottle of champagne on the table and Chris had topped up their glasses, insisting it shouldn't go to waste. Bella couldn't remember much of a conversation, Chris had just reeled off drunken compliments and silly stories and she had giggled a lot.

When the bottle was empty and it was time to go, he had of course suggested they share a cab as they lived in the same part of town. She had fallen back into the cab seat to find his arms around her and without a moment's hesitation she had turned her face up and snogged him all the way home.

Oh God. She closed her eyes but she couldn't shake the memory. It had been so much fun. Despite the night of boozing, he had smelled and tasted good. They had spent the twenty-minute taxi ride entwined in long, probing, teasing kisses.

Even worse, she remembered telling him: 'This isn't really me, Chris, my hormones are on overdrive and I have to mate.'

CRINGE CRINGE. Why could she never have a memory blank like every one else seemed to when they got that drunk?

She had arrived home to Don, legless, coked up to the eyeballs and probably with smeared lipstick and an unbuttoned shirt. Not surprisingly, he had been quietly furious. He had forced her to drink about three gallons of water then sent her to bed.

She had absolutely no intention of saying anything about the snogging unless Don had already guessed and asked her first. A fresh wave of guilt broke over her: there was now an indelible blot on her marriage copybook and they hadn't even been married a year, for God's sake.

It was one thing to have a little crush on someone in the office: quite another to go ramming your tongue down their throat.

She got to work late, harassed and feeling awful. She hurried into her office and flicked on the computer. Among the e-mails waiting for her was:

Bella, I'm out at a client's all day. But I just wanted to let you know I've ordered a whopping bouquet for Susan this morning to atone for our sins. Good plan? Chris

She sat down and sent him a one-word reply.

Genius.

She was sure he would not leave it at that and she was right. Just minutes later, her in-box was flashing.

Oh hello, I'm glad you've finally appeared. I wouldn't have said last night was a complete disaster . . .

Chris, I think we all drank an awful lot. I'm trying not to think about it, I'm not sure I can remember the entire night.

Well that sounds truly pathetic she thought as she hit the send button.

Fine.

She stared at the word on the screen and realized it would be best to leave the conversation there.

'Hi.' Kitty was at the door, looking pale, blotchy and lanky haired in a strangely sedate grey outfit, which meant she must be ill.

'Oh darling,' Bella winced. 'Sit down and I'll pour you some coffee from my lovely little machine over here and you can tell me all about your night of passion with Hector, you evil girl.'

'He is lovely, isn't he?' Kitty said wanly, sinking into the seat.

'Yeah – gorgeous.' Bella hoped she didn't sound too insincere.

'I've fancied him for ages.' Kitty picked up her coffee cup with a trembling hand. 'We had coke and a grope in the Ladies but he didn't come home with me, which I'm taking as a very bad sign. And he's not in yet, so I don't know what to think?'

'Hmm,' said Bella.

'And what about you and Chris?' Kitty added. 'For a married woman, you looked very flirty.'

'I did not!' Bella launched straight in on the defensive. 'We were trying to distract Susan from the fact that two of her staff had *vanished*. Chris is sorting out flowers for her this morning to apologize.'

'He has a point,' said Kitty.

By four in the afternoon, Bella realized her work had been punctuated all day long with thoughts of Chris. He had such an indecently full mouth. She just needed to think about their long kisses to feel a little adrenalin hit.

'I have got to get a grip,' she told herself. '*Just stop this*. I want to have my husband's baby, not an extra-marital fling.'

But she could not silence the little voice in her head that kept telling her this was it – her last chance. Chris was one final opportunity for the wild abandon of a hot affair before she fully embraced motherhood and responsibility.

'But I've already embraced responsibility.' What the hell was this?? Nerves? She was married, she owed it to Don not to sleep around, not even once, not even if there was hardly any chance of him finding out.

Over lunch Kitty had confessed in whispered

giggles to licking coke off Hector's dick in the loos and Bella had felt a stab of jealousy.

Then she thought of Don and felt guilty. Married life was brilliant, but just occasionally she did hanker for the sexual adventure of singledom. Yes, it was like eating McDonald's: you really, really wanted it, you enjoyed most of it, but you felt crap afterwards. Still, she thought marriage would suit her perfectly if she was allowed just the very occasional indiscretion. She would be so very discreet about her indiscretions.

But the flip side was she would have to allow Don to do the same and she knew she could never, ever let him. She'd already warned him if he ever strayed, she'd snip his testicles off with nail scissors.

What on earth was she doing messing around with Chris? For one thing, he was Susan's partner, Bella's immediate boss, and she'd always made it a rule not to sleep with the people she worked with. Even if she was single. *I'm not single*, she reminded herself sternly.

Chapter Four

All the way home, she thought about her ovulating eggs. The weekend was going to be one long 1960s style love-in, John Lennon eat your heart out. It was time to think about Don, and Don alone . . . being in love with Don, having Don's baby.

Chris was a donut on a passing sweet trolley and she was *not* going to eat him. She was going to say No Thank You, I don't think I'll have dessert today . . . or ever again.

It was a baby she wanted now. *Baby*, baby, think baby thoughts. No more sexual hedonism, unless it's with that lovely man wearing your ring on his fourth finger.

Dashing through the supermarket that evening, she'd felt almost out of control when she saw babies and toddlers bundled into trolley seats. She was overwhelmed with the desire to pick them up and squeeze them, push ripe banana into their adorable chubby little hands.

This was becoming weird. Here she was buttoned into her expensive designer suit, zipping home in her successful career girl car, but in the depths of her butter-soft, hideously extravagant leather briefcase was the ovulation predictor kit she was now organizing her life around.

A future without a child now seemed utterly unbearable.

But nothing went to plan and by Sunday she was furious. She was left pacing up and down the flat, barely knowing what to do with herself. Over on the windowsill of the large, airy sitting room she saw her cigarette packet. Only three left, damn.

So much for a love-in. The weekend had been a complete disaster. On Friday evening Don had gone on one of his legendary marathon drinking bouts and there was nothing she could say, shout or even scream down the mobile at him to make him come home.

He hadn't staggered in till the early hours of Saturday morning and then he'd spent most of the day asleep. She had been monumentally angry with him and he couldn't really understand why.

They had gone out for dinner on Saturday night, but Bella had spent most of the meal ranting at him for the night before and it wasn't until Sunday morning that they had finally had make-up sex.

They were still in bed when the phone rang and she knew as soon as Don had reached for a pen that he was being sent out on a job. He'd left for Wales soon after, telling her he could be away till the end of the week. She felt powerless, frustrated and furious. She was going to have to wait another whole month before they could try for a baby again.

She threw herself down on to the sofa and lit up. After a few drags, she decided to phone Tania.

It rang for a few moments before Tania picked up, sounding breathless.

'Hello?'

'Tani.'

'Bella!'

'Are you doing anything this afternoon that you can't get out of?'

'Hmm . . . sex?'

'You can get out of that!'

'Depends. How urgent is it?'

'Pretty urgent. I've been abandoned by my husband for the week and I haven't seen you in a towel for ages.'

'Gym it is, then.'

'When can you get there?'

'Three-ish??'

'I love you, Tan.'

'Sod off, I'll see you later.'

'Byeeeee.'

Tania and Bella's usual routine was a gruelling workout in the gym, followed by a swim, a sauna, then a long, gossipy meal with gin and tonics to start and a bottle of wine to follow, which undid all their hard work.

They had been friends since university where Bella had taken one look at Tania, the only other girl in their maths tutorial group, and fallen in love.

Tania was the most glamorous thing 18-year-old Bella had ever seen. She wore tight, short dresses, had masses of highlighted hair, two boyfriends, a French mother, and contact lenses. She smoked Marlboros, giggled in a tinkly, flirtatious way and drove to class in a scarlet, open-top Beetle.

46

Newly out of a feministy all girls school in Oxford, Bella could not have been more different. She wore jeans, Dr Martens and dark jumpers, accessorized with short hair, glasses and about ten pounds of excess puppy fat. She always took the tube and was virginally single.

Bella had assumed there was absolutely no hope of Tania ever talking to her, let alone becoming a friend. But she'd been wrong. Tania was, like the rest of the class, in awe of Bella's freaky maths genius and determined to get to know her better. Underneath the dweeby, spec-wearing exterior, Tania found Bella a surprisingly funny, upbeat, ambitious kind of girl – ripe for a makeover and had seen her as something of a project.

Tania had taken her to the gym, the hairdresser and even out shopping with her impossibly chic mother, Valerie. Bella still followed Valerie's make-up advice: 'Always Chanel darlings, anything else *rrrruins* the skin – and take it off with cleanser, not this terrible soap.'

By the time Bella left university she was slimmer than Tania, had longer hair, eyes which had been surgically corrected and was madly in love with Daniel, her boyfriend of two years. She also knew exactly where she was going next – straight into a graduate traineeship with Laurence and Co.

Her own parents had been horrified at the transformation, especially her mother. Celia Browning, the wife of an Oxford professor, had put her own academic ambitions on hold to have children. She had settled on a career teaching maths at a very good school but had always felt disappointed with her choice, especially as she'd only managed to have one child and she'd had to watch her husband's stellar academic career from the sidelines.

What she'd always wanted for Bella, who had even more ability than her, was the prestigious university path she'd turned down. But Bella had deserted that for a job in the City! The City! Where you didn't even need a maths O Level to get on. It still made her feel physically ill. No matter how hard she tried to analyse it, she basically didn't understand Bella, had no idea why her gifted daughter had wanted this sort of career. She thought it deeply unsettling that Bella worked shoulder to shoulder with the City sharks, squeezing companies and having people sacked, all in the pursuit of a vastly inflated salary.

She understood Bella's fascination with herself even less, although Celia never mentioned this now. Her daughter's long hair, painted nails, high shoes and short skirts made such a mockery of all the ideals she had tried to instil in her.

Their one argument about this had gone very badly, because Bella had been furious enough to bring up the G-strings. One afternoon when she was about 13 years old, Bella had been poking about in her parents' wardrobes trying on jumpers and jackets. There was never anything sparkly or fun to be found in her mother's side of the cupboards, just grey, black and beige knitted separates and trouser suits. Her schoolmarmish mum had the plainest, frumpiest taste in the world.

Bella had put on one of her father's tweed jackets, turned up the collars, stuck her hands in the pockets and pulled out a pair of pale pink G-strings. On closer examination, she saw they were stretch cotton and unwashed. They were nothing like the sensible white Sloggi briefs her mother kept in the underwear drawer.

With rather stunning naivety, she'd actually shown them to her mother, laughing and teasing her about how uncomfortable they must be.

Celia had snatched the knickers out of her hands and in a shaking voice demanded to know where Bella had found them. When Bella said in her father's jacket pocket, her mother had turned white and without the need for another word, Bella had received her very first painful lesson in her father's fondness for fucking his poetry students.

So, years later, when Bella and her mother had argued furiously about the rights and wrongs of dressing to impress the boys, Bella had of course been angry enough to bring up the G-string incident, telling her mother that if she'd tried a bit harder, maybe her dad wouldn't have looked elsewhere.

It had been an unforgivable thing to say, she'd known that as soon as she'd said it. Her weeping mother had accepted her apology but Bella knew she'd done something she couldn't take back.

Neither of Bella's parents had yet reconciled themselves to her whirlwind marriage to a forty-something tabloid journalist. They had argued and argued against it, racking up monster bills on the telephone from their retirement villa in Italy. They had not come to the wedding, had refused to meet Don, and Bella had not seen them since, although once a month or so they spoke awkwardly on the phone and Bella e-mailed them a little more often than that.

It had not helped Don's case that her father had once ended up in the Sunday tabloids after a disciplinary hearing about an 'improper' relationship with a student. 'Professor Perv' they'd labelled him, of course. And how Celia had rallied to the cause, standing by her man and claiming it was all untrue.

Her father had moved sideways into a different department, just for a term, and once the fuss had died down, Celia had suffered a very quiet nervous breakdown and gone into therapy, which had lasted for years. It was her dad who'd fucked around, but her mother was labelled 'the problem'. The injustice of this still enraged Bella.

So, when she'd moved to London and discovered Tania and a whole new way of life, she'd cheerfully stuck two fingers up to her supposedly liberal-intellectual upbringing and decided to rebel.

After their gym session, Bella and Tania went back to Tania's new flat. All her friend's fussing over paint shades and curtain fabric made Bella realize how much she wanted to have a home of her own. How did she get to be so old without ever owning property, she wondered?

She didn't exactly envy Tania her love life, though. Bella made the mistake of admiring an exquisite gold and diamond bangle Tania was wearing and Tania dissolved into tears.

'What's the matter?' Bella asked, putting an arm round her shoulder.

'Oh darling. It's bloody Greg. This must be about

50

the fifth time he's brought home a pale blue box from Tiffany's and I've thought "Thank you God, he's finally going to propose" ... only to open it and find a bracelet, a brooch, a necklace ... any bloody piece of jewellery you like, apart from a ring.'

'Does he know you want to get married?' Bella felt she had to ask the obvious.

'Well, it's not just something you come out with, is it? I bloody well want to be asked. I don't want to propose to him. It should be damn well obvious I want to marry him. Otherwise, why would I still be with him?'

'Maybe he thinks you're happy not being married. I mean you're not even living together,' Bella said.

'He's the one who insists we have our own flats. He says it's a better investment and he only lives around the corner from this place. That's why I moved.'

There was a pause, then Tania quickly wiped her eyes and tried very hard to stem the flow of tears.

'God, I'm sorry. I hate sounding like some sad woman obsessed with getting a ring on my finger like you used to be,' she joked.

'No I did not,' Bella replied. 'I never wanted to get married at all. It was Don who insisted . . .' *Shut up, shut up, you're not helping*, she told herself.

Spookily Greg and Don were the same age. She'd always wondered if Tania hadn't been in search of a Don of her own when she found Greg. But whereas Don was a free-thinking, rolling stone, rebel 41, Greg was a bloody boring, banking, masses of personal finance plans 41. Maybe Tania craved the security, but he didn't seem to give her that either, and it was weird the way he wasn't even hinting at marriage. Men like him were usually desperate to get all traditional and settle down.

'Let's talk about work,' Tania broke the silence. 'I'm brilliant at work, you know. In fact, I have a client who's looking for a good consultant, I must give you his number.'

Bella got a very good idea of how well Tania's PR company was going when Tania named the client. Hugely impressed, Bella passed the information on to Chris when he came back to the office on Wednesday.

'You realize we're going to be late tonight?' Chris said, as he headed back to his room. 'They need those proposals stitched up by start of play tomorrow.'

'Yeah, it's no problem, I've nothing else planned,' she told him, thinking that it would be their first time alone together since the night in the taxi.

By 8 p.m. everyone else had gone out and Chris asked her to set out papers and plans on the big table in the communal office space while he finished off some other work in his office. She was leaning over to study one of the charts when he came out and walked over to stand right beside her. She didn't look round, but felt the hairs on the back of her neck move.

'I do remember exactly how the office night out ended, you know, and I suspect that you do too,' he said in a low voice. 'I just need to know how you feel, Bella.'

She turned then and looked into the dark eyes riveted on her and somehow the words 'Chris,

I'm married' just did not want to come out.

She parted her lips to say something, but Chris had already moved in and they were kissing, then biting, grabbing at each other, teeth banging together.

Chris broke off from her lips to suck at her neck then moved down, pulling open her blouse buttons. He pushed up against her so she was wedged tightly between his hard-on and the edge of the table.

He was pressing his hips into hers and she was on fire. The blood pounding in her ears overruled every sane objection. She closed her eyes, felt for his belt buckle and could only think about the thrill of having frenzied sex on the office table.

An incredible rush was starting to take hold of her. She gripped the warm skin under his shirt and moved against his erection. 'Oh God,' she heard herself whisper. She could feel nothing but adrenalin surging through her veins, she was that junkie finally giving in.

She unzipped him and put her hand inside, hearing him groan. His hands were under her skirt now, rubbing the skin at the very top of her thighs while he kissed and licked at her mouth.

Her heels lifted off the floor as he slid his fingers under her knickers and moved them around, feeling how wet she was. She was so turned on, she could barely breathe.

As his finger ran up and down her clitoris, she kissed him and tasted coffee. Dizzy with pleasure, she let him lift her onto the table and pull up her skirt.

'Is this OK?' he whispered, pulling her knickers

to one side as he pushed his warm cock up close.

'Oh yeah, yeah,' she murmured and then heard the unmistakable ping of the lift doors opening in the hall. SHIT.

They jumped apart, hurtling back to reality, and scrambled to sort out their clothes as Susan walked in.

Shit, shit, mega shit. Susan must have guessed. How could she have missed it? The two of them must have looked like startled rabbits. SHIT.

However, Susan gave nothing away, she simply said: 'Hello, working hard I hope?' and went into her office, but pointedly left the door ajar.

There was nothing Chris and Bella could do apart from shakily get down to work again. Several hours later, when Chris was on the phone, Bella took the chance to slip out.

The cool night air hit her like a slap in the face. What the fuck am I doing??? Fuck, fuck, almost completely fucked, she thought. Opening the low door of her sleek little car, she flung in her bags before scrambling in, then slammed the door shut and shouted at herself: '*Bella*, you slut. You totally idiotic slut.'

The reality of the situation was beginning to sink in. She had just cheated on Don. Why? What for? A few minutes of tabletop action with one of her *bosses*. Thank God Susan had walked in.

She fired up her engine but for a moment could only see blur in front of her eyes before tears spilled down her cheeks. She was the worst person in the world. 'What is the matter with me? Am I out of my mind?'

Her mobile began to ring, she picked it up and

54

saw the call was from the office. She switched it off and sped out of the car park before Chris could catch up with her.

Somehow by the time she put her trainers on and started pounding the pavement early the next morning, the situation did not seem nearly so gruesome. OK she had come within a hair's breadth of an enormous, big-time, major mistake, but she hadn't had sex with Chris, quite, and now she knew she absolutely should not, *no way*. She was married, committed, trying to get pregnant for God's sake, and anyway, Chris was a boss. It was totally against the rules.

When she got into work, there was of course an e-mail waiting for her.

Bella, I'm out of the office all day today and tomorrow, but could we talk? Is there any chance of meeting for a quick drink tonight? Chris

She was going to have to nip this straight in the bud . . . but very nicely. She opened a new file and started typing.

Chris, what can I say? That was a lot of fun, totally unexpected. But I feel really bad today. Really bad. I'm married. And I'm sorry if I've made you think, well, what can I say?

I love working with you and I would hate to have spoiled that. Can we possibly put last night behind us and be 'just good friends' again? I'll meet you tonight if it would help, but I don't want to give you the wrong idea. Bella.

55

Just minutes after she had hit send, the inbox flashed. She felt a flicker of nervousness as she opened the file. Chris was her boss, after all and she was blowing him out big time.

Friends????? Oh. OK.

I am a bit hurt.

But you are being very sensible. Forget tonight, I'll see you soon.

She sent back a simple 'thanks' and crossed her fingers that things were going to be OK, then she got down to the only thing that would take her mind off all this madness. Work.

Don came home close to midnight on Friday. His story had finally come off and was splashing in the paper tomorrow, so he was in a fantastically good mood. She met him at the front door showered, wrapped up in her silk robe and smelling delicious.

'Hello, fantasy wife,' he said giving her as much of a hug as he could without squashing his armful of goodies.

'Hi, I've missed you loads,' she said, feeling the stab of guilt hit her right on the breastbone.

'This is for us.' He waved a champagne bottle.

'This is for me.' He jiggled his takeaway bag.

'And these are for you.' He held out a scruffy bunch of petrol station roses.

'Thank you. These are for you,' she laughed and pulled open her gown to flash her breasts at him.

He plonked everything down on the floor and moved in for a proper kiss.

After a few moments, he broke away saying, 'It's no use, Bella, I am going to have to eat first, I'm absolutely starving.'

He ate the takeaway in bed, drinking champagne with her and telling her the week's adventures. When he'd finished, he leaned over, kissed her on the forehead and apologized for the weekend before.

'Don, I've already forgotten about it.' He had nothing to apologize for compared with her. But in her experience, unprompted confessions were always a mistake.

'You're so self-contained and self-sufficient,' he said. 'I sometimes forget that you might want me around more. I'm not going to dare suggest that you might "need" me around.'

'Of course I need you,' she said, wrapping herself around him. 'We all need to be loved and held and brought to incredible sexual climax.'

He smiled broadly. Putting the foil dishes on the floor, he said: 'OK, can we start making up now?'

Her dressing gown slid down over her shoulders as he kissed and touched her slowly.

She helped him out of his clothes until they were curled up naked together on the bed where they made love tenderly, looking deep into each other's eyes and Bella realized how much she loved him. What the hell had she been doing? This was where she belonged. Don was her real life action hero, he went to war zones, had even resuscitated someone from a heart attack, for God's sake. Next to Don, most other men seemed pretty tame. Her infatuation with Chris suddenly made her want to laugh.

She also saw that it was crazy to be trying to get

57

pregnant without Don knowing. They needed to figure this out together, they needed to buy a house and anyway, work was about to get very busy again. Two major new clients had been taken on and she was going to be doing at least one of the restructurings herself for the first time.

The next day Bella went into town and bashed her credit card buying a scarily expensive new work suit, just to underline her new resolve.

Chapter Five

It came as something of a shock when she double-checked her dates and there was no doubt about it: her period was five days late.

At lunchtime she slunk out to Boots and bought The Test, feeling rising panic as she handed over the cash and stuffed the box into her briefcase.

By 6 p.m. she couldn't stand the tension any longer, so she e-mailed round the office that she had drinks with a prospective client, and left.

She rushed back with the test burning a hole in her bag all the way home. By the time she finally made it through the door she was so desperate to get this over with that she went straight into the bathroom.

She dumped her briefcase and laptop on the floor, then fished out the Boots bag.

OK, pee on stick, watch result come up one minute later. Not exactly rocket science, then.

So, once the stick was peed on, should she sit watching it for a minute or turn it over and wait? She went with turning it over. She looked at her watch: no second hand, she would have to count.

Suddenly she felt unable to breathe, let alone count. She stood up, pulled up her knickers, smoothed down her skirt and jacket and hung her coat up on the bathroom hook.

Hell, it must be time by now.

As she put her fingers on the stick, she noticed that her hands were trembling. She turned it over and there it was, the second thin blue line that meant yes. She was totally shocked.

She slumped back onto the loo seat with the result in her hands and stared and stared at it. Her mind went blank.

She'd thought she'd wanted a baby . . . but did she really? Now? Starting now . . . possibly arriving in nine, God no, eight months' time? And like this? With Don not knowing? Oh God, this did not feel right at all.

Too shocked to cry, she stuffed the test into its box and went to the bedroom where she hid it in a drawer. She could hear her mobile ringing and went to find her briefcase.

'Hello?' she said, trying to sound bright.

'Hi, hon, it's me,' came Don's voice.

'Hello, are you on your way back?'

'Yeah. What shall we do for supper?'

'I don't know, I haven't thought about it.'

'Is there stuff in the fridge?'

'I'll have a look. How's your day been anyway?' she asked, heading for the kitchen.

'Not too bad. You?'

'Yeah, OK. Right . . . chicken breasts, some peppers, onions. I think we have noodles. Would that do?'

'Fine, I'll see you soon then.'

'Byee.'

'Bye.'

Bella was so distracted that evening, Don wondered if she was OK.

'Just tired,' she kept telling him when he asked. But she seemed too fidgety and restless for a tired person. Finally, she said she was taking a bath and going to bed early, but he noticed she took her laptop with her into the bedroom.

Almost an hour later, he went in to check on her and found her propped up in bed, staring at the screen. 'What's up?' he asked gently. 'Is it work?'

'No, no,' she looked up at him with a surprisingly sombre expression, 'I was just e-mailing Jenna . . . you know, my friend in New York, but I don't know, it's not flowing tonight.' She gave a forced smile.

'How is she?' asked Don.

'Very well. She's got a great new job and she's moving to California and it looks as if her man might be moving with her, but she's a bit scared I suppose. She e-mailed me the other day asking about you and marriage and how would she know if, you know, he was The One . . .' Bella trailed off.

'Ah-ha and you're sitting there stuck for words about us?' Don smiled at her. 'Come on, move over, I'm the wordsmith.'

He sat down beside her. Their conversation had lasted just long enough for Bella to have quietly deleted all the soul-searching about the pregnancy she'd written to Jenna.

'OK.' He pulled the computer into his lap and tapped in his rapid two-fingered type: 'How You Know If It's Love' as a heading, then underneath:

61

'You just know. You'll feel it somewhere between your breastbone and your stomach. No individual details matter: looks, height, hair colour, job description – that person makes you happy, gives you a warm glow,' 'No,' he hit delete. 'That sounds like Ready Brek'. 'Gives you security, comfort,' he typed, 'makes you laugh, makes love like it really matters. You'll go the extra mile for them and you know they'll do it for you.'

'Oh, that's so sweet,' Bella said reading over his shoulder.

'Sweet?' He was smiling at her. 'I set out my philosophy of love and all you can say is sweet?'

'Errr . . .'

'You're embarrassed, aren't you? Do you love me even half as much as I love you?' He was still smiling but she detected an undertow of seriousness.

'Of course I do, Don, of course.'

'That's OK then.'

She put her arms round him and kissed him on the mouth, but she couldn't sum up the courage to tell him.

One week later, she still hadn't told him she was pregnant. She was scared. This was going to be a monumentally big thing for him – his life was about to take an entirely different turn than on the route he had mapped out with her. As she lay in bed beside him, she wondered if she really knew him well enough to guess how he would react.

Almost exactly one year ago now, they'd rushed into marriage at the Chelsea register office. It had been a cool wedding with not a shred of the white or traditional about it. Well, there hadn't been time to arrange all that for a start. As soon as she'd said yes, Don had fixed up the first available date at the registrar's, convinced she might change her mind.

She'd worn a long, tight, wine-coloured lace dress with her hair up. Don was in slightly rumpled black linen and somehow ended up carrying the flowers.

There had been just a small crowd – close friends and as few relatives as they could get away with, made easier by the fact her own parents didn't come. Everyone had taxied to Claridges for a monumental lunch, then Don and Bella had sent the guests on their way so they could start their honeymoon.

In their wonderful room, they had filled the enormous bathtub to the brim with hot water and foam and moved in there for hours swigging gloriously expensive champagne out of the bottle, singing love songs and having giggly sex, trying to avoid impaling each other on the taps or causing too disastrous a tidal wave.

It had been so romantic. Lying in the dark now, Bella couldn't help smiling as she cuddled up close to Don listening to him breathe. Everything about him coming into her life had been romantic, interesting and full of fun.

It was such a fluke they had even met. She had been in a crowded, noisy bar with workmates. A bar she'd never been in before and would never have gone back to. As she had tried to spark up her zillionth fag of the evening, her lighter had died.

She'd tugged at the sleeve of the nearest person to ask for a light. It was Don who'd turned around and glanced at her, then held the look with obvious interest.

She'd lifted her cigarette, raised her eyebrows and said: 'Light?'

His reply, with just a hint of melting Scottish burr, was: 'I knew one day I'd regret not being a smoker.'

She had smiled wide and warm and they had looked each other over approvingly.

'Too bad,' she'd said. 'D'you want to buy me a drink instead?'

'Yes, please,' he'd answered, 'Why didn't I think of that first?'

She'd been unable to stop herself from adding archly: 'It's OK. Most girls don't like a man who's always first.'

They had stood at the bar and talked while the attraction between them built up to bonfire level.

He was clearly gorgeous, intelligent, very interested, ringless. His hand had been round her waist before they had finished their first drink together. She had immediately liked everything about him. He was tall, in a nice suit but he made it look casual with his unbuttoned shirt collar revealing a beaten-up white T-shirt. She'd noticed his clumpy crêpe-soled boots and black plastic diving watch.

He seemed so relaxed and refreshingly individual – a journalist, not another financial clone. She could tell he was way old, in his forties, but it made him more interesting. She'd liked his face, comfortably worn in and full of character. His humour was dark and cynical but he seemed to like her upbeat optimism and she'd never met a man

64

who could quote Machiavelli and Woody Allen back at her.

'God, aren't you a bit young to be a fascist?' he'd asked her with a grin.

'But I'm so attracted to the style, you know, polished leather boots, white marble, geometrically perfect haircuts,' she'd shot back.

They'd looked at each other, laughed and almost kissed right then, but both their mobile phones had gone off at once.

'Whooo . . . synchronicity,' Don had said before answering.

'So what do you do?' she remembered him asking and when she'd answered 'Management consultant', he'd looked utterly appalled.

'Oh God,' he'd said. 'You are quite the City girl, aren't you? So you get paid stacks of money by the big boys to go in and sack people?'

'*Hey!*' she'd rounded on him. 'Just a minute. I've turned loads of companies around that would have gone under costing everyone their jobs. And anyway, I only work for medium-sized finance companies and I have a lot of principles, thank you. What about you? Mr Supposedly Free-Thinking Rebel, you work for Totally Evil Global News Inc!!' she teased. 'And I bet you wear Levi's and Nikes, and look, you're drinking Budweiser and probably do Starbucks three times a day so, hey! Don't talk to me about selling my soul to the big corporations.'

'OK.' He was startled now and pulled a frightened face at her to make her laugh, but it didn't work.

'God,' she'd continued angrily: 'Why do people get so Luddite about big businesses? They're just

65

made up of people, people with mortgages and families and ideas. And if you don't get big companies to change and treat their employees well and not devastate the environment, where do you start?'

'Sorry . . . I'm surprised you've given this so much thought,' he'd said, then wished he hadn't when she answered: 'Why? Because I'm a well-paid girlie??'

'Look I'm impressed . . . it's OK. God, you don't drink Starbucks?' He'd tried to lighten the tone.

'*No.* I make my own coffee!'

'At work?'

'Yeah.'

'I'm very impressed. And you don't wear trainers?'

'No, well, unless they're made in the EU – *don't laugh*! The people who made these shoes,' she'd held out her foot, showing off high-heeled mock snakeskin, 'are entitled to sick pay, trade union membership, a year's maternity leave . . .'

'Ah, but what about the tobacco growers?' he cut in, pointing at her cigarette.

'Well . . . OK, you have spotted my Achilles' heel there. I mean I've tried the ethical, additive-free ones but, just not the same.' She'd taken a hefty drag and smiled at him. He was lovely.

After their final drink, she'd decided to throw to the wind all her advice to herself to stay off men for a while and had asked him: 'So Starbucks drinker, would you like to try my coffee? Very strong espresso, keeps you up all night.'

'Yes please,' he'd said and steered her out of the bar.

They'd kissed for the first time on the pavement outside, then over and over in the back of the cab. She'd been so turned on, she'd found it difficult to unlock the door to her flat. When she finally got it open, they had rushed in and were eating each other up in the hallway, throwing coats, bags and jackets to the floor.

Then Don had slowed down to kiss her with surprising tenderness. Gently he had unbuttoned her blouse and slid her bra straps over her shoulders so he could kiss her nipples. They had made love for the first time standing up in the hall. It was incredibly passionate and yet went so smoothly.

For once she'd been wearing a skirt which wasn't too tight to hitch up, and Don had braces on so his trousers didn't fall down round his ankles.

It could still make her pulse rise if she thought about how helpless, how loose-kneed with lust she'd felt when he had moved a finger expertly between her legs to feel for her clitoris for the very first time.

It was his relaxed assuredness, his complete confidence in himself that she found the most incredible turn-on. He even had a condom on him which he had taken out of his wallet, murmuring 'You must think I'm such a slut' into her ear. And every hair from her ear lobe to her shoulder blade had pricked up with pleasure.

'Likewise,' she'd whispered back, closing her eyes, leaning back, impatient to be kissed fiercely, penetrated, pushed up hard against the wall by such a good-looking, virile man.

He'd lifted her just slightly onto her tiptoes to

take him inside. And as he'd entered her for the first time, she'd let out a sigh of pleasure. For a moment she didn't know what the sensation was, then she realized that he was a breathtakingly perfect fit.

He'd whispered, 'God this feels so right. You're incredible.'

Throughout that fantastic first fuck, in which they had come almost together, she had allowed herself to think the forbidden thought – that she had finally found her match.

Don had stayed with her for the rest of the weekend and had teased her relentlessly about her bare flat.

'There is nothing here, have you just moved in?' he'd asked, looking round on Saturday morning and taking in the sitting room furnished only with a sofa, TV, side table and stack of pink *FT*s and business books.

It was a lovely flat though, two big rooms, large floor to ceiling windows, a galley kitchen, bathroom and a tiny roof terrace.

'Well, five months ago. I'm not here much,' she'd said defensively, knowing he was guessing at her astronomical rent.

'Nope, you're not.' He'd opened her fridge. 'Is that it?!' he'd asked, seeing just yoghurt and oranges.

'I suppose I eat out lots or take away. I'm a complete workaholic, you should know that about me,' she'd answered.

'Should I?' he'd said wrapping his arms around her and gathering her up in a sexy, protective way. 'You mean, if we're going to take this any further.' He'd smiled at her.

'How much further is there to go?' she'd teased back.

He'd answered: 'Oh a lot. A lot further. I really like you.' And she'd felt deliriously happy.

They spent the rest of the weekend talking and talking, in cafés, in bars, in the park, in bed – in between the marathon sex sessions – and both of them felt an amazing connection.

It wasn't that sort of cliché-d liking all the same things, but a fascination for how different they were. Grown-up, cynical rebel versus young, go-ahead, corporate girl. He wasn't at all interested in money, which intrigued her because she aspired to being fantastically rich, which in turn intrigued him. He adored his mother, she . . . well it was complicated. He'd left school at 16, she'd been steeped in over-education since the day she was born.

They were so interested in each other it had felt as if they couldn't ever know enough. A lifetime of talking wouldn't be enough. But when Sunday night finally arrived and Don said he would have to go back to his flat and get ready for the week, she'd had a flicker of doubt. Could this really happen? Would he call? Would they ever see each other again?

Just as she'd prepared to face the melancholy of a Sunday night alone after two unbelievable days like this, he'd said: 'Why don't you come with me? Pack your overnight bag and drive me down.'

She'd flung her work clothes into a holdall before he could change his mind.

Of course he'd been *über*-impressed with her car. 'They don't cost that much,' she'd admitted straight away. 'And I got quite a bit of money on my 21st.' Aaargh. Too late.

'You still have your 21st birthday present?' He'd sounded shocked,' Oh my God, I'm dating a child.'

Oh yes, dear reader, it was only day two and he distinctly said 'dating'. Now it was her turn to be shocked.

'Cars are very important,' she'd told him as they'd pulled out into the road and she'd recovered the power of speech.

'Why?'

'They're like clothes – the outward expression of our inner desires and aspirations.'

'And I thought they were quite a good way to get around.'

'Yeah, right. And let me guess exactly which type of large, chunky off-roader you drive, my friend.'

He was really surprised now.

'See! I'm always right. Some people can guess star signs. I can guess cars. I'm seeing large, dark colour, mega-horsepower, very thirsty jeep-type. I'll go for the classic Cherokee.'

'I must have told you that!'

'You did not!' she was mock indignant now.

Of course, his flat had been the opposite of hers: a low-ceilinged dark basement, crammed full. Every wall was lined with bookcases stuffed not just with books but with old cameras, mini tape recorders, PC disks, candle ends, ornaments, light bulbs, mugs filled with pens, photos, framed and unframed, socks! Jesus, not even her cleaner could help him now, he needed a feng shui expert or maybe a skip.

But it wasn't grubby, thankfully. Doing the

70

guided tour, he'd showed her his room and she'd seen clean white sheets. In the contrastingly spartan bathroom there was evidence that someone had done all the essential cleaning jobs not too long ago.

She admired his hardware – top of the range stereo, widescreen TV and two very sleek computers, 'One's from the office,' he'd explained.

He had made her tea in a patterned china teapot with loose leaves and it was really good, even though she only ever drank coffee. Then he got out an ancient-looking bottle of whisky and they cuddled up on his shabby sofa, with a worn tartan rug flung over it, and got mellow-drunk together.

She'd sat up to light a cigarette and moved to face him, cross-legged, as she smoked it.

'So, what are you like? What do you like to do?' he'd asked.

'Hey big scary journalist,' she'd teased. 'Is this your standard prospective girlfriend interview?'

'Maybe . . .' he'd smiled.

'OK, let me think . . . I mainly work. I love my job. If I'm not working I'm either out eating, drinking or smoking. I go gym-ing or shopping to relax. I used to spend a lot of my spare time having sex with unfamiliar people in unfamiliar places. But I'm trying to cure that habit and apart from the occasional relapse . . .' they'd both laughed, 'I now spend a lot more time reading. Newspapers – but not yours – business books, books from the dodgy "Mind, body, spirit" section. Why am I telling you this?' They'd laughed again.

'I'm not going to pretend I go to the theatre or art shows,' she added. 'Who has time to do that

71

in London? Just tourists and the unemployed.'

'Heretic!' he'd said.

'God . . . I'm always so disappointed by the theatre and postmodern art, or post-postmodern or whatever the hell it is these days, don't get me started!'

'Why do people your age always make me feel so young?' Don had asked. 'You're so grown-up and sensible. I bet you have investments.'

'We didn't all have the luxury of growing up in an economic boom, you know, when teenagers like you could just grow your hair and head off into the sunset in sandals,' she'd said.

When he laughed at this, she'd asked: 'Did anyone you knew at school have their family home repossessed? Didn't think so.'

There was a pause and Bella had changed the subject, not wanting to dwell on how much older he was. 'How long have you owned this place?'

'I've been here two years. I rent it, actually, from a mate.' That had surprised her.

'It's a bit of a hole,' he'd added. 'Damp, the odd mouse, not very warm in the winter. I think I'll move in with you.' This was meant as a joke but they'd looked at each other and just knew it was going to happen.

When she'd reached up to kiss him, he'd responded so passionately that within moments they'd been fumbling with each other's clothes desperate to make love again. And the sex was so good, it was almost a disappointment when it was over and they were too played-out to do it again. Later, she'd told him they should take two weeks to think about it. He'd said she was being wonderfully

72

sensible and that was what he loved about her. The L-word within 48 hours!

Two weeks later he'd moved in – minus most of his stuff. That had been her other condition.

As Bella lay in bed, remembering their first weekend together and the wedding, she knew Don loved her, would love her no matter what. She wondered why she had been so nervous of telling him about the baby. It was time for him to know. She'd tell him tomorrow, on their wedding anniversary.

The next evening, 10 October, they went out for dinner at the restaurant they'd been to on their first proper night out.

Bella decided to wait until she was a couple of glasses of wine down before breaking the news. But then the starters came and she thought she'd hang on a bit longer. Once the waiter had cleared their plates, she took a few more hefty swigs from her glass and brought her cigarettes out of her handbag to steady her nerves.

'You're not going to smoke now, are you?' Don asked with a frown. 'We're in the middle of our meal.'

'Don, we're between courses. Please don't nag. I've had a very long day and I'm just trying to unwind.'

'It's just so anti-social.'

'Oh shut up, will you. I never vowed to give up smoking when I married you, so stop nagging.'

Silence. Oh bloody great, thought Bella, why don't I just start a row? That'll really create the right atmosphere for a pregnancy announcement.

'I'm sorry, Don. Let's talk about something else.'

She took a last long drag and stubbed her cigarette out in the ashtray. 'What do you think about buying a house together?' she asked.

'I think it's a great idea,' he said then reached over and took her hand. 'I know I've always said I was happy renting and I didn't want all the baggage of owning a place, but now I think it would be really nice. I'd like us to have a home.'

'Oh, that's so sweet,' she said.

'I know. Sickly,' he smiled.

She could feel her eyes start to swim. She took a breath and was on the verge ... but the waiter interrupted the moment by arriving with their food.

There was silence between them as they ate the first mouthfuls.

'Delicious,' said Bella.

'Brilliant,' Don agreed with his mouth full.

After another long pause, Don looked up at her and asked: 'Is there a problem at work? You seem really tense tonight.'

'Umm ... no,' she answered. 'It's something else.'

She looked up at him and tried to sound calm: 'There's something I've got to tell you. I'm sorry I haven't told you before, but I've been really worried about how you would take it.'

'OK ...' he was smiling at her, wondering why she looked so deadly serious.

'You've reached the limit on your credit card,' he said, still smiling, then when she didn't laugh, added: 'It can't be that bad. This is me you're talking to, I'm sure we can handle it.'

'Well ...' This was it. She took a deep breath then blurted out: 'I'm pretty sure I'm pregnant. No, make that, I am pregnant.'

74

Nothing but absolute, expressionless silence from Don. Whole minutes seemed to go by, then he said in a quiet voice: 'Christ Almighty. Do you want to keep it?'

Of all the replies she'd anticipated, this had not been one of them.

They sat there motionless, staring at each other, and Bella realized she was close to tears. She asked in a raised voice: 'How could you ask that? Of course I do.'

In confusion, she stood up to leave but Don grabbed her by the wrist and pulled her down into her seat again. He was shouting at her too, but in a sort of whisper: 'Jesus, how do you expect me to react? I can't believe it. How did it happen? I thought you were on the pill.'

She didn't say anything, so he want on: 'I just asked that because you looked so unhappy. I thought you were going to tell me you wanted to . . . terminate. You've always said you didn't want children. You're mad about your job and everything. I mean, have you really thought about what a baby will mean?'

She couldn't bear to hear this any more. She wrenched her wrist free and stood up, hissing at him, 'Yes I have, Don. Yes, it's a surprise but I was beginning to think it was a good one. I'm sorry you don't feel the same way. Fuck . . .'

She picked up her bag and headed for the coat check, trying not to stumble in the blur of tears.

A little later, the waiter went over to the table. He picked up Don's empty plate and Bella's cold, almost untouched one. 'She didn't like it?' he asked with a sympathetic smile.

'No, she didn't like it one little bit,' Don answered. 'I think I'll have a large whisky, please.'

'Of course, sir.'

As he sat in the restaurant drinking, still in a state of considerable shock, Bella was in the back of a taxi. She didn't really want to go home, but she couldn't think of anywhere else she wanted to go either.

Just as the cab approached the flat, she got the driver to pull up outside the wine shop on the corner. She jumped out and went to buy a very expensive bottle of white and 20 Marlboro Lights. She paid with the one credit card in her purse she'd never used before – card number two on Don's account which he made her carry just in case she needed money when all her own cards were maxed – and that made her feel slightly better.

She planned to down a few glasses, have a couple of cigarettes, cry a bit more, then sleep on it. She felt sure Don wouldn't dare approach her again until the morning.

Once she finally fell asleep, she slept for a long time and didn't wake up till late. The bedroom was exactly as she had left it, Don hadn't been in at all. But she could hear the shower running, so he was home.

She lay in bed wondering what they were going to say to each other. She didn't feel angry any more, in fact she felt calm. They were going to work this out: they had to. She tied on her dressing gown and opened the bedroom door. The hall was full of roses, about six enormous bunches of them – red, white, yellow, pink. The sitting room door was open and she could see even more flowers in there.

Roses were crammed into vases, cups, mugs,

teapots, even the kettle. Pink and red carnations had been threaded onto string and pinned to the wall, which looked ridiculous, but she appreciated the sentiment.

Well, kind of. It was a bit cheesy and it did cross her mind to get out the scissors and snip all the heads off to show Don she wasn't going to be mollified by a bunch of flowers, no matter how big. The shower was off now and she decided she might as well go and hear what he had to say first, then decide if the flowers should be decapitated.

Don was standing in the bathroom, dripping wet with a towel round his waist.

As soon as he saw her, he said: 'Sorry, Bella. I'm really sorry. I don't know what else to say.'

'Thank you for the flowers,' she said.

'Oh yes. I had to buy them to get a lift home.'

'What d'you mean?'

'I spent hours walking around town and I got completely lost. I finally met this guy setting up his flower stall and I said I'd buy the lot if he took me and the flowers home. We need more vases, you know.'

She gave a little laugh at this.

Then he added: 'I was walking all night thinking about you and us and . . . a baby.' He moved to put his wet arms around her. 'And I still can't get my head round it.'

That didn't sound good. She waited, wondering if he was going to say anything else.

'I still think of myself as young with so much to do before I settle down. The reality is, I'm going to be 42 next year, I'm married and I'm going to be a father. That's quite a shock.'

'You haven't got the monopoly on being worried, you know,' Bella said.

'I need to think about this.' He put his hand on her hair. 'I mean, I think it's going to be OK. I think it will be fine . . . if you're sure it's what you want.'

'Yeah,' she whispered, 'I think so.'

'Well OK, let's try and get used to the idea.'

'OK, that's fine Don . . . that's fine.' She hugged him tightly.

Chapter Six

She dropped her knees down and stared at a crack in the ceiling, trying to relax as she felt the cold steel go in. How did this whole cervical smear thing start? she wondered. Did women campaign for this? Or did doctors invent them?

God, even root canal work would be better than lying here on an examination couch being terribly polite and civilized as some nurse she'd never met before cranked open her vagina with a speculum and scraped at her with a wooden spatula.

She had finally made it to the doctor's and sitting down on the little chair opposite Dr Wilson's vast desk, she had told him her period was 26 days late and, well, it looked like she was pregnant.

He had looked at her slowly over his glasses obviously trying to decide if she was being funny or merely stupid and said in his usual monotone, 'Hmmm, here's a specimen bottle, shall we check?'

And surprise, surprise, she was definitely still pregnant. About seven weeks, he told her.

Then he weighed and measured her, took her

blood pressure and sat her down for a little 'lifestyle' chat.

She didn't hear anything she didn't already know – fresh fruit and vegetables, moderate exercise, lots of water, folic acid tablets – good. Alcohol, cigarettes, too much stress – bad.

'How much are you smoking a day?' he asked.

'About ten,' she lied.

'Well, you'll have to stop. If you absolutely can't stop, you'll have to cut it to below five. It's very dangerous for the baby, never mind what it's doing to you.'

'Well what about cocaine then?' She felt the mood needed lightening.

He didn't miss a beat, just said, 'We don't recommend it.'

He then asked her which hospital she wanted to go to.

'Hospital?' She was confused.

'For the birth.'

'Oh God. But it's not till next June. Do I have to decide now?'

His reply was a long 'Hmmmmmm.' Followed by: 'No. But it makes it easier for me.'

'Well, you're not the one having the baby, so I'll get back to you on that,' she said, delighted that for once she was going to come out of the doctor's surgery with the upper hand.

But then he had flicked through her notes and said, 'Ah, I see we are due for a smear test. If you let reception know, the nurse will see you in a few minutes.'

The next morning she got up very early to fit in her morning run before going all the way over

80

to Hammersmith for day one at Merris Group.

Merris was her first solo project. She had won the work and Susan had assured her she was ready to handle this contract by herself. Of course she was nervous, make that very nervous, as she pounded along the pavement trying to pump the anxieties out of her system. It was a personal finance company, she reminded herself, her speciality . . . yes, but 'so *old* . . . so *establishment*,' came the little anxious voice. She ran faster to try and blot it out.

It was her job not to be scared, to be confident and absolutely sure of herself otherwise the whole business of advising companies on how to make far-reaching changes just didn't work. Her clients were like wolf packs, they could smell fear a mile off and hunted it down.

After her shower, she donned the armour for battle – serious make-up, a scraped-back bun and her smartest work outfit, white shirt, most expensive black suit, black stockings and high black shoes.

She'd been warned to leave her car behind, because there wasn't much parking space, so she picked up her papers from the stack at the front door and set off down the road to join the throng of cross-town commuters on the tube.

God, she'd forgotten how crowded and warm the trains were even this early in the morning. She took off her coat and managed to squeeze herself into one of the last seats left. Ten minutes later, she was feeling sweaty and nauseous. She put her papers down and closed her eyes, willing the journey to go quickly.

By 8 a.m. she was in Hammersmith feeling

81

unusually dizzy and drained. She could not face the ten-minute walk to the office so hailed a cab. She arrived at the stately-looking building and braced herself for the day ahead.

Come on, Bella, she told herself. Get it together.

Gathering up laptop, briefcase, handbag and coat, she somehow, with a third hand, paid the driver, then clacked up the marble steps and through the revolving door. At reception she announced herself and was told to join the executives upstairs for their breakfast conference.

In the lift she checked herself over in the mirrored wall. She felt queasy and extremely nervous, but thanks to the generous application of cosmetic aid, she looked groomed, professional and moderately beautiful. She took a deep breath and let it out slowly, then the lift pinged open and she headed for the conference room.

Opening the heavy door, she took in a large mahogany-panelled room, an enormous table with twenty or so heads swivelled in her direction and a side buffet heaped with plates of bacon, eggs, kedgeree, fried toast, croissants and steaming pots of coffee.

Nausea rose up in her throat like a hard ball and she broke out in a cold sweat. She could feel beads forming on her top lip and suddenly she knew what this was. Morning sickness. All eyes were fixed upon her and she was rooted to the spot, unable to open her mouth, convinced she was about to throw up on the highly polished parquet floor.

Somehow she managed to swallow the ball down and say: 'Hello everyone. I'm Bella Browning. Where would you like me to sit?'

She wobbled over to her seat while Mr Merris made the introductions. She accepted a cup of tea and as she sipped it she began to feel a tiny bit better. She glanced at the men around the table – all men, all older than her, all definitely thinking, What is this girl going to be able to do for us?

'We'll just run through our usual business first, shall we?' Merris said. 'Give Ms Browning time to get her feet under the table.'

Bella listened carefully, knowing more could be learned about a company in one meeting than in weeks of figure analysis. She easily spotted the people who were good at their job and those who were fudging. Immediately she could tell this was a company dominated by formality and attention to procedure, so she guessed that new ideas, new objectives and goals were needed but were not exactly going to be welcomed with open arms. God, she still felt awful.

When the conference was finally over she was shown to her own small office, where she unpacked her computer and files and made a few calls.

Later on, she managed to get her doctor on the phone but as she'd suspected, he told her it was normal, there was nothing she could take and it would probably wear off in about six weeks or so.

Six weeks!! Six weeks of feeling like this was frightening. And why the hell was it called morning sickness when it seemed to last all day?

She didn't manage to get out of the office until 8 p.m., and day two at Merris got off to an even worse start. She walked into the breakfast conference room and as her gaze fell on the platter of congealing fried eggs, she could barely contain a retch. There was nothing she could do apart from sit down in her chair feeling overwhelmingly sick and weak. When she reached for her teacup, she noticed that her hand was trembling. Even worse, she knew other people had noticed it too.

After conference there was a second long meeting to get through before she could finally hole up in her office. She had barely sat down and lit up a cigarette in the hope of a quick energy buzz when there was a knock at the door and the human resources director, an American called Mitch, appeared and asked if he could come in.

'Yes, of course,' she said and waved him in, fanning smoke around the room. They shook hands and introduced themselves properly then he shut the door behind him, but didn't take up her offer of a seat.

'To be honest,' he said with a serious look, 'I'm here because we're all a bit concerned about you. Forgive me for saying this, but you don't seem very well.'

She suspected she hadn't been hiding it brilliantly. He carried on: 'We do need a consultant, but we need someone who is going to be here for us 110 per cent.'

Bella felt a twinge of irritation now, but carried on listening.

'I'm beginning to wonder if you are the right person for us,' Mitch continued. 'Well, what I mean is, er . . . you seem to have a problem.

'Mitch,' she said, fixing her eyes on him. 'What are you talking about?'

'Well, you've turned up here every morning pale, weak, hands shaking. You only seem to come round after you've been in your office on your own. You know, some of the guys are even hinting at a drink problem.' He gave a brief laugh to distance himself from the suggestion, although it didn't seem *so* far-fetched.

Bella was stunned. It was all she could do to keep her jaw from dropping open. The Merris executives thought that their thousands of pounds a day, A-list consultant was turning up with a hangover and drinking in her office.

There was only one response. She snorted with laughter at Mitch, then added: 'I've never heard anything so ridiculous in my life.'

She put out her cigarette with a single stab and told him: 'I have a perfectly straightforward medical condition I'm not prepared to discuss which will make long tube journeys and greasy breakfasts difficult for a few more weeks. No-one has ever accused me of having a drink problem before and it's certainly not going to start now. I am the most hard-working, 110 per cent person you're ever going to meet. In fact, if you or your colleagues so much as whisper "drink problem" between yourselves again, I'll have you up on a libel charge.'

It was Mitch's turn to look stunned. He realized he was going to have to patch this up pretty quickly.

'Look, er . . .' he fiddled with the knot of his tie, 'I hope you'll accept my apology. Obviously a complete misunderstanding. I'm sure it will be fine for you to come into morning conference a bit later.' He smiled. 'But you should eat something, you know – protein-based breakfast equals better productivity.'

'Oh really!' she said, but he missed her sarcasm.

'Yeah, I thought you'd know that,' he said. 'You're all about improving performance, you should take every little factor on board.'

That was too much.

'How about the fact that people working 12 hours a day, five days a week, tend to under-perform, leave their jobs sooner, take more days off in illness and suffer higher levels of depression,' she shot back at him.

'So, we're in too early for you,' he replied. Ouch, this was getting nasty.

'No,' she answered in a conciliatory tone now. 'I think you all stay too late. From 5 p.m. onwards, hardly anyone in this building does anything constructive. It would probably do you all good to go home to your families.'

'Yes, well . . . that would be nice,' he said with a smile.

'Do you have kids?' she asked because it had recently occurred to her that she didn't know anyone her own age who did.

'Yeah . . . two boys, Mickey five and Joel, three.'

'Nice names,' she said.

'Thank you.'

'I do appreciate the offer of coming in after breakfast. That would work much better for me, thanks,' Bella smiled now.

'Bella,' Mitch smiled back and ran a hand through his sandy hair, 'I don't want us to get off on the wrong foot here. I've looked into the work Prentice and Partners has done recently and you do seem to be able to turn companies around amazingly fast. God knows we need a shake-up, but I have no idea how you'll get this lot to take on anything new.'

'Well, you'll just have to watch and learn.' She arched her eyebrows.

'I look forward to it. Where do you live, by the way?'

'Belsize Park, north London,' she said.

'It's just that Geoff has a driver pick him up from Swiss Cottage every morning, maybe he can collect you en route.'

No more tube. Thank you, God.

The following morning, a sleek black limo pulled up at 7 a.m. A limo! she thought as she climbed in; that will bloody well have to go when the new management plan comes into action.

Geoff, the finance director, was already in the back but fortunately not desperate for conversation. They sat companionably together, reading their *FT*s and passing the odd comment.

On arrival at Merris Group, Geoff went into breakfast while Bella hid in her office for twenty minutes eating yoghurt and drinking water. The sickness was still there, but it was bearable, so for the first time that week she was starting to feel slightly more optimistic about the job ahead of her: turning this dinosaur company around before it became completely extinct.

Later in the day she scrolled through a raft of new e-mails to find a message from Chris:

Darling, how is it going all the way over there in rural Hammersmith? Merris will have to do without your brilliance for a few days because we are off to pitch for work together in Birmingham.

Chris, hello. B'ham?? Really?? I didn't know anything about this. When? Where? Who?

Ah! There you are. Express orders of the boss. Three days of meetings in the next week or so at the wonderful Salwood House Hotel in the country-side. You, me, hard work, fine wines. It's going to be lovely. Client is Bensons. Small finance company over here with a big partner in the States.

OK. Well, phone me next week with the details and I'll sort it out. It better be a good job.

Let's just say if we get this, we'll all be upgrading cars sweetie.

I love my car.

It's so old!!!!!!!!!!!!!!!!!!!!!!

It's a classic. Now go away, some of us have work to do.

Byeeeeee. Looking forward to B'ham.

Oh God, it wasn't exactly hard to work out what he had on his mind . . . and now she had it on her mind as well.

She clicked back to the file she'd been working on and tried to focus.

Chapter Seven

Bella threw herself onto the bed and listened to her heart thudding in her chest. What the hell was she doing? She had wedged a chair under the door handle, not because she was worried that Chris might try and force his way in, but to stop herself from getting out again – well at least not without thinking twice, three times and maybe once again before doing it.

Here she was trapped in luxury, country house hotel splendour with a dark and handsome colleague who was on charm offensive. It was only Wednesday and they were here together until Friday. She didn't trust herself any more; how could she after what had happened?

She had met Chris on the stairs earlier in the evening as they'd come down for dinner. He'd been looking particularly edible in a dark, close-cut suit and fat glossy tie and had leaned over to kiss her on the cheek saying: 'I swear, I'd be soooooo discreet.'

She had answered with a flirtatious laugh and given him the arched eyebrow thing because she didn't want to say 'yes' but still hadn't learned how to say 'no'.

They'd met the clients in the bar and gone through to the dining room where Chris had manoeuvred himself next to her and throughout the exquisite meal had held his hand oh so gently on her leg, running his finger up and down the inside of her thigh, daring to get to the top of her stocking and feel his way along the skin exposed there.

Above the table, she'd been holding her own in a heated financial debate and below, she was considering a red hot invitation. The combination was intoxicating, her conversation was getting faster and more passionate and she was knocking back glass after glass of wine.

After dinner, they'd all retired to the library for brandies, then the clients had gone to hold a phone conference with the American office.

Chris, Bella and another round of drinks were left alone in the quiet room where Bella had sunk back in her leather armchair and was staring into the fire.

'I don't care how long it takes, Bella, I know I'm going to wear you down,' Chris had said to her quietly. 'We could sneak back down here to the fire later on. Imagine the thrill. Someone walking in on two financial superbrains writhing naked on the carpet in unbridled passion.'

She'd laughed, swallowed a sip of brandy, then said, 'It would be against the Code of Conduct, Chris. But would it improve my chances of promotion?'

He'd looked at her, smiling with that soft, expressive mouth: 'Well, if I was a total bastard, I'd say yes. But the truth is, you're probably going to become a partner much sooner than you think. You're a very clever girl.'

'I already know that,' she'd answered.

'And you're bloody sexy as well.'

'Ah ha, I happen to know that too.' She'd drained her glass. 'And use it to full advantage.'

'Can I walk you to your room?' he'd asked and there was no need to guess what he meant.

'Why not?' she'd answered, stepping lightly out of the chair and across the room. She'd walked quickly across the hall and suddenly it had felt like a chase, so she'd run up the huge staircase two steps at a time, hearing Chris start to run after her.

She'd turned down the long corridor and raced for her door, giggling, with Chris belting along close behind her. At the door, she'd turned to face him. They were both breathing hard with effort and excitement.

He'd leaned towards her and they'd started to kiss, just softly on the lips for a moment, then, as she pulled him against her, their mouths had opened hungrily.

She'd pushed her tongue deep, tasting wet warmth and brandy and she'd begun to shudder with the pleasure of it. Her arms were round his waist untucking his shirt, so she could feel the warm, soft skin on his back as he nudged an erection against her and began to unbutton her blouse.

Her eyes closed, she'd leaned her head back and felt him kiss her breasts while her heart pounded almost painfully in her chest and she knew she was very close, very close to the point where it would be impossible to . . .

'Chris, I just can't,' she'd forced herself to say.

'Ssh!' he'd whispered 'Ssh! No, no, no, no . . . You know you don't mean that.'

And he was so right, she didn't mean it. She could, she really could. She just absolutely shouldn't.

'I'm sorry . . . I'm sorry, I do.' She'd said this gently, pulling away from him.

He'd opened his eyes and held her gaze for a long moment, then snapped: 'What is the matter with you? You are going to drive me completely insane.'

Holding her tightly round the waist he looked far too fuckable to turn down, but she had to get a grip: 'I'm sorry, Chris, I'm sorry. I've got to stop doing this. God, I'm married . . . you're my boss. This is ridiculous.'

He hadn't said anything, so she'd added, 'Look, I'm just going to say good night now, I don't want to make things worse.'

His arms had fallen from her waist. 'OK, fine,' he'd said finally. 'Good night it is, then.' He'd turned on his heel and she'd watched him walk down the corridor.

She'd gone into her room where she was lying on the bed now, full of remorse. What is the matter with me? Haven't I messed things up enough already? she thought. She was pregnant, for Christ's sake. Pregnant!! Hello!! Was she completely mad? She wondered if, in the words of Mitch, she needed help.

If she could just be faithful, she'd get to keep Don for ever – it really wasn't such a bad deal, was it?

But the thought of lifelong fidelity scared her. She was like a reformed alcoholic who had to take it one day at a time.

She had been utterly faithful to Daniel, the first love of her life, but he'd broken her heart and since then every man who'd even thought about falling in love with her had been dumped or cheated on. Until Don.

Don had convinced her to take the barriers down and trust him.

But sometimes she wondered if Daniel had taken some non-returnable piece of her heart with him. The scar had healed up nicely but sometimes it ached. It ached for a time when she'd thought love was perfect and unbreakable, not this extremely intricate and complicated machine which needed daily tuning and maintenance or else all kinds of crap was liable to get in there and mess it up.

Christ, she was so tired of always having at least three men in her head – the one she was with, the one she'd left and the one she wanted. It was time to put a little faith in the lovely man she'd married. She'd trusted him, she had to go on trusting him and stop trying to fuck the whole thing up.

It was 1.15 a.m. but she dialled her home number.

'Hello?' came Don's groggy, sleepy voice at the other end of the line.

'Hi, darling,' she said gently. 'Sorry to wake you. I'm really sorry I didn't call you earlier.'

'It's OK,' he said. 'Busy night?'

'Yeah . . . I love you, Don.'

'I love you too. Are you OK?'

'Yeah, I'm fine. I just wanted to hear you. You better go back to sleep.'

They said their goodbyes and rang off. She felt a little better.

The next morning, she woke early and ran, nervous at the prospect of facing Chris again.

Sober grey skirt, pale grey skinny rib jumper and her least frivolous shoes were picked out of her bag. This was definitely a no green signals day. She felt queasy as she went down to breakfast – a mixture of mild morning sickness and nerves.

In the dining room, Chris was already at a table so she went over and said a guarded 'Hello there.'

He smiled back, 'Hello, darling. The scrambled eggs are delicious. Grab some, sit down beside me and tell me what we are going to blind our boys with this morning.'

'Thanks, Chris,' she said. She couldn't help but be grateful for the fact that he was happy to file last night away in the stupid mistake drawer and try to go back to the flirty, matey work relationship they'd had before all this lust started floating to the surface and causing havoc.

The day went well and ended with the two of them in the library together again, but the mood was very different. Surrounded by leather-bound books and wood panelling, Bella felt at ease. Apart from a residual flirtiness, the sexual tension in the air between them had diffused. They were even sitting side by side on the same sofa and it didn't feel dangerous. They were talking work and bitching about the clients.

'They may be brilliant, but they are so dull,' said Bella. 'Their idea of fun is a novelty golf club cover.'

Chris laughed at this, but then turned to her with

a serious face and said, 'Bella, why can't I shake the feeling that you might be the one person in the world who's perfect for me, but I got there too late?'

For a moment she was too surprised to answer, but she realized he was waiting for a reply.

'Erm . . . thank you, that's very nice . . .' she said, 'but I can't be your perfect person, because she'll feel just the same and make herself available no matter what.'

Bella swirled the brandy round in her glass and added: 'I'm married. Liking me is just another symptom of your commitment phobia. I know this because I'm a bit the same.'

'Really?' He was surprised now.

She took a long drag on her cigarette, then said: 'I'm really in love with my husband. He's definitely the best thing that ever happened to me. I want us to have kids, grow old together, the whole thing. But I still haven't got out of the habit of pushing the self-destruct button whenever things are going well.'

She stubbed her butt out into the ashtray to hide her filling eyes and immediately took out another cigarette and lit up again.

'It's OK,' Chris said. 'It never happened, OK? We'll just hit delete. You're happily married with a clear conscience . . . no consequences.'

Bella smiled; it was a nice thought, but the guilt didn't go away quite so easily.

After a long pause, Chris finally said, 'OK, maybe you're right Bella, I'm 34, I've got to sort my life out and find a good woman. And I don't want to be going to her wedding three weeks after I've met her.'

'Ah! I'm sorry . . . I don't know what to say. This is all ridiculously flattering,' she said.

He leaned back with a sigh. 'OK, that's it. I'm going to give up on you, then . . . for the moment anyway.'

Chapter Eight

Bella was sitting in the sauna with Tania. They had managed to drag each other out on this freezing cold, grey December Sunday to get to the gym, and now they were relaxing.

'God, you are filling out, Bella,' Tania said, in the blunt matter-of-fact way that only best friends can get away with. 'Is it all the weights you're doing?'

'No you complete cow, it's because I'm almost four months pregnant.'

Bella was enjoying the look of shock on her friend's face.

'WHAT!!!!!!!!!'

'Yup. I've been absolutely dying to tell you. Don and I are, fingers crossed, going to have a baby. And you better be pleased, because I want you to be godmother.'

'Oh my God. I can't believe it. You and Don . . . Parents!!!' She gave a little shriek, then leaned over to give Bella a big sweaty hug and a kiss.

'That is absolutely amazing. I just can't believe it. You?? Bella, mathematical genius, financial whiz-kid and career girl. You're going to be a mummy.

My God! You're still so young! Bloody hell! What are your plans?'

'Take maternity leave then go back to work.'

'Of course. But it's so brave of you to take on all that extra responsibility. I'm so busy right now, I barely remember to feed my cat.'

'Not helping Tania.'

'God, I'm still in shock. You and Don . . . I can only picture you together in a bar drunk. You're obviously doing a brilliant job of domesticating each other. My God, he's going to be pushing a pram. What does he think about it?'

'He's fine,' Bella answered. 'He's being very mature. I think he's finally realizing he's a grown-up.'

'This is so amazing,' Tania said, 'Where are you having it?'

'I don't know yet.'

'Do you know if it's a girl or a boy?' Tania could barely contain her excitement.

'No, not yet.'

'We'll have to go shopping for gorgeous glamorous maternity clothes for you and cutesy baby things. *Oh my God*, do you know what this means – I'm going to be thinner than you! Yes! Yes! *Yes!*' Tania hugged her again. 'This is going to be so much fun.'

Bella beamed back at her. Tania was taking this much better than expected. Bella had dreaded Tania disapproving or being jealous, or somehow making her feel it would drive a wedge between them.

'Have you told your parents yet?' Tania asked.

'Well no. You're the only person who knows

98

apart from Don, oh and the doctor, obviously.' Shit, she still hadn't rebooked the last cancelled appointment.

'You should tell your mum and dad,' Tania told her.

Bella let out a heavy sigh. 'I know, I know. I'm absolutely dreading it. You know how weird mum is about pregnancies and they still haven't met Don yet. I just don't want to make things worse than they already are.'

'Well, try not to worry about it,' her friend said. 'It will work out, I promise. Grandchildren seem to have this way of resolving all kinds of problems.'

'Ha, well . . . we'll see,' Bella replied.

'Gosh you are looking well. They're obviously taking care of you over at Merris Group.'

This was Susan's idea of a hello when Bella met her for lunch a few days later.

Her boss was obviously desperate to say: Look at the weight you've piled on. Are you eating too many business lunches? Just to make her point, Susan ordered salad. But there was no way Bella could restrain herself, she was permanently starving. She ordered carrot soup with crusty brown bread, then followed with salmon steak, new potatoes drenched in butter and a side salad.

She would have loved to eat dessert too but Susan had looked so horrified at the suggestion, Bella decided to pass.

She had thought a cosy lunch with the boss might have given her the opportunity to break the baby news, but Susan was in a dreadful temper and just wanted to talk shop. She wanted a detailed progress report on Merris Group and then asked Bella about moving over to the Danson's job in the spring, much earlier than planned.

Bella couldn't believe it. How the hell was she to fit maternity leave in? 'I thought Danson's didn't want us in till August at the very earliest?' she asked.

'Well, they've had a rethink,' said Susan. 'They now feel they have the budget to go ahead in May or June. Are you expecting Merris to overrun? Is that the problem?'

Bella tried to fudge it: 'Well, obviously I should be available if Merris doesn't overrun. But you would be best to tell Danson's if they really want me, they should make it August. I suppose I could do some preliminary reports, but get down to it in late July, August. I really want that job, Susan, I worked very hard to get the contract.'

'Merris is never going to run past April. Have you got something else lined up for Spring?' Susan asked sharply.

'Well . . . er . . . there is something I haven't mentioned to you because it is in the very early stages,' she began, but then her courage deserted her 'It's . . . um . . . someone I'm trying to woo over to us and they already have consultants booked in for May/June, so I'm trying to pinch that slot.' She willed herself to shut up, she was making this worse.

'So who's that then?' Susan looked interested.

'Well, I'd rather not say.' For a dangerous moment, Bella thought Susan was going to press the point but instead she dismissed the subject with: 'Well, OK, I'm sure you'll tell me when necessary.'

How right she was.

Susan snapped shut her dinky laptop and flicked her Amex onto the table to pay the bill.

'You're a very able consultant, Bella. You are going to be one of the best. I don't want to lose you. If anyone makes you any offers, please come and talk to me first. In the meantime, you're getting a healthy raise come January and I promise you won't be disappointed with your Christmas bonus.'

Bloody hell, thought Bella. 'Thanks Susan, that means a lot,' she said.

OK, she hadn't told her about the baby, but generally the lunch hadn't gone too badly.

When she got back home that evening, Bella stripped down to her underwear and looked in the mirror. Her breasts were enormous: they were spilling out over the top and sides of her C cups. Her stomach stuck out in an alarming pot belly and her waist had completely disappeared.

She didn't look pregnant, she looked fat and frumpy and she wasn't happy about it at all.

She heard the front door slam. Don was home. 'Bella?' he called.

'I'm in the bedroom.'

'Lucky me.' He stood in the doorway looking at her.

'I'm depressed.' She threw herself down on the bed. 'Look at me, I'm fat all over. My clothes are straining at the seams.'

He flung himself right down beside her.

'Hey, gorgeous,' he said, kissing her mouth

tenderly. 'Look at your cleavage though, it's fantastic.'

He slipped her bra straps down over her shoulder and kissed the tops of her breasts.

'I look fat,' she wailed.

'You look perfect to me and you're doing a great job. You're making a whole new person in there.'

Funny how she hadn't even begun to think of it like that. She wasn't just 'pregnant', she was actually making a baby. It was very weird. She pulled him close and smelled the slightly sweaty, grimy scent of a day's work on him. It was very sexy snogging him when she was naked and he was still dressed in his suit.

'How are you?' she asked.

'Oh, I'm OK, I've got some very nice things I'm going to cook you for supper.'

'Oh yeah. I think your kitchen skills are the sexiest thing about you,' she teased.

'Really . . . well, in that case, I'm going to chop, grate and stir-fry.'

'Oh yeah,' she pretended to pant. 'And what about marinading or casseroling? I'm getting shivers down my spine!'

Her naked body was pressed close up against his and as he tasted his way around her mouth, her hands were undoing his belt. 'What can I do to make you feel better about your lovely body?' he asked.

'Mmmm, I can think of a few things,' she answered.

*　　*　　*

102

On Saturday they went shopping together because she needed new bras to accommodate the increasingly heavy breasts.

Don perched on the little stool inside the changing room with instructions to be quiet. But the sight of his wife slipping in and out of underwear in a semi-public place proved too much to bear. He kept pulling her over, whispering, 'Bella, you have no idea. I'm living out one of my favourite fantasies here.'

For someone hitting 42 next year, he had an impressive sex drive, she thought, looking at the bulge in his trousers.

There she was in the most white and frumpy bra she had ever tried on in her life – welcome to the 'maternity' section – and she suddenly felt the need to thrill Don, to let him know she was still the shockingly sexy girl he'd married.

So she knelt down beside him and unzipped his trousers, freeing the large hard-on inside. Moments later, he came quickly with an impressively quiet gasp.

Bella thought of England and swallowed. Before either of them could say anything, a shop assistant was at the cubicle curtain wanting to know how she was getting on.

As Don fumbled with his zip, Bella stood up and put her head round. 'Haven't you got anything a bit less, well, maternal? These are just hideous,' she said.

The assistant stepped into the cubicle and eyed Don sitting self-consciously in the corner, then she looked at Bella, dressed in a white bra that seemed to stretch from way below her bust all the way up to her collarbone.

'You will need the support over the next few months,' the saleswoman said, adjusting the donkey pannier sized bra cups.

'The breasts get very heavy and if they're not supported, they will droop. We don't recommend underwiring, so you'll have to wear a supportive soft cup.'

'Right,' Bella said, somewhat shaken at the thought of inducing breast droop. 'I'll take two of these monstrosities for day wear then, but I want the nicest, silkiest underwired 34DDs you can find me for special occasions.'

The woman came back with an armful of bright satin and lace. This was more like it.

Bella chose lime green, peach and cappuccino all with matching G-strings, to make up for the horror of the maternity wear.

Don scooped the lot up to take to the till: 'My treat, Bella,' he said, still completely bemused.

Chapter Nine

Bella was in the doctor's waiting room flicking anxiously through old copies of *Tatler*. What for? God knows, she had stacks of files in her bulging briefcase she could be looking through instead. But she was on the verge of being nervous now and she knew she wouldn't be able to concentrate on the finer points of the Merris Group investment return figures.

She was four months pregnant and had been cancelling doctor's appointments almost every week because she had been so busy at work. Finally, overwhelmed with guilt, she'd taken a whole day off to coincide with antenatal day at Dr Wilson's surgery.

But she was fidgety at the amount of time she was wasting.

'Miss Browning,' the receptionist called. 'Dr Wilson is ready for you now.'

She gathered up her handbag and briefcase and strode over to his office, saying 'It's Ms' to the receptionist as she passed.

'Hello, Bella, how are you?' Dr Wilson didn't look up immediately.

'I'm fine, thanks.'

'So . . . Four months pregnant. You're not showing it at all,' he said when he saw her.

'Believe me, my bra is about five sizes bigger and every waistband is straining,' she replied.

'How are you feeling?'

'I'm feeling fine. I'm over the sickness and I feel normal, my usual energetic self.'

'Hmmm,' was his reply. 'OK, you lie on the couch, I'll do a quick examination then I'm going to turn you over to Declan.'

'Who's that?' she said, arranging herself on his couch and lifting her top, so he could feel her stomach.

'Our midwife,' the doctor answered gently squeezing and pressing down on her lower abdomen which felt surprisingly tender.

'Oh right,' she said, wondering why she felt slightly strange at the prospect of a male midwife.

'The midwife will see you now, Mzzzzzzzz Browning,' the receptionist said after Bella had spent another ten long minutes flicking through more magazines in the waiting room then reading all the uplifting notices on the walls: 'How to spot meningitis', 'How to treat a heart attack', 'Saturday appointments are for emergencies only. A cold is not an emergency.'

She opened the door at the end of the corridor and clapped eyes on Declan, who was not at all what she had expected. He was a wiry little elf of a man with short frizzy hair and twinkly eyes.

'Bella Browning. Lovely name,' he said, instantly

revealing which side of the Irish Sea he was born on.

'Hello.' She shook his outstretched hand. 'You don't look nearly old enough for this job.'

'Oh, don't worry, I'm 31. I've been doing this professionally for ten years,' he replied. 'But I actually delivered my first baby when I was 12. Sit down and relax. You're not due for months, so we've plenty of time to get acquainted and go through your options. Now, first of all do you mind explaining exactly what you're doing pitching up here at sixteen weeks, when you should have had a booking appointment with me a month ago?'

'Well, I'm a very busy girl.'

'Yes, you and every other woman who pokes their little Italian shoes into this surgery.' That surprised her. He went on: 'Antenatal care is a serious business, for which you are entitled to official time off work.'

'Yeah, *if* you've told your work you're pregnant and *if* they don't dismiss you on the spot for showing "lack of commitment".' She wondered why this was irritating her so much.

'I'm sure you're aware there are laws against that kind of thing.'

'I'm sure you're aware that there are ways around those laws,' she shot back.

'OK, so let's put a big S for stressed in your book here, shall we?' He turned back the cover of a blue booklet.

'Was the pregnancy planned?' he asked.

'Is that anything to do with you?'

'Look, I'm trying to fill in your maternity book

107

here, this is an official question. You don't have to answer it if you don't want to.'

'Yes, it was planned,' she snapped, still not sure why she felt so angry. She watched him tick the 'yes' box.

They went through the list of questions – age, allergies, illnesses – then he asked if she smoked. To her astonishment, Bella found herself bursting into tears.

When Declan instinctively put an arm round her and asked if she was OK, out it all tumbled – the guilt at telling Don it was an accident, the terrible worry that she would have miscarriage after miscarriage like her mother, not even wanting to tell her mother about the pregnancy because it would upset her. All the fears Bella had not even properly admitted to herself and here she was coughing them out to a complete stranger.

'Have you been pretending to yourself that you're not really pregnant at all?' Declan asked in the kind voice which had made her crack up in the first place.

'Yeah, I suppose so.' She was frantically dabbing at her eyes and trying to stop the tears.

'Smoking too much, because you're so stressed about it?' he asked.

She nodded, starting to weep again.

'Drinking too much?'

She put her head in her hands.

'Look, it's OK.' He patted her back. 'You've got to 16 weeks, that's a really good sign, there's no point worrying about what you've done. But it's time to look after yourself a bit better now. If you can't stop, cut down, OK, and try not to worry about everything so much.'

As she calmed down, they talked about hospitals, screening tests and scans and he rolled up her sleeve to take blood.

When Bella got home that evening, she was determined not to give in to the desire for a drink and ten cigarettes. In the kitchen, she poured an inch of white wine into a tall glass. She swirled it round so it had coated all the sides, then tipped the wine out into the sink. She filled the glass up with ice and soda water and took a sip. Aargh, it was like the ghost of a white wine spritzer, like the drink had died and here she was at its funeral, trying to relive the good times.

But no pain, no gain. She was going to smoke less and drink hardly anything, if it killed her.

Several days later, she was holed up in her tiny office at Merris lost in thought, staring at the graphs on her screen, when her mobile trilled.

She was irritated at the disruption and cursed herself for not putting it onto voicemail.

'Hello.'

'Hello, Bella Browning?'

'This is she.'

'Hello, it's Declan here.'

Her mind was blank. Declan?

'The midwife.'

'Oh yes. Hello, sorry about the other day. I'm really fine, I don't know what . . .' she felt embarrassed.

'Bella, chill out, will you? We need to talk, is now a good time, or should I call back?'

'Now is fine. What is it?'

'We've had the results of your blood tests and I'd like you to come in and discuss them.'

She felt the hairs stand up on the back of her neck.

'Jesus Christ,' she whispered. 'I'm HIV positive.'

'Um, no, I don't think so.' She could hear him turning pages over. 'No, you're not, actually.'

'Oh thank God.' She slumped back in her chair with relief.

'It's the screening test. Look, you really need to come in and see me,' he said.

'Please Declan, just tell me now.'

'Well, it's come back with quite a high possibility . . .' he trailed off, then added, 'I'd really prefer to see you.'

'How high?' she said immediately.

'One in 50 chance of Down's Syndrome.'

'Two per cent? That's small, in fact statistically insignificant,' she replied, trying to convince herself.

'Well, we consider it higher than it should be for your age. There are some steps you can take to check. You can have an amnio or a scan. It would be best if you came in and talked it through.'

'I can't, Declan, we'll have to do this on the phone.' He sounded so serious it was making her scared.

'Well, OK, I'm going to give you my mobile number. I'm on duty tonight anyway, so when you get home and you've put your feet up and chilled out, call me and I'll talk you through it.'

'Thank you.'

'OK, I've got to go now,' he said. 'I'll speak to you later.'

'Bye.' Bella clicked the phone off and looked at

the screen again. The figures were wobbling around and for a moment she couldn't think why. She was about to cry. Quickly she put her head back so the tears wouldn't trail mascara down her cheeks. A 2 per cent chance of Down's Syndrome. What did that mean?

There was a tap at the door, so she pressed her fingers under her eyes to blot the tears away. 'Come in,' she said, hoping she looked normal.

'Hi.' It was Mitch. She waved at the spare seat.

He sat down, then looking at her properly, said, 'Are you OK?'

'Yes, fine. My eyes are tired from looking at the screen all day.'

'No wonder. You are allowed out of here, you know, you can have lunch, you can take your smokes out to the atrium where you will find other, live people.'

'I know. But I have a hell of a lot of work to do. I'm starting to panic I won't get it done in time. I don't want the contract extended.'

'Are things here worse than you expected?'

'I don't know if it would be professional to comment,' she said.

'Can I level with you?' he asked. 'My wife is expecting our third baby in the spring and I'm not a UK resident. If I'm going to need a new job, I want to know so I can start looking now.'

Why was he asking her this? It wasn't fair. It crossed her mind that he was wired up and testing her out for his bosses.

'I really won't know the full situation until I've completed a thorough assessment, then I'll report in detail to the board.'

'Good grief, you sound like a corporate robot. I'm asking you for your opinion.' He looked tired and stressed. He was a nice guy, not the type to get involved with industrial espionage. God, she was getting paranoid.

'Well . . .' she paused. 'Let's just say if Merris was a racehorse, I wouldn't be taking it round the back and shooting it in the head just yet. And that's all I'm saying.'

Mitch burst into relieved laughter. A little too relieved, she thought. If Merris was a racehorse, she'd certainly not be placing any bets on it and she'd be phoning the vet to ask if there was any hope. But then, she was the vet. She was the one who would be recommending either some very expensive treatment or the bullet. The responsibility of her job bore down on her.

When Mitch had gone, her phone rang again. It was Don.

'Hello,' she said. 'I'm getting bugger all done today.'

'Shall I go?'

'No, no I want to talk to you. It's the baby, I got the test results and there's a chance it might have Down's Syndrome.' The words tumbled out.

'What? What test?'

'A blood test they do. There's a 2 per cent chance of Down's Syndrome. They're suggesting we do more tests.'

'OK . . .' he said slowly. 'It's OK. I'm sure it's going to be OK . . . We need some more information about this, don't we?'

'I'm speaking to the midwife tonight.' She realized her heart was beating fast and she was feeling really panicky. 'Can you try and get home early tonight? I'm going to leave soon.'

'Yeah, no problem. I'll be there just after seven unless there's a last-minute hitch. Shall I get some food?'

'Yes please.'

'What do you want?'

'It doesn't matter, Don.'

'OK, see you later, hon. Don't worry – it'll be fine.'

Why did men always say that? He didn't know if it was going to be OK any more than she did.

'Thanks, Don,' she managed. 'Bye.'

She struggled on for another hour, trying to work but finally she powered down the computer. She'd had enough for the day, she couldn't concentrate, her hand was resting on her faint tummy bump. She felt scared and protective and confused.

By the end of the evening, she and Don had reached a decision. She was not going to have an amnio test. Declan had told her it was the only way to be sure the baby was OK but she had argued back that it was madness to assess a 2 per cent risk with a procedure which carried a 1–4 per cent risk of miscarriage.

They would go to the hospital tomorrow for a detailed scan which had an 80 per cent chance of giving them an accurate result.

The next morning, Bella climbed into the limo, said hello to Geoff, then slumped into her seat, too tired and preoccupied to bother with the paper. The

113

awfulness of the decision they could be facing later in the day was too terrible to think about, but she couldn't stop herself.

She felt her stomach flutter in a strange way . . . nerves. It fluttered again and she just knew it was the baby moving. It was one of those magical first time experiences, like a first kiss, first aeroplane ride, first Valentine.

She looked out of the window to make sure Geoff couldn't see the tears welling up in her eyes. She was expecting a baby. A real live little person. It was as if it was dawning on her for the first time.

What if the baby had Down's Syndrome? Was that so bad? Would she really want to give it up? She knew what that meant. An induced labour and giving birth to a tiny, stillborn baby, an unimaginable horror.

'What do you think about these East Asian technology ISAs then?'

'Hmm?' She was startled out of her thoughts by Geoff who was looking at her over the edge of the paper.

'Well, if you've got a few quid spare, sling it in,' she answered. 'Stand back and watch it mushroom to forty times its original value or be wiped out. They're still pretty high risk.'

He didn't say anything else. Just went back to the personal finance page.

Christ, thought Bella, if he spent as much time worrying about the company's finances as he did about his own bank balance, Merris wouldn't be in such a sorry state.

And it was, too. Every day, she ran more figures through the computer and uncovered new areas of decline. The company was running beautifully, smoothly and efficiently but it was going nowhere.

Because it provided pensions, life assurance, illness cover and so on, the coffers were full of mountainous funds, but it barely seemed to have registered that in the past two years the number of new customers had dropped off dramatically. There were no plans in the pipeline to remarket or recreate the financial products Merris sold, no plans to get on-line, and the growth of the fund itself was barely acceptable. With all that money in the bank Merris should be doing something stellar.

She was also seriously worried about a group of pension holders who were taking Merris back to court on appeal next year. If they won this case, the company would be utterly screwed.

This wasn't just her first solo job, it was the first time she'd worked with a company in such bad shape. It was making her very nervous. The whole place was run on such a no-change culture, how could she even begin to chip away at it? She picked at a cracked nail in need of attention.

She'd arranged to meet Don outside the main entrance of the hospital at two o'clock that afternoon. It was ten to two as she stepped out of the cab but, thank God, he was already there.

His coat was buttoned with the collar up against the wind. He was trying to read a broadsheet but it was getting blown about and he was struggling to fold it. She watched him for a moment as he tucked it into a quarter and carried on reading. Then a scowl crossed his face and he took his ringing mobile out of his coat pocket.

At that moment, she absolutely loved him, this tall, capable, independent, clever man.

He spotted her and came running over, mobile still clamped to his head.

With an arm round her he said into the phone, 'I'm sorry, this is important. You'll just have to cut me a couple of hours of slack here. Yup, I'll come back in at five, we'll sort it out then. Right, bye.'

He put his phone back into his pocket, then turned on a smile for her: 'Hello, Bella.' He kissed her on the mouth. 'It's nothing, don't worry about it, some panicking tosser back at the office. Let's just concentrate on this, shall we?'

She was so glad he was there. She had contemplated doing this on her own, but he had insisted on being with her. She slipped her arm through his and they went in, making their way through dreary, fluorescent lit corridors to the ultrasound department.

In the large, institutional beige waiting room, packed with people, an old man was lying on a trolley, the chairs were crammed with heavily pregnant women and slightly pregnant women. In the corner a girl of about 18 or so was sobbing. Three women in green overalls and long white coats were bustling about behind the chaotic reception desk.

Welcome to the hell on earth otherwise known as the NHS, Bella thought grimly.

She handed over her appointment card. It was taken wordlessly and put in a tray on top of a bundle of others.

'If you could take a seat and drink plenty of water, please. You need a full bladder for the scan.'

116

The woman didn't even look up at her, just carried on writing.

Bella knew this and had already glugged back a bottle of Evian on the way over. Her bladder was full. She looked at the room packed with waiting women and realized she might have made a mistake there. Should she go for a pee and start drinking water again? Or wait with her legs crossed and hope it wasn't going to take too long?

She sat down with Don. There was nothing they could say that wasn't going to be of minute interest to everyone else sitting silently in the room.

'I've got all the papers in my bag. D'you want one?' He held her hand and patted it with his fingers. 'It'll be fine,' he added in a whisper.

She reached in and came out with the *Daily Mail*. She was half-heartedly reading through: 'Why I gave up life in a palace for passion with a plumber' when her name was called out.

Her heart jump-started and she felt both cold and sweaty at once. This was really happening, they were going to know in a few minutes. She stood up with Don and gripped his hand.

Her mind was racing. She and Don were in a hospital together – already a first – and they were about to see their baby on a screen and possibly be told that it was mentally handicapped, or special needs, or whatever term you were supposed to use nowadays, before it had even been born. This was unreal. She walked along the lino corridor clutching Don's hand with her heartbeat hammering in her dry throat.

She was ushered into a curtained cubicle with a little bed. A short, smiling Filipino nurse said hello

117

then gestured to the bed. Bella lay down and un-buttoned her blouse and her skirt.

Don seemed to be awkwardly filling up all the available space left. The curtain was hanging over his shoulder and snagging along the rail whenever he moved.

Bella lowered her waistband and was pre-occupied with the prospect of Don turning suddenly and bringing the whole flimsy little contraption down.

'OK, we just put some gel on.' The nurse smiled and squirted a huge quantity of ice cold blue gunk onto Bella's stomach. 'Now we take a look at baby.' She moved the grey handset into place and started sliding it along Bella's greased navel, staring intently at the screen by the side of the bed.

Bella could hardly breathe. Don fixed his eyes on the screen, which was just out of Bella's view. For several long minutes, the nurse looked and slid her handset and said nothing. She pressed a button and the screen made clunking noises.

'I'm just taking some cross-sections for a better look.' This was not reassuring.

More agonizingly long minutes went by. Bella fixed her eyes on Don's face and he broke off from the screen to give her a wan smile.

Finally the nurse turned to look at her: 'I'm sorry' – the word hung in the air and everything after that went into slow motion. Bella watched her lips form the next words: 'Sorry to take so long. I wanted to be sure.'

Bella could feel the blood draining away from her head and cold beads of sweat break out in her armpits.

'Baby looks absolutely normal,' said the nurse. 'We can't guarantee from the scan, but I can see no cause for concern. Let me talk you through it.'

She swivelled the screen to face Bella and Don moved round the bed to stand beside her. She felt for his hand and squeezed it. He squeezed her back. She was trying to feel relief, to run the words 'absolutely normal' over in her mind again, but she still felt a residue of panic.

The nurse ran the handset over her stomach again and a grey and white grainy image flashed up. It looked like the surface of the moon and Bella could see a little astronaut moving about dreamily.

'There is baby, bouncing up and down. You can see the legs and arms.' She pressed a button: 'This is a cross-section of the heart. The four chambers are all normal.'

Amazingly up on the screen was a tiny pulsating heart, contracting and opening at a relentless pace.

'This is a cross-section of the brain, again normal.'

A grey expanse filled the screen. Bella was looking inside the head of her baby before it was born. She felt in awe.

The nurse clicked back to the lunar surface view again. The little astronaut was turning about, carefree and gleeful.

'OK, that's it.' She turned off the monitor and handed Bella a wodge of tissue paper to wipe down her stomach.

'I'll put the report in your maternity book, take it to your midwife who'll go through it again with you, but there's no obvious cause for concern. The Ladies is second on the left,' she added.

How could Bella have forgotten? The dull ache in the pit of her stomach was a bladder shrieking to be emptied.

When she came out after a marathon pee, she and Don hugged hard.

Then he took her arm and led her down the corridor. 'That was one of the most amazing things I've ever experienced,' he said.

'I know,' Bella replied. 'Thank God everything's OK.'

'What would you have done if it wasn't?' asked Don, seeing how pale and shaken she still looked.

'I don't know. I'd like to think we'd have been big enough to say "This was meant to be, let's have this baby" but I don't know.'

'That's OK,' he said and squeezed her round the shoulder. 'I didn't know either. I think we should go and get a drink.'

'I've got to get back.' Bella sounded gloomy.

'Me too, but I think we owe ourselves one.'

'OK.'

Looking down the road in front of the hospital, they could see a pub sign 50 yards ahead.

'That will do.' Don steered her along at a hurried pace and they opened the door on a cosy little pub, quiet after the flurry of lunchtime drinkers and before the evening rush kicked in.

Don went to the bar as Bella sat down on a sofa. She fumbled in her bag for her cigarettes, but just guiltily held the packet in her hands.

Don came back with a glass of white wine and what looked like a double whisky with ice.

'Here we go.' He sat down close beside her and

120

she could smell on his breath that he'd already tossed one back at the bar.

'Should you be smoking?' he asked.

'I'm not. Should you be drinking quadruple whiskies?'

'Aha, caught again. Damn.' He took a sip from his glass. 'I was pretty worried, you know. Up until today, this has been so abstract. You've hardly even got a bump.'

After a pause, he added, 'Christ, I just can't imagine us with a baby, Bella,' and gave a long sigh.

She didn't say anything, so he took another slug of whisky then carried on.

'I'm so unprepared for this. I've never pushed a pram or changed a nappy or held a bottle or even a baby, I don't think. Then suddenly there's all this worry about whether it will be OK.'

'We never asked,' said Bella suddenly. 'We don't even know if it's a girl or a boy.'

'No. Well, anyway. There's all this worry and I realize I am worried. I'm frightened for a baby who hasn't even been born yet but who does exist.'

She put the cigarettes back in her bag. 'I feel that too,' she said. 'But let's not panic. The baby is OK. We will be too.'

She reached for her wine glass and allowed herself a hefty mouthful. It sank straight into her stomach and settled the nervous jangling. She closed her eyes, swallowed again and saw with horror that the glass was empty.

'Better have another,' said Don.

'No. Lime and soda, hon, I really mustn't.'

He came back with a tray loaded with another

double whisky, her soft drink and a second glass of wine, just in case.

'We can't just sit here and get plastered,' Bella reminded him.

'It's solved a lot of problems for me in the past.' Don was smiley and relaxed now, leaning back on the sofa beside her. He unbuttoned his coat, ran his fingers through his hair and looked at her with one eyebrow raised.

'Oh don't give me that look,' she said.

'What look?' he asked, eyebrow still cocked.

'That "I'm sooo bad, you know you want to misbehave with me" look. I said I'd be back.'

'OK, go outside, phone them, tell them you're stuck in traffic and you'll be in early tomorrow.'

'No. No. No. No.' She was smiling at him now.

'OK, I know, we'll have a lovely, relaxing hour here, then we will get in our cabs, go back to our tosspot offices and say we were delayed by aliens who forced us to drink in a faithfully replicated pub in outer space.'

'Go order my cab *now*.' She said it firmly but she wasn't angry with him.

'You're no fun, Bella. But that's why I married you, to stop me degenerating into a drunken bum.'

'I am fun. But only at the right times in the proper places.'

'See?' he said.

He went over to the bar where she heard him say: 'Can we have two cabs in twenty minutes, please? One going east, the other to Hammersmith. Cheers, mate.'

'Twenty minutes?!' she said when he got back.

122

'Shame to waste these. Cheers.' He drained his whisky, as she sipped her soda.

'Are we going to fight over the last one?' He gestured at the wine glass.

'You total soak,' she laughed at him. *Damn!* How could they have forgotten to ask for a picture of the scan?

'It's really time we told our folks about the baby,' he said, halfway down the wine.

'Yeah, I know,' she replied.

Chapter Ten

'Hello?'

'Tania, it's me.'

'Bella! How are you doing?'

'Good, fine. What about you, darling?'

'Oh, surviving. Are we going to meet this weekend? Please say yes.'

'Yes, that's why I'm phoning,' Bella said, 'Can I come round? I've got a dress panic.'

'Really?'

'I've got two Christmas parties to go to this week and I can't get into anything I own without showing off a suspicious bump.'

'Don't tell me no-one knows yet!'

'Well, I'm still only four months, and a little bit.'

'You are such a wimp. So, you're pretending to be sweet but actually you're wanting to borrow a fat frock from your fat friend.'

'Don't say that. You're not fat, you have better clothes than me.'

'Yeah, in a size bigger. Bella, does this mean you still haven't told your parents about the baby?'

'No, I have told them. It went OK, surprisingly OK.'

'See,' Tania couldn't help adding.

The parent phone calls had happened a few evenings ago. Don's mother, Maddie had of course been thrilled and had spoken to Bella at length about morning sickness and backache and warned her to take it easy. She'd made a lovely fuss and couldn't wait to see them both at Christmas.

Then Bella had put the receiver down and toyed with dialling her parents' number for so long that finally Don had picked up the handset and punched it in himself.

'I do spend most of my day making awkward phone calls and persuading people to talk to me,' he told her as the international ringing tone began beeping in his ear.

She'd fled to the other end of the room and sat listening to Don's side of the conversation with a mixture of horror and relief.

'Hello, Professor Browning,' he'd begun. 'This is Don McCartney, Bella's husband. How are you?'

'No, no, she's fine. She's really well. In fact, she's expecting a baby and very nervous about telling you!'

At this point, Bella had buried her face in her hands. It had been excruciating.

'Well, you know,' Don had given a little laugh. 'What with the two of you refusing to meet me and so on . . . I think she's feeling a little awkward.'

There had been a long pause then as Don listened and Bella wondered what the hell her father was saying to him.

Then Don had said: 'I hope so . . . I think it would do us all good to meet up. When are you next over here?'

Bella had looked up to see Don giving her the thumbs up and she heard: 'Great, OK then, I'll put Bella on now,' before the receiver was thrust at her.

'Dad, hello,' she'd managed.

'Hello darling, congratulations,' her father had said, sounding genuinely pleased. 'Is it going well?' he'd asked. 'How far on are you?'

'Four and a half months.'

'Well done, Bella,' he'd said.

There was a little pause and she was grateful that he didn't ask why she hadn't told them sooner.

'Your mother is going to be thrilled,' he'd said.

'Is she, are you sure?'

'Yes, darling . . . She'll phone you as soon as she gets back in.'

Then after a small hesitation, he'd added: 'You know, maybe we've made a bit of a misjudgement . . . about your husband.'

'Don.'

'Well . . . he sounds like a good guy.'

'He is, Dad,' she'd told him and for a moment pictured her father, mother and Don all together round a table chatting, eating, hanging out like a normal family. Maybe it would happen.

But her mother's phone call later in the evening had felt like a dampener. Celia had of course gushed that she was delighted, but had immediately listed the reasons why they couldn't come over until the baby was there: so busy, a lecture tour, building work on the house, looking after the neighbour's property when he was away, etc., etc.

'Maybe you and Don could come and visit us?' she'd asked after what sounded suspiciously like Bella's father talking to her in the background. 'What about Christmas?' she'd added.

'Don's mother is coming here.' Bella was grateful for the excuse. 'We'll see, Mum. We haven't got a lot of time off before the baby's due. But you will come then, won't you?' she asked, wondering what on earth that would be like.

'Of course,' her mother had gushed. 'A grandchild, how exciting!'

But to Bella, even this had sounded somehow insincere.

On the night of the Merris Christmas party, work wound up at 4 p.m. so that everyone could go home and get dressed up. The annual party had always been a ball at the Dorchester for employees, clients and various guests. Bella had been somewhat taken aback to learn it was going ahead this year, but she supposed the board were making every attempt to quell rumours that the company was 'in difficulty'.

Just before she left the office she rang Don, who assured her he was going to get away on time. She was still soaking in the bath when he arrived home, so he came into the bathroom and perched on the loo seat.

'Hello, hon.' He took his glasses off because they were misting up and she could see the tired circles under his eyes. But he still looked lovely, she thought, smiling at him.

'You're gorgeous,' he told her. Her hair was piled on her head, her shoulders were peeping out of a vat of foam and she pointed a toe, with perfectly painted pink toenail, in his direction. He took her foot and began kneading it.

She sank back into the bath and closed her eyes. Don massaged her foot, then leaned over to stroke up her calf. He knelt by the edge of the bath and let his hand run gently down her thigh into the water.

'Don.' Her eyes snapped open, her legs shut. 'We haven't got time for this.'

'There's always time to enjoy yourself,' he smiled.

'Well, I'm not in the mood.' She stood up and reached for a towel.

'Nope, you're certainly not. We haven't had sex for ages,' he muttered.

'Yes we have. We had sex last weekend,' she said as she wrapped the towel round and stepped out of the bath.

'No we didn't.'

'OK, the weekend before that.' She was a bit surprised herself.

'Oh well, that's all right then,' he said irritably.

'I'm sorry, I've been very tired, what with work, being pregnant, the baby scare.'

He was instantly contrite. 'I'm sorry, hon, come here.' He held out his arms and she snuggled in.

'It's OK.' She gave him a light kiss on the lips. 'Come on, let's get ready to party.'

'I'll jump in the shower.'

'OK.'

Tania had lent her a long gold slip dress, which clung to her every curve and bump, but it came with a wonderful floor-length gold taffeta coat she didn't intend to take off, which hid everything.

128

She put on a pink underwired bra, tiny black knickers and hold-ups, then pushed her hair up and applied full-on glamour make-up.

The dress coat was on and she was just sliding into her shoes when Don came through.

'Wow.' He moved in.

'Don't touch, don't kiss or crush.' She pushed him away playfully. 'The cab will be here in fifteen minutes, will you be ready?'

'Yes, ma'am.'

She gave him the once-over as they got into the lift. His dinner suit was secondhand and a bit shabby, he was wearing a not perfectly ironed shirt with a not perfectly tied bow. But that was why he looked so sexy, the aura of just having got out of bed and just dying to seduce you back in clung to him more than to anyone else she'd ever met.

'I totally love you, Don,' she said.

'I totally love you too,' he answered. 'You look fantastic – not at all pregnant.'

The lift doors pinged open and she walked to the taxi, obsessing about whether that meant he wasn't going to find her fantastic when she did look pregnant.

They arrived at the Dorchester just after nine to find a lavish party well under way. Champagne glasses were pressed into their hands and one of the senior execs came over to welcome them.

After the 'hello, how are you? lovely you could comes', they were alone again.

'I think I'll take up a seat at the bar, that's where my type hang out,' Don said.

'Sad old alcoholic soaks,' she teased.

'Ha ha. Now, you go off and network like a good

girl. I think that crowd of boring old farts in the corner are praying that you will go over and talk filthy facts and figures to them.'

'Bella,' one of the men in the group Don was indicating stood up and waved her over. It was Mr Merris himself.

'See you later, hon,' Don said as they parted.

'Bella, I want to introduce you to some of my old cronies,' said Merris. He went round the group making introductions as Bella shook everyone's hand.

'This is Bella Browning, our troubleshooter. She's not just absolutely ravishing, she's also damn clever and that is a compliment, coming from a man who's never put a woman in a top position before.'

Loud chortles from the group. Oh bloody hell, thought Bella, welcome to Jurassic Park.

'Well, we're all equals now, Tony.' She flashed a megawatt smile and deliberately used Merris's first name – something she'd never heard anyone do before, in fact, his first name was Anthony, maybe no-one *ever* called him Tony. That would shut them up.

'Yes, yes of course.' He was even more impressed with her now: what an extraordinary nerve!

'So, you're the type who comes in, has everyone over the age of 40 fired and then calls it a cost-cutting efficiency drive?' asked one of the dinosaurs.

OK, they clearly weren't going to be happy with a nice little chat about sure bet investments or property prices.

'Something like that, except we now prefer to fire everyone over 20 because teenagers are so cheap these days and so good with computers, you'll find they can do everything you need.'

Startled silence, then finally laughter. Phew.

Now she went into her gentle pitch for business, handed out a few cards, then patted Merris on the arm to draw him slightly to one side.

'I'd really appreciate the chance to have a chat with you before the Christmas break. It's very important,' she told him.

'No problem. Now go off and enjoy yourself.'

So she did. She swanned round the room chatting with the people she'd got to know at the company and their guests. She glanced over to the bar where raucous laughter was emanating from the small group which had gathered round Don and was about to go over when Mitch came up and introduced his hugely pregnant wife. Her enormous bosom was cantilevered up close to her chin and the big round belly billowing underneath her ballgown made her look like a large green velvet Easter egg.

'When is it due?' asked Bella.

'February,' said Mrs Mitch.

'Gosh.' Bella was going to be this big in three months' time, it was a terrifying prospect.

'Baby number three, I seem to get bigger and bigger every time. Stomach muscles stretched to the limit, baggy pelvic floor.'

Whoa, this was far too much information.

When she went off in search of the loos, Bella was directed down a shiny yellow corridor with little glass cabinets of expensive trinkets set into the walls. Her heels tapped along the marble floor. This was *such* a plush hotel.

She rounded the corner and walked into Don.

131

'Hello,' they both said at once.

'How's my corporate dynamo?' He sounded nicely pissed.

'I think at least another two jobs are in the bag.' She looked flushed with her own success.

'How sexy. Well, I've got about ten stories. Five usable, two libellous and three utterly unprintable.'

'Have you been talking dirty to the ladies again?' She leaned in to kiss him.

'No, but I can if you want me to.'

He bent down and put his lips over hers. After a long, probing kiss, he moved to her ear and whispered, 'There are no attendants in there, you know.'

'Are you serious?'

'Oh yes.' He kissed her again, scooping her up against him. She could taste champagne on his warm, familiar mouth and she couldn't deny it, she was turned on, but maybe even more importantly she wanted to make up for his 'no sex' crack earlier in the evening.

'Not the Gents, too many people I know might go in there,' she whispered.

'Go and see if anyone is in the Ladies,' he urged.

She opened the pale beech door onto a whole, shiny, peachy little world. It was empty.

She beckoned him in and they rushed into one of the cubicles and banged the door shut. They turned to face each other and burst out laughing.

'I'm getting you back for the bra changing room,' he said, kneeling down in front of her.

'Oh boy,' she replied.

He parted the front of her coat, lifted the filmy gold dress up and let it fall back down over him. Bella shut her eyes and leaned against the wall as she felt him push her tiny knickers to the side and put his mouth against her crotch.

She giggled and he started to lick.

'I want you inside,' she said after a few moments, partly because she did, partly because she didn't want to hang around the cubicle too long.

He stood up and wiped his mouth on the back of his hand before kissing her.

She put one foot up on the edge of the toilet so he could slide in easily.

He felt very good; I might even come, she thought.

'Too much champagne,' Don said by way of explanation as he startled a serious-looking company wife by striding out of the ladies' loos straight into her path. He smiled his extra-dazzling charm smile and she smiled back.

On Friday evening, Bella was getting dressed up again. She wondered why she was feeling anxious. This was office Christmas party night with Susan, Kitty, Chris and Hector. There was to be dinner, champagne, the works and they were all going to behave, especially her.

She was wearing the gold taffeta coat again, but this time with black trousers and boots. It looked surprisingly glamorous and very bump disguising. Don wasn't there to give his opinion, he'd gone to the gym after work.

She had seen Tony Merris in the morning for the private chat and she couldn't really tell how he'd taken her news. She'd listed all her concerns but it had been hard to gauge his reactions. He'd listened carefully and even made a few notes but she couldn't honestly work out if he was surprised by what she was telling him or not.

When she'd suggested that the pension holders might win their appeal case and bring the company to its knees, he had told her that 'friends in the right places' had assured him this would not happen. It was only when she told him that she was going to recommend implementing an emergency action plan well ahead of her full report that he began to look slightly concerned.

'What were you hoping to achieve by calling me in?' she'd asked him.

'Well, I'm very happy with the way the business is run, but I'm aware it's not growing.'

'So you'd be surprised if I told you it is in fact declining and fairly rapidly at that?'

'Hmm.' He'd raised his eyebrows. 'I'd need to see some figures.'

'No problem.' She'd reached into her files and slapped a folder on his desk.

He hadn't picked it up. She'd glanced round the room and noticed the large formal portraits on the walls. 'Your father?' she'd asked, pointing at the one above his desk.

'Yes and that's his father beside him. I'm the third generation in charge here,' he'd said gravely.

'They look pretty fierce,' had been her reply.

To her relief, he'd smiled and said, 'Yes, they were rather. Both naval men, liked to run a tight ship.'

'You run a very tight ship here. Very tight, very formal, very old-fashioned.'

'Is that a problem?' He'd raised his alarmingly bushy grey eyebrows.

'It might be hard to change things.'

'Hmmm,' was his reply.

'May I ask you when you're planning to retire?' She had held her breath and almost crossed her fingers for his reaction.

'Well, that's a little bit presumptuous, young lady.'

'Have you not thought about it at all?'

'I've thought about it, but I haven't decided.'

'It's just . . . please stop me if I'm going too far, but real changes are needed in the organization and I just wonder if you'll be here . . . well if you're going to be . . .' Jesus, should she really be telling the chief executive, the chairman, the grandson of the founder to consider his position?

'Am I the right man for the job? Is that what you're asking me?' He gave a little laugh. 'Well you certainly don't stand on ceremony, do you, Ms Browning?'

She smiled a little and felt she had said enough. She didn't really need to risk her position by spelling out to Anthony Merris that it was time to appoint a new chief executive and sod off to the upper echelons of non-executive directorship.

'I know what you're getting at,' he'd said finally. 'I will give the matter careful thought.'

He had drawn the meeting to a close by suggesting that she draft him a confidential memo on all the matters she'd raised, so he could mull it over during the Christmas break. She'd spent the rest of the day writing it up and making it as bleak as possible in an attempt to spur him into action.

Glancing at her watch now, she saw she still had a little time, so she smoothed down the taffeta coat, lit a guilty cigarette and sat down on the sofa.

She hadn't seen anyone from the office for several weeks now, so she was looking forward to the party, but then the pregnancy secret was a bit of a burden she still did not feel ready to share.

She could see her cab in the street outside, so she flung the cigarette packet into her bag and headed out of the door. They were meeting for dinner in a big, smart restaurant in the West End. She was the last to arrive and was greeted with a chorus of hellos by the gang of four, already seated at the table.

Everyone was dressed up: even Hector wore an unusually impeccable black suit. She sat down, felt instantly relaxed and realized how lovely it was to see them all again, her little office surrogate family.

'Bella! Looking lovely as usual.' This from Chris.

It would be fun to flirt but absolutely nothing else, no way, she promised herself.

Susan was on her right, Hector then Kitty to her left and she was opposite Chris. It was a round table, just slightly too big for everyone to have one group conversation, but that was a good thing. Hector and Kitty were chatting – Kitty trying not to drool – and she, Chris and Susan were no doubt going to talk shop for a while.

Susan wanted to know how Merris was going and Bella outlined the worst of it.

'We can't just tell them that they're in decline,' said Susan. 'You'll have to think of a way of making it look more positive. A shut-down and new start-up, a whole new direction for the company beginning on a small scale, maybe even a takeover or merger. If you're telling them they're on a ship

136

that's going down, in the next breath you'll have to throw them a life raft,' she added.

'I know,' said Bella, 'and I'd really appreciate some input from you. I thought we could maybe meet up over the Christmas break so I could go through it with you and see what ideas you have.'

'Yes, fine,' Susan answered. 'But it will have to be tomorrow, I'm off on my Christmas cruise the day after.'

'Oh lovely,' said Bella thinking, yuck and she'll come back looking all deep brown and leathery.

'Why don't we meet in the office at ten, go through everything, then have a nice lunch?'

'That would be great,' Bella answered.

'Maybe Hector should be asked to have a look. He might come out with some unexpected genius,' Chris put in.

Bella and Susan didn't say anything.

Chris added: 'He's brilliant. Still a bit disorganized . . .'

'And lacking in basic mathematical skills,' Bella added quietly, so Hector couldn't hear.

'But brilliant,' Chris said again. 'He is going straight to the top.'

Bella felt rattled by this. *She* was meant to be the up and coming office star, not barely-out-of-university-unbearably-pompous Hector. Not being childish at all, are we? she ticked herself off and drained her glass. Oh no, now what was she going to drink? Mineral water would be a bit suspicious. She accepted a refill.

'How are you, darling?' She turned her attention to Kitty.

Kitty, squeezed into a tiny silver sequined dress

137

with her hair cut in an extra-short spiky number, was looking sexy, cheeky and hardly bizarre at all.

The mood was mellow. Platefuls of wonderful food arrived as Hector and Chris held court, trying to outdo each other with client anecdotes. Even Susan seemed quite relaxed. There was a nice buzz, Bella thought; Kitty still lusted after Hector and Chris still fancied her. How nice. Now on a third glass of wine, she was starting to feel just a little bit tipsy.

Hector leaned over and whispered in her ear, 'I've brought some stuff with me if you want a dose. Remember the laugh we had last time?'

She giggled and turned back to him, leaning up close to his neat little ear and thinking how nice he smelled, smoky but with an undertone of expensive aftershave and laundry.

'Thanks but I really shouldn't, now that I'm pregnant,' she whispered and they looked at each other in utter amazement: Hector astonished at what she had said, Bella astonished that she'd said it.

'*What??!!*' said Hector, then, 'Did you lot know this?' before she could stop him.

Everyone looked at him. 'Bella's up the duff,' he announced.

Could three people have looked more shocked? She took in the expressions one at a time: Kitty looking delighted-shocked, Chris looking stunned-shocked and Susan looking absolutely furious-shocked.

'That's fantastic!' Kitty spoke first.

'How long have you known?' Chris asked. Hardly surprising.

'When is it due?' from Susan.

138

'Umm, I'm really sorry about this. I didn't mean to say anything until after Christmas. It just slipped out.' She was seriously flustered and glared at Hector, but it was rather lost on him.

'I'm almost halfway there. The baby is due early June . . . ummm.' She was totally rattled, looking at them all staring at her, open-mouthed. 'Don is really pleased,' she added, then, 'And . . . so am I. We had a scan last week and it's looking fine.'

'Boy or girl?' said Kitty excitedly.

'Don't know yet.'

'I just can't see you with a baby, Bella. It's unbelievable', this from Kitty again. Obviously everyone else still didn't know what to say.

'Congratulations,' finally Chris spoke again. Well could she be surprised he was a bit taken aback? By now he'd probably worked out she'd been pregnant in Birmingham.

'Well, we'll have plenty to talk about at lunch tomorrow,' said Susan and made it sound ominous.

Somehow the meal carried on without revolving entirely round Bella and her news. She made it pretty clear she didn't want to talk about it much, politely brushing off Kitty's clumsy questions about maternity leave and what she was planning to do afterwards.

By midnight she was a little drunk, over-anxious and exhausted. Gratefully she clambered into a cab and headed home, wondering how the hell she was going to handle Susan tomorrow.

Chapter Eleven

The square mile that formed the City of London, one of the richest square miles in the world, was eerily deserted on Saturdays. The shops, cafés and bars were closed, the pavements filled Monday to Friday with suits were empty, and the office towers abandoned apart from security guards and the odd weekend visitor like herself.

Bella had dressed down – just a little bit – for the meeting with Susan and as she tapped in the entry code at the front door she wondered nervously how this was going to go.

She was fifteen minutes early, but Susan was already there, in her office with her chair turned to the window. For once she wasn't on the phone.

Bella gave a tentative hello.

The chair swivelled to face her. 'Hello Bella, come in.' Susan's voice was neutral but Bella wondered if she'd made a wardrobe mistake when she saw her boss was in full office gear, with a beige rollneck sweater instead of a blouse as her one concession to informality.

'Hi,' Bella added, somewhat needlessly.

'Sit down.' With a faint smile, Susan gestured to a chair. 'Well, that was quite a bombshell you dropped on us last night. Still, at least you don't have a weight problem.'

What was that? An attempt at a joke? Bella didn't smile, just launched into her planned pitch: 'Susan, I love my job. I love working for you. I'm planning to take a couple of months of maternity leave and come straight back. This is what I've always wanted to do.'

'What, have a baby?' Susan asked.

'No, consult, for the best team in the country.' Bella paused, then added, 'You know I didn't want children when I joined. But I met Don, we got married and my feelings changed. I hope you can understand that.'

'Well, I don't want to be messed around, Bella. Here you are promising me you'll be straight back to work, working just as hard as you do now, but is that realistic?' Susan snapped back.

'I'll make it realistic,' Bella answered.

'We'll have to take you off Danson's.'

Not without a fight, you won't, Bella felt her hackles rise. 'I brought that job in, Susan. They want me to do it. Tell them 1 August and I'll be there. Surely you owe me that?'

Susan tapped long beige nails on the desk and finally said, 'OK August the 1st, but you'll take Hector on the job with you as your number two.'

'Fine.' It was not fine at all, but August was months and months away. She'd worry about that nearer the time.

'OK, well, I'm impressed by your commitment,' said Susan. 'We'll see how it works out.'

141

The subject appeared to be closed, so Bella opened up her files and they began talking about Merris Group.

She listened to Susan and learned. Her boss was as brilliant as ever.

Bella had two whole weeks off for Christmas. She wasn't due back at Merris until 3 January, whereas Don was off just for Christmas Day and 1 January, but she would be too busy to notice, she told herself.

She had drawn up a typically ambitious 'to do' list for her holidays: buy Christmas presents, maternity clothes and a house (well, at least start looking). She also wanted to change hospitals. The ultrasound department had helped her make that decision with its third world waiting room and totally harassed staff. Sod that, she was going private.

Bur first of all, she needed some relaxation, so Tuesday was going to be shopping day. Tania was awarding herself the day off so they could hit town together.

'There's this fabulous maternity shop around here,' Tania assured her when they met for coffee at the start of the day. 'I've already been looking for you.'

Bella took in her friend's recent chunky toffee highlights and bang up to the second manicure. She was the best possible person to take shopping: 'I'm half French,' Tania would declare. 'I don't know the meaning of post-retail guilt. We *need* these things! We *need* to look lovely!'

'Let's do the other stuff first, I just can't see

maternity wear shopping as fun,' Bella said, gloomy at the prospect of getting even bigger.

So they went to Selfridge's and got the Christmas shopping well under way, buying picture frames, candlesticks, rugs, bed linen and books.

Bella cheered up at last when she started shopping for Don. She'd planned to buy him a jumper, but got carried away and bought him the jumper, plus a shirt, plus a new black cashmere overcoat. 'He only ever wears his battered oilskin thing,' she told Tania. 'Oh hell, I'm going to get him a new briefcase as well. It is Christmas.'

'How are we going to carry all this?' Tania asked.

'In a cab,' said Bella.

'Are you as rich as you're making out?'

'Christmas bonus,' grinned Bella.

'Ah-ha, City bitch,' Tania teased.

They hit the maternity shop and wandered round the racks fending off shop assistants.

'Let me just look around for a bit,' Bella told them grumpily. 'God, everything is so twee,' she complained to Tania. 'It's all pink tie cardies and lilac pinafores. I can't turn up for a board meeting in a cardie.'

Bella went to the changing room and was brought one outfit after another.

She flatly refused to try on any pinafores or dungarees: 'Hello, dungarees??' she said sternly. 'They look cute on the under twos. And *no*, I cannot go to work in a pinafore.' She was given a grey jersey skirt suit. It was stretchy, it had no lining, no tailoring, no shoulder pads. It looked like a track suit masquerading as a suit and Bella's gloom deepened.

143

'Well, it's the only type of suit they've got,' Tania told her. 'Try it with this white smock thing. It might not look too bad.'

And it didn't look too awful, she had to admit, although the skirt was a sad, sad, elasticated thing with a front that looked like an empty carrier bag.

'OK, one polyester suit in grey and one in black. Two smock things – one white, one pink. What else can I wear for work?' Bella asked.

'What about this?' One of the assistants brought in a perfectly acceptable long black Lycra tunic with a deep V neck. There was a matching knee-length skirt to wear underneath.

'This is more like it.' Bella slipped it on. She didn't look too bad at all, sort of sexily pregnant. Her desired intention.

'OK, what other colour does it come in?'

'Grey,' said Tania, her image consultant skills rather stretched to the limit.

'Black and grey? This is pregnancy, not mourning. Well, I'll take them both. So, any maternity leather trousers?' This was a joke.

'Yes, as a matter of fact there are,' the assistant surprised her.

'Hurray! I'll have them please. Plus some of the fitted body things and hell, maybe even a pink cardigan.'

She tried everything on again for Don when he got home.

'It's not so bad, is it?'

'I don't know about the suits.'

'You have a point.'

'Have you been whacking your credit cards?'

144

he asked, but not disapprovingly; it was her money, after all. Well, actually it was Mr Visa's but . . .

'Just a bit, but I got my Christmas bonus. It was very good and very deserved.'

'Well don't go over the top with my present, because I don't get a bonus.' He sounded sulky now.

'OK,' she said. Oops too late, she thought.

'Where are we going for Christmas lunch? Do you want to take me and Maddie out somewhere posh?' she asked him, taking a sip of her white wine spritzer and trying to pretend that it tasted nice even though it had only a millimetre of wine in it.

'What about here at home?'

'No no, we're not doing that whole plum pudding and turkey thing just for the three of us sitting at home. What will we do all day?'

'We'll have fun. I always have fun when I'm with you and Mum,' he smiled at her.

'I want to go out. Let's go to a really nice restaurant for Christmas lunch.'

'OK, if you like,' he answered.

'Does that mean you wouldn't like it?'

'I don't mind, Bella, you choose.' He was lying across the sofa and looked like he was about to reach for the TV remote control.

'We have to have a house talk, Don. We are still going to buy a house, aren't we?'

'Yup, that's the plan.' He didn't sound that enthusiastic.

'It's a good investment. I think we should spend as much as we can. We can use the savings for a deposit and furniture, decorating and stuff. Well,

145

we'll have to borrow a bit extra for all that, I suppose.'

She was treading as carefully as she could – note use of 'the' savings, not 'my'. It was a tricky subject because he earned less than her and did not like to be reminded of it. She didn't know exactly how much he earned – they had separate bank accounts – but she knew his tax code. And she knew for a fact he had no savings at all – part of his 'life's too short, I'm still young, everyone's so materialistic' philosophy.

'So how big a mortgage do you have in mind?' He looked up at her.

'Well, we could do four times my salary, but I've found someone who's prepared to lend us three times our joint.'

'So how much is that?' Don asked.

'Well, I'm guestimating for you because I know how coy you are but I'd work it out as . . .' she suddenly felt awkward about coming out with it, so she scribbled the figure on the little pad of Post-Its beside her and passed it to him.

'Da-na,' she tried to make a joke of it.

'Bloody hell,' he said, sitting up. 'That's not far off half a million pounds. What the hell would the monthly repayments be?'

'One and a half times our rent. I've found a very good deal.'

'Bella, I don't want you to bite off more than you can chew. Especially with a baby on the way.'

God, that sounded patronizing.

'Yeah, I know, Don. But I am planning to go straight back to work and I'm expecting them to make me a partner next year and I really want to

146

have a house of my own . . . our own,' ouch, she corrected herself immediately.

'Oh please cheer up.' She went to sit on the sofa beside him. 'This is such an exciting time, new house, new baby. Aren't you excited about it all?'

She cuddled up to him and turned her face to kiss him. He kissed her lightly on the lips then, to her surprise, broke away.

'Bella, I've had a few really stressful days, I'm very tired and I think I'll head off to bed,' he said.

'Oh OK,' she sighed. 'Good night then, I'm going to stay up for a bit, if that's OK.'

'Yeah fine.' He nodded vaguely and stood up to go.

She suspected he was suffering from a classic case of income-related impotence. Never mind, he'd get over it. So she earned a bit more than him, well quite a lot more with bonuses. So what?

She stretched out on the sofa and reached over for her cigarette pack. She shook out the last one and lit up.

Lying there quietly she put her hand on the bump and thought about the baby. She knew there was something perverse about the fact that she only really had the peace and quiet to concentrate on the baby growing and existing inside her when she paused for a cigarette break.

'I'm doing the best I can,' she whispered to the little person down there. 'I'm down to five a day, extra mild, sometimes just two. I really, really hope that's OK with you. I'm very sorry I can't give up for you.'

She breathed the smoke in and out several times, then added: 'You are definitely going to be much smarter than me and not smoke. Mind you, I hope you're not too much smarter than me because I'm pretty clever and I don't want you to be one of those mad, genius types.'

Oh God, she laughed at herself, not that I'm going to be a pushy mother or anything.

Chapter Twelve

On 3 January she was back at her desk at Merris Group. It had been a good holiday, bar a small tantrum over her Christmas presents to Don.

He had given her a pair of small diamond earrings, then been a little less than grateful when she'd given him all her gifts.

He'd said 'Bella, you really shouldn't have,' and meant it. She'd ended up yelling at him, when Maddie was out of the room, that it was her money and if she wanted to spend it on him, she should bloody well be allowed to. They'd smoothed it over later, but it still bothered her that he was upset at her generosity. She hadn't been trying to prove what a big fat wage earner she was or anything. She'd wanted to spoil him, remind him how much she loved him.

Over her fortnight off, her bump had suddenly swelled into a definite, undisguisable entity. She was not going to get away with skirts safety-pinned at the waist and jackets worn open any longer. As she'd stood in front of the wardrobe that morning, she'd had to face the fact that she was going to have to put on one of the horrible jersey suits and break the pregnancy news at Merris.

Not that it would cause any problems; her contract would be over well before her maternity leave kicked in. But it embarrassed her, having to bring her personal life so blatantly into the office, it seemed kind of unprofessional. But what else could she do? Leave the baby in an incubator at home?

Strangely, conference was postponed to the afternoon, so Mitch was the first person to come into her little office and wish her a Happy New Year.

'Hello, Bella, did you have a good holiday?' he asked sticking his head round the door.

She swivelled round in her chair. 'Hello.'

'You look different,' he said. 'What's different about you?'

'I ate too much Christmas pudding,' she said putting her hands round her bump.

'Oh my God, you're pregnant!'

'Well you should know, you've seen it all before.'

'Congratulations. And who may I ask is the lucky man?'

'Mitch! You can ask that at engagements, not conceptions. I'm a happily married woman.'

'There are hidden depths to you I would never have suspected,' he said with a grin.

'I brought Don to the Christmas party.'

'You had sex with *your husband* in the toilets? You are unbelievable.'

'What are you talking about?' She put on her most perplexed and wounded face, but was horrified she had been found out.

150

'The rumour sweeping the office is that you lured a mysterious dark-haired stranger into the ladies' loos at the party.'

She gave her best impersonation of outraged laughter.

'I'm sorry,' Mitch said. 'No-one really believes it. Never mind, the news that you are with child will nip it in the bud. No-one's going to believe that a pregnant woman would have sex with her husband in the toilets even if her life depended on it.'

'Quite.'

'Anyway, I'll catch ya later.'

'Bye.'

He could not get out of the room fast enough. She could practically hear him running down the corridor shouting: 'News just in: Bella in toilet romp pregnancy shock.'

She turned back to her screen. Susan's advice had been to let the board have as much of the bad news as early as possible, along with plenty of practical solutions. That way things should already be improving slightly by the time her final report was due in April.

She scanned through her e-mails and saw one in there from Chris.

Bella, hello. We've not had the chance to talk at all since the Christmas party. I just wanted to congratulate you on your news and tell you I think it's wonderful (OK I'm a little bit surprised, I have to admit. Especially after our . . . well, I know I'm not supposed to mention it.) Anyway, I'd love to have a drink some time, we can talk about how things are going to work while you're away/ when you come back etc. Hope you're keeping really well and don't let the buggers get you down. Chris

Chris. She hadn't thought about him for weeks. A good thing. But it was nice to hear from him and know he was on her side. She typed back:

So glad to hear from you. How about Wed/Thurs night? Bella

Ah yes! There was something else she had to kick off today. She rootled about in her bag for the card she had put in there and soon was deep in conversation with an estate agent.

'And I'm in a real hurry to move,' she added. 'Baby on the way, hectic work schedule, all the usual.'

OK, board meeting, board meeting . . . time to concentrate, she told herself, once she'd put the phone down.

An e-mail dropped from the finance department. The latest reports she had asked for were 'unavailable – files out'.

This was ridiculous, she would have to find out from the finance director himself what the hell was going on. Preparations for the interim report meeting she was holding with the board kept her in the office for almost ten hours, so Don got home well ahead of her.

She messaged him as she climbed onto the tube, so dinner would be ready when she got back. When she finally made it to the flat, he was in the kitchen stirring up chicken with peppers, soy sauce and rice.

'Mmm . . . very macho new man,' she told him, kissing him hello.

'I'm wooing you tonight,' he warned her, smiling and stirring frantically.

'How nice,' she said, thinking, Please no, I *have* to go to bed.

They ate dinner then he insisted she lie down on the sofa while he peeled off her stockings and massaged her feet with oil.

'This is perfect,' she said to him closing her eyes and feeling herself sink to the brink of sleep almost immediately.

'How's work?' he asked.

'It's pretty tough.' She didn't want to elaborate.

'You're doing really well, you know,' he said as he stroked her bump protectively.

'Thanks,' she said, struggling against a yawn. 'I'm sorry I'm so tired all the time.'

'It's OK.' After a pause he added, 'Are we going to get a place with a garden?'

'I hope so,' she said.

'I like the idea of reading the papers in a garden with our little baby playing on a rug.'

'You'll have to mow the lawn,' she warned him with a smile.

'That's OK, I'll mow the lawn. I'm getting very domesticated in my old age.'

'You're really adorable, you know.' She put a hand against the side of his face and watched his eyes. 'Please don't go off and shag anyone else, will you?' She'd meant this to sound jokey but it came out a little pleading.

'Don't be silly, Bella, you're the one.' And when he said things like that, dead serious and holding her gaze, it still made her stomach flip and it renewed her faith that this love affair could last for a very long time.

Chapter Thirteen

Sitting in her tiny office at Merris several weeks later, Bella could feel pinpricks of sweat break through under her arms. Her hands were shaking just slightly. This was it, the interim report, the first meeting with the board to outline her findings.

She was delivering bad news, probably much worse than they expected, but she hoped they would trust her. They had to be sure she was right and that she could get them out of this rapidly accelerating decline.

Her outfit had been carefully chosen that morning to project maximum authority and gravitas: hard to do with a comical bump protruding from your middle. She'd gone for the black fitted skirt and flared top ensemble, along with diamond earrings and gold necklace, then she'd added serious make-up and piled her hair up on her head in the hope that she looked a lot older than 28.

The figures, the reports and the spiel she was going to give them had been replayed over and over in her mind, but she mentally ran through the intro once again.

'You're just nervous,' she told herself, guiltily stubbing out the second cigarette she'd smoked since she got in.

A glance at her watch told her it was eight minutes to nine. Time to get down there. She gathered up her sheaf of papers and left her office.

Once everyone had settled down round the conference table, Merris went through the introductory formalities, then Bella stood up and took in the attentive eyes turned in her direction: 'Gentlemen,' she began, then gave it to them straight.

She started by demonstrating that the funds were showing negligible growth and moved on to show how new business had virtually dried up.

Arms were crossing defensively, mouths were being drawn into tight little lines and she could even hear irritated sighs. She carried on, unfazed, in a quiet, firm voice. Why were there no plans to set up anything on the net? To meet new regulations head on or to prepare for the pension holders going back to court? she asked.

Now everyone, apart from Merris, who'd already heard all this from her, was looking furious and somewhat shocked.

OK – time to swoop down and cheer them up. She started to outline her solutions: new financial products, new marketing initiatives, an on-line service and better strategic planning to deal with the other problems.

'I've spoken to all of you individually and heard a lot of great ideas. It would not take long to get Merris Group back on course,' she said encouragingly. That was mainly a lie, but she might as well try and be a little bit nice.

156

'But I'm sure you are all wondering how this can be financed?' Several heads were nodding vigorously at her.

'Well . . .' She knew her number one suggestion was not going to be popular, 'I think Merris Group needs to bring in a partner or a parent company.' In other words merge or get bought over.

There was a collective wave of shocked in-breaths.

She ran through the other options, not looking up much because she knew their faces would be horrified. Yup – she glanced down again – like patients faced with a rectal examination.

When she'd finished, she sat down and looked squarely at Merris himself.

'Thank you very much, Ms Browning,' he said in an entirely neutral tone. 'Does anyone have any questions?' he added. Surprise, surprise no-one moved. If this bunch had any courage in their convictions, they weren't about to reveal it now.

'Well, perhaps it would be best to discuss this amongst ourselves, and Ms Browning – we'll call you back in if any clarifications are necessary,' Merris said.

'OK.' She stood up, gathered her papers together and tried not to feel hurt. What had she expected? A standing ovation?

Quickly she walked out of the silent room and headed back to her office to wait. This was horrible. Either she would be told 'thank you very much, but we won't be requiring your services further' or the Merris Group executives were going to have to bite a very hard and unpalatable bullet. She sucked down another cigarette, hating herself for it, drank a cup of coffee and waited.

Finally the phone buzzed.

'Hello, Ms Browning?' It was Merris's secretary.

'Yes,' she answered, feeling her heart hammering high up in her chest.

'You're wanted back in the conference room to discuss your report.'

'Thanks, I'll be right there.' She walked along slowly and calmly, not wanting to jump to any conclusions. This could be OK, oh God! Surely they weren't going to ask her back in to fire her? But it was OK. The executives were still in shock and she wasn't sure if they really believed her yet, but at least they were prepared to listen some more.

One of the few uplifts in the very long week that followed was an excited phone call from the estate agent, who promised Bella he had found her new home.

There was also a message on her mobile from Declan, informing her: 'Bella you f***ing useless cow, you haven't been for a check-up for a month. Drag your arse in here next week or you are in so much trouble.'

On Saturday morning she and Don got into his Jeep to go and view the house. She opened the car door, climbed up and surveyed the scene. It was disgusting. The back seat was strewn with newspapers, empty coffee cups and sandwich wrappers. In the front was a tangle of wires – computer extensions, mobile chargers – the ashtray was overflowing and ash was scattered all over the floor and the seats.

'Bloody hell,' said Bella. 'Have you been entertaining again?'

'I tell you what, we'll go via the garage and I'll smarten her up,' Don said.

'Go via the skip, I think you mean.'

'Come on, woman, get in, stop fussing, at least you'll be able to stretch your legs and enjoy the view.'

'I'm perfectly comfortable in my car,' she said clambering up, thankful she was wearing the wipe-clean maternity leathers.

They roared off all the way to the first red light. Don loved to drive fast, which was a bit of a thwarted desire in London. He certainly indulged on the motorways and, even in the tank he drove, seemed to have ratcheted up enough speeding points to be clinging onto his vital licence by a thread.

After a wash and vacuum at the garage, they were running slightly late as they whizzed through north London and into the not very glamorous borough they could soon be calling home. Looking out of the window, Bella took it all in. The high streets full of kebab shops and launderettes, the gloomy tower blocks and council estates which loomed round almost every corner complete with small groups of moody adolescents. Rows of Victorian housing, looking shabby and unloved.

'This can't be right?' She looked at Don.

''Fraid so, we're the second on the left here.'

He turned the car into a long street of tall Victorian terraces which looked grey and grimy. Then they turned left at the bottom and suddenly they were in a lovely little crescent.

The houses here had repainted windows, elegant wooden shutters and brightly coloured doors. The brickwork had been spruced up, railings had been repaired and there were even some jaunty window-boxes.

Bella clocked the cars: a range of new Scenics, Espaces and Golfs. Well, it looked a bit more promising.

Towards the bottom of the road was the large FOR SALE sign.

'This must be it,' said Don, pulling up.

As they got out of the Jeep, the driver's door opened on a car parked right in front of the house.

'Hello, you must be the Brownings.' A young, smartly dressed man was coming towards them with his hand outstretched.

'Bella Browning,' said Bella, shaking his hand, 'and this is Don McCartney, my husband.'

'Hello, I'm Stephen Rennie, so . . . shall I show you round?'

They walked up the steps, Bella noticing the big windows on the basement floor and the glossy wine-coloured front door.

'The owners are away for the weekend, in case you're wondering,' Stephen told them as they entered a vibrant orange hallway. On the left was the big living room painted such a deep navy that it looked strangely dark and old-fashioned despite the huge bay window and multicoloured rugs over the sofas.

In its favour, the room had a lovely old wooden floor. Everything had been neatly tidied and stacked away, but there were obvious kiddie bits all over the place: big boxes crammed full of toys in the corner, a pile of dog-eared books on the coffee table, stacks of Disney videos on a rack beside the TV. The windows at the back of the room overlooked a tiny patch of garden with high ivy-clad walls and a bright swing moving in the breeze.

Bookshelves had been set up in the back of the room and at a glance Bella spotted cookbooks, gardening manuals and more children's books. There was a comfortable armchair beside the open fireplace.

'The fire does work,' said Stephen, following her gaze. 'It looks like it's been used quite recently, in fact.'

Bella heard herself asking all sorts of efficient questions. How old was the central heating system? Would the windows need work done? All that sort of thing. But she felt a strange mixture of excitement and sadness.

She loved not just the house but the whole lifestyle it suggested. It was a warm, family house, cuddly but groovy. It was all kids and dogs and orange and navy. It was a stay-in-bake-cakes-go-out-get-muddy kind of home and although she knew she was never going to be that kind of person, some tiny part of her longed for that.

Oh get a grip, she told herself. Must be the nesty hormones coursing through my bloodstream.

They went up the stairs which were worn and bumpy underneath the blue runner carpet.

The main bedroom was bright pink with an ornate wooden sleigh bed and a beautiful chest of drawers. There was a white fitted wardrobe bulging with clothes. Framed and unframed pictures of two adorable blond boys and their

161

smiley, Sloaney parents were dotted all around the room.

'That's the owners, in case you're wondering,' said Stephen, apparently driven by a need to fill in the long silences as Bella and Don looked around. 'They're moving to the country, Cumbria I think.'

'Hmm,' said Bella. Of course they are, so they can do dogs and wellies and I think I'm going to cry.

'It's a good size of room,' said Don, not risking anything too controversial.

Bella headed into the next-door bedroom. It was a smaller room with a bunk bed, obviously shared by the boys. Everything was brightly painted. Two of the walls were light blue, two were yellow. The chest of drawers and the wardrobes were painted in yellow and blue stripes. Shelves bulged with stuffed toys, trucks, Lego, books and games.

She was feeling very odd now. Here she was looking into other people's lives and she felt a weird combination of regret and longing. She wished she had grown up in a warm, colourful house like this and she wondered if she and Don could ever have such a happy, cosy family life.

The bathroom on the same floor was a cramped sink, loo, shower-in-bath affair. The blue floor carpet was tatty and so were the black and white tiles on the walls, but the bath was a lovely old salvage job.

After looking round the plain third bedroom, they went up a narrow set of creaky stairs to the loft conversion. 'Ah-ha, the home office,' said Don, who got there ahead of her. He was giving nothing away.

The sunny yellow gabled room was crammed with books, pictures, photos, files, papers, all sorts of strange knick-knacks, including an old stuffed salmon – bizarre – a knackered pram and lots of big brown cardboard boxes. There was a long desk with two state of the art computers on it.

Although it was chaotic, the room was totally charming.

'What do the owners do?' asked Bella.

'I'm not quite sure,' Stephen answered. 'Something creative . . . graphic design, media, something like that. So . . . all the way down to the kitchen and the garden now. Shall we?' he asked.

The basement kitchen was just as Bella imagined it would be – antique pine, orange walls, Aga, large round pine table, plants under the windows. It was a country kitchen in the city. Double doors led out into the garden and four pairs of wellie boots were lined up along the wall beside the door.

'And the garden . . .' Stephen unlocked the doors and they stepped out into an unremarkable patch of lawn fringed with untidy bushes and plants. The swing dangled in the chilly breeze. Bella cast her eye round the toys close to the wall of the house: the sandbox shaped like a frog, the faded plastic trike and dirty bucket and spade.

They all looked at each other.

'Is there anything you'd like to see again?' asked Stephen.

'Let's go up to the sitting room,' said Bella.

All carefully wiped the clumps of garden off onto the kitchen mat and traipsed up the rickety stairs. Bella and Don strode round the sitting room, looking out of the windows. The entrance to the park was just four houses along at the end of the road.

Bella sat down on one of the sofas, hoping another angle on the room would reveal something more.

'We'll talk it over then give you a ring,' she told Stephen as they walked down the steps from the front of the house. They said goodbye and Bella and Don climbed back into the Jeep. They watched Stephen manoeuvre out of his parking space and start off down the road before they said anything.

'So,' Bella turned to Don. 'What did you think?'

'You're asking me to go first?' he answered.

'Yup, definitely.'

'OK, well, I'm going to take a chance here and tell you that I really liked it.'

'Don! The whole place needs replastering, re-papering, painting, the wiring looks dodgy, the bathroom has to be replaced, there's probably hundreds of other things wrong . . .' she paused to look at him, 'but I love it. Let's buy it!'

He broke into a smile.

'Unless you think we're rushing into it and we should look at some other places first?' she added.

'Well, this isn't going to be the first thing we've rushed into together, is it? And so far, so good.'

They grinned at each other.

'How much is it?' he asked.

She told him and he said 'Fuck me,' but softly. 'Are you sure you don't want to buy a French château instead?' he added.

'I think the commute might get a bit boring.'

'You're right. Crumbly Victorian terrace in the outer reaches of north London it is, then.'

'There's a tube station just two streets away, you know.'

'Well, that's settled then. Phone Stephen up.'

So she did and by the end of the afternoon their offer had been accepted, lawyers and surveyors had been contacted and there was talk of decorators and moving in by the end of next month.

Bella just hoped their bank accounts could take the strain.

Chapter Fourteen

The mobile text message which read: 'Your baby is going to be on the social services register before it's even born if you don't come and see me NOW!' shook her somewhat.

She picked up the phone and booked herself into Declan's next surgery, then she messaged him back with a simple 'Sorry, love Bella.'

Two days later she walked into his little office.

'Hello stranger,' he said with a friendly grin.

'Hello, someone is losing hundreds of pounds' worth of valuable consulting time while I sit here and have you check my blood pressure,' was her stressed idea of a greeting.

'Calm down, will you. Let's just have a little chat first.'

She told him she was feeling a lot better than the last time they'd met and slightly more tuned into being pregnant. The booze and fags were under control.

He pushed a small pile of books and leaflets towards her. When she groaned, he asked, 'How

166

many centimetres have you got to dilate before you can deliver?'

She had no idea what he was talking about.

'See,' he said. 'Someone as smart as you needs to be informed, so you know what's happening every step of the way, so you don't start swearing and raging at everyone in the delivery room and demanding to speak to your lawyer.'

She laughed at him then and he did the tests. Blood pressure fine, urine fine. He let her listen to the baby's thunderous heartbeat with his stethoscope.

'Any piles yet?' he asked.

She raised an eyebrow.

'You know, on your bottom, causing pain, itching, resulting from constipation.'

'All right, all right, I'm constipated and I've got piles. There, I've never said that to anyone before.'

'Piles are the scourge of pregnancy that no-one tells you about. Everyone has them, no-one mentions them and wait until you've given birth, you'll have a bunch of grapes hanging out of your arse,' he told her with some relish.

'Lovely.'

He advised fibre, lots of water and regular exercise.

'Oh God, isn't there just a cream I could use?'

'Why are you such hard work?' he almost shouted, but with a smile. '*Yes*, but you have to do the other stuff too. Now, we haven't talked about birth or hospitals.'

'Well, I was going to tell you about that.'

'Aha . . .'

167

'I'm going to go private. I've got an appointment at the posh place down the road next week.'

'Oh.' He looked genuinely disappointed.

'I'm sorry,' she said. 'I really like you, Declan. But I couldn't believe the state of the hospital when I went in for the scan. It is filthy and run down and chaotic.'

'The labour ward is a bit better,' he said.

'Oh come on,' she replied. 'If your sister was having a baby and money was no object, you'd send her to the posh one.'

'No, it would be against my deeply held socialist principles. But . . . well . . .' he sighed. 'If you're asking me should every hospital in the country have facilities like the posh one? I'd say yes.'

'Thank you.'

'Well, I suppose that's us then. I hope it goes really well and that you have a lovely baby. You've got all my numbers. If you need any help or you change your mind, just ring or make an appointment here.'

'Thanks, I really appreciate that.'

They said their goodbyes and she stepped out, relieved he hadn't tried to change her mind, but a bit sad that Declan wasn't going to be looking after her any more. He'd been great, he was probably a very good guy to have around during labour.

The following Monday, she had another half-day off to go to her appointment at the private hospital. One advantage of everyone knowing she was pregnant was that she didn't have to make up excuses for the endless time off that being pregnant seemed to involve.

She got into the car – sod the shortage of parking

spaces at Merris, she was driving – and looked herself over in the mirror. Her skin was peachy, sixth month 'bloom', but her hair had gone weird, kind of dried out and a touch wiry. She applied some red lipstick carefully.

The hospital was beautiful, a reception gleaming with marble tiles, gold fittings and whispery staff, just like a smart hotel. But the service had been strangely hotel-like too. A brisk blond midwife had gone through her medical and pregnancy history. She was very efficient, but Bella somehow couldn't see the phrase 'bunch of grapes hanging out of your arse' coming from her lips. In fact, this midwife hadn't mentioned piles once.

She'd had another scan and although it had been lovely to see the baby again, she was passingly annoyed that it had been sprung on her so there was no chance to have Don there.

'We like to have our own report, rather than use data from another hospital,' the midwife had told her. But Bella suspected it was so they could add a few more figures to their already ludicrous bill.

She'd also briefly met the consultant who would be delivering her baby. After a quick preamble, he'd recommended an epidural, telling her, 'For most women, a first labour is more pain than they have ever experienced in their lives, it can be quite a shock.'

Not very reassuring.

Back in her car and about to set off for work, she rummaged around in her handbag for some food. Mmm, a packet of cashew nuts, a bag of ready-to-eat prunes, two cereal bars and a large bottle of water. This constituted lunch. The prunes, which she now tried to eat every day, were actually quite good, but they hadn't had any effect on the piles.

G-strings were now totally out of the question, the damn things bit into her raw, itchy flesh like a torment. She was beginning to learn that at around six months, you had to ditch all efforts to remain sexy and move into F-cup maternity bras and large white pregnancy pants. She thought of the pale pink G-strings in her dad's pocket and shuddered.

Chapter Fifteen

Finally she and Chris were meeting for their dinner. He had blown her out twice and she had cancelled once, but he'd confirmed at six o'clock today that it was still on, so she had taxied into the centre of town to the elegant address he'd chosen.

The waiter led her to a table where Chris was already seated, looking through a stack of documents.

'Bella!' He jumped up when he saw her and gave her a kiss on the cheek. 'Are you drinking?' he asked as the waiter hovered to take an order.

'I'm going to have one glass of Chablis and that will be it,' said Bella, rummaging in her handbag for a cigarette. She lit up, took a long drag and relaxed back into her chair, sighing the smoke out.

'Still smoking then?' said Chris.

'Oh God, please don't,' she answered. 'This is my one cigarette of the day. From now on I'm only going to smoke locked up in the loos.'

'Sorry. I'm still really surprised you're actually pregnant. I mean, you must have been pregnant in

Birmingham.' He lifted his brows and shot her an intrigued smile.

'Of course, I forgot, pregnant women are not supposed to have any interest in sex,' she snapped back, irritated now. 'Bloody men, you think you're so liberated but at the end of the day it's all virgins, mothers and whores and anything in between just confuses you.'

'Er . . . I'm sorry,' he said again. 'You're probably right.'

'You're just repressed, Chris.' She was smiling at him now. 'You only fuck attractive single women you don't know very well. You need some variety.'

'What are you suggesting?' he asked and God, he was so good-looking, he was dangerous.

'Well, maybe a married, heavily pregnant woman you know very well would be a start, but . . . hey, I'm not offering. I've practically given up drinking and smoking, now is not the time to take up infidelity.' She held his gaze for a moment, then looked down at her menu.

'How's work?' he asked.

'Things have just recently got much better,' she answered. 'Merris has told me on the quiet he is going to set up a merger deal soon, so they'll have money to do all the things that need to be done and he's going to hand over to a new chief exec and move into a back seat. About bloody time.'

'Sounds good.'

'Yup.' She blew out a small wisp of smoke. 'Fun this job, isn't it?'

'The best,' he said.

'I'm not giving it up, you know, for the baby.'

'I think you've made that pretty clear. But you might find you can't devote quite so much time to it.'

'I've thought about that. I'm just going to have to be better in the hours that I am around. I think you should up my rate, so people can't afford me ten hours a day.' There was no way Bella was taking a pay cut or going part time after birth: she wanted to put that message out loud and clear.

'Hmm, interesting idea.'

She was annoyed by that: 'Come on, Chris, don't say you don't think I deserve to be a senior partner by the time the Merris job is over?'

'I think you do. You're doing it brilliantly, but . . .' he trailed off.

'But? Susan doesn't agree?'

There was a pause. Bella wondered if she had overstepped the mark. Chris and Susan were partners after all.

'She's very angry with you,' Chris replied. 'She's unreasonably angry. But she is the boss, you'll just have to wait it out and give her a chance to calm down. You might even need to wait until you're back from maternity leave and can prove to her you're just as good as before.'

Bella was about to launch into an angry tirade, but suddenly thought it wouldn't be best politics.

'Let's eat, I'm starving.' She picked up her menu and decided that the business part of the evening was over.

Bella was feeling stressed and in a fairly lousy mood as she drove to the hospital two weeks later for yet another check-up.

173

In less than three months' time the baby would be here, and it felt like pressure, not pleasure. The house sale still hadn't gone through. She wasn't sure if she could wrap Merris up in time, she hadn't read the pregnancy books yet, or the labour guide, or bought any baby stuff or, NAMES, they hadn't done anything about names.

She was so busy playing it all down, telling everyone she was rushing back to work, it wouldn't change her at all . . . blah blah, she kept pushing the whole thing to the back of her mind. Denial – not just a river in Egypt, as they say.

She put one hand on the bump as she whizzed her car into the hospital's car park. There was a lot of movement down there now, she could feel kicks and prods and a weird twirling motion when the baby span around.

Sweeping in through the hospital's gliding doors, she marched over to reception and was told to go straight through. As she turned from the desk, she saw another woman approaching. With long blond hair and an expensive cream trouser suit, she looked vaguely familiar, but Bella couldn't place her and carried on towards the corridor to her appointed consultation room. When she got there, she shook some of her reports out of her briefcase and began to read them.

After thirty-five minutes had gone by, she was extremely irritated that she was still being kept waiting. She could hear someone walking down the corridor but they stopped just short of her room and opened a neighbouring door.

'Was it really her? From *EastEnders*?' said one voice.

'Yes, she's really nice, very down to earth,' came the reply.

'She was a bit early, wasn't she?'

'Yes, but we saw her straight away.' The voice dropped low, but Bella could still hear: 'The other woman just had to wait a bit . . .'

It took Bella a moment to realize the midwives were talking about her, then she felt the blood rush to her face. She pushed her papers into her bag and strode to the doorway.

The midwife standing at the other door swivelled round and looked at her with dismay.

'Well, I've waited quite long enough today, thank you very much,' Bella said sharply. 'I'm sorry my labour won't be featured in *Hello!* magazine. I thought you'd be too professional to care about that. But obviously not.'

Bella might have changed her mind about walking out of the place for good if the nurse had at least apologized, or said something, but she just stood there absolutely silent. So, Bella turned on her heel and marched out down the long corridor, every step ringing in her ears.

At reception she said curtly: 'Due to the treatment I've *not* received today, I'm cancelling my booking with this hospital. Can you send anything outstanding to my home address? Thank you.'

Back in the car, she was surprised to find herself bursting into tears.

What was she going to do now? She'd signed off from the NHS and now she'd pulled out of the private hospital. What was she doing? She was six months pregnant and she hadn't even had the check-up.

She tried holding her head back so the tears wouldn't ruin her make-up, but it was no use. She put her hands over her face and sobbed. She knew there were some takeaway napkins somewhere in the car, she would just have to do a clean-up operation afterwards.

Several minutes of hard sobbing later, she decided to phone Don, who was of course out of town overnight.

She rang his number and after an age heard a very faint, crackly 'Hello?' at the other end.

'Don, Don? Hello. It's me.'

'Hi, Bella.' He sounded lovely, which made her cry again.

'I've just fallen out with the hospital and I'm not going back and I don't know what to do.'

'What?'

Once she'd explained it all to him, he told her he'd ring her back in a few hours from his hotel when he could talk properly. She knew this was the best plan, but she felt gutted. God, why was she being so pathetic? Must be the hormones.

She dialled Tania's number.

'Tania, it's Bella.'

'Hello darling, how are you?'

'In a bit of a state. Can you sneak off for lunch? No-one's going to miss me at work, they're all too busy figuring out how to avoid bankruptcy,' she sniffed hard.

'Antonio's? 1 p.m.?' Tania answered, sensing the urgency.

'I love you,' Bella answered.

'Likewise.'

Bella clicked the phone off and looked at her face

176

in the rear-view mirror. Much worse than she'd hoped. Big red nose, panda eyes, rivulets of mascara and foundation running down her cheeks. She searched for the napkins and her make-up bag and began a repair job.

Lunch with Tania was inspired. In a comfortable Italian restaurant, Tania poured her red wine to 'fortify' her and let her smoke two cigarettes, soothing, 'You go right ahead, you've had a very upsetting morning.'

By contrast, Tania's morning had been very good. She'd finally landed the big account she'd been after for weeks and Greg had booked a trip to Venice to celebrate.

'Maybe this will be it, the big proposal!' she giggled at Bella.

'Oh God, don't you dare come back all depressed if it doesn't happen. Why don't you ask him yourself?' said Bella.

'I can't.' Tania sucked on her cigarette and blew out smoke with the words: 'It's just the one last bastion that I, as an independent woman in charge of my own destiny, can't overcome, storm . . . whatever it is you're supposed to do with bastions.' They burst into laughter together.

'So, how does it feel now, to have this big tummy, this big baby thing sitting in front of you like that?' asked Tania. 'And by the way, you still look unbelievably slim, you cow. You've got lovely big boobs and a glamorous bump and everything else is just the same. Your bum still looks pert, for God's sake. It's disgusting, it should not be allowed. You better have dessert or I'm not paying.'

Bella snorted with laughter again.

'I feel tired and heavy and fat and tearful,' she confessed. 'My hair is all weird and wiry and I'm going to have to start wearing flat shoes because I can feel my spine starting to buckle with all this forward pull—' she cupped her hands round her bulge.

'Are you getting excited about the baby?' Tania asked.

'I don't feel I've really had the chance, at the moment it just feels like a hassle. Work, maternity leave, the bloody hospital. It's causing problem after problem rather than giving me any cause to celebrate,' was Bella's truthful answer.

'Will you let other people deal with some of the problems for a change, Bella? How's Don?' Tania asked, obviously meaning 'why isn't he helping you?'

'He's been away a lot. I think he wants to do all the foreigns he can, while he still has the chance. I don't know, we feel a bit out of touch right now.'

'And what is sex with a bump like?' Tania asked, twirling a forkful of pasta.

'Let's just say there's less sex.'

'Ah.' Tania looked across at Bella, but the subject appeared to be closed. 'I've got a very good idea,' Tania said suddenly. 'Why don't you come down to my parents' house at the weekend?'

'Yeah?'

'Yeah. We'll drive down on Friday after work and we'll have fresh air and pampering. Mum is desperate to see you, now that you're pregnant. She's hoping you're going to make me broody. Anyway, she knows everything about hospitals

178

and midwives and stuff, she'll know what you should do.'

Bella agreed, deciding maybe it would be nice to let someone take care of her for a couple of days.

By 9 p.m. that night, Don still hadn't rung. She'd tried his mobile several times, but only reached the messaging service. She wondered if she should be worried about him but she couldn't get worked up to it, not after just one evening.

She went to bed soon afterwards but half an hour later was woken by him calling from a noisy bar.

'I'm asleep,' she told him grumpily.

'Sorry,' he said. 'It's only 10 p.m.'

'Yeah, well . . .'

'Sorry, Bella. Don't worry, everything's going to be fine.'

'Easy for you to say . . . you aren't carrying around a six-month bump and wondering how the hell this is all going to work out.' She felt angry now.

'Look, go to sleep, it won't seem so bad in the morning. Good night, hon.'

'Bye,' she said and slammed the receiver down.

Chapter Sixteen

Bella had forgotten how fantastically opulent Tania's family home was. It was in the heart of stockbroker belt Kent, a big country house in its own small woodland.

They arrived there in the evening and as they drove up to the house, gravel crunched under the car wheels and vast lit up windows welcomed them in.

Tania's mother, Valerie, was at the door to greet them, hugging and kissing warmly. Ronald was in the enormous sitting room, drinking gin and tonic. He kissed Bella hello and insisted she sit down beside him, because he wanted to hear her City gossip. He was the one who had fired up her enthusiasm for consulting in the first place.

'You are not allowed to talk with Bella all evening, *chérie*. I want to hear all about your pregnancy darling,' Valerie warned from the door.

'Now, what are you drinking, girls? We've got mineral water, cranberry juice, apple, all sorts of soft things in for you, Bella.'

Bella and Tania's eyes met. Valerie was a

respected alternative health writer, it was not going to do to get caught drinking and smoking in your third trimester in her house.

'Cranberry, please,' said Bella.

'Gin and vermouth with a twist,' said Tania.

'Ha ha,' Valerie answered. 'You'll have a white wine and be grateful. In fact you should probably have a cranberry juice and a handful of milk thistle capsules for all the abuse you do to your liver in town.'

It was lovely to be there. Valerie mollycoddled Bella all evening, listening to the story about the hospitals with a great deal of sympathy.

'Well, I have a possible solution for you,' she said when Bella told her she still hadn't made any new arrangements. 'Home birth. I've just interviewed a woman who runs a group of independent midwives in London. You hire the midwife for the whole pregnancy, and in labour she comes to your home.'

Bella was somewhat taken aback.

'God. Is that safe? Is it legal?'

'Oh darling, go read the statistics. Let me get you a book.'

She came back with book, her article on the midwives and the phone number.

'Think it over. Now, tell me all about your new home.'

So Bella did and once Valerie had got over the shock – 'That's how much houses cost in Holloway, darling??' – they got into a whole decorating conversation along with Tania, who lived to decorate.

'I love this room,' said Bella, taking in the rugs,

181

antiques, luscious plants, paintings and all the polished, gleaming things which glittered in the firelight.

'Oh, it's very boring,' Valerie assured her. 'Nice floorboards, very expensive curtains, everything else is white – white walls, white sofas and then all the plants, paintings, things one seems to accumulate.'

'Not very minimal though, is it?' said Tania. Every available space was crammed full and the walls were so laden with paintings, Bella hadn't even registered they were white.

'We've lived here for thirty years, Tania,' said Valerie.

'What makes you think I'm going to be minimal?' Bella asked Tania.

'For a start, you're a mathematician, they're always anal. And secondly, you haven't got any stuff. Your house is going to be a temple to Zen unless you do some serious shopping.'

'Don has stuff. I made him throw out boxes and boxes of stuff before he was allowed into my flat.'

'Yeah, he's got a sofa and a bookcase left, I've been to your place,' Tania teased.

'Well, I was planning to buy a few things,' said Bella.

'You'll have to take me with you. In another month, you are not going to be in a fit state to go alone. By month eight you'll have lost your marbles completely.'

'No I will not!'

'Tell her, Mum.' Tania sounded like a teenager.

'Well, there are so many things to think about,'

Valerie soothed, 'and so many oestrogens and oxytocins buzzing round the system, mental calculations go down the priority list before and after birth.'

'Oh great,' said Bella. 'Like I haven't got enough to worry about.'

'When do you stop working?' Valerie asked.

'I'm working right up to labour day, I hope, then taking about two months off.'

'For a first baby, this is not enough,' Valerie told her rather bluntly.

'Well, I've got a client waiting for me in August and my boss is not exactly brimful of understanding right now,' Bella answered.

'Oh, you are pushing yourself very hard,' Valerie added. 'Just like Tania. Maybe you should take a step back and think about this in the long term. Is a few extra months off now really going to make such a difference to your career in ten years' time? I don't think so.'

Valerie could see by Bella's stormy face she had said too much.

'Think about it, Bella, please.' She patted Bella's arm then stood up and announced: 'Dinner's ready, let's go and eat.'

'Christ, Don, did it ever occur to you that you might have got shot?' she asked, having listened to Don's latest exploits at work when they got together again on Sunday evening. 'And in Bradford, not even Beirut.'

'Well, yes, but I kept telling myself that it wouldn't happen because I've got such a ludicrously big life insurance policy.'

'Have you really? I think I should be told,' she asked teasingly.

'God, that's a point, Bella. In my will at the moment, everything goes to Mum.' He scooped up the last of the sauce from his plate with a piece of bread.

'Better get that changed,' she said. 'I don't want Maddie swanning off to retire in Bermuda while I'm left destitute to care for your infant.'

'*You* destitute – that I would like to see. By destitute, I suppose you mean down to your last technology fund ISA.'

'Ha, ha,' she answered, wishing that were true. They were soon to be mortgaged to the hilt and the very last of her savings were going to be spent on decorators.

'Let's go snog on the sofa,' he said to her when the meal was finished.

'Well, OK, but I'm going on top.'

'Snog, I said. Don't assume I want to go all the way,' he was teasing now.

'One minute of my practised tongue technique and you will be desperate.' She got up from her chair and kissed him all the way over to the sofa where he flung himself down.

'No, not working yet, I think you'll have to try again.' He pulled her over.

She was uncomfortable trying to lie on him and kiss him over the heavy, cumbersome bump. 'Let's go to bed,' she said. 'I can't manoeuvre here.'

They walked through to the bedroom where Don sat down on the edge of the bed and pulled her close. They kissed for a long time then began to undress each other. Neither felt frantically turned on, but there was tenderness in their movements.

Don felt round her outfit for an opening and realized he would have to pull it over her head. He yanked her top clumsily off and left her standing messy haired and rumpled in the most hideous white bra and low slung pants he'd ever seen.

'I know,' she said picking up his disconcerted look. 'Why don't I change into something less comfortable?'

'No, take it all off, I want to see you.'

She unhooked the bra and her heavy breasts dropped down unsupported. The nipples had grown large and a dark raspberry colour.

Her stomach swelled out in front of his face with a strange-looking stretched belly button punctuating the middle. The deep blue veins on her white breasts and stomach were prominent. She pulled off her pants and her pubic hair was tucked away under the bulge, which suddenly flickered.

'God, it moved,' he said anxiously.

'Of course.' She couldn't believe she hadn't shown him this yet. 'Give me your hand,' she said. She put his hand flat against one side. They waited silently for a few moments then he felt a surprisingly sharp blow underneath his palm.

'My God, that is so strong and it's just there, right underneath your skin.'

'Yup,' she smiled.

'That's amazing,' he said. 'It doesn't hurt at all?' She shook her head. 'This is OK, isn't it? Having sex,' he asked.

'Well, let's try.' She smiled at him, sitting there in his boxer shorts, socks, shirt and tie. She knelt down and pulled his shorts and socks off, then leaned into his lap and put her mouth on his erection.

When she pulled herself up to kiss him, she tried to straddle his lap but the bump was in the way.

'Lie down,' he whispered.

She lay on her side and he tucked in close behind her, putting a hand between her legs. She reached back for his cock and slowly worked it inside.

He took hold of her hips and began to move in deeper.

'Oh God,' she gasped, not entirely in pleasure. 'I just don't know if there's room. This feels weird.'

She felt utterly full with him inside and worse, the baby's sharp, solid parts were being pushed about and rearranged. She felt like a sink full of crockery clattering about as someone tried to push more plates in – not exactly passion-inducing.

'Do you want me to come out?' asked Don.

'No, just go really slowly, don't do anything sudden.'

He moved very carefully and it wasn't unpleasant, but it wasn't really sex.

Chapter Seventeen

Completion date on the house had arrived one week earlier than agreed – a minor London miracle, Bella couldn't help thinking as she and Don went to pick up the keys and make the journey up town to their new home. She felt nervous. Christ, they'd just spent an absolute fortune buying property in an area they'd *driven* through.

Don looked relaxed, breezy almost.

Bella was wearing the most glamorous maternity clothes she could muster, black leather trousers and soft white tunic underneath a new grey fur-collared coat. But a seven and a bit month bulge was no longer elegant. She was starting to feel very heavy on her feet and it was some effort to clamber up into the Jeep.

They were visiting the house in the morning, then she was meeting the independent midwife for the first time this afternoon to discuss the home birth option. She'd ummed and ahhed about having Don at the meeting, then decided no, that would probably horrify him more than he deserved at this stage.

He would now look so pained whenever she mentioned birth that she was beginning to worry that he was going to back out of attending her labour.

'Don! You've reported from battlefields,' she'd told him in one heated exchange.

'I've seen people give birth in fields as well,' he'd shot back. 'And it is not pretty. I just don't know if I want to see you in so much pain.'

It was still an unresolved point.

They drove up through town. It was a grey March morning, cold and raining slightly. Her pet hate weather in the world. When they got to the street, it looked much greyer and gloomier than it had done on the day they'd looked round.

Don parked up and got out of the car first. Bella took a few moments to clamber out and lumber up the street after him.

They unlocked their front door and went inside. Don flicked on the hall light and the walls looked unrelentingly orange now that the place was empty and stripped bare. In the dark, sombre navy sitting room there were patches on the walls and on the floorboards where pictures and furniture had been.

Bella looked out of the back window at the rain-sodden garden where yellow flattened grass marked the spot where the swing had been. 'God,' she said to Don. 'It does need some cheering up, doesn't it?' She was trying to sound upbeat, while silently thinking, What have we done?

Upstairs looked no better, especially the pink bedroom, savagely pink now that it was empty, and the children's bedroom with its mismatched walls.

'It feels empty and lonely,' she said to Don, with a slight wobble.

'It'll be fine,' he assured her. 'We need to decorate and put in our own things.'

'Do you still think we've done the right thing?' She needed to hear him say yes.

'Yes. It's a good choice. It's a lovely big house. It's going to be great.' He put his arms around her, 'You're going to feel a lot better once we've christened the place,' he smiled and kissed her nose.

'Now I know you're kidding!' she laughed and pushed him away. 'The only thing I'm going to christen right now is the loo.'

The bathroom was much shabbier than she remembered and cold too. The family must have moved out several days ago because the house was chilled to the brick.

Back down in the kitchen, Don leaned against the Aga as she outlined her decorating plans.

'I want to keep it simple because we've not got long now.' She stroked over the bump. 'I think replaster, paint everything white, strip down and revarnish all the floors, put in a new bathroom and new kitchen.'

He looked at her incredulously. 'That's simple? Bella! That's about eight months of work!!'

'No! Stephen has put me in touch with a team of people who say they can do it in a month,' she answered.

'Can we afford all that on top of the mortgage and an extra month or two renting?' he asked.

Not to mention the deposit, the solicitor's fee, stamp duty . . . she couldn't help adding it all up and the answer was 'No, not really', but she couldn't stand the thought of bringing the baby into a messy, unfinished house. She wanted it all sorted out. She'd get the promotion to partner when she went back to work and then it would be OK. This was just going to be a bit of a struggle for a few months.

'We'll be fine,' she answered. 'I'm going to be a partner by the end of the year,' she assured him.

'This is making me feel strange,' he said, folding his arms across his chest.

'Don –' she was beginning to feel exasperated now – 'You're paying half of the mortgage and we're a couple now. What's mine is yours. Don't say I can't spend money on our home, please.'

'Well, if you're sure it's what you want to do . . .' He looked her in the eye. 'Just don't spend every last penny, Bella, or you'll end up a sad old git like me who has to rely on his wealthy wife.'

'Don!' she smiled. 'Come on, we've got to go. The hippie midwives are coming to see me in an hour.'

'The what?!'

'Sorry, that's what I keep calling them. The independent midwives, the ones who are going to look after me from now on.' She had not had the home birth talk with Don yet. She hadn't made up her mind, so what was the point in worrying him?

'Ah . . .' Long pause. Please don't ask, please don't ask . . . but he did: 'So where are you having the baby now, Bella?'

'Let me speak to them and then we'll go through the options tonight, OK?' She put on her most relaxed, smiling, everything's fine face.

'OK, let's go then.' He glanced around the kitchen which looked dingy and forlorn in the grey light. 'This is a great house, I can't wait to move in.' He was only lying a little bit. It would be fine once it was repainted.

She kissed him on the cheek. 'I love you.'

'Me too,' he said. And they headed home.

Twenty minutes after the arranged time, the doorbell rang. Bella went to the intercom and told Annie Mellor to come up to the third floor. She opened the door to a pleasant-looking, 30-something woman with mousy brown hair gathered into a long waist-length ponytail. She was wearing strange patchwork baggy trousers, suede desert boots, a knee-length anorak and had a straw basket over one shoulder. Bella felt her heart sink: this just really wasn't what she'd expected.

'Hello, I'm Annie.' Annie held out a soft white hand and Bella shook it firmly.

'Come in,' she said, trying not to sound as unimpressed as she felt.

She led Annie into her large sitting room where she perched on one of the two black leather sofas.

'Gosh,' said Annie. 'This is big, isn't it?'

'Can I get you a tea or a coffee?' asked Bella.

'Have you got anything herbal?' Annie asked.

'No.'

'Just water then, please.'

Bella returned with a tall glass of iced water and a cafetière of extra strong, super-caffeinated coffee for herself. She was tempted to have a cigarette as well but decided that would probably scare Annie off completely.

'OK,' said Bella, plonking her tray down on the coffee table. 'I'm considering using your service, so I want you to tell me all about it.'

191

'Well, basically, I will do all your antenatal care . . .'

'Can you come to my office?' Bella chipped in.

'Well, I don't see why not,' said Annie calmly.

'Right.' That was a major Brownie point.

'And then when you are in labour, I'll come to your home and deliver the baby.' This sounded too easy, too much like 'I'll come to your home and deliver your parcel.'

'So . . . how much experience do you have?' Bella asked.

'I'm a fully qualified senior midwife, I've been doing home births for about fifteen years now.' Annie fixed her with a slightly stern look and Bella saw the network of tiny lines around her eyes and mouth and realized she was much older than she at first looked, probably mid-forties.

'Right. And what happens if anything goes wrong?' Bella asked.

'Yes, everyone asks that,' said Annie. 'Obviously, if it's major we rush you to hospital in an ambulance. But our transference rate is about 10 per cent, mainly requests from the mother. Ninety per cent of our babies are delivered naturally without any intervention or even pain relief. You should compare that with the figures at the hospital down the road.'

Aha, figures. Bella was starting to relax.

'We find that women labouring at home with a midwife they know and trust deliver much more safely than if they are whisked off to hospital where all kinds of strangers are prodding and poking at them, strapping them to machines,' Annie said.

192

'So you don't give any drugs at all?' Bella asked.

'We prefer not to. We have a TENS machine on hand but we prefer aromatherapy massage, hot baths or a birthing pool and natural remedies.'

'Well, I've read a home birth book,' Bella said. 'A friend gave it to me, but I just wonder if it isn't all a bit idealistic. It's all smiley happy people having a back rub while babies pop out. What about all the screaming and blood and agony?'

'Well, there's a bit of that too – but birth is not half as bad as they make out on *ER*,' Annie smiled. 'If you're in a good atmosphere with people you know supporting you, it can make all the difference.'

Bella noticed how slight Annie was. Her thin legs were crossed and her desert boots gaped at her bony ankles. She just didn't look strong enough to be a midwife.

'So what do you need for a home birth?' Bella asked. 'We're moving house next month, by the way.'

'All pregnant women are moving house or decorating. It's a rule,' Annie smiled again and Bella smiled back. She was warming to her . . . a little bit.

'First of all we need to talk about your health,' said Annie. 'Truthfully!'

'Right.'

Annie read her way carefully through Bella's maternity notes.

'Are you still drinking and smoking?' she asked.

'I've cut right down.' She did not need another lecture.

'Well you've got to stop, Bella. I can't over-emphasize how bad it is for the baby. Are you doing any exercise?'

'I ran every morning till about month six, now I'm power walking and going to the gym once or twice a week.'

Annie looked a touch horrified and recommended an antenatal yoga class.

Then she asked: 'When do you stop work?'

'I was going to work right up to wire, but the project I'm on might wind up a week or two early, so I might have a bit of extra time off.'

'Good,' Annie said. 'I think you need it, because you've not really had the time to give this baby much thought yet, have you?'

This was said kindly, but Bella felt a little bit stung. She knew it was true and she did feel ready to slow up a bit now, read the books, mooch round the nursery shops and think about names. There and then she decided she was going to give Annie a go. She would get regular antenatal visits in her office, sign up for the yoga classes and mull over a home birth.

Once Annie had left, Bella called Tania for a second opinion.

'You don't think it's just a bit alternative and hippie?' Bella asked.

'Home birth?' Tania answered. 'No, it's ultra modern and cool. *De rigueur* in Notting Hill. The NHS is too PC, private is "Too posh to push", so everyone's having their baby at home.'

'Oh well that's OK then,' Bella said, heavy on the irony. 'God, Tani, this is birth not a fashion statement!'

'Bella, you live in central London, they can get you to hospital in ten minutes flat, I'm sure it will be fine. How's your new house?'

'We went there this morning, it looks empty and sad and depressing.'

'You need to decorate. When can I come and look round?'

They fixed up a date for the weekend.

Bella and Don were eating out with Mel and Jasper that night, so they drove across town crammed cosily into Bella's car.

'I can't believe you can still get into this thing,' Don teased as they sat almost cheek by cheek in the low seats. 'Isn't driving a bit difficult now?'

'No, it's lovely . . . I can whiz around and duck and dive and forget that I'm a great big huge pregnant whale when I'm on dry land.'

'Any more metaphors you'd like to stir into that cocktail?' he teased.

'Oh shut up.' She fired up the engine and reversed out of the space. 'I'm the mathematician, you're the wordsmith. Can we leave it at that?'

'So, who are we going to name our child after?' he asked once they were on the road. 'Wordsmiths or mathematicians?'

'I don't want to name him or her after anyone,' she said. 'I want something totally unique.'

'Oh no . . . not Bellabel Ginseng Algebra Browning!'

She snorted with laughter.

'What about your heroes?' he asked. 'Maybe Benito?'

'Who??'

'Mussolini, of course . . .' he carried on over her protests. 'Woody? For Woody Allen? And what's Einstein's first name again?'

'Frank,' she answered. 'Frank Einstein,' then over his laughter, she asked, 'You want Dylan, don't you? After the great Bob?'

'Yes!' he answered. 'Please, can we?'

'NO! Absolutely no way!'

'Well if we're doing musical heroes, I suppose you'll want Robbie or maybe Ronan . . . or Posh,' he said, so she whacked him on the arm.

'How about Karl . . . after Marx?' was his next suggestion.

'Mark . . .' she said. 'Markie McCartney. Hey! I like that.'

'Hmmm,' he answered. 'And girls?'

'It won't be a girl,' she said with a grin.

'No?'

'No, I just know.'

'You sneaked a peak at your last scan, didn't you?'

'I'm not saying!! I just know.'

'You are a totally devious, cheating woman, Bella,' Don was teasing but stopped when he saw her expression change abruptly. 'What's wrong?' he asked urgently.

'Nothing, nothing . . . sorry. Anxious baby thoughts, that's all. Sorry,' she said, gluing her eyes to the traffic lights in front of them and willing the big hit of Chris guilt to go away.

'It's going to be great,' he said soothingly.

'I hope so,' she answered.

Chapter Eighteen

'Bella, Bella, wake up. Your alarm's been beeping for ages.'

She opened her eyes and looked at Don wearily.

'Oh Christ.' She rolled onto her side and pushed herself up off the bed.

She was heavy and extremely tired. It was impossible to get a full night's sleep now. She had to empty her bladder at least twice a night and despite having pillows between her knees and under her bulge, it was hard to get comfortable.

Still, she had to keep going. It was already April, she was in her eighth month and the Merris deadline had to be met before she could entertain any thoughts of dropping this little load. She cranked herself up and put on her dressing gown, tying the cord over the bump so she looked like a walking Easter egg. She waddled to the bathroom, pinned up her hair, washed her face, slapped some make-up on.

Back in the bedroom she put on large white bra, pants, black maternity support tights, which practically came up to her armpits, then a flapping white shirt and the grey polyester suit and flat shoes.

Don was looking at her from the bed.

'Don't say anything,' she warned him, 'I look like shit, I feel like shit too. The stylish, sexy woman you married has turned into a monster.'

He laughed, but she didn't.

'I hate this, Don, I feel like a whale. I know you're going to make lots of nice reassuring noises but I am a whale.'

Don said: 'I'm your whale mate, then.'

The doorbell rang. It was the taxi. She and Geoff now took a shared minicab to work. It was a posh minicab – plush Rover with driver who could speak English, drive and get them there – but still a minicab, not a limousine.

Geoff didn't say anything to her at all now, just 'Umm' for Good Morning then hid behind his paper.

It always got like this towards the end of the job. Everyone hated you because your criticisms of their work were made public and acted upon. This was the toughest part. It was the natural human 'shoot the messenger' response and she tried not to take it personally, but she always felt a bit hurt when it kicked in.

The baby rolled round in her stomach. She hadn't had time for breakfast and a hard lump of heartburn was stuck in her chest.

'Geoff, I hope you don't mind,' she said. 'We're passing a café in a few moments, I'm going to ask the driver to pull over so I can get something.'

'Ummm.'

'Do you want anything?'

'Ummph.'

God Almighty, she hadn't faced this kind of behaviour since primary two.

She was glad when she was finally in her little office, closeted away from the growing panic enveloping the company. The merger had just been announced, along with Merris's resignation from the chief exec position. Everyone now knew the changes were happening and the anxiety was palpable.

Bella Browning, 28, first solo project, had set this all in motion. She felt badly in need of some re-assurance, so she decided to phone the office.

'Good morning, Prentice and Partners.' She felt better just for hearing that on the other end of the line.

'Kitty, hello, it's Bella.'

'Bella! How are you? We haven't seen you for ages. You must be huge by now. Promise you'll come for Friday drinks?'

'I'll see. I don't know what's happening on Friday yet, I'll try. I've missed you all.'

'It's been so quiet, no-one's been in the office apart from Susan.'

'Is she in now?'

'Yup, I'll try the line, but come and see us on Friday.'

'I'll be there if I can.'

She held for several long minutes. She had barely spoken to Susan since Christmas and she now felt a nervous twinge about it.

'Bella, hello, how are you?' Susan's voice was crisp and professional.

'I'm OK. Well, actually I'm having a bit of a

confidence crisis about Merris. I'd really like to talk you through my final report before I give it, just to make sure it's all right.'

'Of course it is. I have every faith in you, Bella,' Susan answered.

'Is there a good time to phone you later today? I'd really like to just take you through an outline,' Bella persisted.

'That's fine. How about 3.30? But Bella, don't worry, I'm sure it's very good work.'

'Thanks, Susan, I needed to hear that.'

'I'll speak to you later then.'

'Bye.'

She had made the call on her mobile – it was time to be very careful. Now her desk phone was ringing. Janice from Merris's office wanted to know if Bella could go in and see him now.

'I'll be there in ten minutes,' Bella answered thinking *AAAAAArgh* and scrabbling to get some papers together. She could feel her heart thud in her chest and the baby churned around inside her stomach.

She didn't know what this could be about and felt panicky. She took her ten-pack of cigarettes out of her briefcase and lit up with shaking hands.

By the fifth drag, she was starting to feel steady, by the seventh she was toughening up again. Her analysis had been correct, her suggestions good – there was nothing she needed to worry about: if the chairman wanted to hear it from the horse's mouth first, ahead of the board – he was bloody well going to.

Janice showed her into Merris's office. She'd forgotten how old-fashioned it was – wood panelling, portraits of horses and ancestors on the walls, him behind a vast desk in an over-upholstered swivel chair.

Merris, as ever, looked like a dapper politician in a dark three-piece suit, complete with watch chain and tiny yellow carnation bud in the buttonhole. His grey hair was combed back neatly and he fixed his pale blue eyes on her. 'My word Bella, you have torn through us like a hurricane, haven't you?' was his opening gambit.

'No not really,' she said, settling down in the chair he indicated. 'Hurricanes are destructive, I want to help you build something strong for the future.'

'Yes, I appreciate that,' he said, then added: 'I'm very pleased with the merger.'

He told her the very big price he'd achieved. She whistled and he laughed at her.

'Do they know about the appeal case?' she asked.

'They know it's a remote possibility. You're very concerned about that, aren't you?'

'If you lose, it would be a disaster. Well, less of a disaster now you have new partners,' she said.

'We won't lose,' he replied and made it sound like his final word on the subject.

'So,' he continued, 'I'm moving upstairs, which makes me feel a touch sad, but thank you for reminding me that chief executives can't go on for ever. I don't know who's replacing me yet, our new partners will want to have a say in that, but I've called you in here, Ms Browning because I'd like to recommend you for the post of financial director.'

He paused for her reaction, but she didn't make one. She was thinking about Geoff, the current financial director, tutting at her in the taxi and wondered where he would be going, so Merris named his price.

She whistled again.

They looked at each other, then finally she said: 'That's a very generous offer, Mr Merris. But I've got a lot to think about at the moment. I'm five weeks away from giving birth for the first time and to be frank, well, I'm not sure if I have the experience yet.'

That was the clincher. A financial directorship would be very nice and would certainly pay the mortgage but it wasn't in the career plan just yet. She had a lot more consulting to get under her belt first.

But Merris said: 'I wouldn't ask you if I didn't think you could do it,' then added, 'Well I don't expect an answer straight away. Feel free to come back to me any time.'

She smiled at him.

'Now,' he said, 'I am looking forward to your report because I'm expecting you to tell us that the merger and strategies we've put in place, thanks to you, are going to have a very positive effect.'

'Yes,' she said, 'I hope that will encourage everyone.'

'Excellent. Now we may not have the chance for another personal chat before you leave, so I want to tell you how grateful I am for your work. I'll be telling your boss that too. But I'd rather you came and worked for me than anyone else.'

'Well, I'll give it some serious thought.' She smiled at him.

She stood up with the feeling that the meeting was drawing to a close.

'Now—' he opened a drawer and brought out a small exquisitely wrapped box. He stood up and walked round the desk to hand it to her: 'This is a token of my appreciation.'

She took it from him thinking, Jewellery from a client, oops. It struck her as somehow inappropriate.

'Please open it,' he said.

'Right.' She wondered how to handle the situation.

She tugged at the ribbon and lifted the lid on a white teething ring attached to a large solid silver bear. It was quite the most ridiculous gift for a baby ever, but she was still touched at the sentiment.

'Thank you, Mr Merris,' she said, holding out her hand for a businesslike handshake.

'You can call me Tony,' he said shaking her hand firmly and patting her arm. 'In fact, you already have once.'

She blushed slightly.

'Yes, I have, sorry . . . I can be a bit . . .'

'Don't apologize,' he cut in. 'That's what I like about you, Bella. You've got guts. I'm surrounded by yes men and look where it's got me. I think it would do me good to have a "no woman" around.'

'A "no woman", I like that,' she smiled. 'Thank you so much for your support. Now, I'd better go and put that report together.'

'Yes,' he said. 'I look forward to it.'

She swanned out of his office and back to her own, smiling all the way.

At 3.30 p.m. she telephoned Susan to tell her about the latest developments.

'It's gone so well, Susan, he even offered me a job.' She said this lightly to imply there was no question of her taking it.

'And what did you say?' Susan asked.

'I told him I had a lot on my mind right now and I'd get back to him. But I'm with you, Susan. I want to let you know how committed I am, despite the baby.'

'Despite the baby' – she didn't like herself for saying that. Having a baby was not something she should be apologizing about. Hello, this is century 21.

'I appreciate that,' Susan replied. 'Are you handing in the report and finishing up there next week?'

'Yes, probably on Wednesday/Thursday.'

'Well, next Friday we're taking you out for a maternity leave party and as of then you are off. Don't count it as official leave, have the three weeks extra on us. You deserve it.'

Bella felt touched now. 'Thanks,' she said. 'That means a lot.'

The report smacked onto Mr Merris's desk at 8 a.m. the following Wednesday. The eight days it had taken to finish off had passed in a blur and she had worked like a dog.

Most of the weekend had been spent in her dressing gown at the computer compiling the vast amounts of data needed to prove that her recovery strategies were already working, but could be further improved on. She'd barely seen Don, who had been working late as well.

It had been a grind with momentary flashes of inspiration. She wondered about the future of Merris. They were getting an injection of new money and new talent but she did not know if it was going to be enough to really change the thinking there. And she still couldn't be as blasé about the court case as everyone else seemed to be. What if the pension holders won? Merris would be forced to make enormous payouts and its reputation would fold overnight.

Mitch crossed her mind. She had more or less told him it was safe to stay, but now she just didn't know.

On Wednesday afternoon she made her presentation to a surprisingly large audience, not just Merris chiefs but also executives from the new partner company. Her thrust was encouraging but cautious because Merris Group was not out of the woods by a long shot.

She felt horribly self-conscious as she stood in front of them, ridiculously pregnant, bulging at the seams of her foul jersey dress. Could she have been any more of an outsider? Would they take her at all seriously? At the end of the day, that was their problem. She'd done the job she'd been paid to do, she kept reminding herself.

Afterwards, there was a small drinks party, so everyone could shake her hand, ask more questions and thank her for her efforts. Later she was back in her little office, emptying her drawers and packing up, when there was a knock at the door.

Janice came in weighed down with a big bunch of flowers.

'These are from Mr Merris, with compliments,' she said, passing Bella the enormous bouquet. The note attached read: 'Well done, we'd still like you aboard, Tony.'

She was standing in the room, unsure where to put the flowers when there was another knock.

Mitch appeared.

'Whoa, who is your secret admirer?'

'Tony.'

Mitch looked blank.

'Tony Merris.'

'Oh. Really? I'm impressed.' Then he added, 'I'm sorry you're leaving, mainly because all hell is going to break loose here now. I hope.'

'Yeah, I hope so too. It needs a good shake-up, but there's going to be lots more room for good people like you.'

'I hope so.' Then Mitch voiced the concern she expected: 'Do you still think I should stay?'

'I can't answer that. It depends who's doing the reorganization, I've asked them to bring in a lot more new talent. And I'm still worried about the court case . . . if they lose, that's a lot of money.'

'Hmmm.' He didn't give anything away. 'Well anyway, I've got you a present.' He handed her a squishy, wrapped parcel.

'Oh you shouldn't have, now I'm really embarrassed because I haven't got anything for you.'

'It's for the baby,' he added. 'Open it.'

She unwrapped a small, perfectly adorable, blue velvet frog.

'It squeaks and it's machine washable, dads know about that sort of thing.'

'Thanks very much.' She was surprised to feel tears pricking at the back of her eyes. 'How's your wife?' she asked.

'She's doing good, she's very tired because she's got two other little people to run after all day and the baby. But she's well and we're really glad to have got a girl.'

There was a brief silence; they smiled at each other, comfortable with the pause.

'Give me your card, Bella. I'll keep you in touch with what's happening here.'

'Of course.' She dipped into her bag and handed him one.

'Well all the best then,' he said and they shook hands warmly.

'Take care,' she said as he left the room.

So, that was about it. She'd packed up, she'd said her goodbyes. She buzzed reception to get her a cab, then headed out of Merris laden down with bump, bags, laptop, briefcase and the flowers.

As she flopped into the cab seat, Bella took one last look at the revolving swing doors and impressive marble front. She swallowed down the urge to cry as the taxi moved off.

Friday night was much more emotional.

She went out with Susan, Chris, Kitty and Hector for dinner and they made baby jokes and lovely appreciative noises about her all night long.

Finally, as dessert and coffees arrived to the maelstrom of empty wine bottles and overflowing ashtrays on the table, Chris made a jokey speech

207

about her which ended with a silly poem. Everyone collapsed in pissed-up giggles. Fortunately, Kitty brought out a large parcel from under the table.

'Open it,' she urged.

Bella cleared a space and undid the wrapper. Inside was a small mountain of exquisite baby clothes: orange and blue velour babygros, beautiful striped and decorated jackets, rompers, tiny suede shoes, a multicoloured hat with ear-flaps and a bobble and a mobile of little stuffed clowns on ribbons.

'Oh my God,' she said quite overwhelmed. 'You found all these lovely things.'

'Me and Susan,' said Kitty. 'Took a whole afternoon.' That surprised Bella, she tried to picture Susan in a baby shop.

'Oh thank you, thank you so much.' Bella looked up at each of the four faces in turn. 'This is absolutely wonderful. I'm going to cry now.' And she did. At first able to stem the flow with her napkin, then needing to bury her head in Kitty's shoulder for a serious howl.

'Oh God, this is so embarrassing,' she said when she surfaced. 'It's the hormones, I'm starting to go completely mad.'

It was after midnight when she finally kissed them all good night and climbed into a taxi to go home.

Lights were on in the flat and she hoped Don had waited up for her. He was leaving early tomorrow morning on another foreign assignment which he'd promised would be very short as the due date was getting close now.

'Hi,' she called out, opening the front door.

'I'm in here,' he answered and his voice sounded incredibly serious. She walked into the dark sitting room, noticing two large holdalls next to the front door as she passed.

Don was sitting on the sofa in silence, no TV, no music on. He didn't look up at her as she came in. 'I've just found out about the baby,' he said.

'Hello?' she said, wondering what the hell he meant. 'I thought I told you months ago. What on earth do you think this bump is?'

'I'm just so angry with you. How could you do this to me?' He looked round at her now and she saw he was furious.

'What are you talking about??' she asked, totally confused.

'Well, let me explain,' he said. I was having a quiet evening in with not much to do and I happened to see your maternity notes on the shelf. I was just curious, didn't see any harm in reading them . . . didn't have any idea I'd be uncovering your big secret.'

'What do you mean?' she asked, feeling very nervous now.

'Well, either someone's made a mistake, or you intended to get pregnant all along, without bothering to tell me.'

He thrust the booklet out at her and she could clearly see the tick in the 'planned' box. She also saw the handwritten note beside it, 'Folic acid taken for four months before conception.'

'Four months before conception,' Don read out. 'And it never occurred to you, for one moment, to even mention this to me?'

'Jesus,' she whispered. That all seemed so long

209

ago now, she'd completely forgotten about it. 'Can I try and explain?'

'No. Not right now. I'm too angry. I always thought there was something strange about *you* having an accident.' He stood up and rounded on her: 'How could you lie to me about this? Why couldn't you just trust me, like I've always, always trusted you?

'It's so manipulative,' he added furiously. 'You've got it all figured out, haven't you? And I'm just supposed to fit into your big plan.'

'No. Don, I'm sorry, I just didn't think you'd want to . . .'

'No, you know what? I've got to get out of here. I can't listen to this right now,' he cut in. 'I'm going to get a cab over to Rod's and we'll go to the airport together in the morning.'

He stood up and walked past her to the door.

'Don!' she pleaded, she put out a hand to stop him, 'Don, please—' but he brushed her off and went into the hall. He picked up his bags, then walked out without another word, slamming the door.

She slumped down onto the floor, burying her head in the parcel of baby clothes she was still holding, and wept.

Chapter Nineteen

The next morning Bella woke late but felt relieved that at least she had something planned for the day – her first antenatal yoga class.

She felt a lurch of fear whenever she thought about Don and needed distraction from the situation. When it was time to go, she packed her mobile into her bag, just in case he should ring, and drove off to the address she'd been given.

It was a small church hall. In the vestibule she saw a row of socks and shoes leading to an open door where a group of women, many just as pregnant as her, were chatting.

She took off her trainers and socks, and went through to join them.

'Hello, I'm Bella,' she said when everyone looked up at her, 'and I definitely can't put my feet behind my ears.'

Lame gag, but there were smiles and hellos back. This felt very strange. It occurred to her that she had not hung out with other pregnant people before.

The teacher, a slim, wiry-haired woman, took her

details and they settled down for the class. They 'breeeeeeeathed' a lot, they stretched, they practised relaxation techniques and Bella felt that at last she'd found a way to slow down and stay still.

When the two hours was over, she felt calm, happy, rejuvenated. The teacher passed round drinks and biscuits and everyone chatted about babies, birth plans, breast feeding. She suddenly felt fascinated by it all, by the reality of this whole pregnancy state.

'I'm Red by the way,' said the extraordinary-looking woman sitting next to her and Bella said hello, finding it hard to take her eyes off her. Red had skin the colour of chocolate caramel, liquid brown eyes with a halo of gold round the pupil and wild, corkscrew dreadlocks which were unexpectedly ginger.

'When're you due?' Red asked.

'In three weeks,' Bella answered.

'Oh me too . . .' Red cupped her hands round the enormous bump Bella somehow hadn't noticed. 'Not long to go, thank God.' Red added, 'My feet are almost totally flat!' They both smiled.

Back in the car, Bella feeling serene and full of happy, pregnant, yoga thoughts, tried Don's mobile.

It rang for a long time, then diverted to message: 'Hello, Don,' she said. 'It's me, I'd really like to talk to you. I'm so sorry about this. Call me . . . bye.' She clicked off the phone, disappointed.

By bedtime, she was really disappointed. She'd left another message and he still hadn't phoned back.

By Sunday morning, she felt totally depressed.

There was still no reply on Don's mobile. She lay in bed and couldn't face anything, not even making breakfast. She just lay still, staring at the ceiling, wishing she could fall asleep again.

When she finally dozed off, she drifted in and out of dreams of Don and Don holding babies. An insistent hammering and shouting was punctuating the lovely dream; she tried to ignore it and hang onto the image of Don beside her with their baby. But the picture faded and she gradually woke up to the realization that someone really was hammering at the door and calling her name.

'Bella!'

'Bella, are you in there?'

'Are you OK? For God's sake, *Bella!*'

She levered herself slowly out of bed and waddled to the door. She opened it up to see Tania standing there, looking exasperated but hugely relieved.

'Thank fuck for that,' Tania said, 'I thought you'd died or gone into labour or something . . .'

Bella stared at her.

'You weren't at the house. Or answering any of your bloody phones. And I knew you were alone this weekend and . . . when I saw the curtains shut, I just panicked.' Tania was beginning to feel embarrassed now.

Bella was still staring at her.

'The house at twelve. We were supposed to meet there.' Tania held up her hands in total exasperation.

'Were we? Oh God, I completely forgot,' said Bella listlessly.

'Pregnancy, look what it's done to you?' Tania

213

was teasing now. 'You're in bed at 1 p.m., you look absolutely awful and now you've lost your marbles.'

'Yeah, and maybe my husband,' Bella added.

'What!' Tania followed her into the flat and shut the door. 'What the hell's happened?' she demanded, steering Bella into the sitting room.

'We had a huge row. Well, actually . . . we didn't. He's just stormed off on a work trip and not called. I don't know what's going on,' Bella said, wondering why she felt so numb.

'You seem really strange, Bella, are you OK?'

Bella could feel a wave of pins and needles move over her face. She parted her lips and whispered, 'I think I'm going to . . .' before she swayed danger-ously. Somehow Tania managed to move Bella backwards into the sofa before the full weight of a fainting eight-month pregnant woman felled her.

Trying desperately hard not to panic, Tania looked at her friend, lying unconscious and deathly white with her huge stomach moving ominously.

She heaved Bella over onto her side and opened up her buttons. Vaguely remembering some-thing about feet needing to be up, she propped several sofa cushions under them. Then at a total loss, Tania stroked Bella's damp forehead and told her it was going to be OK. Bella's eyelids began to flicker.

'Bella? Can you hear me?' Tania asked.

'Yes,' came the whisper.

'Are you OK? Are you in any pain?'

'No, I'm fine. I think I need something to drink.' Bella still wasn't opening her eyes.

'God, you're scaring me,' said Tania. 'Do you think we should phone for an ambulance?'

'Give me a moment, then we'll ring the midwife.'

This reassured Tania slightly, so she brought Bella a glass of water and held her head as she sipped it down.

Once Bella was able to sit up, Tania made her drink milky, sugary tea and halfway through the mug, Bella realized she was ravenously hungry, so Tania made her toast slathered in butter. As Bella ate and drank, she started to feel better. She rang Annie, who promised to come and check on her later in the afternoon.

When Tania started to quiz her about Don, Bella, somewhat shamefacedly, confessed to the whole 'accidental pregnancy'.

'Is that such a big deal?' her friend asked.

'Well, yeah really. Obviously,' said Bella.

'What do you want to do now?' Tania asked.

'I want to sort it out, I need things to be OK between us again.'

'Is there other stuff going on?' Tania asked.

Bella gave a deep sigh and tried to put the vague unease she'd been feeling lately into words: 'I think he's still a bit terrified of all this. Marriage is one thing, but a mortgage and fatherhood is scaring the shit out of him. And I've been really preoccupied, with work, with the baby . . . with all this house move stuff. I haven't really noticed what's been going on with him or with us.' After another sigh, she added: ' You know Don's dad left when he was tiny. I'm terrified that's what he's programmed to do, on some level.'

215

'Bloody hell,' said Tania. 'How are you going to fix this?'

'I'm not really sure,' Bella answered. 'But I'm going to have to try.'

Tania smiled encouragingly at her.

'Would a cigarette be totally out of the question?' Bella asked, still horribly pale.

'Yup, I'm afraid it would,' Tania answered.

'Will you smoke one for me, then?'

'Well OK, but I'm opening the window and you can't sit right next to me.'

'Spoilsport.'

On Wednesday morning, Bella got up very early, put on the most glamorous pregnancy outfit she could muster and drove to Heathrow to meet Don's 7 a.m. flight, which was, of course, delayed. She wandered round Terminal 3 in a tired daze. With her current bladder situation, drinking a string of café lattes was not an option.

Checking herself over in the bathroom mirror, she was instantly depressed at how enormous she looked, not even her groovy get-up could detract from that. In fact the outfit looked bloody ridiculous, a brightly coloured sarong, high-heeled ankle boots, ouch, and a low-cut clinging top, what was she thinking?? Over this she'd slung her one fantastic item, a brand new mock croc brown leather coat.

She'd gone to town yesterday intending to buy baby things, but it had been way too gloomy. It made her want Don with her even more. They should be choosing cot blanket patterns and types

216

of pram together. So, she'd tried to cheer herself up with the coat.

When the plane finally landed, she stood at the arrivals gate feeling the nerves from hell and scanning every face that went past.

At last she saw him striding along, bag and coat over his shoulder. He was talking to someone else. Damn! She'd forgotten he wouldn't be alone. She couldn't decide whether to wave or wait until he got closer. Then he spotted her and a look of surprise crossed his face.

'Hello Bella! What on earth are you doing here?' He sounded matey, jokey almost. He leaned over and pecked her cheek and she couldn't say any of the things she'd planned, because his colleague was being introduced to her now.

'Rod, this is my wife Bella.'

'How d'you do?' said Rod, shaking her hand.

'Hi,' she answered. 'Good trip?'

'Yeah,' they both replied.

There was an awkward pause, then thankfully Rod said, 'I'm going to shoot off then. Nice to meet you, Bella, see you tomorrow, Don,' and he was gone.

They were left facing each other.

'What are you doing here?' Don asked again.

'I'm your fucking wife, what the fuck do you think I'm doing here? I didn't just happen to be passing.' So, the speech she'd had in mind was undergoing some hasty revisions, as she turned into Reservoir Wife.

'OK,' he said steadily.

'Just how long were you planning to sulk?' she

demanded. 'Were you going to come home today? Or were you going to carry on pretending that I don't exist?'

'I hadn't really got a plan,' he said, still very calm. 'Some of us don't plan every little thing to the nth degree.'

She looked him straight in the eye and felt all her anger dissolve. She loved him and just wanted this to be over, just wanted him back.

'I'm really sorry, Don. I should have told you. It was a really shitty thing to do.' Quietly, she added: 'I'm sorry . . . I really wanted us to have a baby and I was sure you'd say no if I asked.'

'But maybe I'd changed my mind, Bella,' he answered. 'I should have at least had the chance to consider it. Don't you think it would have made a difference, if I'd known how much you wanted this?'

'I'm sorry.'

'I feel you don't trust me.'

'I'm so sorry,' she said again and tears began to slide down her face.

He put his arm on her shoulder. 'What do you want to do, Bella?' he asked.

'I want us to go home,' she sounded tired and sad, 'I want everything to be OK.'

He looked down at the ground: 'I'm sorry I've upset you.'

'Don, I'm eight and a half months pregnant, the theme tune to *Emmerdale* upsets me,' she managed a smile.

He smiled back and they both relaxed a little.

'Please come here,' he said and they hugged as best they could over her huge bulge.

'Shall we go and get a coffee?' he asked into her hair.

'Yeah, OK.' Bladder be damned.

When they were sitting down, he confessed to all the anxieties Bella had suspected.

'I'm sorry.' It was his turn to apologize now. He took a swig of his coffee and she saw how tired he looked: 'It still seems so soon,' he said. 'We've only known each other for a year and a half, now we're buying the house, having a baby. You're charging into all this and I'm wondering if I can handle it.'

'I didn't expect the pregnancy to work out so easily,' she said, 'I thought we'd have to have a few goes. You know what my mother went through.'

He nodded.

'I'm not going to be able to do this without you, Don.' She couldn't bear to meet his eyes, so just stared at the layer of foam dimpling in her untouched cup.

'I know. And I promise I'm going to be here for you, I've been thinking about you non-stop, I've missed you so much,' he squeezed her hand.

'But you didn't even call!'

'I know, I know. I'm so sorry. Once I'm on my high horse, I can never see a way of getting down again.'

'Don! How long would you have left it?' she looked up at him now and tried to smile a little.

'I don't know, Bella. It's terrible. There are some women out there who are still waiting to hear,' he gave a half smile but she looked serious.

'We're about to become parents, Don, we need to tackle all this difficult stuff head on. Even though it's really hard.'

219

'OK, we will. I promise.' He moved his chair over so he could put his arm round her. 'Come here,' he pressed his mouth against hers, tasting her for what felt like the first time in months. She flooded with relief.

'I love your coat,' he said when they finally broke off.

'Thanks. Can we go home now?'

'D'you think I'll get all my stuff in your car?' he asked as they followed the signs to the car park.

'Oh, I brought the Jeep,' she tried to sound casual.

'You brought the Jeep! You must really love me.'

'Yeah, I do,' she answered.

When they got home, they closed the curtains and went to bed for a very tender fuck, lying side by side.

He moved carefully inside her moving his hands over her heavy breasts, enormous taut stomach and down between her legs. She was tensing and trembling against him and just as he came, she cried out 'Oh my God!' and moved his hand onto her stomach where he could feel waves pulsating across it.

'Shit! Are you in labour?!'

'No, I've just had the most incredible orgasm ever. I'm still having it. Whoa . . .' the rippling was slowing down now. Don kept his hand on her stomach for a long time, until it finally stopped.

'I love you,' he said, settling his head back on the pillow but still curled up close behind her with his arm resting on her side.

'I love you too,' she answered.

'I'm going to love the baby,' he added.

'Me too.' She felt tears prick at the back of her

eyes. Not again! She blinked them away and closed her eyes.

Moments later they fell asleep and for the first time in days, both of them slept soundly without any troubling dreams.

Chapter Twenty

As soon as they clapped eyes on the genuine Land Rover three-wheeler, complete with real tyres, sheepskin lining and handbrake, they both knew that this was the pram for them.

'I cannot believe how much money we have spent on a small, unborn baby.' Don was looking fazed in the lift. He had taken a few days off, so they could spend a long weekend finally moving into the house and shopping for furniture and baby things.

One tiny baby seemed to require a mountain of stuff – cradle with all the trimmings, a bath, changing table, towels, vests, rompers, cardigans, assorted clothes Bella could not resist, a car seat and finally – the only thing Don could get excited about – the baby's set of wheels.

'Yeah, well hold on tight, we're going to the kitchen department now,' Bella told him. Poor Don, he had no idea about all that was on her list. They'd rented for years, now they had to furnish a whole house.

The kitchen was granted an enormous stainless steel fridge, a washing machine, a dishwasher,

222

crockery, pots, pans, cutlery, glasses and wine glasses, which all went through on Bella's card as Don began to pale at the running total.

A taxi ride later and they were buying maple wardrobes for the bedroom, an incredibly Parisian-cool leather armchair and a distressed beech kitchen table with six chairs.

'Not half as distressed as I'm going to be when my bill comes in,' Bella joked to Don, as she signed the card slip, and instantly regretted the gag when he didn't smile back.

'Right,' he said as they headed out of the shop. 'That's it, you're not spending any more money. What else do we need?'

'Well, some lamps, some rugs, a coat stand. A new sofa?' She knew she was going out on a limb here.

'OK.' He sounded reasonable. 'Well, I'm getting them.' Before she could object, he added 'No, no, no . . . I don't want to hear it. Bella it's my home too. I'm not your kept man.'

'Can I come with you?' she asked. If he was going to go off and rack up a whole load on his credit card, she felt she should at least guide his choices a little bit.

'No, you have to bundle yourself off into a taxi and get home for your check-up with Annie.'

'OK . . . OK, Don. But you don't have to get everything today,' she told him, kissing him goodbye. 'You know, if you don't see anything you like . . .'

'You mean if I don't see anything you'd like,' he grinned at her.

'No, no, it's your home too.' She tried to really mean this.

223

It was a sunny May afternoon and she was heading back to her new home. She felt happy in the back of the cab, but very tired. Buying the baby clothes had made her feel weird. What was this going to be like? She had spread one of the tiny babygros over her bump and it just didn't seem possible that a real, live baby, this size, was going to come out of there in a matter of weeks . . . *Weeks!!!*

Mostly she felt strangely relaxed about labour, but occasionally she woke up at night covered in sweat having had a dreadful nightmare about blood and agony.

She had pitchforked the home birth issue around and around her mind until she had just had to leave it alone as a decision made which should not be unmade. She repeated the statistics to herself like a mantra and took some solace from the intelligent, reasonable women at the yoga class who were nearly all doing the same. The yoga class was fun. It was nice to be surrounded by other pregnant women and moan about varicose veins, stretch marks and, bugbear of her life, piles.

The front door was open, as usual, because there were always decorators in. Almost every room had now been replastered and painted dazzling white. The floors had been sanded and varnished and the house looked huge, empty and new.

She walked through the hall and upstairs to the bedroom to dump her bags. The mattress they were sleeping on was still unmade from this morning and boxes full of clothes lined the walls. A bulb hung from the ceiling and there was only a sheet pinned over the window, so they kept waking up early with the light.

The new shower, toilet and sink were in the bathroom, plumbed in and working but the walls were still bare plaster and the lino had been ripped up, leaving stained plyboard underneath.

Two of the decorators were replastering in the baby's room. She put her head round the door to say hello.

'Hello, Bella,' said the younger one. 'Bill's down in the kitchen if you want to talk to him.'

Not really. She wanted to lie down flat out on her bed, but she thought she'd better go have a chat. She braced herself for the three flights of stairs down to the kitchen and began waddling.

Bill and two other men were drinking cups of tea when she came in.

'Hello, Bella,' Bill greeted her. 'Don't go giving birth early, this is going to take another week or so. Hopefully we'll get the bathroom finished off at the same time.'

'Well, I think you're safe,' she answered. 'The baby's head hasn't come down yet.'

There was a collective gulping of tea. This was obviously too much information.

She hoped the Aga would look OK in the new stainless steel kitchen. She hadn't had the heart to rip it out and replace it with a steel range. That was the thing about Agas: built-in nostalgia for kitchens you didn't grow up in but kind of wished you had.

Finally lying down on her bed, she called Don. 'Hi, how's it going?' she asked.

'Fine,' he answered. 'Leave me alone, I can handle this!!'

'All right! I'm just checking! Will you bring dinner home? All our kitchen stuff isn't being delivered until tomorrow and anyway, I'm too tired.'

'OK, is Annie there yet?'

'No, she won't be long though.'

'Take care.'

'Bye.'

When Annie arrived and began doing the routine checks, she was concerned at Bella's blood pressure. 'It's slightly up,' she said, looking at Bella lying in an exhausted heap on her bed. 'It's been rising gently, but this is a little bit of a blip. You've got to take it really easy.'

No wonder her blood pressure was up, Bella thought, she'd done more damage to her collateral today than Black Monday . . . ha, ha.

She could feel slight palpitations just at the thought of it.

'Are you OK?' Annie asked.

'Yes, I'm fine. I've definitely overdone it today. I don't think I'll leave the house again.'

'Well, a little walking is fine and your yoga poses, but really nothing more now. It's getting very close.'

'Not in the next two weeks, though?' Bella asked anxiously. 'The kitchen won't be finished.'

'Well, let's hope not. There is running hot and cold in the bathroom if things do start early, isn't there?'

'Yes,' said Bella looking panic-stricken. 'God, Annie, is this really about to happen? I'm not ready.'

Annie smiled at her. 'No-one is ever ready, Bella. You can only be prepared. Prepare to be knocked over, amazed and filled with awe. This is going to bowl you over like nothing ever has done before.'

'Oh no, you're giving me the hippie stuff again, aren't you?' Bella smiled. This had become a standing joke between them. Any time Annie started spouting her natural birth philosophies, Bella dealt with it by teasing her.

Annie wasn't sure what to make of Bella's attitude. She was having a home birth, so on some level she must believe it was a good idea, but she hadn't bought into the whole active birth idea at all. There was no birthing pool, no raspberry leaf tea, no aromatherapy oils burning in the house, no partner learning breathing or massage techniques. Annie hadn't even met Don yet.

'Why did you choose a home birth, Bella?' she asked, venting her curiosity.

'Because it's statistically safe and I wanted a midwife I knew, who could come to my office and home. And . . .' little pause, 'I kind of fell out with the private hospital.'

'Ah.' That explained a bit.

When Annie had gone, Bella took her tiny pack of ten Ultra Super Mega light cigarettes out of her handbag. She propped herself up on pillows and prepared for her three minutes of what used to be happiness but now was a necessary indulgence hugely spoiled by guilt. She clicked on the lighter and inhaled, firing up her cigarette. The yoga breathing had at least been a help here, she could now fill her lungs right up to the brim and get the maximum benefit out of the paltry amount she allowed herself to smoke.

Despite all the compulsively interesting birth books she'd read, squatting in front of the Aga in

227

the small hours of the morning, labour was still a mystery. She felt incredibly well informed, but strangely clueless.

She knew exactly what and why an episiotomy was – OUCH – but no book seemed to offer any description of what labour would actually be like. And she still didn't know the first thing about babies apart from you 'put them to the breast' whenever they cried.

She liked the idea of breastfeeding. She imagined lying in bed beside Don with their little baby between them nuzzling at her breasts. And what the hell was sex going to be like after birth? There was no useful information about that either, just warnings to exercise that pelvic floor.

Don wasn't revealing any details about his shopping trip when he got home that evening and would only say she had to stay in and wait for a delivery the next day.

The van arrived soon after 11 a.m. and three men were needed to haul the most enormous pale tan L-shaped sofa into their sitting room. Jesus! It must have cost a fortune. This was made from a whole herd of Italy's finest designer cows, my God. She was stunned. She hadn't really known what to expect from Don, but certainly something a lot cheaper.

Three very chic lamps and a vast cream sheepskin rug were also delivered. She was really impressed now.

She phoned Don at work.

'Hello?'

'Hello, darling, guess what I'm lying on?'

228

'Bill, the decorator?'

'NO!!! A hugely expensive, wonderfully luxurious *sofa*.'

'Ah-ha. It arrived then. What do you think?'

'Amazing, fantastic . . . bankrupting!' she told him. And not exactly baby-friendly, but she left that out.

It did not take long for Bella to set up home on the sofa. Just days from her due date, she had decided it was finally time to stop working, exercising, trying to look nice, even shopping and nesting. She was too tired, too heavy, too huge. She had put on almost three stone in seven months and her home outfit was shapeless black maternity trousers and one of Don's washed-out tartan shirts. Her feet would only fit into a pair of old sheepskin slippers she'd found behind a wardrobe when they moved.

Prone on the sofa, glued to crap TV or reading decorating magazines, surrounded by grape stalks, digestive biscuit wrappers and empty water bottles, was where Don now expected to find her when he came home from work.

So he was surprised to find the house strangely dark one evening. In a total panic, he realized he could hear something in the bedroom. He ran up the stairs two at a time, heart pounding, convinced he was going to find his wife about to give birth in their brand new bed.

He opened the door and saw Bella lying with the duvet over her, sobbing into the pillow.

'What's the matter?' He rushed over to her side.

'Oh, Don.' She looked up at him with streaming red eyes and nose.

'What's wrong?' he asked urgently.

'I've ruined this house,' she sobbed.

'What do you mean?!'

'It was so lovely. It was full of character and the two lovely boys and two lovely parents and I've ruined it.'

'Oh hon, what's made you think that?' He put his arm around her comfortingly.

'I've stripped it and gutted it and now it feels white and soulless. And our baby's going to grow up in this white soulless place and we'll probably break up because it's so white and empty and it's all my fault,' she sobbed almost hysterically against the pillow again.

'Bella –' he lay down beside her and stroked her hair – 'Bella, you've gone completely bonkers.' He said this as gently and as soothingly as he could. 'The house looks great. It looks airy and light and at the moment any kid would love it because they can charge around without knocking anything over.'

He was hoping to make her laugh a little, but she was still crying hard, so he added: 'If you think it's too white, we'll get the painters back to change the walls. It's not a problem, hon, it's not a problem.'

She looked up at him and he saw how swollen her eyes were with crying.

'I love you,' Don said.

'Are you sure?' she wobbled. 'Are you really going to stay here with me and the baby?'

'Of course I am.' He folded her up into his arms. 'Of course, please don't worry about that. I'm so sorry if I've made you worry about that.'

'But our dads . . .' she tried to restrain her tears

long enough to get the words out. 'Yours left and mine shags around. It's not exactly promising, is it?'

He hugged her harder and didn't say anything for a while, then he answered: 'No-one turns out exactly like their parents, Bella. Let's just give ourselves a chance. You can't promise this will work out and neither can I, but we both really want to try and that's enough.'

'I feel so vulnerable and dependent,' she said in a frightened voice. 'And I hate it.'

He held her for a long time, then kissed her forehead. For a moment she was calm, then she put her face against his chest and burst into tears again. 'Oh God and then there's the kitchen!' she sobbed.

'Bella, it can't be that bad!' he said.

'It is, it's terrible. Come and look.' She heaved herself up and shuffled into the appalling slippers she seemed to wear all the time.

They went down the stairs slowly, Don following his lumbering wife. At the bottom was the kitchen, finished that day, a gleaming, brushed steel tribute to modern kitchen design. A glassy black granite surface glittered in the light of the tiny overhead spots. The walls were crisp white, bordered with a splashback of more glossy black tiles.

The Aga looked a little uncomfortably unfashionable.

'Wow,' said Don. 'I'm impressed.'

Bella just burst into tears again.

'What don't you like about it?' He put his arm around her back.

'I want the old one back. It looked like the kind of place where mums make soup and kids eat biscuits and play with their toys on the floor . . .'

her voice trailed off into another volley of sobs.

'Bella,' he was smiling as he hugged her awkwardly over her mountainous bump, 'you're going to be a great mum. You don't have to bake cakes . . .' Another sob, so he added: 'Unless you want to.'

What should he say next?

'Do you want to replace the doors?' he suggested. 'Maybe you could get wooden doors like the old kitchen?'

'That's a good idea.' She sounded slightly brighter. 'Maybe you're right,' she sniffed. 'Wooden doors.'

She wiped her nose on the back of her sleeve. 'Oh God. I'm sorry,' she said. 'I've got to go and blow my nose and wash my face, I've got to get a grip.'

Chapter Twenty-one

Two days later, all the delivery vans had come and gone, the house was almost complete and Bill had been back personally to change the kitchen doors. He had seemed a bit bemused, but never mind, Bella was deliriously happy with the results.

'It's fantastic,' she told him. 'I don't know what I was thinking of with the stainless steel, so cold and impersonal.'

'Quite tricky to clean too,' he told her. 'You'll be getting grubby little handprints on everything soon.' He gestured to her stomach, now an eye-popping mound which looked far too heavy for her frame to support.

'Any day now then, is it?' he asked.

'It's actually due tomorrow, but the first ones are always late, aren't they? Just as well, there's still a few things left to do.'

She ran through her mental checklist: curtains for all the rooms, more towels and sheets. Don was taking her shopping at the weekend for the final baby bits: nappies, cotton wool, vests.

Bella felt quite sad to see Bill go. He had been

knocking around the place with his workers ever since she moved in. As he drove off in his little blue van she realized it was the first time she'd been alone in the house during the day.

After lunch she fell asleep on the sofa and when she woke up at about four she lay still, feeling the baby stir inside her tummy. Suddenly it made a big movement, almost a roll which came with a loud clicking noise, more like a clunk. She couldn't believe she had just *heard* the baby! What the hell was that? A joint flexing?

She heaved herself down off the bed and stood up. There was a very odd sensation between her legs, like a hard ball pressing down from inside. She took several steps, but it was still there, she had to waddle with her legs apart. The weight was incredible, like a great big pendulum. The baby's head had obviously moved right down, ready to go. But she knew it could still be days away.

When Don got home that night he found Bella in her by now regular position on the sofa, in the black trousers and tartan shirt.

'Hello hon.' She held her arms out to him. 'We have to celebrate tonight, the decorators have moved out and the place is finally ours,' she said.

'Well, I've got chilled white wine, microwavable duck and noodles, ice-cream and about a kilo of grapes,' he said, holding up his shopping bag up.

'I could grow to love you, Mr McCartney,' she answered.

She went to bed early feeling tired and heavier than ever. Her stomach was tingling, there were little ripples of contractions passing up and down it and she could feel it go hard then relax again.

At about four in the morning, she stumbled out of bed to go to the loo. As she sat there she was aware of a strange trickling sensation. Investigating with toilet paper, she found an alarming quantity of mucus spilling out from between her legs.

She had expected 'the show' to be a 'plug' of mucus, not vast bucketfuls of stuff.

The birth was going to happen some time in the next day or two. She felt a small thrill take hold of her, mixed with panic. *Now?? Not yet!!*

She couldn't feel anything – no contractions, nothing different – so she went back to bed.

Just before 6 a.m. she woke to small stitchy pains travelling across her stomach. She lay in bed watching the numbers stack up on the digital alarm clock. The pains lasted just a few minutes. Then at 6.23, they were back . . . and again at 6.57.

Just after 7 a.m. she woke Don.

'You're having a day off today,' she said, amazed at how calm and relaxed she felt.

He opened his eyes and smiled. 'Really?'

Then he sat bolt upright. 'Oh my God, you mean . . . Has it really started?'

'I think so!'

Chapter Twenty-two

'I've got tons of things to do Don, come on, let's get up.' Bella threw back the covers and hauled herself out of bed.

'What do you mean?' he asked nervously. 'You're in labour.'

'Oh God, it won't kick in properly for hours. The bathroom needs a good wash down. All the baby things need to be washed and dried, they're still in their packets. *God*, you have to go out and buy *nappies*!'

He was looking pale with terror.

'For God's sake,' she said, lowering herself slowly down to hug him, 'I'm the one giving birth, remember.'

'Aren't you at all worried?' he asked. She looked at him: stubbly, dishevelled hair, putting on his glasses. Why? As if that would help?

'God no,' she was incredibly calm, 'I weigh so much, the stairs buckle under me, my fingers look like fat sausages, I've had this great mass hanging in front of me for months. I can't wait for it to be out of here—' she pointed at her stomach.

'But it's got to come out through . . .'

'Don! Shut up!'

She pulled on the massive maternity bra and pants: 'Two more things I won't miss about being pregnant,' she said and then as she hoisted herself into the black trousers and tartan shirt, he added: 'And two I won't.'

She padded all the way downstairs to make breakfast in her new kitchen.

The stitchy pains were so mild, she could almost ignore them as she got on with juicing oranges, cutting bread for toast and boiling up a big pot of tea.

She could hear Don showering. When he came down, barefoot, in chinos and a denim shirt, he made a quick call to the office to tell them his paternity leave was starting *now*.

She could tell by his smiles his boss was teasing him mercilessly.

'That's enough,' Don said. 'I'll ring you later . . . yeah, thanks, mate.'

'Do you really think it will arrive today?' Don asked. 'On the due date?'

'Well, it's starting. Who knows how long it will take?'

'That would just be so like you to give birth on the right day. Not early, not late, just exactly on time,' he said and they both laughed.

'Have you called the midwife?' asked Don.

'Let's have breakfast, then I'll speak to her, then we'll clean the bathroom.'

'It's clean, Bella!'

'I want the bathroom and the bedroom extra clean.'

'Well, leave it to me.'

'No, I want to help. Otherwise I'll have nothing to do, just hours and hours of mild labour. Anyway, I feel so energetic!'

'Good grief . . .' he went into TV reporter mode: 'A woman gave birth on her bathroom floor yesterday still clutching a scrubbing brush in her hand. "I just wanted my house to sparkle," said management consultant, Bella Browning, who is currently in talks with the Flash marketing department.'

'Ha ha,' she said and went off to phone Annie.

She had expected Annie to play it cool and offer to come round later. But in fact, she said she would be there in an hour. Bella felt mildly irritated. What would the three of them do all day?

'Honestly, Annie, don't come before twelve. I'll phone you if anything changes,' Bella told her.

They cleaned the bathroom and the bedroom and the kitchen, then Bella made Don hoover the whole house.

The baby clothes were put through the wash and chucked into the tumble drier.

'We haven't got nearly enough,' Bella told Don. 'You'll have to go and buy some more when the baby's here.'

'How will I know what to get?' he said anxiously.

'Just go into baby shop looking clueless and say "newborn baby, about this big." They must be used to it,' she giggled at him.

He kissed her on the mouth. 'This is it, Bella, our last few hours as a couple. It's about to change for ever.'

'Well a shag is out of the question,' she said.

'I know, probably for months.' He hoped this was a joke.

'About six weeks, actually,' she answered.

'Oh my God!'

'Are you sad?' she asked. 'I don't mean about the sex, obviously you're devastated. But about the changing for ever.' She scanned his face.

'No. Well, maybe a bit. I've loved every moment of the two of us. I just hope the three of us is going to be as good.'

'Of course it will be.' She put her arms around him and leaned against his cheek. 'I hope it is too. I love you, Don.' After a pause, she added, 'You are going to get me through this OK, aren't you?'

'Of course.' He stroked her head.

Not long after Don had come back with the nappies and other essential groceries, Annie arrived laden down with bags.

'Hello. Hello, Bella and you must be Don.' Out of breath, she plonked one enormous bright yellow bin bag on the doorstep, then offloaded the holdall she'd had slung over her shoulder.

'Good grief, what is all this stuff?' asked Bella.

'You'll see,' Annie said.

Don picked up the yellow bag.

'If you take that one upstairs, I'll get set out first. Bella, you put the kettle on.' She saw the look on Bella's face and added: 'For tea!'

Annie had asked for a table up in the nursery and she laid out all her equipment there.

'OK,' she called down the stairs, 'Bella, if you can come up, we'll do a little check-up.'

Blood pressure, urine sample, baby's heartbeat, then it was time for the internal. Bella stripped off her trousers and pants and felt uncomfortably exposed as she lay down half naked on her bed. She watched Annie don thin latex gloves and take out a tube labelled VAGINAL EXAMINATION JELLY . . . urgh.

'No-one in the world likes these, do they?' Bella asked, trying to make small talk.

'You'd be surprised,' said Annie. 'Now, just relax.'

'Of course. Why should I be at all tense at the prospect of you jamming a great big latexed hand up my fanny?'

Annie looked at her quite sternly, Bella thought.

Ouch, it was surprisingly painful. She wasn't prepared for that. Either Annie was the clumsiest internal investigator ever or it was something to do with labour.

'OK,' said Annie. 'Only two or three centimetres, so we've a long way to go. Why don't you come down and we'll have a light lunch.'

Annie had brought a flask of homemade vegetable soup, which she was advising Bella to eat. She also filled the teapot with camomile tea bags before pouring the hot water on top.

Don ignored this spartan regime and made rounds of toast smothered in melted cheese with pickle, and strong black coffee.

'Goodness,' Annie couldn't help herself. 'Don't you worry at all about stomach ulcers?'

'No,' said Don with a grin.

Bella's face winced slightly with the pain of another contraction.

'How are you doing?' asked Annie.

240

'It's OK actually, just like a sharp period pain, but then it goes away completely.'

'What would you like to do after lunch?' Annie asked. 'Maybe a walk, or we could do some yoga stretches. Or maybe there's a video you'd like to watch while I give your shoulders a massage?'

'That's a good idea,' said Bella.

'I've brought a lovely video with me called *Birth Lines*.'

'Oh God no, how about Woody Allen?'

Annie said 'Of course,' and Don rolled his eyes.

Bella sat cross-legged in front of Annie who massaged her shoulders with wonderful smelling oil as all three of them watched *Manhattan*. Don kept getting up to pace about the house on some supposed errand or other and Bella would occasionally clutch at her sides and say 'Ohhh, that was sore.'

By the end of the film the contractions were coming every ten minutes and Bella was finding them painful.

Annie ushered her upstairs for another check-up, which revealed a dilation of about four centimetres, then sent her for a hot bath. Don moved a stool inside the bathroom, so he could sit beside Bella and Annie stayed in the nursery so she was around, but not too obtrusive.

After twenty minutes in the bath, Bella got Don to help her out so she could sit on the loo for a bout of crampy, painful diarrhoea.

'Look on the bright side,' she said weakly, climbing back into the bath and turning on the hot tap. 'At least I won't need an enema.'

Don was starting to feel more nervous. This was

really happening. He'd watched women give birth before but in squalid conditions, shouting out words he couldn't understand and it had been like watching a film.

This was Bella, here in the bathroom, in the bath.

Annie came in with a little ball of Plasticine. She stopped up the bath overflow and ran the hot tap again. She tipped in a little oil and the room began to smell of warm summer holidays.

All three of them breathed deeply and felt a little calmer.

Bella was squeezing Don's hand: the pains were shooting up her stomach. She screwed up her eyes and gasped with the intensity of them. But the water was hot and comforting and she tried to relax in between contractions.

Already it was 5 p.m. and soon Annie wanted her out of the bath to do another set of checks.

Bella was irritated by this. Somehow she lumbered out and Don and Annie wrapped a huge towel round her and supported her to the bed. Don went down to the kitchen to throw some food together while Annie performed another painful examination.

'Ouch,' said Bella loudly. 'Can't you be more gentle?'

'I'm sorry,' Annie said then prodded just as hard again. 'OK, about five centimetres now.'

'Five centimetres? Are you sure?' Bella said grumpily. 'This is going to take for ever.'

'Calm down, Bella, some women are slow at the start, then it all rushes out at the end. Just go with the flow. The baby's fine and so are you.'

'It really hurts now,' Bella said.

'Let's try the TENS machine, then come down to the kitchen and have a change of scene.'

Annie dried her thoroughly, then stuck the electrodes onto her back and gave her the little control panel to hold.

'OK, you just push those buttons when you feel a contraction coming on. It stimulates endorphin production,' said Annie. 'Give it a whirl. If you don't like it, we'll take it off.'

Bella pushed down the button and felt a mild flicking on her back. She pressed again and the flicking increased to a sort of stinging pain. She couldn't really see how that was going to help, but at least it was something else to think about. All this waiting was driving her demented.

She was just waiting, waiting for the next contraction and the one after that and for the next hour to pass so she could be a bit closer to getting this over with.

Down in the kitchen, she huddled in an armchair with her control panel and watched Don cook pasta with bolognese sauce.

'Are you going to have some?' he asked Annie.

'I don't eat meat,' she replied.

'Have the pasta with butter and grated Parmesan then. We've got fantastic tomatoes too,' Don said.

'OK. Thank you,' said Annie.

Fantastic tomatoes? thought Bella grumpily. How the hell could he think about tomatoes when she was in this much pain?

'Bella, what can I get you?' Don came over and asked her so kindly, she forgave him immediately.

243

'Just some apple juice please.' She screwed up her face against another contraction and zapped up the counter-effect on her machine. It seemed to block out the intensity by pummelling small electric shocks all over her back.

The pains were bad now: they clamped right round her stomach and back. But then they released and everything felt fine again, felt good in fact.

She was starting to count in the moments when her eyes were screwed up against the pain and she knew the contractions were getting longer. How long could this all go on for? It had been about ten hours since the first twinges. Most first labours took about 12 hours, so there could be as little as two hours to go. Hallelujah!

Two more hours of Annie fussing about and prodding her with those awful latex gloves was about all she could take.

'AAAAAArgh, here comes another one,' a great vice-like grip moved round her stomach and felt as if it was going to squeeze the life out of her. She pushed the button to whack over her back and slowly counted five, four, three, two, one, zero, minus one, minus two, minus three . . . finally the contraction let go of her.

Don was staring at her, fork frozen in mid-air. Annie was eating on blithely. 'We'll finish our supper, then maybe you'd like another massage?' she asked cheerfully. 'Walk around the room a bit, it might help.'

It's all very well for you to say that, you hippie ratbag, Bella thought. She was beginning to feel helplessly furious with the pain, the indignity and most of all with Annie.

Another fierce contraction began and Bella dropped onto all fours on the kitchen floor.

'Owwww!' she felt so stupid, crawling there helplessly.

Don rushed over to her side. 'Hon, are you OK?'

'Of course I'm not fucking OK. It really, really hurts.'

'Come on, Bella,' Annie said briskly. 'Let's get you upstairs, I'll give you a nice relaxing massage.'

'I don't want one,' Bella heard herself say petulantly. 'I want this to stop.'

Somehow, pausing for the contractions that were coming every few minutes, Don and Annie got Bella upstairs into the bedroom.

'OK, let's have another quick look, please,' said Annie lying Bella back on the bed.

Bella groaned.

'Still about five centimetres,' Annie said withdrawing the dreaded glove.

'Jesus,' Bella exclaimed in frustration. 'We're just not getting anywhere.'

'We've got to help you relax and open up. What would help Bella?'

'Less pain,' she snapped. 'Here comes another one . . .' There was a catch of fear in her voice.

She grabbed Don's arm and clung to him, groaning.

'I'll go and get some music,' Annie said, and went out of the room.

When the contraction had passed, Don and Bella's eyes met. He looked anxious to her and she looked frightened to him. That made them both even more worried.

'I'm really scared, Don,' Bella whispered. 'Most

women dilate at a centimetre an hour. That's another five hours to go before I'm ready to push. I can't do this for another five hours.'

Her face looked stricken again: another contraction was on its way. It seized her violently round the middle and gripped her with a pain hotter and more intense than anything she could ever have imagined before this ordeal began.

She was kneeling on the bed with her elbows up on the bottom bedstead clinging to Don who stood on the other side of it. Her face was buried in his chest, her eyes were closed. Then the contraction let go and she breathed again.

Annie came in with a cassette player in one hand and a steaming mug of tea in the other. She went out again and came back with candles, matches and an aromatherapy burner.

The next contraction set in and Bella buried her head in Don's chest again.

When she closed her eyes and felt the pain grip, she knew this was what it was like to be tortured on a medieval rack. Lashed down on a frame, she was being cranked and stretched apart, wrenched open bit by agonizing bit. She was waiting to hear the crack and snap of ligaments being torn apart.

Medieval was the word that kept running through her mind. It was the twenty-first century, but she had chosen a medieval way to give birth. She could have been in hospital with an epidural anaesthetic coursing soothingly through her central nervous system but instead, when she opened her eyes, she saw that Annie had turned down the lights and was lighting candles.

There was the cloying smell of incense in the air

and awful New Age music. Bella began to feel panicky.

Her hair was sticking to her face and neck, droplets of sweat were trickling off the ends and into her eyes, she could feel sweat running freely down her sides, between her breasts.

The contraction was over and Annie was coming towards her with the mug.

'Here we are dear, have a little camomile tea, it will help you to calm down.'

That was too much for Bella: 'Camomile fucking *tea*?' she screamed. 'Do you seriously think that is going to make any difference?'

There was silence in the room. Then Bella moaned because she could feel another contraction cranking up again. It began low down like the cramping pain of a terrible stomach upset and radiated out until she was helplessly overwhelmed by it. She clung to Don and tried to stay afloat.

Suddenly, there was a terrifying bursting sensation and Bella felt as if something had exploded out of her in a rush. Her legs were soaking wet and for a moment she thought the baby must be there.

'That's good,' said Annie. 'The waters have broken.'

Bella came out of the darkness of the contraction to find Annie mopping at the puddle on the bed with a horrible beige, plastic-backed mat.

She laid another mat over the back of Bella's legs. The plastic clung to her sweaty calf muscles, but before she had time to be irritated and move it, another contraction was bearing down on her.

In the depth of it, Bella heard a low animal-like

groaning and wondered what the hell it could be before she realized she was making the noise herself. Christ, this was awful.

Annie went out of the room and as Bella surfaced from the gripping agony and drew in breath, she spoke to Don in an urgent voice. 'Get my handbag, quick.' She pointed at the bag in a corner of the room.

'You can't smoke now, Bella,' Don hissed at her.

'No, no,' Bella said urgently. 'Get the bag!'

He handed it to her and Bella rummaged for her address book. The next contraction was already welling up, she had to be quick.

'Pass the phone,' she urged Don, who in disbelief handed it to her.

'What are you doing?' he asked.

She dialled in the number – Answer, ANSWER – the pain was spreading from the pit of her stomach. The receiver was sliding in her hand, wet with sweat.

'Hello, caller, please leave your message after the tone.'

'Declan, Declan, it's Bella, you've got to help me.' She could hear the groan of pain start to enter her voice, she tried as hard as she could to continue . . . 'Please come round, bring drugs, 18 Park Crescent. I'll pay you whatever you need.'

She dropped the phone and grabbed hold of Don's shirt. He put his arms round her back and hugged her. He had no idea how they were going to get through this. He was starting to feel very afraid.

Annie came back in with a bowl and a face flannel.

248

When the storm of the contraction had passed, she offered to wash Bella down.

Bella realized how much she needed this. The large T-shirt, all she was wearing, was totally sodden and clinging to her. Her hair was completely wet now with salty beads streaming into her face. Her legs were soaked and the plastic mat was sticking claustrophobically on top of them.

Every pore in her entire body was running with sweat.

Annie helped her take the T-shirt off and sponged her face with cool water. She moved on down over Bella's back and legs.

'I'm sorry, Annie,' Bella was wailing now, 'I can't trust you to do this. I don't want this any more . . . candles and shit . . .' Her eyes were swimming with tears and she could feel the low pain starting up again.

She felt like vomiting and began to retch. Racked with fear, she was beginning to think she might die. She buried her head in Don's shirt again and started to concentrate on getting through the pain.

When she closed her eyes, she saw a black ocean swell and her own head bobbing in the enormous bank of water, trying to stay afloat. She was just trying to keep her head above the water and survive, but she had no idea how long she could hang on for.

There was no sign of help and she was so tired of swimming and only very vaguely aware of Don and Annie talking. Way in the distance, she thought she could hear the phone ringing, but it all seemed like a dream she was having while she paddled desperately in this ocean against the black mountainous waves that were trying to drag her down.

At last, it was time to open her eyes and breathe again. The bedroom window had been opened and the sheet was billowing in front of it, sending a cool breeze into the room. The incense and candles had gone, replaced by bright sidelights.

Don was stroking her hair and Annie was prodding about between her legs and listening to the baby's heartbeat with a stethoscope.

'You're both doing fine,' said Annie in a soothing voice. 'Look Bella it's absolutely OK with me if you want someone else here. Just do whatever you need, whatever you want. You have time to go to hospital if you like, Bella, but it will be a very uncomfortable journey.'

'Is Declan coming?' Bella looked up at Don.

'Yes.'

'When?'

'Very soon.'

'Oh thank God.' She was vaguely aware she might be hurting Annie's feelings somewhat but she knew she couldn't really care about that right now.

Declan was coming. The fresh air hit her and she began to feel slightly stronger and thirsty.

'Annie, could I have a drink? There's apple juice in the fridge.'

'Of course.'

Annie bustled out and Bella sat back on her heels and tried to rest and breathe but the pain was there, cranking up again.

'Oh Don,' she moaned and held out her arms so he could gather her up and somehow get her through this.

She was amazed at how much agony her body

250

could endure. Hours ago she'd thought the pain was as much as she could bear, but each contraction since then had upped the level again and yet again and harder and longer, trying to squeeze the life out of her and still she was surviving somehow. It was becoming a relentless storm with no clear beginning or end to the contractions. It felt as if hours had passed yet it also seemed barely twenty minutes since she had been in the bath thinking labour was OK.

Outside it had grown dark and she was aware of more people coming into the room. At one point she opened her eyes and saw Declan, or was she just imagining it? She managed to smile at him but had to close her eyes and groan again.

But it was him. He was really talking to her in his lovely Irish accent.

'Bella, hello, how are you doing? Come on my love, open your eyes and look at me for a moment.'

With enormous concentration, she prised open her eyes.

Her arms were still wrapped round Don, but Declan had his hands round her face now and looked into her eyes.

'Bella, you're doing fine. It's just taking a long time to happen, so you're getting tired and a bit discouraged. Now I'm here, with my good friend Zena, to help you. Annie is here too and together we're going to help you do this. You are a strong, tough old girl, Bella. I know you can do this. You've got your lovely husband here holding onto you for dear life. We are all here for you. We are not going to let you down. OK?'

'OK,' she managed to whisper.

'Now, gas and air. I promise this will really, really help.'

He passed her up a flat white plastic tube. 'Put this in your mouth and take a deep breath,' he said.

A blast of cold parchingly dry air hit the back of her throat. She wanted to cough but sucked in again and again.

She pushed the tube away as her face now felt strangely numb and she felt sick to the pit of her stomach.

'No, no, no . . . I feel sick,' she wailed.

She could hear Declan: 'Keep going, I promise, it will be fine.'

She put the tube to her lips again, everything was starting to blur in a dark red melting pot of pain. Declan's reassuring words felt like a repeating mantra which had been going on for hours.

She knew it was night time, but there were flashes of bright light when she opened her eyes. When she closed them, she was in a sea of hot red liquid pain.

'We've got to get her up.' Declan's voice sounded far away in the distance, she was still focused on the tiny head, bobbing in the waves, dipping under in the hot sea. God, she just wanted to rest, just wanted this to be over.

She felt strong arms under her armpits wrenching her out of the sea.

They were trying to make her stand on dry land, but her legs weren't working.

'Bella! Bella!' It was Don with a hint of panic in his voice. She thought she would like to see Don, where the hell was he?

There was cool water on her face and running down her back. She opened her eyes.

Don was standing in front of her, holding her up, Declan was at her side.

She opened her eyes wide and was aware of the terrible, clear pain. They were holding her up, defying the force between her legs, which was dragging her down. She felt her knees buckle with the effort, but still they held her up.

She made a primeval, guttural scream as she felt an enormous weight crash down against the whole band of muscle from her belly button down round to her anus. An irresistible force was urging her to push it out although it went against every instinct of pain avoidance and self-preservation. Her hip joints were screaming at the very edge of their sockets.

And she had to push, knowing it was ripping her in half. Her anus was being pushed inside out. There was a wrecking ball inside her pelvis crushing and destroying everything in its path.

It was coming down, it was coming out.

She was squatting on her knees despite Don and Declan hauling against her.

She could hear roars and screams of agony, which she knew she was making, but her mind was in a small still place. She was alone and quiet in the eye of the storm. Small logical thoughts were forming there: This is it, the baby is coming out. It's almost over. We're nearly there. I've just done a crap on the bedroom floor. I hope someone's put plastic sheeting down.

The arms pulled her up so she was kneeling on

the bed, Don was in front of her, so she automatically flung her arms around his chest. Everyone else was bustling about behind her. There was an immense burning and a tearing sensation so violent she thought she heard it, then the pain peaked – white hot searing pain and silent screaming. And then it was over.

She sank forward into Don. Oh thank God, thank God, thank God. It was over, she was still alive, she'd got through it.

Don was hugging her head into his chest.

'Oh Bella,' he sounded croaky. 'There's the baby.'

God, the baby, she'd totally forgotten about the baby. She turned her head and saw an enormous purple baby, with two little tubes in its nose, which Declan was deftly manipulating.

She collapsed into an awkward heap on the bed, blood spilling out from between her legs and was handed this big, slippery solid baby.

She just looked for a long moment, then managed to whisper, 'Hello.'

The eyes opened and Bella looked into them and somehow in the same moment noticed she was holding a boy. He smelt briny, as if he'd been plucked from the sea.

'Hello there,' she whispered. 'Hello Markie.'

Don's face was next to hers and they were both gazing at this extraordinary new person.

His dark eyes latched onto hers in an unblinking, steady gaze. They were the deepest, darkest pools of wonder she'd ever looked down into. She was just astonished they had managed to make something so perfect.

The baby put a tiny hand up against his face and

254

Bella took in the fingers with perfect little purple nails and wrinkles round the joints and dimples on the knuckles.

'My God Bella, he's just amazing,' Don whispered beside her.

Bella looked round and noticed three other faces close by watching them quietly.

She smiled and they all smiled back at her.

She looked back at the baby. 'Just perfect, so perfect,' she said falling back in elated exhaustion against the pillows someone had propped behind her.

Chapter Twenty-three

'OK, Bella, we've still got some work to do here.'
Declan sounded brisk.

The cord was cut, then Declan handed Markie
over to Annie for a wash while he busied himself
with delivering the placenta.

When the enormous lump of raw liver slid out
from between her legs, Bella saw she was sitting on
a damp and bloody plastic sheet. She was naked
and her legs were smeared with blood, dried
blood and traces of shit. Her fingernails were dark
with dried blood, her hair was soaked, blood was
pooling between her legs and she was beginning to
shiver.

Don was over by the baby bath taking pictures.

'I'm really sorry, Bella, but we're going to have to
do stitches now,' said Declan.

'You're kidding,' she managed.

'I'll hand you over to Zena, a wonder with a
needle. We'll give you a jab first, then you better
have the gas and air to hand.'

Bella sucked furiously at the gas cylinder as Zena

cleaned then began to stitch at the long tear on her perineum.

Bella's face contorted with pain. She could not believe how much she'd had to endure in one night. A deep stoic resignation began to settle over her. If someone had come in and said they were here to pull out her back teeth, she would have accepted it as her lot.

'You know why it's called labour now,' said Zena in a gentle Caribbean accent as she worked away on an interminable number of stitches. 'It's women's work, no man would be able to take this.'

Bella smiled at her weakly in between gulps from the gas cylinder. She wasn't sure if the gas helped at all but at least it gave her something to do other than scream.

Finally it was over. Markie was dried and dressed and Zena helped Bella hobble into the bathroom for a warm deep bath.

Bella sank into it. She looked down at her body. Somehow, on the edge of the deepest exhaustion, she found the energy to be pleased that her stomach was so amazingly flat.

OK it looked like a strange wrinkled, deflated soufflé, but it was flattish. She could see over it, she could bend. Her breasts were absolutely enormous, especially in comparison to this flat stomach.

Between her legs everything felt oddly sensation-less and tightly strung together. How the hell was she going to pee? Let alone . . . she didn't want to think about that. There were piles the size of houses rubbing painfully between her buttocks.

She could hear vigorous crying coming from the

bedroom, so she raised herself carefully out of the bath, she dried off with a towel and slipped on the clean nightshirt hanging on the back of the door.

The bedroom had been transformed. New clean sheets and pillowcases were on the bed, Markie's little cot had been brought through. The lighting was dim with just one sidelight and a few candles.

Zena was tying up plastic rubbish bags and Declan was scribbling in Bella's maternity notebook, while Don sat on the bed holding the crying baby.

Bella went over and picked Markie up awkwardly, letting his head loll back. 'Sh, sh sh,' she soothed.

'OK,' said Declan. 'Let's help you get him latched on.'

She sat back against the mountain of pillows and opened her nightshirt. Markie immediately turned to her breast. Very matter-of-factly, Declan pinched up her nipple and pushed it into the baby's little open mouth. He sucked vigorously.

'Well, he's off,' said Declan. 'No problem at all. Your only trouble might be making enough milk for that baby, do you know how much he weighed? Ten pounds and three ounces. For your build, that is enormous. No wonder we had a job getting him out.'

Bella watched her son's little mouth chomp up and down on a breast bigger than his head.

'It was absolute hell. I am never, ever doing that again,' she said, at last feeling just a little bit like herself again.

Declan laughed. 'I've heard that before. The second one is always easier.'

'Yeah right,' she said. 'You just say that to keep yourself in a job.'

She looked at Don: he was exhausted with huge damp patches under the arms of his shirt. 'I'm sorry hon, we can never ever have sex again, even in six months' time, when the wounds have finally healed,' she said.

'Nonsense,' said Declan. 'Give her a month Don, then put on your best gear and she'll be gagging for it. But lubricate,' he added.

'Enough!' said Bella in horror. 'I'm never having sex again. That is final.'

As she leaned over and kissed Don, the baby unlatched and scrabbled frantically to get his lips back round the nipple.

'Oh no,' said Bella, breaking off her kiss. She turned Markie round and let him have a go at the other side.

Don kept an arm round her. He had never felt so relieved in his life. Bella and his son were alive. They were safe and well in the bend of his arm, and he didn't think he would ever feel so grateful for anything ever again. It had been terrifying. About twenty minutes before Markie was finally born, Don had heard Declan make the calls to check that an ambulance was available and to warn the hospital that an emergency C-section could be on its way.

Annie came in with tea but Don said, 'Bugger tea, I've got champagne downstairs,' and he set off to get it.

'I'd really like the tea first,' Bella quietly told Annie.

'I'm sure, dear. And there's a big jug of diluted

259

apple juice here for you as well. Do you want some toast or something?'

Bella thought about the hideous piles and said 'No, thanks. And, by the way, I want to say thank you, I'm sorry I was so awful to you.'

'Bella, it's fine. I got worried too that nothing was happening and I think you felt that. You did the right thing and it's all worked out.'

Annie looked down at the little face buried deep in Bella's breasts.

'Look at that,' she said with a smile. 'Hopefully he'll sleep for a long time tonight and give you both some rest.'

'What time is it?' Bella asked.

'Three-thirty in the morning. Markie was born at 2.15 a.m. precisely. So you were in labour for about 21 hours. That's a long time.'

'Damn right,' said Bella.

Several glasses of champagne later, it was time for everyone to go and leave the three of them alone together. The three of us: Bella kept trying the words out in her mind. They sounded strange.

Declan had left her a huge bottle of extra-strong painkillers after insisting she take two. Annie had disapproved and promised to come round in the morning with a breast milk friendly alternative.

Bella had taken the pills. Her whole genital area was starting to throb and painful contractions still racked her stomach. She longed for sleep.

Don came up to the room after he had seen everyone out of the door.

He looked at the picture before him of Bella and baby and felt his heart swell to encompass this.

Bella was a mother and they had a new baby to care for.

The baby had fallen asleep in her arms. 'The baby' – he still seemed too new to have a name.

Bella put him down in his cradle at the side of the bed.

Don undressed and pulled on a T-shirt and some shorts. He climbed into bed beside Bella and held her close. 'I am so proud of you,' he said.

'So am I,' she answered with a smile. 'That was hell on earth. I thought I was going to die.'

He didn't say anything, just wrapped his arms around her even more tightly. Finally, he leaned over to switch off the light and realized how enormously tired he was.

Bella rolled over so she could lie looking at her tiny son in his little crib beside her. Her son: the word resonated in her mind.

In the gloom she could see that he wasn't sleeping any more, his eyes were open and fixed on hers. She felt overwhelmed with love. Don was on one side of her and this wonderful new baby was on the other. Nothing had ever felt so perfect and so complete before.

She tried to sleep, but felt too overcome. She kept opening her eyes just to check on the tiny person lying brand new beside her.

And it seemed to Bella that every time she opened her eyes, those small dark ones were looking back at her, gazing in wonder at her and this whole new world.

261

Chapter Twenty-four

Don made all the phone calls and handled the hourly delivery of flowers while Bella lay in bed like a worn-out princess with Markie snuggled up beside her.

'Tania's coming round later,' Don said, poking his head round the door, amazed to find Bella finally awake: 'There's no stopping her.'

'Oh, it's OK,' Bella whispered, 'When I said no visitors today, I meant apart from her.'

'And Mum and your parents have sent the most amazing flowers. D'you feel up to calling them? They're all waiting by the phone.'

'Yeah, of course,' Bella answered, feeling guilty that she would rather speak to Don's mum than her own.

Don went over to look at the baby again. He was lying on his back fast asleep with his head turned to the side and his arms up beside his ears in a still life Highland fling.

He had a white cotton hat on with a knotted top but his face looked too old for such a babyish thing.

He looked like an ancient Buddha, not sleeping, merely closing his eyes in meditation.

'Has he been awake again?'

'No,' said Bella. 'Not since seven. I think they do that for a day or two, sleep it off.'

'How are you?' He looked at her pale face and the deep dark circles round her eyes.

'Not too bad. I'm exhausted, I can't walk, I'm still getting contractions and my tits feel like lead balloons but these are keeping me happy—' she nodded at the big bottle of hospital-strength painkillers Declan had left her.

'Remember to hide them when Annie comes round or she'll take them away.'

'Over my dead body.'

'Have you changed his nappy?'

'God no!' Bella looked appalled. 'It's been on for hours.'

'OK . . . what do we need?'

They set up a towel on the bed. Don brought in a bowl of lukewarm water, cotton wool balls and a new nappy as instructed.

He lifted Markie onto the towel and he and Bella fumbled with the hundred tiny popper buttons on his babygro and the velcro on his nappy straps. Markie was disgusted to be so rudely awoken. He balled up his tiny fists and began to howl so violently that his body shook and his face changed from red to purple.

Bella opened the tiny nappy: it looked bone dry, so she peered down more closely and was aware that her cheek was wet. She moved back in surprise as Markie's teeny willy sprayed about in all

263

directions. In an elegant arch he wet the duvet, his babygro and his own face. This made him cry even more frantically.

Bella and Don were in a horrified panic. He dabbed at the baby's face with the edge of the towel and Bella picked the little bundle up and cuddled him to try and stop his piteous wailing.

'OK,' she tried to sound calm. 'We'll need a new vest and babygro.'

Don brought them in to Bella on the bed and they looked at each other with apprehension. Markie was still purple and crying fiercely.

Two grown-ups, one who had covered wars, the other who had fought in her fair share of boardroom battles, were just beginning to get an inkling of how truly helpless they were in the field of baby rearing.

Changing Markie for the first time ever was horrific. He battled with his legs and arms and roared at them in terror. His parents, terrified they were going to break him, touched him gently and gingerly but he acted as if he was being tortured. Finally, when it was all over, Bella lifted him up to her breasts and let him nuzzle. At last there was silence.

'Oh my God,' Don sighed, then he looked at Bella. After a moment of relieved silence, they collapsed into giggles which got more and more hysterical.

'He peed in your face . . .' roared Don in between belly laughs.

'Your expression, when you came in with the vest . . .' Bella was laughing so hard that Markie lost his grip and squawked until she'd latched him on again.

'How does it feel?' Don gestured to his son

clamped tightly onto his wife's breast, when they had finally calmed down.

'I don't really feel anything apart from his little jaws going chomp, chomp, chomp.'

'How do you know he's getting enough?'

'Because Annie told me he'll howl the house down when he's hungry, not lie in his crib asleep – normal survival rules.'

'I'm glad you're so sussed,' he told her.

'Oh God, I'm so not, Don. I'm terrified! But we'll just have to muddle through, learning the ropes on the job.'

'Are you sure you don't want anything to eat?'

'Believe me if your exit points felt like mine, you wouldn't want anything either.'

He didn't need to know more.

'OK,' she said when Markie had drunk his fill, 'Let's call the folks.'

Don sat up on the bed beside her as she punched in her parents' number.

'Hello Mum, it's me,' she said when her mother picked up.

'Bella! How are you? We're so proud of you.' Well that was a first, Bella couldn't help thinking.

'Just spare me the details,' her mother added. 'Don said it went on for hours. I don't want to know, I really don't . . . but then you would insist on doing it at home. But you are OK now, aren't you? And little . . . Mark?' She said the baby's name in that 'Please tell me I'm wrong' sort of voice.

'Markie,' Bella answered.

'Oh yes, I'm sure he's a little Markie now, but later . . . anyway, is he utterly lovely and perfect?'

'He's beautiful,' she said and slipped her hand

into Don's. 'You should come and see him, Mum.' She held her breath for the reply.

'Well . . . it will be hard for me, Bella' – and here we go, Bella thought. 'I've had nothing to do with babies since you were small because of what I've been through,' her mother continued. 'I know it's going to trigger a lot of difficult feelings. I've bought a book about becoming a grandmother and I'm trying to prepare myself for the rush of emotions. All the pain and sadness of losing five little babies, it's all going to come flooding back.'

As she listened, Bella thought how strange it was that her mother seemed so emotionally open and yet only ever managed to push her away. Whatever Bella did, her mother could only experience it in terms of how it affected her – even giving birth, for God's sake.

When the call was finally over, Bella banged the receiver down, relieved that her mother had given herself an excuse not to visit for months now and furious with her for it at the same time.

After that, it was a pleasure to have Don's lovely mum, Maddie, on the other end of the line saying all the right things.

'Well done, Bella, Don is so proud of you, I've never heard anything like it. And so am I . . . Markie, what an adorable name, goes so well with McCartney . . . I'm coming down as soon as I can sort out some cover and only if you want me. Maybe you want a little time to yourselves first of all? . . . Now back to bed, make sure you rest as much as you can.'

She fell asleep again not long after. Her last image was the bank of purple, yellow, pink and white blossom forming in the bedroom. Don had run out of vases and was now using buckets, bowls, whatever he could lay his hands on. It reminded her of the night she'd told him she was pregnant.

Her last thought before falling into the doze was: Twenty-one hours! Ten pounds and three ounces! Bloody hell, it was little short of a miracle that they were both alive.

Tania arrived much later when the sun was starting to set on Markie's first day. She rushed into the bedroom and woke Bella with a kiss.

'Oh congratulations, you fantastically clever girl,' she gushed, leaning into the crib and trying to get a good sniff of the sleeping bundle inside.

'Look at him, he's absolutely gorgeous.'

'No he's not,' Bella said groggily. 'He looks like a miniature Chinese Winston Churchill.'

'Actually, now you mention it . . . Shut up, Bella. He's adorable. I'll have him if you don't want him.'

'If you think I went through all that just so I could be your surrogate mother . . .' Bella was smiling now.

'Was it really bad?'

'*Bad??!* I'm sorry, I'm not joining in the postnatal mum conspiracy to keep childless women in the dark. It was appalling, it was awful, it was much, much more excruciating agony than I could ever have imagined. Went on for much longer than humanly bearable and is just barbaric in every way. Next time – Caesarean or at the very least, the full epidural works.'

Tania looked at her in horror.

'Oh my God, you're not pregnant are you?' Bella asked.

267

'No,' said Tania. 'But I might reconsider that plan now,' then she burst out: 'But he's so gorgeous, I want one!!'

She rustled around in the glossy shopping bags she'd brought and pulled out a huge, plush teddy bear. They both burst into laughter.

'Oh my God,' said Bella, 'it's so big, he'll be frightened of it.'

'He'll grow into it. It's so cute. And look at these.' She tipped out an array of jewel bright baby clothes.

'Baby Kenzo,' she said. 'Aren't they fantastic?'

'Oh wow,' said Bella. 'You really shouldn't have.'

'Nonsense. I'm his fairy godmother. Now for you, fairy princess . . .' She opened another bag and out slid a huge, fat bottle of lavishly expensive aromatherapy foam bath.

'Thank you very much,' said Bella. 'As soon as the stitches have healed, I will indulge.'

Tania pulled a face: 'How many?'

'An unspeakable amount. I've told Don we can never have sex again.'

'Oh God. That means you won't need my final present.'

Bella laughed, curious now.

Tania brought out a shoebox. Inside were pale green strappy snakeskin shoes with vertiginously high heels.

'Good grief,' said Bella shocked at Tania's extravagance.

'Well, I worried you might not get back into your clothes just yet, so I thought these would make you feel foxy again.'

Tania was surprised to find her friend choked with tears.

They put their arms round each other and Bella sobbed.

'I'm sorry,' Bella said as soon as she could. 'It must be the hormones. Thank you very much.'

'It's a pleasure, honey,' Tania smiled and got paper hankies out of her handbag. 'I brought supper as well, Japanese . . . sushi, broth, all your favourite things. I'll go down and heat them, then Don and I will come and eat by your bedside with you.'

When a steaming bowl of noodly broth was put in front of her with a large hunk of buttered bread, Bella realized she was ravenous. She was going to have to eat and worry about passing the consequences when it happened.

'My mum says you have to have someone come and stay and look after you for a while,' Tania said biting down on a piece of rice and sushi. 'She says she's going to come if you haven't got anyone else!'

Bella laughed: 'That's very sweet. I think Maddie's visiting soon, Don's mum, so that will be good. But Don is off for two weeks, so we'll be fine. I'm sure I'll feel back to normal by then.'

She heard herself saying this but wondered if it was true. She was shocked at her condition and her injuries. Just two days ago, she could clean floors, walk round the block, make love: now she was barely able to shuffle to the bathroom. And she was in so much pain. Her breasts ached, her uterus was still contracting in sharp spasms, especially when the baby breastfed, and her stitches and piles . . . well, best take another painkiller and try and forget about it.

She felt as if the entire area between her legs had

269

been stapled shut. It was bruised and swollen and an exploratory feel of the damage had not been reassuring. In between a dense weave of hair matted with congealed blood were hulking great stitches, which, thank God were supposed to dissolve rather than need tweezing out when the wounds had healed.

She had torn almost to her anus; only a large bulbous pile seemed to have stopped the path of the rip. And she hadn't been prepared for the bleeding either. Annie had brought round maternity pads the size of mattresses earlier in the day and told her to bathe in water with lavender oil when it all got too uncomfortable.

Jesus, Bella had just never expected this amount of damage. She felt injured, war wounded and everyone was smiling and sending flowers and congratulating her as if she'd just won an award. Get well cards and sympathy would be slightly more appropriate. Maybe she should design a new range: 'It's a boy! Fifteen stitches, wow you must be feeling sore!'

But she had her reward, didn't she? Markie was sound asleep in his bed again, oblivious to the chat going on around him in the room.

Tania was stroking his downy head and watching his chest rise and fall and Don was gazing at him too as he spooned noodles into his mouth.

The baby was a magical presence, no doubt about it. They were all transfixed by this tiny being whose beautiful blue-veined eyelids were fluttering in sleep like butterfly wings.

Chapter Twenty-five

It was close to 2 a.m. when Bella was ripped out of deep sleep by her baby's ferocious wailing. She turned on the sidelight. Don had woken up too.

She lifted her screaming son out of his crib and put him against her breast. He sucked like hell and it really, really hurt. She gritted her teeth and watched his jaw moving up and down. 'Oh God—' she turned to Don. 'This is so painful. I don't think I can let him drink much more.'

Her bleary-eyed husband mumbled something sympathetic.

Bella put her finger down to Markie's mouth to break the suction and took him off. He burst into desperate screams again. Quickly she put him back on her other breast. She watched the little face working up and down and tried not to think about the horrible rubbed raw pain coming from her nipples.

After about three minutes, she swapped sides again, then several minutes later she swapped back. She couldn't take it any more. Surely, he must have had enough by now. She broke him off again and was horrified to hear his anguished cries.

She rocked him a little bit, then put him back in his crib. Maybe he was just tired and needed to go back to sleep now.

He screamed furiously at her down there and balled up his little fists. Maybe he needed a new nappy. She picked him up and stumbled through to the bathroom with him, she undid the rompers and opened the tiny nappy while the pink legs kicked against her and Markie screamed so hard that his jaw was trembling.

In the nappy was a small solid black mess. Bella filled with relief. OK, as soon as this was changed he'd settle down and feel much better.

She fumbled her way through the nappy change and headed back to the bedroom. Don was already half asleep. Bella put Markie into the crib and he screamed even harder. She patted him and spoke gently to him, but he was inconsolable.

'I don't know what it is,' Bella turned to Don.

'Turn out the lights, I'm sure he'll settle down,' Don mumbled.

In darkness they lay listening to the anguished crying. Bella felt so tired she could barely move and yet the crying pierced her to the core and it was impossible to just lie there and listen to it.

She leaned over and scooped Markie out of his crib again. She rocked him in her arms – no change – she hauled herself out of bed and began to hobble painfully round the room holding Markie up against her shoulder and patting his back.

An age later, he finally stopped crying against her shoulder. She leaned over the crib to put him down and the wailing started up again.

'Oh no!' she cried in desperation and sank onto the bed, 'I can't feed him again, it's too sore,' she wailed. 'And I've got to get some *sleep*!'

Don dragged himself out: 'Let me have a go.'

He picked up the screaming baby and walked round the bed with him, then he started singing something indecipherable and astonishingly tuneless. Bella watched the digital minutes stack up on the bedside clock. It took sixteen minutes, until 3.08 a.m. before Markie was asleep again.

Don eased him into the crib, then collapsed back onto the bed. Less than three hours later, they were woken again by the wail of a hungry baby.

After four more nights like this, Bella began to wonder how she was going to survive. She felt dizzy and ill with tiredness. Her head was pounding and more than anything else in the world she wanted to sleep, but she felt so desperately needed by this tiny, helpless baby. Her nipples hurt excruciatingly as Markie drank and she was balancing him awkwardly against her as she couldn't even sit up properly because her stitches and piles were so painful.

Don had fallen straight back to sleep beside her and it was impossible not to fill up with rage. Bastard, she thought, how dare he not have to stay awake and breastfeed? He could damn well wind and change the nappy and then change the outfit which usually got puked on just when the nappy changing was over.

She looked into the little eyes which were wide open and fixed on her and at the furrowed brow and tiny, perfect fingernails and she knew she was completely, helplessly, hopelessly in love. Markie was making her life utter, utter hell but she loved him, adored him, felt totally captivated by him.

Oh great, she thought. Just the kind of dependent relationship I've been trying to avoid for ten years and here I am desperate to please a needy, greedy, ungrateful little man.

She stroked his cheek: 'You are,' she said gently, 'a needy, greedy, ungrateful little man.' The baby sucked contentedly.

She took Don's advice and went back to bed in the middle of the morning once Markie had been fed again and gone back to sleep. As she walked up the stairs, she had to face the fact that finally she was going to have to go to the loo, and not just for a pee.

Christ. What if the stitches ripped? Or everything tore? Or she passed out with the pain? She was going to have to be brave and find out what the score was.

She sat herself down on the toilet seat and waited. She was hit with an absolutely searing pain but within seconds it was over. Hardly childbirth then, she thought to herself. She wiped and was surprised to find the toilet paper covered in bright red blood. She looked into the bowl and the white porcelain sides were splattered with blood droplets. Oh God. Gingerly she felt down. Stitches all seemed to be in place. Anus was ringed with a bleeding spongy mass. God, there must be something she could do about this. The technological advantages of living in the twenty-first century had to include not having to put up with horrendous post-partum piles.

She went into the bedroom and collapsed on the

bed. She felt as if she had only just fallen into a jumbled sleep when Don was at her bedside holding a red, screaming Markie.

'What's the matter?' Bella asked, shaken out of exhaustion by anxiety about her baby.

'He's just hungry. He's been awake for about forty-five minutes, but I've been carrying him around, trying to distract him so you could sleep for longer.'

'Thanks, Don.' She glanced up at him. His eyes were ringed too and he was sprouting a healthy coat of stubble. 'Why don't you go for a shower while I feed him?' she said.

'OK. Then I'll make some lunch, shall I?'

'Yeah, thanks.'

She didn't look up again, he noticed. Her eyes were fixed on Markie as she lifted her T-shirt and placed her nipple in the ravenous mouth.

Don was ashamed to feel a wave of jealousy pass over him. He was jealous that Markie had all Bella's attention but also jealous that Bella was everything Markie needed. He felt left out of the intimate circle of two. It was also strangely arousing to see his son's tiny lips suck at the large rosy pink nipples. Bella looked beautiful. Buxom and blossoming and just perfect. How was he ever going to last another . . . *five and a half weeks* without sex?'

'Oh God,' he groaned.

'What's the matter?' She asked while the baby suckled on, unperturbed.

'I've just remembered how long it is before we can have sex again.'

She laughed now for what felt like the first time in days. 'Forget it, Don! We are never having sex

275

again! They've stapled me shut and even if they hadn't, I am never, ever going through childbirth again. So I'll need medical documents to prove your vasectomy has been a complete success before letting you near.'

They both laughed now and wondered how much of that was true.

Don made lunch and later on, he made supper. He was a pretty domesticated man, but the household was deteriorating round them fast. The bedroom laundry basket was overflowing with tiny vests and babygros stained bright yellow with baby crap. How could something so small produce so much vivid waste product? he wondered, taking care to handle the clothes by the edges.

The kitchen was grubby and cluttered with dirty dishes; everywhere needed to be hoovered.

Don could hear Markie upstairs in the bathroom wailing all the way through his evening bath. That was bound to upset Bella. He suddenly felt exhausted and decided to nip out and finally get some newspapers in. The walk would clear his head.

Chapter Twenty-six

Bella had her laptop out and was trying to engage her brain just long enough to write her New York friend, Jenna, an e-mail.

My dear darling Jen, My seventeen day old baby is finally asleep and I have just enough energy left to sprawl out on the sofa and type you a note. Thank you so much for the lovely outfit which arrived yesterday. It's just gorgeous, perfect . . . thank you. Markie has worn it for about 20 seconds but now it's back in the wash basket covered in projectile vomit. Ah the joys of motherhood!

I'm sort of hanging in here – battered, bruised, a bit weepy and totally, totally beyond the limit of human endurance tired. I have never been so tired.

I am going to hit the next person who tells me 'don't worry, the first six weeks are the worst' because I'm thinking SIX WEEKS – I cannot survive another six DAYS of this!!

Breastfeeding – lovely concept – hurts like hell, plus I look like a chunky, frumpy, brunette Dolly Parton. Only industrial size painkillers are getting me through the stitches, post-partum piles situation but, hey, I don't want to put you off or anything . . . are you still brooding on the broody question?

How is Ritchie doing? I hope you are considering a visit soon so I can inspect this man and you can come and worship at the shrine of Markie.

Don is OK, despite me turning into the baggy shirted, slipper wearing harpy from hell who nearly screamed the house down when he suggested going off to Italy for a week to 'work' on some football tournament.

Markie is of course adorable, adorable, just a million times lovelier than I could ever have imagined. But so much work, much worse than expected . . . I'm such an amateur it terrifies me – I can't even steer the buggy properly. I feel a bit helpless and out of control and I'm very worried about how I'm going to make all this work. But I keep telling myself I'll figure it out somehow . . . hopefully soon. Take care cupcake, love you, Bella xxx

She hit send then closed up the computer and tried to fall asleep.

By the afternoon, she felt strong enough to take Markie out for a walk when he was fed and ready for a sleep. She put him into a new nappy, sleepsuit and cardigan, then laid him down in the buggy. That had only taken about forty minutes – a new world record time.

She dragged the buggy down the front door steps, cursing every single one of them. This had all been much easier when Don was around. But he was already back at work.

It still felt strange to walk along the road pushing this great big thing along. The sun broke out from behind a cloud and Markie, dazzled, began to cry. She pulled up the hood and it only partially covered his face, so she moved him gently up the pram until he was in shade again, still crying. She spoke to him soothingly as they moved on down the road and finally he fell asleep and she felt herself relax a little.

The nearest high street was shabby and run down with a grotty-looking shopping centre at one end, then a handful of chain stores, interspersed with kebab shops and taxi offices. Scabby market stalls selling cheap handbags and underwear were pitched up against the pavement.

She went to Boots first where she headed for the aisle with nappies and all the other postnatal products.

Wow, I'm an entirely separate consumer group, she couldn't help noticing. Extra-large sanitary towels, cracked-nipple cream, nipple guards, haemorrhoid cream, she piled the lot into her basket. Add a packet of super-strength painkillers, a bottle of wine, and maybe she would get through the evening after all.

As she paid at the till, Markie started to stir. By the time she got back outside, he was bawling miserably and she knew she had to feed him . . . where?? There was no bench or seat in sight and anyway, would she really be happy whipping up her top here? Plus there was the wind chill factor to consider. She headed for the baby shop at the far end of the street.

Markie was red in the face and howling by the time she got there. She hurried through the shop straight for the tweely labelled 'Mummy's Room' which had a bench, several changing mats, a sink, a grotty cartoon character frieze on the wall and an overpowering stench of dirty nappies. No wonder new mums got depression, this looked like the perfect venue for a postnatal suicide.

She bent over the buggy to lift out her screaming son and as her fingers reached behind him, they slid into warm wetness. She lifted him up and he and the sheepskin-lined buggy were covered in slimy yellow crap.

'Oh God,' she cursed under her breath.

She hadn't brought anything with her: no wipes, no change of clothes, no cloths, it was another Amateur Mum moment.

She put Markie down on one of the changing mats. He was waving his fists and bawling. No wonder, starving and covered in poo, not a good scene.

Stay calm, she told herself. There was a drum of paper towel on the wall so she pulled off about six feet from the roll and bundled Markie up in it. That would do while she fed him; they would begin the damage limitation exercise afterwards.

The staff were somewhat bemused to see a harassed and obviously brand new mother come out of the changing room holding a baby swaddled in yellow-stained paper towel.

Bella scanned the shelves and got vests, babygros and a large box of wipes. She picked out a black duffle changing bag, paid for the lot at the till and went back into the Mummy's Room for some time. When she came out again her baby was re-dressed and lying in his buggy on a wad of paper towel. The bulging duffle bag was slung over her shoulder.

On the walk home she tried to laugh about it but she felt hopeless and weak. God, how useless was she? She couldn't even take her baby round the block without turning it into a major crisis. She could feel tears welling up at the back of her eyes. This was just nothing like she'd imagined. All her baby daydreams had been about sitting in a sunny garden with a darling baby fast asleep in his pram. Instead the weather was cold and grey and he cried most of the time and she felt shattered and totally wound up.

Her mobile trilled in her pocket.

She clicked it open and was astonished to hear Kitty: Kitty asking her if she wanted the mail accumulating in the office to be sent to her or if she was coming in. It felt like greetings from another planet and served only to ignite her anxiety about the countdown on her time with her son.

She had six more weeks of being with her gorgeous little boy 24 hours a day and then she had to hand him over and get back to work, or else she would lose her place and anyway they had a mountainous mortgage now which they could not pay without her salary.

Chapter Twenty-seven

'Hello?' Don's voice sounded irritable.

'Don?' Bella was in tears again and there were frantic screams in the background.

'What's the matter, hon?' He tried to sound sympathetic.

'He won't stop crying,' she sobbed. 'I don't know what to do, I've fed him, I've changed him, maybe there's something wrong with him.'

'Have you winded him?'

'Of course.' She was beginning to sound angry now.

'Maybe he's just tired, Bella. I'm sure he's fine.'

'Tired?' she shouted. 'Of course he's bloody tired, he's been up since 6 a.m. and it's now eleven but he'll only sleep with my nipple in his mouth. I can't take any more of this. I need to tidy up, I need to have a bath, I need some sleep, I'm going to go insane.' She was practically screaming now.

'Bella,' Don's voice was angry too, 'I'm at work, I can't help you right now, calm down, go for a walk or something. I've got more important things to do than listen to this.' Shit, he regretted the words as soon as he'd said them.

All he could hear was his son's inconsolable wailing then a venomous 'Fuck you' before Bella slammed the phone down. 'Go for a walk' – she was too exhausted to walk the length of the room. She threw herself down on the sofa and howled with her baby.

Don sat at his desk wondering what to do. Was his wife bashing his son's head against the wall right now? Should he phone her back? Should he phone social services? He decided to phone his mum.

'I think it's definitely time for you to come down and help, Mum, if you can,' he said as soon as the fond hellos were over.

'Don, I'd love to, I've been dying for you to ask, I didn't want to impose.'

He was already feeling much calmer at the sound of her voice.

'How are you both getting on? I've been worrying about you.'

'It's absolute murder,' he was surprised to hear himself say.

'Oh dear,' Maddie said sympathetically. 'How's Bella coping?'

'Not very well right now,' Don answered. That was putting it mildly.

'Well, she's been such an independent girl for so long now. It must be a shock to be at the beck and call of a baby.'

'When can you come?' he asked, thinking she'd probably missed the last flight out of Inverness today. But maybe he could get her on the first plane in the morning.

'When do you want me?'

'Tomorrow? I can organize a flight.' He knew how desperate he must sound and felt a bit embarrassed.

'Don't be ridiculous, Don. You need to warn Bella. I'll come at the weekend. Are you phoning from work?' she asked sharply.

'Yes.'

'What on earth are you doing there? Your son isn't even three weeks old.'

'I had to get back.'

'What utter nonsense,' she said. 'Take the next three days off and I'll be there on Saturday. In fact, if you don't take the next three days off, I'm not going to come, is that clear?'

'I'll see what I can do,' he mumbled.

'Don McCartney, you should be ashamed of yourself.'

Once the call was over, Don arranged the time off, despite the news editor's raised eyebrows, and he left work that evening as early as he could.

He still hadn't dared to phone Bella back and wasn't quite sure what to expect when he opened the front door.

Bella was obviously giving Markie his evening bath, because there was frantic crying coming from the bathroom. Don went into the sitting room and flicked on the TV to the championship match he'd been hoping to watch.

He took off his shoes and glanced round the room. It looked extraordinary. There were cloths and pieces of kitchen towel in little heaps all over the floor. In one pile he spotted a yellow stained vest and several yellowish rolled-up nappies. Plates, one with a half-eaten cheese sandwich, and mugs half full of cold tea littered the area round the sofa. The beautiful leather sofa had an unmistakable yellow stain on it. Christ.

It was time to go upstairs and say hello. He took off his coat and carefully hung it up in the hall before heading up the stairs.

Opening the bathroom door, he saw Bella had Markie cuddled in a towel on the changing mat. He was shrieking and she was trying to talk to him soothingly as she struggled to put on a nappy.

She looked awful, her face was pale and blotchy with red-rimmed eyes, her hair was lank and fixed up messily on her head. She was wearing his old tracksuit bottoms with the hideous tartan shirt. The shoulders were stained with white patches of vomit and he could see patches of damp around her breasts when she turned round to look at him.

'Hi,' he said gently.

She didn't say anything back.

'I've taken the rest of the week off so I can help you, and Maddie would like to come down at the weekend.'

'Fine,' she said simply and turned back to Markie.

'Does he need a feed now?'

'Yes, no doubt,' she snapped back.

'Well when he's finished, why don't I take him and you can have a bath or a nap and I'll order some curry in if you like.'

'OK.' She didn't add anything more or look round at him again.

285

'All right, I'll go downstairs and tidy up a bit.'

She still didn't reply, so he left the room.

About forty-five minutes later, Bella came down with Markie. He was nuzzled up against her shoulder looking dreamy.

'OK, you're in charge,' she said, handing him over gently to Don.

She went out of the room and Markie started to grizzle. Don put him up against his shoulder and started to walk round the room trying to keep one eye on the football match – bloody hell, a penalty kick.

He stood still to watch the kick and could hear the soft choking noise which meant his son was puking on his shoulder. With some distaste, he looked over at the lumpy white vomit on his best work shirt. Where were the cloths?

He searched the room and realized he had tidied them all away, he would have to go into the kitchen. From the hallway he could hear the cheers, damn, a goal. Damn, damn, damn, he should be there. He should be in Italy right now, not dealing with baby sick.

Bella was standing naked in the bathroom waiting for her bath to fill. She looked at herself in the full-length mirror and the sight was utterly depressing. Her breasts were huge sagging marrows with silvery stretch marks streaked across them. Her stomach was unmarked but it looked deflated with crinkly skin covering a horribly large mound of wobbly flab. She turned around and saw with horror that her bum appeared to have dropped by five inches and there was a layer of unyielding cellulite sitting all round her thighs.

She sighed and tried to think happy thoughts. A bath, a long, hot, relaxing bath and she would feel better. She opened the bottle of fantastically expensive bath foam from Tania and leaned over the taps to tip it in.

The liquid hit the running tap water and bounced, spitting a blob back, which landed squarely in her right eye. It stung like hell. She rushed to the sink and tried to wash it out. AAARGH, her eye was smarting. She rinsed and rinsed then looked up in the mirror to see her eyeball, bright red and watering.

For a moment, she thought she was going to dissolve into tears for the millionth time that day, but she suddenly saw the funny side and began to laugh hysterically. She could feel her stitches strain as she drew breath and laughed again.

God, this was a nightmare. No wonder nobody warned you, no-one would have children.

She crawled into the bath and leaned back to relax, but now that the water was off she could hear Markie howling downstairs. OK, from now on baths were out, she would have to relax in the shower, where she wouldn't be able to hear him.

With a heavy heart, Don had decided to abandon the football entirely and take Markie for a walk outside. He had finally managed to work the little howling bundle into his zip-up suit and then into the buggy when Markie vomited again all over his clothes and the buggy.

Oh God, Don groaned to himself, how do people do this? How do they manage with a baby, with a toddler, with two children . . . three? This baby was going to be dependent on them for the next sixteen years at least. Sixteen years!! He pictured Markie as a little schoolboy, as a 12-year-old, as a sulky teenager and he felt gripped by a vague panic, he didn't know if he could handle this. Was this what he wanted? To go through all that stuff again: swings, sandpits, playground bullying, school football matches, homework, first dates, wet dreams, driving lessons, but this time as a dad?

He looked at the baby, crying now with vomit in a pool beside his face and on his jacket. God this was going to be really, really hard.

For a moment Don thought about his own dad and wondered what part of it all had caused him to walk out of the door for ever.

Chapter Twenty-eight

Maddie's visit was life-saving. She breezed in on a cloud of Crabtree and Evelyn Gardenia and diagnosed the cause of Markie's long screaming sessions at once: 'He's absolutely starving, Bella. He's enormous. You can't possibly feed him all by yourself, not until you get some proper rest.'

Bella was happy to agree, so Maddie had barely dropped her bags in her room before she rushed out to buy baby milk, a sterilizer and bottles.

Once Markie had drunk Bella dry, he greedily sucked down several ounces of bottle milk and fell into a deep sleep which was to last for an astonishing six hours.

'You see.' There was no note of triumph in Maddie's voice, she was just happy she could help. It had been a shock to see Bella looking so exhausted and unwell.

With an enormous pot of tea, Maddie held court in the sitting room: 'I know baby care nowadays is very different from my day and just as well, I was in the maternity hospital for a month and only allowed to see Don every four hours and not at all during the night but, if you ask me, it's gone too far the other way now, it's all home birth and breast-feeding on demand and doing things naturally and that's all very well if you're a tribeswoman with a whole tribe to support you—' she took a breath.

'But Bella, you poor dear, you can't even walk properly yet. You need total rest and relaxation. Don't you dare feel guilty about giving Markie a top-up of bottle milk. Now I'll make some more tea and then off to bed with you.'

Maddie went back down to the kitchen and Don and Bella were left on the sofa looking at each other. Markie was in the carrycot in the corner of the room still sound asleep.

Bella smiled.

'She's quite a girl,' Don said, smiling too. 'You better do what she tells you.'

'I feel awful,' Bella confessed.

'You look awful too,' Don added, but kindly and with a grin.

'Thanks a lot.' She considered hurling a sofa cushion at him, but didn't have the strength. 'If I could wish for one thing in the world right now, it would be for you to have the breasts, so you could feed him 24 hours a day and see just how hellish it is.'

'You're doing a great job, Bella.'

'You lie. I'm the worst mother on the face of the planet, I was starving my baby and I wouldn't even have known because I haven't had the strength to take him to the baby clinic yet. He's probably already on the at risk register.'

'Bella! Go to sleep, hon,' Don ordered. 'Just go now!'

'Thanks,' she said. She got up and walked to the door.

He looked at the baggy grey tracksuit trousers, drooping round her bum. God, she had to get some new clothes, this was depressing.

'Don, give the girl a chance!' Maddie fired back at him when he mentioned it to her. 'She needs rest, more rest and your love and care and attention – not to be told she's looking frumpy. For goodness sake, give her time to adjust to this. You hardly look like Kirk Douglas yourself. A shave wouldn't go amiss and maybe you should think about reacquainting yourself with the ironing board. There's a stack of housework to be done and you will be the one doing it when I go back home.'

'How long are you going to stay for, Mum?'

'A week. I think that's as long as any woman wants her mother-in-law around.'

'OK. That's great.'

'Right.' She drained the last of her cup: 'The whole place needs a good hoovering, so Don, you do that while I dust, then we're going to tackle the windows.'

He'd had six hours of fragmented sleep the night before and was desperate to join Bella upstairs in their cool, white haven of a bedroom, but his mother was right, the house was a mess.

Markie didn't wake up until close to six o'clock. Don distracted him for a little then brought him upstairs to Bella.

She was curled up in the bed, still fast asleep. He placed Markie down on the duvet close beside her so that the baby would be the first thing she saw when she woke up. Markie lay on his back and gave

291

a little gurgle. Bella's eyes opened and focused on the baby. She smiled an intensely loving smile that gave Don a lump in his throat.

Then she looked up and saw him standing there and smiled the same smile at him too.

'You've been asleep for hours,' he whispered. 'You look much better.'

'Thank God. I feel better. Has Markie just woken up?'

'He woke up about half an hour ago, but he's starting to get hungry now.'

'How long did he sleep for?'

'Almost six hours!'

'That's amazing!! Have I been asleep for five then?'

'Yeah, Maddie and I have renovated the entire house and she's now busy making a "nourishing stew for tea",' he mimicked her singsong Scottish accent.

'How sweet of you both.' Bella still sounded dreamy.

She sat up in the bed and held Markie in her arms. She lifted her T-shirt and Don glimpsed the luscious creamy white breasts with big, pert nipples before Markie hungrily clamped on. He sat there watching and inhaling the milky, sweaty, sweet smell coming from them and realized he was totally turned on. He could hear the baby sucking noisily at her breast and God, he wanted her. He sat close beside her and kissed her on the cheek as together they watched the baby's jaw moving up and down.

'Where are you going?' Bella asked as he finally got up to leave the room.

'For another cold shower,' he joked.

She gave a little laugh. Men. Absolutely obsessed with sex. She stroked her son's tiny, downy soft head and tried to remember what sex was all about, but she just couldn't.

Maddie cleaned and cooked and looked after Markie for as much time as she could, but it was hard to wrestle him away from Bella.

'Go to your room!' Maddie would order Bella. 'I don't care if you're not sleepy, go and read a magazine, file your nails, have a bath . . . just rest. You'll be sorry when I'm gone.'

'I will be very sorry,' Bella told her one morning over what felt like her seventeenth cup of tea. 'I've got so much to organize, I haven't done anything about finding a nanny, or a cleaner. We'll really need a cleaner when I go back to work.'

There was a pause and Maddie looked up, surprised to see Bella's eyes filling with tears.

'Whatever's the matter, dear?' she asked gently.

'I'm really confused about it all. Oh it's nothing,' Bella sipped at her tea, fighting back the urge to cry. 'Just the hormones, isn't it? Makes you feel like this.'

'It's normal to feel worried about going back to work. Of course it's normal, you're handing over your precious little boy to someone else,' Maddie said.

At that Bella couldn't hold back any more. She burst into fierce sobs.

'I don't want to do it, Maddie. I want to be here with him . . .' Maddie put an arm round her.

In between sobs, Bella said: 'But I loved my job, I don't want to give it up. I just want the impossible

293

. . . I want Markie to not exist for the time I'm working then be here when I get home. I can't bear the idea of him crying and needing me when I'm not around, how will I be able to work thinking about him?'

Maddie cuddled her close and asked, 'Can you take a bit more time off to work this out?'

'Not really, no,' Bella answered, thinking about the Danson's contract for the first time in weeks.

'Can you do some work from home? Or maybe go part-time for a bit?' Maddie asked.

'I don't think so. Anyway we need the money. The mortgage on this place is astronomical and Don's never going to get a pay rise and we've borrowed loads of money to do it up and furnish it. Oh shit, shit, shit.'

Maddie hugged Bella hard and tried to sound comforting, but she felt worried. She'd never seen her daughter-in-law like this before. Bella always had everything figured out, this was so unlike her.

'You've got to find a lovely nanny Bella, that's your top priority,' Maddie said. 'And get comfortable with her before you go back. Then go back with an open mind and see how it goes. If you hate it, have a rethink. You can change jobs or move to a smaller house, whatever is going to make you all happy.'

Bella wiped her tears and Maddie added, 'Have you talked to Don about all this?'

'No, he's terrified as it is, if I tell him I'm scared, he'll just take off altogether.' Damn, damn, Bella could have kicked herself.

'Just because his father walked out on us does not mean Don is going to do the same, Bella,' Maddie said. 'I've brought him up to be a good man and he won't let you down, but be careful not to shut him out.'

There was an uneasy silence at the kitchen table, then Maddie decided to change the subject. 'Well, the two of you are going out on Saturday night. I won't hear any objections, you are going to scrub up and go off somewhere nice.'

Well, it was a reasonable idea, although the prospect of having to scrub up was making Bella feel mildly panicky. She went upstairs to look in the wardrobe. There was no way she was putting on her maternity clothes again, that would just be admitting defeat, but she was never going to get her enormous bust or flabby stomach into any of her old things.

There was still the Heathrow outfit. A sarong didn't technically count as a maternity skirt and she could wear the green sandals from Tania.

She decided to give her friend a call.

'Bella, hello! How's the little pooky pie?' Tania asked.

'He's fine. He cries a lot and feeds non-stop and goes through 200 nappies and items of clothing a day.'

'And how about Markie?' Tania joked.

'Ha ha. How are you? And Greg?'

'I'm fine, he's the same old . . . gone off to see his parents *again*. I still haven't met them . . . live in the country somewhere. You know, I don't even have their address or phone number.'

'How do you speak to him when he's there?'

'On the mobile . . . when he remembers to turn it on.'

Bella was beginning to wonder how long Tania, Greg and the no-proposal situation could go on for.

'You need to ditch him, find a nice man and have babies, Tania,' she joked, realizing as she said it how much she needed a friend with a baby right now.'

'Hmm. Anyway, are you chatting or do you want to arrange something?'

'Do you want to come and cuddle and kiss with my baby next weekend?' Bella asked.

'But I don't fancy Don at all!' was Tania's answer.

'Ha, ha. Actually, that's a real shame because he's gagging for sex and if you could just service him for a few months I wouldn't consider that infidelity at all because you're family.'

'Better incest than infidelity, that's nice.'

'Please shut me up, my mind has gone since birth.'

'What's 84 times 169?' Tania asked her.

'14,196,' Bella shot right back.

'Is it? Well if you're right, that strange bit of your brain is still working, so good, you still have a job to go to.'

'I hope so.' She said this cheerfully, but wondered if she meant it.

Chapter Twenty-nine

They took a cab to the restaurant and Bella felt weird and uneasy leaving the house without Markie. She'd given him an hour-long feed before they left, barely leaving herself enough time to get changed and made up.

He hadn't been asleep but had snuggled quite contentedly in his granny's arms.

'Just go,' Maddie had shooed her away. 'He'll be absolutely fine, he's going to fall fast asleep and if he wakes up before you're back, I'll give him some bottle milk. Now *go* and *enjoy yourselves*.'

Sitting in the back of the cab, Bella looked down at her outfit. God her boobs were enormous, but they didn't look glamorous, just matronly, trussed up in a nursing bra closely akin to scaffolding.

At least her feet, in the shoes from Tania, looked sexy and so did her husband.

She smiled at him and folded her arms under her breasts. 'I look like the Queen,' she said mournfully.

'You look great, just calm down,' Don said, looking round at her. 'I love your hair.'

'What? Washed and brushed?'

'It looks nice.'

When they got to the restaurant and were shown to their table, Bella's unease had blossomed into full-blown nervousness. She took her mobile out of her bag and placed it on the table, checking there was a good signal.

'What are we going to drink, then?' Don said cheerfully, picking up the wine list.

'Well, I can't have much, goes into the milk, and anyway, I've got to get up later.'

Don didn't say anything. He watched her fiddle with her phone and cutlery and wished she would relax.

'Do you think we should ring up and check?' she said finally.

'No,' Don answered firmly. 'Maddie will phone if there's a problem. We'll probably just wake him up if we call.'

'Mmm.' Bella looked round the room distractedly.

'Bella,' Don took hold of her hand and looked at her face. 'Bella, look at me. I'm here with you tonight, this is "us" time, Markie is fine, can you please stop worrying, just for a little, tiny bit?'

'Yes,' she said. 'Yes, you're right, what shall we eat?' She picked up the menu and tried to concentrate although her stomach was churning and she couldn't imagine how she was going to eat anything.

When the first course arrived, she asked Don about his work because she knew he would talk and she could pretend to listen.

By the time the main course was there, she could feel her heart pounding, she was so anxious.

'I'm going to have to phone, Don,' she said suddenly, interrupting his story.

'It's OK, I'll do it,' he said. She was relieved she hadn't seen any flicker of annoyance cross his face.

'I'll go into the lobby where it's quieter.' He got up and walked over to the double doors.

Moments later he came back to the table, smiling. 'He's still sleeping, he fell asleep ten minutes after we left and he hasn't stirred. OK, are you going to start enjoying yourself now?'

He poured himself another generous top-up of wine but didn't offer her anything as she had barely touched the glass in front of her.

Halfway through her plateful, she wondered if Don had phoned at all. God, what an idiot she was, he'd probably stood in the lobby and not even bothered because if Markie had been crying, well it would just have spoiled the meal, wouldn't it?

'Bella, for God's sake. By the look on your face, you'd think our son was in hospital not snuggled up in his bed.' Don sounded exasperated now. 'Why don't you just have a cigarette or something? Christ, I thought this would be fun.'

She had not had a cigarette since Markie was born. Her conscience had finally overriden her urge to smoke. 'I don't want nicotine in my breast milk,' she said.

'It never worried you when you were pregnant,' Don answered sharply.

'But he's here now, he's not an abstract baby, he's a real one, I couldn't do anything that might hurt him.' She felt her eyes fill with tears and she just longed to hold her baby. Her breasts were tingling strangely, she wanted to be with him, feeding him and cuddling him. 'I want to go home,' she said, a tear spilling over onto her cheek. 'I'm sorry, I'm just not ready for this.'

Don knocked back his glass and refilled it, draining the last of the wine from the bottle.

'OK,' he said 'I'll get the bill.'

They were home at 10 p.m., just an hour and a half after they'd left. Bella went straight upstairs to bed, and took Markie, who was still asleep, up with her.

Don stayed downstairs with his mother and opened a bottle of whisky.

When Markie woke at 1 a.m., Bella sat up, switched on the sidelight and fed him. As the baby suckled, Bella watched Don fast asleep beside her. He had not even stirred whereas Markie's smallest cry woke her from deep sleep.

At 6 a.m., when Bella was woken up by Markie again, Don still slept on soundly. Markie wasn't ready to go back down straight away, so Bella got up. As she put on a dressing gown, she looked over at her sleeping husband and felt a fresh wave of resentment break over her. She had thought they were going to be ultra modern and share the parenting equally. But it was obvious to her that breastfeeding was letting Don off lightly.

Don was already back at work, he slept soundly all night and wanted to go out for dinner and have sex and the relationship they'd had before the baby. She was the one who felt that everything had changed for ever and she felt bitterly angry that he couldn't see that.

She and Markie were the couple now, Don was the third party. It was Markie she was attuned to,

Markie she wanted to make happy and needed to be with. Don felt like just another demand on her time and emotions and she was so physically exhausted, she could barely cope with the baby's demands.

Right now, she couldn't feel anything apart from the mildest affection for Don. Whereas for the baby snuggled against her shoulder she felt the fiercest, most possessive love, passion and need.

She took Markie downstairs. Maddie joined them soon after 7 a.m. and put the kettle on.

'I've had a lovely time, Bella, but I bet you're looking forward to having the house to yourselves again.'

'Not really,' Bella said with a smile. 'You've been wonderful. Thank you so much for coming down.'

'I'm sorry if I packed you off for a night out before you were ready for it,' Maddie added.

'Don't be,' said Bella. 'You weren't to know, neither was I really. I think Don's a bit angry with me though.'

'Och, he'll get over it.' Maddie poured boiling water into the teapot and brought it over to the table. 'But don't leave it too long before you go out again,' she added. 'You and Don need each other too.'

'Hmmm. Shall we take a walk round the park after breakfast?' Bella tried to sound breezy. 'It's not too bad, a bit of greenery at least,' she added. This was about the nicest thing that could be said about the park. It was a dismal stretch of urban grassland bisected with tarred paths and furnished with grimy benches, concrete litter-bins and piles of dog dirt.

She had wheeled the buggy around it several times and it never cheered her up, in fact it made her depressed. Litter blew about the grass, she had once spotted a used condom lying under the bench and she had never seen any other mothers or children playing there. People just came to the place to shag and let their dogs crap.

It continued to amaze her that so much money had only bought her a house in this unremarkable part of town. OK, the houses in her street were lovely, but the high street was dire, the park was a pit and there was nowhere to go. No coffee shops – ha, that was a joke – no bookshop, no cinema, no duck pond, no swings for Christ's sake, just a branch of Mothercare. Is that what she was supposed to do all day now that she had a baby? Go to Mothercare and Boots and hang out?

She and Maddie put on their coats, bundled Markie into his pram and opened the door on another unseasonably grey and cold June day.

'Goodness,' said Maddie as she helped lift Markie's pram down the steps. 'It's like November out here.'

Chapter Thirty

Bella sat at the kitchen table watching the cold wind shake at a bush in the garden. Tears were streaming down her cheeks but she didn't care, didn't even really notice. She was exhausted but couldn't imagine going back to bed. Markie would wake up as soon as she fell asleep anyway.

She'd been up since before 5 a.m., feeding, changing, winding, sterilizing bottles for the top-up feeds, tidying up the house, feeding, changing, winding, feeding, changing, winding. It was one long endless cycle. Markie was crying less, but not sleeping for the luxurious long naps he had settled into when Maddie was here. Bella blamed herself, what was she doing wrong? In the four days since Maddie had left, Markie had somehow wound himself up again.

Her nights were wildly interrupted and she was barely making up for the lost sleep with catnaps during the day. As soon as Markie fell asleep, she rushed round the house, tidying up, getting dressed, doing all the things she didn't have time to do when he was awake. Then just as she lay down and started to relax, he would wake up again. It was like living with a ruthless torturer, except she loved him hopelessly, was driven to despair when he was unhappy. The most sophisticated torture of all.

Why could she not get this together? Christ, she was still in her dressing gown at 2 p.m., she should probably eat something . . . She brushed the tears from her face and wondered if there was anything in the fridge she could face.

Then she heard the doorbell. Who on earth was that? There was no time to change, she would have to answer it as she was.

She went upstairs and considered looking through the peephole first, but then decided 'oh bugger it, who cares?' and swung the door open.

There on the step was Red from the yoga class. Bella had totally forgotten they'd swapped numbers and addresses and said they'd keep in touch.

'Hello,' Red said, cracking a wide smile which showed beautiful white teeth against her dark skin. 'I thought I'd come round to show mine off and see yours.'

She looked just jealous-making lovely, in a tight sports top and wide-legged trousers and trainers, her long ringlets fanning out in the wind. She had a tartan papoose strapped across her front and Bella could just see the hat on the little baby snuggled inside.

'Hello.' Bella smiled broadly back, surprised at how glad she was to see this woman. 'Come in, the place is a mess . . . I'm a mess, sorry.'

'Sorry?!!' said Red, incredulously. 'Don't ever

apologize. The first six weeks are an absolute hell. Just be thankful everyone's still alive.'

Bella burst out laughing.

'Don't,' Red said, laughing as well. 'The pelvic floors can't take it yet, we'll pee ourselves.'

This just made them laugh even more. Bella began to feel quite hysterical, tears were forming in the corner of her eyes and oh God, she was about to cry *again*.

She started to sob and Red put an arm round her. 'I'm so sorry, I wish I'd come sooner,' she said.

'Don't be silly,' Bella managed after a few more moments. 'We don't even know each other very well.'

'Well, yeah, but I've been here before and I should have thought about you.' She squeezed Bella's arm affectionately. 'Come on, let's get some tea. Gorgeous house, by the way.'

'Thanks,' Bella said gratefully and they headed downstairs.

'This is Ellie.' Red patted the little hat buried deep down in the papoose. 'Born May 25th, 10.32 a.m., six pounds, nine ounces, after a four-hour labour, epidural, no tear, thank you God, but second babies are easier,' said Red.

'Oh yeah,' Bella said. 'I'd forgotten you already have another one. How old is . . . ?'

'He. Jamie is three,' answered Red. 'He's with his dad this afternoon,' she said as she settled into a chair. 'Come on, I want all your gory details.'

Bella busied herself with the kettle and realized she was starving: 'Do you want a sandwich?'

'Oh yes please,' said Red. 'Isn't breastfeeding the

best? An excuse to eat even more food than when you're pregnant.'

'Brie, ham, pâté or peanut butter?' said Bella looking into the fridge.

'Yes please,' said Red with a giggle.

When they were sitting down with tea and big plates of food in front of them, Bella gave Red her labour low-down and didn't spare any little detail. It took about half an hour. Bella was amazed the babies were still sleeping.

'It was so much pain,' she said. 'I could never have imagined how much pain it was. I didn't feel I'd been warned either.'

'I don't think anyone wants to tell pregnant women, in case they spend nine months in a state of panic,' Red said, then added: 'Well actually, I could have told you. I did the all-natural home birth thing the first time, but it was so Godawful I told Sandy I was only going to have another one under general anaesthetic. The epidural was our compromise,' she said in between big mouthfuls, 'and it was fab, no comparison with bloody gas and air. I think they give you that mouthpiece just to stop you screaming. It doesn't have any effect at all.'

They both cackled.

'How are you doing now?' Red asked.

'I'm just so tired,' Bella confessed. 'I didn't know I'd be awake most of the night, every night . . . because feeding takes so long and he doesn't want to go back to sleep afterwards.'

'I know,' Red added. 'You've just got to sleep in the day, sod the housework, sod the cooking, let the whole place fall in around you. You must sleep! Or else you will go loopy loop, stare at the walls, crack up big time.'

'I think I'm already close,' Bella answered.

'You're back at work really soon, aren't you, you brave woman. What do you do again?' Red asked.

'I'm a management consultant. I'm supposedly back in three weeks' time, but I haven't done anything about a nanny. I don't know where to start and I can't face it.' Bella sounded almost tearful again.

'It's OK,' said Red. 'Everything you're feeling is normal. You'll be fine.' She gave an encouraging grin. 'Just give yourself some time.'

'That's the one thing I don't have.' Bella stared down into her tea. 'What do you do?' She looked up at Red.

'I'm an accountant . . . part-time accountant,' said Red. 'Well, when Jamie was born, I went back to work full time, but I found it impossible. I hardly saw him, I hardly saw Sandy because he was working so hard and all three of us were exhausted.

'We struggled on for about half a year, then jacked it in and downsized,' she continued. 'We sold the house, got a little flat round here and Sandy and I now run our own business together from home. He does most of it and I help out when I can.'

Red took a gulp of tea then added, 'I've told him absolutely nothing doing until Ellie is at least five months old. I really believe in breastfeeding, it's good for the baby, establishes immunity and everything but it's *terrible* for the mother, so exhausting and such a bind. You can't leave them for more than four hours max and even then you worry all the time. How are you managing with it?'

307

'It's getting better. I give Markie bottle top-ups as well,' Bella told her. 'I'm just hoping he'll take bottle milk in the day and breast milk at night when I go back to work.'

'Good for you,' said Red. 'I've never managed to get one baby to take as much as a sip from a bottle. But don't you dare feel guilty if you have to give up breastfeeding once you're back, you might find it's just too much. I mean, I was a lunatic, working all day, breastfeeding all night!'

Bella felt a surge of relief to hear someone else being honest about how hard this all was. It felt wonderfully bonding and conspiratorial.

Red added: 'I wouldn't say it's impossible working full time in London with a baby but it's really, really hard. What does your partner do?'

'Don's a journalist,' Bella answered.

'Oh yikes!' said Red. 'So not around very much?'

'Well, it's not too bad. Long hours, but he's not usually out of town more than a week every month.'

Bella could see the little lights rising on the baby monitor. Markie was starting to stir and she leapt up to get him.

'Oh God, he's enormous,' exclaimed Red when Bella brought him down to the kitchen. 'I'm amazed you can sit down.'

'Only on cushions!' Bella laughed and began feeding him.

When Ellie started to stir, Red didn't even take her out of the sling, just deftly lifted her top, twanged open a patterned, colourful, actually quite pretty nursing bra, Bella couldn't help noticing –

308

and her hungry baby latched on, leaving Red with both hands free to cradle her cup of tea.

'I like your outfit,' said Bella. 'I can't get into anything apart from Don's old stuff. I refuse to wear my maternity things again.'

Red laughed: 'Go buy yourself some new sports gear, that's my tip. It's very stretchy and covered in logos and stripes which detract from all the lumps and bumps. And I think it looks a bit more racy than leggings and a T-shirt, the uniform of new mums across the western world.'

It was Bella's turn to laugh: 'And what about work clothes? What did you do when you went back?'

'I did wear some maternity things, cunningly disguised,' Red confessed. 'But I bought a couple of suits, two or three sizes up and then just had them altered when I got back to normal.'

'I don't know if I'll ever get back to normal,' Bella said looking down at her stomach ruefully.

'You're joking, right?' said Red. 'You are about to become the busiest woman on the planet. You will never sit down, eat properly or get the chance to laze ever again. The pounds will fall off, in fact you'll have to try and eat extra if you carry on breastfeeding.'

Bella didn't really believe her, but it was nice to hear it anyway.

'I'm going to have to go,' Red said finally. 'This is my address and phone number, in case you've lost them—' she handed Bella a bright red business card. 'Just come round or phone, any time, I'd love to see you.'

They headed upstairs and as Bella opened the door she felt childishly pleased when Red gave her an affectionate kiss on the cheek as she left.

Markie had fallen into a doze again and Bella went upstairs, inspired to find a new outfit. But there was nothing in the wardrobe she could hope to get into so she donned the tracksuit trousers and tartan shirt again. Depressingly hideous.

But she washed her face, brushed her hair, put on lipstick and felt surprisingly better. OK, sod the housework, the most important item on the agenda was finding a nanny. In the sitting room, she found the phone book and began dialling.

Several phone calls later, she was totally disheartened again. Everyone she had spoken to had been appalled she'd left it so late. She basically wanted a nanny who could start in two weeks' time. All said they would put her on their lists, but could promise nothing.

She punched in another number.

Instead of a deep sigh in response to her request, a slightly more human-sounding woman said, 'Oh dear, has someone let you down?'

'Yes, I'm afraid so,' Bella fibbed.

'You poor thing, it's so awful when that happens. Luckily for you, we prefer to keep a waiting list of nannies rather than mummies. Do you need someone this week?'

'Well, no, the start date would be in two weeks' time. I go back in three weeks' time, but obviously I want to find the right person.'

'Of course. We've only got one girl experienced with babies ready to start at the moment, but let me tell you all about her and we'll arrange a meeting.'

Bella felt a wave of relief and anxiety pass over her. OK, she might be able to solve the nanny problem after all but that meant she really could be going back to work in just *three weeks*.

She thought about her little son sucking contentedly at her breast and felt an overwhelming sadness at the thought of giving him up. Her eyes were pricking, Christ, she was not going to allow herself to cry again. Heading back down to the kitchen, she tried to keep Maddie's words in her mind. She would go back with an open mind and see how it went. If she had to change her plans, so be it.

Chapter Thirty-one

Bella was dimly aware of the alarm in her dream for a long time before she managed to drag herself back to the surface and open her eyes. Her sleep was so fractured now, every nap led to the deepest, most complicated dream sequence.

Don had taken Markie downstairs after his 6 a.m. feed to allow her to sleep in until eight. But now she had to get up and get ready. Today was nanny interview day.

After she'd washed and leaned over the top of the stairs to make sure she couldn't hear frantic howling, she came back to the bedroom. The usual problem of what to wear loomed large today. It had only occurred to Bella this morning that this wasn't just about her liking the nanny: the nanny had to like her too.

She opened her wardrobe but closed it in despair after a few moments and tried Don's. There she found a white shirt, which did at least button up over her chest, and a pair of camel-coloured jeans. She pulled them on, rolled up the bottoms and

312

looked at herself in the mirror. Frumpy but not hideous, it would have to do.

She added earrings, her diamond pendant, lipstick and even a squirt of perfume. It was a slight improvement.

'Bella!' said Don with a smile when she came into the kitchen. 'You look nice.'

'No, I don't,' she snapped.

'OK, nicer,' he said. 'Christ, I'm just trying to be friendly.'

'Nicer than what?' She was so tired, she didn't have the energy to be anything apart from irritable.

'Well, nicer than in my old track suit. Look I'm not saying any more. Everything I say just seems to make things worse.' He turned to Markie who was lying on his sheepskin rug on the floor gurgling.

'I'm sure he smiled at me a minute ago,' Don said, waving a rattle over his son.

'Did he?' Bella rushed over. If Markie was going to start smiling, he damn well better smile at her first. 'Hello hon, how are you today?' she cooed at him. Markie locked eyes with her and smiled.

'*See!!*' Bella and Don said in unison, then laughed.

'Wow, he's smiling at five weeks, I think that's early,' Bella said, gazing at her son.

'Oh no,' Don groaned. 'He was supposed to have your looks and *my* IQ!'

Bella managed a laugh at this, then sat down and ate some cereal, her mind on all the things she wanted to do in the house before the nanny arrived at 10 a.m. She was glad Don had taken the morning off to help her make this decision.

Bella was still breastfeeding in the immaculately

tidy sitting room when the doorbell rang at ten to ten.

Don jumped up to get the door and Bella could hear polite hellos before Don ushered the nanny into the room.

'Hello, I'm Joanne,' said the solidly built girl heading towards her with an outstretched hand.

Bella juggled Markie for a moment, then managed to reach Joanne's hand.

'Hello, Bella Browning, pleased to meet you. Please sit down.' She was surprised at how quickly her brisk, business tone had kicked in, even with a baby clamped onto her nipple.

'And this must be Mark,' said Joanne sitting down on the edge of the one armchair.

'Markie, we call him Markie,' said Bella, glancing down at the fuzzy little head nuzzling at her.

Looking up again, she took Joanne in. She was unredeemably plain, squarely built with pale, freckly skin, watery blue eyes and short mousy brown hair. She had a large nose and thin lips and was wearing no-nonsense navy blue trousers, a white blouse and a navy blazer with gold buttons.

Well, look on the bright side, Bella thought to herself. Don isn't going to shag her.

They spoke about Joanne's last job, which was perfect previous experience, two years looking after a little boy from babyhood until he went off to nursery.

Then Joanne asked Bella questions while Don made coffee.

'Have you got him into any sort of routine yet?' she asked.

'Errrr, well, he wakes up at about 6 a.m. for a

314

feed,' Bella answered. 'And he's usually awake till about eightish, then we both go back to bed for a snack feed then a nap. From about 10 a.m. he feeds every two and a half to three hours and his naps in between feeds vary from none to the full three hours...umm...he has his last feed at 9 p.m. when I go to bed, then Don looks after him till he falls asleep about an hour later.' She knew this was not a routine, just daily chaos.

'He wakes up at about two and then six in the morning...' she added, 'and then off we go again. It's not much of a routine yet, I know...' Bella trailed off.

'Well, it's not bad for...five weeks he is now?'

'Yes.'

'So you're managing to get enough sleep?'

'Well, just about enough to keep sane,' Bella smiled.

'And does he take a bottle as well?'

'Yup, he got a lot of top-up feeds from a bottle until a few days ago, then suddenly he didn't seem so hungry.'

'So we'll have to get him really happy with the bottle before you go back. Are you giving up breast-feeding?' Joanne asked.

'I don't want to just yet. I think I'll try and do a morning and evening feed for as long as I can,' Bella replied.

Joanne looked doubtful. 'It makes it very hard for the baby to detach from you,' she said matter-of-factly.

I should bloody well hope so, Bella thought, I don't want him to detach.

'Well, I'm not setting anything in stone, I'll have

315

to see how it goes,' she said, suddenly anxious that Joanne was going to turn them down.

They covered some more ground. Joanne was slightly taken aback by the hours: 8 a.m. till 8 p.m. Monday to Friday.

'That's a 60 hour week,' she pointed out.

'Well, most nights I hope to be here at 7.30 p.m. but I want to make sure I'm covered if I'm later,' said Bella.

'I don't mind doing those hours to start with until we're all settled in, but then you'll really have to think about giving me a three-day weekend and finding someone else for Monday or Friday,' Joanne said, then added: 'And I won't be able to do any regular evening babysitting.

This was not the attitude Bella had expected at a first interview. She thought about her own first job and how she had worked almost every waking hour.

'It's a very tiring, demanding job looking after a small baby,' Joanne said by way of explanation.

Well yes, thought Bella, but not so bad if you've been able to sleep the night before.

Don returned with coffees and put Joanne more at ease with general chatty questions about where she was from and how she got into being a nanny.

He followed that up with: 'Can you cook?'

'Yes,' Joanne answered. 'But obviously that won't be one of my duties here, will it?'

'Well, it could be,' Bella wobbled. 'If you wanted it to be . . .'

'I'd rather not,' said Joanne with unarguable finality.

'Will I have the use of a car?' she asked.

'Not immediately,' Don answered, trying to imagine Bella letting someone else drive her Mercedes. 'But we'll look into it for the future.'

Bella was horrified. She didn't want Markie to be driven anywhere without her.

It was time to wind this up, she decided.

'It's been lovely meeting you Joanne,' she said with a slightly forced smile. 'We're going to talk this over together, call your references if we may and I will get back to you on Monday, if that suits.'

'Yes, no problem at all,' said Joanne, picking up a bulging navy handbag and standing up. She shook hands with them both and bent over to gently stroke Markie's head before leaving the house.

As soon as the door had shut, Bella and Don turned to each other.

'Well, what did you think?' Don asked first.

'No way. Just no way,' Bella answered.

'You're joking?' Don asked, exasperated. 'I thought she seemed really nice.'

'What!? She wasn't going to stick her finger out one little bit. I can't have someone who works to rule looking after my baby. What if he's awake for an hour longer in the day than she'd estimated, would she just ignore him?'

'Bella, what are you talking about? She wanted to clarify her hours, which are bloody long, and make sure she doesn't get lumbered with all our house-work and cooking. I think that's fair enough.'

There was a pause as the two looked at each other.

'She seemed like a nice, caring person and she certainly knows what she's letting herself in for, she's done this before,' Don said. 'Anyway, have you got any alternative?' he added. 'Your start date is less than three weeks away and this is your only candidate.'

Oh no, Bella was looking tearful again.

'Look,' he said putting an arm round her. 'Why don't you phone the family she was with before and ask them before you make a decision? Then, if you like, you can put her on trial for a month. If it's not working out, look for someone else when you're back at work.'

Bella sniffed hard.

'You should be enjoying this time,' Don hugged her against him, 'not filling it with anxieties about nannies and going back. I'm sure it's going to work out fine,' he added. 'You kept telling me when you were pregnant that this was what you wanted. It'll be fine.'

'I don't want to leave him,' Bella heard herself wail against Don's chest. 'He's so small and he needs me and I just haven't figured this whole thing out yet.'

Don held her tightly and didn't say anything for a while. Then in his most soothing voice, he said, 'Bella, just suck it and see, hon. Go back and see how it works out. You loved your job, I just don't believe you'd be happy without it. You've got to start thinking about how you're going to make this work, not blow every hurdle up out of all proportion.'

She knew he was right, but she was still crying.

Chapter Thirty-two

Joanne was hired on the basis of the absolutely glowing report from her last employer and Bella now had one last week on her own with Markie. Next week, Joanne would start and the week after, she would be back. Back at Prentice, starting on the Danson's project. It seemed unreal.

This morning, Bella had woken up with an agenda. This was be nice to Don day. She was going to do the supermarket run, very superficially clean round the house, cook him dinner and who knows, they might even have sex. It had been six weeks, after all.

She packed Markie into his car seat and left him rocking in the hall while she to-ed and fro-ed to her tiny car with all the equipment: one bottle of warmed milk in a thermos, one bottle of cooled, boiled water in case he got thirsty, a change of clothes, sunhat, parasol, nappies, wipes, muslin cloths for wiping up vomit, the changing bag, her handbag, buggy, sunscreens for the car windows . . . this was a nightmare, how was she going to fit all this in?

She crammed the buggy into the boot, squashed the changing bag into the space under the passenger seat and piled the extra nappies, bottles and dummies into the glove compartment and squeezed it shut.

When she went back for Markie, she smelled the unmistakable smell of dirty nappy and with a groan felt her determination to go out draining away. But she changed him, put him back in the car seat, fumbled the seat into the car and *finally* they were off, Bella, like every half-demented brand new mother, driving with one hand on the steering wheel and the other shading her howling little son's eyes from the sunshine.

When Don came home that evening, he found his wife and his son out in the garden, enjoying the last of the day's sun, Bella in a deckchair, Markie lying on his sheepskin rug. They were both freshly bathed and changed. Bella's hair was still wet, but she looked nice, in a clean white T-shirt (his) and a sarong and sandals.

The kitchen was unusually tidy and it actually smelled as if something was cooking.

'Hello!' he kissed them both, adding, 'Have I walked through a time fault and come out in the 1950s? Baby on the lawn, the wife in a skirt, dinner in the oven.'

'Ha, ha . . .' Bella answered, 'I'm being nice to you – for a change.' She smiled at him and he kissed her again.

The evening was so warm, they ate the simple meal of baked potatoes, ham and salad out in the garden. Bella lit candles on the garden table and poured out ice cold white wine.

Markie astonished them both by falling fast asleep straight after his 9 p.m. feed, so Bella carried him upstairs then switched on the intercom so she could go back out to the garden. When she sat back down in her deckchair, Don moved his chair behind hers. He began to rub her neck and rumple her hair, which she loved.

'How are you doing?' he asked.

'Fine,' she said. 'It's nice to see you, I feel as if I haven't seen you for ages. Are you OK?'

'Yeah,' he answered and as she felt his strong thumbs circle at the base of her neck, she let her head fall forward and closed her eyes.

After a few moments, Don said: 'So . . . Markie is asleep . . . and you're not. I don't suppose you'd want to go inside and, you know . . . cuddle up?'

She turned round to look at him and gave a sly grin. 'Don't you mean go inside and hump like an animal?'

'Hey, I'm trying to be sensitive and understanding here!' He smiled back and couldn't help running a finger down her nose and onto her lips.

'Have we even snogged since he arrived?' she asked.

Don shook his head sadly.

'That's disgraceful,' she said and got out of the chair.

She blew out the candles, then took his hand and led him into the kitchen. She turned to him in the open doorway and pulled him close for a kiss. He tasted warm and wine-flavoured; she pushed her tongue deeper into his mouth and moved her hands through his hair.

321

He kissed back for several long minutes but kept his hands anchored firmly round her waist. He wasn't going up to her breasts or down to her pants without written permission. He held her tightly and concentrated on the kissing.

Then Bella took him by surprise by throwing her T-shirt off over her head. Quickly she unhooked the matronly white nursing bra underneath and tossed it to the side.

He cupped his hands round breasts which felt heavy and solid. 'Are you OK?' he whispered.

'I'm fine, I've missed you . . .' this in a teasing voice as she pulled his shirt out of his trousers.

'Where are we going to go?' he asked in such a throaty I'm-so-ready-to-fuck-you voice that she suddenly flicked from 'this could be fun' to 'take me now'.

Their kisses became long, hot and devouring.

'Kitchen table?' she broke off to say. 'No, I'll get squashed. Kitchen wall?'

'Ah ha.' He steered her until she was backed up against the wall then they kissed again. As she unzipped him, he moved his hands down to the fabric of her skirt.

He felt through the folds to her pants and pulled them aside. Their eyes were open and he watched her closely. 'Just tell me what to do,' he whispered, feeling how encouragingly wet she was.

'Slide your finger into me,' she whispered back. It felt OK, it felt good. She smiled at him and licked his mouth, feeling his stiff hard-on flicker in her hands.

'You're a lovely man,' she said.

She pulled her pants down, unknotted her skirt so it fell on the floor, then guided him slowly inside.

322

She felt a ring of pain at the opening and nothing but numbness beyond that.

He moved against her and they looked at each other. Where was he?

'Are you really in?' she asked.

'Yeah,' he said.

'I can hardly feel you.'

'Let me move a bit.' He moved his cock almost all the way out and pushed back in again.

'Ow!' Bella's head fell back against the wall.

'Sorry.'

'Oh God, is this it?' Bella asked, sounding upset. 'Is this what sex is going to be like now? It feels like a sharp pencil in a shoebox. No offence, Don,' she added.

'Ermm . . . none taken.'

'Does it feel OK for you?' she asked.

'Well . . . it's different, but it's still good,' he reassured her. 'I take it you don't want me to carry on here?'

'No, no, I'm sorry. I'm totally depressed. It's obviously something else no-one wants to tell you about, having a baby ruins your sex life for ever,' she said.

Don moved out of her and tilted her chin up with his hand.

'Maybe it doesn't, Bella.' He kissed her on the cheek. 'Maybe things move back into place slowly. It's OK. I'm not going anywhere,' he kissed her again. 'Come on, I'm sure it's going to be fine. Anyway, there are lots of other things we can do . . .'

But for her the moment had well and truly gone. 'Yeah, like the washing up!' she answered.

*   *   *

Bella phoned her new friend the next morning, as soon as she had the chance.

'Red, hello, it's Bella.'

'Oh hello! How's it going?' Red sounded glad to hear her, although she was speaking above chaotic baby and toddler noise.

'Fine, I was going to come round this afternoon, if you're about?'

'Yes, that would be lovely. How about 4, 4.30ish, so we can all have a nap first?'

'Perfect,' answered Bella. 'Look there's one thing I have to ask, it can't wait.'

'Yes?' Red was intrigued.

'Sex? Does everything stay this baggy for good?'

There was a momentary pause and Bella suddenly wondered if Red didn't know how to break the bad news.

But then Red broke into cackles of laughter. 'Blimey!' she said. 'I'm impressed. I'm planning to milk it for at least another month.'

'Pelvic floor exercises,' she added. 'That's probably what you need. No-one ever does them and things do bounce back eventually, but I suppose you could use them to hurry it up.'

'So will it really be the same as it was? I want the truth,' Bella asked, hating the fact that she sounded so anxious.

'Do enough exercises and it will probably be better,' Red laughed, 'Anyway, I'll see you later, which will be lovely.'

'OK, thanks. Bye.'

'Bye,' she squeezed in and tried to hold for ten . . . where had those muscles gone?

Chapter Thirty-three

Red opened the door looking just annoyingly good: glowing face, tumbling hair.

'Hello!' she said enthusiastically and came down the steps in her bare feet to help Bella up with the buggy. Bella noticed that her toenails were French manicured – her toenails!! How did she find the time to do this stuff?

'God you always look so well, it's very irritating!' Bella said.

'Thank you, I think! You look much better than the last time I saw you,' Red replied.

'Still room for improvement though.' Bella looked down at her outfit, more of Don's clothes, this time a faded blue T-shirt and grey drawstring shorts. Revolting.

'Oh, he's asleep,' Red said looking down at Markie as they came in the door. 'Shall we leave him in the hall?'

'Yeah, that's fine,' said Bella.

'Come in,' said Red and pointed Bella in the direction of the sitting room.

She walked in and was surprised to find the

quaintest little room this side of *Little House on the Prairie*. The walls were covered in faded flowery wallpaper, the sofa and armchairs were large and chintzy. Dark, antique furniture was crammed into every available space and there were toys and books and balls and cars everywhere.

On the one available square inch of floor, a little black-haired boy was squatting down, drawing.

'Jamie, this is Bella, say hello,' said Red.

'Hello,' said Jamie without looking up.

'He's going through an intense drawing thing at the moment,' said Red. 'Actually maybe we should sit in the kitchen, it's not so calamitously untidy.'

She led Bella into a red kitchen, again crammed to bursting with table, chairs, a pine dresser, bunches of herbs, bookshelves, a drinks cabinet.

Bella pulled up a chair at the table and estimated there were at least fifty little cars and trucks scattered across the surface.

'It's a bit different from your lovely Zen home!' said Red, spotting Bella's wry look at the table.

'Oh no, it's lovely,' Bella said, feeling caught out.

'Believe me,' Red put on the kettle and hunted for clean mugs, 'I would love to live in your house, but it's just impossible, I'd drive Jamie and Sandy insane asking them to tidy up all the time . . . and then both Sandy's parents and my mum died in the last couple of years and we couldn't bear to give their furniture away so we've tried to fit most of it in . . . and we never got round to redecorating after we moved in . . .' she tailed off.

So Bella said: 'Stop it! It looks really homely. I kind of rattle around in my place and worry if it's too white. It will probably look really cold and clinical in the winter.'

'Well homes seem to evolve around you, never quite the way you planned them,' Red said, bumping mugs down on the table in front of them. 'Anyway, how are you?' She sat down and propped a hand under her chin, looking Bella squarely in the face. 'And the truth please, not the "I'm a new mum and I'm coping" version!'

'Not too bad,' Bella answered. 'The nanny starts next week and I'm going back for my first half-day on Friday, then work proper the Monday afterwards. Yikes.'

'I'm glad you found a nanny, is she lovely?'

'Ummm. To be honest I didn't really like her at first but her references were good and I thought, well, we'll do a month's trial and see how we go.'

'Sounds fine. Are you looking forward to going back?'

'Not yet.' Bella sighed, she felt complicated about this. 'I think I'll be OK once I'm there. I'm just so worried about Markie. I worry about how he'll adjust and that he's going to miss me the whole time.'

'You'll have to wait and see,' said Red. 'You'll only know once you're back. Try not to fret about it too much.'

'Right now, I really envy you, Red,' Bella said. 'But don't you miss work just a tiny bit?'

'Well, I do work part time to remind myself how boring accountancy is, but you know what I miss?' she said. 'I miss the whole getting dressed up, going to the office, meetings, colleagues, team effort sort of thing. And I miss the way I could forget about everything else in my life and just work, you never get that feeling when you work part time, especially from home. But as soon as you're a mum, everything becomes a compromise.'

She put the teapot down in front of them and loaded two spoons of sugar into her cup.

'But, you know,' she went on, 'I really wanted to be with my son and now the baby, more than I wanted to be at work, so it made sense to leave. But the flip side is, at the moment I don't have nearly as much money or the "Gosh how impressive" status that went with the job.'

She sipped her tea adding, 'No-one in the world considers motherhood a good job or an important one. How can it be highly rated when most women like us hire someone else to do it for a fraction of our salaries?'

Bella was silent.

'I'm sorry,' said Red. 'I'm being very tactless, you've got me banging on about my favourite topic.'

'Don't worry, I'm interested,' said Bella.

'Well, as I said it's a compromise. I like being at home, teaching Jamie how to draw, reading to him, building sand castles, all those small things that are so important to him, and I'll be able to breastfeed Ellie for ages. But it's a sacrifice to stay at home – financially, careerwise, statuswise. I've just learned to live with that – for the moment,' she added with some emphasis. 'Maybe I'll feel different in a few years' time and want to go back. I just keep telling myself that life is long and childhoods are pretty short really.'

'Right,' Red smacked her palm onto the tabletop. 'Here endeth the lesson for today.'

They both smiled.

'I just don't know how I'm going to have the energy to do it all,' Bella said. 'I'm functioning reasonably at the moment because I sleep for two to three hours in the afternoon. But in a week's time, that's going to be over.'

'I don't know, Bella. Maybe you'll have to get the nanny to stay over, so she can do some of the night feeds,' said Red.

'She's made it pretty clear she doesn't want to do that.'

'Look, try not to worry about it. You'll have to figure out what's going to work for you when you get back,' Red soothed. 'If I have one tip, it's just try not to be too extreme.'

'What d'you mean?' Bella asked.

'I started out a workaholic career mum, put Jamie in the kind of nursery where they teach French and maths from three months and we got through the nights with Calpol abuse. But it made me utterly wretched, so what happened? I went to the other extreme . . . quit work, became the mad organic puree-ing, breastfeeding till he was two, co-sleeping supermum. And surprise, surprise, I didn't feel any better.'

'I'm trying to find a balance this time round. But everyone is different,' she added quickly. 'All kinds of arrangements work.'

'Hmm . . .' said Bella, feeling slightly panic stricken. Did she have any idea what she was getting herself into here?

Jamie came into the kitchen.

'Hello sweetpea,' said Red, and her little son scrambled onto her lap.

'Like some juicy please,' piped the little voice.

'Of course.' Red got up and, holding Jamie under one arm, with impressive biceps, Bella noticed, she deftly rinsed out a beaker and filled it up with apple juice from the fridge diluted with water.

Jamie sat on her lap and gulped it down.

'You've got to come upstairs and meet Sandy,' she said when Jamie had finished.

'Oh, he's here is he?' Bella was certainly interested in meeting Red's other half.

'Yeah, he's always here, slaving away in the office.'

Red led her up the tiny, narrow staircase to the top floor and pushed open one of the two doors.

'I've brought Bella up to say hello,' said Red and a head turned round from the large computer screen which dominated the small floral room.

'Hello,' said Sandy with a wide smile. Well, well, thought Bella taking in this surprisingly young and utterly gorgeous man with dishevelled jet black hair and dark eyes, dressed in chinos and a floppy blue sweatshirt.

'Hello there,' she answered, deeply regretting her outfit, particularly the shorts.

'I'm sorry I'm so busy, otherwise I'd come down and be sociable,' he said and grinned again.

'We'll leave you to it,' Red told him after a few pleasantries had been exchanged.

'I'll meet you properly some other time, I hope,' said Sandy as they backed out of the room.

'Wow,' Bella grinned at Red on the way back down the stairs. 'He's a real dish.'

Red giggled. 'I know and *five* years younger than me. I still can't believe my luck.'

'So don't tell me – he's 25?'

'No,' Red looked incredulous. '29.'

'Bloody hell,' said Bella. 'You are looking good for your age.'

'How old are you anyway?' Red asked, smiling at the compliment.

'Twenty-nine as well and I know, I look ancient.'

Red laughed, then a baby started crying. For a moment they listened, then Bella knew it wasn't hers. Weird, she thought, how you could tell the difference.

They went back into the kitchen where Red fed Ellie and Bella topped up their teas.

On Sunday, Bella, Don and Markie were out together for a supposedly nice, relaxing lunch. But it was not nice or relaxing. Markie had been crying and fussing ever since they sat down.

Bella had fumbled with her shirt and bra and given Markie his first ever public breastfeed – feeling strangely embarrassed considering she was someone who hadn't shrunk from sex in public places – but it didn't settle Markie. As they waited for their order to arrive, he began to howl.

Bella could see irritated customers twitch their Sunday papers and scowl and the worst thing was she knew she'd done exactly the same, in this very café when she used to come here on Sundays with Don from their little flat round the corner.

She felt upset and angry. She offered Markie a drink of water, another feed, but he turned his head away and didn't want anything, just grizzled and cried.

Don sighed, which upset her even more.

'I'll take him out for a bit, maybe the change of air will help,' she said, getting up.

'I'll get them to wait with your food till you come back,' he answered.

'How big of you,' Bella snapped.

After pacing up and down the street for twenty minutes with Markie crying against her shoulder, she decided to go back in and eat something.

'What do you think it is?' Don asked as she came back in.

'I don't know, Don,' she said, feeling totally stressed. 'Maybe he's just a bit tense, like me.'

'Look, you sit down and I'll take him out in the buggy, maybe he'll fall asleep. We can't let him howl the place down.'

Bella felt like a traitor handing over her wailing son. Don tucked him into the buggy and wheeled him out. She felt as if every head in the restaurant was turned on her.

Now, when she glanced around, she saw there were lots of babies here but they were all sitting contentedly in their prams and car seats, gurgling and watching their parents happily. What was the matter with her son? She felt a tear sliding down her cheek. He always needed all her attention, all the time.

She never seemed to be able to just put him down and let him watch happily. Christ, she was obviously the most tense, uptight, crap mother in the world, creating the most tense, uptight and miserable baby in the world. More tears splashed down onto her scrambled eggs and smoked salmon. She wiped them away and tried to concentrate on eating something.

She'd been finished for ages when she finally saw Don coming back into the restaurant. He was pushing the buggy and smiling at her, surely a sign that Markie was asleep.

He wheeled over and sat down wearily in the chair. Bella immediately looked into the buggy to check her sleeping baby.

'He cried for ages, poor little guy, but then he did finally drop off,' said Don. 'Thank God, I can now have a few moments of peace, with my wife.'

He looked at her and put his hand over hers: 'Hello,' he said smiling into her face. 'Remember me? I'm the person you used to spend lots of time with until that little munchkin came along.'

She laughed. 'Don't call him a munchkin!'

'He is, though, all he does is go munch, munch, munch on your breasts – which I never get to play with any more – or waaaaaaaah a lot.

'Poor Bella. Are you OK?' he added.

'I'm tired,' she answered, rubbing her hands over her face. 'I feel like I'm going to be tired for ever now, I'll never ever have enough sleep ever again and I'm worried about what going back to work will be like.'

'It will be fine, Bella,' Don soothed. 'You're you at work, that's your natural habitat. It's the baby part, being at home, breastfeeding and being bawled at all day that's strange to you. That's why you feel so weird.' He smiled at her.

'One week back at the job, axing staff, blood-letting, and you'll be your old self again. I'm expecting you to drop a stone and have worn me out by the end of the month.'

'Right,' she said grimly. 'Remind me to get you

that book . . . What Not to Say to New Mothers Unless You Want to Get Kneed in the Balls Very Very Hard.' She took her hand out of his.

'Bella! I'm joking, but yeah, there's some truth in it. I'm sorry, I want things back to normal a bit. I want you back to normal. You're just so wrapped up in this, there's no room for anything else. Christ, you haven't even bought any clothes that fit you. I can't believe you're wearing my trousers and shirt again.'

'Oh sod off,' she said and looked away. Tears were welling up in her eyes again. God! She hated herself for all this self-pity, but she couldn't seem to stop it.

'I'm sorry,' he said, 'I feel left out. There's just not much I can do for Markie. Walk him about in the pram, that's about it. He's not really at a terribly interesting age, I can't play football with him yet.'

Don thought he was being light-hearted, but Bella took every word as a slap in the face.

'Jesus, Don . . .' she looked at him with eyes brimful of tears. 'You could speak to him and sing to him or carry him around, or hold him in front of flowers in the garden or shake a rattle over his head . . . or persuade him to drink out of a bottle or . . . there's just a hundred things you could do. But let's face it, you're not interested . . .' Her tears were slipping down and she spat out the last words with droplets of saliva. 'You didn't want him in the first place, that's what you really want to say, isn't it?'

'Just calm down,' he said urgently. 'I'm sorry. I'm sorry . . .' he held her arm. 'I'm really glad he's here. I'm really glad you got me to do this. I think he's wonderful.'

334

She felt a little better for hearing him say this so passionately.

But then Don added: 'I'm just a bit overwhelmed at how much things have changed. I feel I haven't got any time to myself at home, you certainly don't have any time and there's just nothing left for us.'

'Well too bad, Don,' she stormed. 'We're adults. I expect you to be able to look after yourself now. Markie is six weeks old, he can't.'

There was an uncomfortable silence.

Then Bella said simply: 'I'd like to go home now please.'

Don motioned to the waiter and asked for the bill.

They drove home in silence. Unusually, Markie hadn't woken for the transition from buggy to car seat and was sleeping in the back. Bella looked out of the window and watched the chic streets of glamorous north London gradually grow shabby as they headed to their part of town, further north-east.

Christ, why had they moved to such a big house so far away from anything interesting? Why hadn't they just gone for a lovely two-bedroomed flat nearer civilization? They'd borrowed an absolute fortune for a Georgian terraced house in urban wasteland. What had she been thinking?

She began to feel even more miserable. What the hell were they going to do for the rest of the day? Just babysit and argue. Nothing was fun any more, just effort.

Chapter Thirty-four

Bella was standing in front of the bathroom mirror, nervous as hell, trying to apply make-up properly – for work. She couldn't believe it had come round so quickly. It was already Friday. And was that a hint of double chin? Good grief.

Nanny Joanne was out for a stroll with Markie, and Bella was heading for the *office*.

She'd decided to go in for an afternoon catch-up session with everyone before she moved straight into the work at Danson's on Monday morning.

She saw her hand trembling as she applied mascara and she had a dry feeling in her mouth. She couldn't decide if she was nervous or excited. She was looking forward to seeing everyone again and hearing the gossip. If only she could shake the guilt and anxiety about leaving her baby.

In the bedroom, she changed into one of the new, size bloody 14, suits and shirts she'd bought yesterday in the two hours Joanne had forced her to go out of the house and leave Markie alone.

She put on the dark knee-length skirt and white shirt, no point wearing the jacket, it was

27 degrees outside. God her bust was enormous. A post-partum bulge sat uncomfortably below the waistband of her skirt. She looked like every other out of condition mum and it made her deeply depressed.

She put on stockings and her highest heels, shocked at how excruciatingly uncomfortable they were, but in her eyes it didn't make up for the lumps and bumps. At least her hair was gleamingly clean and neatly put up. She decided on diamond earrings for morale, and she'd put on red lipstick in the car.

OK, almost ready to go. Bella looked through her briefcase, untouched for two months. She poked about inside. Everything she needed was there and ah ha, in the zip-up compartment at the side was a packet of Marlboro Lights and her gold lighter. Suddenly she felt as if she was looking at the answer to her prayers.

She picked up the bag and ran down to the garden. Perching on the edge of the iron table she pulled out a cigarette and lit up. The smoke filled her mouth and touched the back of her throat, oh yes . . . yes . . . yes, she'd definitely missed these more than sex. She spent a few dreamy moments enjoying every breath of smoke then finally stubbed the last inch of cigarette out with her heel on the lawn and went back into the house to pick up her bag, car keys, jacket.

Right, she thought, checking herself out in the hall mirror, this was it. Goodbye maternity leave, hello working mother.

She shut the front door and locked it, feeling a momentary panic about whether or not Joanne

337

would have remembered her keys. Oh shut up, she told herself, are you trying to become the most neurotic woman on the planet? Of course Joanne has her keys.

She walked to the car enjoying the click of her high heels on the pavement and the clunk as she opened the car lock. She clambered in awkwardly, totally unused to the skirt, and damn, smudged oil onto her leg. Automatically she leaned over to the glove compartment and popped the button.

A pile of nappies cascaded to the floor, followed by a baby bottle full of water, a squeaky toy and a dummy. For a moment she had to blink very hard, but the tears were averted.

No, there was not a single pair of stockings left in the drawer. She re-examined the smudge. Well, it wasn't so bad, she could live with it.

She fired up the engine and drove out into the street. It felt good to be driving on her own again, without a bump or a baby. Actually, it felt brilliant. She dodged into the traffic, put on her sunglasses, buzzed the roof down and flicked through her CDs. Girl guitar rock with the volume up loud.

It was of course Kitty she saw first when she walked out of the lift and through the double doors into the office.

'Hi,' Kitty, in something fluorescent green, mouthed silently with a big smile, waving excitedly, because she was on the phone.

No-one else was in the reception area and for a moment Bella couldn't decide whether to knock on everyone's doors or go into her own office.

She decided to check out her room first.

She pushed open the door and was amazed to see Hector sitting in her chair with his feet up on the desk as he chatted on the phone. The room smelled like a café, so obviously he was using her coffee machine too. Coffee!! She'd somehow forgotten about coffee and spent her entire maternity leave drinking tea.

Hector's eyebrows shot up when he saw her.

'Actually,' he said into the receiver, 'something rather urgent has just come in, I'm going to have to call you back. Sorry. Bye then.'

He put the phone down, stood up and smiled at her, holding out his hand. 'Hello, Bella, welcome back,' he said, 'I do hope you'll forgive me for using your office while you were away.'

'And my coffee machine,' she cut in, noticing how well dressed he was; he was obviously sharpening up big time.

'Oh no, is that yours too, I am sorry,' he replied. 'Makes wonderful coffee, though. In fact, would you like a cup?'

'Piss off, Hector!' She was trying to joke off the irritation she felt at finding a usurper in her office space. 'You just moved yourself in, the moment my back was turned!'

There was a small silence and she began to wonder what else of hers he'd moved into.

'I'm looking forward to Danson's,' he said. Hell, she had totally forgotten Susan's decision months ago that she would have to take Hector along with her on the job.

'Oh yes,' Bella managed to say.

'The project manager on Danson's side was at Cambridge with me. I've had lunch with him to talk about it, sounds very interesting.'

This was even worse news.

'Hmm,' she said. 'Who else is in today?'

'Oh hasn't Kitty buzzed everyone for you?' Hector asked.

'Yes,' came Kitty's voice from the door.

'Hello Mummy,' she said holding out her arms to Bella. As Bella hugged her, she could see Susan and Chris coming out of their offices to greet her.

'Hello, darling,' said Chris when it was his turn. He squeezed her in his arms and kissed both her cheeks.

'Hello. Well done,' said Susan and for a split second they stood facing each other without moving, then Susan leaned forward and gave her a dainty hug and peck on the cheek.

'So,' said Susan, 'tell us all about him. Is he cute and adorable and I hope you've brought pictures.'

Well, this was an unexpected show of interest.

'Well, funnily enough . . .' said Bella opening up her bag, and everyone laughed.

She'd been very restrained and had only brought an envelope of about ten pictures.

'Oh he's gorgeous,' said Kitty.

'Lovely eyes,' said Susan. 'Looks like you, Bella.'

The boys were more sheepish.

'I'm sorry, he looks like Chairman Mao in this one,' said Chris holding up a photo of Markie's face.

'Chris!' Kitty smacked him on the arm.

'So, Susan, has anyone got any work to do or are we adjourning to the pub?' asked Chris.

'We are adjourning,' said Susan.

'But it's only two o'clock,' Bella reminded them. 'I *want* to do some work!'

'But this is a very special day,' said Chris. 'We've got our hot shot back.' He put his arm round her and added, 'And can I just say, fantastic breasts.'

Another round of laughter.

So the office phones got diverted to Kitty's mobile and they went to the pub across the road for drinks and work gossip and a bit of baby gossip too. She didn't want to make their eyes glaze over, so stuck to horrific labour details served with a slice of humour.

'And then, when I'm in the most pain you can experience without passing out or dying or something, Don and the midwife – *Declan* – start discussing which match they thought was the best they'd seen that week. Was it the Man U last minute equalizer or the Bayern Munich v. InterMilan championship decider?' she joked.

'And pretty soon after that I gave birth to something the size of a sofa. All I can say girls is "don't try this at home" – next time I'm doing the drugs.'

She sipped her white wine and soda and drew heartily on her fifth cigarette. She felt relaxed and civilized and back to normal, as Don had told her she would.

But by six o'clock, she was feeling twitchy about Markie and Joanne. This was the longest Markie had been without her and her breasts were enlarging by the minute. Chris had barely been able to keep his eyes off them. They were starting to feel hot and sore: it was time to go home.

She said fond goodbyes and headed for the car

feeling happy and light-headed. This was going to work, it was going to be fine.

When she got back home at 6.45 p.m. Markie was asleep and Joanne was straightening up the kitchen. 'Hi,' said Bella, plonking her bag and keys down on the kitchen table. 'Give me the full run-down.'

'He was fine,' said Joanne. 'He's not really happy with the bottle yet. He drank a little milk and spent some of the time feeling unsettled, but he fell fast asleep about an hour ago. Don't worry, we're getting used to each other and it's going to be OK.'

'Thanks,' said Bella. 'Thanks for doing the kitchen. Do you want a drink or something? I'm going to have a glass of wine.'

'I'm fine,' Joanne answered. 'I'll be off if that's OK with you? Do you want me here a bit early on Monday, as it's your first day?'

'That would be great. That's very kind of you. About 7.45 a.m. would be perfect.'

'OK, see you then. Bye, Markie,' she said leaning over the carrycot.

'Bye Joanne,' said Bella.

She poured out the wine then stood over her son's cot. He was curled up on his side fast asleep with his little fists bunched up close to his mouth.

She couldn't resist picking him up. He stirred, turning his head instinctively to her breasts, so she undid her blouse and bra and he latched on and began to drink, not even opening his eyes.

She stroked his cheek tenderly. He was just perfect, and this was going to work.

Chapter Thirty-five

Hector and Bella were in a glossy little office buried in the heart of the Danson's Corporation having a celebratory coffee. They had just pulled off a very slick presentation together and felt they deserved to pat themselves on the back.

The Danson's job would be fun, provided Hector wasn't too major a pain in the arse. It was a healthy, profitable company just wanting to trim back costs, get some fresh ideas and step up turnover. The kind of thing Bella could wrap up in two months, tops, but still very lucrative for Prentice and Partners.

'You look tired,' Hector said.

'Tired? Ha! Tired is for wimps.' She inhaled the steam coming from her coffee. 'I'm just going to have to get used to functioning on this level of sleep deprivation. I went to bed at 9.30 p.m. last night. I was up at 12.30, then 3 a.m., then got up at 6.30. Only women are tough enough to take this on a nightly basis.'

'Are you missing the baby?'

'Markie? In a funny way, no,' she answered. 'Because I don't associate him with work at all. But

343

when I think about him, then I just want to be with him. It's like when you're first in love, you know, when you want to hold someone and look at them and be with them and make them smile all the time and watch them sleeping. Yeah, I'm obsessed.' Shut up now Bella, she told herself.

'Hmmm,' Hector answered.

'Anyway,' she said, trying to snap back into work mode. 'This morning went really well. I think they love us.'

'Yeah,' he said. 'This should be a nice easy one for you to get back into the swing of things.'

'I'm not out of the swing of things!' she exclaimed.

'So what new ideas are we going to hit them with then?' he asked.

As well as all the usual cost-cutting and evaluation, she wanted to tackle the levels of stress and poor communication in the company with lots of 'touchy-feely' stuff . . . a shorter working day, breakfast stations, informal brainstorming meetings, parental leave and even a crèche.

'Are you sure you're not letting the baby get to you here?' Hector asked.

'No,' she told him. 'I'm not the only person in the world with a child, you know.'

Hector didn't make any further comment, so Bella outlined the first round of data to be analysed.

After several hours of steady work, it was obvious she was going to have to deal with the excess milk now starting to leak out of the zeppelin-like breasts sitting in front of her. She was also going to have to phone home, she couldn't hold out any longer.

'I'm off to pump out breast milk for a bit,' she told Hector. 'I hope you don't think that's too weird.'

'Right,' he said.

Perched on a chair in the ladies' loo, she undid her bra and cupped the pump over a solid, throbbing breast. She squeezed the trigger steadily and watched the pale, bluey-white milk spurt out into the bottle.

Of course she was thinking about her son as she did this. She wondered what he was doing right now, was he asleep, curled up in a dear little huddle? Was he looking round, flickering smiles? Or was he drinking out of a bottle, wishing he could cuddle up and feed from his mummy? With that thought she felt tears prick the back of her eyes. God, she did really miss him.

Work felt surreal, like it was no longer the real thing, but an elaborate game, a way to spend time before getting back to reality. Markie was reality for her now, not coming up with money-saving schemes and gimmicks for some multimillion-pound organization.

She rinsed her gadgets, packed them into the black bag and dialled home on the mobile as she walked back down the corridor.

'Hello.' Bella heard Joanne's voice, then listened closely and could hear Markie crying in the background.

'Hello, Joanne, it's Bella. I wanted to see how everything was going.'

'Well, he's a bit unsettled. He's barely taken anything from the bottle all morning and now he's hungry and tired.'

'Oh dear,' Bella's heart sank to her shoes at the

sound of the pitiful wailing in the background. 'What are you going to do?' she asked Joanne, not sure herself what would be best.

'Well, I think I'll take him out for a bit. Hopefully, he'll fall asleep then feel more like drinking something later when he's had a nap.'

'OK, just phone me if there's anything I can do,' Bella said, but she felt helpless.

'Don't worry about him,' said Joanne. 'We'll get settled down and into a routine soon.'

'OK . . .' she tried not to sound as anxious as she felt. 'OK, I'll try and be there about six-ish. See you later.'

'Yeah, bye,' said Joanne, hanging up.

She kept a brave face through lunch with Hector and several Danson's execs, but by the afternoon, time was dragging and she was desperate to go home.

At five, she told Hector she was going to have to go: 'I'll take some of the sheets with me to do on the computer later and I'll be on my phone if you need me, but I really need to go, it's Markie's first day,' she explained.

'Yes, of course,' he told her. 'It's a shame though, I'm meeting my friend, you know Peter Garvy, for a drink after work, and he'd hoped you could come.'

'No, drinks after work are going to be out of the question for a while, tell him I'll do lunch this week,' she answered, trying to firmly squash down the feelings of guilt this conversation was inducing.

Hector's friend was not the trainee she'd expected, he was one of the senior members of their liaison team at Danson's. She really did not want Hector having cosy little meetings with him while she was seen to be leaving the office at five. Shit. But she had to go.

Once she was in the car, she told herself to get a grip. She was the senior person on this job and she remembered her fighting talk to Chris when she was pregnant. She'd aimed to up her day rate so people wouldn't want her hanging round their offices for too long. She and Susan really needed to have that talk about her promotion to partner or, at the very least, a pay rise.

She hadn't spoken to Don all day, so speed-dialled him on the mobile.

'Hello,' he answered almost immediately, sounding terse and stressed as usual.

'Hello, Don, it's me.'

'Bella. Hello, what can I do for you?'

'Don! It's my first day back at work. Aren't you going to ask how it's going?'

'Oh God! I've been really busy, hon. I've been in court on the Mitchell trial.'

'Oh.'

'How is it going?' he asked.

'Well, fine for me, but I don't think Markie is having a very nice time. When I phoned at lunchtime, he was howling his head off and he hadn't drunk anything all morning.'

'He'll be fine,' Don said. 'Try not to worry about him.'

'I'm heading home a bit early to see him,' she said.

'OK. Why don't you sort yourself out for dinner? I'm going to be late, about nine, ten-ish.'

'Right. I might not see you then, I might be in bed,' she said, feeling annoyed about this.

'Let's speak later hon, I've got to go.'

'OK, bye then.'

After a frantically impatient drive home, through snarled-up roads, Bella ran up the steps to the house, desperate to see her baby. She opened the front door and could already make out his wailing.

Rushing into the sitting room, she found Joanne cradling her son who was red-faced and inconsolable. She scooped him up into her arms and plonked herself down on the sofa. As she struggled with her buttons and bra hook, Markie was already quietening down and had turned his head towards her to drink.

Only when he'd latched onto her breast did he open his eyes to look at her for the first time.

'Has he been like this all day?' Bella asked.

'I'm afraid so. He had a good long sleep in the afternoon, but he's been crying almost non-stop since four.'

'Oh God.' Bella flooded with guilt.

'I can't get him to drink out of the bottle. Well, no more than a few sips. He won't even take water. I'm worried he'll dehydrate in this heat.' Joanne sounded rattled.

'What about the survival instinct?' Bella said. 'I thought babies were programmed to eat or drink something when they were hungry.'

'You'd have thought so,' said Joanne.

'He's not going to starve himself to death without me, is he?' Bella asked.

'No, I don't think so,' said Joanne. 'But he's going

348

to have some very uncomfortable hours waiting for you to get home.'

'Oh God,' Bella said again.

'Look, things will probably be much better in a week or two. We can't give up yet.' Joanne's sensible and reassuring tone kicked in. 'Why don't I make you a cup of tea before I go? You must be tired.'

'Thanks,' said Bella. Yes she was tired. Sunk deep into the sofa, she wondered where she was going to find the strength to get up.

An hour later, with Markie cuddled up to her, dozing and feeding on and off, she knew she did not have the strength to move. She ordered in a Chinese takeaway from the phone beside her and clicked onto a TV news channel to wait. She was planning to eat dinner, have a bath with Markie in his carrycot beside her, then go straight to bed with him. Sod the work she'd brought home from the office.

She'd decided Markie should just sleep and feed next to her all night, it might let her get some more sleep than switching on the light, getting him out of his bed for a proper meal of both breasts then trying to settle him back down to sleep, which always took ages.

Her head hit the pillow just after 9 p.m., ridiculously early, but she felt as if she was finally crawling to bed at 2 a.m. after a hard day's work and a night on the town.

It was a very disturbed night. Don woke her up when he came to bed at midnight. Markie then seemed to wake her almost hourly to feed.

Finally at 6 a.m., there wasn't any point in

pretending to be asleep, so she decided she might as well get up. She looked at her husband, so sound asleep in bed he didn't even stir, then picked up her baby and headed to the sitting room. Together, they watched the news and had breakfast.

By the time Joanne arrived, Bella was ready, made up, hair up. She had changed into her suit at the very last minute in case of baby vomit. Don was still in bed.

'Just ignore my husband wandering around,' Bella told Joanne. 'He's probably got a late start or something.'

'Markie looks happy today,' said Joanne, seeing him gurgling on the sitting room floor.

'Yeah and he's full of food, because he's been stuffing his face all night.'

'Oh dear,' said Joanne. 'That's a bit hard on you.'

'Hmm. There's plenty of breast milk in the fridge for you to try with today. And he needs a change and some new clothes. I just haven't had the chance, or the energy,' she confessed.

'OK, off you go. We'll be fine, don't worry about us.'

Bella picked her son up and kissed and held him. 'Goodbye sweetheart, see you soon.'

As soon as she put him down again, he began to cry.

She left the house with a wrench.

350

Chapter Thirty-six

Bella called home on Friday morning and could once again barely listen to Joanne for the sound of her son's raw howls in the background.

All week Markie had cried for most of the time she wasn't at home. He was refusing to drink anything at all now and she had the eeriest feeling when she came home at night that he was withdrawing from her. He seemed to turn away, he wasn't looking at her for as long, he merely ate and slept when she was around, he didn't seem to want to interact with her and he hadn't smiled at her since Wednesday.

Joanne sounded tense and harassed now, she obviously no longer knew what to do to try and distract this baby from his misery.

'Why don't you bring him in to see me?' Bella asked now. She knew it was not a good idea, not a practical one, but she hoped that somehow they could all wring some relief from it. Markie and Bella could have some breastfeeding time, then Markie would sleep all afternoon because he was full and

Joanne would have the distraction of a day trip to the office.

'Yes, why don't we do that?' Joanne sounded quite cheered up at the prospect.

At 1 p.m. on the dot, Bella was buzzed by reception and she told them to show her visitors up. She'd warned Hector, who had gone off for lunch early so she would have some privacy.

Joanne arrived with Markie strapped up in a baby carrier.

'I hope you don't mind me using one of these, buggies are such a hassle on the tube,' she explained as she came into the room.

'No, no,' said Bella.

'Very nice office,' Joanne added.

'Yes. I'm on assignment here. How's he doing?' Bella looked anxiously over at the little head she could see at the top of the carrier.

'He's fallen into a doze, he's so exhausted with crying, but I'm sure he'll wake up at the prospect of lunch.'

'This is just terrible,' Bella told her.

'He's so attached to breastfeeding,' said Joanne. 'I've never seen anything like it. You should have had him on the bottle from the off. Most women going back to work so soon do that.'

'But breast milk is so good for them. No-one ever warned me that this might happen.'

Bella took her son from Joanne's lap. His hair was plastered against his head with sweat and his babygro was damp. His face looked flushed.

'He's a bit hot, Joanne,' Bella said, cradling him in her arms.

'It's very hot outside and I got hot on the journey.

Sorry, I should have thought of that,' she replied.

Markie stirred against Bella and instinctively latched on. As soon as he started to suck properly, Bella felt herself relax. Maybe Joanne could bring him in every lunch break? Maybe that would be how they could get through the next few weeks. Surely that was all it was going to take for him to get used to the bottle, get used to this new set-up where she wasn't around for most of the day?

She felt the heavy weight of guilt in her heart as she looked at the little cheek moving up and down just a few inches from her face.

Markie fed from both sides slowly. When he was finally stuffed full, he broke off. Bella looked at the white dribble of milk running down his chin. He was fast asleep. She stroked him tenderly on her lap. It felt such a betrayal to be sending him home asleep. He would wake up and not even understand where he had been and where she had gone.

She hooked up her bra and tucked in her blouse. There was a knock at the door.

'Come in,' she said, assuming it was Hector.

The door opened and she was horrified to see Tom Proctor, the group FD she'd had sacked from AMP last year. The one who'd phoned her up just to tell her she was a cunt. God, she still remembered that awful conversation word for word.

'Well, well, it is you again.' There was no hiding the contempt in his voice. 'I didn't think I could be quite this unlucky but there we go, once the shit has hit the fan, it gets everywhere.'

She didn't see why she should reply to this.

'Having a little crèche meeting, are we?' he asked with a sneer.

'No actually, there isn't a crèche at Danson's.' How dare he try and make her feel guilty about seeing her son. 'Are you going to be working with us, Mr Proctor?' She tried to make this sound civil.

'I bloody hope not,' he replied. 'I'm going to do all I can to get you parasites drummed out of the building.'

'And what is your position here now?' she asked, trying to keep the panic she felt out of her voice.

'Yes, I bet you're bloody anxious to know that, aren't you? But I think I'll keep you guessing Mzzz Browning. So watch your back.'

With that he slammed the door and was gone.

Bella looked at Joanne and caught the appalled expression on her face.

'Don't worry about him,' she said, trying to hide how shaken she was. 'He's an arse. I'm sure if he was in any position to get rid of me, he'd have said. He's just trying to rattle me.' She hoped this was true.

We have a contract with them, we have a half a million pound contract, she was reminding herself.

It was time for Joanne to leave. Bella kissed her baby on the forehead and handed him over, feeling like a traitor. Joanne buckled him back into the carrier and he was in such a deep, satiated sleep, he didn't even stir.

'See you later,' her nanny said, gathering up her things and heading for the door.

'Bye and thanks for bringing him.' Bella watched the door shut behind them and suddenly felt a little weak and wobbly.

Her mobile began to ring, so distractedly she went over to her desk and picked it up, just as

Hector came back into the office from lunch.

'Hello,' she said into her phone.

'Hello Bella?' She didn't recognize the voice.

'Yes, who's that?' she asked.

'No, I don't suppose you'd remember.' It was an American accent, clipped and cold.

'Mitch! How are you?' she said fondly.

'How the fuck do you think I am? I've just been sacked. Merris lost the court case and the company's been bought over by a bunch of money-grabbing vultures. No-one is to blame for this more than you and I can't believe you didn't warn me.'

She was stunned.

Mitch continued furiously: 'I asked you Bella, I came to your office to see you. I told you I had a baby on the way. Surely you could at least have warned me?'

Bella felt as if she had been slapped in the face or winded and all the fight drained out of her.

She didn't want to spout all the usual stuff – that the company was going down the pan, that Mitch would have lost his job anyway, that she had been Merris's only chance. Maybe Mitch was right, maybe she had cocked it up for them all. Most of all, she knew she did not want to be the one taking all this shit all the time.

'Haven't you got anything to say?' he asked.

'I'm sorry,' she mumbled, 'I didn't know.'

'Yeah, well it's a bit late for sorry. It's a bit fucking late for that.'

There was a long pause.

'Is that really all you can say?' he asked, even more furious that she wasn't giving him the chance for a proper fight.

'Yes,' she whispered.

Mitch hung up.

'Oh fuck,' she said under her breath.

'Who was that?' asked Hector.

'Someone from Merris Group. He was a bit upset,' she mumbled. 'I didn't know they lost the court case.'

'Yeah. It was big news a couple of weeks ago,' Hector answered. 'Never mind. You should have just given him your famous line – sod off to the country and restore antique furniture,' Hector said with a laugh and was astonished to see Bella bursting into tears.

'Oh come on, Bella, get it together,' he said, 'or people are really going to think you're not up to the job.'

Stung by the remark, she knew at once that Hector didn't think she was up to it and she wondered who else he'd told.

Hiding in the Ladies, she lit a cigarette and took a deep drag. OK, she told herself, two more hours of work then I'm out of here. Maybe Markie won't even have woken up. But when she rang home on her mobile on the way out of the office, the loud screaming in the background told her otherwise.

'Hang on in there, Joanne, I'm getting into my car, I'll be back in forty minutes.'

Except she wasn't, she got stuck in a long traffic jam full of angry overheated drivers blaring their horns and swearing at each other. Her breasts were hard and hot and oozing milk onto her sticky, sweaty shirt. She clicked the button to pull up the roof of her car so she could cry without attracting too many stares. What a complete, fucking night-mare of a day.

Finally she got home and collapsed on the sofa with her baby.

Joanne fetched cold drinks from the kitchen, while Markie sucked frantically. 'I've made us something to eat,' she said, handing Bella a tall iced fruit juice.

'Oh thank you.' Bella felt pathetically grateful. Joanne had tidied the sitting room as well, despite her earlier warnings about refusing to do house-work. No wonder, it had been revolting, dustballs building up in the corner, takeaway dishes from four nights in a row.

Bloody Don, shouldn't he be helping with some of this? Instead he'd come in late every evening and she'd been away before he was up in the morning.

Bella nibbled at her luscious chicken sandwich crammed with slithery tomatoes and mustard may-onnaise and occasionally glanced over at Joanne eating hers. There wasn't much to say. Joanne had had a terrible day, Bella was shattered. They were both hoping things would work out better next week.

'I really appreciate how hard this is for you at the moment,' Bella said. 'I hope it will get easier.'

'Me too, we'll wait and see how it goes,' Joanne answered.

Soon after her sandwich, she left and Bella and Markie were alone.

Bella stroked his cheek and cuddled him close to her. Propped up on pillows on the sofa, she fell fast asleep with Markie in her arms.

It was 10.30 p.m. when he began to cry. Her eyes

opened and she was momentarily startled to see an unfamiliar ceiling and set of curtains, then realized she was in the sitting room.

She looked at the baby snuggled up against her chest. His face was pink and marked with the folds of her clothes and he was bathed in sweat from sleeping so close beside her. There was also a tell-tale feeling of wetness on his back, oh yuck, she could see yellow goo seeping out of his nappy. She decided to take him upstairs where they could both peel off for a bath together before bed.

By contrast, the next day, Saturday, was perfect. Once Don had surfaced from his lie-in, he looked after them both. He did the babysitting, cooking and tidying. Markie was calm and contented all day, he ate well, he slept for long stretches, leaving Bella free to lounge around the house and relax.

She lay on the sofa, watching sunlight stream into the room and she felt pleased with how lovely it looked, snowy white with gauzy curtains stirring in the breeze and big pools of light on the elegant blond floor.

By Sunday morning, she felt so calm and rested that when the call came for Don to go off on a job for a day or two, she took it in her stride. She considered phoning Red or Tania for company, realizing that she hadn't spoken to Tania in weeks. But somehow, the day passed and she didn't get round to it. Funny how the idea of phoning Mel, Lucy or Jaz seemed almost ridiculous now. What would they talk about? Her old friends wouldn't be at all interested in Markie.

She played with her son, dangling things above his head and watching him reach out his little hands. He was so surprised with his hands, he opened and closed them in amazement and startled when they moved back and touched him. Bella watched him with utter devotion and he rewarded her with long, adoring looks and the occasional fluttering smile. By Sunday night, she knew she did not want to go back to work, could not go back for another week like the one they had all suffered.

The work for the next month at Danson's was basic figure analysis, there was no reason why she couldn't do it from home. Hector could e-mail it all over to her daily. He could call her whenever he needed to, hell they could have a meeting every couple of days if necessary, but basically, she would be at home.

She could feed Markie whenever he was hungry and Joanne could look after him while she worked.

The more Bella thought about it, the more perfect a solution it seemed. Why hadn't they arranged this from the start? Just naivety. She hadn't know what a nine-week-old baby was like and neither had her office.

It was time to let them know.

Chapter Thirty-seven

On Monday morning, Bella put on her work suit and high heels and headed for the office. She thought she might as well stick with plan A until everyone knew about her plan B.

In the car at 8.05 a.m. she decided to try Susan before she drove into the morning traffic. She dialled her direct line.

'Hello,' came the reply, before a second ring had sounded.

'Susan, hello, it's Bella.'

'Oh hello, Bella. I've been thinking about you. How are you coping?'

'I'm fine, sort of. Have you got any time today? Lunch or after work when we could have a quick meet?'

There was a pause, Susan no doubt checking her overstuffed diary for a bite-sized chunk of opportunity.

'No, I'm totally booked up. You're speaking to me in the freest moment I'm going to have all day.'

Oh well, here goes, thought Bella, taking a deep breath.

'I'm going to suggest doing my share of the Danson's work from home for the next few weeks. I haven't spoken to Hector or Danson's yet, I wanted to clear this with you first.'

No response. Bella thought she'd better just carry on: 'Hector and I can communicate by e-mail and phone and we'll have regular meetings. I really don't think it will pose any problems.'

'What's brought this on?' Susan asked.

'Well, I have a full-time nanny, but my son is still unsettled, really upset about me being away all day, Susan. He's still breastfeeding and he needs me around.'

She tried not to sound too emotional as she said those words.

Utter silence from Susan. Bella waited a moment then began to wonder if she should say something else.

Finally Susan spoke. 'Well,' she said, 'I have lots of other things you can do for me from home, Bella. But if that's where you want to base yourself for the time being, Hector will do the Danson's job on his own, closely supervised by Chris.'

Bella couldn't believe it. She was stunned, too shocked to do anything but gasp for breath.

'Does that sound OK?' Susan said lightly.

'No it bloody well does not!' Bella was surprised at the anger in her own voice. 'Hector!' she exclaimed. 'I can't believe I'm hearing this. This is a half a million pound contract, which I won for you, remember. I have given up a whole month of maternity leave to come back and work on it and all I'm asking for is a little bit of flexibility here. Hector is the most junior person in the office, he was my assistant on the job.'

Susan's voice came back, calm and controlled. 'Don't have a girlie fit on me, Bella. Yes, half a million pounds is at stake here, I can't take a risk. Hector told me on Friday you didn't seem to be ready to come back yet. He said you were tearful, leaving early, unable to attend key meetings. And there's some senior exec there you have a problem with, apparently.'

Bella was distraught, the little shit had completely stitched her up.

'Go home and think this over for a day or two if you like,' Susan continued before she could challenge Hector's version of events, 'but I'm sure you'll see I'm right. I've got lots of work to keep you busy with, I can't let you risk our reputation by sending you out to clients before you're back to full strength.'

Bella could not believe what she was hearing. She was being demoted to Hector's position and he was waiting in the wings to snatch up her job. Her prized job, the one she had fought so hard to get.

'I should have been promoted after my work with Merris, Susan,' she said, surprised at how calm she suddenly felt. 'Instead, you're going to demote me because I've had a baby.'

'I'm not demoting you,' Susan cut in.

'If you make Hector the number one on the Danson's job, you'll leave me with no option but to resign.' She realized she was deadly serious.

'For Christ's sake, Bella, don't be so melodramatic. You're obviously tired and postnatal, don't do anything you're going to regret.'

Bella was speechless with anger.

Susan spoke again, angry too now: 'Resign! Don't be ridiculous. Of course you're not going to resign. This is your dream job, the one you were born to do, you're not going to sit at home pureéing carrots, you'll go up the wall.'

There was a long pause, then Bella began to speak, only recognizing the truth of her words as she said them. 'You know what? I am going to resign. It's not ridiculous. Leaving my two-month-old baby alone all day with a stranger is ridiculous, thank you for helping me to see that.'

There was a long silence on the line, then Susan stormed: 'Bella? Bella? Don't even think about putting the phone down now, Bella. If you hang up, your job here is finished. I mean it, I will not re-negotiate with you . . . Bella?'

Bella held the phone away from her ear and clicked the end call button.

She stared at the little hung-up phone symbol on the green screen in disbelief.

Her message symbol was flashing, so she called it up and looked at a wonderfully inappropriate text note from Don: 'Dn't let the bugrs get u dwn. Luv u D.'

Christ. She dangled her car key in her hand and wondered what to do. She couldn't face going back home just yet, she needed some time to think. She decided to head over to the café beside their old flat.

During the fifteen-minute drive she replayed Susan's words over and over: 'You're obviously tired and postnatal' . . . 'You're not going to sit at home pureéing carrots.' She was so furious, it was hard to drive straight.

But she had *resigned*. She felt her stomach lurch at the full implications. No more Danson's, no more Prentice, no more Chris, Kitty, no more big salary. But on the other hand no more leaving Markie behind . . . well, for the moment. God, she needed to think this through.

In the café she drank a succession of lattes and smoked her way through five cigarettes. It didn't really make things any clearer, but she felt calmer in a sort of caffeined up, nicotine buzz kind of way.

OK, she'd resigned from Prentice, she would take a couple of months off to be at home with Markie full time, then she would get another job. Hell, she could still take up Merris on his offer; well, if he had a company left to run. She shuddered at the thought of the phone call from Mitch.

Suddenly she really wanted to speak to Chris about all this, so dialled him up on the mobile.

His reaction to the news was a hardly surprising: '*What?!!!!*'

'I had a bit of a run in with Susan this morning,' she explained. 'And anyway, I've left.'

'Bella! What the hell happened?'

'All I wanted was to do the Danson's work from home. I thought that would be perfectly feasible. But she said she'd give Danson's to Hector and give me "other things" to do.'

'Oh God . . . so you took the huff?'

'Chris!' Bella felt very defensive. 'I was really insulted she didn't believe I could do it. And she was offering the contract I won to that creep. He

364

phoned her up on Friday and told her I wasn't up to it.'

'Jesus,' Chris let out a long sigh. 'But are you happy about this? Do you really want to leave?'

'I didn't feel I had any choice, Chris. I don't know. I'll have to think about it. I just want to be with my son right now.'

'Look . . . maybe you need some time off, time to think this over,' he said. 'Why don't you leave it a few days then phone her back? I'm sure something can be worked out. Bella . . .' Chris was almost pleading with her now. 'You don't really want to leave, do you?'

All at once Bella felt exhausted, far too tired to deal with all this, so tired she just didn't care any more.

'I don't know Chris,' she managed. 'You're right, I'm not in the best frame of mind to make any decisions. I need to go home, get some sleep.'

'I'll phone you. Take care.'

'OK thanks, you know, you're a really nice guy,' she added.

'Thanks, bye, bye,' said Chris.

'Bye,' she answered.

She had to get home. She paid up and headed for the car then drove back, wondering what the hell she was going to tell Don.

As she let herself into the house, she could hear Markie's desperate cries coming all the way from upstairs but also the TV on in the sitting room. She walked in and saw Joanne lying on the sofa watching breakfast television.

Joanne turned round to her, open mouthed.

'Well, you're fired,' Bella said simply.

'There's nothing I can do with him to make him feel better, I've had to leave him to cry himself to sleep,' she said by way of explanation, quickly getting to her feet.

Bella was white with fury, but controlled. 'I don't care,' she said. 'It's not what I would do and I need a nanny who will do things my way, or Markie will never be happy.'

Joanne's face flushed, she picked up her bag and her jacket. She looked up at Bella, obviously wanting to say something before she left the house.

'You should have bottle-fed him from the start. The situation you're in now is unfair on him and unfair on me,' she said in a raised voice.

'Thank you, Joanne,' Bella said grimly, 'you can go now. I'll settle up with you through the agency.'

Bella stood rooted to the spot in the sitting room until she heard the furious slam of the front door, then she ran upstairs to her son.

He was lying on his back in the cradle beside their bed. His face was red and creased with howling and his furious fists were waving about in the air.

God, how could Joanne have left him like this? Bella scooped him up and slumped onto the bed. Propping pillows behind her back, she hurried to feed him.

Afterwards, they both fell into a doze.

Bella was woken by the trilling of her mobile. Gently she laid Markie in his crib and ran out into the hall. Hell, where had she put it?

The trilling stopped and then the house phone rang.

Aha, she knew what was coming next.

She ran back into the bedroom to pick up.

'Bella?' It was Don, sounding anxious.

'Yes.'

'Is everything OK? I couldn't get you on your mobile so I just tried this number on the off-chance.'

'Everything's fine,' she said. 'I've resigned from my job and fired the nanny, otherwise everything's just fine.'

Don swore. He'd been able to tell from her weird tone of voice that this was not a joke.

Bella held the phone tightly and wondered what was coming next.

'OK,' he said, very tense now. 'What happened?'

Bella gave him a sketchy outline of her quarrel with Susan, then Joanne's dismissal.

'Right,' Don said. 'I can come back this evening, I think I probably should. There are obviously a few things you need to talk through.'

It was the right answer. 'Thanks, that would be really good,' she said.

He promised to be home by seven.

'Drive safely,' she pleaded, imagining him bowling the Jeep all the way down the fast lane of the M6 in his rush to get home.

Don was surprised to come back to such a peaceful house: he'd worked himself up into a state about Bella on the drive home. He'd expected to find her hysterical and on the verge of suicide with a screaming baby in her arms. Instead, she was snuggled up on the sofa watching TV with Markie asleep at her breast. She'd had a bath and her damp hair was coiled up on her head.

They kissed hello. She smelled clean and flowery and milky, whereas he was unshaven, grubby and reeked unmistakably of the greasy café he'd spent the afternoon in.

'You look incredibly calm,' said Don, sitting down on the sofa beside them, 'I was expecting you both to be having tantrums.'

'I am very calm,' she said, smiling at him. 'I need to take some more time off to be with Markie, then I'll have no problem finding another job.'

'Well, OK,' he answered. 'You seem to have made up your mind. Don't you want to keep a slot open with Prentice? I'm sure you could patch things up.'

'Maybe, but not right now. I've got a point to make to Susan.'

'Right . . . and that point is?' He felt irritated by her now.

'That she can't have everything her own way.'

'I wonder who else needs to learn that lesson,' he said quietly.

Bella rounded on him. 'Just fuck off, Don. This is my life. I'm allowed to make my own decisions.'

'Of course you are, Bella,' he retorted. 'I just don't want to see you toss your career away for a few more weeks of playing the good mother.'

'What the hell does that mean?' she asked furiously.

'You worked your arse off to get that job and you loved it. I can't believe you've just thrown it away over a petty argument.'

'Petty? She won't let me work from home. She won't let me be here with a two-month-old baby who needs me.'

'She said you could work from home, just on different stuff,' he reminded her.

'She was going to give Hector my job!' Bella

shouted and Markie woke up with a start and began to cry.

'Oh well that's a perfectly logical reason to resign, wounded pride,' Don replied.

'Just fuck off,' Bella said, for the second time. 'And go and have a shower, you smell revolting.'

Don stormed out of the room and Bella was left feeding Markie again so that he could settle back down into sleep. She was very hurt and angry. She'd taken a huge step, albeit without any fore-thought, and she needed Don's support. He'd always supported everything she'd done before, made her feel confident and understood and fantastic. Now, she felt unsure and damn furious with him.

Don, standing under a hot, soapy shower, was in no better a mood. He'd been away for two days and quite frankly wished he hadn't bothered coming back. He was nostalgic for the homecomings they used to have. He remembered eating takeaways in bed and fantastic sex. Their relationship was now turning into everything he'd dreaded about married life, everything he didn't want – rowing, screaming baby, chaotic home, sexual frustration.

For the first time ever, he felt bored with Bella. She had always been so much fun – interesting, daring, outrageous. This was all so mundane and now stressful as well. Just how the hell did she think they could afford the mortgage without her salary?

Bella was wondering exactly the same when the phone rang.

It was Tania, but Bella could feel only mildly enthusiastic.

'Hi, how's it going?' her friend asked.

369

'Well . . . I quit my job today.'

'Really? You've had a better offer? You cow, you better not be earning more money than me.'

'Ha ha. No, I've decided to stay at home for a couple of months, look after Markie and get a new job after that,' Bella explained.

'Oh my God! Now I'm really shocked!' Tania laughed. 'What are you going to do all day? And what will you live on?'

'The answer to your first question is a fuck of a lot,' Bella was frosty now. 'And I'm going to live on my savings,' she lied. 'And my husband, if I still have one. It's only two months, for God's sake, just no shopping for a few weeks.'

'How boring,' Tania groaned. 'I wanted to ask you over on Saturday, just you and me. We could have a girlie good time, shop, drink cappuccinos, maybe go for a massage or something. I've had such a stressful week, and I want to talk to you about Greg.'

'Tania,' Bella cut in, 'I've got a small, breast-feeding baby, I can't spend a day without him. Anyway I don't want to,' she huffed.

There was no response from Tania, so Bella said: 'I'm sorry. Why don't you come over? I'll make you lunch, then we can take Markie to the Heath and have a long walk.'

'God, Bella, you're in danger of turning into a surburban housewife,' Tania joked.

'Well at least I'm not some sad Bridget Jones,' Bella snapped. 'Why don't you just phone me back when you've grown up?' With that she slammed down the phone.

She threw herself back down on the sofa and lay looking at her son asleep in his carrycot.

Good going, she told herself. At this rate I'll have no career, no husband and no friends. A little part of her also thought, So what? My son loves me, I just want to be with him.

She stroked the little fuzzy head.

Chapter Thirty-eight

Bella stood up very slowly to move her sleeping baby from her arms into his bed. She put him down with tiny, careful movements, but as soon as his head touched the mattress, he woke and began to cry.

She let out a curse of frustration. Damn, damn, damn. For the third time, she was going to have to sit down and put him back on her breast until he fell asleep, then try and move him. She felt furious with him. Why couldn't he fall asleep without a nipple in his mouth? Why wouldn't he leave her alone for just half an hour so she could do something for herself, clear up the breakfast dishes, take a shower, lie on the sofa in peace. She needed to be left alone, just for a few minutes.

He was so tired, she knew she should just put him down and let him howl until he fell asleep, but she couldn't bear to do it. He had cried and cried and cried the times she had tried before and in the end she had always given in, picked him up and comforted him with her breasts again.

Every single one of the plethora of babycare

books she had surrounded herself with recently had advised her that feeding a baby to sleep was a bad plan, but it had become too entrenched now. Markie was four and a half months old. This was how he went to sleep, morning, noon, night, middle of the night. She didn't know how she could break the cycle. The fact that it was all her fault made her feel even worse about it.

She picked the baby up roughly. 'Damn you!' she shouted. He cried even harder with fright.

'I'm sorry, I'm sorry,' she soothed him up against her shoulder and felt like crying herself.

She lay on the sofa and put Markie beside her so that he could latch on. He had barely swallowed a few mouthfuls before he had fallen asleep again. His lips smacked as they broke off from her nipple and to her infuriation, the noise woke him up and he quickly started to suck again.

Finally, ten minutes later he fell soundly asleep. She didn't dare to move him. If he woke up again, she was in danger of shaking him, smacking him or doing something that she would have found just unthinkable before. Now, with a thousand tiny frustrations heaped on her every single day and night, she knew anyone could hurt their child, if they were pushed far enough.

And she was very close to that line. She was absolutely exhausted. Every day, she was functioning on just six or seven fractured hours of sleep, she had dark double bags under her eyes and her skin looked grey. She had just enough energy to get through the day and nothing in reserve. She had taken on way too much. She was doing all the baby care, all day long, all the breastfeeding, day and night. Don was there to cook her dinner some evenings and he helped out at the weekends, but otherwise, she was totally unsupported.

Right now, she just couldn't see a way out of the situation. She couldn't bear to get any childcare sorted out while she wasn't working because of guilt at the expense and because she still hated the thought of handing Markie over to anyone after the last experience.

But she knew she wasn't going to get any aspect of her life back together until she had some time and some energy.

And what the hell was she going to work as anyway?? She couldn't be a part-time consultant. It wasn't that sort of job and even if she could think of a way of going part time, she might as well throw her ambition in the bin.

Where was the solution?? All these questions and anxieties were whirling round her head in such an unanswerable frenzy, it was beginning to make her very depressed.

The day before, she'd made the mistake of thinking company would cheer her up and she'd met Mel and Lucy for lunch in the City but the obvious gulf between what she once was and what she'd now become had just depressed her even further.

She'd turned up at the smart restaurant in Don's jeans and a shirt, with a changing bag on her back, lugging a baby in a car seat. Mel and Lucy were in exquisite designer suits, with Fendi bags, kitten heels, long nails and tiny mobile phones.

Markie had been perfect. She'd propped him up into the restaurant's high chair – an unexpected miracle – where he'd mouthed on pieces of bread as

Mel and Lucy had cooed over him adoringly, even though Bella forbade them both from smoking within 50 yards of him and Lucy had cuddled him just a little bit too hard so he'd landed a blob of sick on her jacket.

But the questions about what her plans were had been hard to answer because she just didn't know.

'Well, you know, in another couple of months he'll drink from a beaker and eat more solids, so I'll be able to leave him with someone else for a bit,' she'd heard herself say, but she was mentally adding, but not all day, no way.

'God, how are you surviving without a salary?' Mel had asked, genuinely curious.

With a lurch, Bella thought about the mountainous overdraft, the credit cards racked up to the hilt, and said: 'Oh you know, I've got a bit saved up to tide me over for a while . . .'

'Do you spend the day doing lovely stuff?' – this from Lucy – 'Going round parks, art galleries, deli shopping, it must be so relaxing not having to go to work. God, it must be fabulous.'

Bella pictured herself endlessly breastfeeding day and night, dodging dog shit with the buggy, trawling round Boots and dealing with the trauma of a screaming baby when she was out with no place to feed or change him and said, 'Hmmm, yeah,' vaguely.

'Don't you miss work a bit?' asked Mel.

She'd looked at the two of them, perfectly dressed, perfectly made up, about to go back to their vastly well paid jobs, then afterwards maybe on to a noisy cocktail party. On Saturday they could sleep in all morning, read the papers, go out for lunch, see a film, have a facial, buy expensive new clothes, book holidays. Shit. Shit. Shit. She missed it all desperately.

Then Markie happily waved a bread crust in his fat fist; he was giggling and drool was running down his chubby chin onto the bib she'd tied round his neck. She adored him, felt her heart ache just looking at him.

'I don't know,' she sighed. 'I miss lots of things about work, the buzz, the power trip, the money, that feeling of purpose every morning. God,' she managed a laugh, 'I can't believe I used to go jogging *every* morning! But I'm just besotted with him. I don't want to miss anything. I don't want to make him unhappy and I want to do everything right.' As she said this, she wished she could think of a way to somehow have both lives, but it seemed utterly impossible.

'Have you spoken to Susan, since you . . . em?' Lucy asked awkwardly.

'No,' Bella said.

'What about doing two or three days a week. Susan would definitely take you back, wouldn't she?' Lucy asked.

'Ermm . . . I don't know, I keep meaning to speak to her. God, I don't know.'

Lucy and Mel had felt slightly at a loss. This was Bella, the girl who'd always had it all figured out before, who'd got the fab job first, who'd got married first, who'd now had a baby, *first*. It was unsettling to see her like this, looking crap, sounding vague and anxious.

On the walk back to her car, Bella looked round at the streets which had been her backdrop for so many years. She felt like an outsider. Everyone who pushed past her was in a suit and in a hurry, Markie was bumped about in his car seat as the City's workers raced past back to their offices to make more money.

There was a smartly suited couple kissing passionately on the street corner and she watched them break apart laughing as their mobiles went off together. 'Synchronicity,' Don's voice was in her head. That had happened the first night they met . . . about one hundred years ago.

Now, one entirely uneventful day later, she was back at home with Markie finally asleep on the sofa – snuggled right up against the back, so even she, the most anxious mother in the world, couldn't worry about him rolling off. She plugged in the baby monitor and left the room with the listening device in her hand.

Downstairs in the kitchen, she opened all the windows and lit up a cigarette. She inhaled right down to the bottom of her lungs and felt the wonderful tingling buzz, she put her lips round the butt and sucked in again. It was warm and comforting and wonderful. 'Good old Marlboro, that's what I say,' she said out loud in a voice made husky with the lungful of smoke she was exhaling.

'Talking to myself,' she said out loud again. 'An interesting new development. Obviously the first sign that I'm about to go completely bonkers.'

She stubbed her cigarette out in the tiny bronze ashtray and went upstairs to sort out another load for the washing machine.

God, she was bored. She was becoming a slave to an endless round of domestic chores. The washing had to be done, the kitchen sink had to be cleaned, the shower plug unblocked. There were 101 little tasks she could occupy herself with all day long but what for? The clothes and sink would get dirty again, the plug would gum up. It was merely a version of digging holes and filling them in again. A way of making her feel she was busy.

'Oh shut up,' she told herself, 'this is getting very black.'

But then the little voice said: 'You used to get pissed in all night bars, drag strange men home to bed, do boardroom presentations so good they turned you on . . . now you shop for baby vests. SHUT UP, BELLA.'

But it was boring and she was boring.

'He managed to roll over onto his tummy today and he lifted himself up with his arms. He was so pleased with himself, he giggled and squeaked. And he was pointing at me and going "Ah, ah". I'm sure he was trying to say Ma Ma. It's just really exciting,' she heard herself say to Don at supper that evening. She sounded like an idiot.

When she'd finished her bath, she went through to the bedroom and found Don waiting for her on the bed. He looked nice, still tanned although it was the end of autumn now. His thick hair was overgrown and in need of a cut, she liked it like that.

'Hi Bella,' he said gently and she knew that look.

'Oh boy,' she said with a smile. 'You can try, hon, but I'm very tired, it will be like raising the dead.'

'Come here,' he held out his arms. 'Let's just cuddle up.'

'Yeah, you say that, but I know you mean "let's have a shag".'

'Bella! Stop being so defensive and get over here!'

She kept her thick white dressing gown wrapped tightly round her and lay carefully on the bed beside him. He rolled onto his side and wrapped her up in his arms, squeezing her so hard, her large milky breasts hurt.

He aimed for her mouth and kissed her, reaching between her lips with his tongue. God, she struggled against the urge to push him away. She really wasn't in the mood. Why so full on straight away? Couldn't he kiss her neck first? Or her forehead?

She broke away and kissed his cheek, neck, ear, anything to get away from the closeness of a mouth on mouth kiss.

He opened her dressing gown and fondled her breasts, but to her they felt heavy and manhandled. His hand moved down to between her legs as she unzipped him and took his erection between her hands. She'd decided to just do this.

Poor Don, he was a nice guy, he was working really hard and they hadn't had sex for weeks. She would do it for him, she knew it would be quite nice for her too, but she was just a million miles away from being really turned on by this.

He was kissing her on the mouth again, ugh. She broke off and moved down the bed to lick his penis. Bizarrely, that felt much less personal.

She carried on for as long as he would let her, hoping it might reduce the portion of sex coming right up.

Don pulled her on top of him and said breathlessly, 'What's the current contraception situation?'

'Condoms,' she answered, 'In the drawer with KY Jelly . . . the scar is still quite uncomfortable.' Oh the romance.

'OK,' he said, turning to the drawer. She moved off him so he could sit up and fumble about with cellophane wrappers and foil, then the condom and finally the jelly.

'Are you OK?' he asked turning round to her.

She leaned down and kissed his face while he rubbed grease onto his rubber-clad penis. She kissed the small, soft apples of his cheeks and reminded herself that she loved this man. She put her hands into his hair and took him inside her.

It felt good, she felt snug and almost muscular inside, he felt just right again.

He closed his eyes.

She moved to his rhythm, enjoying it but not wanting to lose control. She focused on the bedstead in front of her and felt him cup his hands round her breasts. They felt heavy and sagging. It was painful even to bounce gently on top of him without the ten-ton breasts crashing up and down against her ribcage. She glanced down at her wobbly tummy and immediately regretted it. This was not her body, she just couldn't feel sexy with it.

Don was slowly working up to an orgasm beneath her and, with some detachment, she watched his face change from tension, screwed-up eyes and locked jaw to pleasure and relief.

He opened his eyes and looked at her: 'You weren't there, were you?' He said this kindly, with a smile.

'Well . . . I was there a bit,' she confessed. 'It was nice.'

'Oh God, nice.' He was only smiling a little. 'We've reached the "nice sex" stage. You know what comes next, don't you? The "no sex" stage. The "Not tonight darling, I'd rather have a lovely cup of tea" stage.'

'Don't, Don.' She moved off and lay beside him. 'I'm sorry. I'm not in the mood.'

'You're never in the mood,' he said.

'Please don't. You're just going to have to give me a chance here. I'm looking after a baby 24 hours a day, I'm *tired*. Anyway, we've been together for two years now.' She was starting to sound angry.

'What's that got to do with it?' he asked.

'Well, that's when people go off the boil a bit.'

'Bella, you pessimist!' He cuddled her up in his arms and decided to joke her out of this: 'I'm intending to still fancy you when you're 50. Obviously, feel free to get the necessary plastic surgery and designer corsetry required.'

She whacked him over the head.

'Ha ha. Now leave me alone. I've got to get some sleep.'

'OK.' He kissed her on the lips. 'Good night. Just try and relax, we're OK. You're going to be OK soon.'

She didn't answer. There was no way she was kicking off a discussion about the baby/job/working dilemma right now. She couldn't face it. She did not want to talk about it.

Chapter Thirty-nine

She was curled up in front of the telly, feeding Markie one dreary, grey afternoon when the phone rang. She reached over to get it from the table jammed right beside the sofa arm.

'Hello, Bella?' for a moment she didn't recognize the voice and hesitated.

'It's Red, I just wondered if you were still alive?'

'Oh hello Red, how are you doing?'

'I'm good. How are you? Is this not an odd time for you to be home? I was expecting to leave a message on your machine, or with your nanny.'

'Oh God, have I not told you about all that?'

'No . . .' Red sounded intrigued.

'I resigned . . . and I fired the nanny.'

'Oh my God, really? When did all this happen?'

'Err . . . Markie was two months old and, God, he's coming up for six months now.'

'How come you haven't called me? We could have had lots of lovely baby-mum times together.'

'I'm sorry . . . I just felt a bit, you know,' Bella felt a lump forming in her throat.

'Bored, lonely, exhausted, depressed . . . suicidal? I know.'

'No, I'm fine, honestly. I'm really enjoying being with him.'

'Yes of course, that too.' There was real understanding in Red's voice, which was making Bella's lump even more painful.

'What about coming back to yoga class with me on Saturdays?' Red suggested. 'There's a postnatal class too, you know.'

'No . . . no, I can't go back there,' Bella sounded tearful. 'I was so different back then, I don't want them to see me like this.'

'Like what, Bella?' Red asked. 'Maybe you should come along and see that everyone else is feeling like you – shattered, uncertain about the next move.'

'I can't.'

'Well, another suggestion then. Why don't I come and babysit for you one evening?'

'Thanks, but I don't think that would work.'

'Why not?'

'He falls asleep at the breast and sometimes he wakes up just an hour or so later for a top-up. If he didn't get it, he'd howl himself sick until I came back.'

'Well, just go to the pub round the corner. You've got to get out of the house without him, trust me. You're going to go stir crazy.'

I already am, Bella thought, but said: 'I'll think about it, Red, I promise.'

'OK, sorry Bella, I'm not wanting to bully you or anything, d'you want to meet up or come round?

I've got some free afternoons a bit later in the week. And there's a baby-toddler group we can go to on Fridays.'

'Thanks, Red,' she said. 'How are you anyway?'

They chatted on for a bit and when Bella put the receiver down, she felt a little better. Maybe she would load Markie up into the car tomorrow and go to a park a bit further afield.

She tried to enjoy their park trips, but the truth was, he was just too small still. He sat propped up in his buggy and watched things with interest, but she looked enviously at the groups of mothers sitting chatting on benches in the play areas while they watched their toddlers climb over the slides and dig in the sand pit.

It would be much more fun when Markie was older. The baby stage seemed such a thankless grind. God, she immediately felt guilty at that thought. It wasn't thankless, he smiled at her, he giggled at her, he looked at her with utter adoration and was upset even when she went out of the room. Her son's unconditional love for her was over-whelming.

The following weekend, Bella watched the rain running steadily down the window. The sky was steely grey and even though it was only 4.30, it was starting to get dark. Bloody November, she'd always hated November and she was beginning to hate Sundays too.

All three of them had been cooped up inside the house all day, not able to go out for a walk and not getting it together to go anywhere in the car. She felt as if she and Don had worked split shifts all day long – he had looked after Markie while she slept in, she had kept the baby amused while Don read every paper printed in Britain that day. Then when Markie had his afternoon nap they had tidied the house together, put on laundry and Don had done the supermarket run. God, it didn't come more domesticated than this. She looked out of the window now and watched the rain, feeling bored beyond belief.

What would she give for some time to herself, time away from all this? When she was still a teenager she had backpacked round eastern Europe on her own, now she was stuck in a house in a shitty part of north London. Make that stuck on a sofa, in a house in a shitty part of north London. How had she let her horizons close in around her like this?

She desperately wanted to be alone, but she desperately didn't want to leave Markie. It made no sense that these two emotions should be wrestling in her mind like this. She wanted to un-make him, so that he and his relentless demands didn't exist, just for a weekend.

She fantasized about what she would do: go to an airport and take a flight to New York so she could roam around a loud, noisy, brash city and stay up all night without worrying about the 6 a.m. wake-up call the next morning. Or maybe go somewhere quiet and clean and green. Finland. She'd always wanted to go there.

She wanted adventure and change and above all to be by herself to think her life through. She needed mental free time, time not to think: Are there enough nappies and clean clothes left? Are the pears ripe enough to mash? Is he old enough to try live yoghurt? Will a bread crust choke him? All the million things that took up all her thoughts every day now that just hadn't been there before.

She used to be able to think about work and Don and holidays and the future. Now she was too busy.

What the hell was she going to do next? Up till now her life had run according to the game plan. She had known exactly where she was going and how she was going to get there; now suddenly at 29 she was in freefall.

She was not going back to the 9–5, ha, more like the 8–8. She was not going back to screwing companies for massive amounts of money just so she could get people like Mitch fired. It was too bloody and too soul-destroying and what was she going to tell her son when he asked 'Mummy what do you do?' 'Well, darling, I am the axeman, the bean counter, the cost-cutter, the men in grey suits, the bloodletter.'

But the money had been nice, the power, the status, the respect had all been very nice. She didn't have any of those things now.

'Right, Bella.' Don plonked some sort of noodly chicken concoction on the table in front of her when she came back down from putting Markie to bed. 'We are going to have a proper talk over dinner tonight. I've left you to your own devices long enough and now I need to know what is going on. You've been like a weird space cadet for weeks.'

She sat down, picked up her fork and tasted his meal. 'Hmmm, very nice,' she said, wondering where the hell to begin.

'I know, never mind that . . .' He looked up at her with a serious bordering on angry face. 'Our son is almost six months old and you are still at home, still breastfeeding him all day long, not making any calls, not organizing any childcare, not earning any money . . . you know we can't afford to go on like this.'

Bella looked up at him with big, brimming eyes and did not know what to say. She couldn't begin to express her own wretchedness at the situation: Well Don, the answer is to make Markie not exist for a few days so I can go to Finland and have a rest and come up with some brilliant new plan. That wasn't going to work.

'What's the matter, Bella?' his tone had softened. 'I just don't recognize you. You're so vague and undecided. I don't think you're really happy being here all day long with Markie, but you can't seem to snap out of it.'

'Snap out of it?' She felt angry now.

'Well yes. You're just mooching about here feeling sorry for yourself. You could easily get any other job you wanted, but you haven't tried. You could easily find another nanny, but you haven't tried. Jesus, you haven't even bothered to buy anything that fits you, you just skulk about here in my old clothes. You look awful.' Don regretted that as soon as he had said it. But there it was, he couldn't take it back and anyway, maybe he'd been far too nice to her for too long. Maybe it was time to get tough.

'*Don*, I haven't bought anything because I'm not earning any money,' she shouted.

'I'm well aware of that,' he shouted back. 'What the hell do you think we are going to pay the mortgage with next month? I'm at my overdraft limit and your account must be in meltdown. Just what are you thinking? If you want to spend the next few years at home being a housewife, then we'll have to sell the house and move to a small flat. But that's not why I married you.'

'What is that supposed to mean?' She was furious now.

'I never wanted to be married to someone who stayed home and cooked and did the cleaning and talked about the kids all evening. It's so fucking dull. I thought you were the absolute opposite of that and I feel like I've been tricked.'

'*You've* been tricked?! How the fuck do you think I feel?' Her tears were spilling out now, she was so angry and so hurt. 'I never knew what this would be like. I didn't ask for a baby who would only breastfeed, who would howl the house down whenever I left him. I didn't ask to feel this bad and this tired and this *pissed off* with everything.'

Words suddenly couldn't express her rage and frustration, so she flipped over her dinner plate, spilling food all over the table and ran upstairs.

Lying sobbing on the bed, she heard the front door slam. Good. Don had gone out, she hoped he didn't come back.

Once she had cried herself out, she went and washed her face in the bathroom.

That evening, she started to think about what it would be like to leave Don. Where would she and Markie go? How would she pay for it? Jesus. She could sell the car. She'd have to get a job first. She went into Markie's room and checked on him. He was lying on his back with his hands thrown up and out beside his head. He looked blissfully peaceful.

Far too hyped up to sleep, she went down to the kitchen, opened a bottle of wine and took out her cigarettes.

Two fags down, she felt steadier. She picked up the phone and dialled Tania's number. Unbelievable that she hadn't spoken to her for months now. She'd been so rude to her the last time, and never found the time or inclination to make up.

The answering machine picked up and Bella clicked off her phone. She couldn't leave Tania a message, she'd have to speak to her in person.

Who the hell else could she call? She lit another cigarette and thought for a moment, staring at the telephone keypad,

Aha. Speed dial seven.

After a few rings, that oh-so-missed voice answered.

'Hello?'

'Hello Chris, it's Bella.'

'Bella! Hello. Bloody hell. I thought you'd died or something.' He sounded so pleased to hear her, it made her stomach flip.

'You never wrote, you never called,' she teased.

'No, I didn't. Sorry, that was really, really crap of me. Bad boy.'

'How are things?' she asked.

'Terrible,' he answered. 'Danson's went ape when they heard you were off the job. Threatened to bring you in on a personal contract, then Susan threatened them with breach of contract . . . blah blah. I've been working like a dog, because Hector, well he's just a conceited, scheming bastard. I take back all the nice things I've ever said about him. And we miss you. It's like a leg lopped off, the phone constantly rings with people asking for you and we've all been told to say you're not working for us or anyone else, you're simply not available.'

Bella was amazed to hear all this.

'But that's not true, is it?' Chris asked. 'What are you doing? Have you taken the plunge and set up on your own?'

'Err . . . well, to be honest no. I'm having a bit of a maternity . . . em . . . sabbatical.'

'Really?' He sounded surprised.

'Well, the next move is important for me, I don't want to rush into anything. 'It was funny to hear that sort of career-y, work thing creep right back into her voice.

'No, you're absolutely right,' he said, then added: 'Susan is desperate for you to come back. She's too proud to come to you, but she would bite your hand off if you offered, probably any terms you liked.'

'Partner?'

'I'm sure. I'd probably get sacked to make room for you.'

'Ha ha.'

'How's your son anyway?'

So Bella told him, trying not to go on for too long.

'He sounds lovely,' said Chris. 'Are you enjoying being at home?'

'Mostly. But it's very tiring and I worry a lot that everyone thinks I've dropped off the face of the planet. You know that whole corporate culture of taking your mobile into the delivery room and rushing back to work before your stitches have healed.'

'Don't be silly,' said Chris. 'No-one's forgotten you, Bella. If anything, your mysterious disappearance has got even more people clamouring for your services.'

'Do you ever have any qualms about the job we do, Chris?' she asked, surprising herself.

'Oh-oh conscience time. No not really, we usually do quickly what would have happened much more slowly and bloodily over the long term.'

'Hmmm,' she answered, wondering if she believed that line any more, 'I think it would do me good to see you.'

'I'd love to – when and where? I'm free!'

'No hot dates at the moment then?' she teased.

'No.'

They settled on Sunday, her house, 8 p.m.

'It'll be great to see Don again,' Chris added, because he wanted to know if Don was going to be there, but he didn't want to ask straight out.

'No, you won't see him, he's off to Africa for about ten days, civil war refugees or something,' He was leaving tomorrow morning. She wondered if they would have a chance to make up before then and if she wanted to.

'So just you and me then,' Chris said in a way that made her wonder . . .

'Well, you, me and, hopefully, a sleeping baby,' she laughed.

Chapter Forty

In the morning, she and Don were polite to each other, but there was no big making-up scene. Don had spent the night on the couch after an evening in the pub and woken with a grotty hangover.

He packed his bags as Bella made breakfast for herself and Markie. Don only wanted coffee. Her son was eating porridge with mashed banana and he mouthed at little pieces of bread while she sat down to fresh orange juice, cereal and two slices of toast.

The ring at the doorbell meant Don's taxi was early. She could hear him cursing in the hallway. He went out to say he wasn't ready yet.

Five minutes later he appeared in the kitchen, wearing the long, waxed overcoat she loved him in, with a bag slung over his shoulder.

'OK, I'll say goodbye then,' he said rather stiffly.

He leaned over Markie sitting in his high chair and gave him a kiss: 'Take care my little buddy,' he said. The baby patted him on the cheek.

He came up to Bella and put his arms round her: 'Look after him for me and take care of yourself. I'm sorry we rowed last night, but I can't take back what I said. I think you need to get your head together,' he said. 'I want to help you, but you won't tell me how I can help you.'

'Right, I get the message,' she replied.

'I really don't want to leave on a bad note,' he said. 'But it's work. I have to go and I want to go. I'm sorry.'

'It's OK, Don, I'll be fine, it's just ten days, isn't it?'

'We've not got a definite return date yet, but it shouldn't be more than two weeks.' He leaned down, kissed her quickly on the mouth, and said 'Take care, I'll call you,' then he left.

'Bye,' she said and when she heard the front door slam she wished she'd been big enough to tell him to take care too. Take care wasn't 'I love you', they were both still too angry for that, but it was at least 'I really care about you'.

Two hours later, Markie had finally gone down for his morning nap when the phone rang. Bella rushed over and snatched the receiver up before the ringing woke him.

She was surprised to hear Don's voice.

He'd taken the wrong laptop to the airport. He could still use the one he'd taken, but he asked her to access a file on the laptop at home and pull out the contact numbers he needed for the trip. She found his computer in the sitting room and once it was up and running she called him back.

He talked her through the passwords until she'd opened the right file, then he took down the numbers and said goodbye, telling her to take care again. This time she said it back.

She hung up and decided to e-mail the file over to him and maybe put a conciliatory little note at the bottom.

She prepared her message then plugged the computer into the phone socket and hit send. As it exited the basket, she was left looking at the list of stored mail and she saw 'S.Sewell@nota.Virgin.net re: trip.'

S. Sewell could only be Simone Sewell, the tabloid harpy from hell Don had been seeing on and off over several years until he'd met Bella. She was a news reporter on his rival paper and she'd taken up the L.A. correspondent job not long after Bella and Don's engagement.

Bella clicked open the message, all it said was 'Looking forward to it.' But as she scrolled down, the story unfolded – all Simone's recent messages to and from Don were enclosed on the file.

Simone was back. She'd been made chief reporter on her paper, so now she and Don were direct rivals. She was going on the same civil war story and would be meeting him at the airport. Their first encounter in two years. Simone had sent the tasteful message: 'The child-bride has a baby now, so you must be gasping for a good grown-up shag,' along with a few choice reminiscences of their earlier adventures on the road together.

Bella read through them, thinking that a rain-filled ditch in Cumbria during a police hunt for an abducted toddler wouldn't have been her number one location for a sexual encounter, no matter how irresistible Don was.

She shut down the computer. Her hands were shaking and she could hear blood pounding in her

394

ears. This would not be nearly so worrying if Don had at least mentioned Simone and if he hadn't had to leave home in the middle of a decidedly rocky patch.

'FUCK!!' she shouted out loud, 'Fuck, fuck, fuck.' She had no idea what to do. Should she phone Don and ask him what the hell was going on? Should she bundle Markie up and follow him on the first flight out there? No, that was ridiculous.

Unfortunately, her deepest insecurity now triggered, dinner with Chris was taking on a whole new meaning.

Rifling through the phone book, she booked a hair appointment at one of the most expensive salons in London, then began to make elaborate preparations for Sunday night.

Don opened his eyes and focused on an unfamiliar ceiling. His arm felt numb and he turned to see Simone's bleach-blond 40-year-old head lying on it. He eased it out from under her neck, managing not to wake her up.

Jesus, Simone.

He hadn't seen or heard from her for over two years, yet she had kissed him on the mouth and with her tongue when they'd met at Heathrow and he'd been jolted with a surprise shudder of lust, although the time in LA had not been kind to her.

Her skin was now a dark, dried-out tan, her nails had sprouted to inch-long, candy pink talons and she ended every sentence with a really irritating 'yunno?'

She was still single, of course, still totally neurotic about her career and it was obvious, now she was back, that she had every intention of rekindling their affair.

Their liaison had begun four years ago when she'd joined her paper. It had been a torrid on-off, hot-cold, sex and newspaper centred relationship complete with stealing exclusives from each other and snatching opportunities to fuck on the job. It had been thrilling in parts, immensely stressful, and after just an hour on the plane with her, drinking lukewarm in-flight champagne, he remembered exactly why he'd finally ended it on meeting Bella.

Bella, Bella . . . his beautiful, young Bella, who thought she was so tough and City-slick. To Don she'd seemed fresh, untainted and positively dewy-eyed. All that enthusiasm – for work, for life, for him! Finally, someone who hadn't been fucked up the arse by life one hundred times over like Simone and all the other women he seemed to hang around with back then.

He had listened to Simone cracking her hard-nosed, sarcastic gags on the plane, eaten up with bitterness and totally cynical, and he remembered how she'd laughed in his face whenever he'd tried to say anything really nice to her, whenever he'd tried to get in under that bulletproof shell. He could have become just like that, but thank God he'd met his girl – the gorgeous, sexy, razor-sharp girl asking him for a light. The one who had trusted him enough to let down her guard and fall in love.

Poor Bella. He sat up in bed now and rubbed his hand over three days of stubble. She'd had no idea what had hit her when the baby arrived and he'd left her to it, all the anxiety about money driving him to work harder, longer and away from home. He needed to take a holiday and give her a break.

This week had been hell, covering really grim shit from a place on the very outskirts of civilization. Now it had all turned nasty, and he and eight other journalists were holed up in the last two available hotel bedrooms waiting for a ride out.

He looked at his watch: 8.15 a.m. The plane was due in two hours. If he got good connecting flights, he would hopefully be back in London late, late Sunday, early Monday. He longed to be at home, to wrap Bella and his tiny son up in his arms and tell them it was going to be OK. He was going to make it OK.

Simone was stirring, he looked over and saw her eyes open. She yawned, stretched her arms out over her head and grinned at him.

'There's still time to change your mind, yunno?' she said and under the covers, he felt her hand reach for his belt buckle. 'They're going to say we did it anyway.' She nodded at the two photographers still comatose in sleeping bags on the floor.

'Thanks, but no thanks,' he said and moved her hand away.

'Well, well, respect to the child-bride,' Simone said. 'She's finally reined you in, yunno?'

'Her name's Bella,' Don replied. 'Let's just stick to Bella.'

He threw back the cover and, already dressed in trousers and a T-shirt, he got out of bed and pulled on his boots.

'I'm going to see if I can find some coffee in this place,' he said.

The haircut was fantastic, easily worth the eye-watering bill. Bella's mass of long, dark brown hair had been transformed into a sleek, layered, shoulder-length bob, shot through with ginger and caramel highlights. A heavy fringe had been cut into the front, which managed to make her look 19 again.

By Sunday night, her fridge was crammed with delicious food and very expensive wine, a new outfit was hanging out ready on the wardrobe door and the house was tidy and gleaming, filled with luscious fresh flowers and candles.

She had put Markie to bed early, so she would have a full half-hour to get ready. It still felt strange that he slept in his own little room now, but she'd decided to move him out three nights ago, so she could reclaim the bedroom.

Drying off after a quick shower, she covered herself in fragrant cream, then put on a little make-up. Back in the bedroom, she picked out her best underwear: suspenders, lace G-string, an under-wired bra which she was going to spill out of.

She had no idea if she had the nerve to seduce Chris or not, all she knew was that planning it like this had been the most fun she'd had in ages.

She rolled on nude lace-topped stockings, struggling to see over the cartoon cleavage she'd given herself, and hooked them into place. On top went a new slinky skirt, slit from ankle to mid-thigh, a fitted emerald green shirt, unbuttoned low, and the green strappy shoes.

She had just applied the lipstick, squirt of perfume and checked herself approvingly in the mirror when the doorbell rang. A shot of excitement hit her and she raced down the stairs.

She opened the front door and there he was, still eat-me-with-a-spoon handsome.

'Hello!' She leaned in close to kiss him on both cheeks. 'Lovely to see you.'

'Hi, you look stunning,' he said with a grin, closing the door behind him.

So did he. She'd never seen him out of a suit before, but here he was in cords with an open-necked shirt which showed his smooth olive skin. His hair was longer than usual with a hint of curl and he had a soft navy jumper tied over his shoulders.

'Come in.' She led him into the sitting room.

Chris handed her a bunch of heavy pink roses and a bottle of champagne, so cold the glass was wet. It slid a little in her hand.

'Thank you, you're such a gentleman. Shall we?' She waggled the bottle at him.

'I think so.' He raised his eyebrow, smiled and they held each other's gaze for a long moment.

She watched him peel off the foil and put deft thumbs to the cork. He nudged it out slowly and it made an expensive pop.

'Glasses?' he asked.

'Oh yeah.' She went to get champagne flutes from the kitchen, then curled herself into the sofa, putting her green-sandalled feet up, and watching him carefully pour out their drink.

They clinked glasses and sipped, then he sat down on the other side of the L-shaped sofa, within touching distance of her feet.

'I love your hair,' he said.

'Thanks.'

'Susan knows I'm here tonight,' he said, surprising her.

'Oh really? What did she say?'

'She wants a full report on what your plans are. She knows you're not working. Well, she thinks she'd know about it if you were.'

'And what are you going to tell her?'

'Whatever you want me to, boss,' Chris answered.

Bella took a deep sip from her glass and lit up a cigarette. 'D'you want one?' she asked.

'Think I will, actually.' She tossed him the packet, liking the fact that he smoked only very occasionally, just to keep her company.

As she sat up to light him, he leaned his face close over her hands, so she could feel his warm breath on her fingers. She had to stop herself from touching him.

'So . . .' he said blowing smoke out, 'what are you going to do next?'

'I'm figuring it out,' she answered.

'What do you want to do, Bella?'

'Well, a three-day week for a start,' she said. 'But a three-day week that doesn't kill off all my prospects – something lucrative, but a bit more worthy, and something that feels as if it has a future. I'm sick of batting from contract to contract.'

'That's quite a long list,' he said.

'Every problem can be solved if you spend long enough trying to find the solution,' she said, aware that she didn't have much longer to solve this at all.

'Well . . . I'm looking forward to it,' he said,

then asked: 'What do you want me to tell Susan?'

'That I'm sorry we fell out and I'll be in touch with her soon, when I've got a clearer idea of what I'm going to do next,' Bella replied, deciding it might be a good thing to mend some bridges. 'Will she be OK with that?'

'Yeah.'

They talked animatedly on the sofa, Chris filling her in on all the latest work news, and when the champagne bottle was empty, she took him downstairs for some food.

'What a great kitchen,' Chris said as he stepped down the final stair into the cosy cavern Bella had laboured to create.

The table was laid with crystal glasses, candles and flowers. The lighting was low and the garden lights were on, making the room look far bigger and more glamorous than it really was.

'Thanks . . . take a seat, open another bottle.' Bella handed him the wine and served the first course.

They ate slowly, still talking about work and office gossip. The wine bottle was already two-thirds down and it occurred to Bella that she hadn't drunk this much for over a year, but she felt fine. She felt good.

'I'm not feeling very hungry,' she told Chris. 'Shall we have another cigarette?'

Conspiratorially they lit up together, giggling about it: 'This is what I call the inter-course cigarette,' she joked, feeling herself slip into full on flirt mode.

'We need more wine,' he said and got up to get a bottle from the fridge.

'Oh my God, how come I don't feel drunk yet?'

she asked when she'd got through another large glassful.

'Maybe you're having too much fun,' he answered, tilting his head so a thick lock of black hair bounced down over his forehead and for a moment, she felt slain with lust.

'Are you trying to get me drunk, Chris?' she asked when the power of speech had returned.

'No, no, no,' he was smiling at her. 'Although you're very nice drunk.'

'Oh boy.' She smiled back at him.

'You always know when you really, really fancy someone, because the most unappealing things about them become sexy,' he said, topping up their glasses again.

'Such as?' She knew this was dangerous, dangerous water, but she had her boots on and was wading on out there.

'I'm feeling really quite turned on by those damp patches on your blouse,' he said.

She looked down to see two large wet marks, where her breasts had leaked, and burst out into shrieks of laughter. He began to laugh too and for a few moments, they were overcome with hilarity.

That was when she realized how pissed she was.

'OK, your turn,' he said when they had calmed down a little. 'What's the least appealing thing about me?'

She looked at him closely, trying not to giggle. Two of his white front teeth were snagged . . . adorable. He had a bristling middle eyebrow . . . gorgeous. She looked at him for a very long time and couldn't see anything to complain about.

'You see,' he said finally. 'You really fancy me.'

'Yeah,' she answered.

He leaned over and kissed her hard on the mouth. She opened her lips and let him, thinking only about how strange and interesting a different mouth is, when you've been with one person for so long.

The kiss went on and on. Her eyes were tightly closed and their knees were bumping together. She felt his arms around her lifting her to her feet so they could get closer. He risked pulling her in tightly to him, so she could feel how turned on he was.

Finally, he broke off and looked at her, seeing how pink and swollen her lips were already from the intensity of the kissing.

'Are you OK with this?' he asked.

'Oh yeah,' she whispered and latched onto his mouth again. Then she kissed his neck and felt his pulse throbbing under her lips.

'Where do you want this to go?' she heard him ask.

'The bedroom,' she answered, the head rush of lust and alcohol ruling out any indecision.

They moved up the kitchen stairs and in the hall they kissed, licked and touched each other all over again. He undid the buttons of her blouse and let it fall to the floor. He pushed a nipple out of the tight lace bra and put his mouth against it. Licking round it and biting on the very tip, he whispered: 'It tastes sweet.'

She crashed a kiss onto his mouth and to her horror, he lifted her up and ran to the stairs.

'Chris!' she cried. 'You can't do this!'

She closed her eyes and tried to enjoy the ride.

Chris was struggling as they got to the top of the steps and she had fallen so low in his arms, he was practically dragging her up. He stumbled and fell on top of her.

'Ouch,' she giggled as she lay under him.

'God, sorry.' He saw she was OK and locked his mouth on top of hers. Kissing him hard, she reached for his belt and fumbled to unbuckle it, then unzipped his trousers and felt for his cock.

He put his hands on her thighs under her skirt, then hooked his fingers round her pants and peeled them down her legs. He placed one hand over her naked crotch and held it still, so she could feel the heat radiating from his palm. On the brink of distraction that he wasn't moving it, wasn't feeling her, she pushed down into his hand, meltingly wet.

Their lips were locked together and both her hands were stroking his cock, feeling the long hardness of it, rubbing against the rim and the little opening at the top.

'Come to my room,' she whispered. Of course she'd said 'my room', the thought flickered through her mind.

'Is that OK?' Chris whispered back.

She stood up and led him in by the hand, her heart thudding in her chest.

The room was lit only by the street lamp outside the window, the curtains hadn't been drawn. Snowy new sheets, duvet and pillows were piled up on the iron bed.

Bella pulled off her skirt and sat down in bra, stockings, suspenders and high heels. She enjoyed seeing the effect this had on him. He tugged off his clothes, not taking his eyes from her. Bella looked at the smooth, hairless chest, firm stomach and quivering cock.

Chris knelt at the edge of the bed and pulled her hips to his face.

She closed her eyes and lay back, letting him bury his face between her legs. She could feel herself coming almost immediately, but it didn't do anything to slake her thirst.

'Please fuck me,' she said.

'Do you have anything?' She could hear the urgency in his voice.

'Table beside you, top drawer,' she said.

He pulled out the drawer and found the packet of condoms, open with several left inside. He tore one open and slid it into place.

'You'll need the KY too,' she said, then added: 'Stitches,' by way of explanation.

'Oh,' he said and fumbled for the tube. He squeezed some out into his hand and rubbed it over his condomed penis, which was not quite as hard as it had been.

She stretched out her arms for him and he wondered where to wipe his jellied hand.

He placed it down on the duvet and tried a surreptitious wipe as he carefully crawled up towards her, covering her body with his.

After a long, probing kiss, he noticed how still she was lying, underneath him. He opened his eyes and looked at her face. She was looking at him very seriously. The desire and the drunkenness which had spurred her on to do this was fast dissolving and she was left feeling very naked under a strange body.

'Oh dear,' he said and rolled off onto his side. He propped his face up on one hand and looked at her, lying on her back on the big bed. They were both suddenly very sober and very serious.

'It's OK,' he said.

'It's not OK, it's not OK at all . . .' she sounded angry. 'I thought this would make me feel better, but it doesn't.'

'I'm really sorry, this is my fault,' he said. 'I feel like I've taken advantage of you.'

'No, no.' She was surprised to feel tears forming in her eyes. 'No. I think I meant this to happen . . . I'm really frightened that Don's having an affair. And I somehow thought if I could get even, it wouldn't hurt so much . . . And do you have to be so good-looking?' she added.

'I'm really sorry,' he said again and sat up on the bed.

She sat up too now. 'I've got to speak to him and find out what the hell's gone wrong with our marriage.' She was wiping tears from her face. 'I've been so down, it's hardly surprising he's gone off with someone else.'

'Hey, it can't be all your fault.' Chris put an arm round her, wondering distractedly how he was going to dispose of the condom scrunched up in his other hand.

She put her wet face on his bare shoulder and he felt her breasts brush his chest: 'I'm in love with you, Bella,' he said, taking himself completely by surprise – in fact he didn't even know if this was true.

'No you're not,' she said, but she looked up at him and gave a half-smile. 'You really care about me and

406

you lust after me. And I feel the same about you.'

With some relief, he realized she was right.

'Shit,' she sighed. 'We really shouldn't have done this.'

'No,' he said. 'Well, we haven't . . . not technically. Actually I'm not sure I could have managed.'

'Attack of conscience?' she asked.

'Bella, I've got your husband's condom in my hand.'

Before she could even laugh in response to this, she heard a thin wail coming from next door.

They had woken the baby.

'Oh bugger,' said Bella, reaching for her dressing gown.

Chris stood up and turned away from her, suddenly self-conscious and needing to get back into his clothes. 'I should probably go,' he said.

'Are you sure?' she asked. 'There's lots of food downstairs.'

'Well . . .'

'Go and eat some of the curry, I'll settle Markie down then come and join you.'

Once her son was asleep again, she stripped off her underwear and stockings and let them fall in a heap on the bedroom floor, then in her dressing gown and slippers and went downstairs.

She ate a plateful of curry with Chris and they both drank water. Feeling totally sobered, they talked very safely about favourite curry recipes and cooking until it was time for Chris to call a cab and leave.

'Thanks for dinner,' he said at the door, putting a hand on her shoulder.

'Yeah, and the rest.' Bella gave a wan smile.

'It's OK.'

They kissed on the cheeks.

'I'm really sorry I've loaded all this on you,' she said. 'It's a good thing you're such a nice guy.' She gave him a grateful hug.

'It's really OK,' he said and kissed her forehead. 'Call me if I can do anything and call Susan soon. OK?'

'Yeah,' she said. 'You're a star.'

'Good night.'

'Good night.'

She locked the front door and stood alone in the hallway. God, she was exhausted. She decided to blow out the candles and go straight to bed. She could tidy up in the morning, she had nothing else planned.

In a light, dozing sleep very early the next morning, she thought she heard the sound of the front door unlocking.

She opened her eyes and looked at the alarm 5:41 a.m. She closed her eyes again then heard bags being set down in the hall.

BAGS!!!! Jesus Christ!

She was awake now, bolt upright in bed, her heart pounding. There was the rustle of a waxed coat being taken off and she heard the sitting room door creak open.

She knew what he would see in the sitting room – candles, flowers still wrapped in paper and two empty champagne glasses. She heard Don's heavy tread on the stairs down to the kitchen, where he would find the table still laid out with dinner for

408

two, complete with lipsticked butts in the ashtray and too many empty wine bottles.

He was back in the hall now, probably picking up her blouse. Fuck, fuck, fuck . . . she heard him coming fast up the stairs, two at a time. Frozen to the spot, she saw her stockings and suspenders lying on the floor as the bedroom door swung open.

Chapter Forty-one

'What the hell is going on?' Don's face was stony white.

'Well . . . well . . .' she answered, trying not to panic, 'I was about to ask you the very same bloody thing.'

'What the hell does that mean?' he shouted.

She stared at him in silence.

'Who the fuck was here last night?' he asked.

'And why would you care?' she answered.

'I'm your husband, in case you hadn't noticed.'

'Well, you certainly haven't been acting like one.'

'Just what the hell is going on, Bella?' he asked again. 'Your pants are hanging from the banisters.' His fury was barely under control, especially as he had just seen the pile of lace and stockings on the floor beside the bed.

'Well you start, Don. Did you have a nice little reconnaissance trip with Simone? Simone "you must be gasping for a grown-up shag" Sewell.'

'Jesus Christ, Bella.' For a moment, he looked like he might laugh.

She was slightly thrown off her stride by this.

'I finished with Simone when we met, you know that. But she's back over here, she works in my business, she's a die-hard flirt and you'll just have to live with it. I've made it clear to her I'm not interested.'

'Oh.'

'But just what have you been doing?' he stormed. 'Have you gone out of your mind?'

'Well, what the hell are you doing back anyway?' She threw the question at him, still avoiding his. 'You don't call for five days in a row then turn up on the doorstep.'

'Sorry to spoil your fun. I've just been airlifted out of a war zone by the UN. I thought you'd get a nice surprise!' he shouted.

'Oh.'

Don put his hands on his hips and squared up to her. He looked grey and exhausted, his black moleskin trousers were splashed with mud and his pale green shirt was stained, he hadn't shaved for days. But she saw only the man she loved most in the world and like a dreamer waking up to reality, she realized what a monumental mistake she had made.

'Your clothes are scattered all over the house, there's last night's candlelit dinner for two in the kitchen – am I going to get an explanation? And don't you dare lie to me.' She had never seen him so angry.

She hung her head, she couldn't face looking at him. 'Chris was here,' she said finally, 'We ... things got a bit ...' this was really hard. Fighting the lump in her throat, she said, 'I almost slept with him, but I changed my mind.'

Don turned his head towards the window and swallowed hard. He felt as if he had been kicked in the balls.

'Chris from work?' he asked.

'Yes,' she whispered.

Don folded his arms and kept his gaze fixed on the window.

There was a long silence. She looked up at him and was distraught to see that he was trying not to cry.

'It was a huge mistake,' she pleaded. 'I just felt lonely and unloved and unattractive and I thought you were sleeping with someone else and he seemed like the antidote. Don, I really miss you . . .' she broke off to choke down a sob. 'I miss the way we used to be.'

'Christ. I've got to get some sleep,' was his reply in a strained voice. He turned on his heel and walked out of the room. Bella could hear him take the stairs up to the attic. So he was going to sleep on the sofa up there. The hellishly uncomfortable sofa in that cold, unheated room.

She felt so sorry for him and so full of regret. For a moment she just wanted to howl, but then she decided not to give in to it.

She couldn't feel sorry for herself any longer, this was all her fault. She'd wanted the baby, she'd got pregnant without telling him, she was the one who hadn't been able to handle it all, she was the one who'd pushed Don away, read his mail, seduced Chris . . . JESUS. What a mess. She could hear Markie stirring in his room.

It was late afternoon before Don came downstairs. Bella had already tidied the house and taken Markie out to the park and the supermarket and come back home again. She was stacking the lunch dishes into the dishwasher and Markie was sitting in his high chair messing with the slop of food in front of him when Don came in.

'Hello,' Bella said.

Don didn't answer but bent over Markie in his chair. 'Hi there, little guy,' he said tenderly.

Markie stretched out his gooey hands towards him and Don looked touched.

'Are you eating yourself now? That's very clever.' He picked up Markie's spoon and scooped up a bit of the fruit purée.

'Bella. I've decided to move out for a bit,' he said as he guided the spoon into Markie's mouth.

Bella stood rooted to the spot.

'I think it will give us both some time to think things through and work out where we go from here,' he said.

'No, it will not give me time.' She was furious with him for this. 'It leaves me stuck with the baby 24 hours a day.'

'So, maybe you'll finally sort out some childcare,' he shot back.

'And just where are you planning to go?' she asked.

'To Mike's place, he's got a spare room, it's fine with him.'

How dare he sound so calm about this. 'How is moving to a bachelor pad with your mate going to solve our marital problems exactly?' she demanded.

'Well, maybe you should have thought of that before you shagged your boss,' was his furious reply. 'I don't think solving problems was top of your agenda last night, was it?'

'Well, it certainly solved a few problems,' she shouted back.

'And what's that supposed to mean?'

'Oh never mind . . . just walk out Don, just turn your back on me and on your son. Go on, just pack your bags and leave – I hope it makes you feel a whole lot better. You're just selfish and immature and totally unable to deal with any responsibility.'

'What about you?' he shouted back. Markie was staring at them without making a sound. 'You're such a control freak, you can't trust anyone else to take care of our son, yes *our* son . . . not even me . . . no-one else is good enough. What are you going to do, Bella? Look after him every single day until he's torn from your arms to go to school?'

'Just shut up!' she screamed. 'Just shut up and leave us alone.'

'I'll be back tomorrow afternoon to see him. You are not going to take him away from me, Bella.' Don's voice was more controlled and threatening now.

He turned out of the room and headed upstairs, leaving Bella to collapse into the chair beside Markie.

The baby was laughing now, this had all been a big dramatic show for him, not a frightening scene.

'I'm sorry,' she whispered to him, picking up the spoon and feeding him some more. 'I'm so sorry.' Tears were pricking her eyes but she didn't want to cry until Don was out of here.

Ten minutes later, she heard him in the hallway.

'Three p.m. tomorrow, you better let me see Markie or I warn you, Bella, I'm calling a solicitor,' he said loudly from the top of the kitchen stairs.

She didn't answer. The front door slammed shut heavily. Jesus Christ, how had it come to this? She picked her baby up out of his high chair and cuddled him close while her tears fell freely.

The day dragged on and on after that. Markie's routine – changing, feeding, walk, nap, changing, feeding, bath – meant she had to keep going but she felt as if she could break down hysterically at any moment.

God, she had to get out of here, out of this house where everything had gone so wrong. She had fucked everything up – her career, her marriage . . . and how would all this affect her son? She was probably going to fuck him up too. She slapped her hand against the wall, furious with herself.

She had to get out of here.

Markie was clean and fed, it was 7.30 p.m. so he was getting sleepy. She wrapped him up warmly in snowsuit and blankets and put him in the buggy with the raincover over. She put on her thick winter coat and they headed out.

The street was dark and slick with light rain, but glowing orange in the street lamps.

She walked to the end of the road and wondered what the hell to do. Go to a pub? Were babies allowed? Go somewhere in the car? Where? Where? Where? Christ, she felt on the brink of insanity. If she'd been on her own, she would race off in the car and drink herself to oblivion somewhere very chic and expensive. But she was stuck.

She found herself trudging off in the direction of Red's house, not sure if she really wanted to ring Red's bell at this time of night and dump all this on her. It wasn't like they even knew each other well.

But she didn't really know who else to turn to. Tania had never called to make up . . . Jenna was on the other side of the planet . . . Mel and Lucy wouldn't understand . . . Chris was a whole load of trouble. Jesus. And she never ran into anyone else now that she'd moved. Red was the only person she knew round here.

Christ, no wonder mothers ended up on Prozac and Valium. Did everyone think they'd vanished off the face of the planet just because they'd stopped working and hanging out in bars?

She was in Red's street. She looked down at Markie, who was mesmerized by the streetlights. He was wonderful now. The long, inexplicable screams had finally worn off and he was a giggly delight to have around with his boundless wonder at the world. The lights were on at Red's so she took a deep breath and rang the doorbell.

There was a long wait before Sandy answered the door.

'Hello,' he said with a hint of surprise in his voice.

'Hello,' she said. 'I know it's probably not a good time, I was just passing and wanted to say hello . . . is Red . . . I mean, if she's . . . ?'

'Come in, come in – it's always a good time.' Sandy cut her off.

'Red!' he bellowed from the door. 'It's Bella.'

Bella was just grateful he'd remembered her name.

416

Red called down from upstairs: 'Hello Bella! Sandy, come up and take over, will you?'

He bounded up the stairs and a few moments later Red came down, damp and dishevelled.

'Hi – rescued from bathtime – how nice!' she said, swooping down and kissing Bella on the cheek. 'Your hair looks fantastic, by the way.'

'Thanks,' said Bella. 'Just send me away if it's not a good time.'

'You're fine, let me take your coat, come in. Hello, Markie,' she said peering through the raincover.

Bella followed her into the kitchen, which was as cheerily chaotic as before.

'Tea, coffee or no, let's have wine,' Red smiled and held up an already opened bottle of white.

'Good idea.' Bella unstrapped Markie from the buggy and sat down, holding him on her knee. He immediately put out his hands to reach for the toy cars on the table.

'So, how've you been?' Red asked, bringing out glasses.

'Dreadful, couldn't be worse.' Bella said this with a sort of manic smile.

'Oh dear.' Red sat down and poured. 'What's happened?'

'I'm totally depressed, I've fucked up my career and slept with one of my bosses . . . well as good as . . . and now my husband's found out and left.' She had no idea why she was smiling at Red as she told her this.

'Ah,' Red took a deep sip of the wine. So did Bella.

'So . . .' Red said after a while, 'what are you going to do now?'

'Well, I was planning to wallow in self-pity for a bit,' Bella answered.

'No, you'll just get even more depressed. How bad is it on the husband front? Has he really gone? Or can you sort things out? I mean, do you want to sort things out?' Red asked.

'Yeah,' Bella said quietly, 'I really do. But I don't know what he's thinking.'

'When did all this happen?'

'Well, he left today,' Bella sighed and hoped she wasn't going to cry again.

'Oh boy,' said Red. 'You probably both need to cool down a bit.'

'Things just haven't been the same between us since Markie was born,' Bella said.

Red snorted: 'Of course they haven't. There's a big, crying, needy baby between you.' She smiled at Markie, who giggled back at her. 'Isn't there?' she said to him. 'You've got to adjust . . . it takes ages. I used to keep a bag packed under the bed all the time when Jamie was tiny, I was so fed up.' She laughed at the memory of it. 'And the one time I did actually run off to my mum's, she sent me straight back, bless her.'

'Red, I don't think I'm a very nice person,' Bella blurted out. 'I don't think I deserve Don, or Markie, or my brilliant career . . . well the one that I had.' She gave a half-smile, but now she really wanted to cry, or at least smoke.

'Oh boy,' Red topped up Bella's wine glass. 'Don't be ridiculous. You must have worked so hard to get your job and I know how well you've been looking after Markie. Now you just need to

418

turn your attention to Don and yourself. Be nice to yourself.'

'I don't know what there is to like about me.' Bella put her nose on top of her son's head and felt a tear slide down her face, she watched it glistening on top of Markie's hair.

'Bella!' Red was smiling warmly at her. 'When you first burst into that yoga class, you were this sort of infectious surge of energy and determination . . . and you're funny and lovely looking . . . everyone wants a piece of you. You're just a bit down and worn out. You need time and rest and a bit of inner peace, man.'

Bella smiled back at her, lump-in-the-throat grateful for this pep talk. 'I'm very glad I met you,' she said. 'You're so together.'

'Well, thanks but don't beat yourself up about it, it's taken me three years to sort the motherhood thing out . . . a bit . . .' Red drained the last of the wine into their glasses, then got up to look for another bottle.

'What do you really want to do next? Have you thought about it?' she asked.

'Yeah, endlessly,' Bella answered. 'It goes batting round and round my head. I know what I want, I just can't figure out how to get it – a part-time job which somehow pays more than my last one, and is going somewhere, really nice childcare for Markie . . . oh and I want him to sleep through the night and only breastfeed twice a day. Then I want Don back the way he was before we had Markie, but also a devoted father.' Bella gave a small laugh. 'Bit of a long list.'

419

'Not really,' said Red. 'Don probably doesn't want anything radically different – you back the way you were, working, more available to him, but also a devoted mother. Think of all you've been through as . . . adjusting.'

'But I don't know if he'll forgive me for what I've done,' said Bella.

'Was it a one-off, one night stand?' Red asked.

'Emmm . . . kind of. In my head it was,' Bella answered.

'Well, all you can do is try and explain that to Don.'

There was a pause.

'How long have you been married?' Bella asked.

'Oh for ever,' Red said. 'Six years now. And some things get easier and some get harder,' she added. 'Actually, I think being married and having kids is a lot like eating a healthy diet and going to the gym – you know it's really good for you, but sometimes it's completely dull and you can't be bothered.'

They both laughed at this.

'But it's really hard to get it all right,' Bella said. 'You just need to take your eye off the ball and the whole thing messes up.'

'Mmm,' Red nodded. 'And admit to me, before you were married, you had the lovely wedding fantasy, didn't you . . . You in the dress and flowers and the handsome man at the altar?'

Bella was smiling and nodding.

'Then,' Red continued, 'as soon as that ring was on your finger, I bet you started having the funeral fantasy? You know, the one where you're in a beautiful black suit with a hat and a veil and you're devastated but still young and . . . free!!'

Bella was open-mouthed, feigning indignation: '*Red!!* I can't believe I'm telling you this, but . . . *yes!*'

They collapsed into giggles.

'I suppose it's just human nature,' Bella said finally. 'That grass is greener feeling.'

'Count your blessings, child,' Red said, putting on a voice. 'That's what my mum always said and she had a point. Anyway,' she added, 'I can help with baby things. You can pump me for advice on that.'

So they talked weaning, sleeping through the night and childcare for a bit and Bella agreed to go and meet Red's childminder.

Sandy appeared at the door: 'Red, the babies want a night-night kiss from you.'

'OK.' She stood up. 'Have another glass of wine, Bella, I'll be down in a second.'

'No, it's OK,' Bella stood up as well. 'I've really got to go, get Markie to bed.' He was dozing, almost asleep in her arms.

'What time does he usually go?' Red asked.

'Eight-ish, so this is late for him.'

'OK, well I'm coming round at seven tomorrow so we can sort the sleeping problem out.'

'Oh God.'

'Trust me, I'm a mother!' Red laughed.

The three of them said their goodbyes and Bella headed home wishing she'd accepted Sandy's offer of a lift as the rain began to beat down heavily. She ran the final lap to the house, bouncing Markie about in his buggy. She was soaking wet and laughing when she got into the hallway and feeling much better for the evening out of the house.

When Markie was tucked up in bed, Bella tried to

call Don. She dialled his mobile number and it rang
for a few moments but then clicked onto voicemail.

'Don, hon, I'm really sorry,' she said. 'I love
you . . .' At a loss for anything else to add, she put
the receiver down.

Chapter Forty-two

Red's childminder Sylvia was lovely, as Bella found out when she went round the next day.

Ellie was already there, crawling after a squeaky ball, and Markie wriggled about in Bella's arms until she put him down on the floor, so he could try to crawl after it too.

Sylvia wanted two babies to look after, she said, because they could play together and keep each other company.

'I just want to do one or two mornings a week to start with,' Bella said, barely believing she would be able to do it, leave her son here with this woman who seemed nice but was still a stranger.

'We'll start gradually, that's no problem, you just arrange the hours and pay the hourly rate – then we'll all be happy, won't we?' Sylvia directed this question at Markie who was now up again bouncing happily on her knee. 'When do you want to start?' she asked with a smile.

'Errrr ... shall I bring him for two hours tomorrow and you can see how you get along,' Bella heard herself say ... thinking, Oh God, what am I doing?

'Yes, that's fine.'

When she left Sylvia's, Bella felt a euphoric sort of panic. Oh my God, could she handle this?

As she was lifting the buggy up the stairs to her front door, her mobile went off. She scrabbled to get it out of the changing bag, hoping it would be Don.

It was.

'Oh hon,' she said, fumbling to open the door without tipping Markie down the stairs. 'I'm really sorry. I'm really, really sorry . . .' She pushed the buggy into the hall and sat down on the floor.

'Look,' Don said, 'I'm phoning because I'm not going to be able to come today.'

'OK,' Bella said, dreading that this meant he didn't want to see her yet.

'My stupid, stupid fucking job,' he said angrily. 'I was supposed to get some leave, but I've now been given this piece of crap to chase down on the south coast for a couple of days.'

'Oh,' she said, feeling a crash of disappointment. He was going away again, they weren't going to see each other for days and they wouldn't be able to sort anything out.

'I'm still so angry with you,' Don added.

'I love you,' she said, 'I really love you, Don. I can't believe how stupid I've been.' She was close to tears now, he could hear it. 'I couldn't bear to lose you hon, please . . .'

He gave a long sigh, then said: 'I'm going to stay away till the weekend. I think we both need the time to calm down and think things through.'

'If it's what you want,' she said. 'But promise me you'll come at the weekend.'

'OK.'

'Tell me about Markie,' he said, changing tack, 'I really miss him.'

'He's gorgeous,' she said, trying to swallow down her tears. 'He's wearing an adorable red cardigan and woolly hat. He's sitting up in his buggy looking at me. His eyes are going to be dark like mine, I'm afraid.'

'That's nice,' said Don, 'I like dark eyes.'

'I wish he'd got yours, I like yours best,' she said. 'And his new favourite toy is the bunch of house keys which is a bit scary because I keep thinking he's going to drop them in a drain when we're out.'

'We should leave some spares with your friend round the corner.'

'You are so sensible!' she managed a slight laugh.

'Just because you're such a wild child,' he said.

'Don, please, I'm never going to do anything like that again.'

There was a pause before he said, 'OK, I have to go, Bella. I'll call you and I'll be there at the weekend.'

'Take care,' she said.

'Bye,' he answered simply.

She clicked off the phone and unloaded Markie from the buggy, carrying him down to the kitchen. She still couldn't really tell what her husband was thinking. He was still angry, but she took the 'I like dark eyes' comment as a good sign. God listen to me, I'm like some stupid teenager, she thought.

She had mixed feelings herself – she wanted Don back, no doubt about that, but the Don who'd bought out a flower stall for her, who'd rushed her to the register office in a passionate leap of faith, who'd held onto her when she was giving birth and willed her to survive.

At 7 p.m. on the dot that evening, Red arrived to help put Markie to bed without a breastfeed. She had assured Bella that it could be done and he would sleep much better for it. But Bella didn't believe her.

'Hello,' Red breezed in with a kiss and a clinking carrier bag. 'Essential supplies,' she explained.

'My God, I feel like I'm letting a witch into my house,' Bella joked nervously. 'Are you going to put a spell on my son?'

'No!' Red snorted, following her into the sitting room. 'Trust me, I absolutely promise this will work, every night from now on.'

She slapped her coat over the back of a chair and put her bag up on the coffee table, spotting a framed photo there.

'God, your dad is so young looking . . . doesn't he look handsome holding Markie!' she said.

Bella laughed out loud. 'You are about to be so embarrassed!'

'No!! It's not?'

Bella nodded vigorously. 'Oh yeah.'

'Well he's very good-looking, but . . . er . . . quite a bit older than you.'

'Thirteen years,' Bella answered. 'He went grey really young, but I think it's sexy, obviously I have a father complex or something.'

'Right . . .' Red put the photo down and emptied out her bag of goodies: 'For you – a choice of comfort aids: bottle of red, a bottle of white, a family

426

pack of Pringles and ten Marlboro Lights, because I suspect you smoke, am I right?'

Bella nodded.

'Also some lavender oil, to keep both of you calm and finally –' Red fished the last thing from her bag – 'this is for you, Markie.' She pulled out a little beige towelling bunny with long, dangly ears.

'Thank you.' Bella was really touched by all this.

Markie grabbed the bunny with his hands and giggled.

'OK, we've got bath, feed and story time to fit in before bed at eight on the dot. Lead the way,' Red told Bella.

After his bath, Markie was breastfed downstairs on the sofa with the TV on loud and the lights turned up to ensure he didn't fall asleep.

Finally, he'd eaten his fill and was looking dopily tired.

'Now take him upstairs,' commanded Red. 'Read him a nice little book on your knee, then dim the lights, lie him in his cot with his little bunny and say "Good night" really nicely and *leave* when he's still awake. *And no cheating.*'

'He'll just howl the house down and I won't be able to stand it,' Bella insisted.

'We will not leave him, I promise. Trust me.'

'OK, OK, I'll give it a go, but I'm giving in if it gets too awful.'

'OK.'

When Bella settled Markie down in the cot, he kicked off his blanket with a giggle, and looked wide awake again. But she stroked his little forehead and said 'Night, night,' then stepped out of the room, leaving the light on low.

There was silence for a moment, then a surprised cry.

By the time Bella got downstairs to Red, muffled roars were coming from the baby monitor in her hand.

'OK.' Red pulled out an alarm clock from her coat pocket and handed Bella a glass of wine.

'Sit down here for two minutes, we'll time it, two minutes, that's all. Then you can go to the door of Markie's room and tell him it's OK, you're just downstairs, then leave.'

'Right,' Bella said dubiously.

She gulped at her wine then went upstairs again and did exactly as she was told. Markie stopped crying for the few moments she was at the door but bellowed with renewed vigour when she left.

'Bloody hell,' she told Red when she got back down. 'Do you really expect him to fall asleep like this?'

'He will, trust me.' Bella urged her to finish her wine, poured her another glass and opened the crisps. 'OK,' she said. 'You've got to wait five minutes now.'

Bella didn't feel she could argue.

They sat for five minutes, Bella slugging back the wine, munching the crisps absent-mindedly and staring grimly at the monitor. The row of green and red lights rose and fell on the monitor, Markie was screaming his head off.

'OK,' Red said as the clock hand nudged towards the five-minute mark. 'Just do exactly the same again, poke your head round the door and speak to him, then leave.'

Bella was shocked when she saw Markie this

428

time, he was bright red and his hair was matted to his head with sweat. He looked furious and didn't stop screaming when he saw her. She spoke as soothingly as she could, then came down the stairs quickly.

'Are you sure he's going to be OK?' she asked Red anxiously. 'He looks really hot.'

'He'll be fine, now light up,' Red said proffering a cigarette. 'You've got to deal with the full ten-minute wait this time.'

'Oh Jeez.' Bella drew in a deep breath of smoke. She fixed her eyes on the alarm clock, which seemed to be standing absolutely still.

'You're sure this is working?'

'The clock? Of course!' Red answered.

Somewhere around minute seven, Markie's cries began to grow a little bit less desperate, then abruptly they stopped.

Bella looked at the monitor. She went out into the hall . . . silence. What!? He must be lying in his cot wondering what to do next to get her attention.

Red looked at her and smiled triumphantly.

'He's going to start up again in a second,' Bella told her.

'He is asleep, fast, sound asleep,' said Red. 'Believe me, if he had an ounce of strength left, he'd still be bawling at the top of his lungs.'

Bella turned the monitor up to full volume: she could hear the quiet rustle of her son's breath.

'I don't believe it!' she was astonished that her baby could actually go to sleep without being breastfed, rocked, walked, patted or soothed in some way.

'And I bet he doesn't wake up again till the

429

morning,' Red said. 'Because he's learned to fall asleep without you.'

'In one lesson?!'

'Well, it might take a few nights, we'll see,' Red replied. 'Tomorrow night, just do the same and soon you'll be able to put him down without a squeak.'

'OK.' Bella was still unconvinced. 'Can I go and check him?'

'No! He's fine . . . OK, you can go in five minutes. Meanwhile, let's not waste the wine,' Red answered.

They drank the best part of the two bottles and Bella smoked seven cigarettes. OOPS. But it was a laugh. It was a girlie laugh, well more a mummy laugh.

They talked organic baby milks, stopping breast-feeding, favourite purées and Bella felt at least some of her anxieties about Markie were allayed.

Then they got more personal and talked about themselves. The origin of Red's unique colouring was explained: she was part Polish, part English with a generous measure of Jamaican.

'So,' Red topped up their glasses. 'When did you meet Don? And how?'

Bella told her, reminding herself what a whirl-wind romance it had been.

'God, you two didn't hang about, did you?' was Red's verdict.

'We just knew it was right and that we were ready . . . I suppose,' Bella answered, then stumbled on, 'Everything has always been really full-on between us. What's happening now is weird. I just don't know what he's thinking.'

430

'I really hope you guys will be OK,' Red said.

'Hmmm.' Bella took a long drag on her cigarette and thought about her husband. She *had* to get herself together and get him back.

It was time for Red to go. As she slipped on her coat, she asked: 'So is Markie going to Sylvia's tomorrow?'

'Yes . . . I think so.' Bella still wasn't sure if she could bring herself to do it.

'We have to go out, to distract you, otherwise you'll just sit here worrying about him and phoning Sylvia up every ten minutes to listen for wailing in the background.'

'Yes, I suppose you're right. Don't you have work?'

'I can make an exception.'

'Where can we go in two hours?'

'We'll go to the shopping centre and the market down the road,' answered Red.

Bella raised her eyebrows. She couldn't see any reason to go there.

'Bella! You've obviously been far too snobbish to notice the good stuff there,' Red teased her. 'It will be fun, I'll meet you at Sylvia's when you drop Markie off.'

They were at the door now. 'OK,' said Bella, 'I'll see you there, 10 a.m. tomorrow. Thanks for tonight, Red,' Bella said and kissed her on the cheek.

'I'm glad to help, OK!' Red smiled.

Chapter Forty-three

The sound of crying woke Bella – as it had done for the past seven months. She opened her eyes and looked at daylight filtering in through the white curtains. Daylight?!! She leaned over to look at the clock – 7.26 a.m.! She was waking up from the first full night's sleep she'd had since her son was born. Apart from the incredible weight of the full breasts lying on top of her chest like bricks, it felt *amazing*!

She went through to Markie's room and bent down to pick him up out of his bed. He smiled and giggled at her, stretching up his chubby hands. She took him back to bed with her and they curled up together, Markie latching on ravenously to feed.

He gazed up at her with his brow furrowed and she just adored him. This was the only time he lay quiet in her arms now, he had grown into such a wriggly, inquisitive little thing. She would miss feeding him so much.

She spent the next two hours in a mild panic – breakfast, changing, dressing, packing one hundred assorted bits and pieces into Markie's bag, so that he wouldn't be without his favourite drink, snack, toy, whatever else she thought he needed to survive two whole hours at Sylvia's without her. She packed a sheet of paper into his bag with her home number, her mobile, her bleeper, Don's mobile, Don's work number. You're being ridiculous, she kept telling herself. *Relax*.

Finally, they were ready to go. She whizzed Markie, his buggy and the bulging changing bag out of the door and over to Sylvia's house.

Red was there waiting for her and Bella was able to hand Markie over without feeling too awful about it. She babbled out a torrent of instructions to Sylvia about drink times and nap times, despite her impression that Sylvia was listening but probably not going to worry about it too much.

'She thinks I'm totally neurotic, doesn't she?' Bella asked Red as they walked away from the house.

'And who could blame her?' Red teased, then added: 'Don't be too hard on yourself. You'll learn to let go bit by bit.'

Bella fumbled in her handbag for a cigarette. She lit up and inhaled.

'Feel better?' asked Red.

'Yes, a bit. Do you fancy a drive to the high street?'

'Well, it's more environmentally friendly to walk – but if you really want to . . .'

Red was very impressed with Bella's car.

'God! How come I've never noticed this outside your house before?'

They climbed in and Bella revved the engine up.

By the time Bella was parking dextrously in the shopping centre car park, Red was talking about work.

'Couldn't you go part time, or work from home . . . set up on your own like I did?'

'Well,' said Bella as they headed down the grimy staircase towards the shops, 'these things are all possibilities, I'm just trying to get my head round them.'

'OK,' said Bella as they got to the bottom and surveyed the scene: stalls selling limp vegetables, a tatty supermarket, a branch of Woolworth's and a discount jewellers. 'Where do you want to go?'

'We're heading for the café, but not until we've trawled round the amazing clothes shops. Follow me!'

Bella wondered what the hell Red could mean. All she could see were the crappy cheap chains with prices plastered on the windows. Red was making a beeline for one of them. 'You cannot be serious,' said Bella.

'Come on!' said Red.

Once they were in, Red scanned the racks like a pro. 'OK Bella, we are finally getting you out of your leggings and rugby shirt and propelling you into the twenty-first century.'

Bella was looking through the stuff and laughing. 'Sequined denim?? You can't make me do this!'

'Look, perfectly acceptable grey combat trousers . . . £8 on the sale rail . . . padded waistcoat £12, T-shirts, a fiver, customized jeans, denim skirt . . . black three-quarter sleeved shirt . . . blah, blah, blah. Bella you are going to come out of here a new woman . . . for less than 50 quid.'

They went to the changing room with armfuls of stuff.

'Oh my God, it's a size 16,' wailed Bella pulling on a remarkably close-fitting shirt.

'The sizes are wincey here,' Red said. 'That's how they save money – use less material.'

'Yeah that and child labour in third world countries.'

'No, this lot are OK. The stuff's mainly made in Morocco and Portugal.'

'OK, well, I'm leaving my social conscience at the door. How come your stomach is so flat already?' Bella asked, eyeing Red up in the long, narrow mirror installed presumably to make women think they looked long and narrow too.

'Gym twice a week. I've gone since Ellie was tiny,' came the smug reply.

'Ah! I remember the gym. I still have membership for the really poncey one, down in Belsize Park.'

'Well, go!' Red replied. 'If you don't go when you stop feeding, you'll be tying your tits up in a bow. They'll have a crèche, you know.'

'Yeah, I know, I just couldn't bear to leave him in there.'

'But you're getting over that, aren't you? Looks very good,' Red nodded at Bella in the sporty, grey trousers and a tight red long-sleeved T-shirt with a flower on the front.

'Is it mutton dressed as the proverbial?'

'No! It's Seattle fashion . . . downsized, home-worker, computer nerd. You've got to get some trainers.'

'What about this?' Red asked, modelling a

435

spray-on denim skirt embroidered with multi-coloured flowers. 'Hot off the catwalk. This is real designer diffusion . . . never mind DKNY, Emporio and all that . . . they're just trying to keep up. This stuff is knocked off and in the shops three days after the shows.'

'How do you know all this?' said Bella, trying on a fuzzy white zip-up jacket made of long curls of acrylic wool: 'Ha ha, look at this. Outrageous!' she laughed.

'This chain is my biggest client,' Red answered her.

'Really!'

'The chief exec made almost a million last year on bonuses alone.'

'Wow. Do you get a discount?' Bella joked.

She liked all the shiny anorak fabric stuff. She was thinking how wonderfully wipe clean it would be and went for it big time, deciding on a pair of beige trousers, the grey ones and a long black skirt, all in the same shiny, crackly stuff with drawstrings and plastic buckles.

Then she got three long-sleeved T-shirts with wild designs on the front and a short silvery grey anorak lined with fleece. Red made her buy an over the shoulder rucksacky thing, teasing her that a mock croc kelly bag just wouldn't go with her new outfits.

The total bill was less then a week's groceries, so Bella paid without any accompanying feelings of guilt.

'Boots next,' said Red, who'd bought a couple of tops.

They went to Boots and browsed about the make-up stands like schoolgirls.

'You can't buy red nail polish. It's the most boring shade in the world,' Red insisted.

'Well, I'm not buying green!' said Bella.

'Why not?'

'It's so teenage.'

'So? You're only late twenties, not 100. You don't need to wear camel and dress like your mother just yet.'

'Hmmm. Well what about silver grey? It will go with my anorak.'

'I think there's a daring side to your nature just waiting to be unearthed.'

'No, believe me, I've spent years trying to bury it.'

'Really! But you always look quite . . . conservative.'

'Yeah, fashion was never my thing, just recreational drugs and casual sex.'

'Maybe you should channel your need to shock into something a little less harmful.'

'Like green nail polish?'

'Try it!' Red laughed.

There was time for coffee in an organic, vegetarian, ceramic mug kind of place tucked round the back of the centre which no, Bella had never noticed before.

'I usually do Mothercare and the cute little baby shop, then I'm out of here.' Her face suddenly looked pained.

'Stop it,' said Red sipping her frothy coffee. 'You were thinking about Markie, weren't you?'

437

'Yes, but only because I haven't thought about him since we got here.'

'Good.'

'But I haven't even been to the baby shop,' Bella said, picking her phone out of her bag and double-checking for messages.

'They are fine,' Red said firmly.

And when Bella was back at Sylvia's house thirty-five minutes later, it was obvious that Red was right. Markie was fast asleep in his buggy and Ellie was playing with the baby Lego in the middle of the sitting room floor.

'He's been good as gold,' Sylvia told her.

Bella wheeled Markie home while Ellie stayed on with Sylvia because Red had gone home to do some work.

Work . . . Bella mused to herself as she pushed her sleeping baby along the road . . . work?? She couldn't deny she was a bit jealous of Red. She would be sitting in her little office, making calls, using all those cool, logical parts of her brain and earning *money*.

A whole massive part of the stress situation with Don would be eased if she was earning a good whack again. The overdraft was beyond maximum and realistically, if she didn't have a job very, very soon, they would have to put the house on the market. That thought instantly depressed her.

She got in, unzipped Markie's coat and loosened his hat, then left him to doze in the hall.

She took the bags from the morning's shopping trip upstairs and decided to cheer herself up with a quick try on. On went the long skirt, with the deep slit up the front, then she pulled on socks and her gym trainers and one of the new long-sleeved T-shirts. She put the silver anorak on top and laughed at herself in the mirror.

It was very different, but comfortable and kind of cool – she looked at her old clothes lying in a heap on the floor – why had she skulked about in that crap for so long?

Internet geek chic. She looked in the mirror and Red's comment about it being the ultimate diffusion fashion came to mind.

Diffusion, brand names for less . . . internet chic. She had the strange, exhilarating feeling that something was coming together in her head . . . then bing! The pieces slid into place and she had the most amazingly good idea.

'Oh my God!' she said out loud. 'That's it! That is it! Brilliant!'

She sat down on the bed and her thoughts raced. It was so good her hands were trembling and it could not wait. She picked up the phone and speed-dialled three.

A very familiar voice answered: 'Good afternoon, Prentice and Partners, Kitty speaking, how may I help you?'

'Kits!' she almost shouted.

'BELLA! Hello, how are you?' Kitty answered excitedly, then in a whisper added: 'What's happened Bella? No-one will tell me anything. I've just got to say you're unavailable for work right now.'

'You could have phoned!'

'Yeah, well, but I didn't want to impose.'

'*Impose*! I'm rattling round the house with a new baby staving off nervous breakdown central and

439

you're worried about imposing! Jesus, Kitty. What would the sisterhood say?'

'God, I'm sorry, Bella. I never thought about it like that.'

'Well . . .'

'Are you coming back?' Kitty cut in.

'We'll see. How is everyone anyway?'

'Good, same as usual, we've got a new girl and she's a total bitch, 24 or something.'

'Hector isn't a partner, is he?' Bella tried not to squeak.

'Oh God no, he got a written warning from Susan last week.'

'Really?' This was good. She suddenly realized how much she'd missed them and all the daily intrigue.

'How is Susan . . . and Chris?' Poor old Chris.

'Susan is pining for you, I think.' Kitty's voice was conspiratorially low. 'Chris is really quiet, maybe he's pining for you too!'

'I miss you all, as well,' said Bella, feeling a rush of guilt about Chris.

'How's your little son?' Kitty asked.

'Oh he's great. Anyway, I want to see Susan, but turn up kind of unannounced, when she's there and not seeing anyone else.'

'Well . . .' she could hear Kitty tapping her way through Susan's agenda, 'your best bet is early morning, Thursday or Friday.'

'OK, well I think Friday will be best. Will you ring me if anything changes and she's not available then?'

'Yeah sure. But *tell me* . . . what is this about?'

440

'I can't . . . not just yet. But I promise, you'll be the first to know if Susan goes for it.'

'Bella!'

'I have to go now. See you Friday.'

'OK, be like that then! Bye.'

'Bye.'

Bella took a deep breath and speed-dialled four. There was something else she really had to sort out as well. The ringing tone hummed in her ear, twice, three times, she could feel her resolve draining away, maybe this wasn't a good time . . . maybe she would leave this till the evening.

But then there was a brisk 'Hello?' at the other end.

'Hello Tania, it's Bella.'

'Bella?! God . . . hello!' There was a tiny pause, so Bella launched in.

'I'm really sorry I was so awful, Tania. I don't know why it's taken me so long to phone you back. I'm really sorry.'

'I'm sorry too,' Tania said. 'Oh I'm so glad you've phoned. I wanted to phone too. It's OK, we were both very stressed bunnies . . . you with the baby, me with Greg.'

'Greg? What happened?' Bella asked.

'I can't believe you don't know about all this,' Tania replied.

'About all what?'

'He's married.'

'*What!!!?*'

'Yup,' Tania continued. 'All those weekends with his parents and not wanting us to live together . . . turns out he's already got a wife and three kids.'

'Oh my God!' Bella was stunned, even she hadn't seen that one coming.

'Yeah, I found out . . . well it's a bloody long story. I was phoning you that night to tell you how suspicious I was.'

'Oh God,' Bella cut in, 'I'm so, so sorry. I thought I had the biggest problems in the world at the time and obviously I didn't.' Christ, she thought, that was months ago. How had Tania got through all this without her? She was so angry with herself that she hadn't been there, hadn't been the shoulder for her friend to cry on.

'How are you doing?' Bella asked.

'Not too bad. I was miserable as sin for weeks. But on the up side I lost about a stone, so I look good. I just worked like a demon, which kept me busy, and redecorated the flat . . . and bought a new car.'

'No! Not a . . .'

'A brand new, shiny red Ferrari.' Tania cut in.

'Cow!' said Bella then added sincerely, 'I can't believe you didn't phone me.'

'I couldn't handle it, Bella – there you are all married and happy and babied up and I'm starting out single *again*.'

'Oh yeah,' said Bella. 'It's been bliss all the way. I resigned from my job, Don and I are having a trial separation, we're practically broke, but thank God, thank God, my son is finally sleeping through the night.'

'*What*?' It was Tania's turn to be shocked.

'Yeah, it's this amazing thing where you put them in bed awake and they cry at first but then they fall asleep by themselves and . . .'

442

'Not the *baby*!' Tania was practically shrieking now. 'You and Don are separated??'

'Yeah, but hopefully not for long. It's been really, really stressful and I kind of slept with my boss but I hope he might forgive me . . .'

'What! Slow down, you're babbling, girl.'

'Do you have time for the whole thing?'

'Well if you could give me the short version now, then maybe we could meet on Saturday and you can tell me the full saga.'

After Bella's quick outlining of events, they arranged to meet on Saturday morning.

'At the gym please,' Bella said. 'I have to go back there, I still look like a blancmange.'

'Ha, ha, ha, ha – I'm slim and slinky,' sang Tania. 'It's role reversal time.'

'Double cow! What's the point in being friends with you if you're going to look better than me?' Bella said, delighted that she and Tania were straight back in best friend mode again.

'*Bitch*!' Tania shrieked. 'Get your flabby arse in gear. No wonder your man's looking elsewhere.'

'He's not!' Bella screamed down the phone. 'I'm the one who looked and I didn't like what I saw . . . well actually, it wasn't bad . . .'

'Bella! You are a mother now. You have to behave responsibly,' Tania said in mock-shock.

'I'm dying to see you,' Bella replied. 'Shall we say 10.30ish? We'll do a class, then sauna, then long lunch?' She was thinking, Four hours away from my son . . . I can cope, I will cope. Don can look after him . . . he can cope, he will cope . . .

'Perfect. I'll see you there.'

'Tania, I've really missed you,' Bella said.

'Me too,' Tania answered. 'Let's be best friends for ever and ever.'

'OK,' Bella laughed. 'See you Saturday.'

'Byeee.'

Chapter Forty-four

Don called at nine-ish as he had done every evening since he'd left the house. The calls were short and they mainly talked about Markie, who was a neutral, safe topic.

It was the third time she'd put Markie to bed without a breastfeed and he had only cried for seven and a half minutes.

'I'm sleeping like a dog,' she told Don. 'I go to bed at ten and don't wake up until Markie stirs at seven, it's just bliss. I feel like a normal, sane person again, it's amazing.'

'Are you still breastfeeding?'

'Yeah, three feeds a day, which is really nice for us.'

'Good, and the childminder is working out OK?'

'She's really lovely. She's going to take him for two full mornings tomorrow and Friday.'

'Wow, what have you got planned?'

'Totally top, top secret. I'll tell you about it on Saturday. You are going to come on Saturday, aren't you?'

'Yes,' he said and didn't elaborate.

'I'm planning to go to the gym in the morning to meet Tania, because I thought you'd want some time on your own with Markie and then hopefully he'll sleep in the afternoon and we'll be able to talk a bit.'

'That's fine, Bella,' he said, then added: 'You're going to the gym? To meet Tania? Well . . .' he'd been about to say 'you're almost back to your old self' but checked himself. There wasn't any going back, she was becoming her new self. Bella with baby. He wasn't sure how he fitted into that yet, but that was what they had to work out.

'Is that OK?' she asked, as he'd paused for a long time.

'It's fine, it's good. I really miss Markie,' he said. 'I can't wait to see him.'

'Yeah.' She decided not to add 'I really miss you' because if he didn't say it back, she would be heart-broken.

'OK,' he said. 'I better go then, good night, Bella.' She detected a vein of tenderness in those words which comforted her.

'Good night, hon.'

She clicked off the phone and wandered upstairs to see her son. She tiptoed into the room and looked at him in the dim glow of the night light. He was on his side with his hands curled up in front of him, he felt warm and slightly damp to touch, still sweaty from his little cry at bedtime.

His chubby cheeks were rosy and impossibly long eyelashes curled down onto them. She listened to his gentle breathing and leaned over to inhale his sweet, warm butter smell. He was perfect. She'd never felt anything like this, so full up with love. It was calming and grounding and heart-expanding.

Somehow, there was going to be room in her heart for all this baby love and for Don too and for loving her job and her friends and, she really should face it, her parents.

She'd thought at first that Markie was going to use up all her love and there wouldn't be any left for anyone else. But she was learning that Markie had opened up the floodgates. She'd made this incredible amount of extra love in her life for him and now she was going to spread it about. Soften up a bit . . . smell the roses . . . hug trees.

She could feel her eyes grow dim and watery again. I'm turning into a complete sap, she thought . . . and I quite like it.

She stroked her little boy on the head then left the room.

Downstairs, she threw together a quick supper, then went up into the attic office taking her laptop with her. She had the plan, now she needed to research it.

Three hours later, she finally went to bed, tired but very excited. This was going to work.

The next morning Bella drove into town once she had dropped Markie off at Sylvia's. If she was to face Susan tomorrow, she needed to psyche herself up for it. She was going to present a radical new plan so she felt it was fitting to have a radical new image to go with it.

Combat trousers and kaleidoscope tops were fine for home, but the new work look was going to have to be a little more sober.

No more tight skirts, high heels, stockings and cleavage. What did she have to prove? She was married with a baby, she knew she was attractive and damn good at her job. It was time to get on with it. She now wanted sleek, streamlined, professional. There was no reason for her office clothes to 'work' at a cocktail party any more either. Once she'd put in the hours, she was going home.

Anyway, she was online, she was on the phone – why the hell did she need to be at the office all day long?

She put the car into an underground garage and headed out onto Regent Street. It was early December, cold but blue-skied and crisp and not quite ten o'clock, so the shop doors were only just opening and the pavements were quiet.

An hour later, after careful consultation with a good shop assistant, Bella had found exactly the right thing: a long, lean, light grey trouser suit, which looked perfect with her shorter hair. She looked at her reflection in the mirror and couldn't believe how much younger and fitter she looked. The suit shoulders were narrow and unpadded, the jacket skimmed down to mid-thigh and the trousers were fluid without being wide.

Underneath, she had on a grey knitted silk sleeveless top, cut straight at the top. No more cleavage but bare arms instead, it was still sexy but in a kind of sporty way. She decided on the same top in bottle green as well.

Her new coat was a black nylon mac, knee length with a tartan lining. Now she decided on a new briefcase as well – shiny nylon black, big enough for a laptop, mobile, car keys and a few nappies – what else did anyone need?

The whole lot was wrapped up for her in glossy

blue bags. She handed over her card without flinching because as of tomorrow she was going to have a brand new job. She was sure of it.

Several shops later and she'd bought two new pairs of shoes, futuristic loafers in black and grey leather with low, trainer-like moulded rubber soles – cool.

Then came new make-up: sludgy green eye shadow, brownish lipstick. Then new underwear. She explained the still breastfeeding situation to the assistant, who suggested a grey jersey crop top sports bra and matching hot pants.

Bella looked at herself in the mirror and began to see the outline of the figure she'd once had. The breasts were still over-heavy, but the tummy was diminishing. She would get there.

It was already heading for 12.30, so she had time for a quick sandwich before she raced back to Sylvia's for 1.30.

She spent the afternoon playing with Markie, then after she'd given him supper, a bath and tucked him up in bed, she got down to work again.

Poor old Susan, she had no idea what was about to hit her.

Chapter Forty-five

It was time to go for it, Bella told herself, as she strode up to the elevator, which would take her to Prentice and Partners for the first time in five months.

She punched the button and the doors pinged open. Once she was inside, she could feel her hands shaking slightly so she tightened her grasp on her briefcase and tried to slow her breathing right down. This was going to work, there was no way it couldn't.

Ping. She was out on the fourth floor lobby, she walked towards the glass double doors and could see Kitty taking off her coat on the other side. Bella smiled and tried to relax. This was her office, this was her job. It was going to be OK.

She stepped in, it was 8.25 a.m. so just Kitty and Susan should be around.

'Hello,' she said to Kitty.

Kitty looked up and stared: 'My God, you look completely different!'

'But good,' said Bella.

'Yes, very good. Very *moderne*. Gimme a hug, it's lovely to see you.'

They hugged and kissed.

'Is she here?' Bella said this quietly; she didn't want to spoil Susan's surprise.

Kitty nodded and picked up the phone.

'Hi, Susan,' she said. 'There's an unscheduled visitor here for you . . . but I'm pretty sure you'll want to see her.'

After a momentary pause, Susan's office door opened.

For a few seconds, her face registered just surprise, then she smiled, half held out her arms and said, 'Bella, my God. Welcome back!'

'Hang on a minute,' Bella grinned. 'I've just walked in the door. I think we might need to talk first.'

'Yes, of course, come in.' Susan motioned with her arms, then added: 'Kitty, can you bring us some coffee, please? And hold all my calls. Come in, Bella.'

Bella hadn't known what to expect from Susan, but this was a very good start.

She walked into the small office and was surprised to see it had been revamped. There was a compact desk at the window now, with a tiny laptop and silver mobile phone on top and below it nested a small set of sleek chrome drawers on wheels. The room was mainly taken up by three vast brown leather armchairs grouped around a low coffee table.

'It's the new, we're all equals, touchy-feely, twenty-first-century thing, do you like it?' Susan asked, pointing her into a chair.

'It's fab,' said Bella, sitting down in the squashy leather and feeling very at ease in her new clothes. No skirt to ride too high, no uncomfortable heels to hoick up her knees at an awkward angle.

'You look great,' said Susan, perching in her chair because of her skirt and heels. 'I love your hair . . . and is that *green* nail polish?'

'Yeah . . . thanks,' said Bella. She was wondering if she should apologize first or if Susan was going to.

There was a pause as the two women looked at each other and smiled.

'About the way I left . . .' Bella began. 'I am sorry about it, but I think I had a point. I'm not saying I was right, but I was making a point which you should have taken on board.'

'I think that's fair,' Susan replied. 'I didn't want you to go, I'm sorry I reacted so strongly. I don't want you to go, in fact I'd love to have you back.'

'I really want to be back, Susan,' Bella said. 'But not in my old role, I've changed too much.'

Susan didn't say anything; she was waiting for Bella to explain.

'I can't put the job first the way I did before,' Bella continued. 'I think that might be quite hard for you to understand. I mean, I want to do a really good job for you, but I don't want to rule the universe the way I did before.' They smiled at each other. 'My son comes first. If there's ever a choice between work and baby, he's going to win. But that shouldn't mean I can't work.'

Bella looked hard at Susan to try and read her reaction, then carried on with her pitch: 'I'm a very capable person, I've got a lot of ability I know you can use for the hours in the week I'm willing to devote to work.'

Kitty knocked and came in with the coffee, which was perfect because Bella knew Susan was thinking hard about what she was about to suggest – and whatever scenario Susan was imagining, Bella knew her own plan would beat it right into the ground.

Kitty poured out two cups, saying, 'Nice shoes,' to Bella to break the silence.

'Thanks, they're my time management shoes,' Bella joked. 'Instead of going to the gym, I'm going to jog home from work.'

'So,' said Susan, once Kitty had closed the door, 'what have you got in mind?'

'I want to run the new Prentice and Partners internet arm.'

'Go on.' Susan's eyebrows were raised but she was listening.

'Your company is going to run the first on-line consultancy for small businesses. Turnover of less than 5 million a year.

'People will log on, answer a detailed questionnaire and get an initial plan of action back from us – for free. If they want more advice, they can have consultancy sessions on-line or over the phone at an agreed rate.

'It's designer diffusion, the Prentice brand off-the-peg for the small guys who really need it. Obviously you can sell advertising on the site to tons of linked financial services – banks, lenders, insurers etc., etc.'

'Goodness,' said Susan raising her coffee cup. 'Do you think it will make money?'

'I'm willing to bet it will make pots of money,' said Bella, hardly able to contain her enthusiasm for the scheme. 'You'll have to employ new staff to keep up with the demand. It's the mass market, Susan, tens of thousands of small hits a year instead of five big deals. It's also incredible advertising for you. You're going to look like the most forward-thinking company in the game.'

'But we're giving out advice for free.' Susan almost winced at the thought.

'I know, scary concept, but the whole lure is that you get something really good for nothing, so you pay for more. Anyway, the advertising will pay for all the people who log on for the free stuff and then disappear.'

'Have you got a business plan for this?' Susan asked.

'Of course,' said Bella with a smile. 'I'll e-mail you.'

Susan laughed, then asked, 'How are you going to have time to run it?'

'Well, I've got a minder for Markie four mornings a week, when I'll log on and do most of the work, from home mainly,' Bella said. 'Because that gives me an extra ninety minutes of time I'd otherwise spend in the car.

'I can log on again in the evenings to keep on top of it and I'll meet people here in the office when it's needed, which isn't going to be more than a couple of times a month.'

'You've got it all figured out,' said Susan with a smile. 'Why do I feel as if I'm going to have to let you have a go at this?'

'Well . . .' said Bella still smiling, 'it's either give

in or I take you to industrial tribunal for construc-tive dismissal during maternity leave.'

'Ouch . . . that would look bad . . . woman boss and everything.'

'Very bad,' Bella agreed.

'Bella, I'm really proud of you,' Susan said finally. 'You remind me of myself at your age, but I think you've made better choices.'

'Susan!' Bella cut in. 'You're running your own internationally successful company. That was a good call.'

'Yes, but I never had a child.'

Bella heard surprising regret in those words and realized this was the first time Susan had ever told her anything personal about herself.

'I kept putting it off for the next promotion, the next good job, the next big client and suddenly I'm 48 and it's not going to happen now,' Susan continued. 'And you know, on some level I'm quite glad, because I don't think I would have achieved all this with a family. But I'm sorry if I reacted badly to your pregnancy – I'm probably a bit hung up about the whole thing, a bit regretful for myself.'

'I'm sorry,' said Bella. 'We've been fed a whole lot of crap about careers and babies and I don't think you can have it all. You can have some of it, some of the time, if you're lucky and work really hard.'

'You see, you've made good choices,' Susan said, then added with a smile, 'But won't you miss walking into the big boys' offices and telling them it's OK, you're here to sort things out?'

'Ah well . . . probably a bit,' Bella replied. 'But I can always come back to that later. I'd really like to try and make this new idea work.'

'Who do you want to help you set it up?' asked Susan. 'Chris?'

'No. I think Chris and I had better stick to our separate empires for the moment. What about the new girl?'

'Milly? You've heard about her then?'

'Yeah. I'll meet her and see if we can get on. Hector . . . well,' Bella wanted to be ultra tactful. 'He's not my type.'

'I'm not sure if he's mine either,' Susan said. 'Hire someone new if you like, a computer nerd. We could soon need a bigger office,' she added, with what sounded suspiciously like enthusiasm.

'Maybe I'll get another mum who also wants her desk to be at home. Oh and I know this great American guy . . .' Bella suddenly remembered Mitch and wondered if he would take her call.

'Well you choose,' said Susan.

'Err, we haven't discussed . . .'

'Money?' said Susan putting her cup down.

'I'm working fewer hours, but I'm not working part time. I'm afraid this is not going to be a chance for you to slash my wages,' Bella said, trying to sound firm.

'Relax, this is a fantastic new venture,' Susan answered. 'I'll raise you by 20 per cent, make you a partner in our new internet arm and give you a 35 per cent profit share in that department.'

'Forty-five per cent,' Bella said straight away.

'You certainly haven't lost your balls, have you?' Susan replied. 'OK, forty.'

'Done.' Bella held out her hand and Susan shook it, then Bella jumped up from her seat and said 'Yeeeeeeees!' punching the air.

Susan, standing up too now, looked at her in disbelief but Bella clasped her in a hug. 'It's the new, touchy-feely, twenty-first-century thing, do you like it?' she giggled, squeezing Susan hard.

'Oh my God,' Susan gasped. 'Trousers, trainers . . . green nail varnish . . . you've gone completely mad.'

They both laughed, Bella feeling ridiculously happy. This was going to work, she was going to repay Susan a hundred times over for this chance.

'So, when do you want to start?' Susan asked.

'I'll come in and meet the new girl next week and work out if we need to hire someone else. Then I want a couple of months behind the scenes before we do the massive, pull out all the stops launch, say in February/March. Oh and I'm assuming I get the usual Christmas fortnight off . . .'

'OK,' said Susan, raising her eyebrows. 'I'll start paying you in a week's time then.'

'Yes please,' said Bella. 'Otherwise, I'll be repossessed.'

'You better keep in close touch,' Susan warned.

'I will. This is going to be fantastic, I'm really, really excited.'

'OK, keep your cool, I'll hear from you soon.'

They were standing beside Susan's door now.

'One other thing,' Bella added with a gleam in her eye.

'Ye-ees?' Susan was wary.

'I have to take you shopping, Susan, you need modernizing. You know the couture suit, padded shoulder, stiff hair thing . . . it's so over.' Bella crossed her fingers behind her back, hoping she hadn't gone too far.

But Susan burst into laughter. 'We'll see, Bella. Bring me in a bottle of the green nail polish . . . maybe I'll start there.'

Susan's mobile began to trill as Bella opened the door. 'Bye and thank you Susan, from the bottom of my heart and all that. You won't regret this.'

Susan had the phone in her hand and managed a quick 'I hope not! Bye,' before she answered with a brisk: 'Hello, Susan Prentice . . .'

Bella closed the door and was in the main office. It didn't look as if anyone else was in yet.

Kitty looked up: 'So, are you going to tell all? Are you back?'

'I'm kind of back in a week's time, but I can't tell you anything yet,' Bella grinned broadly.

'But you promised, you ratbag.'

'It's so exciting!'

'What the hell can be exciting enough about work to shout out yippeee like an idiot in front of Susan?'

'It wasn't yippeee it was yeeeees,' said Bella, adding, 'I like your outfit,' at Kitty's ripped camouflage trousers and neon orange plastic top.

'Oh my God. You must have had a nervous breakdown!'

'Something like that . . . but I'm starting to feel much better. Really good, in fact. I'll see you soon Kits, take care.' Bella was heading for the front door.

'You can't just go without telling me *anything*!' Kitty called after her.

'Oh yes I can.' Bella smiled mischievously.

When the lift pinged her out on the ground floor, Bella opened her briefcase and took out her packet of cigarettes.

458

She was shaking one out when she realized what she was doing. She was smoking to celebrate, but then she also smoked when she was depressed, she smoked when she was happy, she smoked when she was drinking, she smoked when she wasn't. Basically, she spent all day long giving herself excuses to smoke.

She crushed the lid closed, crumpling the three cigarettes which were jutting out of the packet and tossed the lot into the bin beside the main door. Then she strode out of the office, enjoying the long, comfortable strides she could take in her trousers and flat shoes.

Chapter Forty-six

Bella and Markie were still sitting at the kitchen table over breakfast on Saturday morning when she heard the front door opening upstairs.

Don called out: 'Hello, it's me,' in the hallway and Bella ran up the stairs to meet him.

She bounded up and flung her arms round him, kissing him on the lips without worrying about whether she should or not.

'Blimey,' he said, pulling back from her. 'You look . . . extraordinary.'

'Extraordinary good . . . or extraordinary bad?' she asked as he held her at arm's length and clocked the trainers, rustling grey nylon trousers and tight pink and silver top with flared sleeves.

'Good, good . . . I think. I like it, I'm getting used to it . . . You look very sexy,' he said finally and couldn't help pulling her in for another kiss.

'And the hair?!' he said suddenly. 'When did you do that?'

'Weeks ago, but you've been too angry to notice,' she answered.

'It looks great,' he said, deciding not to get into the 'why I was angry' discussion just yet.

They were interrupted by impatient squawks from the kitchen.

'He's in his high chair,' Bella explained, so they both went downstairs. She noticed Don didn't have his bags with him and felt a lurch of disappointment, but what did she really expect – that he could have forgiven and forgotten what had happened just six days ago?

Don headed straight for Markie and plucked him out of his chair in an easy movement, swinging him into the air.

'Hello, how's my big boy?' he said, beaming. 'You've got so big, in just a week.'

Markie giggled, stretched out with his hands and landed a long trail of drool on Don's face.

'Teething,' said Bella as Don brought the baby down quickly with a 'Yeurgh,' and wiped his face with his hand. 'Tea?' she asked. 'Toast? We're just finishing up.'

'Yeah, that would be great. I came early because I thought Markie might need time to get used to me again and . . . Mike probably wants the place to himself for the day.'

'Yeah,' said Bella. The moving back question hung in the air, but neither of them dared to touch it just yet.

'How is Mike?' she asked. She liked Don's news editor.

'He's well, he's going to retire,' Don answered.

'Really? He's only 50-odd, isn't he?'

'Fifty-six, but it's a hard job, plus ex-wife number

two is back in Scotland with the kids, so he's thinking about moving up there because he never sees them.'

Don had spent most of his evenings this week listening to an over-stressed, late-middle-aged man spilling out his regret at having always put his career before his family. The irony of the situation had not been lost on him.

'Anyway, how've you been?' Don settled into a chair with his son bouncing on his knee, trying to pull off his glasses.

'Good,' said Bella. 'Very good, bought some new clothes, got a lovely childminder, Markie's sleeping through the night, got a new job – busy week.' She turned to pour boiling water into the teapot, so Don couldn't see her smiling.

'Bloody hell,' said Don 'New job?!!' He paused, waiting for an explanation.

Bella brought the teapot and cups to the table, saying: 'OK, sit tight and I'll tell you the whole thing.'

So she did, starting all the way back at the cheap shop with the diffused clothes for computer geeks.

He listened intently with growing admiration.

'So,' she said when she'd finished, 'Pretty good huh? So I'll now be earning more than you but working less. Is that a turn-on or what?' she joked but then quickly carried on talking because she couldn't bear for him not to answer. 'Now, I really have to go or I'm going to be late, Markie's food is in the fridge all anally labelled with when you feed it to him and how much, etc. etc. . . . Have loads of fun. I've got the mobile for any panics.' She kissed them in turn, picked up her gym bag and hurried

462

to the door, before she could change her mind about leaving Markie in the care of his dad for a whole morning.

Don was left speechless and a bit awed by her exiting whirlwind.

Once the front door slammed, Markie looked up at him and said: 'Da, da,' quite distinctly and Don was surprised to feel tears prick the back of his eyes.

'Hello Markie,' he said gently. 'I love you.' He hugged the tiny boy close.

Right, he thought to himself, time for a walk in the park. Where was Markie's snowsuit? And sling thing? And shoes, did he wear shoes? Should he pack a snack, when did Markie next expect some food? How come he didn't know any of these things?? He'd been a useless git, but that was going to change.

'OK son,' he said and patted the baby's head. 'time for a stroll. Hello there, this is your dad talking. The one who's going to teach you about cars, football, girls, keeping a clean bat . . . that sort of thing.'

Markie turned his big head and blinked; he looked a bit like a baby owl thought Don, but he was cute . . . And he's mine, he thought with a strangely joyous swell of pride.

Bella was just climbing out of her car in the gym's car park when an outrageously bright red Ferrari pulled up not far away.

'Hello darling!' Tania called out of the open window.

'Bloody hell! It's lovely!' shouted Bella as she walked towards the car. Both women were grinning at each other.

'Urban grunge?' Tania shouted back. 'God, Bella, I never thought you'd go for that. A silver anorak!!?'

'It's comfortable and cheap,' Bella countered. 'Anyway, get out of the car, let's see the new you.'

Tania threw open the door and stepped out in high-heeled ankle boots, tight black leather trousers and a tiny red sweater. She had huge sunglasses perched on top of her head.

'Oh my God!' Bella exclaimed. 'It's Liz Hurley.'

'I'm much younger than her!' Tania said in mock horror.

'Of course you are, anyone can see that.'

'Come here,' Bella held out her arms.

They hugged and Bella said, 'I love you.'

'Yeuck,' said Tania breaking away. 'My friend has been kidnapped by aliens and replaced with an American teenager.'

'Shut up, you're so uptight,' Bella laughed. 'Let's go work out.'

'I bet you've given up smoking as well,' Tania said as they headed up the gym steps.

'Yup,' Bella answered.

'Will you stop talking like that? What's happened to you, have you been on-line too long?'

'Yup . . . and it's going to get worse,' she hinted.

After an hour and a half of hard effort, they decided to collapse in the sauna together.

'Has it been really rough?' Bella asked her friend as they lay back in the heat.

'Yeah, it has really,' Tania answered. 'I felt so betrayed and so furious . . . furious with him and furious with myself for being so *stupid*. When I think about it now . . . it just seems so obvious. I mean, I wasn't misreading the signs, Bella, I was walking past massive billboards which spelled it out and turning my head the other way. Jesus. But you know, after two weeks of hysterical sobbing, smoking, insomnia and unrelenting grief, normal break-up rules had to apply.'

'You threw everything out?'

'Yup and sold the jewellery and tore up the photos and erased his numbers from all my files and changed the locks and did everything just right.'

'I'm so proud of you,' said Bella. 'Have you had transition man sex yet.'

'Yeah, actually,' Tania laughed.

'And was it the best ever?'

'Yeah, but I cried in the morning.'

'Well, men who don't make you cry in the morning are hard to find,' Bella said and thought about her husband.

'And how are things with Don?' Tania asked, guessing why she'd started staring off into the distance.

'I think they're going to be OK. I hope so. I really love him and if I've screwed this up, it won't just be me who suffers, but Markie as well,' she answered.

'Oh God.' Tania sat up and looked at her friend. 'I'm sorry, Bella. You'll just have to tell him, you know, how you made a big mistake.'

'Yeah ... very big mistake.'

'I'm sorry I haven't been around.'

'Me too,' said Bella. 'But I'm sort of glad we fell out though, because we've never done that before and it really, really used to bug me that I couldn't say what I thought in case we argued.'

'What! You want to fall out again?'

'No, I just know now that if we do, we'll get over it, but a bit quicker next time! I mean, if we don't argue, we're just sociable acquaintances, we're not really blood, gut and tears friends, are we?'

'So what have you been longing to say to me all this time?' Tania dared her.

'Oh loads of stuff!'

'Well go on then.'

'You're kidding, you really want to hear this?' Bella grinned.

'Bring it on out, if you think you're hard enough,' Tania teased.

'All right then . . . I thought Greg was really boring and you deserved someone better.'

'OK,' Tania said.

'And I think you sometimes act like too much of a ditz when you're actually a really smart, really great person.'

Tania smiled.

'And I'm so jealous you have a lovely brother . . . and a fantastic mum and dad who gave you enough money to start up your own business and buy a flat . . . and you're obsessed with fashion, which is tedious . . . but you know what annoys me the most, you never think you look good in anything, that drives me up the wall . . . Please stop me now,' Bella laughed. 'See? I could have let this out gradually over the years but now it's all gushing out in one colossal friendship-destroying tidal wave.'

'*Bitch*!' Tania said in mock horror: 'What about you!? Ms Smug Smarty Pants Perfect, you're so good at picking out people's faults and bossing them around, you do it for a living.'

'A damn good one,' Bella interrupted.

'Shut up, this is my rant! And you think your dress taste is so spot on, when in fact it's just really boring . . .'

'Hey, what about the silver anorak!'

'And how dare you get married first and have a baby first and always get every man you've ever wanted just by flaunting your cleavage and dropping your knickers. I hope you've learned your lesson this time, Bella.'

'Ouch,' Bella said soberly.

'And . . . and I was so jealous of you and Daniel at university,' Tania blurted out.

'*Daniel*!!' This was news. 'You can't be jealous of Daniel, we were together for three and a half years, we were a couple, we were in love!'

'Of course I can be jealous. He was so lovely and played Hamlet and let's face it, every girl in the place wanted him and I still can't believe you got him.'

'Oh God, you can't be jealous? We hung out with you all the time, don't tell me you were pining away for him because you weren't! And anyway aren't you forgetting all the trauma at the end of that?'

'You left him,' Tania said, as if Bella needed to be reminded.

'But he cheated.'

'But he wanted you to forgive him Bella, just like you want Don to forgive you.'

'Jesus,' Bella felt irrationally angry, 'it was nothing like this.'

'If I ask you something, do you promise to answer truthfully?' Tania said, after a pause.

'No,' said Bella sulkily.

'Well, I'm asking anyway. Do you love Don as much as you loved Daniel?'

'No,' Bella said without hesitation.

'Oh my God!' Tania was shocked.

'I'm a grown-up now,' Bella said calmly. 'I loved Daniel unconditionally. It wasn't very good for either of us. I think Don and I are better at treading that line between dependence and independence,' she tried to explain. 'Between us it's: "I love you, I want to be with you, but treat me badly and I'll . . . reconsider".' It was hard to say that because she knew Don was reconsidering right now . . . knew she had been reconsidering in the weeks before the night with Chris.

'So why did you play away with someone else then?' Tania was not treading lightly today.

Bella hugged her knees up to her chest and rested her face on them: 'Christ I don't know, because I could . . . because he was there.'

'What's that?' Tania asked. 'The Mount Everest defence, "because it was there" – that's just bloody stupid.'

They both started to giggle, then laugh, then became quite hysterical.

'Come on,' said Tania finally. 'We've got to get out of here, it's so bloody hot, we've probably got heatstroke.'

They had a quick lunch together because Bella was starting to fret about Markie and when they kissed goodbye, Tania wished her good luck and promised her everything was going to be OK.

Bella wished she could be so sure; she felt horribly anxious and stirred up.

When she got back to the house, she opened the

front door as quietly as she could. If Markie was asleep, she didn't want to wake him, so she tiptoed in.

She could hear a football match on in the sitting room, and Don making the odd comment: 'Nice one' and 'You must be joking!'

She looked in to see Don lying full-length across the sofa with Markie propped up against his chest. They were both engrossed in the match. It was just heart-wringingly cute.

'Hello,' she said from the door, and when the two heads swivelled round, she momentarily wondered which face to look at first. She shot a quick smile at Don, then beamed at her little son who was laughing and holding out his arms for her.

'Hi darling, how are you? Would you like a cuddle?'

'Yes, please,' said Don.

She laughed and ran over to pick Markie up. Don clicked off the TV with a 'Rubbish game anyway,' and sat up.

'How's it been?' she asked, cuddling Markie against her and noticing that Don was wearing a different top.

'Good, fine mainly. Don't go into the bathroom just yet, I haven't had a chance to clean up.'

Bella raised her eyebrows.

'I took him out in his sling thing and when we got back, well, there was a severe nappy overflow. My God . . .' Don began to laugh, 'there was crap everywhere, all over Markie, all over the sling, all over me.'

Bella gave a snort: 'Yup, it's a learning curve.'

'But, you know, we've had a nice time. He's a

really great little guy. I love the way he flaps his arms when he's excited, which is about three times a minute.' Don smiled.

'Has he had a nap?' she asked.

'He nodded off for about ten minutes in the sling, but woke up when we came back in, so not really,' he answered.

'OK,' she said. 'Let's take you upstairs for a nice feed and a snooze.' She kissed Markie on his chubby cheeks.

'Can I come?' asked Don.

'If you like,' she said, surprised by the request.

In the bedroom, Bella lay down on the bed. Propped up on the mound of pillows she turned onto her side, lifted her top, unzipped her bra and snuggled Markie up close against her full breasts.

Don lay down on the bed behind her and leaned on his elbow so he could watch.

Markie took her nipple in his mouth and began to tug hard, his jaw working up and down. She waited a few moments for the warm, tingling rush of milk and saw Markie close his eyes in bliss as it arrived.

A trickle of milk ran out down the side of his chin.

Don's head moved to rest on her shoulder, so he could watch the little face pressed close against the soft, creamy mound of skin. He felt a gush of love and lust.

As Markie sucked hard against her, Bella felt the distinct connection between nipples and clitoris that made breastfeeding such a pleasure.

Don's warm breath was against her neck and she longed for him. He smelled of unfamiliar soap and clean laundry. He shifted slightly so he was closer

470

against her and his keys and pocketful of change jangled as he moved.

She curved her back so she was pressed against him and he kissed her neck. She shivered and let her eyes close, so he kissed gently again.

Markie had stopped sucking, so Bella moved to loosen her other breast and put it into the drowsy baby's mouth. He began to suck again slowly and Don placed small, soft kisses on her neck and licked at her with his warm tongue.

He laid his hand on the curve of her waist then stroked down her side. She was overwhelmingly happy to feel a hard erection against her.

Don moved a hand to the waistband of her trousers and pulled open the drawstring. Then he felt his way down to her wet, swollen clitoris.

She parted her lips with a sigh as he made contact. Her baby was still sucking hard on her nipple and Don was moving his finger slowly up and down between her legs. It felt blissfully good.

She felt wet and slippery and desperate for him as he slid one finger inside her.

'Is this allowed?' she whispered urgently.

'I don't know,' Don whispered back . . . 'Shall we wait until he's asleep?'

'He's nearly there,' she whispered.

She heard Don unzip his trousers and she felt his warm, hard dick press against her buttocks.

Markie's mouth slid off her nipple and she could see he was sound asleep. She moved him slightly away from her on the bed, then rushed to pull off her trousers.

Don grasped her hips in his hands, pulled her back onto his cock and pushed inside.

471

He kissed the back of her neck, keeping one damp hand against her clitoris and moving strongly inside her.

'Oh God,' she gasped. 'I'm going to come really quickly.'

'Me too,' he said. 'Is it OK?'

She knew it wasn't really but she couldn't bear to have him pull out the condom box and realize there was one less in there than last time.

'Yeah,' she gasped and felt the warm rush and shuddering of her own approaching orgasm. He thrust strongly through it and she came, trickling breast milk, just before his long sigh of pleasure.

They were sweaty and sated and he threw his arm round her and pressed his face into the back of her neck. 'Oh, that was nice,' he whispered.

'Yeah,' she answered and they lay still for a few moments with him gradually shrinking inside her.

When he had pulled out, she turned around to face him. 'Don?' She looked into his eyes and tried to read the answer to this question before she asked it: 'Do you still love me?'

He placed a hand on her cheek and answered, 'Yeah, of course.'

'What about you?' he asked. 'Do you love me?'

'Yes,' she answered.

'But don't think I wasn't angry,' he added. 'Christ, I was furious . . . but I've come to the conclusion that I can forgive *a little* infidelity here,' his finger brushed her pubic bone, 'so long as there is none here,' he pressed his finger to her breastbone.

'I'm so sorry. You're the one, and I know that now,' she whispered.

'Do you want to be married to me?' he asked.

'I do,' she said.

'Do you want to bring up a baby with me?'

'I do.'

'Will you try and keep me unto yourself, forsaking all others?'

'God yes.' She blinked and a tear slid down her nose and hung on the end.

He licked it off.

'I'm sorry I wasn't more help with Markie,' he said. 'It all got a bit much for you. I'm going to do a lot more, be around a lot more. I'm booking some holiday, for a start.'

She hugged her arms round his back and pushed her wet face into his shoulder: 'I'm sorry I didn't think about you . . . I was so wrapped up in the baby and losing my job and everything . . .' She began to cry against him, 'I love you, Markie loves you too. I promise I'll be so good if you take me back.'

'Bella, it's OK,' he soothed. 'It's not a question of taking you back. I never imagined it working out any other way.'

'I love you,' she said again.

'I love you too,' he answered.

'Are you going to move back in today?' she asked.

'Yeah, my things are in the car but . . .'

'Oh dear . . .' she said. '"But" doesn't sound good.'

'I've probably got another two-week foreign coming up very soon. I'm so sorry, I've already said I'll do it, but I promise, I'm taking two weeks off at Christmas.'

'What do you think about going to Italy for Christmas?' she said, surprising herself.

He was taken aback too. 'Don't your parents live there?!' he asked.

'Yeeees . . . I'm not suggesting we go and stay with them for a fortnight. But I think we should visit.'

'OK,' said Don. 'This is something of a breakthrough.'

She didn't say anything more about it, just smiled at him. They stayed cuddled up on the bed together, not speaking, for a long time.

Finally Bella sat up and said: 'I'm starving, shall we go and make bacon sandwiches?'

'Fantastic,' he said. 'Are you going to put Markie in his cot?'

She looked at him with her eyebrows raised.

'Here, why don't I try?' he added quickly. 'Just don't blame me if he wakes up.'

'But it'll be your fault!!'

Chapter Forty-seven

Bella was ensconced in her little attic office where she had been working hard since Markie went to Sylvia's at 8.45 a.m.

She liked the bright yellow eyrie a lot more now. She'd put in new shelves, a filing cabinet, a desk and chair and a cappuccino maker. Once she closed the door at the top of the stairs, she found it easy to forget about her baby and the rest of the house and slip straight into work mode.

Prentice had given her a spanking new computer with all the bits and a tiny silver mobile just like Susan's. Bella had been amused when everything had arrived in boxes labelled 'Bella's Baby'.

She was concentrating hard on the proposals up on the screen in front of her, when a sharp ring at the doorbell startled her.

Oh God! She really could not cope with another Jehovah's Witness, meter reader or carpet shampoo salesman. She stayed put in her chair, hoping they would go away. There was another long, loud ring. Bugger. She closed the file and stomped down the two flights of stairs.

She turned the catch, swung the door open and saw Don, tired, crumpled, with a large bag over his shoulder.

'Hello gorgeous,' he said with a big grin. 'I've lost my keys.'

'Hello!!' she cried. 'I didn't think you were back till this evening.' They hugged and kissed hard on the doorstep. She hadn't seen him for two weeks and she'd missed him like hell.

'Nice coat,' she said as he stepped inside. She laid her cheek on his shoulder and smelled his neck, then kissed it.

'Yeah, my wife gave it to me. Don't tell her I've come here to see you first.' He grinned and they kissed mouth to mouth again.

'You look really tired. D'you want to go downstairs and have coffee?' she asked.

'No, no, I'm fine. Markie isn't here then?'

'No, he's at Sylvia's until one. How was the trip?'

'Bloody awful, but never mind, it was my last one.' He gave her a teasing smile and twined his hands behind her waist.

'What?' She pulled back to look at him.

'Well . . . I've got something to tell you . . .' he paused, enjoying the suspense. 'I've just been made news editor.'

'No!!' She was really shocked now. 'You're kidding!!'

'I'm not.' Don looked very pleased with himself. 'I just heard this morning. I told them I wasn't going to do it because the hours are so long, so they came back with an even better offer and said I could do four days a week, starting in January.'

'My God! Are you happy?' she asked, somewhat needlessly.

'I'm bloody thrilled,' he said with a smile.

'No more foreigns, though . . .' she said, sure he would miss them.

But he surprised her by saying 'Thank fuck for that!' with a laugh.

'Well, congratulations. Four days a week – that's amazing.'

'So . . .' he said 'What about you?'

'Well . . . I've got some news too actually.' She locked her eyes onto his, very intently. 'It's going to shock you a bit.' She sounded nervous and he started to feel nervous too.

'I've just found out I'm pregnant again. By complete accident, and that's true this time,' she added.

'Oh my God!' he gasped, then put his arms around her. Resting his chin on her shoulder, he let out a low whistle and said, 'God, Bella.'

'It must have been that Saturday. I was so glad you were back . . . I didn't really think about . . .'

'Oh yes,' he cut in. 'That was very hot.' He looked at her tenderly. 'It's a sign,' he smiled. 'We're meant to be.'

She hugged him close. 'Thank you Don,' she whispered and felt tears well up.

'God,' he said again and wiped her cheeks with his thumb. 'Everything's going to be OK, I promise . . . and I definitely need the coffee now.'

As they walked across the hall to the kitchen stairs, she suddenly stopped him to ask with a smile, 'Just a minute . . . has any news editor you've ever known stayed married?'

'No, but I see that as a challenge,' he answered, smiling back.

'And are you going to be earning more than me now?'

'Just a tiny, tiny bit more, I think. But no bonuses . . . so . . .'

'So that's all right then!!' She laughed and turned him round so she could kiss him on the mouth.

'Mmmm . . .' she said. 'Just you, me, a hallway . . . it's like old times.'

'Just what exactly do you have in mind, Mrs McCartney?'

Unbuttoning his coat and letting it fall on the floor, she answered, 'Why don't I just show you, Mr Browning?'

THE END

DID THE EARTH MOVE?
Carmen Reid

Meet Eve: 4 kids, 1 hectic job, 2 complicated exes and a lot on her mind.

Like, is sex with **the vet** better than no sex at all?

Is she too old to shop at **Topshop** or dye her hair pink?

Are **violets** the new geraniums?

What the hell is in the **fridge** for summer?

And, most important of all, has she let the **love of her life** get away too easily?

Did the Earth Move? is a sexy, thought-provoking and wildly entertaining novel from the bestselling author of *Three in a Bed*.

'Full of love, hope and a dash of sadness. A great summer read'
Sunday Mirror

A fabulous read. A sexy read. A Carmen Reid.

9780552155809

CORGI BOOKS

THE PERSONAL SHOPPER
Carmen Reid

Meet Annie Valentine: stylish, savvy, multi-tasker extraordinaire.

As a personal shopper in a swanky London fashion emporium, Annie can re-style and re-invent her clients from head to toe. In fact, this super-skilled dresser can be relied on to solve everyone's problems … except her own.

Although she's busy being a single mum to stroppy teen Lana and painfully shy Owen, there's a gap in Annie's wardrobe, sorry, life, for a new man. But finding the perfect partner is turning out to be so much trickier than finding the perfect pair of shoes.

Can she source a genuine classic? A lifelong investment? Will she end up with someone from the sale rail, who'll have to be returned? Or maybe, just maybe, there'll be someone new in this season who could be the one …

A fabulous read. A sexy read. A Carmen Reid.

'If you love shopping as much as you love a great read, try this. Wonderful!'
Katie Fforde

9780552154819

CORGI BOOKS

Far from the Tree

Also by DeBerry Grant and available
from Bantam Books

Tryin' to Sleep in the Bed You Made

FAR FROM THE TREE

DeBerry Grant

BANTAM BOOKS

LONDON · NEW YORK · TORONTO · SYDNEY · AUCKLAND

FAR FROM THE TREE
A BANTAM BOOK: 0 553 81333 1

First publication in Great Britain

PRINTING HISTORY
Bantam Books edition published 2001

1 3 5 7 9 10 8 6 4 2

Set in 10.5/12pt Plantin by
Phoenix Typesetting, Ilkley, West Yorkshire

Bantam Books are published by Transworld Publishers,
61–63 Uxbridge Road, London W5 5SA,
a division of The Random House Group Ltd,
in Australia by Random House Australia (Pty) Ltd,
20 Alfred Street, Milsons Point, Sydney, NSW 2061, Australia,
in New Zealand by Random House New Zealand Ltd,
18 Poland Road, Glenfield, Auckland 10, New Zealand
and in South Africa by Random House (Pty) Ltd,
Endulini, 5a Jubilee Road, Parktown 2193, South Africa.

Reproduced, printed and bound in Great Britain by
Cox & Wyman Ltd, Reading, Berks.

To the memory of Emma Clatin Hammond, Emma Horne DeBerry, and Emma Williams Cameron, our grandmothers – the roots that nourished our tree

WE GRATEFULLY ACKNOWLEDGE

Hiram L. Bell III: Thank you for lettin' me be myself again . . . and again. – D.G.

Robert L. Gore, Jr, for thirty years of friendship and encouragement, and for never letting me forget how blessed I am, and The Good Doctor, for your persistence. Without it I would have missed much. – VDB.

Lisa A. Nicholas, M.D., for assistance with our medical questions.

Anthony Cofrancesco for his help with information about the Buffalo Public Schools.

Lisa Quarles for her take on being a young, struggling performer.

Andrea Cirillo for her encouragement and advice (XOXOXO).

Jennifer Enderlin for letting us take our time.

Always, Gloria Hammond Frye, Juanita Cameron DeBerry, and the late John L. DeBerry II for the right stuff.

Alexis, Lauren and Jordan, Brian, Christine and Arielle, the future.

And all our family members and friends whose continuous love and support is surely the grace of the Creator at work.

PROLOGUE

'. . . dwellin' on the past won't change
nothin' now.'

Wish I never heard of Prosper, North Carolina! Odella
Womack sucked on her bottom lip and stifled the sob
that rippled just below the surface. She held a smoky
blue taffeta dress in her arms, hugged it like she hoped
it would hug her back as she tried to shake the flashes
of that night in the house on Little Pond Road. The
night that haunted her days and robbed her of sleep.
*Ain't nobody ever gon' make me come back to this no-
'count town!*

The floorboards creaked, and Odella shivered as
she paced the narrow space between her cot and the
storeroom shelves. A naked lightbulb hanging from
the ceiling cast harsh, hot light on the cluttered room.
She could taste the thick hot smell of coffee, old
onions, and fried everything – porgies, chicken, pork
chops, and hair – that passed for air in the rickety,
narrow building shared by Pal's Kitchen and Lucille's
Beauty Parlor. But she couldn't complain. *If Hambone
and Lucille hadn't let me stay here, after . . . after . . . I
don't know what I woulda done.*

Odella could still feel Henry's spit sting her face
with each bitter word he'd spewed. *'I'll get you, gal.'*

9

Her half brother had skinned his lip back against his teeth and snarled like a cornered, rabid dog. '*You won't know when, but I'll kill you, and Will too, if I have to. You understand me?*'

Still clutching the dress, Odella sank to the bed and rocked herself. *It's gon' be awright.* She buried her face in the iridescent fabric and caught a whiff of Lester's sweet, musky cologne. Without meaning to she started to hum her part of the harmony they had sung so well together, let the music soothe her for a minute, then suddenly she tossed the dress aside like it burned her to touch it. *What the hell am I singin' about? Lyin' son of a . . .* She turned away, determined to stomp out that fire before it flared up again. *Dreamin' ain't got me nothin' but trouble. I gotta be strong . . . like Mama was.* Odella stood, steadied her rubbery legs. *And dwellin' on the past won't change nothin' now.*

'You almost ready, Odella? Car's all packed up 'cept for your bag.' It was ten till dawn, but Will sounded wide awake and raring to go. 'You know we supposed to be at the justice of the peace by eight o'clock.'

I gotta stop this foolishness. 'In a minute!' she called. And with a sigh that said good-bye, Odella hurriedly folded the dress around her shattered feelings and dropped it in the butterscotch leather valise, beside the rag doll her mother had given her so long ago. She ran fingers over the doll's woolly black hair, almost pulled it out of the bag, but stopped. *What do I need with a toy?! I'm about to be Mrs Odella Frazier.*

That name sounded so strange, like it couldn't possibly belong to her. Odella had never put her name with Will's before, but she'd tried on Lester's

10

many times. It had even tickled her when Lester tacked his first name onto hers and gave her a stage name because he said all hit singers had made-up names. Now, Odella refused to look at the home-made pasteboard sign that was stuck in the pocket of the suitcase lid, but she saw it in her mind's eye any-way: 'Sat'day Nite Only. Johnny DuPree. Featuring Della Lester.' Those words used to make her heart fly. *We goin' all the way to the top. That's what Lester used to say.*

Odella shook her head to clear her thoughts. *And it wasn't nothin' but a bunch a mess.* 'Odella – No – Della – Della Frazier. Mrs Will Frazier.' She said it aloud, as if to convince herself, because that's how it was going to be. *A new name for a new start.*

Odella didn't know how long she'd been staring into the suitcase, but she jumped when one fat tear-drop plopped on the bodice of the dress, then another. *How'm I gon' marry this man? I can't even make a biscuit!* Odella wiped her face with the heel of her hand, then closed up the bag and shoved it under the cot because she wouldn't be needing the things that belonged to her old life anymore.

Will's a good man. Strong. Honest. Takes care of things . . . like Papa. Odella rolled her white cotton night-gown and put it in her battered blue suitcase, closed it up, and sat it by the door. *Will saved me – twice now.* She straightened the seams of her stockings and stepped into her gray tweed skirt. She used to get up in the middle of the night to rub the silver fox collar of the jacket that went with it. The suit had been a gift from Lester, and she thought twice about wearing it to marry Will but it was the best-looking outfit she had. It made her feel grown. *Grown enough for this?*

11

At eighteen, Odella had seen enough to make her feel older – some days. Brown as bourbon, she was near tall as most men, with long lean legs, which she happened to think were her best feature. Nobody ever called her mannish, but pretty didn't fit either. She had a strong, square jaw and eyes that turned down at the corners, just a little, making her look sad sometimes, even if she wasn't. But her face came alive when she sang. People were startled when she opened her mouth, and a voice pure as rain and strong as a hurricane filled the room. Odella was imposing, more mountain than foothill, more river than stream; she wasn't the ribbon or the bow or the pretty wrapping paper. Odella was the whole package, she just didn't know it.

'You ain't gone and chickened out, have you?' Hambone called to her from the kitchen on the other side of the dingy flowered curtain where he was getting ready for the first morning customers at Pal's.

'I ain't studyin' you, Hambone!' She propped her hand mirror on the shelf against the red and black Luzianne coffee cans, stooped down and combed through the tight rows of hard curls Lucille had put in last night with her smallest curling iron, so they'd last. They had pretended like it was a regular hairdresser visit so neither one had to face good-bye.

For the weeks Odella had stayed in the storeroom, she'd watched Lucille and Hambone like a hawk. They seemed to be as different as day and a potato, but every spare moment they'd be huddled up together, talking, laughing, acting like they preferred each other's company to anybody else in the world. *That's just how Will and me are gon' be.* She put on her jacket, buttoned it to the top, but didn't allow

12

herself to fondle the dense, soft fur this time.

I know me and Will gon' have a better life than the one we'd have in this town! 'I'm ready!' A deep sigh escaped as Odella picked up the blue suitcase, pushed open the curtain, and walked through the doorway.

1

'You can't cut your dresses by my pattern.'

'Ma?!' Ronnie leaned against the blue Formica counter and shuffled the hodgepodge of dishes in the cabinet. 'Where's my mug?' Even though she'd been away for years, there was something about being in the kitchen at home that made her sound like she was nine years old. She looked over her shoulder at her mother.

Della sat at the dinette table, head in hand, staring into her lukewarm cup of coffee like she was searching for something she'd misplaced a long time ago.

Ma is really out of it. Ronnie had been torn up since she got the call about her Daddy – and getting through this long, sad day had sucked her dry. In between her own tears and grief, she wondered how her mother could act so calm. *Not that she ever goes to pieces. Ma's just strong, I guess.* Ronnie stretched to reach the top shelf and tugged at her little bit of skirt, trying to keep her butt covered. 'You know the one, Ma, with the Esso tiger on it?'

Della's expression never changed.

'You mean the Exxon tiger? I haven't seen that cup since . . . maybe since before I left for college, Aunt

15

Ronnie.' Niki left the bag of garbage she was tying and opened another cabinet to look.

'There are a hundred mugs here!' Celeste backed against the swinging door and came in toting an armload of platters and serving bowls. 'Use one of them!' Her tone was sharp as barbed wire. She set the stack on the counter and examined a gold-rimmed plate. 'Humph! Friends call themselves helping you, but these are still greasy, Mother.' She looked across the room for an acknowledgment, but Della stayed in her own world.

'Do you mind if I drink *my* tea out of the cup I want to?' Ronnie slid a foil-wrapped pound cake, a stack of paper plates, and a shrink-wrapped fruit basket out of the way and hoisted herself up on the counter. 'You know that mug has been my favorite ever since . . .' Ronnie's voice caught in her throat. '. . . Ever since Daddy brought it home.'

'Daddy died five days ago and you just showed up yesterday, so don't come telling me about how much some cup means to you!' Celeste rolled up her sleeves, dropped her pearls inside her blouse.

'You haven't seen your sister in a long time, Ma.' Niki spoke in a hush as she stepped between her mother and her aunt. 'Maybe you don't want to argue . . .'

'I do not need you to tell me what I want, Nicole. Maybe *you* could finish taking out the garbage some time tonight!'

Niki just barely turned her head before she rolled her eyes. 'Right, Ma!'

'And you might sit on kitchen counters in New York, but we don't do that here!' Celeste reached in the pantry and snatched the apron.

16

Ronnie crossed her legs defiantly.

'Fine. Sit there. But I have work to do.' Celeste turned the hot water on full force. 'Of course, helping out would be of no interest to you.'

'Get over yourself,' Ronnie barked, then jumped down from the counter. 'This has been a hard day, and I'm exhausted . . .'

'Exhausted?!' Celeste gripped the sink with both hands to keep from throwing the plates at her sister. 'You flew in here yesterday like the queen bee, acting like everybody was supposed to stop what they were doing and buzz around you.'

'I did not!'

'You have no idea what we've been through this week! All the planning, the arrangements. Funerals don't just happen!' Celeste took aim and launched a laser beam of anger. 'And where were you?'

'I got here as soon as I could!' Ronnie's red-rimmed eyes filled with tears.

'Don't start that again!' Celeste snapped.

The bickering finally penetrated Della's haze. She left her long-ago memories of leaving Prosper at the bottom of her coffee cup and looked up at her daughters.

'You don't understand,' Ronnie sniffled. 'I didn't see him for so long, and now . . .'

'Whose fault is that? Nobody stopped you from visiting,' Celeste snapped. 'You barely call. We could all be dead . . .'

'Celeste!' Della fired a warning shot.

'I'm sorry, but it's the truth.' Celeste planted her hands on her narrow hips.

'That's a lie,' Ronnie sputtered.

'That's enough!' Della's look could have cut glass.

17

'I . . . I couldn't get here any sooner,' Ronnie whimpered.

'Why not? Your father died! Is your so-called *acting* career more important than that?!' Celeste demanded, then sucked her teeth, turned around, and attacked a platter with a soapy sponge. 'You might fool other people into thinking you're the dutiful daughter, but I know better!'

'Aw right, both of y'all.' Della rubbed her thumb over the chip in her coffee cup. 'Everybody's had enough today. The dishes can wait. I'm not plannin' for company tomorrow.'

'It won't take me long. You never know who might stop by.' Celeste put the wet platter in the dish rack and picked up a bowl.

'I said leave 'em.'

'Fine.' Celeste wiped her hands on her apron. 'I'll go put the folding chairs away.'

Della watched her first born storm out of the kitchen. *As headstrong as she ever was!*

The morning she realized she was pregnant, Della awoke to the tippy-tap of sleet against the windows. It was still dark, and the heat wasn't up good when she rolled out of bed to fix Will's breakfast and his lunch bucket. She lit the oven, popped open a canister of ready-made biscuits. That's when she felt the tickle that started deep inside. At first she felt foolish, wanting to laugh for no good reason. And then she knew.

Will was almost done eating when she told him. He stopped, the syrup dripping from his biscuit, and gave her the biggest, silliest grin she'd ever seen on his face. There was plenty of food in the house, but that night he came in with an armload of groceries

18

because he wanted to make sure his babies ate good.

Della stayed happy the whole nine months, and no matter what people said about carrying high or low, or whether she craved salt or sweet, she knew this was a girl, her daughter. The only thing that would have made her happier was if her own mother could have been there with her, crocheting baby blankets, telling her what it would be like.

Contrary to the horror stories about labor she'd heard from young mothers on the Michigan Avenue bus and grandmas in the Broadway Market, Celeste came into the world in a rush that was over only five hours after it started. However, the bliss ended not long after the baby came. Della was expecting a pudgy, brown cherub, but Celeste was that pinky-beige newborn shade, bald as a cue ball, and all spindly arms and legs. She was almost scared to hold her child, but when the nurse laid daughter in mother's arms, Della felt her heart swell with a new kind of love. As soon as they got home, though, the colic started. No matter what formula Della tried, Celeste puked it up. Her piercing, vibrating cries made Della feel frazzled, but the doctor assured her nothing was wrong; some babies were just fussy. So Della would walk the floor with her, bouncing, singing, whatever she thought of to make it better, but mostly Celeste cried until she fell asleep. By then Della would be exhausted, but she'd put Celeste down on the bed and lie next to her so she could feel her warmth, inhale that baby-sweet scent, play with her fingers and toes, and pray for her to grow out of this difficult stage. But colic led to teething, earaches, and colds, all of which kept Celeste cranky.

As a toddler Celeste didn't care much for cuddling.

She'd squirm out of her mother's hugs, push away from her kisses. Della craved more, and what made it even harder was that Celeste was the spitting image of Della's mother, Annie. Celeste turned out to be that red-brown that people say comes from Indian blood in the family. She had Annie's delicate build, petite, with slim, long hands and feet. Her face was wide at the forehead and cheeks, tapering to a point at her chin, and she had a slow, sweet smile that could catch you off guard when she revealed it. A sliver of brow framed deep-set, old folks eyes. Della always thought she was too serious to be a child. She'd sit at the table, drawing, with a crayon tightly clenched in her fingers, her forehead furrowed, her mouth tense with attention. Della knew Celeste wore that same expression now.

'Grandma, did you see the hat Miz Godfrey had on at church this morning?' Niki wanted to neutralize the atmosphere. 'I think some sparrow is still looking for home.' She tied up the trash bag.

'I bet she got that at Dixie Hats about 1962.' Della swallowed a gulp of cold coffee.

Ronnie blew her nose on a paper towel. 'At least she took it off when she got here. Y'all need to tell her straw is not a fall fashion accessory.' Hands still shaky, she took a cup and saucer from the cabinet and turned on the burner under the kettle.

'Katherine wears that hat to everything, weddin's, christenin's, funerals . . .' The word echoed off the sunflowered wallpaper and hung awkwardly in the air.

This time last week, nobody dreamed there'd be a funeral for Will Frazier, least of all Will. He loved to brag about his full head of hair, and he'd happily compare biceps with 'knuckleheads young enough to

20

be my *grand*kids.' But Della had buried her husband over at Forest Lawn today.

Nobody could get over how awful it was, him being electrocuted, of all things, working on one of the rentals he bought and maintained so proudly for years. There were whole blocks in the Fruit Belt that still held on to their dignity because Will and Della owned houses there. Shorty Mayo, his handyman and right arm, was so broken up he cried until Della gave in and had the funeral procession drive past the fourteen doubles Will had acquired through the years. Shorty swore Will would rest better that way.

When they got to Buffalo in the fall of 'fifty-seven, Will and Della rented the lower half of a tiny, gray frame house on Emslie Street and stepped on the first rung of the neighborhood ladder. A German family had the upper, and Della and Will had a good laugh about how in Prosper you had to go clear across town to see White people. Right away Will got a good-paying job at the steel plant, and within the year he had saved up enough to buy the house. Almost immediately the Steinbachs moved. Living in the same house was okay, but paying rent to a colored man was another story. Will shrugged it off, mentioned the vacancy at the plant, and easily found new renters. Every year he added a new property, and after three he moved the family up a step to a white clapboard single with forest green trim and a wide front porch on Chester Street in Cold Springs. Whenever he wasn't shoveling coal at the plant, Will was tinkering on one of those houses, painting, repairing, putting out folks who didn't pay or who thought that since they gave him their money order by the fifteenth, most of the time, they had the right to tear up the place.

Ten years in he finally moved his family to the house he'd been driving by to visit ever since he saw a Black family go in the front door. Hamlin Park was a solid middle-class community, home to doctors, teachers, preachers, assembly-line workers, and undertakers. Had been for years. Hard work was the price of admission. Magnificent elms, oaks, and maples lined the sidewalks and made the substantial brick and wood homes look elegant. Nobody had peeling paint or raggedy curtains at the windows. Front and back lawns were carefully mowed and weeded on Saturday mornings, rows of boxy hedges marked property lines, and driveways led to two-car garages. Will bought it from his dentist when he moved to North Buffalo. The Craftsman-style house had a mustard-colored brick front and a roof that swooped dramatically over the porch. Will used to tease the girls that he would take them up there in the winter and teach them how to ski. The mirrored basement had a wet bar, red leatherette banquettes, and a pool table, and Will swore it looked better than half the watering holes he frequented on Friday nights. Celeste and Ronnie had their own rooms and a swing set out back. There was a sewing room for Della, and Will finished the attic, added a bathroom, and made the top floor his office. And whenever he came up the walk and put his key in the door he felt proud. This was a long way from his family's rented shack in Prosper, North Carolina.

After twenty years, Will figured he'd left enough sweat by the coke oven and retired to manage his empire full-time. Even though he still worked hard, there was no time clock, no blistering heat, and nobody on his back. It had been that way for the last twenty-four years and would have continued if a faulty ground wire and a puddle on the floor hadn't changed everything.

Ronnie stopped pushing cans of cling peaches and soup around another shelf and looked at her mother. 'I swear I got here as soon as I could, Ma.' Celeste always knew the fastest way to make Ronnie feel like two cents' worth of nothing, even if she didn't show it. Tonight was no exception.

'I know you did. Ain't no need to talk this into the ground.' Della absentmindedly flicked crumbs off the bust of the green flowered duster she'd stuck on after visitors had gone.

'Okay, Mamacita.' Ronnie doused a tea bag with hot water. When she got home yesterday she was shocked by how much older her mother looked. The sprinkling of gray at Della's hairline had sprouted into a fuzzy ring around her face, and she moved slower than she used to. Ronnie piped up before the silence was too thick. 'Where's the honey? Somebody told me it wouldn't collect on my hips as fast as sugar.' She flipped the hair of her dark auburn human-hair fall, the one she trimmed herself so it hung straight down her back and the bangs dusted her brows à la super-model. She wore it when she hadn't quite made it to the hairdresser to get her extensions tightened. Hands on hips, she flashed a honey-dripping smile and batted her eyelashes. 'Girls my age have to work to keep it together, you know.'

'Girls your age. Ain't that nothin'.' Della mashed stray cracker crumbs off the table with her middle finger and sprinkled them in an empty plate.

'Sugar or honey, makes no dif. It all goes to the same place.' Niki still had on the tangerine knit dress she

23

had worn because her granddaddy liked it so much. She had worn it for her graduation from Cornell, and he said it made her stand out in the crowd, like she should. Her mother didn't see it as an appropriate tribute, and they were still only half speaking.

'I knew it sounded too good to be true.' Ronnie squeezed her tea bag against the spoon, flopped it in the sink, then looked up at Niki. 'And I can't believe I'm getting nutrition advice from you. Look at you. I swear you were just a little pipsqueak, but I haven't seen you in . . .'

'Four years.' Della knew exactly. Ronnie had been scarce ever since she first left home right after high school, and over the last seventeen years her visits had gotten fewer and farther between.

'It can't be, can it?' Ronnie shook her head, looked off for a moment. She couldn't believe it had been that long since she'd seen her dad, and now . . . 'And now you're bigger than me.' She turned back to Niki. 'And got the nerve to be managing a hotel restaurant. I'm scared a you.'

'Assistant manager, and it's just the café, not the caviar and wine list restaurant.'

'Well, I'm proud. Doin' your thing, movin' to Atlanta. I know your mother had a cow when you told her that.' Ronnie continued her cabinet search.

'A cow? How 'bout the herd!' Niki set the trash bag by the back door, listened for approaching footsteps. 'You should hear her.' One hand on her hip, she waved the other back and forth, underscoring her words. '"Why do you want to live all the way down there? Restaurants? Any fool can work in a restaurant! You're smart, Nicole. You should apply to law school.

24

At least get your M.B.A." Blah, blah, blah. She won't give it a rest.'

'That's my sister, Celeste the Magnificent, all-seeing, all-knowing.' Ronnie plunked the remaining half of a five-pound sack of sugar on the counter and fished behind the boxes of cake mix and chocolate pudding. 'You made it through the worst of it. How bad can she annoy you a thousand miles away?'

Niki pulled a new garbage bag from the box, flapped it open, and lined the can. 'Yeah, but I'm afraid I've got something to tell her that's gonna fire her up again.' She paused. She wasn't planning to bring this up, but now she could feel the question marks aimed at her. Besides, these seemed calmer waters to test. She sighed, dropped her voice. 'I want to quit my job and go to culinary school. I want to be a chef.'

'Oh shi–oot. Is that all?! What's wrong with that? It's in the same field.' Ronnie opened the refrigerator and examined the bottles on the door.

'You don't get it. To my mother I'm a *manager*. At least she can tell people I'm in charge and that I'm planning to run a major international hotel conglomerate someday. A chef? I might as well tell her I'm flipping burgers.'

'Move and let me find this honey before you have the whole kitchen upside down.' Della planted her fists on the table, lifted herself out of the seat, and shuffled slowly across the room. Her big toe had poked through her panty hose.

Ronnie rested her hands on Niki's shoulders. 'It's your life. If it makes you happy, she'll have to fix herself to deal with it.'

Della could hardly keep from grinning. 'Umph. Look who's givin' advice.'

'They won't have to pay for it.' Niki had had this conversation a hundred times in her head, knew all the arguments. 'I'll work part-time and . . .'

'Don't sweat this, Nik. Celeste did what she wanted. She can't run you too. Isn't that right, Moms?'

'You can't cut your dresses by my pattern. That's how some folks used to put it.' Della stopped in front of Niki, hesitated a beat. 'Your great-grandma was a cook. Best for miles around.'

Where did that come from? Ronnie cocked her head to one side. 'How come you never told me that?'

'There's a lot you don't know.'

Ronnie arched one eyebrow. 'So what happened with you? The cooking gene skipped a generation?'

'Girl, move on out the way. If I got any honey, it'll be here.' Della shifted jars of garlic salt, onion powder, and other seasonings on the shelf above the sink. 'And if it skipped one generation, it sure skipped two.'

'Mama, you have hurt my feelings.'

'Wasn't the first time, and it won't be the last.' Della finally found the sticky jar and handed it to Ronnie. 'I don't know when I *have* used this.' Most of the thick sap had crystallized.

Ronnie held it in her fingertips, draped the other arm over Della's shoulder. 'No offense, but you couldn't even pass this off on a bee.' They all laughed.

And in the darkened kitchen window, Della caught the reflection of three generations, all variations on a theme.

Tall like her father and the tawny gold of a lioness,

Niki's microbraids shot back from the arrowhead of a widow's peak that made her slug several classmates when she was seven 'cause she got sick of them calling her Eddie Munster. To the disappointment of her mother, Niki had preferred soccer to ballet lessons. Even now, she got up at dawn most mornings and ran, just to feel herself slice through the wind, the sweat trickling down her back. It made her feel strong and free. As lively, eager, and flighty as twenty-three ought to be, what was gospel today might be history tomorrow, but Niki was ready to be baptized in life. Not a sprinkling on the forehead baptism, but full immersion, drenched with experience.

Della was amazed by how much her granddaughter had matured in the few months she'd been on her own and working. Her brown eyes seemed keener, more alive, her lips riper. It seemed only a little while ago that Niki had been sitting in the middle of the kitchen floor, playing with the pots and pans she dragged out of the cupboard. Now she was a woman. *Not as grown as she thinks, but you can't tell nobody that. Nobody could tell me. Ronnie either.*

Ronnie had always bobbed when other people weaved and somehow made it work. She came into the world two weeks late and after forty-six hours of labor, presented her butt first. She stopped wailing the moment she laid her eyes on Della and grinned, gummy and drooling, as if to say, 'Now wasn't I worth it?' And Della, exhausted, sweaty, and sore, grinned back. From the time she was four, when she asked Santa for a credit card and said she'd take care of the rest, Della knew her baby girl was two steps ahead of her and everybody else. Ronnie – because by first grade she'd stopped answering to Veronica – was smart, fearless, and funny, a taxing combination from a mother's point of view, but some days Della marveled that she had given birth to such a wonder.

And when Ronnie announced that right after high school she was going to New York to be a model and an actress, she made you believe it was undisputed truth. She'd been building up to it all along. Right from her debut as an angel in the Sunday school Christmas pageant, Della knew her child was hooked on the charge that only applause gives you. Sure, Ronnie was young, but some flowers bloom in spring, and although Della couldn't tell her how to make it happen, she was sure Ronnie would find her way. And she did. Della just worried sometimes if what Ronnie found was really what she'd been looking for.

Ronnie's legs seemed to start at her armpits, so she looked long, but she was only middling tall. And just like Della, there wasn't much meat on those pins. Della said she didn't sit still long enough for the weight to catch up with her, but by the time Ronnie was thirteen she had enough curve in her sweaters and swerve in her skirts to cause men who had known her from baby booties to sneak a peek. Ronnie was the spicy brown of nutmeg with smooth, clear skin and a face that couldn't help but say what was on her mind. Her dark eyes slanted up at the corners, accentuated by the sharp angle of her cheekbones and by keen, arching brows. She had her father's square chin and his plush lips.

But she always had my tongue. Della looked away when it came to her own reflection. For the last twenty years she'd watched the face looking back in the mirror morph into someone unrecognizable to herself. Someone with creases and droopy jowls, low-slung breasts, jiggly upper arms, and too much belly. Now she felt stumpy and dumpy. *And who's lookin', anyway?*

'Mother, where are your slippers?' Celeste charged back into the room and zeroed in on her mother's stocking feet.

'I need some air.' Niki grabbed the garbage and headed out the back door.

'My feet are fine. Now there's somethin' I wanna do, while it's on my mind. Both of you go on and sit down before you get into it again.' Della led the way to the table. Ronnie motioned Celeste ahead with a hand flourish, which Celeste answered with sucked teeth, but she grudgingly went first. They sat on opposite sides of their mother.

Della reached in her housecoat pocket and brought out two frayed blue savings bank passbooks. She pulled off a stray thread, twirled it in her fingers, looked at her daughters. 'I remember when your father opened these. You were around nine and fourteen, I guess. Just old enough to start gettin' in your own messes, he said.' She chuckled to herself. 'He was big on makin' sure there was money tucked aside for hard times. He wanted to make sure you had a little cushion too.'

'Daddy was always lookin' out for us.' There was a hitch in Ronnie's voice. She held her mug tight to steady her hands.

Celeste fingered her pearls and cast a wary eye on her sister.

'Yeah, he sure was puddin' when it came to the two of you.' Della handed them each a bankbook. 'Anyway, you never did get yourselves in trouble. Leastways none you told us about. You've been grown

29

for a long time now, so I figure you can hold on to your own rainy day stash, or do what you want with it.'

Celeste laid hers on the table, covered it with her palms, and bit the inside of her cheek to stay composed. She'd done it so often over the past few days that it was raw.

Ronnie quickly opened the cover. It was a joint account, she and her father. She turned the pages until she found the last entry, May 23, 1984. The balance came to $10,367.54. She closed it, held it to her heart. Tears splattered her cheeks.

Della looked at her daughters. 'They're both the same. I don't know what else he left you but . . .'

'How can he be gone?' Ronnie rocked back and forth in her seat, the tears coming faster.

Celeste drummed her fingers on the table. 'Oh, spare me the performance! You couldn't wait two seconds to see how much was in there!'

'I never asked Daddy and Ma for a dime, and you know it!' A fringe of Ronnie's hair stuck to her wet cheek.

'She acts like she's the only one with feelings!' Celeste shot back.

'Celeste, leave it alone!' Della reached over, patted Ronnie's arm.

'Why did this have to happen?' Ronnie folded her arms on the table, laid her head on them, and bawled.

'It's all right, baby.' Della wrapped her arm around Ronnie's shoulder and held her.

'I don't believe this.' Celeste got up and walked to the other side of the room to keep from exploding. She paced, trying to suck down the rest of what she had to say. Through the window she saw the flash of headlights pulling into the driveway and prayed it was

30

Everett so she could get the hell out of here before she had to listen to one more word of her sister's sniveling. Standing on her tiptoes to look out the window, she saw Niki waiting on the steps and Everett unfolding from the car. 'Thank God,' she said under her breath and hurried to the hall closet, where she snatched her suit jacket, pocketbook, and Niki's leather backpack to save time. All Celeste wanted was to get out of this house.

'Does Mrs Godfrey ever stop talking?' Everett held the back door open for Niki as they came into the kitchen. 'And where on earth did she find that hat?' Niki looked up at her father and stifled a giggle. You knew Everett was tall when you saw him, but it wasn't until you got up close that you realized how big he was. When they were dating, Celeste's girl-friends used to ride her about the tall men who were wasted on little bitty women. Everett was the golden brown of single malt scotch, with a voice and a manner that were just as mellow. By the time he met Celeste, when he was a second-year med student at the University of Buffalo and she a college junior, he already had the mustache and goatee. He had a serious 'fro too, round like a mushroom; now all he had left was half a halo. The sleeves of Everett's black mock turtleneck were pushed up to his elbows. He and Celeste had had words about his attire this morning. He didn't wear ties anymore, decided they were pretentious and unnecessary. Will certainly knew that, so Everett saw no reason to wear one to his funeral.

Celeste met them at the back door, handed Niki her bag. 'I'm ready. Let's go.'

Everett saw Ronnie and Della huddled together.

'Why don't we stay for a while?' he said softly to Celeste.

She shook her head and scowled. 'Be back tomorrow,' she announced.

Della looked up and nodded, and Celeste was out the door.

2

'No good-byes. Just gone.'

Celeste let herself in the Volvo, which she insisted they take instead of the rattletrap four-wheel-drive monstrosity Everett couldn't seem to part with. By the time Niki and Everett came out, she had already steamed up the windows.

Everett paused a moment, looked at the night sky before he got in. 'So many stars. Your dad got a nice welcome.' He turned on the ignition, backed out into the street.

'My mother acts like it's just another day. For God's sake, her husband is dead. You think she'd show some emotion. And I am sick to death of my sister!' Arms folded and legs crossed tighter than a Scout knot, Celeste fumed. 'She manages to make every situation revolve around her!'

'Sick to *death*? You have such a way with words.' Niki cleared the fog from her window with her palm.

'Don't mock me, Nicole. I am in no mood.'

'Aunt Ronnie expresses what she feels. What's wrong with that, Ma?'

'I *hate* it when you call me *Ma*! Don't call me anything if that's all you can say!'

33

'Fine!' Niki slumped against the seatback and stared out the window.

'And that skirt she had on was a disgrace. I have wider belts. This was her father's funeral, not some damn disco!' Celeste grumbled to no one in particular.

Everett glanced sidelong at his wife but decided to leave it alone. He knew there was no right answer for Celeste when she was like this. It had been a long, drawn-out day, and he had his own wounds to tend. He liked his father-in-law from the first time they met. Celeste was carrying on about Everett being a medical student. Will looked him over and said, 'They let *you* practice medicine?' Everett told him yeah, and he was gonna keep practicing till he got it right. Will chuckled, handed him a beer. They watched the Bills, and they'd been buddies ever since. If he had the time, Everett still pitched in, over Celeste's objections, when Will needed an extra set of hands to work on one of his houses. Sometimes it felt good to Everett just to be the guy holding the ladder, instead of the one who was supposed to have the answers. He wished he'd been helping out the day of the accident.

They rode the rest of the way to Amherst in silence. Back when Celeste had finally convinced Everett they needed more space because of the baby, and it was time to abandon the crowded one-bedroom apartment near the hospital and buy a house, she insisted they move to the suburbs. She saw their three-bedroom cedar shingle, split-level ranch as a starter home. Problem was, twenty years later they were still in it. Even when Everett's peers joined lucrative private practices, took their long green out to the lavish new developments and built mansionettes, he wasn't interested. He thought they already had a great house, Niki liked her schools, and he preferred working at the North Star Family Clinic he had founded. His salary wasn't as big, but he found the work rewarding. It's what he always told Celeste he wanted to do when they were dating, and she'd go to his apartment and cook big pots of spaghetti and jar sauce with dry meatballs and wait up until two thirty in the morning when he finally got off duty so they could eat together. She would light the red candles she had wedged in the tops of old Mateus bottles so the wax dripped down the sides in free-form ribbons. Everett would come in all wound up about some procedure he had finally been able to use and how it had made the difference for a patient. He'd tell her that's why he was in medicine, not for the big bucks. Celeste would tell him how righteous that was, gaze at him in the twinkling light, and think she'd explode if he didn't put those big hands around her soon. Everett's goals had remained noble as the years wore on, but Celeste seemed to have forgotten how righteous she once thought they were. Between his salary and her pay as a guidance counselor they had a nice life, but somewhere along the line Celeste had started blaming him for not wanting more.

As soon as the car stopped in the driveway, Celeste made a beeline for the bottle of chardonnay in the fridge and poured herself a healthy glass by the light from inside. She had a headache that would kill a horse. She shut the door so the room was dark again, took a swig. It stung the raw place inside her cheek. *How could Daddy be gone?* She slid onto the banquette in the breakfast nook. Moonlight shone through the window, bounced off the table. At the funeral Ronnie had cried, moaned, and all but collapsed by the open coffin. She had to be helped to her seat and fanned so she wouldn't swoon. But what did Ronnie really know about their father? Did she know he still liked the peanut butter sandwich cookies and grape soda they thought was so nasty when they were kids? Or that he was considering selling most of his houses because some of the tenants were too rough for him to mess with now, and that it made him sad because he'd spent so much of his life tending to them? Or that he wished he knew how to make Della happy again? *Like anybody could make her happy.* Celeste emptied her wine glass, wasn't wasted enough, got up for a refill.

Your daddy's rich, and your ma is good-lookin'. Celeste sang the words in her head as the sound of Everett and Niki's piano playing drifted in from the living room. Niki first learned scales and 'Greensleeves' sitting on her father's lap. They still played together, four hands on the piano. Celeste filled the glass to the rim this time, took a few sips so she wouldn't spill it, then sat back down, closed her eyes, propped her head against the window frame.

She hadn't gone up for a final viewing. Celeste wanted to remember her daddy her way. In the back-yard, mopping barbecue sauce on a slab of ribs with one hand and sweat off his forehead with the other. During the reception he and Della gave after Celeste announced she and Everett had eloped, Will led her upstairs to her old bedroom and made sure she knew that even though she was another man's wife now, she would always be his baby. She had always felt more

36

like his baby than her mother's. *And he's gone and left me here with her. What am I supposed to do now?* Tears leaked from the corners of her eyes, down her neck. Celeste didn't know how long she had been sitting that way, when the kitchen lights flicked on. She squinted, shaded her eyes from the brightness.

'I didn't know you were in here. Thought you'd gone to bed.' Everett got an ice cream sandwich out of the freezer.

Celeste meant to tell him that she was on her way. That she'd stopped off for some wine, that he and Niki sounded good together. She meant to say that, but all that came out was a muffled whimper, then waves of tears. Everett sat beside her, held her until they subsided, steadied her as they walked to the bedroom. His hands were sure as he helped her undress, get into a nightgown, and by the time she lay down, her back curved against his chest, Celeste felt calmer. His breathing was always slower than hers, so she deepened her breaths to match his. It had been a long time since they fell asleep this way. Their schedules didn't seem to mesh anymore, especially since Niki had been gone.

Oh, they were very socially active. Celeste still loved receiving the creamy vellum envelopes that read 'Dr & Mrs Everett English' in lovely script. They attended openings at the Albright-Knox Gallery, galas at the Studio Arena Theater, and chaired fund-raisers for their local NAACP chapter. Celeste and Everett were A-list cocktail party guests because they were such good minglers, always ready with an entertaining anecdote or an intriguing perspective on current events. And they looked so good together. She'd been dealt a hand full of fives and sixes in life, but with persistence and constant attention to detail, Celeste had done all right.

So the weekends were generally inked in well in advance, but their five-days-a-week lives didn't intersect much. Celeste had her after-school routines. Tuesdays she stayed late to advise the prom committee. Thursdays were her standing four-thirty hair appointment, so her precision cropped hair looked exactly the same at all times. She attended sorority meetings and library board meetings. By seven or so she'd be home, broil some sole or a chicken breast or pick at leftovers. Lately she turned in around nine thirty, with a book and some sherry. Half the time Everett didn't get home before that. He'd get tied up checking on patients, reviewing charts, completing paperwork, or speaking to some community group about the warning signs of high blood pressure or the importance of mammograms and self-examination in breast cancer detection. Celeste didn't bother getting up when she heard his keys jingle in the door. Eventually he'd poke his head in the bedroom to talk for a minute, then he'd busy himself down the hall in his office, reading journals, or logged on the computer. Sometimes he stayed downstairs, noodling at the piano, enjoying his 'live at the Blue Note' fantasy. She'd rouse a little when he'd drop his clothes in a pile by the side of the bed and get under the covers around two A.M., sometimes later. And more and more he didn't make it to bed at all. On her four A.M. bathroom run she'd shuffle down the hall and find him sprawled on the brown velour sofa across from his desk. She always felt a fist in her guts, like somebody had a handful of her intestines, but it was just that they were both so busy. They still had so much in common, what difference did it make where they slept? The next morning, the routine would start all over again.

But tonight Celeste felt calm pressed into the curve of Everett's body. She let the stress of the day pass from her and fell into a deep sleep.

At 3:12 A.M. Celeste woke up feeling too warm under the comforter. She pushed it off, reached for Everett, and shivered when she felt the empty space beside her.

Della straightened the covers on her side of the unmade bed, piled up her pillows, and sat down. Three-fifteen was a little later than she usually stayed up, but not much. Her nighttime supplies littered the crocheted coverlet on the other side: puzzle books, *Jet*, *Ebony*, *Life*, the TV remote, unread sections of Sunday's paper, a blue acrylic snack tray, her everyday pocketbook, a deck of cards, Chapstick. She slipped her legs under the sheet.

Della had stood in the doorway of Ronnie's room a long time, watching her sleep. Ronnie slept like the dead, had since she was little. Della remembered the time the house across the street caught fire in the middle of the night. There were sirens screaming, all sorts of commotion, and Ronnie never budged. From the look of things, that hadn't changed. The whole time Della watched, the only movement was the steady rise and fall of the pink chenille bedspread. She worried about Ronnie, which was nothing new. Della worried about both her daughters, but since they'd been grown she kept her concerns to herself. They wouldn't have listened, anyway. This was a rare

39

opportunity to worry in person for as long as she wanted.

Della wished Ronnie had seen her father more recently, not because he didn't understand that the life she had chosen didn't leave much room for stops in western New York, but because Della wasn't sure Ronnie understood that as long as she was happy, Will had been happy and proud. *Nothin' to be done about it now.*

Della reached over for the tray and settled it on her lap. She picked up the red deck of playing cards, fanned them with her thumb. She couldn't help feeling like Will was upstairs, asleep, like always. They hadn't actually shared a bed in years, ten, twelve. It wasn't planned or deliberate, not this time. Way back when the girls were teens he started showering and shaving up in his attic bathroom because there was too much commotion sharing the room with three females, and this way nobody bugged him about whisker fuzz in the sink or how he left the toilet seat. Eventually his clothes migrated up there too because he said Della didn't leave him enough space for a pair of drawers. When he retired he kept all his gadgets and whatnot up there too, and when he wasn't working he'd spend hours fooling with them, then fall asleep in the recliner with the TV set going. One day he just stopped waking up and coming downstairs. At first he used to visit Della's bed from time to time, but that had petered out a while back. She didn't think she'd ever hear herself say it, but after so many years all that bumpin' and rootin' around had stopped being a whole lot of fun. She was relieved not to hear his buzz saw snoring, or to have to wrestle for covers. Will had a mushy mattress the way he liked, and they'd meet over breakfast every morning. It was their routine. Della knew Celeste and Ronnie hadn't approved of the situation, like they had any say-so in the matter. It worked okay for the folks involved, and Della didn't see any reason to explain, especially not to her *children*. There were plenty of things she figured they didn't need to know.

Della shuffled the deck for a long time, dealt out a game of solitaire. The cool night air felt good on her bare arms. She always wore those sleeveless cotton nightgowns in pink or yellow, with the teensy ribbon tied in a bow at the yoke. She examined her up-cards, moved the ace of diamonds up top, the two of clubs on the three of diamonds, ten of clubs on the jack of hearts. Nothing in the last week had been regular, not Ronnie sleeping in her old room, not folks in and out of the house, laughing too loud or talking in whispers, or Celeste digging through Will's closet for his good navy suit. Della was tired of the phone ringing. Sick of sympathies and condolences, of folks looking at her with pity, asking how she was bearing up, what she was going to do, what she needed. She needed for all this foolishness to stop so she could get back to something like normal because now her life felt unfamiliar.

Della had been waiting for something to come over her for almost a week now. Will's death had been a big . . . well . . . shock. That last morning was the same as usual. She'd put on a pot of coffee and gotten ready for work. By the time she was ready for a cup, Will was dressed and finishing his second mug, light and sweet, with a bowl of toasted oats and skim milk because he had to watch his cholesterol. He drove her to work, like every morning since he'd retired, pecked her cheek, said he'd be back at quitting time.

Della was sorting through a stack of learner's permit applications when Everett showed up at her desk at the Department of Motor Vehicles late afternoon, looking pained. A friend of his was in the ER when they brought Will in and gave Everett a call. And that was that. No grim diagnoses, or tubes or monitors. No decisions. No warning. No good-byes. Just gone.

She counted off cards in threes: four of clubs, five of hearts, five of spades. Della thought solitaire was a lot like life: a whole lot of shuffling, but mostly the cards don't go your way. She put the three of clubs on the four of hearts, put the ace of clubs up top. Snatches of the obituary Celeste had read at the funeral drifted through Della's head. '. . . *leaves behind his devoted wife of forty-four years, Della Womack Frazier . . .*' *Forty-four years*. That was a whole lifetime, and she'd known him longer, ever since another hasty funeral left her world upside down. *No point dragging all that up*. As far as Della was concerned, you couldn't change the past, so there was no reason to look back at it. She needed to look ahead, to what she was going to do with all those houses and to how she was going to get back on schedule, now that a big chunk of the last fifty years was gone.

3

'. . . sleight-of-hand fame . . .'

'It's twelve noon straight up, sunny and forty-two degrees in Newark,' the pilot announced as the plane smacked the runway, bounced and heaved down to land speed. *And two weeks after Daddy* . . . The pilot couldn't add that detail, and Ronnie couldn't finish the thought. She hadn't even figured out how to say it. *Died? Passed?* So she maneuvered around the exact words, just as she had maneuvered around spending any more time than absolutely required around Celeste. *Always actin' like she knows it all.* Whenever Ronnie thought of their funeral night fight it set her teeth on edge. *I'd a been home the next day if* . . . She didn't even like admitting to herself that she was stone broke and so in debt to her friends there wasn't anybody else to borrow from. She had to wait for her paycheck so she could buy a plane ticket. She certainly wasn't going to tell Celeste that.

She shifted impatiently in her seat, crossed and recrossed her legs at the ankles, and felt a corner of the check she had folded and slipped into her black suede boot. *I hope I can get this to the bank before two. The sooner it clears* . . . Ronnie looked around for a flight attendant, then jammed her empty paper cup in

43

the seat pocket and stifled a yawn. She still could not believe this morning. It was bad enough that her period had come early again, complete with hot, pulsing cramps that kept her awake half the night, but then her mother actually came in her room at six, flashing the ceiling light off and on and barking orders like when Ronnie was in school. She hated it then. One of the best things about leaving home was no Della alarm. *Ma must be havin' flashbacks.* Ronnie could have screamed. But she kept a lid on it and didn't bother to point out that the airport was only fifteen minutes away, or that she counted a mad dash through the terminal as exercise. Because unlike Celeste, Ronnie chose her battles carefully, and this one wasn't worth the hassle. Besides, she was ready to make her exit.

So she had downed four aspirin, thrown herself in a cold shower, stuffed her clothes in her bag, swilled three cups of Della's watery coffee because she was out of tea, and played with a bowl of oatmeal. *Only thing she didn't do was braid my hair and check my homework.* They were headed for Buffalo International by eight thirty for an eleven o'clock flight because her mother, who had no flyer miles, frequent or otherwise, thought it was a good idea. 'Better safe than sorry,' Della had said, then checked the window and door locks for the second time as she recounted the story of the house in the next block that had been burglarized year before last. 'Cleaned them out in broad daylight.' Della had a hard-luck story for every occasion, so Ronnie just nodded sympathetically and started her lift-off countdown while Della secured the perimeter.

Della had putt-putted along the highway seemingly

oblivious to the rush-hour traffic that zipped by the big, gray waterbug on wheels that Will had bought because he liked his cars substantial. 'Maybe this winter will be like last year. We didn't have much snow at all.' Ronnie thought the city looked and smelled like it was wrapped in an old, wet wool overcoat. She had stared out the window at the ominous gray clouds to keep from screaming, 'It's weather, Ma. It'll be whatever it's gonna be,' but her time at home reminded her that winter weather was an endless source of conversation in western New York. Dire predictions, wise prognostications, hopeful dreams, and stories of triumph were a common denominator. Like subway stories in New York, everybody had 'em and everybody shared 'em. Snow was a safe, neutral subject, perfect for that awkward silence between people's sympathetic recollections of Will Frazier. So for nine days Ronnie heard 'em. Lake effect. The ice boom. The Snow Belt. Winter words. Words she grew up with but had long ago shoveled to the back of her mind.

Della's good-bye had come with the usual warning to be careful and a reminder to call when she got in. Ronnie had leaned across the bench seat to hug her, which usually felt good because Della was soft and cuddly. Those hugs stuck to Ronnie's ribs, but this time a wave of sadness came over her, and it was all she could do to get out of the car before she went down in the undertow. Then Della reached in the backseat, handed Ronnie a shopping bag groaning with foil packets of ham, chicken, and pound cake. They could both be spared the 'You're too thin. Are you eating right?' speech. 'All that food shouldn't go to waste,' Della told her. '*I'll* never finish it.'

Two weeks ago it would have been 'we,' and there and then Ronnie decided that what her mother's life would be like now was another thing she wasn't prepared to consider yet. Next week Della would go back to work and . . . *And what?* Not that her parents had been lovey-dovey. Not that she knew exactly *what* they'd been to each other. Except there. They'd always been there.

'Please keep your seats until the fasten seat belt sign has been turned off,' the flight attendant's voice crackled over the loudspeaker.

'Are we taxiing to the damn George Washington Bridge?' It was out of Ronnie's mouth before she knew it. Other passengers chuckled in agreement. The whole flight only took fifty minutes. It seemed like it was taking that long to get to the gate, and Ronnie was too through. She leaned forward, clacking her heels on the floor like a flamenco dancer, waiting for the *ding* that meant she could spring for her bag. Finally, the cabin lights came up. Ronnie snatched her carry-on from the overhead and inched down the aisle with the rest of the cattle. Nine days. The longest she'd been home in seventeen years.

Ronnie slipped on her faux tortoise street-vendor diva shades, but only partially to dim the bright October sunlight that glinted through the windows. The concourse bustled with folks racing to get where they were going, but since she hadn't hit the real city, she wasn't required to up her pace yet. *Everybody looks so . . . so damn happy. Actin' like they* want *to be here. It's Newark Airport, for God's sake!* Still stiff from the crowded flight, she walked slowly through the terminal. *I feel like crap.* Ronnie resented coach and always cast a jaundiced eye as she passed the lucky few

46

comfortably ensconced in the wide leather seats of first class. She'd had the privilege of the other side of the curtain only once. She'd been up for a sitcom and her then agent had somehow finagled her a first-class ticket to L.A. No one in the cabin was exempt from her profiling. For six hours she regaled them with tales of her adventures in the 'business.' Some of the stories were actually true, they'd just happened to someone else. The rest she had made up out of the thin air at thirty thousand feet.

Ronnie snaked through the squadron of livery-car drivers who chatted among themselves while holding signs with the name of their next fare. *Humph. One day.* By the time she reached baggage claim her aggressive edge was closer to the surface, bringing with it her need for a cigarette. She elbowed to the front of the carousel and snatched her duffel, which was now minus a strap. Disgusted, she examined the damage as the crowd scrambled around her. *They'll laugh in my face if I make a claim for this ratty old piece of shit.*

Dragging the black nylon bag by its one good handle, Ronnie made her way outside to the bus line. Until she got to the bank, that check in her boot was just a piece of paper, and she was tapped out. She thought about asking Celeste for a small loan, but it wasn't worth the lecture. From the time they were kids, Celeste kept a stash – just in case. To Ronnie, money meant a good time *now*. A candy bar. A 45 record. A movie. Because what is there besides the moment and the memory?

Ronnie fished in her purse for her smokes and started a mental list of all the good times her windfall would provide. *At least I can pay my rent on time for a change.* Before she lit up, the driver reached for her

47

bag to stow it in the belly of the bus. 'Could you put it over there?' She pointed to a corner in the front, flashed her chemically whitened smile. *So I don't have to wait two years for you to find it when we get to the city.*

'Anything for you, dearie.'

'Thanks!' *Spare me.* She climbed aboard and took a seat up front next to an old man listening to headphones because he didn't look like he'd give her any lip. The tinted windows didn't let in much light, but Ronnie kept her shades on anyway.

No one knew how shaky Ronnie's life was, because Ronnie never let on. Never. She hadn't actually earned a living as a model or an actress in years. She barely earned a living, period. The folks at home thought . . . *What did they think exactly?* What she wanted them to. To her parents, their friends and neighbors, she was a star, a celebrity. After all, she'd lived in Paris and Milan and Tokyo. They didn't know that the tiny hotel rooms she shared with dozens of other wanna-bes were only a notch above hovel. They'd seen her in their Kmart circular. Not since 1988, but for them it was like yesterday. And her cigarette billboard was longer ago. For months it had guarded the Jefferson ramp onto the Kensington Expressway, but whenever she was home, no one would let her forget it.

That was back before she had an agent, when she'd been naive enough to believe the photographer when he told her that being the girl in the pink jacket, leaning on a toboggan, puffing a menthol was her ticket to stardom. He was so easygoing, so mellow. She was new; he had national magazine credits. So he taught her how to work to the camera and to the light, and she was an eager pupil. The excitement in his voice made her believe he really hadn't seen anyone in a long time who made the shot pop like she did. And no one had ever looked at Ronnie so intensely. It was as though he could see through the lens directly into her eyes and right into her soul. It had been a scorching August day, but she actually enjoyed spending hours in the un-air-conditioned studio, bundled in hot ski clothes, cavorting in fake snow, a cigarette poised jauntily between her fingers.

When his assistant and the hair and makeup guy finally left and he asked her to stay, Ronnie felt an excited tingle. So it seemed perfectly natural for her to lounge on the leather sofa while he put on some smooth tunes, turned the lights down low, poured her a glass of wine. And, oh, by the way, 'Just sign the release. It's standard,' he had said. Ronnie scribbled her name without thinking twice. She drank in the cabernet and his philosophy of photography, felt honored when he showed her his portfolio of art pictures even though she didn't really get the blurry black-and-white abstractions. At first it was even okay when he held her face and kissed her.

He just wouldn't stop.

She said, 'No.'

He said, 'Come on, baby.'

She said, 'No!'

He said, 'You know you want it,' and pressed harder.

She said, 'Stop!' and tried to wriggle out of his grasp.

He didn't. He held her down, covered her mouth with his, and didn't say anything else until he was finished. Then he stood up and zipped. 'Later,' he said.

Ronnie straightened her clothes and hair in the hall-way and walked out into the anonymous Manhattan twilight feeling dazed, raw, and somehow responsible. Too stunned to cry, she concentrated on fighting back the bile that bubbled in the back of her throat, putting one foot in front of the other and remembering how to get back to her residence hotel. She didn't tell anybody because she didn't know anybody to tell, not anybody who would care, or believe her or do anything about it. Telling her father never crossed her mind. He'd come bring her home where he could protect her. All Ronnie wanted was to put her head in her mother's lap and boohoo until she felt relief, but this wasn't a scraped knee, this was sex, and they didn't talk about that. Not in so many words, but Della had made it clear that Ronnie knew right from wrong and that was that. So if she was supposed to be grown enough to live on her own, then she should have seen the squeeze play coming.

To this day, Ronnie still hadn't said anything.

Three months after, she got a five-hundred-dollar check in the mail for what she later found out should have been a ten grand payday. She'd been screwed, any way you put it. Not to mention the nicotine jones she still had.

And then the billboard showed up that winter and taunted her from rooftops and bus shelters. Looking up at her own bright-eyed, smiling face made her want to vomit, but it made her family proud. When she went home for the holidays, her father made her pose for snapshots under the billboard. Only she could see the sadness in her eyes when she looked at the picture.

But as a result of the campaign, she got an agent to

50

take her on, and by the time she made two appearances during the third season of *The Cosby Show*, Ronnie's star status was assured. 'Damn! My baby workin' with Bill Cosby!' She could hear her daddy's pride over the phone. Will boasted to all his tenants, 'My daughter, the one who's an actress in New York, yeah she and Bill are tight.' He called him Bill, as if Ronnie's brief association made *him* a friend as well. She didn't have the heart to tell him that since she didn't have any scenes with Mr Cosby, she hadn't even met him on the set.

Even Celeste had been a little impressed. Della seemed to be too, but the only thing she said was, 'Are you still havin' fun?' Ronnie had shrugged it off as some of her mother's weird gloom and doom. Since when did Della care about fun? Had she had any since 1969? Of course Ronnie was having the time of her life. It was what she dreamed about, wasn't it?

And as for men, she'd figured that out too. Never get caught off guard. Never believe they're sincere. Never show them who you really are.

These days, pretty much all that came her way was extra work on soaps and movies here and there, when they needed a Black face in the background. She couldn't even pay her SAG dues with what she earned for those shows, and even she couldn't fix her mouth to call it acting anymore. And as far as modeling, she hadn't done a print ad in five years. There was the occasional trade show at the Javits. Automobiles, computers, didn't make any difference. She'd stand in killer heels, wearing something skimpy and tight, and smile at strangers for twelve hours. She quit waiting tables a few years ago because that was too big a cliché, but her steadiest gig, the one that accounted for most of the income on her income taxes, was her Thursday nights and all day Saturdays and Sundays behind the Sable Shades makeup counter in Macy's. *Sable Shades, rich enough to be you.* She'd been sent on the casting for the line's debut ads a few years back. Nothing came of that, but Ronnie had figured if there was anything she'd learned from the business, it was how to beat a face, so she got herself a job as a 'beauty consultant.' Folks at home didn't know that, though. They still compared Ronnie stories and ate up her sleight-of-hand fame like they ate chicken wings. She'd heard it a hundred times between the wake and the funeral, from church members who remembered giving her father extra sale circulars after service, or from classmates she didn't remember who could cite chapter and verse of her career. She'd set out to become a household name, which she was, but only in the households of people she knew. People who'd restricted their dreams to fit comfortably within the limits of the world where they lived. Ronnie had become their ray of limelight, and she wanted to shine for them, so she became a master of illusion. But she was painfully aware of the trapdoors and secret compartments, and when the smoke cleared she still hadn't fulfilled the dreams she carried with her the first time she left home.

As the bus barreled along the Jersey Turnpike, Ronnie craved a cigarette. She shifted in her seat, caught the old man in the seat next to her staring at her legs. *Ain't that nothin'.* She flipped her trench coat over her knees. She wasn't glad to be back, just anxious to be away from that home and family stuff death drops on you in your hour of bereavement. The stuff that doesn't have jack to do with the dearly departed. It was her mother who seemed to float through the week like she was mildly annoyed at the inconvenience, and her darling sister who seemed to relish the respectability of mourning, that had gotten on Ronnie's reserve nerve. It was all too close, and it got harder every day to keep up the front. Questions. Too many of 'em. Three days at home was usually her max. She could make it all work for that long.

Ronnie could see a patch of light at the end of the Lincoln Tunnel. She was back to her life, such as it was. She could return to her days spent ritually traipsing to castings and auditions. She'd dress to suit the part, read the copy, and smile pretty as she exited stage right. 'Thanks. We'll let you know.' She heard it in her sleep. At this point hope was pretty hard to come by, but Ronnie had perfected the role of Veronica Frazier, her stage name, worked so hard trying to be who people thought she was, she had no time to think about whether it was still fun.

Ronnie was off the bus at Port Authority before the brakes had stopped squealing. 'Baby, I'll carry that bag anywhere you wanna go.' The man's grungy fatigues looked like they'd seen action. He quickened his steps to try and fall in beside Ronnie. She threw her hand up in a stop sign, turned her head, and never broke stride.

He stopped and let her pass. 'That sorry-assed wig must be too tight.' The retort smacked her in the back of the head and she felt the adrenaline surge. *Welcome home.* She needed that kick in the attitude to navigate the terminal and fend off the ersatz 'door' men, eager to get her a taxi, for a small gratuity, thank you. *I should take the train.* But the thought of dragging her raggedy, one-handled suitcase down into the subway to catch the shuttle, then changing for the ride uptown was too dismal. She'd still have to lug her load another four blocks. *What could it be, ten bucks? Fifteen?* By the time her frantic waving had snared a taxi on Eighth Avenue, the sun had disappeared behind a cloud and the sky threatened rain, but Ronnie still had her shades on.

Home, Alfred. 'Seventy-fifth and York.' Ronnie gave the driver her cross streets. One of her first New York lessons was that only out-of-towners gave a cab driver an actual address as soon as they got in. The taxi headed east on Forty-second Street. *Home?* Although she'd lived in Manhattan a long time, Ronnie didn't really think of it as home. She'd had enough addresses and phone numbers to fill a page in the Manhattan phone book. Her current sub-sublet was just one more. All part of her glamorous, nomadic lifestyle, her parents thought. She'd overheard her father, for whom a trip to Rochester was an adventure, brag about that too. 'Yeah, Ronnie has lived all over New York. Knows it like the back of her hand.' When her mother asked if she didn't get tired of moving, Ronnie told her it was exciting. 'I need new surroundings to stimulate me. Besides, this apartment is closer to the subway, drugstore, acting class . . .' But what Ronnie never had was a lease or a utility bill in her own name. Della and Will never visited her, but then they'd never been invited. Celeste came once on a teacher's convention when, luckily, Ronnie was apartment sitting in a high-rise on West Fifty-seventh Street. Ronnie bought a few frames at Lamston's and put family photos on display around the place. Celeste really bought the act, even complimented Ronnie on her taste. A couple of years later, Everett came to town to deliver a paper at Columbia Presbyterian and brought Niki with him. They stayed at the Plaza, and for two days Ronnie showed them the New York they thought she lived in. Her secret was safe. No one knew how far her ends had to go before they'd meet.

The taxi turned up First Avenue, swerved to avoid taking out a bike messenger. *Oh yeah, the bank.* 'Make that Seventy-ninth and First,' Ronnie shouted through the Plexiglas partition, then reached down and tugged off her left boot. Years ago, at the end of her six weeks in Tokyo, the agency paid her in cash, nine thousand U.S. dollars. A fifteen-year-old model from West Virginia showed her how to stuff the money in her boots. On her customs form, Ronnie declared a hundred dollars. She had felt like a secret agent.

Inside the bank, Ronnie filled out a deposit slip so she'd get five hundred dollars back and dragged her luggage to the teller window. A young woman with bad skin and very long blue and yellow striped nails examined the draft, then pushed it back toward Ronnie with the eraser of her pencil. 'You'll have to get this authorized by an officer.'

'I have an account here.' Ronnie pulled out her miffed executive act. 'This is a bank check made out to me.'

The teller pointed the pencil toward the row of desks across the room. 'It's from out of town. Some-one has to initial it.'

Yep. I'm officially back. New York City. If something is simple, they make it difficult. If it's difficult, they make it impossible. Ronnie recalled how the branch manager at her parents' bank addressed her mother by name,

55

asked about her health, and offered condolences. While they were waiting for the check to be drawn up, the woman shared a story about how Will recommended a good plumber and how much she and her husband appreciated it. *But you're not in Kansas anymore, Dorothy.* Ronnie, prepared for battle, hoisted her suitcase and scanned the suits hoping for a friendly face. *Thank God.* She spied a brother in the far corner. Brooks Brothers pin stripe, rep tie, no facial hair, no jewelry. She sauntered closer. The brass nameplate on his desk read R. Phillip Dade. *Ugh. One of those.* But Ronnie cleared her throat, focused her 'sincere' smiling eyes, the look she used for young mother auditions, in his direction. On cue, R. Phillip looked up, took off his rimless glasses. Ronnie kicked up the wattage aimed in his direction.

'I'm truly sorry for the inconvenience, Ms Frazier, but your funds should be clear in five to seven business days.'

Did you have that whiny voice before they hired you, or did it come with the nameplate? 'This is not acceptable.' She didn't want to sound desperate. 'Can't you release a portion of this?'

'This isn't a local check, you see. If you had the money in your account to cover it, we could . . .'

'If I had the money in my account we wouldn't be having this conversation, would we?' *You pompous ass.* Ronnie knew there was nothing left but to save face and retreat.

'Bank policy. I wish I could do something to help.'

'Well, Mr Dade, I need to deposit this for convenience sake, but I will be taking my business to another bank.' *Right. So* they *can send me bounced check notices.* She turned on her heels and sauntered back to the teller with all the righteous indignation she could muster. And to add insult to injury, by the time she came out of the bank the sky had opened up and all the cabs that clogged the street twenty minutes ago had vanished. *It's only five blocks in the rain with a broken suitcase.* It was all getting funny now. She hoisted the bag on her head and amused herself on the walk home watching passersby try to look at her without really looking.

Ronnie stopped at the mailbox. Half was junk mail, the other half she was sure had 'final notice' printed across a bill for some amount she couldn't pay yet. *What are they gonna do? Shoot me?* She trudged up the stairs and heard the voice on the answering machine as she turned the three locks and opened the door. 'If you've already sent your payment, please disregard this message.' *Shit!* Home. A fourth-floor walk-up studio, smaller than her bedroom in Buffalo, for which she had the privilege of paying eleven hundred ninety-five dollars a month, not including utilities. Of course, it *was* furnished, which meant there was a lumpy double bed with a Campari poster on the wall where the headboard should have been. A dark, rickety dresser that looked like somebody's grandmother must have thrown it out stood on the opposite wall. Only the top drawer had been empty, so Ronnie kept her underwear there and used her luggage to store the rest of her clothes. One of the two small closets was jammed with boxes that Ronnie guessed belonged to the leaseholder. The other had a slow leak and she wasn't sure where the water came from. There was an eat-in kitchen, which meant there was enough room to stand at the counter and eat in it. Ronnie had opened the cabinet under the sink once, heard scurrying feet, and never opened it again. The bathroom was in keeping with the rest of the decor, aged tile and rust. Truth was the place gave her the willies, which is why she spent as little time as possible there. But that's what New York was about, wasn't it? Being out and about. Besides, at least she didn't have roommates, 'cause you never knew what horror show *that* would be. She'd been here nearly a year, long enough to know the address and phone without checking her address book. The apartment belonged to a friend of a friend of someone she met on an audition. He had temporarily relocated to Brazil but wasn't ready to give up his shoe box on the Upper East Side. Ronnie never met him. The arrangements were made over the phone; the keys came FedEx.

Welcome home. Ronnie dropped her wet bag by the door, tossed her mail in the wicker basket, yanked off her soaked, squishy boots. *These are over.* She chucked them in the trash and stuck her feet in the formerly white canvas tennis sneakers she used as slippers. Her wig was matted to her head, she was wet down to her bra, the pain in her belly was back, she was tired and hungry. That's when she realized that somewhere between Buffalo and here she'd lost her care package from home. 'Damn!' She knew there was only half a sesame bagel, some ketchup, and leftover split pea soup in the refrigerator, and she didn't want to know what that had turned into in her absence. 'Damn! Damn! Damn!' She felt herself coming unglued, and that was more loose pieces than she wanted to deal with, so she turned on the combination radio, tape player, and three-inch TV to mask the sound of the toilet that always ran. A soothing piano melody came over the radio, and she used that little bit of calm to get herself out of her soggy clothes and wrapped in a terry cloth robe she'd swiped ages ago from a suite at the George V in Paris where she had a gosee. A few drags of menthol and she was composed enough to call Della. After all, it wouldn't do to burst out in tears and say, 'My life is shit!' which was a feeling Ronnie wasn't prepared to acknowledge to herself and definitely not to her mother. 'The flight was a breeze. Yeah everything is great here. Fabulous actually . . . Gotta go, Ma . . . phone calls to return, appointments to reschedule. Call ya soon!'

The DJ said it was 4:37, but Ronnie curled up on the bed and slept all night.

When she assumed her post behind the Sable Shades counter the next morning, wearing the required fashion-black above-the-knee skirt, turtleneck, opaque hose, and gold cardigan with the interlocking double S logo, Ronnie had rebounded. Her life was still hung together with chewing gum, paper clips, and spit, but at least this felt normal. On the M32 bus to work she had gone over next week's casting calls in *Back Stage* and *Show Business* and circled the ones that seemed right. It would only be a week till the check cleared. *The beauty shop. Rent. A new head shot and mailing. A little shopping.* She had things to look forward to. *Thank you, Daddy!*

Ronnie liked to say she worked at the Sables Shades counter to prepare for her own sitcom. The Veronica Frazier Show, *or should I use Ronnie?* She even kept notes, intended to write a TV treatment one day. Truth was she kind of liked the gig. It was a relatively new cosmetics line, and competition was stiff. Fashion Fair and Naomi Sims had a loyal following. Iman was gaining a nice toehold. Sable Shades was

59

the new kid on the block, and Ronnie liked the team spirit and the products. She had worked for an hour, gingerly removing the sticky little tags that said 'sample, not for resale' from the array of bottles, jars, and pots she'd sent to Niki last Christmas because she wanted to send her niece something nice. Who'd ever know?

In the locker room she caught up with gossip from employees and from models who had cologne sample duty. Ronnie had been booked for that job a few times, but it was a real dog. You assault innocent shoppers with perfume you know stinks, and they don't pay you enough to take the abuse. Ronnie was nervous when she signed in and saw that Marilyn Ellis, her supervisor, had scheduled a lunch meeting with her. Ronnie knew it was to chew her out for the extended absence, *blah blah blah*. But in the meantime, Ronnie's charm turned passing shoppers into prospective customers. Her skill and how-to banter as she applied foundation and powder, brushed brows into shape, or highlighted a cheekbone turned those prospects into sales. She was good. She knew it.

Fortunately, the morning was busy and profitable. She did makeovers for a bride, her mother, and her two bridesmaids, and they bought the whole package from cleanser to mascara. *Ka-ching*. But it was more than the money. Ronnie felt good because each of them looked better than when she sat down in the chair.

'Glad you're back.' Marilyn perched on the chair across from Ronnie, who had been waiting, and took her menu from the waiter in the court jester's hat. Marilyn was small enough to shop in juniors, but her style was far more chignon and pumps. She used

60

Essential Ebony, the darkest foundation in the line, but even without it her skin glowed.

Could we skip the small talk and get to the point? Ronnie had her ain't-too-proud-to-beg speech in her hip pocket because she really wanted to keep this job. 'I am too. I'm sorry I was away so long. It's just that . . .'

'Unfortunately, it happens to all of us sooner or later. How's your mother handling it?'

She's being so nice. Ronnie was not prepared for this. 'Uh, she's okay. My sister lives in Buffalo too, so that helps.' *Helps who?* Ronnie could hear Celeste and Della at each other.

'Listen, Ronnie, let me get to the point.' Marilyn laid the menu down, leaned across the table like she had a secret to share.

Here it comes.

'We want you full-time.'

'Are you serious?! I knew I was history.'

'Oh, no. While you were gone it became apparent that working just twenty hours a week your sales account for more dollar volume than any other Sable rep. This is a new company, so there's lots of room for growth. We're looking to expand the line into other markets across the country. You could make supervisor in less than a year. It would be a salaried position, plus commissions, which means you can really clean up. You'd have benefits, vacations.'

A job? Me? 'Marilyn, I don't know what to say.' *This cannot be why I spent all these years bustin' my chops.* 'I'm really flattered, but . . .' *Shit, I haven't had health insurance since I left home. And a vacation?* 'You know I work part-time to keep my days for auditions. When the right call comes I need to be free to go.' *When was*

61

the last time that happened? 'I like Sables Shades, but for me it's a paycheck, not a future.'

'Don't say no. Think about it. We want you on board, Ronnie.' Marilyn picked up the menu. 'Let's order.'

Ronnie was almost too tense to eat, but this would probably be her meal for the day, and it was a freebie.

'So I told her I'd think about it.' And Ronnie had thought about it. More often than she wanted to, but right now she was happy the check had cleared, the rent was paid, and LaVonne was putting the finishing touches on her weave.

LaVonne spoke to Ronnie's reflection in the mirror. 'She really thought you wanted some lousy ass full-time job at Macy's? Girlfriend better get real. See, that's what's the matter with us. The sister should be encouragin' you to follow your dreams, you know. Not tempting you to sell out. Did you hear about Téa? She got herself a series, girl. Prime time. I think she's a cop or somethin'. Packed up and moved to Hollywood. She called me looking for somebody to keep her naps in order out there.'

Téa got that show? They were the same type, and Ronnie always ran into her at auditions, like the one for this series. 'Good for her.' But Téa had been getting the callbacks.

'Ta da! Only her hairdresser knows for sure!' LaVonne spun the chair around and handed Ronnie the mirror. It was long, flowing, and fabulous. No one could tell it wasn't nature made. LaVonne was the best. The wigs could go back in the closet. Ronnie happily made out the check for eight hundred dollars, which included her model discount.

LaVonne's was on West Fifty-seventh, across the street from the building where Ronnie had been staying when Celeste came to visit. Ronnie looked up at the towering structure, remembered the twenty-four-hour doormen who never failed to speak to her by name. 'How's it going, Miss Frazier?' 'Need a cab, Miss Frazier?' She loved it and she wanted it again. She strolled along Fifty-seventh toward Fifth, hair blowing in the autumn breeze. She had a really great audition this week, three scheduled for next, and a callback for a commercial this afternoon. Her rent and most of her bills were paid, she had money in the bank, and she was going to a party tonight. She felt like herself again. Ronnie waited for the light and ignored the young brother in the yellow down jacket who stared at her and licked his lips. *But you're right. I look good!*

Who could ask for anything more? Ronnie sang to herself. *Girl Crazy*. It was her first big role in a school play, a musical with real costumes and scenery. Before the show was cast, she made her mother buy the album. Della fussed about wasting money, but Ronnie listened to Judy Garland belt out that song until she had it down pat. Ronnie didn't have the best voice, as the drama teacher pointed out at the audition, but she had the best delivery.

From the time she was eight and sat in the audience watching Celeste in the Richmond Speaking Contest, Ronnie was mesmerized. On the day of the citywide oratorical competition, Celeste walked onto the stage wearing her Sunday best, navy blue Jonathan Logan double-knit dress with the brass buttons and white stockings instead of her usual kneesocks. Ronnie, in a flowered cotton skirt Della had made, white blouse, and anklets, sat between her parents wishing that she should would wake up the next day and be in eighth grade too. She thought Celeste looked so sophisticated. Celeste began, "'The Creation.'" She paused, then continued, 'by James Weldon Johnson,' and her voice, rich and round, filled the auditorium, and Ronnie watched with her mouth open. Celeste enunciated each syllable of the dramatic poem, and when she was finished, the audience broke into applause. All those people clapping for her sister. Ronnie was so excited she jumped to her feet cheering and waving at Celeste. Della had to yank her down in her seat. Afterward they went to Howard Johnson's for ice cream sundaes, and Ronnie tried to tell Celeste how great she was and that the judges were wrong not to pick her. Celeste just rolled her eyes and kept stirring her melting ice cream, but that didn't matter to Ronnie. She was inspired. She wanted people to clap for her too.

Then Ronnie had asked how come they spelled sundae with an *e*. Celeste said, 'Boy you are really stupid!' 'I'm not stupid!' Ronnie shot back. 'Stupid people pretend they know everything, like you!' Will and Della stopped them before a full-fledged fight broke out, and they rode home, each wedged in a corner of the backseat, glaring at each other. Celeste went to her room, and they never talked about the contest again. Ronnie remembered it like it was yesterday.

That began Ronnie's real pursuit of stardom. She was so sure and determined that Will and Della couldn't tell he no. So she took tap at Miss Barbara's School of Dance and drama classes at the Langston Hughes Center. She learned modeling and deportment at June II. Ronnie progressed from Sunday school pageants, where every child who tried out got a role, to performing in plays at the African Cultural Center. What Ronnie lacked in talent she made up for with enthusiasm and energy, which got her as far as New York.

After high school, she convinced her father to give her the money he would have spent on her first year in college to try out Manhattan. If she made it, the money was hers, free and clear. If she couldn't take care of herself after the first year, she promised to come home, go to school, *and* get a job to pay him back. Della convinced Will it was a fair deal. Father and daughter shook on it. Celeste told them they were crazy. Ronnie took the Greyhound to the city, moved into the Martha Washington Hotel for Women, and started making the rounds. Agents, go-sees, auditions. 'Too short.' 'Too curvy.' 'Too ethnic.' 'Would you shave your head?' 'Do you have a wig?' She got a few nibbles, met some photographers. Then she lost her personal and professional cherry for that cigarette ad. After that she actually made it to Europe and back, but it had all been hit-or-miss. Her enthusiasm wasn't enough to make up for the elusive 'it' she seemed to lack. The A-list girls, Iman, Beverly, Mounia, Magic, Sheila, worked all the time. The B-list girls worked when the A's weren't available. C's got the A and B leftovers, and then there was everybody else. At TV auditions the names changed to Jasmine, Janet, and Robin, but the story was the same. Ronnie was still in New York, drifting somewhere between C and everybody else. It just wasn't as easy as it used to be. Or as much fun. And she wasn't as young as she used to be, either.

But today was a good day. Ronnie turned down

Fifth Avenue and slowed her pace to allow for a little window shopping. The black mink bomber trimmed in leather made her stop. The mannequin posed right next to the big red SALE sign, and for a second Ronnie's reflection in the glass made it look like she was already wearing it. It was definitely her. Not over the top and tacky like that hideous red fox number her friend Kayla had been so proud of, or uptight and pretentious like the boring little ranch mink Celeste had worn to the funeral even though it wasn't *that* cold. SALE. Ronnie looked in the window another few seconds. *If I get that commercial.*

She continued down Fifth and entered the smoked glass building for the callback. Ronnie took two spins through the revolving doors, cranking up her energy. It made the building service guys laugh. *Yes! I got the power.* She was a few minutes early for her two forty-five call time, so she paced the lobby, getting into character, focusing, transforming herself into the young entrepreneur whose business got a boost when she switched to FlexTime Long Distance Service. Ronnie wore the same black trousers, red silk twin set, and gold button earrings she'd worn to the audition and she felt like she had 'it.' *And my hair looks two hundred percent better.*

Ronnie always felt more confident at second readings because it meant they already liked what she could do, so she was free to do it better. At two forty she rode the elevator up, followed the sign pointing the way to the FlexTime callbacks. Before she could sign in she was greeted by the same ad exec who made her feel so comfortable before.

'We're ready for you.' The woman was round and brown with short-cropped hair.

The woman's vibe was definitely large and in charge, but she was also very encouraging at the audition. Ronnie felt her confidence growing as she was ushered into the taping room. She shook hands firmly with the men seated next to the video camera, then took her place across the room, behind the white line. The copy was printed on an easel placed in her line of vision, but she knew it by heart. 'FlexTime lets me do business anytime!' Ronnie's heart pumped like a runner who knew she had the race won. When she got the signal she slated her name and gave them two different readings. First she did her 'mellow, unquestionably Black but not street' rendition, followed by her 'so crisp and clear I could be from anywhere and nobody would know I'm Black' version. Ronnie saw them taking notes, heard whispering behind the camera. The whole thing took two minutes, but the account exec walked her to the door, gave her a wink and a thumbs-up. Ronnie was flying.

And she was still up when she arrived downtown that night for the party. She had changed clothes six times before settling on black leather pants and a skintight, sheer brown tank that made her look topless until you got real close. She stepped off the elevator, put on her pleasantly disinterested smile, and casually searched the cavernous space for her friend Kayla, who'd convinced Ronnie this was *the* event of the week. Kayla, whose real name was Margaret, was an in-between, like Ronnie, still struggling to make her life work out the way she planned it nearly twenty years ago. She had a high-pitched voice that she figured would make her perfect for cartoons, but the voice-over thing hadn't panned out yet. She had recently cut her hair skull short and gotten new head shots to shake it up a little. Never one to miss an opportunity to charm the person who could turn her career around, she made it her business to know what was happening, when, and how to get in.

Ronnie was midmakeover on Thursday night when Kayla dropped by the Sable Shades counter to give her the scoop. 'The loft belongs to Michael somebody. He's some kinda investment banker or broker or something. Anyway, he made a whole heap of money in the stock market and his uncle or somebody is the mayor of . . . Atlanta, I think. I'm not sure. So this guy, the one with the loft, not the mayor, just got married to a singer who used to work with Quincy. Her brother is what's his name, you know he used to play for the Knicks, but anyway she just got a lead role in . . . *Rent*, yeah, I think that's it. And her new hubby is throwing this party to celebrate his bride's good fortune with a hundred or so of their closest friends. I heard Wesley might stop by. He's shooting a movie here, you know.'

Ronnie always added an hour to whatever time Kayla said they'd meet, but even that plus the forty-five minutes it took her to find a taxi and get down here apparently wasn't enough. She adjusted her new Prada bag on her shoulder, took a glass of champagne from the passing waiter, sipped, and continued to search the sea of faces. Ronnie dug out her cigarettes, glanced around for an ashtray, then noticed no one was smoking.

'They make it really hard for us. You have to go outside or up on the roof.' The nasal voice behind her was vaguely familiar. Ronnie turned. The face was familiar too. Pecan brown, bland, rimless glasses. At

68

first she couldn't place him. Brooks Brothers pin stripe, rep tie. When Ronnie figured it out, she didn't let him know.

'I know you – Veronica Frazier.' He grinned. 'R. Phillip Dade. From the bank.'

Ronnie feigned puzzlement for a beat to take him down a notch. 'Oh? . . . Yes . . . I remember.' She only gave him her sixty-watt smile this time. 'Small world.'

'I'm going up for a smoke. I'd be delighted to have your company.'

Ronnie looked at her watch. She didn't want to miss Kayla. 'I'm meeting someone who's . . .' She was dying for a butt. 'Uh . . . never mind.' *Let her wait for me for a change. Besides this'll be amusing.* 'Why not?'

Ronnie weaved through the crowd behind him to the bustling kitchen, which was bigger than her whole apartment, then out a steel door, up a short flight of stairs, onto the roof, into the night air. Trees and shrubs lined walkways that led off in several different directions. 'Each resident has a private area,' R. Phillip said. They emerged into a garden Ronnie could instantly imagine in the summertime, but right now it was really cold. She crossed her arms over her chest 'cause she knew her nips already stood at attention. A slice of moon hung over the Flatiron Building. *Wow.* But she maintained her cool, perched casually on the end of a cedar bench, and took out her pack. R. Phillip put an orange flame to the tip almost before she got the filter to her lips. Ronnie cupped her hand around his to protect the fire from the wind. His hands were soft, a little doughy, but warm.

'It's windproof.' He lit his own cigarette and snapped the gold lighter closed.

'Convenient.' Ronnie tried to figure out whether she meant that to sound as snide as it did. 'I wouldn't have taken you for a smoker.'

'I'm not. I'm a quitter!' He chuckled at his own lame humor. 'About every six months, I give them up for a while. Then one day I look down and I'm holding a lit one. I never remember exactly how it happens.'

'Convenient.' Ronnie said it again.

'Look. I'm sorry I couldn't help you at the bank. I . . .'

'Don't be. It was no big deal.' *Yeah. It was no problem avoiding my bill collectors a little longer. And scrounging around in coat pockets and old purses for change and tokens.* 'It's lovely up here.'

'They had a great cookout last Fourth of July. Terrific for watching the fireworks.' He took a drag. 'So, you're friends with Mike and Felice?' He phrased it as a question, but she knew the answer was really the password. He wanted to make sure she belonged. She'd make him wait. 'Mike went to Morehouse with my older brother,' he offered, still waiting for Ronnie to reveal her connection. 'And we're all fraternity brothers.'

Ass. 'Ah. Old friends. That's great. It's so hard to make new ones in this town.' *Just a little longer.*

'Are you Greek?'

'No. I was never interested in pledging.' *I didn't go to college either, you jerk.* 'My sister did, though. I guess I'm not much of a joiner.' Ronnie could hear the wheels turning, and before he could ask her about her sister, she crushed her cigarette under her heel and stood to leave. 'My friend must be wondering where I am by now.' *Okay.* 'She and Felice have the same

70

voice coach. And they were on one of the soaps together. *All My Children* maybe?' *No names.* Ronnie had no idea where or how Kayla heard about this party. But her story sounded good. She knew R. Phillip would buy it. *Now he knows I'm a mongrel, but I have a professional connection to his crowd.* Ronnie knew the type. She wasn't really 'one of them,' but there were always exceptions.

'So from what I can see, I bet you're an actress as well.' R. Phillip gave Ronnie a thorough, not even subtle once-over and grinned dumbly.

They were always ready to grant some sort of temporary pedigree for her. 'Yes. Yes, I am.' She smiled her 'you'll be lucky to know me when I'm famous' smile. *How long will it take?*

'So, have I seen you in anything?'

'Maybe.' She shivered against the cool breeze and hugged her arms around herself. 'I've done some commercials, a few films, nothing major – yet.' *Come on, Mr Dade. Ask me out. You know you want to. You're intrigued. I'm 'different from other women you know.'* These guys were always good for dinner at some new, expensive, hard-to-get-into restaurant. They spent lots of money and liked arm candy to show off, but years ago Ronnie had imposed a one-date limit. She'd use them, they'd use her, no fuss, no muss, no expectations. It worked very well. *If he starts another sentence with 'so,' I might strangle him right here on this roof.*

'So, I was wondering if I could call you sometime? Let me make up for what happened at the bank.'

Bingo!

'There's this great new restaurant! Reservations are impossible to get, but a buddy of mine knows . . .'

Thank you very much! The streak continues! Ronnie

71

acted surprised, then smiled pleasantly. 'Um . . . ah . . . sure. You certainly have my number.' *And boy do I ever have yours. And you, sir, are not my type.*

Of course Ronnie didn't know what that even meant. Over the years her type had changed almost as often as her address. She started her jock block in high school, and it lasted through her first two years in New York when she decided that while their bodies were hard, so were their heads. It was followed immediately by the deep, soul-searching, writer-actor and by the *way I have even less than you* phase. She rebounded to the TV news/sports guys but quickly tired of not being the cute one. That led to the corporately mobile, leverage my way to the top brother spate, where R. Phillip would have fit quite nicely. This moved her directly into her older men with money moment, which didn't last any longer than the 'it's only angina could you hand me my pills' date. At least one 'real' boyfriend emerged from most of these periods. Ronnie would pin her hopes that this might be the one. Then she'd want too much and he'd offer too little, or she'd find somebody else's underwear, or money missing from her purse. And the same pin that held the hopes usually popped the bubble. So two years ago, fed up with the pickings and deciding her type didn't exist, Ronnie declared a moratorium. It had been a long, dry spell, but R. Phillip, while he might be useful, wasn't the one to break it.

She reached out her hand and touched his sleeve, but it was so brief and light R. Phillip almost thought he'd imagined it. Ronnie eased away. 'I'd better get back.' She disappeared down the path toward the stairs and added some bounce to her step because she knew he was watching.

Kayla had been a no-show at the party, and Ronnie was on her way out the door when she called two days later. 'Sorry, girl. I was on my way, then Buster called me. You know Buster. I dated him last year for a while.' Ronnie played with the stack of mail by the phone while Kayla rattled on. 'Anyway, he used to do the weather on Channel Five, and now he's doing sports in Miami but he still knows e-v-e-r-y-body.' Ronnie didn't like mail. It was usually people asking for money she didn't have. It put her in a bad mood, so she didn't like to open it. Besides, she'd paid most of her bills. 'So Buster invited me to a screening of that new Will Smith flick. *And* to the private party after. I know you know I told you I cut Buster loose 'cause he's one tired, boring motherfruther, but I had to go to this. You'll never guess who was there!'

'I can't talk, Kayla. I got another callback for that phone company gig. I'll call you later.' And even though they always shared information, just in case one of them heard about a casting the other hadn't, Ronnie didn't tell her about the audition for a sitcom pilot she was going to after that.

'Thanks for coming by, Ronnie. This campaign is quite extensive. The client wanted to see you one more time.' The ad exec's words echoed in Ronnie's head as she rode down in the elevator. 'In order to be sure.' On the corner she checked the address for her next appointment and headed up Fifth. *National ad. Major market rollout. Residuals. BIG residuals. Spokesperson! I could be the FlexTime lady. Like James Earl Jones. I could be* the brand! *I could be in a Super Bowl commercial!* Ronnie sailed along the street, her feet barely touching the pavement, oblivious to everything but the story in her head until she found herself smack in front of that mink bomber jacket again. Her next audition was in the same building, and the jacket was still there. *This has to mean something.* She rationalized. *It's a sign. I've never been to a call here in seventeen years.*

It fit like it was custom made for her. *Another sign.* She wrote out the check and waited while they called the bank to verify her funds. She'd have enough to tide her over. There would be a few weeks before the residuals started, but she'd have her day rate for shooting the ad right away. *Wait till I tell Ma and Da* – Ronnie stopped the thought cold. *Ma'll share the news with sister dear. I'll call Nik myself.*

Ronnie wore the jacket home. She felt so good she opened a bottle of merlot and plowed through the wicker basket of mail. Five or six pieces in, she saw the stamp and the postmark. Rio de Janeiro, Brasil. He was coming back in six weeks and wanted his apartment. *Perfect, 'cause I am tired of this shit hole. Maybe I'll use a broker this time. That's a first.* The phone rang as Ronnie counted her chickens and piled her eggs in the basket.

'Glad you left us your home number. I didn't want to leave the message on your service. I wanted you to hear it from me.'

Yes! Finally! I'm the FlexTime Girl! Ronnie spooned honey into her tea.

'It was close. They really loved you . . .' Ronnie stopped stirring, her spoon suspended midair. '. . . But the client made the final decision. They got hung up on your hair being different.' She didn't hear the rest.

The spoon landed on the receipt for her jacket,

which sat on top of the mail on the kitchen counter. FINAL SALE. No Refunds. No Returns. No Exchanges. Drops of tea splattered onto her checkbook, which lay open next to the mail. The balance hardly covered next month's rent, let alone first and last months' security and key money for a new place. Ronnie's basket full of unhatched eggs crashed to the floor along with her cup of tea.

4

'. . . running into a brick wall only hurts you.'

Here we go. Deep breath. Celeste shifted all of the plastic grocery bags to one hand, propped the screen door open with her foot. She dug past the date book, wallet, and coupons in her purse, found the *F* key ring, and fumbled with the locks on her parents' back door. Will had been dead for six months, but she still thought of it as her parents' house. She'd taken to stopping by a few times a week to check, because somebody had to.

'You wouldn't need so many locks if you'd sell this place and move out where we are. It's much safer, Mother.' Celeste fussed up the stairs and into the kitchen. 'Mother!? Where are you?' She put the bags on the counter and peeked in the living room. It could have been a lovely room, with the fireplace and honey oak mantel, but her mother was never more creative than the oatmeal and gold tweed Herculon sofa and love seat that sat on sculptured pea green carpet with the nap worn flat. As a kid, Celeste used to be embarrassed when the neighbors would come over because their homes looked so much more polished. *Daddy was so ambitious. Think where they could have gone if Mother had tried, even a little.* Celeste hung her coat in the hall closet. 'Mother!?'

'I heard you the first and second times.' Della trudged up the back steps from the basement, lugging a full laundry basket.

'Let me take that.' Celeste reached for the basket.

Della shooed her away. 'I wash clothes when you're not around, you know.'

Unfazed, Celeste plowed ahead. 'You could have a washer and dryer right in your apartment *and* no stairs! Wouldn't that be great?' She reached in the drawer, pulled out an apron, and shook it out in front of her. 'This looks awful.' Her lips tightly pinched, she examined spots and stains that no amount of washing would eliminate. 'Where are the new aprons I bought you?'

'They'll end up just like that one.'

'That's not the point. They'd look nice now.' Celeste waited for her mother to tell her where the aprons were or go get one. But Della didn't move a muscle. Finally, Celeste slipped the scuzzy one on over her teal suit and started unpacking her bounty. 'Did you see those boys hanging out on the corner by the Clifton house? Someone should call the police. This neighborhood is not what it used to be.'

'No, I guess it's not.' Della put the basket down by the door. 'Things change.' She flipped the stairway light off. 'But *those* boys live in that house now. Moved in last month. I hired 'em to clean up the yard, now that the snow's finally gone.' She pulled back the curtain, looked out the window, and smiled to herself. 'Um-hm. Did a nice job, didn't they?'

'They might be all right, but they could be little hoodlums waiting to rob you. You can't be too careful

77

these days.' Celeste carried twenty boxes of spaghetti to the pantry.

'What the devil?'

'I was at the store this morning . . .'

'What else is new?' Della asked sarcastically. She knew her daughter's Saturday ritual began with a seven A.M. trip to the supermarket. Whether it was Top's or Wegman's depended on the sales, which she would have carefully researched and organized her shopping list accordingly. As a rule, by nine she had completed her shopping, picked up and dropped off dry cleaning, filled up the tank, had her car washed, and was back home putting her groceries away. Having crossed several items off her to-do list gave her a feeling of great satisfaction and, to some extent, comfort. That left the rest of her day free. Free for steering committee meetings, annoying her mother, sales at the mall, Women's Day committee meetings, annoying her mother, outlet shopping in Pennsylvania, sorority meetings, Literacy Volunteers, and annoying her mother.

'It was a great sale, Mother.'

'I'm sure it was.'

'Maybe I'll put this on now.' She held up a huge ham.

'What am I gon' do with that? It'll take me six months to eat it! There's only one of me, you know.' Della jammed her hands into the pockets of her duster.

Does she have to say that all the time? Celeste faced the counter so only the cabinets registered her annoyed expression.

'Besides, I buy my own groceries. Do I look like I'm starvin'?'

'Well, I don't think you're eating right.' Celeste opened the refrigerator, moved the plastic sherbet container of fruit cocktail and the leftover half of a chicken pot pie to make room for the ham, then opened the crisper drawer. 'Look at this lettuce and celery. They're turning to slime.' She reached for an empty grocery bag, deposited the offending produce. 'And why aren't you dressed? I ordered all those jogging suits for you to wear! Are you sick?' She gawked at Della's coffee coat.

'I dress to go to work. I don't jog, and I don't need to impress anybody around here, unlike some people.' Della rolled her eyes at Celeste's suit. 'I know you didn't get all done up to bring me a ham and some spaghetti.' Della handed her a paper towel to wipe up the slime juice.

'I'm meeting Lydia later. We're going to select the flowers for the benefit.'

'That woman won't ever be your friend, Celeste. No matter how many ways you turn yourself inside out.' And Della had watched Celeste try to impress people she thought were important, had more money or higher social standing her whole life. When Celeste was young, the one or two invitations she'd receive to Doctor or Attorney so-and-so's daughter's birthday party were more exciting than Christmas. She'd go into her stash of hoarded allowance and buy a gift that was far too expensive, an angora sweater or a charm bracelet. Other kids brought a record, or a bottle of Love's Lemon Fresh. Celeste's present never received the ooohs and aaahs she hoped for. It would stand out like a neon sign that blinked 'I'm trying.' The hand-written thank-you note always followed in a few days, but she never got the phone call to 'come over and

79

hang out,' or 'wanna go to Santora's for pizza?' that meant she was accepted. She was still trying.

'Don't be ridiculous. Of course she's my friend. We've vacationed together for years!'

Della recognized a stalemate and changed the subject. 'Did your sister give you her new address and phone number?'

'Oh. She's moved again? Isn't that twice since Christmas?' Celeste replied, then changed the subject back. 'You need to get out more.' She opened the milk carton, took a sniff, screwed up her face, then poured the contents down the drain and added the container to her plastic bag. 'You should come to church tomorrow. Reverend Walters . . .'

'I don't *feel* like going to church.' Della didn't hold much with religion, hadn't since she was a teenager. Will was a staunch churchgoer, and she'd go now and then to please him. It wasn't that she wasn't a believer, quite the contrary, but Della was convinced long ago that the destiny of her soul was between her and the Lord, and she neither needed nor wanted to share her feelings with anyone else, much less a bunch of meddlesome busybodies. 'And for your information, I get out of here every day. Or doesn't going to work count?' Della got the pad and pencil by the phone, copied Ronnie's new address from the Chapman Brothers Funeral Home calendar where she'd written it. 'You weren't worried about how much I got out before your father passed. Why is it so important now?' She ripped the page from the spiral, handed it to Celeste. 'Here. Just in case.'

'I don't even copy them in my book anymore.' Celeste took the paper, pinched off jagged edges as she spoke. 'And it's different now. You shouldn't spend so much time by yourself. It isn't good.' She took a breath, tried to sound like her plan was spur of the moment instead of carefully thought out. 'Okay. Forget about tomorrow, but come to Easter service with us next week. We're not going away. My husband says he's too busy at the clinic.' She propped an elbow on the open refrigerator door. 'I don't know how Everett can stand that awful place. If I'm sick of it, surely he must be.'

'He started it. What are the chances he's gon' leave? And where is he? Why aren't you with him instead of annoyin' me?'

Celeste closed the refrigerator, looked away quickly. 'He's . . . uh . . . I don't know, playing tennis or something. I'll see him back at the house.'

Della noticed the missed beat but didn't call attention to it. She'd had a feeling something wasn't right there for a long time. But it wasn't her place to say so.

'I made sure he's not working next Sunday.' Celeste recovered and returned to her script. 'We'll pick you up, and I know! We'll go shopping during the week! You could really use some new dresses. And we'll have brunch on Sunday at Fanny's or maybe E. B. Green's. I'll make reservations.'

Della sat down at the table, popped open a can of honey-roasted peanuts, and waited for Celeste's sudden gust of wind to blow over.

Celeste got her date book out of her purse, slipped Ronnie's newest new address inside, then flipped to her schedule for the week. 'How's Wednesday? I'll come by your job after school and we'll go to the Galleria. It'll be mobbed. Everyone's having Easter sales, you know, but it's the nicest mall.' Celeste penciled in the date, closed her book. 'Wednesday it is.'

81

'Did you hear me say yes?'

'But . . .'

'But I'm not goin' shoppin' this week, so you can take out your little book and your eraser. And lunch or brunch or whatever next Sunday would be nice, but don't do it on my account.'

'Everett and I are going anyway!'

'Okay. Thank you.' Della poured a handful of nuts. 'You got any more plans for my time?'

Celeste paused. 'Not exactly.' She'd sidled up to this talk before, but Della had managed to slip away. This time Celeste was loaded for bear, and she planned to come away with an answer even if she got clawed in the process. 'I hate to bring this up . . .'

'Then don't.'

Why does she give me such a hard time? Celeste took a deep breath. 'Even if you won't move out of here, you have to think about selling some of those houses.' She knew this had to be brief and to the point. 'It's way too much for you to be bothered with.'

Della cut her eyes at Celeste, returned to her peanuts.

Celeste hated it when her mother wouldn't dignify her with an answer. It made her feel four feet tall and eleven years old. 'I know Mr Shorty is looking after them, and you trust him, but he's getting old too.' She furrowed her brow. 'I drove past the house on Verplanck this week. One of the side windows is broken.' Celeste waited for some kind of response, walked back to the refrigerator when she didn't get one. 'You're only delaying the inevitable. How are you going go keep up with all that property? You haven't even gone through Daddy's clothes yet, have you? I saw that ancient plaid sport coat of his in the

82

closet just now. Someone less fortunate can use . . .'

'Leave that jacket right where it is,' Della snapped. She had planned to give the jacket away thirty years ago, until Ronnie found that note folded up in the pocket. It had hung there ever since, to remind him that she might have forgiven, but she never forgot.

'Okay. But I can go through the rest of his things, bag them up for the City Mission. I think it'll make you feel better.'

'I feel fine, but go ahead since it's worryin' you.'

Makes it sound like she's doin' me a favor. Celeste took out the ham again, snatched a roaster from the cabinet by the stove, struggled to keep the mad out of her voice. 'Well, you went through his papers and things to file taxes, didn't you?'

Della squared her shoulders, assumed her immovable object pose. Truth was, she'd planned to tackle the attic many a Saturday morning, or Thursday night, had her hand on the knob, but she never turned it. She knew it was past time for income tax, but she'd rather take a spanking than be up there sorting through his papers and clothes that smelled of him, wading through too many yesterdays.

'You didn't, did you?! Mother! What am I going to do with you!?' Celeste's voice hit the high spike. 'Why didn't you say something before now?'

'Do whatever you want, Celeste, and leave me the hell alone.' Della got up, retrieved her laundry basket, and headed out of the kitchen.

Celeste's hands shook, so she steadied herself with the routine tasks of cooking. She rinsed the ham, squeezed on some syrup, shoved it in the oven, just like Della always did it. In one of her grief-counseling

83

books she'd read about a man who kept his dead wife's false teeth in a jar on the kitchen windowsill for over a year. Used to drive his son crazy. Then one day the man just threw them away. When he was ready to let her go, he did. Until then he needed something to hang on to. Maybe that's what her mother was doing. At any rate, she'd outlasted her this time. *She'll see I'm right about this.*

After grabbing her reading glasses from her purse, Celeste walked quietly upstairs, past Della in her sewing room, which Celeste and Ronnie had dubbed Della's House of Style when they were kids. In one of their few joint efforts the girls had ganged up to persuade Della that her 'original creations' made them look like rejects. Even their father helped plead their case. Della's feelings were hurt, but she turned her hand to her own wardrobe and over the years had made herself hundreds of smock tops, all pullovers since she never mastered the art of the buttonhole. And she made curtains. Every room in the house had seasonal changes of window dressing.

Celeste opened the attic door to Will's World. She and Ronnie had stopped calling it that when the name came too close to the truth. His room always smelled of Old Spice and shoe polish. It still did, a little. Right after the accident, she and Ronnie had picked up socks, stacked papers, gathered towels from the bathroom, stripped the narrow single bed that stood forlornly in the far corner. The task was too sad to stay at for long. Besides, she and Ronnie were on each other's nerves in no time. Celeste hadn't been up here more than once or twice since October. She meant to, but the holidays were busy as usual, and she had been preparing herself for the assistant principal's interview. If she could move one more notch up the pay scale, maybe she could convince Everett they could afford to buy their own summer place instead of always renting or waiting for an invite.

Celeste had expected the room to be cold. Empty, unused, and dead meant cold somehow. *It's warmer than downstairs.* She took off the apron and her jacket, draped them on the hook on the back of the door where her father's snap-brim cap used to hang. She stood in the splash of sunlight coming through the skylight, looked around. There was no Della presence up here. To Celeste it didn't seem deliberate, but gradual, the way continents that used to be joined had slowly, imperceptibly separated until there were oceans between them. Up here Della was a million miles away. *When did they start drifting away from each other?*

The room was arranged with comfort and convenience in mind. Not particularly macho, although she had flushed and fumbled when she stumbled on the stash of skin magazines under his bed. Will's entertainment center was actually a double set of deep mahogany bookshelves, built-ins he'd removed from a house on Florida Street after he noticed long, charred scars from cigarettes laid on the shelves and left to burn. They stood on either side of his megascreen television. The upper shelves held two VCRs, a couple of camcorders, a short-wave radio, an electronic weather station, and stereo components, including his latest toy, a CD player that held one hundred disks. Lower shelves were crowded with repair manuals, how-to books, and catalogs of every variety. Will loved himself some gadgets, and he believed in shopping the easy way. Celeste could hear him. 'Why should I go to the store, when they'll bring what I want right to my door?'

Celeste examined the photos he had arranged on the middle shelves. Everett, arm around Celeste, who held baby Niki, giggling at the stuffed dog wrapped in her arms. Ronnie grinning five feet wide on her Expressway billboard. Celeste picked up the faded family portrait taken in the snow, in front of the house on Chester Street. Will held a shovel over his shoulder. One of Della's hands rested on her very pregnant belly, the other held hands with a decidedly grim-faced Celeste. She tried to remember that day, or who was behind the camera, but nothing came to mind. *They look so young.* She could feel tears collecting so she put it down, turned away.

The midnight blue leather sofa, ordered straight from the Penney's catalog, had a recliner at one corner and pull-out end tables. Celeste ran her hand across the rings left by countless cans of Genesee beer, picked up the remote, clicked on the TV. *Just for a little company.* Stock car races on ESPN. *The last channel he watched.* Celeste shook off the feeling of disquiet, continued to surf until she settled on a decorating show. She figured she'd start with his papers because getting the taxes filed was the most pressing issue, so she went to her father's desk.

The thing was massive, longer and wider than the dining room table and made from heavy, dark-stained oak. It had taken him, Mr Shorty, and the next-door neighbor all afternoon to get it up the stairs. There were carved gargoyles on the corners, and brass lion heads with bared teeth opened the drawers. Celeste remembered thinking it was the most hideous thing she'd ever seen. He'd found it at the flea market out in Clarence, and the dealer claimed it came from a castle in England. Her father didn't care whose palace it was from. He liked that it was solid and big enough to hold the paperwork, leases, receipts, deeds, mortgages, repair estimates for all the properties he already owned and would have plenty of space left over for those he planned to acquire.

A brand-new PC sat boldly in the middle of the huge old desk, flanked by the cordless phone and answering machine on one side and the fax machine on the other. It seemed an awkward meeting of the past and the future. Will could preach about the importance of keeping up with the times. 'We don't drive horse and buggy nomore, neither,' he'd say. Celeste reached across a stack of CD-ROMs and removed a fax from the machine. An estimate for a new roof for – she couldn't make out the property address. *He must have requested this before* . . . Celeste blinked back a tear, went to the cabinet by the door. On the shelf along with the boxes of Salada and Swiss Miss and a jar of store brand instant coffee sat Ronnie's faded Esso Gasoline mug. The tiger's grinning face had faded to an orange smudge. Celeste took it out, dropped in a tea bag, and filled it with water from the five-gallon cooler in the corner. She popped it in the microwave and waited. The tea would be an elixir to ward off the haints that lay in wait for her among her father's things.

An hour later, her mug was empty. She'd gone through all but two of the drawers on the right side of the desk, and the stack of paper she was currently sorting rested in her lap. Sitting in Will's oversized swivel chair, with the reading glasses she hated balanced precariously on the tip of her nose, Celeste felt like a detective, plowing through her father's history. Most of Will's files were orderly. Each property had a folder that contained the deed, bills, receipts, and records for the house. Celeste had made four neat piles on the desk in front of her. The first contained papers that pertained to their income taxes. Fortunately she found the name of Will's accountant and planned to call him Monday morning. Next came 'Ask Mr Shorty,' 'Ask Mother,' and 'File.' A fifth pile contained odd bits of memorabilia she'd unearthed. Matchbooks from the Humboldt Inn, construction paper birthday cards she and Ronnie had made eons ago, a crystal teardrop earring, the receipt for the Autumn Haze mink jacket he'd bought Della one Christmas. Ronnie was barely toddling. Celeste could still see her father's chest poked out in his flannel robe, still hear him saying, 'The whole coat is fur, not just the collar.' She remembered begging her mother to let her try it on. Della draped the fur over her daughter's narrow shoulders, and the bottom dragged the floor. When Della got all dressed up and put that jacket on, Celeste used to think she looked like a movie star. *What ever happened to those days?*

The smoky-sweet aroma of the ham had worked its way upstairs, but Celeste was too deep in another world to pay attention. She dropped a January 1969 bill from Iroquois Gas into the already overflowing wastebasket, reached for another folder.

Little Pond Road? Where's that? Celeste ran Buffalo streets through her brain, but Little Pond didn't ring a bell. She flipped through the folder. The house had been painted a year ago. Will had bought a new stove and refrigerator too, but she noticed they were more expensive than the ones he usually put in the units.

And where is Gaston Appliance? She examined the deed. *Prosper, North Carolina? Is he kidding? What kind of name is Prosper?* She thought a moment, had a vague notion that Della and Will were born there, but nobody ever brought it up. Neither one had much of an accent except on the odd word like *po*-lice or *ho*-tel so you'd forget they were born somewhere else. Their move North had pretty much been a one-way deal. There were no summertime excursions to visit relatives or even rushed car trips to bury the dead. During all the funeral preparations there was never a discussion of taking her father back home. *To Prosper, North Carolina?* Buffalo had become his home. Will's brothers and sisters had all moved away from home too. Detroit. Indianapolis. St. Louis. Camden. *Why on earth would Daddy buy property down there? And not tell me?* Celeste flipped the pages. *Deeded to: Will Frazier, Celeste Frazier English, and Veronica Frazier by Odella Womack Frazier? What the . . . ?* None of this made sense. Stapled to the back was a small manila envelope. Inside she found two keys.

'Mother!' Celeste ran down the stairs and found Della still in the sewing room, sitting on the old vinyl hassock by the window, surrounded by shelves of fabric for future projects and plastic trash bags full of yarn. She didn't knit or crochet, but she'd been 'plannin' to learn' for more than twenty years, so she stocked up on skeins of yarn in every possible hue whenever she found a good sale.

'Do you know about this?' Celeste thrust the deed at her mother.

Della gave the paper a cursory glance, sucked her teeth. 'Oh for cryin' out loud.' She turned away. 'Wish I'd a tore that mess up before your father ever saw it.'

89

'Torn it up?! Why would you do that?!' Celeste's voice grew louder with each utterance. 'Whose house was this?!'

'Don't you use that tone to me.' Della shot her a look.

Celeste yielded, dropped her eyes momentarily before she spoke. 'I'm sorry. I didn't mean to yell, but . . .'

'I'm a tell you this just once, so you better listen good.' Della took a breath. 'You listenin'?'

'Yes ma'am.'

'That house and land belonged to my daddy. It came to me a couple a years back. I told Will I didn't care what he did with it, I didn't want it. When I left Prosper I said I was never goin' back and I meant it. I know he sent Shorty down to look the house over, and that's all I know. So now it belongs to you and your sister. Y'all best figure out how to sell it.'

'Our grandfather's house? I didn't even know his name! All you ever said is that he and your mother died when you were young.' Celeste's heart was racing. 'Then you married Daddy and moved here.' Over the years Della's story never varied, and more probing only netted a bad attitude. Della never talked about any old days, good, bad, or indifferent, so finally Celeste had stopped asking. But this was a house, solid, substantial. *Real* estate. *She's gotta tell me something.* 'Well what does it look like?'

'You heard what I said. Now I'm through with this conversation.' Della picked up a skein of red yarn.

'But Mother, I . . .' Della's intense glare interrupted her. Celeste stood her ground a long moment, then realized that running into a brick wall only hurts you.

She backed out of the room, made it halfway down

90

the stairs, then had to sit and regroup. It was like she'd won the grand prize, but nobody else seemed to want it. *I'm not gonna let her make me feel bad about inheriting a house.* Celeste leafed through the papers in her lap. They showed ownership of forty-five acres. *It's probably a swamp. That would be perfect. Whatever it is, it's one more thing for me to take care of.* The piercing bleat of the smoke alarm shocked her back to reality, and she went running to check on the long forgotten ham.

Della heard it too, but the alarm going off in her head was louder. Besides, she didn't want that ham in the first place. No more than she had wanted to go and live at Little Pond Road.

MONDAY, DECEMBER 27, 1948
CADYSVILLE, NORTH CAROLINA

'*MAMA!*' Odella's howl heaved itself against the ponderous December clouds and the pelting rain, silencing the somber, prayerful moans of the mourners.

They had been packed in the white frame church all morning, singing and praising and shouting loud enough to wake the dead. Usually Odella sang in the choir, because she had a voice that was big and rich as a grown woman's, but on this day she sat in the first pew, rocking, her hands balled up in the lap of her white cotton dress. All through the service she prayed for her sweet mama to get up out of that box, because this could not be.

Nothing had made sense since she got called out of class, how many days ago? She'd been staring studiously at the open reader in front of her because she'd already finished the story, but Ruthetta Buttons, the girl she shared the desk and book with, was still inching her finger along the page. So Odella kept her head bowed because the last time she got caught daydreaming she received a lecture about the burden of being 'Aunt Haggar's chilren' and the teacher predicted her wasted future as another 'no-count colored gal' who wouldn't finish fifth grade, much less go on to A&T and make something of herself. 'I was puttin' my 'magination to work, like you said,' Odella had answered in defense. She was rewarded by a whipping with the willow switch that always stood, a silent warning, against the slate board.

'Odella, get your things and come on up here. You're needed at home.'

The teacher's voice had startled her. 'Yes'm.' She quickly gathered her belongings, happy because she figured that somehow her mama had extra time off.

At twenty-six, Odella's mother, Annie, had a reputation as one of the best cooks for counties around. Annie's mother had been a good cook, but Annie had a special gift. She could fix anything, from beef Wellington and baked Alaska to fried catfish and sweet potato pie, and have people licking their lips, their fingers, and wishing they could lick the plate.

Sometimes Annie took Odella with her on small jobs, a birthday luncheon or a christening brunch if it was nearby. Odella would watch her mother take charge of the kitchen and the household help. 'We'll need that silver tureen. And make sure it's polished. These string beans aren't fresh enough, try that market over on Salisbury Street.' People scurried to do her bidding because they knew without her there was no party. When she was eight, Odella told her mother she wanted to be a cook just like her. Annie about bit her head off. 'You'll do no such thing! I want something better than slaving over a hot stove for you!' Annie's grandmother had dropped dead in front of the stove on the plantation where she'd stayed after emancipation. Annie's mother worked as a cook six and a half days a week for thirty-seven years. Annie had come far enough to set her own workdays, but she didn't want *her* daughter in anybody's kitchen. So Annie showed her how to set a table from salad forks to fish knives and demitasse spoons, how to hold china up to the light to tell if it's really fine, and the proper way to pour tea, but never how to cook.

Between Thanksgiving and Christmas, Annie Williams's culinary services were in great demand by wealthy white families in Charlotte, and Annie made a good portion of her living in that month. She catered dinner parties and such the rest of the year, and together with the money she got from Odella's father, the two of them did just fine.

Odella liked it because her mother was home most of the time, and not grouchy and dead tired like her schoolmates' mothers who worked sharecropping, or in the mills or poultry plants. And Odella loved everything about Annie, from the way she plaited her hair in two straight rows down the back of her head to the way she sang 'The Sandman's Comin'' when she tucked her in at night.

Odella still curled up with Susie, the first rag doll her mother gave her. She was a cast-off toy with wide eyes, loopy black wool hair, and a dotted swiss dress. Annie had soaked her in tea for a week to make her brown-skinned. Odella adored the sugar cookies Annie baked shaped in the letters to spell out Odella Womack, and on her way home from school she would gather Queen Anne's lace and her mother would make them both crowns. Odella loved nothing more than to sit for hours, just the two of them, with slabs of Annie's homemade raisin bread and steaming cups of tea and milk, poring over glossy, color photos in the magazines Annie would bring from the homes where she worked. They'd drink in the unimagined possibilities life offered and plan their getaway from Cadysville to Australia or Bali or California because the pictures looked so beautiful. Even though she made Odella study her schoolwork, complete her chores, and mind her elders, Annie was fun.

So this year, like all the others, Odella and Annie had their own special Thanksgiving dinner, with roast goose and wild rice stuffing, collards from the garden, and fresh coconut cake for dessert, on the third Thursday in November instead of the fourth. Annie was feeling a little poorly, so when they'd cleaned up the kitchen she brewed some hog's hoof tea, then rubbed goose grease and camphor on her chest, which she wrapped in flannel, and got in bed under a heavy quilt to sweat it out. Despite the pungent smell and the hot, heavy quilts, Odella begged to sleep with her mother. Annie, afraid Odella would catch her cold, refused. But during the night Odella crawled under the covers to be near her and Annie didn't have the heart to put her out, so she spent the night circled in her mother's arms.

The next morning Annie left for Charlotte. She wasn't due back until Christmas Eve because she flat-out refused to work Christmas Day, then she'd be gone again till the day after New Year's. Odella stayed with Miz Cora and her children during that time. It was the longest six weeks Odella could imagine, and she was just starting to get excited because there were only four days left until she'd see her mama, but now she'd come early.

Waiting outside the two-room school was not Annie but Miz Cora, rocking side to side and wringing her hands. She didn't say a word, didn't even look at Odella directly, just hurried her to the old blue Ford. Odella knew something was wrong, but she was too scared to ask what.

Pastor Malone was waiting when they got to Miz Cora's. He went all around Robin Hood's barn, clearing his throat, looking up at the ceiling for the words to tell Odella that Annie had been called to be with her heavenly Father. Odella looked at him like he had three heads, and all of them were on fire. Then she all but called him a liar and refused to listen to him or anybody else who tried to tell her some nonsense about her mother being dead.

Christmas Eve Odella sneaked out of Miz Cora's house and waited on the porch at home. Waited all night in the spindle-back rocker, bundled in the old brown Pullman blanket that stayed folded in the seat. 'You are my sunshine, my only sunshine,' Odella sang in a whisper through the long, lonesome night. It was the first song she learned from her mama, and they always sang it together. 'Please don't take my sunshine away.' So she shivered and rocked and sang, because Annie always came home on Christmas Eve.

At first light Christmas morning Miz Cora found her, shivering, fingernails blue, eyes swollen and crusty from crying. That's when Odella knew she'd never see Annie again, and she felt like she'd been sucked up by a tornado and hurled off the edge of the world. She couldn't see, or feel, or hear, not even her own earth-shattering screams. Two days after that they dressed her in white and took her to the funeral.

And now the mourners ringed Annie's grave in the small churchyard, trying as best they could to protect themselves from the relentless downpour. Odella gripped the clod of earth Miz Cora gave her to sprinkle on her mother's coffin so tightly it dribbled through her fingers. Couldn't anybody see that Annie had taken all the air and sunshine with her and that right now all Odella wanted was to go with her too?

'Mama, don't leave me!' She flung herself on the ground and crawled in the red mud toward the gaping hole. 'Mama, please!' She felt hands snatch at her, tasted the dirt on her lips. Odella kicked, squirmed, hollered, and would not be moved. Then two huge hands grabbed her by the upper arms, lifted her to her feet, held on until the struggle went out of her.

'Looka here, Odella, ain't nothing to be done.' Usually Odell Womack's voice boomed, but he spoke gently to her, looked like he'd lost his last friend too. She grabbed two fistfuls of his tweed coat, buried her face in it, and cried, both her tears and the ones Odell couldn't shed. He stood there and let her, one hand resting on her shoulder, while the preacher pronounced Annie's ashes to ashes, accompanied by a weary, resigned hum from the congregation.

Odell was no stranger to his child. Three or four times a year Odella would come home after class and find him sitting at the table. Annie always cooked something extra-special those days. She wore clothes she usually saved for Sundays, and she looked even happier than she usually did. And he always brought something for Odella, whether it was a toy, a new dress, or a piece of money. She called him Papa, at least when nobody else was around, and he was the biggest man she'd ever seen, definitely bigger than anybody in Cadysville. Only thing she could think to compare him to were the hickory trees in the woods behind the house. When she was little she'd climb up his long sturdy legs and he'd stretch out his strong arms, like branches, for her to swing on. Then she'd sit on his knee, eyes wide, and listen while he told her a tale about Nat Turner or Paul Bunyan or Harriet Tubman and make it sound like he'd been right by their side. Then he'd keep company with Annie for a bit out on the porch, squeeze some folded bills into her hand, and he'd be gone. After Odella turned eight, there were no more laps or hugs. Odell kept more space between them. 'You too big for all that now,' he had said.

There'd been plenty of speculation around Cadysville the last few days about what Odell should do now that Annie had passed on. People in town had always had something to say about his keeping a full-time family in Prosper and a part-time family here. Never said it to his face, though. And he didn't slink around acting like he cared about their approval. He made no bones about the fact that Odella was his child. He couldn't have denied her if he had wanted. She was strong and sturdy, a sapling to Odell's tree, not birdlike, lighter than air, like Annie.

When the preacher had stopped speaking, Odell pried his daughter's hands from his coat. Mud streaked her white dress and Annie's good black wool coat that Miz Cora had made her wear. It had caked under her nails, smudged her face. He handed Odella his handkerchief, and she barely had the strength to reach for it.

'Come on.' His wide, callused hand swallowed her small, clenched one. It was the color and texture of a razor strop and felt tough and sturdy as resoled shoes. 'We goin' home.'

Home.

The word terrified Odella, and she trembled from someplace deep that didn't seem to have a bottom. What home? How could it be home if she didn't know where it was or what it looked like? If there was no Annie?

Odell picked her up and carried her to his car, a new green Pontiac, parked by the side of the road. He had found a blanket in the trunk for Odella to wrap up in. She was so cold, wet, and upset when she climbed in the car that her teeth chattered almost as loud as the flip-flop of the windshield wipers. When he drove off she craned her neck to see out the window, but in a moment they were on the interstate, headed away from her familiar, everyday, toward Prosper, and what?

'I went by the house, packed up your stuff. It's in the trunk.'

Odella wondered what he had brought and what she'd never see again, like the big milky green glass bowl with a chip in the rim that Annie wouldn't throw out because she liked the feel of it tucked under her arm when she mixed up a cake. Or the new white coverlet she was crocheting for Odella's bed. 'Uh . . . Did you get . . . the . . . there was some . . .'

'Spit it out, girl! You gotta speak up if you want anybody to know what's on your mind.'

'There was some magazines . . .'

98

'Them old ones, stacked up in the corner? Naw. Wasn't no cause to take that mess.'

Odella bit her lip. It was like the dreams shared over those pages got left behind too, to be thrown away with the rest of the trash. Her mother was gone, there was no going back for her, and nothing would ever be the same.

She stared at the white line in the road for miles, occasionally sneaking a glimpse of her father, but only when she was sure he wouldn't notice.

'That's cotton over there,' he nodded at a field as they passed. 'When I was a boy I used to pick it till my fingers bled.'

'Oh,' was all Odella could manage. She was having a hard enough time wrapping her mind around her father right here in the present, driving her to *his* house. She couldn't begin to imagine what he used to do.

Odell leaned to one side, wrestled a pack of Lucky Strikes and a matchbook out of his pants pocket, and struck a match with his thumbnail. Not a word passed between them for the next twenty miles, and the hypnotic, stutter-thump of the windshield wipers and the sizzle of tires on wet road put Odella in a trance. When Odell finally cleared his throat, she jumped.

'My wife, her name is Ethiopia.'

'Uh . . . Yessuh.'

'She knows about you, knows you're comin'.' He took a hard drag on his cigarette. Hardly any smoke escaped. 'You're always welcome in my house, Odella. Do you understand that?'

Odella's head bobbed up and down. She picked at the dirt under her nails.

Odell kept his eyes forward. 'I can't hear you nod your head.'

'Yessuh,' she said, all the while trying to picture these other people Annie told her she would never meet. On one of his visits Odella had asked him why he couldn't just stay with them. That night Annie had explained that her father had a wife and son, who lived in another town. She made it sound far away, like the places in the magazines, except where they were driving now still looked about the same as Cadysville. Odella had wanted to know why he got to have two families. 'He had that family before he had us,' Annie said. And to nobody in particular she added, 'We had love. It was just too late.' Annie sounded sad for a moment, but then she hugged Odella and added, 'He's a good and loyal man. I never wished for more than that. And he takes care of us, so don't you never hold that against him. You hear?' Odella had heard, but it was only words until now. She stole another quick peek. Odell had stiff, bristly hairs sticking out of his ears and a splatter of little brown moles along his jaw.

Silence for twenty more miles.

'She said you can call her mama . . .'

'No! . . . I mean I can't . . . It's just . . .'

'It's all right. You'll figure something out. Looka here, there's some sandwiches in that paper sack on the floor.'

Odella fished out two brown paper parcels, each with a slab of ham between two slices of bread. He ate and she sat with hers in her lap for forty more miles.

'See that church over there.' Odell's long leathery finger pointed past her. 'Built with bricks from my yard. Got the biggest brickyard in the county. You know that, don't you?'

'Yessuh.' Annie had explained what he did for a living. Odella just couldn't quite figure out how anybody *made* bricks.

'You don't have to say *yessuh* every time I speak to you, Odella. This ain't the army. I'm your father. Your brother Henry's fifteen, and I don't think he's ever said *yessuh* to me unless he was tryin' to avoid a whippin'. I don't know what to . . . say about him. He's . . . Don't let him push you around, that's all.' Odell's voice trailed off, but not before Odella could hear the sadness.

The next time Odell spoke they were turning off the highway. 'House's at the end of the road. We'll be there in a minute.'

The rain had stopped, and what was left of the daylight slipped quietly through the curtain of towering, longleaf pines that lined the narrow dirt road. Odella couldn't make out neighboring houses or anything else through the trees, except more trees.

Odell stopped the car. 'This is it.' He got out, opened the trunk, and grabbed the battered blue suitcase that had been Annie's. Odella just stared. He came around and held the door open for her. 'Come on, girl, get on outta there. I'm sure Ethiopia's got supper waitin'.'

The big white house loomed in front of her as they started up the brick walkway that led to the wide front porch. Odella couldn't believe how many windows there were, didn't think colored lived in places like this. The small, neat house she'd grown up in had three rooms and a little patch of yard in front and in back where Annie managed to grow vegetables and even a few flowers. It was nice by Cadysville standards, but Annie had cooked for people who lived in houses like this.

Odell caught her gawking and smiled a little. He was proud of his house, owned it and the surrounding forty-five acres free and clear. People in town thought it was funny that the brickman's house was made of wood.

'*That her?*' The voice was a loud whisper.

Odella looked around, but there was no one behind her.

'*Guess so,*' another voice answered.

She fixed her eyes on the porch.

'*Ain't she kinda big to be ten?*'

'*Looks like she been rollin' in the slop pen.*'

'*Y'all need to stop.*'

A dark green porch swing hung from thick chains and swayed like a ghost just got up, but there was no one there either.

'*You think she even know how to read?*'

'*She real country, ain't she?*'

Odella caught a head as it popped back around the side of the house.

'Don't pay them no mind.' Odell looked toward the far side of the house. 'That's Henry and them fools he hang around with.' Odell put the suitcase down and squatted beside Odella. 'I don't s'pect this gon' be easy for you, but this life ain't easy for none a us. I'm real sorry 'bout your mama, but this here's your home now. You gon' have to learn to stand up for yo'self 'cause I won't always be around neither.' He lifted her chin. 'Don't you never let nobody run you. You understand me, Odella?'

'Yessuh. I mean, yes, Papa.'

'Henry! Come on 'round here, boy, and carry this bag on in the house. Lester! Will! Y'all best be gettin' home. I'm sho you done caused enough trouble for one day.'

Three boys emerged from behind the huge azalea bush at the far end of the porch.

'Evenin', Mr Womack.' The boy was nearly tall as Odell and the kind of rich red-brown that made you think he might actually have been molded from Carolina clay. He tucked in his shirt and wiped his palm on his dungarees before extending it to Odell.

'Will.' Odell nodded, shook his hand.

'That supper smells mighty good, Mr Womack.' The next boy shoved his hands in his pockets, hunched his shoulders, and winked at her father.

'I'm sure Henry will tell you all about it tomorrow, Lester.'

'Hey. You must be Odella. Heard you was comin'.' Lester grinned at her. She peeked at him from behind her father. Lester wasn't as tall as Will, and he was lean, more muscle than bulk. She thought he was the color of devil's food cake with a smooth, sweet voice.

Odella figured the smallest one was Henry. He was narrow as a band of baling wire, and he glared at Odella, his black eyes cold and hard.

Odella felt a shiver creep up her spine, but she didn't show it.

'Mind your manners, boy.' Odell's words implied the threat.

Henry stared a moment longer. 'Hey.' His voice was as flat and empty as the gesture.

Odella, remembering her father's words, met his gaze and held it.

'You plannin' to look this bag into the house?' Odell said.

Henry snatched the suitcase and stomped down the path.

Odella wanted to run all the way back to Cadysville, and it took every ounce of determination she had left to put one foot in front of the other and follow Henry and Odell into that house.

Della hadn't moved. She still sat on the vinyl hassock in her sewing room, housecoat stuck to the backs of her thighs, damp from sitting so long on the plastic. Miles of yarn lay tangled about her feet. *And I'm not goin' back to Prosper. Not ever again.*

5

'If you don't shake up your life, all the good
stuff settles on the bottom.'

'It's so sweet he left you all that property, but what in
the world are you going to do with forty-five acres
in the middle of nowhere?' Lydia Kendall had worked
on her prep-school accent so studiously it sounded
almost natural. 'I looked at that outfit. It was too – I
don't know – too something for me.' She smiled
benevolently at Celeste. 'But it suits you.' In her navy
blazer, white shirt, and jeans, Lydia looked casually
understated, and suddenly Celeste felt way overdone
for a Saturday afternoon in her teal silk suit, pearls,
heels, and hose.

'Thanks.' *Why did I change my clothes?* 'Everett and
I are going to dinner,' she lied. 'I won't have time to
change.'

Lydia moved a bowl of roses aside and flipped the
florist's sample book open on the counter between
them. 'Let's agree. No carnations. They're so – ordinary.' She absentmindedly twirled the dime-sized
diamond on her ring finger.

'Agreed.' *As long as you agree to stop flipping that ring
around.* Thornton gave it to her for their twenty-fifth
anniversary and Lydia nicknamed it Plymouth Rock

105

because she said it was proof her ancestors had finally arrived. Since then she'd taken to wearing bright red nail polish and had done everything short of learning American Sign Language to keep her hands on display. Celeste was way over it. Not that the band of diamonds surrounding her own finger was a cereal box prize. It had blown her away when Everett presented it to her after a champagne toast on their twentieth anniversary. She even muffled the tiny voice in her head that said, 'It's about time.' But it wasn't Plymouth Rock.

'I'm sure we can find something more interesting than carnations. The flowers they did for your friend Mimi's son's wedding were breathtaking.' Celeste admired Lydia's sense of style, her flair for entertaining, and her direct connections to everybody in Buffalo who mattered. It's what Celeste aspired to, which is why she roped Lydia into the planning committee for Everett's clinic's annual fund-raiser. This was only the third year, and Celeste was determined to make it into one of the class events of the spring social season, a gathering people put on their calendar for the second Saturday in June, year after year.

'Honey, the flowers were the best thing about that wedding. The bride and her family are so – common. I know at least six girls, beautiful, smart, accomplished, I could have set him up with, but he drags this – thing home. I mean she had braids standing all over her head and had the nerve to put a headpiece on top of *that*. It looked like a swarm of snakes under that veil.' Lydia pushed some stray hairs from her steel gray pageboy behind her ear with her third finger, left hand. 'They'll be divorced in a year. Mark my words.'

Celeste wanted to redirect the conversation. She wasn't too happy with Niki's braids either and had conveniently forgotten to mention her displeasure to Lydia, who always had an immediate, take-no-prisoners assessment of any situation. Sometimes it was exactly the kick Celeste needed to make her take action, but she wasn't interested in that kind of commentary about her baby. Celeste made it her policy never to tell Lydia anything she didn't want to hear repeated, with dramatic embellishments. She knew Lydia couldn't carry a secret across the street in a Tupperware container without spilling it. That was just Lydia.

'You know, I'm still a little flustered. Finding that deed was such a shock. Daddy left all the other property to Mother in his will, but this came out of nowhere. I mean, I don't know how, but Mother had forgotten all about it. Doesn't even know how long it's been in the family.'

'Hmm. And nobody even *visited* this place?'

'Well – no.' As she raced from Della's house to meet Lydia on time, Celeste had rehearsed this conversation about her inheritance. Lydia was supposed to be impressed, at least a little, but it wasn't quite working out. 'Daddy was having some restoration done before he . . .'

'You can't really expect much from that. I mean it's probably a house, you know, four walls and some plumbing, maybe, but if it was so charming they would have stayed, don't you think? At least gone back to see the place once in a while.'

'Well – I guess – But with so much land Ev and I could build . . .'

'Oh, what about these!' Lydia pointed to an impressive arrangement of white lilies and roses, accented with trailing ivy. 'So simple. So elegant.'

'And so expensive, I'm sure. This is a fund-raiser, remember. The clinic is supposed to make money.' Celeste came up with the idea for an event after listening to Everett complain for the zillionth time about how tight the funding had become for low-income medical care. He was touched that she took on such a big challenge. All the planning and networking made her feel important, never mind that the pressure of wanting it to be perfect gave her sleepless nights and hives. The payoff was that it seemed to raise her profile around town. And her picture in the *Buffalo News*, presenting the board of the North Star Family Clinic with a ceremonial check, made her feel like a real philanthropist. It also meant her parents got to see her since she couldn't persuade Della to attend. They wrote a generous check, but her mother said she couldn't be bothered with all that mess.

'Just once I'd like to plan an event that didn't have to make a profit. Wouldn't it be fun to do a flawless affair instead of always planning on the cheap?' Lydia shivered with glee at the possibility.

'You'll have to wait for one of the twins to get married for that.'

'Not even. Lorna will elope with some fool who calls himself an artist, because she's "in love" and has her head stuck up in the clouds. I mean, how could you do that to your parents? Can you imagine the phone call? "I'm fine. And by the way, I got married last week." '

Celeste smiled tightly and offered no comment. After all, she and Everett had eloped. He wasn't into the pomp. She wanted to avoid the trying circumstances involved in planning such an important event with her mother because she was afraid the festivities would be too tacky for words.

'And Leticia never takes my advice. What a little witch she is if everything isn't exactly *her* way. She was impossible at her cotillion. Sometimes I think how lucky you were that Nicole chose not to debut.' Lydia shook her head in exasperation. 'We'll mark this page. Just to ask about the lilies.'

Choosing to ignore the little zinger about Niki declining to be a debutante, Celeste nodded. Her eyes were directed at the sample book, but her head was still focused on the Womack Estate, which is what the property had become in her mind. 'The house is on Little Pond Road so I'm hoping the name means we're by some water. I haven't had the chance to look at a map yet, but it would be fabulous if it's somewhere near the beach. Maybe Wilmington . . .'

'Thorny and I have stayed all along that coast. If it's anywhere you want to be, I should have heard of it, and believe me, I'd remember Prosper.'

Celeste looked crestfallen.

Lydia's eyes brightened as the lightbulb went on in her head. 'But you know, if you're lucky there'll be some development nearby, an industrial park or something. There's a lot of that going on down there. What you should do is sell the land and buy something you and Everett really want, on the Vineyard or Sag Harbor. Someplace where you can really entertain. We've been toying with the idea for years, but we just can't decide where to buy. Thorny keeps saying we have friends all over, we should just pick a place. If we get bored in a few years we can sell it. Oh, speaking of vacation homes, did you get my message about the house in Highland Beach?'

'Shoot. I forgot to mention it to Everett.'

'This cottage is really special. And what a view of Chesapeake Bay! It makes me feel calm just thinking about it. It's been in my friend's family since the turn of the century when her great-great-grandfather on her mother's side had it built.'

I guess that's a lot different from forty-five acres in Prosper. 'Sounds perfect.' Celeste turned some more pages without really looking.

'They're spending this summer with their son and daughter-in-law in Tuscany, so they won't be using it, but they won't rent to just anyone. They gave me first dibs, but if we don't scoop it up, we'll lose it.'

'I'll let you know by Monday. Promise.'

The Kendalls and the Englishes had been vacationing together since their kids were in fourth grade. Celeste and Lydia had accompanied the class on a trip to the Museum of Science and hit it off. Their husbands were both at the beginning of their careers, Everett as a physician, Thornton a CPA. Lydia had twin daughters, but she seemed to have it so together. Celeste learned a lot from her, things she would never dream of asking Della, like where the best families sent their kids to camp or how to tell really fine china. Thornton made partner at his firm, and the Kendalls had the goods to show for it. Celeste tried to keep up, but she usually felt like an also-ran.

'I was wondering if you two would be interested in doing a whole month this year? It's a little steep. Ten thousand dollars each couple, but they'd rather do it that way. I mean, I guess I could find another couple to take two weeks, but . . .'

'No. No, a month would be good.' *It's not a rainy day, but I'm sure Daddy wouldn't mind if I used the money he left me for this.* 'My husband never takes that much time because he thinks North Star would close up without him, but I could use a rest. It's been such a hard year, and in the middle of it all I'm interviewing for assistant principal in a few weeks. Then I'll be on pins and needles until I hear.'

'I love ambition.'

'I love the paycheck.'

'Let's hear it for getting paid!' Lydia lifted a pink rose from the vase and held it like a champagne flute.

Celeste grabbed a flower too, and they toasted. *And maybe I can get Niki to join me for a week or two. Like we used to.*

After two hours of wrangling with Lydia and the florist, Celeste was pleased with the arrangements they'd worked out. There would be a bowl at the center of each table with ten separate nosegays. That way, everyone would have flowers to take home at the end of the evening. Celeste was proud she came up with the idea and that Lydia and the florist both thought it was brilliant. And the day had been productive. She'd crossed all seventeen items off her to-do list.

When Celeste drove into her block, she was usually annoyed to see Everett's heap in the driveway. She wished he at least had the decency to hide it in the garage, but today she was glad to see the outline in the evening light because it meant he was home. She hurried into the house, because despite Lydia's wet blanket, she was still excited about her discovery.

Confused too. It would have been so much easier if it was the Frazier family house. She was sure there wouldn't have been all the secrecy. Repeating the details to Everett would make them feel more real.

Celeste went in and laid the yellow tulips she'd bought at the florist on the kitchen table. She heard water running and went down the hall toward the bathroom.

'Hel-lo!'

Everett cracked the door. 'Hey! Be out in a few. I got something to show you.'

'And I've got something to tell you.' She peeked in the den, expecting the usual sprawl of newspapers and medical journals to neaten but was surprised to find that he'd been rummaging through a box of old photos. The ones from back when they first met. *What prompted the trip down memory lane?* She sat in his favorite old tweedy club chair, the one from their first apartment that he wouldn't let her reupholster or throw out because it was comfortable just the way it was. She sifted through the piles of pictures in the old sneaker box sitting on the ottoman and came up with one of Everett, sitting on the hood of his prize yellow 'sixty-nine Triumph Spitfire. The one he'd still have if she hadn't convinced him there was no room for three cars with a two-car garage. Everett had one foot up on the chrome bumper, his elbow propped on his knee, and he rubbed his goatee, looking very deep. Celeste remembered taking it about three weeks after they met. It was late fall and you could tell it was windy because his gigunda 'fro and the long fringes on his brown suede jacket blew to one side. Everett looked dead at the camera, his black eyes like pools with no shallow end. The look used to give

112

her chills. It had from the first time she saw him.

Celeste had been hanging out between classes, eating french fries and gravy and talking trash with a girlfriend down in the Rat on UB's campus. She about gave herself whiplash doing a double take when she saw him, and she couldn't take her eyes off him as he bopped across the room. He was long, lean, and confident, and Celeste thought he moved like he belonged anywhere he chose to be. By the time he plopped his tray down on the table across from them she was hot and heavy into a very raunchy fantasy that took place upstairs in one of the listening rooms where, for an hour at a time, students routinely appreciated much more than music behind locked doors in soundproof privacy. Celeste always thought it beat the hell out of a backseat because while she majored in education, she'd minored in men, and as she liked to tell her girlfriends, she wanted to do plenty of research for her thesis. Before she could hunch her friend, Everett had fixed her in his sights. He held her gaze for a long, slow, disarming moment before he looked down and started reading the big textbook he had with him. Celeste burned with embarrassment because she felt like he knew exactly what was on her mind, which was usually the way she liked it, but not this time.

When Celeste rose to leave, she purposely avoided looking in his direction, but she took her sweet time, hoping he'd look up from his book. She wanted to give him ample opportunity to notice her in her bell-bottom hip-hugger jeans. It was the first time she'd worn the white turtleneck that clung like a second skin and stopped just at her belly button, revealing an inch-wide ribbon of skin at her waist. She'd left the house with her jacket closed so her mother wouldn't see it. Celeste may have been old enough to vote, but Della still maintained veto power in the wardrobe department.

By the time Celeste reached for the door, his hand beat hers to the knob. 'I wanted to introduce myself, since we already had a conversation back there,' is what he said. Celeste had felt her skin flush hot, and she could barely babble her name. She might have fallen in love with him right there.

'Whatdya think?' Now Everett leaned against the door frame, his bath towel a sarong at his waist, arms folded across his chest like a big, brown genie.

Celeste's eyes opened like saucers. 'What did you do to yourself?'

'I was examining a little boy, seven years old, this morning. He grinned at me and said I looked just like his grandpa. And you know what? I might be as old as his grandpa, but the look had to go.' Everett had shaved his receding rim, leaving a shiny dome. He grinned as he rubbed the stubble on his chin. 'I'm growing the beard again too. I figure if I can't have hair on top . . .'

'You could have warned me!' She got up and stood, hands on hips, in front of him.

'Warned you? I didn't know till the razor was in my hand. Come on, Celeste. It's no big deal.' Everett playfully grabbed at one of her hands. 'Give it a rub. Maybe you'll get your wish.'

'You think this is a joke, don't you?'

'Well, it'll look a little funny till my scalp color browns up like the rest of me, but . . .'

'You know that's not what I mean.'

'If you're gonna try to run that dignified BS on me again, save it.' Right after they got married Celeste went on a campaign to change Everett's hair. She carried on about how he'd look more professional, command more respect from peers and patients, if he shaved his beard and trimmed his mane down to size. It's not that she didn't like his Afro. It just wasn't dignified enough for *Dr* English. She figured it was a wife's job to look out for her husband's interests. Her mother never seemed to do that for her dad, and Celeste vowed she would be different. After a while Everett gave in and they never spoke about it again. 'If somebody's planning to give me a hard time, nothing I do with my hair will change that.'

'Have it your way, Everett.' She tried to slip past him, but he put his hands on her shoulders to hold her. With the distraction of hair gone, his eyes seemed even more intense.

'I got this flash a few months back.' He licked his lips, looked for the right words. 'Tomorrow ain't promised. If you don't shake up your life, all the good stuff settles on the bottom.'

Celeste looked up at him a long moment. Moist warmth radiated from him and he smelled fresh, like a walk in the woods. There were still moments when she felt the same pull she had more than twenty years ago. Like the moon on the ocean, irresistible. Undeniable. Used to be a time they would already have been in it. They'd have found a chair to even the height. She'd straddle his lap and they would devour each other, her arms straining to meet around his wide back, his smooth, hot hands squeezing her, kneading her. 'When did you add philosopher to your credentials?'

'Yeah. Cool.' Everett retracted the drawbridge of his arms. 'Just call me Socrates.'

Celeste could feel him watch her walk back to the kitchen. It made her crazy that Everett got these ideas in his head and just *did* them without planning or advance warning. She was so pissed off she didn't even notice how he looked shaved clean. It was too big a shock, and she'd had enough of those for one day. And she had too much on her mind for a roll in the hay if that's what he was thinking one of her wishes might be.

After rummaging through the cabinet, Celeste chose a green glass vase for the yellow tulips. For the last eleven years sex for them had been more about need and convenience than passion. There were still moments. Niki's graduation weekend they shared a lusty joy that kept them all over each other, before convocation, after commencement, and any other five minutes they could steal. But for the most part, neither expected the need to be reciprocal or the convenience mutual.

The fault line in their marriage appeared eleven years ago and caused a major quake. Everett was an attending at Buffalo General when he was recruited by a group that was looking for another internist to join their private practice. Celeste never heard his doubts. Thought he was just having normal jitters when he worried that if they made an offer and he took it he'd be selling out and putting his dream of opening a clinic on hold forever. Yes, she knew he always talked about medicine as a mission, a way to help those who needed it the most, but it only made sense to her that he would take advantage of the chance to move up in his profession. Who wanted to stay at the bottom of the barrel if they could climb out?

Fresh out of the classroom and into the guidance

116

office, Celeste was doing her part to keep them upwardly mobile. Never mind that sometimes she hated the paperwork and the administrative hassles. She missed watching ninth graders gain new insights about the world or themselves after reading *Black Boy* or *Catcher in the Rye*, but guidance counselor was a step up on the food chain. She figured Everett would see his choice the same way and do his part to assure that Dr and Mrs English would assume their appropriate and expected place and reap the benefits money and position offered.

Armed with visions of a luxurious home, lavish vacations, a fancy car, and quitting her job to do charity work, Celeste went into high gear, preparing him to look the part of a prosperous physician for his interview. She steamed, brushed, and fussed over his one suit, a blue double-breasted chalk stripe she had convinced him he needed. She bought him a shirt so it would be bright white, then starched and ironed it for an hour until it was a gleaming breastplate. And she picked out a new silk foulard tie for luck.

The outfit triggered the first rumbles. Everett said he was a doctor, not a corporate lawyer. He didn't see the need for such formality. Celeste told him it was an interview, not triage, but that was minor compared to the upheaval that occurred when they asked him to come on board and he turned them down.

It was like Celeste's brain seized and she had lost comprehension of her mother tongue. He couldn't possibly have said what it sounded like he said, which was no. For weeks they fought like heavyweights in a title bout, each punch intended as a knockout. They argued before Niki got up in the morning and after she went to bed at night. Once, when they were driving to the library, Niki asked Celeste if they were getting a divorce. Celeste had never actually allowed herself to say that word, not even think it. Hearing it aloud, in Niki's small voice, cut Celeste to the bone. It was unimaginable. After all, she had caught one of the good guys. The one other women told her they wanted to clone. She wasn't a big enough fool to let that walk away, so she did her best to assure Niki that her parents would never split up and what would make her say something so silly? After that, they only argued when Niki wasn't home; Celeste still felt too cheated to let it rest.

But no matter how rank the situation got at home, she maintained her composure in public. This was a private battle. No one needed to know there was trouble in Oz. It went without saying she would never tell Lydia, because this news was not for broadcast. And Celeste wasn't about to tell Della, because she had thought their marriage was a bad idea from the beginning.

Celeste and Everett had eloped on Christmas Eve and made the announcement during dessert and coffee on Christmas Day. While she and her mother were cleaning up the kitchen, Della stopped scouring the roaster and out of nowhere asked if Celeste really loved that man or whether she liked the idea of being married to a doctor. Celeste was so incensed that she got her coat right then and they left. The climate stayed chilly until Nicole was on the way.

About a month into the hostilities, Everett got an offer that he did accept. Came home one night and told Celeste he was spending six months at a medical facility in Benin, like it was around the corner and down the block. He said the hard part about being in

West Africa would be not seeing Niki, but he hoped the time apart from Celeste would give them both some breathing room and a little perspective. It couldn't make things any worse than they already were.

Was he ever wrong. Celeste carried on so bad that he stayed at the hospital a few days until she could speak in something other than a screech. The drama didn't change his mind, though.

Everett left the country to stony silence. The good news was that he'd provided Celeste with a plausible excuse for his absence. They weren't separated. He was working abroad. His salary was deposited directly into their joint account. He wrote Celeste and Niki regularly and phoned home twice a month. Celeste spoke to him mostly in monosyllables and only long enough for Niki to get on the line.

For the first few months of the cooling-off period, Celeste was so angry it left a bad taste in her mouth. So mad that she felt she deserved anything that made her feel better. She bought clothes, cut her hair from a middle-of-the-road, midlength nonstyle to a short, asymmetrical do with more pizzazz. People commented on how good she looked, and all the attention kept her distracted for a while.

Toward the end of his season overseas, Celeste had to admit, at least to herself, that she was scared and lonely. She missed Everett's wisecracks, his long, square, hairy toes, his cooking, which was really much better than hers. Celeste missed the passion Everett brought to living, from his big, loud grizzly bear stretch when he first sat up in bed in the morning to deep caring for his patients and his adoration of his daughter. She missed the intensity he radiated when they held hands.

When Everett walked back through the door at the end of his stint, Celeste was planning to maintain her cool, but a force she couldn't resist pulled her up out of her chair, across the room, and into his arms.

They talked into the morning like they used to, about what he had done and seen. Everett loved her haircut. Celeste loved the way the sun had kissed his skin to a burnished brown glow. And they loved each other, wanted to try to salvage their marriage, get back to where they started. Then, in the spirit of beginning fresh, Everett confessed that shortly after he left, while he was angry and resentful, he had a fling with another doctor in the program. He explained how his transgression only showed him how much he really wanted what he already had and asked her to forgive him. Celeste cried quiet, wounded tears and let him suffer for nearly a week before she told him she was taking the high road and that she'd found it in her heart to forgive him. But she left out the part about her own extracurricular involvement with an assistant principal at her school. Everett's confession became Celeste's moral vindication, convinced her that his wrong made hers right.

The rekindled flame stayed lit for a while, but it sputtered when Everett turned down another lucrative offer in favor of opening the North Star Clinic. Celeste was proud of his accomplishments. She just wished they had a little more to show for them.

Everett, wearing baggy gray sweats and a white terry cloth sweatband around his head, dropped his gear bag on the kitchen floor and headed for the refrigerator.

'You want something to eat?' Celeste draped her jacket on a kitchen chair.

'I'll grab a snack. I'm going to the gym to scare up a racquetball game. I don't get many free Saturday evenings.'

'You should have Satur*days* free too. You spend so much time at North . . .'

'This conversation is tired, Celeste. Give it a rest.' The edge was sharp in Everett's voice.

'Okay. All right.' Celeste retreated. 'Is it hot in here?'

'I don't know. Check the thermostat.' He snatched an orange and an apple from the vegetable bin.

She reached in the cupboard for a can of tomato soup, watched him a moment as he peeled the orange over the sink. 'Maybe you do look younger with your head like that. I didn't mean to jump on you. I was just startled.'

'Peace.' He held up the two-fingered salute. 'I needed a change, that's all.' He popped an orange section in his mouth, put the fruit on the counter, and reached for a paper towel.

'I still haven't told you my news.' Celeste got a small bowl and put Everett's orange in it, then wiped the counter.

Everett watched her and smirked.

'What?'

'Nothing. Tell me.'

Celeste recounted her discovery of the deed and Della's abrupt reaction while she warmed her soup.

'Secrets in the attic, huh? That's some wild stuff. What did Ronnie have to say?'

'Humph. Ronnie? Mother told me my sister has

moved yet again. I mean, what is with her? It's like she's never grown up.' Celeste poured her soup into a bowl. 'I'll call her when I've figured out what we need to do.'

'Don't you think she should be involved in this figuring process?'

'Ronnie doesn't have a real job, she can't keep an apartment. Why would I think she'd have any clue about what to do with this property?' Celeste waved the spoon for emphasis. 'For God's sake, Everett, she can hardly keep her phone turned on.'

'This is her decision as much as it is yours. Both names are on that deed.' Everett propped his elbows on the counter, bit into his apple.

'Whose side are you on?!' Celeste got saltines from the white metal tin that said 'Crackers' in blue letters. She put a few on a bread plate.

'This has nothing to do with sides. The property is deeded to both of you.' Everett roughed up the stubble on his chin.

'I'm not saying it isn't, but Ronnie has no business sense and clearly no sense of family. How could she go four years without seeing her parents? It's disgraceful! I don't think she's capable of making an informed decision about this, and as far as I'm concerned she has forfeited her say-so. She isn't responsible. Period.'

'Strong words. Suit yourself, but don't forget she's a grown woman, not just your baby sister. You're gonna make this into a feud.'

'I'll take my chances. We're not exactly bosom buddies as it is.' She got a glass for some wine and straightened sage, one of the herb prints grouped on the wall.

'Are you gonna go see this place? School's out all next week. You could fly down.'

'No time. I'm booked up here. My committee needs to finalize the menu for your clinic fund-raiser, and I've got a few more articles to read before the assistant principal interview.' And Celeste wasn't ready for Prosper yet. The lifetime absence of a family history allowed her to create one that suited her notions of her ancestors, of life in the South. She had elaborate pictures of suffering and injustice, sacrifice and heroism. Besides, her father always said they left because there was nothing in the town for a Black man but hard times and old age. No telling what she'd find there now. *If Daddy had just mentioned it to me.*

Celeste headed to the pantry and got a bottle of merlot. 'I thought we could drive to Prosper before our vacation this summer. Oh, I've been meaning to tell you, Lydia has access to this fabulous home in Highland Beach . . .'

'I told you months ago I didn't want to go on vacation with the Kendalls again. I'm not interested in another two-week dose of them. How long have we been doing this? Ten, eleven years?' He dropped his peels and cores down the garbage disposal, gave them a quick buzz. 'We have to listen to them brag about their newest new car or about their fab-u-lous cruise and all the important people, in addition to themselves, who were on it. We don't do this for Nik anymore, not that she ever enjoyed it as much as you wanted her to. Can't blame her. The Kendall twins were always obnoxious.'

'They weren't that bad. Besides, they don't come anymore, and this place sounds fantastic.' Celeste launched into her spiel.

Everett shook his head. 'I'm sick of Thornton cheating on his golf score.' Everett rubbed his palms together. 'And I know she's your running buddy, but frankly I could live without Lydia.'

'She's helping me a lot on the clinic benefit, you know.' Celeste sidestepped the issue. *This always happens. He'll be happy to go by June.*

'And North Star appreciates her efforts.' Everett's eyes brightened with a sly, seductive sparkle. He sidled next to Celeste. 'How about a romantic holiday for two in the south of France? We could have a little Beaujolais, a little *déjeuner*, a little matinée, oui? Or would Switzerland tickle your toes? I showed you the article about the jazz festivals in Nice and Montreux. We could explore by day, dig the tunes by night, maybe take a little side trip to Italy or Spain.' He pulled her close.

'Oooh, don't put those sticky hands all over me.' Celeste lifted his hand off her shoulder, plunked it on the counter.

'I remember when you used to like it.' Everett picked up his gym bag.

'You'll mess up my blouse.'

'Never mind. Later.' And was out the door.

Celeste wrestled the rest of the weekend with what to tell Lydia. By Monday morning, when she snagged a third cup of coffee in the faculty room and headed for the guidance suite, she still hadn't made up her mind. It was such a great opportunity to meet a new group of people. *Everett was just mad because I fussed about his haircut.* She unlocked the door to her first-floor office and flipped on the light. *I gotta call maintenance again.* The fluorescent bulb hummed and flickered. She put down her insulated mug and her purse, got her agenda out of her purple and gold canvas school tote bag, and added it to today's to-do list. There were fifteen items so far. The first, 'Confirm Highland Beach.' *What am I going to do?*

Celeste's office was anything but picture-perfect. Battered beige file cabinets lined one wall, and piled on top of them was a jumble of papers, college and technical school brochures, catalogs, and videos. The windowsills were heaped with folders, attendance records, old aptitude test booklets, and career guides. But unlike at home, the way her office looked mattered less than what she accomplished while in it. Celeste had her own pretty awful counselling experience when she'd been in high school, one that changed her forever. Celeste's grades weren't spectacular, but they weren't awful either. She knew she had to buckle down and bring them up because she wanted to go to college and be a teacher. After her initial session in the guidance office, she was advised to forget about preparing for the SATs and to consider a nurse's aid training program upon graduation. When she got back to her homeroom she saw that every Black girl in her class had the nurse's aid brochures, while the White girls had booklets on college entrance exams and pamphlets from various universities. Celeste made up her mind she *would* be a teacher and that it would always be about the students. When she finally became a counselor she decided it was pretty much the only place in the school where the kids were dealt with as individuals, not just part of biology class of Homeroom 317. Celeste did her best with each and every one of them, and her kids did well. Whether they went on to the Ivy League or to the post office, in some way, large or small, they benefited from the time Mrs English spent with them.

Celeste picked up the receiver.

'Do you have a minute, Mrs English?' Joey Tsang appeared at her door.

'Sure. You're not trying to get out of your history class, are you?' She winked at him, put down the phone. Joey had spent a great part of the first grading period trying in vain to convince her that the curriculum was outmoded and that three years of history was enough for anyone who wasn't planning to be a historian or go to work for PBS.

'No. I'm goin'. I swear! I just wanted to say – uh – thanks. I know you didn't have to meet with my parents like you did, but it really made the difference.'

Both of Joey's parents taught at SUNYAB, his father engineering, and his mother physics. They expected Joey to follow in their footsteps, but his true love was music. Joey wanted to be a composer, he didn't want to go to MIT. Celeste, convinced that love combined with ability made for a fulfilling and worthwhile career choice, encouraged him to follow his heart. She agreed to meet with Joey and his parents, and they'd left not fully convinced but at least able to see Joey's point of view. Joey was Celeste's first student to be accepted at Juilliard.

'Just doing my job, kiddo!'

'It was more than that. And I wanted you to know how much it meant to me.'

These moments were rare, but they're what made Celeste love her job. She'd savor this on the bad days. The day she lost another fifteen-year-old to unplanned pregnancy, or the day one of the boys she thought she'd gotten through to was arrested in study hall. This was a moment she'd frame and hang on her wall.

'You're more than welcome. Now get out of here before you're late.' She shooed him out the door.

Celeste still had a smile on her face as she dialed Lydia's number. 'Hey, it's me.' She took a deep breath, bit her lip. 'Of course we're in. We wouldn't let the good times start without us.'

6

'Always is over.'

Spring passed in a blur of events for the Englishes. Celeste had the last-minute rush of students still trying to get admitted to college and counseling sessions with those in danger of flunking courses. For a switch, she herself was reduced to anxiously wondering if she'd get the call that told her she'd be assigned as an assistant principal in the fall. The uncertainty reminded her of why her college-bound seniors bounced off the walls from January until April.

In May, Celeste's prom committee pulled off a lovely affair and everything was in place for North Star's event. She'd even found the perfect dress, a white sheath with a lace overslip and sleeves. Celeste wondered if it looked a little 'mother of the bride,' but Lydia had been with her when she picked it out and assured her it was very elegant. Celeste had put Prosper on the back burner, and she hadn't told Ronnie there was a pot on yet.

On the Friday of Memorial Day weekend, Celeste was in a great mood. The official teachers' countdown to the end of the semester had begun, and after school she stopped off at Cole's, the local faculty watering hole, to celebrate. She left the restaurant feeling mellow and strolled to her car, soaking up the warm, late-day sun. The promise of summer and two months of freedom hung sweetly in the air. *If Everett gets home at a reasonable hour, I'll throw a couple of steaks on the grill. That'll be a nice change.* Celeste looked forward to the full slate of parties and barbecues for the weekend, but she'd forgotten the last time they actually ate dinner together in the house.

Driving down Parkside past the zoo, Celeste noticed the giraffes gnawing on tree leaves in the distance. She smiled as she remembered how Niki used to wonder how long it took for their food to get all the way from their mouths to their stomachs. *I wish Niki had come up for the weekend.* Celeste had offered to send a plane ticket, but Nicole begged off, said she had to work, promised she'd come home for the North Star fund-raiser. She missed the details of Niki's life. What dress she bought, where she was going on Saturday night and who was going with her. Celeste called once a week, Tuesday morning since that was Niki's day off. It was usually a 'Hi. I'm fine. I'm busy. Nothing's new. Bye.' conversation that left Celeste feeling left out, wanting more. Niki hadn't been home since the funeral, not even for Christmas. That was hard. It was Celeste's first Christmas without both her father and her daughter. Della never was big on Christmas, not even when Ronnie and Celeste were little. It was Celeste's favorite time of year, but Della hung over it like a big, gloomy rain cloud over a picnic, threatening to spoil her fun at any moment. From the time Celeste was grown and on her own she celebrated with all the trimmings. So she decided to carry on with her usual traditions. She put Christmas trees in the living room and dining room and covered them with so many ornaments you could barely see the green. She decked banisters, archways, and mantels with pine garlands, red velvet bows, and twinkling white lights, and each window in the house had a glowing golden star. She and Everett had hosted their annual Christmas Eve supper, but a lot of the spirit was missing.

Celeste ditched her shoes at the back door and stepped into the white terry cloth scuffs she had waiting. She defrosted two T-bones in the microwave, put them in a bowl with Italian dressing to marinate, then collected her shoes and marched upstairs to take a shower. She figured school maintenance had sent up too much heat for such warm weather. Why else was she hot and sticky all day?

The first thing Celeste noticed in the bedroom were the blue jeans balled up on the floor on Everett's side of the bed. *He never puts things away.* She made a face and scooped them up. He'd actually made it to bed last night, although Celeste was too tired to talk or do anything else when he got under the covers. He was still a night owl like he had been since she met him. On the other hand, after Niki was born Celeste went back to being a morning bird like she had always been before she dated Everett. When he used to complain that she had vowed to love, honor, and keep company, she would bring out her iron-clad excuse: she needed her rest to keep up with the baby. Nothing had changed after the baby was grown though.

Celeste dropped the pants in the hamper and got undressed. It felt good to get out of her blue blouse and gray skirt, better to peel off her hose and her no-nonsense beige bra and panties. She had a lingerie drawer full of serious underwear. As usual she didn't look down as she slipped into her pink and white striped robe. In the bathroom she zipped past the mirror as she put on the shower cap, adjusted the water to semi-scalding, and waited until the steam drifted over the shower curtain. She stepped in and moaned as the hot water pelted her shoulders. Then she grabbed the deodorant soap and got down to business.

Bringing Nicole into the world had made Celeste feel officially grown. After all, she was old enough to be somebody's mother, but she never got over what it did to her body. She had rubbed lotions, creams, cocoa butter, and lard on her belly, but nothing got rid of the rippling stretch marks that marred what had been smooth, taut skin. Her breasts had gone from tangy apples to droopy pears. And what had been a spandex-tight love fit between her and Everett had become more like a baggy kneesock. B.C. – Before Childbirth – Celeste like to flaunt her stuff in bikinis and clingy dresses, and tease Everett, telling him she was naked and warm under her sundress hours before he could do anything about it. A.D. – After Delivery – he used to tell her she was as hot a mama as she ever was, but she figured it was what he had to say. Besides, she didn't have time to worry about such frivolous things. Celeste was a mother.

Della had passed on lots of baby care tidbits, most of which Celeste discarded as old-fashioned, but never said two words to her daughter about the radical changes to her physique. So Celeste had been prepared for diaper changing, bottle sterilizing, and no

131

sleep, but not to surrender her sassy shape. At twenty-three? It made her mad, but she couldn't admit it. Who could she be mad at? Certainly not her darling baby, her gift from heaven, her daughter.

Celeste was soaping her thighs and composing a mental timetable for Saturday when a knock on the door made her jump.

'How 'bout some company?' Everett came in and closed the door.

'You scared me to death! What are you doing home so . . .'

Everett pulled back the curtain. He was already undressed for the occasion. 'Are those goose bumps from fear, or because I'm here?'

She smirked. 'Very funny. I was about to get out.'

'Then I got here just in time.'

'Everett, there's no room.'

'I'm sure you missed a spot.' He grinned and got in. Everett closed his eyes and let the water run over his head. 'Oh yeah.'

Celeste shimmied past him so Everett was closest to the spray. 'This is a surprise. The sun is still up and you're home.' Despite her bark, Celeste's stomach flip-flopped as she watched the water gloss his body.

'You've got steaks out. You're plannin' to *cook*?' His eyes sparkled mischievously.

'Touché.' They gazed at each other a long moment. A subtle vibration radiated through Celeste's body. Before she could stop herself she reached up and rubbed slow circles over his chest hair with the bar of soap until he was covered in lather from shoulders to waist and her vibrations deepened. 'No meeting tonight?'

'Umm. Not one. And I played hooky most of the

afternoon.' Eyes closed again, he directed her hand down toward another clump of hair.

'You know I'm obligated to report this to your truant officer,' Celeste purred as she kept circling.

'Can I make a plea for leniency?' He pulled her close so the shower sprayed them both.

'On what grounds?' Love in the afternoon wasn't on her list of things to do, but she was about to go with the flow for a change.

'How about that I spent the time with a travel agent and I got a stack of brochures for places to take us on one hellafied vacation?'

Celeste's mouth suddenly felt dry as the bottom of an old shoe. More than a month had passed since she gave Lydia the okay, but she still hadn't worked their Highland Beach rental casually into conversation with her husband. Now she worked to keep her voice smooth. Head resting on his arm, she stared at the white tile. 'Hmm. What did you have in mind?' *And please let it be August.*

'You, me, good food, beautiful surroundings, and a whole lotta jazz.' He led her in a slow, hip-rolling dance to the music of his voice. 'There are a bunch of festivals to choose from in July and I'm ready to get on the plane right now.' His hands slid up and down her back.

Uh-oh. Celeste's good vibrations stopped abruptly, crushed by the lump of lead that landed in her guts. Her hips stopped swaying and Everett opened his eyes.

'What's the matter?'

'Nothing. You're gonna get my hair all wet.' She edged herself away.

'Come on, Celeste.'

Her body wanted to stay, but Celeste's head screamed *What am I gonna do?* so loud she had to pay attention. 'I'll meet you in the bedroom. Promise.'

Everett cocked his head to the side, took a deep breath. 'As long as you keep on the same outfit you're wearing. I like it.'

'Deal.' She was still damp when she pulled on her robe and trotted down to the kitchen. She poured a glass of wine, took a slurp, topped it off, then poured a second glass and carried them back to the bedroom. Everett wasn't much of a drinker, but she hoped it would soften him up for a vacation with a slightly different beat.

Celeste found a bulging manila envelope in the middle of their bed. It seemed to throb as she sat at arm's length, looking at it and trying to think clearly. She took another swallow of wine for confidence, then picked it up, unwound the figure eight of string that held the flap closed, and let the color travel brochures fall in a heap on the bed. She swirled them with both hands, picked one at random. *What am I going to tell him?* She stared blankly at the cover.

'The travel agent stayed at that hotel, says it's a classy joint.' Everett stood in front of her, still drying his hairy chest.

Celeste sipped her wine. 'I brought up a glass for you.'

'In a minute. Right now I see something I'd rather have.' He sat beside her, tried to pull her into an embrace. Celeste was as pliable as a two-by-four. 'Come here and let me ease your mind some.'

I wish you could. 'Everett, I kind of already made plans for our vacation.'

He sat back. 'You planned a vacation and didn't *tell*

134

me? Oh! It's a surprise right? You're gonna pick me up at the clinic with my bags packed and . . .'

'Not exactly. It kept slipping my mind.' That felt lame as soon as it left her lips, but Celeste had no choice but to plow on. 'It was a great opportunity – so I accepted the rental in Highland . . .'

'No you didn't.' Everett shot to the other side of the room. Hands on hips, he stared at the floor. The smooth contours of his face turned to granite and Celeste felt static in the air, like right before a storm. They hadn't argued in a long time, but Celeste braced herself as he banged open a dresser drawer, grabbed some briefs, and put them on. 'Please tell me you didn't do that, Celeste.' He opened the closet, snatched some chinos off a hanger.

'It was getting late, and we hadn't made any plans. I didn't want us to get caught without anything.'

Everett stopped in his tracks, glanced up at Celeste, then let out a big, whooping belly laugh.

'What's so funny?' Everett's laugh unnerved her.

He had to catch his breath to talk. 'So you booked the one place I specifically said I *didn't* want to go! That's good. That's really good, Celeste.' Everett's eyes stayed locked on her as he stepped into his pants.

Celeste wasn't sure if they were fighting or making up, but the laughter stung. 'I know what you said, Everett, but we always take a rental with . . .'

'Always is over,' he snapped. 'And you should have listened to me, because I'm not going.'

'Oh come on, Ev. I can't go alone. Lydia and Thornton would have a field day with that.'

'If you had paid even a little attention to what I said, you would know I don't give a shit what they think.'

'You're overreacting. It's not the last vacation we'll

135

take. We can go to your little jazz thing or whatever next year.' Celeste felt her world wobble.

Everett stared at her like he'd never seen her before, then he grinned, shook his head. 'My "little jazz thing." That about sums it up. You obviously don't care what I have to say.'

'That not true . . .' She gripped the side of the bed to keep her balance.

'I'm not even gonna argue with you, Celeste, because if I give you enough time, you'll make this whole thing my fault.' He hurriedly pulled on a denim shirt, buttoned it lopsided. 'I've tried everything I know how to do – Half the time I feel like some kinda show dog. You parade me around and collect points, or ribbons, whatever you get for a good performance.' He shoved his feet into sneakers, knelt to lace them.

Celeste stood up, hoping to regain her footing. She picked up his towel from the bed, folded it, and held it to her chest. 'We can always cancel. It's late for them to find another couple, but . . .'

'It's not just the vacation! It's the way our marriage has been for years. You go along your merry way making plans that suit some idea you have of the perfect life. You don't give me or anybody else credit for having sense, and how fortunate we poor fools are to have you to show us the way.'

'I never said . . .'

'You're right. You never came out and said I was a disappointment to you, but your message is loud and clear. Well, I can't do this anymore.' He stood and looked her square in the eyes. 'I'm outta here, Celeste.'

'Fine. When you get back we can . . .'

'I don't mean for a walk around the block. I mean I want a divorce.'

All Celeste could hear was her heart pounding. It felt like a long time before she could make her lips move. 'You don't mean that.'

Everett got his wallet off the dresser, shoved it in his pocket. 'Do you even hear yourself? This would be funny, if it wasn't. I almost walked many times before, but something always stopped me. Niki, or the way I remembered you, back in the day. I don't know who you are anymore.' He moved toward the door, then stopped. 'The last time I had my bags packed, your father died. I couldn't go then. Wouldn't. We're family. It was a crisis. After that I decided to give us one more chance, but I'm through with it. I see life and death regularly as part of my job description, but when your father died, that was a personal reminder that life can be over faster than you can scratch your ear. Any time. Any day. It's too short not to enjoy every moment, and I've just been going through the motions here. This may be enough for you, but it's not enough for me.'

'Who is it this time?' Celeste hissed, grasping wildly at anything to keep her balance.

'Bingo! I've been waiting for your ace in the hole. It's been more than a damn decade, but you can make it feel like yesterday. I hate to disappoint you, but it's not about anybody else. It's about what we're not any-more.' Everett sounded hollow, tired. 'Maybe we never were.'

'What kind of example is this for Niki?'

'It's time for you to stop hiding behind Niki. In case you hadn't noticed, she's a woman. And believe me, this won't come as a surprise to her. She lived here, remember? We can tell her when she's home in a couple of weeks. I won't mention it to anyone until then.'

'Tell her what!? This is crazy, Everett. Are you having a breakdown or something?'

Everett closed his eyes, shook his head, then turned and left the room.

Celeste stood, paralyzed, her hands balled into fists, her body quaking. She heard the back door close, heard Everett start the car and drive off. *He can't leave me.* The voice in her head started small, but it swelled, sending her into a frenzy. She flung the towel in her arms and knocked her empty glass off the nightstand. It was like the sound of shattered glass flipped a switch in her head. She drank down the wine she brought for Everett, then smashed the glass against the closet door. *He can't leave me!* Celeste ripped covers off the bed, tossing travel brochures like confetti. Twirling in the tangle of sheets and blankets, she knocked down the clothes valet she bought but he never used, upended a brass floor lamp. Its frosted glass globe exploded when it hit the wall, splintered into a million shards. 'He can't leave me!' She didn't realize she was yelling. Celeste whirled like a cyclone, touching down at random, leaving destruction in her wake, until she got tangled in the drapes and fell, yanking the rod down with a crash. Celeste landed in a heap, wet with sweat like she'd just come out of the shower. She curled up in a ball and sobbed until she fell asleep.

It was dark when Celeste woke up, feeling like freeze-dried hell. Only the mayhem around her kept her from writing off the afternoon as a bad dream. She got to her feet, found the light switch, shuddered at the wreckage. She stayed up half the night, methodically cleaning up the mess, feeling soothed as she restored order.

The next morning Celeste jammed last night's uncooked steaks down the garbage disposal and made an extra-strong pot of coffee. She was on her second cup when Everett came down from his study and into the kitchen, still wearing his clothes from the day before.

'Are you feeling better?' Celeste's sarcasm was thick as peach nectar.

'I feel fine. As a matter of fact, better than I have in a long time.' Everett poured a cup of coffee.

'The Hills' cookout starts at three.' Celeste planned to treat the disturbance as only a test of the emergency broadcast system. No need to prepare for fallout. She was going back to her schedule.

'Have a good time.' Everett spooned sugar in his coffee.

'If you still want to talk about this nonsense, we can. I'm willing to forget what happened . . .'

'I'm not. I meant everything I said. And this nonsense is my life. It's about time I got on with it.' He disappeared down the hall.

'This'll blow over, Everett!'

Everett kept walking.

Celeste did go to the barbecue. She extended Everett's apologies, said he had an emergency at the clinic. The next two weeks went by pretty much like normal; she went her way, he went his. Celeste filled every waking moment with busywork: rearranging closets, handling last-minute details for the banquet, getting Niki's room ready for her visit, buying her mother groceries and cleaning products Della said she didn't need. She couldn't stay around her mother too long. For some reason Della kept asking Celeste if everything was okay. She'd find some drawer to search through or shelf to dust so she didn't have to look her mother in the eye while she said, 'I'm fine. It's just been so busy.' Then she'd ask Della for the sixteenth time if she'd reconsider going to the North Star fund-raiser, so Della could say no again.

In the midst of her swirl of activities, when Celeste had a few unscheduled minutes, her heart would pound like a drum, but it would pass. She was not going to let Everett's tantrum get to her. She figured two weeks was enough time for whatever little midlife crisis he was having to pass, and if nothing else, Niki's arrival would snap him out of it.

Niki chattered the whole way home from the airport. Celeste had planned that they would go out for lunch, but Niki insisted on cooking. After a short detour to the grocery store, she whipped up smoked salmon and Gruyère omelets with asparagus vinaigrette, garnished beautifully with cherry tomatoes and cilantro. Everett raved, and Celeste was just about to breathe a sigh of relief when Niki put down her fork.

'I'm leaving Atlanta. This job was fine for right out of school, in fact it's been great. It's given me the chance to really be on the inside of the restaurant business and helped me to know what I want. I'm going back to school.'

'Grad school?! How wonderful! Isn't that wonderful, Ev?' Celeste moved forward in her chair, bubbling with excitement. 'Where have you been accepted? Oh, I hope it's somewhere nearby. Atlanta is fine, but it's so far away from us.'

Everett shot Celeste a look.

'It's upstate New York, not far from the city – but it's not exactly graduate school.' Nicole took one last deep breath before spilling all her beans. 'I've enrolled in the CIA.' She caught her mother's quizzical look. 'The Culinary Institute of America. I'm going to be a chef.'

'You're what?!' Celeste's hand went up to her chest to hold her heart in place.

'I love food. I love cooking and I'm good at it. Every spare moment I had at the restaurant, I'd hang out in the kitchen, dying to take off my suit, roll up my sleeves, and grab a sauté pan. I learned the business side of running a restaurant, which is good. It'll be very helpful when I have my own place, but . . .'

'We didn't spend all that money on an education so you could become a cook!' Celeste nearly lunged across the table.

'I didn't say a cook, I said a chef.' Niki held her ground.

'Don't insult me, Nicole! How dare you think that you can waste your time and your life that way? Are you insane?' Celeste screeched.

'Cut the hysterics, Celeste. Nicole has found what she loves to do in life. Some people never do. She's lucky.' He turned to his daughter. 'And I know you'll be the best chef in the world!'

'How can you sit there like nothing is wrong?' Celeste jumped up, waving her arms like a traffic cop. 'Your daughter is throwing her life away! And you're telling her it's all right! Has everyone in this house lost their grip except me?!'

'It's my life, Ma. It's the only one I have. If I don't do this, I know I'll regret it. I may be only twenty-three, but I've figured out that I only want to regret the things I do. Not the things I never tried.' She looked at her father. 'You always told me I could do anything, be anything. This is what I want to be.'

'I won't listen to this anymore! I'm going upstairs to get ready for tonight.' Celeste started out of the kitchen.

'We have something to tell you too, Nik.'

She froze. 'Surely you're kidding, Everett!?'

'Sit back down, Celeste, or do you want me to do this alone?'

Celeste didn't move a muscle.

'Do what?' Niki looked back and forth between her father and her mother's back.

Everett waited a few seconds, reached for Niki's hand.

Celeste prayed that Everett wouldn't say what she knew was coming.

'There's no good or easy way to say this, baby.' Everett looked at Celeste, then back at Nicole. 'You know your mother and I have been – well, it hasn't been good for a long time. We've talked about it and decided we need to be apart.'

'So you're getting divorced, huh?' Niki looked as though she'd been waiting for that shoe to drop for years.

'We haven't gotten that far.' He spoke to Niki but he watched Celeste. 'We've just agreed that what we have isn't healthy, and it hasn't been a good example for you, either. We apologize for that. We love you, both of us. And we've always wanted only what's best for you. You're grown now. A woman with a mind and life of her own.' He dropped his eyes to the floor, then looked at Niki. 'Now it's time to do what's best for us.'

Celeste wanted to spit. This was best for him, not for her. Until now Everett's words were like a bad dream, disturbing but easily forgotten. But hearing him say it out loud, to their child, that was too real, and she wanted to make it go away. 'Nothing is final, Niki. Your father is just upset right now so you don't have to feel . . .'

'Stop telling me what to feel, Ma!' Niki's eyes blazed. 'You're always tryin' to tell somebody what to think, what to do, where to go! Then you don't understand why nobody can *live* with you.'

The words splattered over Celeste like shrapnel. Staring straight ahead, it was all she could do to put one foot in front of the other and leave the room.

The third annual North Star benefit was a huge success and raised more money than ever, but Celeste barely remembered the evening. She spent it smiling too brightly, talking too cheerfully, and staying on the opposite side of the room from Everett. Lydia's antenna was up too. She kept shooting Celeste sideways glances and asking if everything was all right, but Celeste managed to evade her – barely. It was the hardest act Celeste ever put on.

The three of them drove home in silence. Niki and Everett retired to their rooms. Celeste brought the wine bottle and a glass up to bed because this had all been too painful and she wanted to forget it ever happened, but no matter how hard she drank, she couldn't sleep. She knew that now, since he had told Nicole, Everett would be ready for the next step, and she had to stop it. At least long enough to figure out what to do next. She tossed and turned and sweated. The semester was over in two weeks. She should be leaving for Maryland, but that was out of the question. She didn't know what she was going to tell Lydia and Thornton yet; she'd have to make up some lie. But she needed a place to go where she could be alone and think this through. Some way to stop Everett from surveying the real estate pages for an apartment.

Morning edged around the window shades before she thought of Prosper.

By the time Celeste dragged herself downstairs, Niki had already left for the airport to change her ticket and catch the next thing flying back to Atlanta, which Celeste blamed on Everett. And for the rest of the weekend Celeste stewed and steamed alternately at Everett for being irrational and at Niki for being a stubborn, ungrateful brat. Celeste didn't even go to church, and she never missed the Sunday after the North Star benefit. She'd show up early and stay long after service, smiling like a bride and basking in compliments from church members on what a beautiful affair it had been. But she didn't have the heart to put up a front. What energy she did have was devoted to finding a way to get her husband and her daughter to come to their senses before their decisions became public. Before Lydia found out, which was in essence the same thing.

By first period on Monday, Celeste was just plain evil and she stayed that way all week. Coworkers and students blamed her foul mood on end of the year pressures and stayed out of her path.

At home the week was no better. She wouldn't go downstairs in the morning until Everett left for the clinic, and although she was always wide awake when he returned each night, she'd pretend to be asleep. She quickly checked the 'will not attend' box on the invitations that appeared in the mail and made hasty excuses for those that arrived via telephone. Most of the time she let the machine pick up, but she stood by, ready to snatch the receiver in case it was Niki, calling to say she had changed her mind. But Niki didn't call.

By the time Friday dawned, Celeste had made up her mind. Before she left for work she had made plane reservations for North Carolina, leaving as soon as school was over. Now she had to tell her mother.

For a hot second Celeste considered hiding her little excursion to Prosper from Della, but she'd never even gone on a long weekend without leaving her mother a detailed itinerary. Not that Della had once used the 'in case of emergency' phone numbers. Of course, she still hadn't told Ronnie about their little inheritance, either, but that was a simple phone call. If Ronnie's phone wasn't disconnected again, that is. But after their one and only conversation on the subject, Celeste knew her mother would be a tough customer.

'Mother?!' Celeste trotted up the back steps, trying to keep the grease that had soaked through the pizza box from getting on her blouse. 'I brought a surprise!' She'd stayed in her office late, buried under paperwork, but when the custodian had stopped by her office a third time, mop in hand, she knew she couldn't delay her visit to Della any longer. *Dreading a thing is worse than doing it. That's what Daddy used to say.* She pulled an old cookie sheet from the cabinet, put three slices on it, and slipped the pan into the oven.

Della shuffled into the kitchen. 'You'd a sure been surprised if I hadn't been here.' She spied the telltale half box from Bocce's. 'And I *might* have already eaten,' she said, knowing full well her plate of cheese and saltines sitting upstairs on a snack table didn't compare.

'You're right.' Celeste didn't want the fight to start this soon. 'I should've called first, but it was Friday and I just felt like some pizza. Everett is working late, as usual, and I know how much you like this.'

Della examined the box. 'Humph! Bet you didn't go . . .'

'Yes I did. All the way down to Clinton Street.' Celeste had counted on getting extra points for going out of her way to the original pizzeria instead of one of the branches. Della swore she could tell the difference, and if pizza the way her mother liked it would make some inroads on this Prosper business, it was worth the inconvenience. 'It'll be hot in a couple of minutes.' Celeste grabbed two plates from the shelf.

'I don't know the last time I had some Bocce's.' Della took two pale yellow paper napkins from the holder on the table and folded them in half. 'Might not have been since Will passed,' she said more to herself than to Celeste.

Friday night pizza used to be a Frazier family tradition. A couple of years after Will started at the steel plant, he decided to try this concoction his coworkers raved about. Until then the only 'Eye-talian' food Will and Della knew from Prosper was spaghetti. So he stopped by the place they'd recommended and brought home a pepperoni pizza pie. It was love at first bite. Della even pinched off small pieces of the tomatoey crust and fed them to baby Celeste, who was teething. From then on, Will brought home pizza on Friday night.

146

'This sure hit the spot.' Della bit into her second slice.

'Glad you like it.' Celeste watched her mother dab at the corner of her mouth with the napkin. 'And I'm so glad the school year is over next week. It's been a hard one.' She put down the sliver of pepperoni she had squeezed between her thumb and index finger and wiped her hands. 'I – uh – I've been thinking about getting away for a few days or so.'

'Y'all usually take a trip. I thought you were goin' somewhere with your *friend* Lydia and her husband.'

'Later. This would be a little getaway just for me. I could really use some time to myself. You know, recharge the old batteries. You want the other slice?'

'Uh-huh.' Della took another bite.

Celeste got up and went to the oven. 'I thought it made sense to go down to Prosper and take a look at the house.'

Celeste's back was to her mother, but she felt the frosty stare, the chill that fell over the kitchen like a new Ice Age, suspending everything in one terrible, final moment. She stood frozen in place. 'I'll let Ronnie know I'm going,' Celeste ventured weakly. She half expected to see wispy clouds of breath as she spoke. 'When I get back we can decide what to do with it.'

Della shoved her plate away and pushed herself up from the table. 'Humph! I shoulda known you were up to somethin'. Comin' in here with somethin' I *actually like* instead of somethin' you think I should want.' Infused with an energy she didn't usually feel this time of day, Della nearly sprinted from the kitchen.

'How can you say that?' Celeste was quick on her

147

mother's heels. 'Anybody else would be glad her child wanted to see where she came from.'

Della whirled around so fast that Celeste nearly tripped over her own feet trying to stop. 'Didn't you hear what I said when you found that deed?!' Della's low growl made Celeste take a step backward. 'Or did you just decide to go 'head and do what *you* want like usual?'

'It's what Daddy would have wanted me to do, and you know it!'

Della turned back around and proceeded down the hall. 'I don't know no such thing! What I do know is that you are bound and determined to stick your nose where it don't belong!'

'Then tell me what's so bad about this place, why I shouldn't go,' Celeste shouted as Della started up the stairs.

On the sixth step Della stood stock-still. She spoke without turning around. 'Celeste Anne, don't let your age make you forget I'm your mother. I don't *have* to tell you a damn thing!'

7

'One last shot.'

'Save your sorry-assed reasons, Celeste!' Ronnie spat into the cordless phone. She had to convey the venom without the volume because she wasn't sure who was home, and there was no reason for her roommates to know her business. 'You didn't tell me about the house because *you* decided *you* know best! . . . No! You're wrong! Period!' Smoke from Ronnie's cigarette curled around her head like storm clouds. Her stomach had been churning and griping before the phone call. Most of the night, in fact. Since before dawn she'd shuffled back and forth between the bathroom and the bed. Several megadoses of Advil later, her cramps had finally quieted to a dull roar. She was just drifting off for a nap when the phone rang, and Celeste got her riled up again. 'You make this sound like you found a pencil I lost! . . . And what have *you* done about it in the last three months? Not a damn thing!' The strident *beep-beep-beep* of a truck in reverse, seven stories below, drifted through the open window and underscored Ronnie's argument.

Ronnie puffed furiously and countered Celeste's version of events. 'Maybe *you* didn't have the time to go down there until now, but did it ever occur to you that I might?' Anger made sitting impossible, so Ronnie climbed up out of the broken-down sofa, stuck her feet in her sneakers, because she never put a bare toe on the grimy, worn industrial tile floors in the loft, and stalked into the kitchen. 'Nobody asked you to decide what my schedule would allow! We could have listed with a broker by phone. Might even have a buyer by now.' Ronnie ground her cigarette out in the already full Altoids tin-cum-ashtray sitting on the fifties-era red Formica dinette table. She bent to empty the tin into the trash, but there wasn't space for another butt, and she had sworn she wasn't taking out the garbage again before somebody else did. 'Cut the sentimental crap! Since when are you so interested in our family history?! And what do you expect to find in Proper, South Carolina, that Mama and Daddy . . . Fine. *Prosper, North* Carolina. Whatever. If there was anything important there, don't you think they would have got it by now?! . . . What do you mean Ma won't talk about it? . . . That's crazy! . . . Maybe she won't talk to you . . .' Ronnie grabbed a plastic stirrer from a coffee-stained white paper bag abandoned on the kitchen counter. She perched on one of the rickety, orange vinyl chairs and folded and refolded the small plastic stick into jagged peaks.

'So now I'm supposed to be grateful that you're gonna go straighten it all out!?' The little straw sprang free from Ronnie's hand and flew across the room. 'You wouldn't even be telling me now except you might need my signature for something.' Ronnie tromped out of the kitchen, plopped back down on the sofa, then jumped up again and went to close the window against the wail of sirens from the street.

'Thank God Daddy put my name on the deed. But then, he had your number.' She balanced precariously on the narrow sill. 'You figure out what it means, Celeste, I'm through talkin' . . . Oh yes I *can* hang up!' Ronnie clicked off, then tossed the phone across the room onto the sofa. *Ma's father's house? My whole family is whacked.* She felt a twinge in her belly again, like somebody pinched her hard from the inside. She looked at her watch. It wasn't time for more pills yet.

What kind of idiot does she think I am? Ronnie didn't know if she was madder at Celeste for not telling her or at herself because Celeste was probably right. *I can barely handle me.*

After that big commercial fell through last fall and Ronnie had to vacate the Seventy-fifth Street apartment for the returning caballero, every part of her life seemed in a race straight down the tubes. She was back to bill-paying roulette, where only the lucky few were chosen each month. Her agent disappeared owing her for two bookings, no forwarding phone or address. She hadn't found a new one willing to take her on yet and hadn't been on a decent audition in months. *It's my own damn fault. I blew ten thousand dollars like the candles on a birthday cake.*

The one good thing about the latest dump she called an address was that most of the time nobody was around. She'd been on West Twenty-fifth Street four months. It was a share: living room, pass-through kitchen, two bedrooms, one bathroom. Four people more or less, depending on who stayed elsewhere and who dragged someone home with them. It was in one of those uniquely Manhattan buildings, zoned commercial/residential, which meant that no tenant could whine because the fourth floor was running a catering business from her apartment, or because the occupant on ten lived in his graphic arts studio. The upshot was you could do pretty much whatever you wanted within your four walls as long as you paid the rent.

Ronnie had met the guy who held the lease, a self-styled fashion designer who went by the name Rake, while she was hanging out at a photo studio with Kayla. The photographer was one in an endless series of Kayla's exes, but they had at least stayed friendly enough that he did her new head shot for free when she agreed to pose for some artful nudes. Ronnie and Kayla were weeding through chromes at the light box while Rake, a six-foot-four-inch exclamation point with platinum locks and sixteen visible piercings, attempted to convince the guy to shoot some of his designs for just the cost of film and processing. In a warp-speed harangue, Rake predicted the photographer would be able to ride his coattails to the cover of *WWD* and *Vogue*, fame and fortune. Ronnie and Kayla had been knocking themselves out laughing on the QT but they pulled on their straight faces when he approached. Somehow, in the midst of his raving, Rake had overhead Ronnie bitching about having her bags packed with nowhere to move. He said he'd just lost a roomie, and she could have the spot if she was interested. Ronnie turned the idea over for about two seconds. He looked a little orbital, but she'd definitely seen worse. The location was convenient. The rent was reasonable. And the photographer knew him, right? This was Ronnie's best offer. Actually, her only offer. He was a fashion designer after all, how bad could it be?

The apartment did have a view of sorts. The living room window looked out on a double-decker outdoor garage, but if you leaned out you could see the Empire State Building. Rake had the larger bedroom, at least that's what Ronnie had heard; she'd never seen it. He kept the door locked, and he had no visitors. The other was shared by Melise and Lucy, two girls Ronnie swore didn't look old enough to be out of high school. They were both five foot dust, brown-skinned with hair shaved down to scalp and helium voices. If they weren't sharing a wardrobe, they had very similar tastes in skin-tight clothes, and they had each mastered a look of perpetual boredom. Together Ronnie spoke about six words to them a week, and so far neither had been home on the same night. When Ronnie first moved in, she wondered what would happen if they mixed up their schedules and showed up at the same time, but she didn't give it much thought. She never paid enough attention to remember which was who; she thought of them as Mel-Lucy.

As the latecomer, Ronnie slept in the living room on a sofa bed. The arms and back of the powder blue monstrosity had been shredded by some long-ago cat and it smelled permanently of Chinese food. The first few nights she fell asleep and dreamed about moo shu and egg rolls. Ronnie kept her stuff in a big suitcase and one of those flowered cardboard chests of drawers in the front closet. She didn't kid herself; the place was a pit, but it was only temporary. Just until she got on her feet again.

Ronnie had calculated that from what they all paid in rent, Rake lived for free, which allowed him to buy the sheets of latex and rolls of plastic, from which he created the 'Rake Down Chic' look. His creations, basics for the astral epoch he called them, looked like Deep Space Nine meets dominatrix. Ronnie found out firsthand how much they felt like instruments of torture when she bartered down her rent by modeling in a show he held at midnight on a Wednesday in May, behind a warehouse just off the West Side Highway.

Even her social life sucked. She'd gone out with R. Phillip a few times, enough to cajole him, after several glasses of wine, to reveal that the *R* stood for Rudolph. It was all she could do to keep from making reindeer jokes. He always took Ronnie to fabulous places, and she always had a boring time, but once he realized that all he was getting for the price of dinner was her company, the phone calls dropped off sharply. She decided he'd found a suitably attractive somebody, with better credentials and a more open admissions policy, to show off to his pretentious friends. No big loss. They had left it friendly enough. When she moved and changed bank branches, yet again, he even made a phone call to somebody he knew and arranged for her to handle Ronnie right away, no lines, no waiting, like she had more than $1.37 to deposit. Ronnie decided he liked hooking people up. It made him feel like a junior wheeler-dealer. And they still went out once in a while, last minute, like his prime candidate must have canceled. He had called Sunday to invite her to some museum reception on Tuesday. She gave him a hard time, just for practice, but she accepted because, hey, it was better than sitting around the apartment.

Ronnie still had her usual quotient of wine and hors d'oeuvres evenings. She did her fair share of talking trash, but the truth was she figured she'd heard every line and could answer them back like a champ. Nobody got over on Ronnie, not anymore. She had decided the sampler pack of male companions suited her needs; there was lots to choose from, no main course to get bored with, and there were no leftovers. But for all her bravado, she didn't part with her digits very often. She had too much important stuff to get straight and no time to be chasing after some man like she watched Kayla do. It just wasn't a priority.

She still had a few steady clients, trade shows, showroom gigs, and photographers who booked her directly because she charged them half the going rate, but she had to stand on her head to collect. If it weren't for Sable Shades, she couldn't have made it this far. Twice, she screwed up her courage to ask Marilyn Ellis if the job offer with the company was still open, but although she swung some extra hours on Monday night, she couldn't bring herself to ask for full-time. What would people say? You remember Ronnie? Ronnie Frazier? She's selling cosmetics now. Ronnie couldn't bear the ordinariness of it. She was supposed to be somebody. She couldn't give up, although it was hard some days to remember exactly what she would be losing.

Ronnie stood and opened the window again. *How come Ma never told us about this house?* Summer was only a week old, but the heat already had that thick, oily feel she had come to know in the city. Except for Rake's room, the apartment had no air conditioning. Ronnie gathered her hair off her neck. She was overdue for a visit to LaVonne, but it wasn't in the budget this week. She poked her head out the window, hoping to catch a breeze. *Prosper? That's a sick joke!* She squatted, rested her arms on the sill, and watched

155

the midday traffic clog Twenty-sixth Street. *It's like Daddy's givin' me another chance. And this time I absolutely, positively will not screw up.* She watched a bike messenger dart between two trucks, zip past a startled pedestrian. *That much land ought to be worth something. Enough to get me settled in L.A. maybe? I can pay for some acting classes. I haven't studied in so long — too long. Celeste can build a monument on her half if she wants to. I'm gonna finance myself a fresh start. One last shot.* She pulled her head back in the apartment, got up, and brushed the soot off her hands.

I need a map. She glanced around, then laughed out loud. *Like I could just go to the bookshelf and grab an atlas. The only thing to read around here is a takeout menu.* Ronnie popped two more Advil, washed them down with a swig of diet iced tea, and made a mental note to pick up more. *Damn, that was a 250-pill bottle. Didn't I just buy it?* Then she snatched her white shirt from the back of the sofa and threw it on over her leggings and tank top because she didn't feel like listening to the nonsense she'd hear on the street otherwise. She grabbed her purse. If she left now she'd have time to browse in the big bookstore on Sixth Avenue before she needed to come back and get dressed for work. *A first step toward my future success.*

Ronnie got on the elevator and joined a black-haired girl who wore a black leather vest, black lipstick, two safety pins in her right eyebrow, and a bright yellow Walkman. She rocked to her tunes, eyes closed, and appeared oblivious to Ronnie's presence. Ronnie waited a few seconds, but none of the buttons were lit, so she pushed *G* and the doors finally closed. *Airhead.* She dug around in her bag for the roll of antacids to help quiet her stomach. *I hate this building.*

The car stopped two floors down, and an elderly man carrying a white toy poodle got on. He huddled in a corner and whispered in an unintelligible stream to his little red-eyed dog. Ronnie jammed her shades on and rolled her eyes. *Please don't let another fool get in here.* When the gears ground to a halt at the ground floor and the doors clanged open, she made a dash for the door. Through the glass she saw mystery roommate number one. Or was it two? *Melise? Lucy?* She got out of a white panel van with a rheumy looking guy wearing spattered painter's pants and a denim shirt with the sleeves cut out. He slammed the door and the van drove off. *Glad I'm leavin'.* Ronnie nodded, flipped the door open wide enough for them to catch if they wanted to, and was on her way.

In five minutes she was in the air-conditioned cool of the bookstore. *No wonder people hang out here. Tables, chairs, sofas?* She didn't remember the last time she'd been in a bookstore, certainly not since they started looking like dens. Ronnie inhaled the scent of cinnamon and chocolate, surveyed the seemingly endless rows of books. *I need a damn compass.* She got directions at the information desk and followed the instructions to the travel section with a growing sense of excitement. After collecting an armload of books that had something about North Carolina in the title, she parked herself in an empty chair and dug in.

Tar Heel State, Blue Ridge Mountains, population 7,000,000. In the whole state!? My block has more people than that. She thumbed through the volumes, scanned maps. No Prosper. She got to a book sealed in cellophane and could feel a fold-out map in back. She looked around, checked for clerks on the prowl, then punctured the wrapping with her thumbnail, opened

157

out the map. In the index she got the coordinates, then scanned and squinted. *There it is.* Prosper was printed in the tiniest, lightest type. It was surrounded by towns with names like Peedee and Peachland. *Are they serious?* The nearest 'real' city was Charlotte. Remembering her fourth-grade geography, Ronnie checked the legend, measured the distance between Prosper and Charlotte between her thumb and forefinger. *That's more than an hour away!* She checked the rest of her books for Prosper highlights, but unlike Duck, Cullowhee, and Swan City, all of which had enough going for them to warrant inclusion in one book or another, Prosper appeared to be completely unremarkable. *Great. It's probably right up there with Mayberry.* Ronnie left her books on the table. *What if I go down there too? To look after my interests, get this process moving? Celeste might not like it, but she couldn't stop me – if I wanted to go.*

By the time she turned on her block, she'd decided to call and check the airfare when she got off work. *And I bet I can get Ma to tell me more about this place than she told Celeste.* Ronnie had a little space left before she maxed out her charge card, and this seemed like a good investment. She started composing her speech to ask Marilyn for the time off. Fortunately, her ride up in the elevator was solitary. She'd have just enough time to shower and change into her Sable Shades getup.

'What the . . .' The prickly feeling started at the top of Ronnie's head and snaked down her spine. She stood in the open doorway, trying to comprehend the damage. Cans and broken jars from the kitchen cabinets spilled onto the counter, littered the floor. A sack of flour had burst and dusted the mess with a layer of white. All the drawers had been yanked out and ditched in a corner.

Fear made her want to run, but she was rooted in place. Then she caught sight of Rake, splayed on the couch, holding his head like it would fall off.

'Are you all right?' She hurried inside.

'Aw man – they cleaned me out,' he wailed.

Broken glass crunched under Ronnie's feet as she walked through the kitchen. It was hot in the loft, but she was suddenly cold, about to shiver. 'What the hell happened?!' She stepped over the medicine chest, which had been ripped out and abandoned in the middle of the floor. A lot had happened to her since she left home, but she'd never had a break-in.

When she got up close, Rake didn't look hurt, but the rest of the apartment had been worked over. Tables and chairs overturned, lamps broken, the heavy metal fire door to Rake's room hung precariously from one hinge. Ronnie sank down on the sofa next to him. She couldn't raise her voice above a whisper. 'What the hell happened?'

'Somebody broke in.' His voice was flat.

'Did you walk in on 'em?'

'Naw. I wish I had. There would have been bloodshed.'

'Save it, Rake. How long have you been waiting for the cops? You didn't touch anything, did you?' Ronnie's eyes darted around the room. 'Thank God I wasn't here!'

Rake just stared at the ceiling.

Ronnie noticed that the TV and VCR were still there. *Probably too old to fence.* 'What did they take?' She did a mental inventory. She had on her real jewelry, her watch, a pair of gold hoop earrings, and a matching gold ring and bracelet she'd ordered off cable in the middle of the night. She didn't have anything else in the apartment but clothes, and no self-respecting burglar would waste his time on . . . *Shit! My jacket!* She'd meant to put it in storage, looked up a few places, even called for prices, but she put it off, left it wrapped in tissue paper in one of her suitcases. She stared down the hall, saw the closet door ajar, and she knew. She couldn't feel her legs as she got up to check. The clothes that had been in the bag were dumped on the floor and the empty suitcase propped the door open. She kicked it, then dropped to her knees, deflated. 'My mink jacket's gone!'

'I'm sorry. I didn't check anywhere but my . . . I didn't know . . .'

'I'm callin' the cops again.' Ronnie jumped up and dug the portable out from between the couch cushions where she'd thrown it. 'I'll say I think they're still . . .'

'Don't!' Rake sounded panicked.

'It's the middle of the damn day! They should be here by now.' She started to punch in the numbers, but Rake grabbed Ronnie's wrist and snatched the phone. 'Ow! Get your hands off . . .'

'No cops, Ronnie.'

'We've been ripped off! What do you expect me to . . .'

'No cops. I can't tell what they stole.'

'You got so much crap in there you can't figure out what's missing?' Ronnie headed toward Rake's gaping door. She was surprised by the plush ambiance. The faux marble walls were covered with sketches and clippings from fashion magazines, secured by clear pushpins. A huge oval gilt mirror hung over the maple dresser, which matched his king-size headboard. Aside from the obvious looting, the room looked as traditional as Rake did not. The green plaid bedspread hung askew on his bed, pillows and shams tossed aside. *This boy even has drapes!* Two towering bookshelves lay toppled and splintered, the trophies, plaques, bolts of fabric, sample cards, and actual books strewn across the room. She walked farther in, drawn by the contradiction. The TV, VCR, DVD player and stereo, all state-of-the-art, had not been touched. His dressmaker's dummy lay on its side, but his work table and industrial sewing machine were intact too. Ronnie noticed that the door to what she assumed was a closet, as well as all the molding around the jamb, were splintered, like they'd been chewed up. 'What the . . .' She found a room, at least the size of the other bedroom, with walls lined with aluminum foil and track lights and spots crisscrossing the ceiling. Wooden planks elevated the floor, and some kind of water tank and hose system occupied a corner. Shelves like bleachers were lined with big, plastic flowerpots, some of them overturned, all of them empty. There wasn't a leaf in sight.

He came in behind her. 'You shouldn't be in here.'

Ronnie whirled around. 'You're growin' weed in here?!' She shook with anger. 'Oh my God, I'm livin' with a damn drug dealer! You coulda gotten me arrested – or killed, Rake! Are you crazy?!'

Rake backed away from her tirade, stumbled on the bed, and plopped down. 'Naw, Ron, it wasn't like that. I swear.' He talked to the floor. 'I used to just grow for myself – and couple of friends – once in a while – I was gonna finance my own show.'

'Is that how you found out?' She pointed to the

alarm pad by the door. *I've been sharing an apartment with a guy who alarms his room?!*

'I had to get it. My roommate situation is so . . . there's a lot of traffic through here. Anyway, the security company beeped me.'

'See how much good that did!' She shoved his shoulder, hard. *How could I be so stupid? Again!*

'For all I know, *you* had something to do with it.' He sat up and stared hard.

'You're not gonna blame this on me!' *Why wouldn't he? He doesn't know any more about me than I know about him. Not a damn thing.* 'Talk to your little friends Melise and Lucy.'

'They're not my friends. I met 'em at a club.'

Great. 'One of them was coming in with some skeevy guy when I left.'

'Look, I don't give a shit, all right! Get the hell outta my room, and if you tell anybody . . .'

'What?!' Ronnie stood up to him, but suddenly she was aware how much she didn't want to know what. She didn't know Rake had a marijuana truck farm in his room, and she didn't know what else he'd do either. She just wanted to leave, but where did she have to go besides the Sables Shades counter? 'Damn! I gotta go to work.'

The tears were streaming by the time she got to the bathroom. She put the lid down, sat on the toilet, and sobbed. *What am I gonna do?* Ronnie didn't have much time to wallow in it. She pulled herself together, did her face from memory since the mirror was gone, all except eyeliner because her hands weren't steady enough, and she was behind the Sable Shades counter only twenty minutes late. Fortunately she had no makeovers, so she concentrated on ringing up the

162

merchandise and bagging it without bursting into tears. The time weighed heavily because she knew that after the store closed she had nowhere to go except back to the loft, and for the first time in her life she was afraid to go home. So when she got out onto Thirty-fourth Street, she started walking. Nowhere in particular, just one foot, then the other, crossing wherever the light was in her favor, trying to shape some coherent plan out of ashes.

Kayla told Ronnie that if she needed a squat she was always welcome. 'You know Mama won't mind. She likes you,' Kayla had said.

Ronnie was afraid of what Kayla's mother was like if she *didn't* like somebody. To Ronnie, Kayla's situation was nearly as bad as her own. She still lived in Brooklyn with her mother, grandmother, and two younger sisters and their five kids. Or, as Ronnie thought of them, the witch, grand wizard, two harpies, and their evil spawn. A few years back, after a party in Fort Green, Ronnie had been too wasted to go home, and Kayla insisted she spend the night. Ronnie had been appalled at the way they spoke to each other, cursing as soon as not, children included. It made her and Celeste look like sweet and sweeter. She had no idea how Kayla put up with the anger and chaos.

Besides, this was not a story she planned to share with her flighty friend just yet. Repeating it aloud would amplify the nightmare, and the volume was already deafening. And Kayla was still in the Hamptons for a long weekend, anyway; some friend had a share and she considered the island fertile hunting ground.

By the time Ronnie got to Thirty-eighth Street, the

'what if' game had taken over. *What if they do come back? What if the police find out about Rake's enterprise and think I'm part of it? What am I gonna do?* She stopped at Bryant Park. Nestled in this valley between skyscrapers, a crowd had gathered, enjoying the balmy night; people lounged on the lawn in folding chairs, stretched out on blankets with gourmet munchies and wine, or balanced on squares of folded newspaper watching *Some Like It Hot* al fresco, projected on a huge screen. That's the kind of thing she had always loved about the city, the thrill of moonlit movies, the sense that all things are possible if you just find the right corner to turn.

Ronnie sank to a bench, just vacated by two men and a woman conversing in animated German. She couldn't see stars; they were rare on a clear night. Even the moon was reduced to a bright glow showing through the haze. The park walkways still bustled with briefcase-toting yuppies, tourists out to soak up as much of the city as they could in six days and seven nights, and rollerbladers jockeying with skateboarders for sidewalk space. Ronnie marveled at a limber red-haired girl who twisted and spun with the same agility and fearless abandon as the boys around her. The girl came to a dead stop, flipped her board up into her hand, and tucked it under her arm in a motion so slick Ronnie wasn't sure she'd actually seen it. *She's got a whole life ahead of her. When will she stop enjoying it?*

Ronnie hadn't walked far, but she was exhausted. She hadn't intended to walk in the opposite direction from her apartment, but then she really didn't know what she intended to do. About anything. The weight of her day, of her life was pressing down on her. Her shoulders slumped from the load. And the soles of her

164

feet burned. *Stupid sandals!* They were cheap and meant to be cute, not walking shoes. She wiggled her toes, hoping a little air would help cool the fire. A burst of laughter erupted from the audience and was swallowed by the night. She thought it was funny that this little bit of green encircled by concrete and granite was referred to as a park. Back in Buffalo they'd probably call it a square. It definitely wasn't a real park like Ellicott Creek or Chestnut Ridge, with hills, streams, birds, and room to run. A fragment of a memory darted across Ronnie's mind. She was seven or eight, running full out through the park with a water balloon, laughing wildly. One of her braids had come undone and she had on brand-new Keds. They were so white. Celeste was chasing her. Then it was gone, quick as it came. Ronnie closed her eyes a second, tried to get it back, but when she opened them again, tears had replaced the memory. Blinking, she looked away, brushed her cheeks with her hand. Fortunately no one was paying attention to her, because only nut jobs and losers sat on park benches crying. She tilted her head back to stem the tide and tuned in to the buzz of streetlights, traffic, and so many people with so much energy rushing by one another with conviction, purpose. The heartbeat of New York. *I'm so tired.* The charge, the excitement of being in the greatest city in the world, used to fuel her days. Anything could happen here. The possibilities were as vast as her hopes and dreams. The city used to get her up, keep her going, and put her to bed so she could do it all over again. But now that all felt like a story that happened to someone else a long, long time ago. She had tried, kept her end of what had always been a one-sided deal. New York had become another broken promise. *Maybe I'm losing my edge. Or maybe I've just lost my grip!* The rustle of a newspaper and a grunt snatched her back to park view. He sat on the bench opposite hers, the *Post* open across his lap, right hand moving up and down like a piston, his game of pocket pool well under way.

I gotta get outta here.

8

'. . . a few square miles of raggedy road and broken dreams . . .'

'Now this limited power of attorney, it means you can sign the papers for me, but only for this one closing, is that right, uh, Mr Dawkins?' Even though Arthur Jr had taken over the practice from his father more than ten years ago, Della still had trouble calling him anything but Chunk, which is what the senior Dawkins had nicknamed him when he was little. First time Della saw him he was a five-year-old chunk of chocolate, working diligently at stapling the papers and licking the envelopes Arthur Sr's secretary would hand him to keep him occupied. That was back when she and Will bought their very first house, and through the years, all of their legal affairs had been handled by father or son. Della saw no reason to change that.

'Uh, yes. That's exactly right.' Even in the simplest situations Arthur chose his words carefully, like he had deliberated over six other words before choosing the most precisely correct one. 'Then I can execute all the necessary documents. You won't even have to be present for the closing. I will, of course, forward you the check immediately.'

The house on Minnesota was the tenth one Will had bought and the first she'd arranged to sell. Della wasn't keen on watching the change of hands. It was for a good cause, though. She wanted to make sure Niki had whatever money she needed to go to chef school.

'As for giving money to your granddaughter, you're allowed to make a gift of up to ten thousand dollars a year to a family member without any tax repercussions. If that works out for the both of you, I'd suggest handling it that way. We can make some stipulation in your will that this be continued, but I don't see the need to set up a trust.'

'Once we get this house squared away, I'll come in to talk about my will.' *My Will. That used to mean something completely different.* Della knew Celeste was right about getting rid of the houses. She just wanted to do it in her own time and in her own way, without Celeste any further in her business than she already was.

'This'll only take a second.'

Della watched as he turned to his computer and input some information. She thought Arthur Jr had grown into a fine man, but she always had a feeling he would. And he'd done a fine job of growing the business. He took it from a solo practice working out of a storefront to a suite in a small office building he encouraged his father to buy. Chunk supervised the renovations, then he beat the bushes for new business. Now he had five attorneys working for him.

And Arthur Jr had his own family now. On the wall behind his desk, among the framed degrees and citations, hung a smiling portrait of his wife and their three sons. But back when he and Celeste were teens,

Della had picked him as the perfect match for her oldest daughter. She thought they were a lot alike: both serious, persistent, levelheaded. He knew he wanted to be a lawyer early on, and even back in the days of ripped bell-bottom blue jeans, platforms, and love beads, he dressed more sensibly, like a professional man. Della thought they'd complement each other, and every once in a while she couldn't help but imagine a church wedding and beautiful grandbabies, not that it was any of her business. At one point she sensed ol' Chunk was sweet on Celeste too. At least that's what it seemed like to her. If he was around the office when his father had papers for Will, Arthur Jr would volunteer to deliver them in person. Della would do everything short of fixing lemonade and cookies and sitting the two of them out on the porch swing to encourage them together. Arthur didn't help his own case much. He was slow to make a move. Celeste dismissed him as way too boring. The more Della talked him up, the harder Celeste shot him down, until finally Della gave up. It's not that there was anything wrong with Everett. Della loved him to death; she was just never convinced he could make Celeste happy.

Not that Della cared at this moment if Celeste or Ronnie was happy. Right now she was furious at both of them.

Arthur reached behind his desk, plucked the document from the laser printer, tucked it in an envelope, and handed it to Della. 'Take these home and read them over. Call me if you have any questions. Otherwise, sign both copies, send them back, and we'll be all set.'

Della took the envelope without looking at it. 'One

more thing – It's about some land down south that was left to me.' She hated to be like this, but as far as she was concerned Celeste and Ronnie had driven her to it. She didn't begrudge them the money. They could sell the property, split the proceeds, and that would be the end of it. But now they were both heading to Prosper to poke their noses where they didn't belong, and neither one seemed to care that it was against Della's wishes. So she made up her mind that she didn't care what she had to do to stop them. Della began to explain the situation, which jogged Arthur's memory. He brought her files up on the computer, read for a moment.

'The difficulty is that legally, it's not your land anymore.' Arthur took off his glasses, threw them on his desk, squeezed his forehead in his hand. 'I mean, I take it you grew up there, and you must feel some – attachment. But once you signed it over to Mr Frazier, it was legally his to dispose of, and he certainly did that in a lawful way.'

Della's eyes glazed with hurt and anger. She zipped and unzipped her pocketbook as she thought. 'What if I buy it back from them?'

'That would be fine, as long as you three can agree on terms.'

'And if they won't sell it to me, I can take them out of my will, can't I?'

'Mrs Frazier, I – this is rather drastic.'

'That doesn't answer my question.'

'Well, technically, yes, you could disinherit one or both of your children. It usually creates quite a problem. You'd give them grounds to challenge the will. They'll end up with other attorneys involved, it usually drags on, stirs up bad feeling. Nobody really wins. I don't know what, uh, situation, brought this about, but if you give it some time, I'm sure . . .'

'I ain't got time.' She stood and left the office.

Della ran the rest of her errands wearing a sour puss. She chewed out a grocery clerk because they were out of the sale ice cream, and when the checkout line tried her patience she pushed her whole cart of food to one side and left the store.

At the beauty shop she didn't have two words to add to the round of gossip. Della was too aggravated to work her word puzzles, so she closed the magazine on her lap, sat under the dryer, and steamed at Will for starting this whole mess. And what gave her children the right to dig around in her life without an invitation? *Goin' a thousand miles out of the way to kick a sleeping dog. Then question me about why I'm upset!*

With a flowered head scarf tied over her rows of fresh, hard curls, Della left the shop and carried her bad attitude home with her. She wandered through the house for a time, too fidgety to sit in one place for long. It was dinnertime, but talking to a lawyer about her own children had taken her appetite. *If my mother had ever asked me not to do something . . .* Della stood at the kitchen counter, ripping open mail. Half of it was junk, still addressed to Will.

Hesitantly, Della stepped into the rays of amber evening sun that flooded the living room. She stood in front of the piano, lost in thought. As far as she was concerned, Prosper was a few square miles of raggedy road and broken dreams. *Lord only knows what it's like now.* She pulled out the bench, sat down, and flipped the lid. Tentatively, she ran the back of her index finger over the keys, playing a quiet glissando that stopped at middle C, where her hands fell naturally into place. The simple melody flowed from her effortlessly, like it had waited a long time to be released. Della's whole body seemed to carry the music, swell with it, glide on it. As she continued to play, she embellished the tune, hummed the harmony. Finally she opened her mouth to sing. Her voice cracked and stopped her cold.

SUNDAY, APRIL 23, 1950
PROSPER, NORTH CAROLINA

'So your father tells me you sing, Odella. Is that true?' Mrs Garland clasped her hands and rested them on her enormous blue and white flowered bosom.

Odella looked over at her father, who nodded. 'I guess so, ma'am.'

'You were in the choir over in Cadysville?' Mrs Garland spoke in the same thin, warbly soprano as she sang. 'What part did you sing?' She turned her mouth down, tucked her chin in, and her face melted into the thick fleshy rolls around her neck.

'Ma'am?' Odella folded and unfolded her church bulletin. Mrs Garland made her nervous. She had a mustache and a mole that moved when she talked, and Odella was usually so busy watching them she had a hard time paying attention to what Mrs Garland said. Besides, she didn't want to talk about singing today. Service had been particularly long. It was nearly three o'clock, Reverend Garland had preached two hours nonstop, and she just wanted to go home, take off her dress, and go down to the pond. Once she discovered the wide, still pool, it quickly became her favorite spot. She liked to be alone and think about

172

stuff, and the fact that Henry hated it made the location all the more appealing.

This morning, before they left for church, her father knocked on her door. He sat on the edge of the bed, adjusted the crease in his freshly pressed trousers. 'It's time you joined in things a little. You been here a while now. Your mama told me what a good voice you have so I decided to speak to Mrs Garland after church. I'm sure she'd welcome you in her choir.' Odella knew it was fruitless to protest, and although she never mentioned it to anyone, she did miss her music.

Two years ago, when Odella came to Prosper, her father said he'd give her time to settle in and get adjusted to her new life. 'And give these folks time to get adjusted to you.' He predicted accurately that she'd be a curiosity for a while. And she had been for most of the first year. There had been a constant parade of visitors stopping by the house on some pretext or another, but all they really wanted was a good closeup look at Odell Womack's outside child. She'd hide in the woods and hear them whispering as they walked up the road on their way back to town. 'Well, she looks jus' like him.' 'How can Ethiopia stand it?' 'Right in her face. Um, um, um.' Odella stayed to herself, did as she was told, and spoke when spoken to.

That philosophy worked with her father's square-faced wife as well. Ethiopia was always polite, but Odella felt more like a boarder than family, which was just fine with her. She had no use for Miz Ethiopia either. There was no point in her even pretending to be motherly, because the simple fact was she could never be Annie.

The only person she couldn't easily sidestep was Henry. He kept his rancor in check when others were around to the point that Odella had heard people comment on how mature it was of Henry to welcome his half-blood kin. But when they were alone he'd unleash his pent-up humiliation. Henry viewed her mere presence as an affront to his mother. And that she was named for Odell and he was not was daily kindling to Henry's smoldering rage. He'd trip her, accidentally on purpose, tear up her school assignments, track mud into the house after she'd finished mopping so she'd have to do it again, and dare her to run to Odell. 'He's a damn mangy dog, just like you.' Odella dealt with his pranks and name-calling, as long as he left her mother out of it. One day he started to bad-mouth Annie, and she took after him with a mop handle. He didn't do it again.

Odella looked up at the beamed ceiling and rocked back and forth on the heels of her black patent leather Mary Janes. She wished she was somewhere else. Twelve, going on thirteen, as she told folks when they asked her age, was such an awkward stage between girl and woman. She was neither and both. Odella felt like she grew taller while she slept, and dungarees that had fit a few days ago seemed to have shrunk overnight. It was like her whole body had a secret pact she wasn't privy to. Blouses that she wore to school didn't button anymore, thanks to newly sprouted breasts. Her skirts suddenly became too loose in the waist and too tight across her hips. She hunched her shoulders in an effort to conceal her chest and appear shorter until Odell made her stop. A few days later she came home from school and discovered a pile of new clothes on her bed. At the bottom of the pile, under the dresses, sweaters, and skirts, were two brassieres, two girdles, a box of sanitary napkins, and a pamphlet entitled 'Your New Body.' Miz Ethiopia, as she called her father's wife, when she had no choice but to use a name, asked her if she found everything. Odella nodded and that was that. But none of that helped how she felt about growing up and out, so Odella wished for Annie and tried to figure out what to do with herself.

'Stop fidgeting, child, and answer my question.' Genevieve Garland huffed and puffed, her mammoth breasts rolled like the mighty Jordan. She was a formidable woman, at least twice the size of her husband, but they were quite suited to each other. Samuel and Genevieve took everything about life seriously, and Faith Chapel Colored Methodist Episcopal Church was their life.

'I sang whatever they needed me to, ma'am.' Odella didn't like either one of them. They may have been good, but they weren't nice, especially to her. She longed for her church back home.

'Come now. You have to be a soprano or an alto. Maybe your old choir didn't make such distinctions.' She looked down her nose and over her glasses at Odella. 'But in this choir we do. Most of our members read music too.' Her intent was clear.

'Odella.' She could hear the warning in her father's voice. 'Answer Miz Garland.'

'I guess I do both, ma'am.'

'Humph.' Mrs Garland moved her considerable bulk over to the piano and plopped down on the stool, which disappeared beneath the overhang. 'We'll just see about that. Come on over here.'

Reluctantly, Odella went to stand beside her. As

175

she did every Sunday, before every song, Genevieve Garland made an elaborate show of limbering her fingers before she began to play. She started and nodded at Odella, who followed her scales note for note. Mrs Garland moved up an octave then down one. She changed keys, and Odella sang, almost intuiting where the music would go next. Mrs Garland finished and glared at Odella over her glasses.

A few folks who were still milling about outside the small white building, complimenting the pastor on his sermon, catching up on news, and getting their weekly dose of gossip, poked their heads back in the door.

'Maybe it would be better if I sang a whole song, ma'am.' Odella found comfort in the sound of her own voice. She hadn't sung in so long she'd forgotten how good it felt. 'Ma'am?' Odella nodded slightly toward the piano. It took Mrs Garland a moment to realize that Odella wanted her to get up, that she would play for herself. The rickety upright in the corner of the sanctuary groaned as Mrs Garland leaned on it and hoisted herself off the stool. She stepped away, folded her arms across her expansive chest, and waited.

Odella sat gingerly on the stool, looked at Mrs Garland, then over at Odell who was having a hard time hiding his smile. Odella put her hands on the keys, closed her eyes, and opened her mouth. 'Precious Lord, take my hand. Lead me on . . .' Odella lit up the rafters with her body full of voice, and anybody who was still outside drifted back in. Will and Lester dragged Henry inside and stood in the rear of the church. Others, including Odell, Ethiopia, and Reverend Garland, took seats in the pews. By the time Odella got to the last stanza, she was accompanied by a chorus of 'Amen,' 'Lord ha' mercy,' and 'Thank you, Jesus.'

'We hold choir practice on Saturday afternoon,' Mrs Garland said matter-of-factly and dabbed at the trickle of sweat at her temple with a tiny blue hankie.

'Yes, ma'am.' Odella got up and looked at her father, who beamed and nodded his head approvingly.

Lester left Will and Henry standing in the doorway and headed up the aisle to meet Odella. A long and lean sixteen, Lester moved with the lazy lope of a trotter. 'How come you didn't tell nobody you could sing like that, Odee?' He stopped in front of her.

Although Henry remained as hateful as he was the day they met, she eventually got on well with Will and Lester, which only made Henry more unpleasant. Will was protective and always stood up for her, and she and Lester quickly became sparring partners, trading wisecracks and insults. Odella spent a lot of her time at the pond wishing they were her brothers instead of Henry.

''Cause nobody didn't ask, and don't call me Odee,' Odella shot back.

'You got a smart answer for everything, don't you, Odee?'

Odella caught herself short of sticking out her tongue. They were, after all, still in church, and she didn't want to know what kind of sin Reverend and Mrs Garland would call that.

'Well answer me this. You wanna do a duet sometime? We'd sound pretty good together.'

Lester Wilson was the best baritone for miles around. Even though he had just turned sixteen, he sang most of the male leads and solos in the Faith Chapel choir. Sometimes he'd even sing at other churches, and they'd take up a special collection and give him the money.

'I sound pretty good by myself –' Odella couldn't let him know how tickled she was that he was asking her to sing with him. '– But I'll think about it.' She flashed him a big fake smile, walked outside, and found herself surrounded by church members waiting to pat her on the back. Lester went past her and rejoined Henry and Will. The three of them made it a habit to walk home from church. Odella gave Lester another cheesy grin and climbed in the backseat of her father's car.

'Didn't know you played the piano too,' Odell said as they pulled away from the church. Her father's wife said nothing. 'Were you taking lessons back in Cadysville?'

'No, Papa. I just play what I hear.'

'Well, we'll look into some lessons.'

Two weeks later and right before her lessons began, Odella came home and found a shiny, black spinet piano in the living room. Her stepmother asked if she'd seen it. Odella nodded, and that was that.

If her piano lessons were magical, learning to connect what she heard with a written note was alchemy. Turning the sounds in her head into music on a page came as naturally as breathing. She loved going to Mrs Yarbrough's house for her lessons. She didn't have to be told to practice, although sometimes she had to be asked to stop. Wednesday afternoons were her favorite. Miz Ethiopia and her Sunshine Ladies from church visited the sick and shut-in. And Henry almost never came straight home from school, so Odella would run all the way, knowing she had at least two hours when she could play anything she wanted, any way she wanted. That's when she'd sound out the songs she listened to on the radio instead of hymns and waltzes.

Eyes closed, she was thumping out the melody to 'Is You Is or Is You Ain't My Baby' with her right hand when she felt the pain shoot up her arm. She hollered, looked down at her throbbing fingers mashed between the lid and the keys, then up into Henry's face. 'You don't play no nasty music in *my* mother's house,' he snarled.

When Odell came home, saw her swollen hand, and asked her what happened, she watched Henry's eyes narrow malevolently and said simply that the lid fell. Her father put a latch on the piano to ensure the accident wouldn't repeat itself. Odella couldn't play the piano for weeks.

When did it get dark? The street lamp in front of the house had come on. Della rubbed her right hand absently, then she slammed down the piano lid. A dissonant burst of notes lingered on the air.

Della didn't want to know how time had passed in Prosper, but one way or another, it looked like she was about to find out.

9

'My life. My rules. Right?'

'Of course, Mrs English. I'll let Ms English know you're here.' The young man behind the ornate Regency-style desk at the entrance to Les Fleurs stashed a stack of thickly bound, gold-tasseled menus in their wall rack, picked up the phone, and punched in an extension. After a murmured conversation he hung up.

'She's in a meeting with a new purveyor, but she said she'll be with you as soon as she can.' He gestured toward a brocade settee by a towering palm tree. 'Can I get you anything while you wait?'

'No. Thank you.' *Ms English is in a meeting with a purveyor. I hope her penmanship has improved. She'll never be able to read her notes.* Celeste sat gingerly on the edge, trying to avoid getting wet circles on her clothes. Her blouse was soaked under her linen jacket. The silk felt clammy against her back. Late June in Atlanta was much hotter than she was used to. On the ride from the airport, Celeste was sweating like a pig while her taxi driver seemed perfectly comfortable with the window only open a crack. It wasn't quite noon when they pulled in front of the hotel, but she was ready for another shower. *How can Niki stand this heat?*

Celeste shifted slightly to her left, directly in the path of an air-conditioning vent. The cool blast refreshed her. Most of the restaurant tables were still empty. Paintings of lavish floral arrangements and formal gardens decorated the walls. Servers busied themselves checking the contents of salt and pepper shakers, examining flatware, and refolding napkins. *This is casual dining? Nicole never said it was so elaborate.*

A nattily dressed elderly couple stopped at the display case outside the restaurant to look over the lunch menu. They held hands and whispered to each other before moving on. *They're so sweet. I always thought Everett and I . . .*

Celeste forced her brain to make a U-turn. She took out her agenda, crossed 'take cab to airport 6 A.M.,' 'switch flight,' and 'get plane at 7:45' off her to-do list. She had managed to convince herself that she decided last night, while she wrestled in bed, unable to sleep, to reroute her flight through Atlanta. That it was a spontaneous decision just to spend a day with her daughter, not a detour that had been on her mind for weeks. Otherwise she'd have to admit this visit was one of the many land mines in her life and that she was running out of safe places to step. That she didn't tell Niki sooner because she was afraid she'd find some excuse to keep her mother away. And that the whole Prosper episode felt like one big booby trap, with a hair trigger.

Down to the last Della refused to speak on the subject, and she grew more evil about it the closer Celeste got to departure. *I wish Daddy had sold the place and left me out of it.* She tried not to hope too hard that she could convince Nicole to go with her to North Carolina, even for a day or two. Somehow Celeste imagined the house was in the boonies, down a dirt road, with no phone, and Niki's company always made her feel better. And she'd have another shot at talking some sense into her child, at making Niki see that stirring pots in somebody's kitchen was not a step on the path to a successful career. Celeste and Niki had struggled through a few fast phone conversations after her short visit. When they spoke they avoided two subjects completely, Niki's decision and Everett's impending departure. Celeste hadn't even told her daughter about her great-grandfather's house until last week.

Celeste added 'call NC hotel and change arrival' to her list. She had tied herself in square knots during the last few weeks, trying to keep her life together. Once she realized that Everett thought he was serious about leaving, her first challenge had been to convince him not to go before school was out. She appealed to his sympathetic, understanding nature. 'You know it's the busiest time of the year for me. I can't handle all the pressure at school and this at the same time. You owe me at least that much.' His answer still rang in her ears. 'I'll hang out a little longer because you asked, but don't run it into the ground. Right now I owe myself more than I owe you.'

By the end of June, Celeste pleaded for another extension and asked him not to move out until she got back from Prosper. 'I authorized work on the new roof Daddy got bids on. I have to go check on it.'

At the last possible moment, when she'd given up

hope of changing Everett's mind, Celeste called the Kendalls to postpone their arrival in Highland Beach. She told Lydia that she had to go to Prosper right away because Ronnie was pressuring her about the house. Lydia said she understood completely. 'Family can get so ugly when it comes to money. But I hope you can get here for some part of the month. It would be a shame to waste ten thousand dollars.' Celeste could have kicked herself for blowing all that money, but it wouldn't matter if she could stall Everett long enough for him to come to his senses and put this divorce business behind them.

Celeste watched Niki approach, carrying a maroon leather binder under her arm. Her braids, bundled into a chignon, and the creamy sheath, gold choker, and black patent pumps clearly said 'I'm in charge here.' *She looks so grown up.* Niki glanced down as she passed a table set for four, then whispered to a passing waiter, who immediately cleared the service plates. She waved at Celeste, then stopped a moment to examine the enormous floral arrangement in the center of the room. At the desk she conferred briefly with the young maître d' before continuing on to her mother.

'You look so professional!' Celeste stood, held out her hands, and offered Niki her cheek.

'Hi.' Nicole obliged, gave her mother a quick kiss. 'Sorry to keep you waiting.' The older couple Celeste had seen earlier entered the restaurant. Niki instantly diverted her gaze from Celeste to the guests. 'Welcome to Les Fleurs. Eric will be . . .'

'Right here, Ms English.' The maître d' appeared, menus in hand.

'Enjoy your meal,' Niki said as he escorted the early lunchers to a table.

Celeste felt almost teary-eyed, watching her baby take charge.

Niki returned her attention to her mother. 'Are you okay? Is something wrong?'

'Everything is fine.'

Niki searched her mother's face. 'This visit is really unexpected.' *And you're not a spur-of-the-moment kinda babe.* Her mother's call caught Niki as she was brushing her teeth and trying to get out the door. All morning she'd been bracing for the approaching storm.

'And I know I'm barging in on your life, but it's only for a day. I leave tomorrow for Charlotte. I thought we might . . .'

'Just a sec, Ma.'

Celeste cringed at the 'Ma,' looked to see if anyone had heard. When she turned back, Niki had gone to speak to a small, distinguished man in a tan suit. He was shorter than Niki by several inches, and Celeste was amused when he took a step back so he didn't have to lift his head to talk to her. Celeste knew that trick. She used it herself. Niki opened the notebook she carried, flipped through several sheets of paper before handing one to the man.

Niki crossed the room to Celeste in three long strides. 'Ma, I can't talk now. That's the hotel manager, and I have to meet with him about – never mind what it's about. I'll see you back at my place around six thirty.' *So I can find out exactly why you're here.* Nicole reached in the pocket of her dress. 'Here. It's my spare.' She handed her mother a key. 'You have the address?'

'Uh-huh.' Celeste was surprised by the thoroughness of Niki's caretaking.

'It's not far. I'll have them get you a cab. Where's your luggage?'

'I checked it with the bellman. I was hoping you could get away for a little shopping. That's a great mall across the street!'

'Not today. I'm swamped. Make yourself at home.' Niki looped her arm through her mother's and started toward the door of the restaurant. *Damn! I didn't make my bed. I wasn't expecting the inspector general. But it's my house.*

To make or not to make had been a struggle between mother and daughter since five-year-old Niki asked why she had to make her bed if she was just going to mess it up all over again. Celeste told her that nice little girls wanted their beds to look pretty. Without hesitation Niki said, 'I guess I'm not that nice,' but she was forced to comply anyway.

When she turned twelve, Niki started keeping her bedroom door closed and her bed unmade. Celeste had a fit, accused her of being defiant and disobedient, and grounded her. Everett came to the rescue, cautioning Celeste to give Niki some slack because considering what some of their friends were going through with their children, this was minor. Celeste grudgingly gave in, but when Everett took off for Benin, she reneged and the battle raged again. When Everett called home, Niki told on her mother, but Everett, already on the outs with Celeste and emotionally overwhelmed by the work he was doing, didn't have the will or strength to fight Celeste from the other side of the world. He told Niki to try and get along with her mother. Niki started making her bed again, but she still kept the door closed.

'I'll call the bell captain. Your bags and a taxi will

be waiting when you get to the door.' Niki pecked her mother on the cheek and picked up the phone. *She's gonna freak when she gets there.*

Celeste set her suitcase by the front door. *I wish she hadn't taken a first-floor unit. It's so easy to break in.* She had to admit it was a lovely, well-manicured complex, ten minutes from the hotel. *But you never know.*

Celeste sighed at the mound of shoes abandoned in the foyer. *How can she leave these lying around? It's the first thing you see.* She matched them in pairs and made neat rows of shoes on the floor of the coat closet. Rays of sunlight sliced through the vertical blinds, making zebra stripes on the creamy carpet. When Everett and Celeste came down to help Niki get settled, Celeste had offered to stay and help decorate. Her feelings got hurt by how quickly Niki said no, but except for a boom box, her electronic keyboard, and a white chaise lounge that clearly belonged on the patio, the room was empty. Then she saw the neat rows of boxes lining the hallway, and her heart skipped a beat. *She's really planning to move! I hope she hasn't given notice yet.* Celeste felt the sweat trickle down the center of her back. She took off her jacket, dropped it across her suitcase, and turned on the AC before continuing the invasion.

What on earth possessed her? A galaxy of candles in crimson glass holders dotted the floor of Niki's bedroom. Smack in the middle sat the rumpled bed, on big industrial wheels no less, enclosed by a veil of gauzy white fabric that draped from the ceiling and puddled on the floor. The same fabric framed the large window. *It's a fire hazard, for goodness sake!* Celeste tiptoed into the room. *And it's much too*

186

– dramatic. A mirrored room divider stood in a corner, diagonally across from the bed, and two huge posters of lush purple orchids dominated one of the walls. The whole thing made Celeste feel squirmy, so before she could give any more thought to what scene her daughter was setting, she tucked the red sheets in as best she could, fluffed the leopard print comforter, and piled the stack of red and black pillows where she thought the head of the bed should be, then took off for the kitchen in search of dishes to wash.

She was surprised to find the kitchen immaculate. There was not a spoon in the sink, the stove sparkled. Blender, mixer, toaster, microwave, knife block, a tiny television, and cookbooks for a variety of cuisines lined the countertops. She opened cupboard doors to find them well organized and fully stocked, and the cabinets below held a collection of pots and pans, like the ones Celeste had looked at a few years ago and decided were far too expensive to actually cook in. Niki's, however, were not for show. They had been seasoned.

Celeste poured a glass of iced tea from the pitcher in the refrigerator and took a seat in the dining area on one of the violet Parsons chairs surrounding the black lacquered table. She held the cool glass to her temples a moment before taking a swallow. There was nothing in Niki's apartment that Celeste would have chosen for her. *It's like this place belongs to a stranger.* Through the sliding glass door to the patio she gazed at the dancing shadows cast by the magnolia tree on the other side of the brick. The twelve o'clock sun had slipped a bit to the west, and Celeste decided to finish her tea outside. She stretched out in the twin to the chair in the living room, put her glass on the fieldstones stacked table-high next to it, then kicked off her shoes.

Why didn't I see this coming? Celeste remembered the first dish Niki cooked from scratch. She was ten or eleven when she decided to make muffins from a recipe she found in one of Celeste's magazines. She laid out all her ingredients, measured precisely, followed the instructions exactly, and proudly set the table for Saturday breakfast. They tasted awful. 'Why would they print directions for nasty food?' Niki was incensed, and for the next several weeks she tinkered with the recipe, adding ingredients, adjusting amounts, consulting Celeste's cookbooks. They ate muffins for breakfast for a month, and Niki kept a diligent record of what worked and what didn't. Eventually she came up with Nicole's Blueberry Crumb Muffins, and they were moist and delicious. She proclaimed that recipe the first one in the *Nicole English Cookbook* and she promised there would be no bad food in it. Everett bought a brown leather book with blank pages, had the name embossed in gilt letters on the front, and presented it to her.

I wonder if Nik still has that silly book? Everett should never have encouraged her that way. Okay. She's good in the kitchen, better than I am for sure, but it's hardly a reasonable career for a girl with her background! She has so many other options!

Celeste wasn't sure how long she'd been stretched out. She may even have dozed off awhile, but she was hot again and her head throbbed. She grabbed her shoes and glanced at her watch on her way to the kitchen. *Where'd the time go? Nik should be home before long.* Celeste dumped the contents of her glass in the sink and let the water run. *I'll find something for this head, then I'll take a shower. We can go to dinner – some-place really nice – maybe Niki's restaurant.* Celeste filled her glass and started the search for aspirin. She opened all the cabinets in the kitchen, and although she found several bottles of vitamins and herbal supplements, she didn't come across anything that would relieve the pounding in her head. *Nik knows we always keep aspirin in the kitchen. Why doesn't she have any in here? It's certainly more convenient.* Celeste headed to the bathroom.

She opened the medicine chest and her eyes went right to the snapshot taped inside. A man she'd never seen before stood behind Niki, his arms around her waist. He wore a chef's jacket, and his toque sat on top of dreadlocks secured back with a rubberband. 'We'll make beautiful food together!' was written across the bottom of the photo. *That's where she got this ridiculous idea!* The man was definitely older than Niki, but no matter how closely she examined the picture, Celeste couldn't tell by how much. She *could* tell that her headache had gotten worse. It took a huge effort to take her eyes off the smiling couple and resume her search for painkillers. *Oh my—* Celeste snatched the box from the shelf. *Reservoir tip. Ultra thin. Like wearing nothing.* She dropped the box like it bit her, and condoms littered the sink. She didn't mean to count them, but eight were gone and her brain felt like it would spray out of her ears like a geyser. She could hear Everett saying, 'In case you haven't noticed, Niki is a woman.' But a well-used box of condoms, the fantasy suite bedroom, and lover boy's picture was just too damn grown for her little girl.

Celeste didn't hear Niki come in the apartment.

She just looked up and her daughter was standing by her side. Celeste's mouth went dry.

'Find everything you need?' Niki laughed and turned to leave.

'I – uh – I – I – certainly don't need these. And for your information, I was looking for aspirin. I have an excruciating—' *Where did it go?* 'I had a headache, that's all.' Celeste tightened her upper lip, jammed the foil-wrapped packets back in the box. Then she turned the hot water on full blast and washed her hands like she was scrubbing for surgery.

Niki waited for her to finish, then moved aside the first-aid cream and the box of bandages. 'Here you go.' She exchanged the bottle for the box, replaced it on the shelf, and closed the medicine cabinet door.

Celeste clutched the bottle so tightly she was afraid the childproof cap would pop off. 'Thank you.' *My head doesn't even hurt anymore.* She pushed past Niki and headed down the hall. *But I have to take them now or she'll think I was just being nosy.*

Niki joined her in the kitchen. 'I thought I'd fix us dinner tonight.' *Or just slit my wrists.* 'Just the two of us! We haven't done that in ages.' *Which is probably why we're both still breathing.* 'That'll be fun.'

I won't say a word. Celeste shook two tablets into her hand, tossed them back, and took a swig of water. *There. They can't hurt. An ounce of prevention . . .*

'Did you get some rest?' Niki started removing the contents of the shopping bags she'd left on the counter.

'I don't know – I mean – yes, I did. Thank you.' Celeste put her glass down. 'Can I do anything to help?'

'Pick out a bottle of wine and pour me a glass.' Niki

opened a cabinet door Celeste hadn't, revealing a full wine rack. 'I'm pretty fried. My boss is a real asshole.' Niki heard it as soon as it came out of her mouth. *Shit. I shouldn't have said that.*

Celeste cleared her throat but didn't remark.

For a moment Niki didn't know what to say. *Why do I feel like I did something wrong?* She'd never cursed in front of her parents. *I'm in my own kitchen. In my own home. My life. My rules. Right?* She sounded unconvincing, even to herself. She took a sauté pan from a lower cabinet and reached for the box of rice she'd brought home.

'Wouldn't it be more convenient if you kept your canned goods down there and your pots and pans by the . . .'

'I like them exactly where they are. How are we coming with the wine, Ma?'

'My goodness. This is quite a selection. I mean for one person.' Celeste pulled a bottle at random.

'I don't usually drink alone.' Niki took a plastic bag of shrimp to the sink.

'I can see that.' She didn't mean it to slip out. It just did.

I'm not gonna bite. Niki tore into the bag. 'Choose any wine you like. Fumé blanc might be nice with the . . .'

'How can you leave those – things around like that?' Celeste slammed the bottle of pinot grigio on the counter.

'Like what, Ma?' Niki dried her hands on a dishtowel, took the bottle, and yanked a corkscrew from the drawer. 'In *my* bathroom? In *my* medicine cabinet?' She stabbed the point into the cork. 'Tell me, would you rather I *didn't* use condoms? Now

191

there's a really bright idea.' Niki turned the screw.

'Nicole! How can you talk like that? You weren't raised that way!'

'Gimme a break.' Nicole kept screwing. 'Are you trying to tell me you and Dad didn't have sex until after you got married?' The cork made a self-satisfied pop as it escaped. She laid down the corkscrew and grabbed two glasses. 'I read about the seventies. He probably wasn't even the first, but that's cool.'

'That's none of your business! And this isn't about your father and me.' *And how many times I was worried that I was pregnant.* Celeste unscrewed the cork from the end of the opener and rolled it between her fingers. 'This is about – What's his name, Nicole?'

'Brian. But that doesn't really matter does it? This is about sex. Isn't it, Mother?' Niki filled each glass halfway. 'I have a job. I have my own address, my own car. I'm an adult. And I *am* having sex.' *I can't believe I said that.* 'With one man who happens to mean a lot to me. Is it forever? I don't know. I haven't gotten that far yet.' *Okay. The gloves are off. Let's just put it all out there and see where the dust settles.* 'So now you've had your questions answered. I have one for you.' Niki lifted her glass to her lips, took a deep swallow. 'Just why did you come, Ma? To snoop around in my life? Or to tell me I'm wrong to want what *I* want instead of what you want for me!?' Niki reached for the cutting board and a head of garlic from a basket on the counter.

Celeste could barely keep the liquid from sloshing out of her glass. 'It looks like I have to come snooping, as you put it, to find out what you're doing. You're obviously moving, but I wouldn't know that . . .'

'I told you my plans in May. What do you want, a

minute-by-minute account? Okay. I'm shipping my stuff next week. Then Brian and I are driving to Hyde Park. He's up there now, looking for an . . .'

'And when were you planning to tell me you'll be living with this man?!'

Not until I had to. 'When I found the right time.'

'This – this Brian has obviously made you forget who you are.'

'No, Mother.' Niki removed a knife from the rack. 'Brian accepts who I am, which is more than I can say for you! You're the one who can't understand.'

'I understand he's about to make you screw up your life. Is that what you want?!' As soon as she said it, Celeste heard Della so clearly she expected to turn around and see her. *'I don't care if he's God's gift to medicine! You keep hanging around with this man all hours, you'll flunk out of school, Celeste. Is that what you want?'*

'What?' Niki started chopping and followed her mother's eyes.

'Nothing – never mind – how old is he, Nicole?'

'You don't get it, do you? This has nothing to do with Brian!' Niki's kitchen was a good size, but it seemed to be getting smaller. 'And I still don't know why you came. I know you can fly nonstop to Charlotte.'

'Your father and I have worked too hard . . .'

'My father is proud of me and what I'm doing. And your grandmother had her own catering business, back in the forties. Her *own* business, Ma. That's what I want.'

'What are you talking about?!'

'Grandma told me.'

'Your grandmother must be losing her mind along

193

with the rest of you. She never said anything about her mother being a cook, much less running a business.'

Niki picked up the wall phone. 'You wanna call her?' She held it out to Celeste. 'If it makes you feel any better, Ronnie didn't know either.'

Celeste knew when not to take a dare. 'Besides, this is your life. Not some fabricated ancient history!'

'You're right, Ma. It is my life. It's like Ronnie said when Papa died, you did what you wanted with your life. This one is mine.'

'When Papa died?! You told Ronnie back then and you didn't tell me?! How could you, Nicole? How could you embarrass me like that?'

'That's all you care about, isn't it? Well, see these!' She pointed to the knives. 'The best chefs use them. Dad sent 'em! And my tuition? Grandma asked how much I needed.'

'Oh, did she?' *Thank you for finding another way to go behind my back, Mother.* Celeste chewed the inside of her cheek.

'Ronnie said if I get an externship in New York, I can stay with her, rent free . . .'

'She can't keep a roof over her own head,' Celeste hissed.

'Why can't you accept that this is what *I* want? Me. Nicole Yvonne English.' Niki patted her chest for emphasis. 'I love food, Ma. Everything about it. The colors and textures of fresh produce in the market make me happy.' She picked a bunch of frilly greens up off the counter. 'This is cilantro.' She stuck her nose in, took a whiff. 'It smells better to me than perfume. I love the way shallots make a recipe taste different from onions or scallions. I love inventing new dishes. You know, I've been working on one, so

194

I thought I'd make it for you tonight. And I was hoping you'd like it and we'd have a nice meal and talk, but that doesn't seem like what you had planned. I mean you act like I want to sell heroin!' Niki walked the kitchen in small circles, came to a stop. 'I don't know why Dad didn't leave before now. He should've stayed in Benin. Maybe she would have made him happy!'

Celeste sunk her fingers into Niki's arm like vise grips and shook. 'How dare you!? You don't know what you're talking about!'

Niki pulled free. 'At first I'd put my headphones on and go in my closet because I couldn't stand to hear you two argue. Then I decided if I knew what you were fighting about, when I grew up I'd know what not to do! I heard him ask you for forgive him. It's the first time I heard Daddy cry.'

Celeste met Niki's defiant gaze but said nothing.

'I kept waiting – waiting for you to tell Daddy you did the same thing.' Niki didn't take her eyes off her mother. 'But you didn't.'

Celeste's head snapped back like she'd been slapped. She spoke in a low, slow rumble. 'What are you talking about?'

'Mr Weeks. Wasn't that his name?'

How could she know? Celeste's jaw dropped.

'From your old school.'

I was so careful— 'I have no idea what . . .'

'Come on, Ma. I was twelve. Not exactly the sharpest pin in the cushion, but I wasn't dumb or blind. I didn't really even know what sex was. We'd had the egg and sperm talk, but that wasn't sex. Sex was the sighs, the long looks, like in the movies. Like you and Mr Weeks.'

195

'That doesn't deserve an answer.' *I don't have one.* Celeste put her glass on the counter before she dropped it.

Niki was way past the deep end, so she figured she'd just keep stroking. 'You were working at school that summer and Mr Weeks would come by supposedly to talk about some school stuff. I didn't think anything of it until one night. I'd already gone to bed, but I went to the kitchen to get some water. You two were on the sofa. His arm was around you. Then you kissed . . .'

'Stop it!'

Niki finished her glass of wine, poured another, took a swallow. 'After that I could see it all the time. You had all the signs. Giggly, gooey and glowy. I knew what you were doing was wrong because it wasn't Daddy. But it was romantic, and I liked the way *you* were then. You didn't pick at me the way you always did. You were like – I don't know, but I wanted to feel what you were feeling. I used to wish you'd be like that with Daddy, but you weren't, and it only got worse when he came home.' She folded her arms across her chest. 'After that you two just fought all the time. And you – you were so mean, and spiteful – and I hated you. I asked him once if you were gonna get a divorce. He said he didn't know.'

At this moment, a knife would have felt more merciful to Celeste. 'He said what!?'

'It took a while, but it looks like he's finally made up his mind.'

'You just wait until chef boy comes home one day and says he's quitting his job and opening a soup kitchen! Then you talk to me.' Celeste was trembling. 'I won't discuss this anymore.'

'Have it your way. I just know that when Daddy poured his heart out, told you he'd done wrong, you kept your little secret.'

Celeste stormed from the kitchen and into the living room, but there was no place to hide. No shadowy corners or soft surfaces, no cushions or drapes. There was nothing to sink into, nowhere to shelter herself in the bare room. 'And since you hate me so much, I won't stay . . .'

'Don't be so hysterical, Ma. Where are you gonna go? A hotel?' Niki chuckled at the irony as she followed her mother into the living room. *I know I'm gonna pay for this. Maybe I should have just booked her a room.*

'Well, clearly you wouldn't have someone you think so little of spend the night in your house.'

'Chill, Mother. I'm not gonna tell Daddy. Your secret is safe.'

They never ate. Celeste spent the night tossing and turning, alone and adrift in Niki's floating bed. Niki slept on the chaise in the living room. And the next morning didn't come soon enough for either one of them.

As soon as Niki came to a stop in front of the terminal at Hartsfield, Celeste waved for a skycap. When Niki pulled off, Celeste was rummaging in her purse for the tip, so shaken she didn't know where to look for her own wallet.

The balance of power in their relationship was shifting, and Celeste couldn't get her footing.

10

'At ease, Gomer.'

'Ms Frazier?'

'Yes.' Ronnie had looked right past him in the crowd at the gate. She was expecting someone cut from the same cloth as R. Phillip. *Not Gomer dressed for gym class.*

'Douglas Pryce.' He extended his hand and smiled broadly, his thick brush of mustache turning up at the corners of his lips.

Ronnie cast a disapproving eye on the shorts, polo shirt, crew socks, and sneakers. She managed half a smile as she shook his outstretched hand. *This must be Rudy's little payback for not givin' him any.* After the drug bust in her apartment left her needing to escape from New York, Ronnie called R. Phillip to back out of their date. She left out the small detail about the break-in and not knowing where the hell she was going to live. Having to dispose of property she inherited was enough reason for him. True to form, he said he went to college with a guy whose family handled real estate in the Charlotte area. By the next morning Phillip had made the connection and arranged for his friend to meet Ronnie at the airport. It was a good thing too. She hadn't figured out how she was going to get from Charlotte Douglas International to Prosper.

'Call me Doug.' He caught her checking his outfit. 'I coach a girls' softball team. Our game ran late.' His dark eyes flashed like sparklers on the Fourth of July, and Douglas Pryce had the whitest teeth she'd ever seen.

Toothpaste commercial. He certainly wasn't drool-on-yourself gorgeous, not by Ronnie's standards. Tall and rangy, his shirt fit smoothly over a body that showed he did more than paperwork. Doug's hair was close cropped, and like his mustache was sprinkled with gray, although you couldn't tell by looking at him if he was twenty-two or a hundred and two. But there was something about his face. His bold features looked like they'd been chiseled from burnished walnut. They kept her gaze a moment longer than she intended. *Not my type. No edge.* But her type or not, she was planning to make Douglas her new best friend. At least until they got this property sold. 'How'd you recognize me?' *Here comes the lame line. 'Phillip told me you were gorgeous' or some BS. I can flirt with him a little—*

'Black clothes. You New Yorkers wear 'em like a badge.' Doug didn't bite, didn't even give her a once-over before he reached out a sinewy arm and grabbed her carry-on. 'This way.' He touched her back just long enough to indicate the direction they were heading.

Ronnie flinched slightly. His touch caught her off guard. 'Oh. Is that so?' *It beats hell out of looking like a Boy Scout.* Ronnie was prepared to deflect the advance, not defend her wardrobe. She lifted her sunglasses from the top of her head, hooked them at the neck of her oversized black silk sweater, shoved her hand in the pocket of her black jeans, and listened to the click of her black leather ankle boots on the granite floor as they walked through the airport. Doug's sneakers squeaked. His stride was long but unhurried. *Why should I worry about a man who probably couldn't dress himself right on a bet?* She couldn't imagine Doug in a hand-tailored suit, or flying first class. Not that it mattered. Not that he mattered. This was only her natural radar at work, and he was too insignificant to cause a blip on the screen.

'I mean, people down here wear black, but not like you folks.' He grinned.

She didn't grin back. *Did he read that somewhere?* 'It makes life simple when I travel.' *Probably not a big consideration for you.*

Doug seemed not to notice her displeasure. 'Do you have a bag checked?'

'This is it. My sister and I will only be here a few days. Especially since, your boss – your mother, right?' *That should sting.* 'She said you had a buyer already lined up. We can take care of our business and be on our way.' She wanted to walk ahead to speed this up, but since she didn't know where they were headed, she had to downshift to follow his lazy zigzag through the terminal. Ronnie noticed there were lots of people coming and going, but nobody raced around, looking one step away from a breakdown.

'So it seems. I must confess I hadn't heard of Prosper until you called. I haven't been back long. But Edna Pryce keeps her finger on the real estate pulse of southwestern North Carolina. She's been at it forty years, and nobody does it better, as they say. It's through those doors.' He nodded the direction.

'That's enough of the commercial. Truthfully, if she says she's got a buyer, you can consider the deal done.'

'Glad to hear it.' The sliding doors opened to the balmy night. Ronnie was surprised by the hint of flowers in the warm, soft air. There was no trace of the tingle, the yin and yang tug of the power surge and energy drain that fired her up in the city, kept her running, no matter what. 'The sooner I can get back the better.' *Because this deal is my ticket to finally getting my life together.*

'The greater Charlotte area is really booming . . .'

'Don't know about Charlotte *or* Prosper.' *Don't want to either.* 'Never been down here, and frankly, I'm not planning to be back.' *I don't mean to sound like a snob – Yes I do.*

'Then I'll save the Chamber of Commerce speech.' He shifted the bag to his other hand. 'It's not bad here. Not bad at all.' Doug sounded like he was trying to convince himself. He stopped at a shiny, champagne colored four-wheel drive parked at the curb.

At least it's not a pickup truck. 'Convenient. At La Guardia it would have been towed.' She stood at his side while he dug in his pocket for keys. *He smells like – not like Dolce & Gabbana or Gaultier. What is that? Zest or Irish Spring.* 'Humph.' Her reaction, barely audible, slipped out. Men in Ronnie's world smelled like they thought money should smell, not like soap.

'I'm not used to this either. Head of airport security is a cousin. I wouldn't leave it here all day, but this comes in handy when I'm cutting it close, like tonight.' He opened the door.

Ronnie sighed and climbed in. *Will I have to listen to*

201

stories about his million country cousins all the way there?

Doug tossed her bag in back, went around, and got in the other side. 'I was hoping to take you by the house as soon as you got here, but your flight got in too late.'

'Cause it was the cheap fare. Charlotte by way of Pittsburgh.

'You won't be able to see anything now. We made arrangements to have the power turned on, but it won't happen until tomorrow. So I'll just drop you at your hotel. Uh, I need you to buckle up.'

'Why? You plannin' to run this baby off the road?'

'It's not my driving I worry about.' He flipped on the headlights and waited.

It was clear he wasn't moving until she fastened her seat belt, so Ronnie reached around for the strap. The back appeared to be the storage locker for the softball team. *No wonder it smells like french fries and sweat in here.* 'How long a drive do we have?' *In a stinky car.*

'Little over an hour. Do you want to grab something to eat?'

'Uh. No. I'm fine.' Her cramps were still hanging around, and the last thing she wanted was food.

They headed for the airport exit. 'I realize it's a little messy in here, but it was faster than stopping to get my company car.'

'No problem. I appreciate the ride.' Ronnie looked out the window. The night sky was inky and spangled with stars. The motorist in the right lane slowed, flashed headlights. Doug waved an acknowledgment and merged into the steady stream of traffic on Route 74. She searched her purse for her cigarettes, stuck one between her lips and examined the dashboard. 'Is there a lighter in here?'

'Yes, but I have to ask you not to smoke.'

'Isn't tobacco the state flower or something?' Ronnie shoved the pack down in her bag.

'This Tar Heel doesn't go near the stuff.'

Great. He probably doesn't drink or swear either.

Doug concentrated on the road and drove like he planned to shave as much off of that hour as possible. *I thought salesmen liked to talk. This one doesn't have much to say unless it's required.* Ronnie was in no mood for silence. She spent the bulk of her flight chatting with her seatmate, a young actuary from Vancouver, excited about being flown down for an interview. He had a ton of questions about living in the States, and Ronnie was all too happy to play the expert because it kept her from thinking about what a screwed-up mess her life was at the moment.

Staying in that snake pit of an apartment for the few days before her flight took most of her strength. Before heading to the airport, she'd packed her stuff and moved it to Kayla's mother's basement, having no idea where her next oasis would be, trying hard to ignore the fear that only mirages lay ahead. This struck her as a new low. For the first time in her life she had no official address, just an answering service phone number.

And it took the rest of her strength not to call home and cry to her mother that this was too hard and she couldn't do it anymore. Those feelings might have spilled out when she called Buffalo to see what Della would tell her about Prosper, but it was not a warm and fuzzy phone call. Ronnie got a hot earful of Della's displeasure. Her mother made it clear she felt Ronnie had no business down there. 'It is business, Ma. Celeste is going down so I need to protect my . . .'

Click. Ronnie called back every fifteen minutes for the rest of the evening, but Della never picked up the phone. It was a nice little guilt trip that Ronnie packed next to her toiletry bag, and all of it jumped out and bit her if she had too much time for her own thoughts. *He doesn't even play the radio.* 'What did you mean back there when you said you weren't used to having parking privileges? Did your cousin just get the job?' *Not that I really care.*

'No. He's been there for years. I moved back six months ago.'

'From?'

Doug paused, like he didn't want to answer. 'L.A.'

Damn. I didn't ask his bank account number. 'So, were you in the business?'

'Real estate? No. I . . .'

'Show business. Movies. Is there any other business out there?'

'That's right, Phillip did say you were an actress or something, right? I don't even remember the last time I went to the movies.' Doug went back to the business of driving.

Ronnie had expected some comment about her occupation. Men usually wanted to know what movie they'd seen her in, or how she got into her parts. She was having trouble figuring out which of her roles to play with Douglas Pryce. *He probably likes talking about himself.* 'So – what *did* you do?'

'I was a reporter. *L.A. Times.*' Doug sped up and whipped around a slow-moving sedan.

Ronnie grabbed the dashboard to steady herself. 'You coulda been a cab driver.'

He glanced at her and grinned. 'I still forget this isn't the freeway.'

'What on earth made you move back here?' Ronnie heard her snob again. 'I didn't mean that the way it sounded. You're right. It doesn't look so bad – Of course it *is* dark out! Only kidding!' She chuckled, he didn't. 'But why leave La La Land for this?'

He shrugged. 'My mother's had a few health problems. My kids are grown and on their own. Seemed like the time.'

Ronnie examined his hands on the steering wheel. *No ring.* She hated married men who didn't wear identifying jewelry. They usually had some jive excuse about how it interfered with their work, or they claimed not to wear jewelry. But in Ronnie's experience, those guys thought they had special dispensation to eat their cake, some of yours, and still have a slice laying in the cut. Like the guy she met while she was profiling at a gallery opening. He said he wasn't with his wife. It wasn't until several months down the line that Ronnie found out he and wifey-poo were still married, just not *together* at the gallery that night. And she was too through when he had the nerve to argue that technically he was telling the truth. Personally, she thought the married ones should have a brand, on their foreheads preferably, front and center where they couldn't hide it, because she had no interest in barking up somebody else's tree. 'How does your wife like it here?'

'She died four years ago.'

Ronnie's stomach did a queasy flip-flop. 'Oh. I'm . . .'

'No harm.' He never took his eyes off the road. 'My mother eats and breathes real estate. If she can smell a deal, nothing will stop her. She's wanted me to join the business my whole life. And I spent my whole life resisting.' He shrugged his shoulders. 'Who wants to work for his mother? But her glaucoma didn't respond to treatment and she's not getting any younger. I needed a change. It seemed like this might work for both of us.'

'Is it?'

'Too early to tell.' He opened his window and took a deep breath. 'So what made you and your sister decide to sell this property after all? I understand it's been vacant for several years, and the owner of record never responded to letters.'

'We never heard of it until a few weeks ago.' Ronnie explained what she knew about the place and how she and Celeste came to own it.

'I guess all families have their mysteries.'

'I don't know about all that. I'm just glad we can take care of this quickly. I'm sure Celeste will be pleased.'

'You haven't told her we've spoken? That we have a buyer?'

'Like I said, we only found out about this a few weeks ago. I've been crazy busy.' *Trying to figure out what to do about my drug dealer landlord.* 'And so has Celeste. It's hard to keep up.' She had no intention of letting him know how little she and Celeste talked about this. That her sister had known for months and hadn't mentioned it. Ronnie decided to switch to another subject. 'So how long have you known Rudy? Oops! Sorry. My little joke. Phillip.'

'His brother John and I were in school together. Phillip started the year we graduated, and I haven't thought about him since then. I wouldn't exactly say we were best buds.'

'So he called you outta nowhere?'

'John and I have stayed somewhat in touch since Morehouse, and we alums have tried to maintain a kind of network. If at all possible, requests are honored, favors granted, exceptions made. Period. No questions. If it's impossible, we do the best we can.'

'That must be – I don't know – kinda reassuring? Knowing that there's all that help out there?'

'It's useful once in a while, like a fraternity but without the secret handshake. More like being from the old neighborhood. Kinda Morehouse homeboys!' His laugh was deep and robust. Genuine.

Ronnie noticed he didn't look to see if she was laughing too. It didn't matter. He enjoyed his own humor. Her father used to laugh that way, full out. Even at his own corny jokes. Okay. *This is the part where he asks for my pedigree.* Ronnie sat up straighter, squared her shoulders, and waited for him to grill her about her background.

'So your family never visited here? No summers down south with the relatives?'

'We had friends who did.' *Hmm. No third degree.* 'A girl I went to elementary school with used to come back full of stories about milking cows and collecting eggs with her cousins on her aunt and uncle's farm. It sounded so exotic to me. All I had was camp.'

'Exotic, huh? I grew up in Charlotte, but we'd spend a lot of time in the country during the summers. My grandparents had a place. My mother thought it was a good experience for me and my sister, but they used to work us like field hands. You know, cows can be mean if you don't have the right touch, and chickens will peck you till you're bloody unless you're careful. I used to be glad for school to start, which was

207

probably the point.' Doug reached an arm around the back of his seat, grabbed a squeeze bottle of water from the floor. 'They're kinda warm, but would you like one?'

'That's quite all right.'

He took a long swallow. 'I drove out to look your place over yesterday. Prosper itself appears pretty typical. Small southern town full of personal history and mystery. A lot has probably changed since your family left and a lot is likely the same as forty years ago. Population hasn't fluctuated, one way or the other, more than a hundred people in over sixty years. Depending on who's counting, the racial mix is about even. There's a brand-new Winn Dixie, and a small radio station. The house was fairly large for its time, not many that big owned by us. And you've got a good-sized piece of land. The inlet is pretty overgrown down your end. Looks more like marshlands. But it lets out into a good-sized lake. People have boats and docks on the other side.' Doug turned his head and yawned.

Must be past his bedtime. Much as she couldn't admit it, Ronnie wanted to keep him talking because his voice was soothing, resonant, like a saxophone in a smoky room.

'It's pretty isolated from the town.' Doug flicked the turn signal. 'Otherwise the offer might be higher, but I guess it's like found money.'

'It was a pleasant little surprise.' Ronnie wasn't interested in discussing how crucial this 'found money' was. Her half of the $193,000 offered for the house and land was more money than she had hoped for.

They pulled into the tiny parking lot of the T ee T p Motel & Inn. The two-story cinder-block box couldn't have had more than twenty rooms, half on the ground level facing the scenic parking spaces and the others upstairs off a concrete walkway with a wrought-iron railing. *No wonder the rates were so cheap.*

'I know what you're thinking.'

'You can't possibly.' A flash of her ransacked apartment and Rake's empty, foil-lined closet streaked through her mind. *My luck is holding. Nobody can pick a place like I can.*

'It's not bad – really. Clean. Quiet. The rooms are really – uh.' He started to laugh. 'There's no need my trying to make this more than it is. You can see it's not the Ritz.' He stopped the car in front of the motel office, a separate structure with a log cabin facade.

'Thanks for giving me some credit.' Ronnie got out. Her footsteps on the gravel seemed nearly as loud as the buzz and crackle of the neon sign, sans the *r* and *o*. Doug came around beside her. 'Is this the only place to stay around here?'

'This is it. There are others closer to Charlotte, but this will make it easier to take care of your business. You and your sister will need to spend a fair amount of time disposing of the contents of the house.'

'Contents?'

'Seems that everything was left to the new owner, so even though nobody ever came to claim the place or clean it out, the taxes have been paid so nothing's been moved or sold.'

'Great,' Ronnie mumbled. Warily, she followed Doug up the plank stairs to the office. 'Listen, do you think your buyer will want the furniture and stuff too? It would save us a lot of trouble – and time.' She noticed a hand-lettered sign taped to the window. 'Free Cable in Every Room.'

Doug held the door open. 'There's never enough of it, is there? Time.'

Ronnie felt like the comment was from a different conversation, but she didn't want to know who it was meant for.

'We can ask if they're interested in the contents. I might not have an answer by the time I pick you up tomorrow, but we'll get to work on it.' He led the way to the desk.

While Ronnie filled out the registration form, Doug made small talk with the clerk. She offered her anemic Visa card as guarantee, but even at these rates, a week's stay would eat up what remained of available charging privileges. *But when I leave here, these days will be over, for good.* Once she was checked in, Doug walked her back to the building, handed over her bag at the bottom of the concrete stairs.

'Can we get an early start in the morning?' Ronnie knew if she wasn't ahead of the game by the time Celeste arrived, she'd never get to play.

'I have a meeting first thing, but I can be here by eight thirty. We can have breakfast on the way if you like.'

He doesn't think that's early? 'No problem.'

Doug gave her a card. 'This has the office numbers, but it's easier to reach me on the cell.'

'Okay, then. Guess I'll, uh, head up to my suite.' Ronnie trudged up the concrete steps. He waited downstairs until she unlocked her room and turned on the light. She gave him a little salute. *At ease, Gomer.* Then went inside.

The sweet, cool night air stayed outside. Ronnie sucked in a nose full of the hot, deodorized-sanitized air. *Have they opened a window in the last thirty-five years?* She locked the door, put the chain on, then turned around and took in the small room in a glance. *Okay. So it's not hideous. A little on the tacky side, but I've stayed in worse. Who am I kidding? I've lived in worse. Wait till Celeste gets a load of it, though.* Ronnie walked the ten feet to the other side of the room, turned the air conditioner on high, and smirked at the thought of her sister's reaction. Then the walls rumbled. *What the—?* She held her breath, stood stock-still but ready to run. It happened again. This time a groan and rumble followed by a crash. Then she heard the whine of a motor. *Ice machine. Perfect.* She thought about calling for another room, but she'd seen food and toiletry vending machines at the other end. *What's the dif?*

She kicked off her boots and flopped across the double bed, exhausted. When she reached for the remote, she discovered it was attached to a swivel and bolted to the bedside table along with a clock radio and telephone. *Who'd want to steal this crap?* Ronnie sucked her teeth and aimed at the set. Her first click brought the eleven o'clock news; so did the second and third. She zipped past golf, infomercials, music videos, and settled on an ancient episode of *Benson*. *I'll get undressed and wash my face when this is over.* Ronnie tucked both anorexic pillows under her head.

'Mom and Dad'll never know.' Voices filtered in from somewhere Ronnie couldn't place. *What the—?* She awoke with a start, the TV still playing. *Where the hell am I?* Ronnie was cold, dry-mouthed, with a stiff neck and a backache. She blinked to unstick her eyes and focus. *Oh yeah. The Inn at Hicks-ville.* The clock radio by the bed read 4:37. She sat up, massaged her neck, and stared at the screen. One of the identical cousins was slathered in cold cream, pretending to be the other one. Then both girls dissolved in a fit of giggles. When she was little, Ronnie used to watch the show after school and wish that she and her sister could have fun together like Patty and Cathy. But that never happened. Celeste was older and never seemed to think of Ronnie as much more than a nuisance she was forced to put up with because of her parents' misbegotten biological urge. Ronnie shook off a twinge of sadness. *Can't miss what you never had.* She turned down the AC, peeled off her clothes. *And I bet we'll have goo-gobs of fun when she gets here.* Ronnie padded to the bathroom and was back in bed before she was awake enough to really start thinking. Eight-thirty would be here soon enough.

11

'You never know what a day will bring.'

Doug Pryce called her room at 8:29.

Damn, why couldn't he be late like everybody else?
Ronnie was finishing the last touches to her hair and
makeup. Not that she was getting done up, just
making sure that Doug or anybody else would never
mistake her for a local. And after a night's sleep she
felt ready to find out what made this man tick. It
was a modest challenge, just to make her stay more
interesting. *He should wait a few minutes.* Casual chic
was the order of the day, so she wore her same black
jeans, a tailored white shirt, and black low-heeled
sandals. When she locked the door behind her fifteen
minutes later, her no-makeup makeup was perfect,
and her hair was in a low ponytail with the grown-out
edges smoothed under a wide, black hair band.

He dressed up today. Doug, wearing khakis and a
pink polo shirt, leaned against a dark green sedan with
a gold Pryce Real Estate logo on the door. *Charlotte
by way of L.A. What more should I expect?* He seemed
to be talking back to his *Observer* as he read, but he
closed the paper and looked up in her direction when
he heard her footsteps. Ronnie slipped on her sunglasses and her smile as she walked down the stairs.

'Morning.' Doug was pleasant, but he wasn't talking to her.

Ronnie looked over to see whom Doug had spoken to and swallowed her smile.

'Uh – Good morn – Ronnie, what are you doing here!?' Celeste lost her grip on the large suitcase she pulled behind her. 'How did you know where I was staying?'

'It came to me in a vision.' Ronnie stopped next to Doug.

'Who's he? Last night's company?' Celeste's jaw locked in her teacher-on-a-mission position, and her upper lip clamped tightly to her lower one, forming an airtight seal.

'I'll pretend you didn't say that, especially in front of someone you haven't met yet. Good morning, sister dear. How was your trip?' Ronnie tossed her purse over her shoulder, shifted her weight to one hip, slid her hand in the front pocket of her jeans, and waited. Celeste looked a little rough around the edges, more like a day-old version of her usual neat, crisp self.

'My trip?!' Celeste hissed.

The game was on. Ronnie knew the rules and had her own strategy. She could play as well as Celeste. After all, they'd had years of practice. 'I thought you'd already be here when I checked in. It's the only motel in town, you know. Well, I guess this is sort of town.' She waved her hand, presenting the highway, the truck stop across the road with the faded red sign that read 'EAT & Hot Showers,' and the crumbling building on the other side of the Tree Top Inn. 'And this is Doug Pryce.'

214

'And?' Celeste tugged the pull strap and made her suitcase heel. 'You still haven't answered my question.'

'I'm not sure which question you're referring to, but Doug is a real estate agent, before you embarrass yourself any more.'

Celeste sputtered. 'Why is he here? Who asked him to . . .'

'*I* asked his company to handle the sale for us. We have a mutual friend in New York. A banker. Isn't that the most wonderful coincidence?'

Doug followed the volley between the two sisters like the center court action at the U.S. Open. He'd had a grandmother, mother, wife, and a daughter, and through trial and error he had learned when his two cents was welcome, but this looked like one of those times it was best to keep his change in his pocket. 'Listen. I'll come back a little later. You two catch up. Ms Frazier, call when you're ready to go out to the house.' He started toward his car.

Ronnie trotted to catch up. 'Doug?' She took hold of his arm and walked with him. 'Sorry about that. My sister is a little intense.' The firmness of his arm surprised her.

'No apology necessary. Call when you need me.'

'Sure.' She walked backward a few steps, watching him duck in, then turned and marched back toward Celeste, who had wheeled her bag to one of the room doors and was fumbling with the key.

'You really showed your ass, didn't you?'

'What do you mean showing up like this?' Celeste snapped.

'Like what? Like I have some interest and some

215

say-so in what happens here? Like this house and land is half mine, whether you like it or not? Maybe that's what I mean by showing up!'

'I never said it wasn't half yours.' *First Everett, then Niki, and now this.* 'And besides, that isn't the point!'

'What is? That you're in charge and you've already talked to another realtor?'

'No – it's not—' *Why didn't I think of looking for one before I got here?* 'What if we don't want to sell it?'

'Right.' Ronnie shifted her weight to the other hip and cocked her head to the side. 'I got it. You and Everett are planning to relocate. He'll start a new clinic, maybe make house calls too! And you'll teach in the one-room school! Give me a break, Celeste. You barely find Buffalo sophisticated enough for you. How on earth would you manage a place like this? Wait till you see your room!' Ronnie snorted.

'This has nothing to do with Everett!!' Celeste snapped.

'Does anybody have anything to do with it besides you?' *Damn. She's really on a short one this morning.* Ronnie noticed a man wearing dungarees with a pressed crease and a woman in a lavender pants suit looking in their direction and whispering. 'And you might wanna lower your voice, unless you're planning to make this a town meeting.'

'This is a legacy from our grandfather,' Celeste hissed.

'Oh, yeah. Trust me, Celeste, inheriting property in Podunk, North Carolina, from some long-lost grampa we never heard of won't move you one rung higher on the social ladder! I bet you're already calling it the Womack Estate!' Ronnie folded her arms across her chest like a shield.

'Social standing is irrelevant.'

'Since when? This is me. Remember.'

'I'm going to put this away, and then I'm driving out to see the place.' Celeste looked at the numbers on the lower doors, then started toward her room.

'And you're gonna leave me standing here? I don't think so. Okay. We won't call Doug until later, but I *am* going with you.'

'The man at the car rental said to make a *right* turn onto this road and it was three or four miles to Prosper.' Celeste flipped the visor down to block the sun, which appeared to be directly in their path, like it was the destination. 'He said I'd have to get more specific directions once I got to town.'

'We've gone at least ten miles and we haven't passed it yet.' Ronnie scrutinized the map she had spread open across her lap and over the dashboard. It fluttered and rattled, blown by the air conditioner vents. She circled a spot with her stump of pencil. 'Celeste, Prosper is in the other direction. You must have heard him wrong.'

'I did not hear him wrong. I . . .'

'Fine. He didn't know what he was talking about. He was confused. He wanted you to get lost. Who gives a shit? The bottom line is we're going the wrong way.'

Celeste pulled onto the shoulder and stopped. 'Let me see that.'

Ronnie cut her eyes but handed over the map without further comment. First, Celeste dug her reading glasses out of her purse. Ignoring Ronnie's markings, she traced her index finger along the route from the airport to the motel, then along the way they had just come. Ronnie drummed her fingers impatiently on the armrest and watched tiny beads of perspiration pop out on Celeste's upper lip.

'Could you not do that?' Celeste looked over her glasses at her sister.

'For cryin' out – I'll try not to breathe too loud either. Just look at the map.'

Finally Celeste dragged her finger back the other direction, landed smack in the spot where Ronnie had drawn a circle around the town of Prosper. Methodically, Celeste refolded the map, tossed it on the dashboard. She tugged out of her taupe linen jacket, chucked it in the back-seat, then checked her mirrors and without a word swung a U-turn. Ronnie rolled her eyes, shrugged her shoulders, and watched the same scenery go by, this time from the other side of the road. When they passed the Tree Top Inn, she chuckled to herself and Celeste humphed.

Sure enough, three miles in, just past the Mid-State Brickworks, they saw the sign: 'Welcome to Prosper, the Little Town with the Big Heart. Pop. 3,800.' Except for a Hardees, a junkyard, and a radio tower, they didn't see much else for another mile or so. Then the highway became Albermarle Avenue, an oak-shaded thoroughfare that led to the center of town. A few folks ambled along a sidewalk bordered with low hedges, petunias, and marigolds. Willows and crape myrtle graced the deep green grass in front of First Baptist Church.

'Looks like a movie set, doesn't it?' Ronnie craned her neck to look back at the town hall, a quaint, pillared white limestone building that sat watch directly across from a pocket-sized park, complete with a bandstand. 'Smalltown, USA.'

218

'I need a cup of coffee.' It was pretty surprising to Celeste too, but she wouldn't give Ronnie the satisfaction of agreeing with her. 'And we have to get directions to the house.'

'If you slow down, maybe I can find a – Let's see, there's the post office, People's Hardware, Eckerd Drugs, Zion A.M.E. Church,' Ronnie recited the signs along Albermarle. 'Hutchinson's Copy Shop, First Presbyterian, JD's Fish Market, Bob's Photography, Lucille's Beauty Studio, Trinity Baptist. Damn! They sure have a lot of churches! And who knows what's down the side streets?'

'I could do without the travelogue.'

'Okay. There's a place called Pal's over there, and Mickey D's is across the street. You can get coffee in either one, probably directions too. Take your pick.'

Celeste eased into a spot at the curb and checked for the parking regulation signs. There weren't any. They got out, Celeste grabbed her jacket from the backseat, locked the car, and looked back and forth between the two choices. The only sound was the hollow clink of the rope against the flagpole in front of the Elks Lodge.

'This is not life and death.' Ronnie crossed the street toward Pal's. 'Let's try the local cuisine.'

Celeste would have fussed, but Ronnie was almost in the door.

'Morning.' The hefty, moon-faced man greeted her with a quick nod and a hitch of his suspenders. He was the color of a just-peeled russet potato with a bristle of nappy red hair and freckles everywhere he had skin.

'Hi,' Ronnie answered. The smoky smell of bacon

219

reminded her she'd skipped dinner. 'I just realized I'm starving.'

'I guarantee you won't be when you leave.' The man looked at Ronnie intently, like he was trying to place her. He picked up a menu, looked again. Ronnie was used to it. Sometimes she went into her actress rap, other times she just let them wonder. Before she decided, Celeste came in the door behind her.

'Two, no smoking please. We're in a bit of a hurry.'

'Chill, Celeste. It's under control.'

'Have a seat anywhere you like. The breakfast rush is over. How about that booth by the window? It'll give you a fine view of our little town. I can tell y'all not from 'round here.' He seated them and signaled the waitress, who hurried over with a steaming coffee pot.

'Ma'am?' The young Jheri-curled girl held the pot aloft in front of Celeste.

'Please.' Just the smell of the coffee made her feel better.

'Ma'am?' The waitress smiled at Ronnie.

'Tea please.' Ronnie hated being called ma'am. It made her feel older than she wanted to, like she was somebody's mother. Ronnie looked closely at the teenager, realized she was easily old enough to be that girl's mother. She shivered and shook off the thought.

'Be right back.'

Celeste heaped two spoonfuls of sugar into her mug. 'Do you mind telling me why you decided to come? It's really not necessary. I'm sure you have something better to do with your time.' She blew on the surface of the hot liquid, took a cautious sip, then a deep gulp.

'I wanted to see it for myself. You do, don't you? Why wouldn't I?'

The waitress returned with a tea bag, a small pot of hot water, and sliced lemons. 'Let me know whenever you're ready to order.'

'And that's why you called a real estate agent?! You never asked if I wanted to sell. You didn't even have the courtesy to tell me you were coming! You just show up!' She banged the mug down.

'Like you would've welcomed my company!' Ronnie dunked her tea bag in the pot and closed the lid. She continued in a syrupy drawl. 'And if we're discussing a lack of courtesy, let's talk about how you conveniently forgot to tell me about my inheritance until it suited you.' Ronnie ditched the drawl. 'I'm personally sick of this conversation, so let's drop it.' Ronnie picked up her menu and blocked her view of Celeste with it. She wasn't sure if she wanted more than tea and toast, but she studied the specials anyway and was tickled to find one of her father's favorites, porgies, grits, and biscuits, listed. Della had never been able to make grits that didn't look and taste like wallpaper paste, but Will could turn out a mighty fine meal if he put his mind to it. He'd come in from Reisner's Fish Market early on a Saturday morning and get out the big cast-iron frying pan, the spider, he called it. The kitchen was directly below Ronnie's bedroom, and she'd hear him through the register, humming to himself while he cleaned fish. It gave her the creeps to watch that part, but when she heard the sizzle of the first one hitting the grease she'd put on her slippers and bound down the back stairs to join him. She'd set the table, pour the orange juice, and when the platter was heaped with crispy brown fish, the grits were bubbling just right, and the biscuits were ready to come out of the oven, she'd call her mother and Celeste to breakfast.

'Remember how Daddy used to fix this?' Ronnie pointed to the menu.

'Oh, yeah. He'd smell up the whole house with those stupid things. Why is it so hot in here?' Celeste fanned herself with the menu.

'It's not. Maybe all your heat is under your collar.'

'Maybe you should shut up.' Celeste sounded just like she did when she was fifteen and Ronnie was ten. She took another swallow of coffee and looked over the rim of her cup, past her sister. The beefy man was standing by the cash register, talking with great animation to a woman whose head barely reached his elbow. She was black as blue and narrow as a nail, with a soft cloud of snow white hair. Her small hand rested on his meaty arm. His big, round head bobbed and nodded in their direction. Celeste sipped her coffee, pretended not to notice them.

'I'm tellin' you, Lucille. The one with the long hair—'

'Lord, Hambone, that ain't her hair.'

'It's on her head. That makes it hers in my book. Just look at her.'

'You haven't seen a face in the last forty-four years that didn't remind you of somebody you seen somewhere!'

'Ain't but so many combinations of noses and eyes and lips. They bound to repeat. But that's not what I'm talkin' about now. That girl sittin' over there look for all the world like . . .'

'I guess if you look real hard, she favor her some.' Lucille unlooped her arm from her husband's, put her hand on her narrow waist. 'But she don't disturb the air in a room the way Odella used to.'

'All's I'm sayin' is . . .'

'You been talkin' since you opened your eyes at five o'clock this mornin'! Ain't you said enough?'

He leaned over and hunched her gently. 'Now you know we did a little more than talk this morn . . .'

'Hush up, Hambone!' She slapped his arm playfully. ''Fore somebody hear you talkin' that mess!'

'Probably wouldn't believe it!' He winked at her.

'I'm goin' across the street. I got Marvella Peoples at ten.' She stood on her tiptoes, kissed him bye, and swatted his hand away from her butt.

They have to be older than Mother and – Celeste watched Hambone walk her to the door and wait by the window while she crossed the street. When she got to the door of the beauty parlor, she turned and waved, like it was their daily ritual. *Did I ever see Mother and Daddy act like that?* A long-forgotten image of Everett patting her behind as she bent over Niki's crib washed over Celeste, thrusting her into the past. She pushed back and shoved the memory away.

'They already have a buyer.'

Just as she pushed Everett away that morning. 'A what?!'

'Cash money.'

'That's all it comes down to for you isn't it? Money? And I know you're always broke, I don't care what you tell them at home. What makes you think this would be any different? You'd just blow it all.' Celeste conveniently forgot how her little nest egg had cracked. 'Isn't that how it goes, Ron? Well, I'm not sure I want – uh – that we should sell this land.'

'What the hell else are we gonna do with it?' Of course, like always, Ronnie needed the money. But she'd be damned if she'd give her sister the satisfaction of being right. 'Be serious, Celeste. You know you want to sell it. You're just mad because I contacted a realtor and you didn't have anything to do with it. You should be happy. They're the biggest Black agency in North Carolina. I wasn't sneaking around trying to pull something behind your back. I *knew* you were gonna be here. I found us some help and got here first, that's all.'

'We never discussed it, so from where I sit it looks exactly like you were going behind my back.'

Ronnie threw up her hands. 'If you'd climb down off your high horse you'd see a whole lot better!'

Celeste waved the waitress over.

'Ready to order?' She smiled slightly.

'The check please.' Celeste reached for her jacket and purse. 'I'm trying to find a house around here. Do you think you could help me?'

The girl giggled, but Celeste's stony look stopped her cold. 'Sorry, ma'am. But if you turn me 'round three times, I get lost walkin' to the door. I'll get Mr Anderson for you.' She scribbled on her pad, tore off the sheet, and put it facedown on the table in front of Celeste.

Ronnie grabbed the check, turned it over. Eighty cents and 'Have a nice day' were written neatly in pencil.

'I'll take that.' Hambone reached out, and the slip of paper disappeared in his massive hand. 'Can't charge nice visitors like you ladies for a little mornin' coffee.' He smiled and his freckles formed a different design on his wide face. 'I hear you need directions.'

'The house used to belong to Odell Womack,' Celeste said.

224

'I knew it! I knew it!' He slapped his thigh. 'I told Lucille. You gotta be Odella and Will's girls. Right? Am I right?' He grinned from ear to ear. 'Lordy, Lordy. It's been a helluva long time, but I knowed you right away.' He looked at Ronnie. 'You look so much like your mother. I gotta call Lucille.' He shouted across the restaurant. 'Mary! Mary!' The waitress hurried in from the kitchen. 'Call the beauty parlor. Right now! Tell Miz Lucille I said to get over here. Quick.' He turned back to Ronnie and Celeste. 'Lord. Where are my manners? Y'all don't know me from Adam.' He reached for Celeste's hand. 'George Anderson. Ever'body calls me Hambone!' He laughed heartily and worked her arm like a pump handle. 'Just look at you! Both of you! Umph, umph, umph! I don't hardly know what to say.'

Celeste was ready to scream. Even simple acts, like stopping for coffee, led to surprises, and she didn't have time to digest before the next tidbit was rammed down her throat. 'Celeste English. And this is my sister.'

'I can introduce myself.' Ronnie stretched out her arm. 'Veronica *Lucille* Frazier.'

'Veronica *Lucille*? Is that right?!'

'That's right!' *I wonder if—* 'But ever'body calls me Ronnie. And I'm happy to meet you, Hambone!' She grinned. She liked this man when she first walked through the door, and it made her happy to know he thought she looked like Della, even though Ronnie didn't quite see it. After all, Della was so – dowdy. *But maybe she used to be different.* 'So you knew Ma and Daddy?'

'Knew 'em? Watched 'em grow up. Your mama even lived with me and Lucille for a spell. What a

225

spitfire! She was some gal, your ma. Loved herself a good time.'

Celeste and Ronnie looked at each other like they had just heard there *was* a Santa Claus.

Ma?! Ronnie toyed with the notion that her mother had been 'some gal.'

'We wasn't sure your daddy could hold onto her! He had more than a bit of tamin' to do. And heaven knows, she had a stubborn streak a mile wide.'

Mother? You got the stubborn part right. But a good time? Celeste was sure he had confused Della with someone else.

'Didn't take no stuff from nobody. But I guess Will musta done all right! How they doin? They come with you? Your ma ain't been back since she left. Will was here in 'sixty-three or 'sixty-four.' Hambone looked up to think. 'Can't remember which. He come again in 'sixty-nine. That I'm sure of 'cause it was the summer we had that "giant leap for mankind." Couldn't nobody talk about much else. Your daddy watched 'em walk on the moon right here with us. Well, across the street. We used to be over there where Lucille's shop is now.' He gestured out the window.

Celeste instantly pulled up her memory of that night in July. *And we watched in front of that old Philco portable in their bedroom. Daddy wasn't there. Mother said he had to go away for a few days – take care of some business. We ate fish sticks for dinner that night. They were burned on the outside but still icy and wet in the middle. When Daddy came back, we got a new stove. We got a color TV that summer too.*

'Daddy died in October.' It was the first time Ronnie had said it out loud.

Hambone's face fell. 'Oh, Lord. I am so, so sorry.'

Ronnie knew his sorrow was real. 'Your mama?' he asked tentatively.

'Fine. She's fine,' Celeste answered. 'So you know where the house is? We'd really like to get out there.'

'Was a time when ever'body in this county and the next could tell you where the Womack place was, but that was a long time ago. When your granddaddy was livin'.' Hambone shook his head. 'Umph. Umph. Umph. Time sure do slip away from you.' He looked up when he heard the door open.

'What in the world is the matter with you, George?' Lucille wore a blue nylon smock. Several combs stuck out of her pocket, and hair clips dangled from her collar. A wad of waxy, yellow grease hung off the back of her hand.

'See! I told you she reminded me of Odella! These her and Will's girls!' Full of self-satisfaction, he folded his arms over his ample belly and gave Lucille a 'so there' shake of his head.

'Well, well, well.' Lucille wiped her hands on her top and held her arms open.

Ronnie got up first to accept Lucille's bony embrace. She wasn't in the habit of hugging strangers – she wouldn't have lasted two minutes in New York if she had been – but neither of these people seemed like a stranger.

'Lord, child, you feel just like her. She had a fire deep down in her too, burnin' her up. You couldn't see it right off if you wasn't payin' attention, but you could sho'nuff feel it.' She patted Ronnie's back with her bony hand. 'Some folks didn't understand that.' Lucille released Ronnie from her wiry grip and beckoned to Celeste, who stood as expected. 'You must be the firstborn.'

'Yes, ma'am.' Celeste was startled to hear herself say that.

Celeste fit a little more comfortably in the fold of Lucille's arms. 'Welcome home, child. Welcome home. Let me look at you.' Still gripping Celeste's shoulders, she moved back a couple of steps. 'Look at 'em, Hambone. Ain't this something? Lord. You never know what a day will bring. How's your mama and daddy?'

'Will passed last fall,' Hambone said solemnly.

'He calls us all when He's ready. But Della. How she doin'?'

'She's fine, Mrs Anderson. Still in Buffalo. Not far from me and my husband,' Celeste answered.

'I don't suppose she's plannin' to meet you two here,' Lucille said.

'No – That doesn't seem likely.'

'Said she wasn't never comin' back, and she's bein' true to her word. She left somethin' with me way back then. Figured she'd call for it when she was ready. She never did. Hmm – Anyways, glad y'all come to see about the old homeplace. It's time. Was a man out there a couple a years ago workin' on it, but it's been empty a long while. Not good for a house to have no life in it for too long a spell. It can't settle on its foundation. Settlin' don't always work out too good for people, but a house – a house should never stop settlin'.'

Ronnie smiled at the wisdom of Lucille's down-home philosophy. Ronnie seemed more comfortable than Celeste standing on the threshold of the past. Celeste seemed awkward in the warm gush of strange familiarity.

'Yes, Lucille, they're looking for the house, and if

228

you be quiet long enough, I'll tell them how to get there.'

'Y'all stayin' at the Tree Top? You have to come by our house for supper. Shoot! I got two late customers tonight, but Sunday? We'd be honored if you'd join us.' She hunched her husband. 'Wouldn't we, Hambone?'

'Yes sirree. We sure would.' He tugged on his suspenders for the umpteenth time.

'If I don't get back Marvella's gon' come after me with my own straightening comb! I can't wait to talk with y'all some more. I 'spect a lot's happened in forty years.'

Two and a half miles down Albermarle Road, as instructed, they made the right at an old barn, right again at a rusty old truck with bushes growing out of the grill.

Towering longleaf pines lined the single-lane strip.

'You sure wouldn't know this was Little Pond Road unless somebody told you.' Ronnie propped her head on her arms in the open window and peered through the trees. 'But I guess if you come down this road you know where you're going.' She couldn't make out neighboring houses or anything else through the trees, except more trees.

Celeste looked straight ahead and eased the car tentatively over the rocks and ruts. She prayed there were no oncoming cars because there didn't appear to be room to pass. For a change, their silence seemed more anxious than testy as they waited to see what lay at the end of the road.

12

'Let's get this show on the road.'

'This must be it.' Celeste slowed to a stop where the deep, wild grass swallowed the single lane.

'Wow!' Ronnie felt like she'd unwrapped a wonderful surprise on Christmas morning. A grin took over her face as she stepped out of the car, too engrossed to close the door.

'I was expecting a shack from the way Mother's been carrying on.' Celeste closed Ronnie's car door, then minced cautiously through the weeds and wild flowers that had overrun the elaborately patterned brick walkway. She stood next to Ronnie, dangling her purse at her side, wishing she'd changed into pants and sneakers.

The big, white clapboard house loomed in front of them, impressive in its abandoned, lifeless silence. It had refused to be engulfed by the surrounding knee-high grass or the hulking bushes that had grown unchecked and were themselves a tangle of vines, leaves, and tiny flowers. On the porch, a weathered green swing dangled from the ceiling by rusted chains, and two wicker armchairs leaned upside down against the wooden railing like they were kneeling at an altar, in prayer. The past met up with the present at the front steps, which were concrete and obviously new like the shingled roof, the wooden banisters primed in gray but not yet painted.

A bird chattered in the nearby woods, and a gentle, cooling breeze rustled the leaves, but perspiration ran from Celeste's hairline down her neck and into her blouse. She wiped at her forehead with the back of her hand. 'My, my.' She inched forward but stopped, feeling like she was trespassing. Dark, wet circles had spread under her armpits and sweat trickled down the backs of her thighs. A low-level vibration started at the top of her head and traveled south to the soles of her feet. *I wish Everett was here.* A pang of loss hit her where she'd been feeling only annoyance and anger. Right now she didn't want to lash out at her husband. She wanted his hand to hold. Celeste clinched her pocketbook tightly into the curve of her waist and took another step forward.

Ronnie shaded her eyes and counted the eight windows across the front of the house looking back at them. 'This is way cool! Ma really lived here when she was little, can you believe it?' She waved away a bee, then moved toward the side of the house, using her hands and her strides to cut through the tall grass. For the first time the property was more than a winning lottery ticket to her.

'Ronnie! Where are you going? You don't know what's back . . .' But she had already disappeared from view. Momentarily dismissing thoughts of snakes and Lyme disease, Celeste took tentative steps along the path that Ronnie had walked and peeked around the corner of the house. 'Ronnie!'

'Right here.' She had circled once around and came up behind Celeste. 'You should see all this stuff. There's a porch out back too. And a shed, and some kind of big brick fireplace. Farther back there's another shed or something. Do you think it was a chicken coop? I can just see Ma with her basket, gathering eggs . . .'

'Don't you know anything could be back there? Are you crazy?'

'What? Lions? Come on, Celeste.' She doubled back toward the front door. 'Are you worried about me, or is my big sister ascared to be out here by herself?' Ronnie teased Celeste in baby talk.

'Don't be ridiculous!' Celeste couldn't admit she was glad not to be alone. She trailed behind Ronnie up the front steps.

Ronnie cupped her hands beside her eyes and peered through the oval window in the door. 'I looked for the lake out back, but . . .'

'There is water! I was hoping – from the street name.'

'Doug says it's kind of a little cove or something, but it lets out into a bigger lake. Can you believe none of the windows are broken out?' She looked over at Celeste. 'He also said all the furniture and stuff is still in here. So where's the key? Let's get this show on the road.'

Celeste opened her purse and removed the small manila envelope that had been stapled to the deed.

'Maybe we'll find some things from Ma's spit-fire days! Isn't that what Hambone called her? I'm dyin' to rag on Ma about that.' Ronnie watched Celeste's hand tremble as she shook two keys into her palm. 'Here, I'll do it.' Before Celeste could object, Ronnie had grabbed one, and the door was open. She had expected it to creak and groan, like a haunted house. Instead it swung wide without a peep.

But Celeste heard a *whoosh*, like the noise from opening a vacuum-sealed coffee can, or Pandora's box. She felt it too. 'Did you hear that?'

'What?'

Celeste held her breath a moment. 'Nothing.'

Ronnie shrugged and walked in. The house smelled of brittle paper, musty clothes, and old furniture sealed away and forgotten. 'Doug said the lights would be on today. Not that we need them.' Dust motes danced on rays of sunlight that streaked across the living room and into the foyer. Ronnie hesitated a moment, as if passing through the beams would set off some alarm, but curiosity made her plunge ahead. 'Look at this!' To the left and right of the hall, bulky, sheet-draped hulks of furniture floated, like specters, on islands of faded rose and ivy bordered rugs. 'It's like a movie!' Celeste hung back. 'Don't tell me you're afraid of ghosts!' Ronnie cackled.

'No!' At least not the ones who prowled graveyards after midnight and walked through walls. Celeste feared the phantoms who had recently come to haunt her life, some dead, like the grandmother and grandfather she knew nothing about, and the father she thought she knew so well. Then there were the living, like her mother, who was proving to be a bigger mystery than Celeste had imagined, and Everett, whose spirit she seemed to have lost somewhere along the last twenty-four years. Sweat dripped down her back, and goosebumps sprouted on her arms. This was too much to swallow, too much to digest, but Celeste screamed silently and walked into the living room anyway.

'Right,' Ronnie snorted and looked around.

'It's weird – all this stuff still being here. And it belongs to us.'

'Is that all you can think about? What you get out of the deal?'

'No! It was a thought, all right? You're not the only one who has them! Anyway, Doug said the taxes were paid, but nobody showed up to claim anything.'

'I know Daddy had work done. Maybe he was planning to clean it out later.' Celeste glanced around her. 'Get it ready to sell since his wife . . .'

'You mean your mother, or aren't you claiming her today?'

'Do I have a choice?' Celeste frowned. 'I mean, why is she so dead-set against this place? I could see if it was a shack, but this is a nice house.'

'I bet you'd be too through if it *was* a shack. That would be so beneath you.'

'Don't be ridiculous! Besides, we need to get started.' Celeste took out a spiral-bound pad. 'We should catalog whatever we find.'

'We have to *see* what's here before we do anything.'

'I think . . .'

'Do what you want. I'm exploring.' Ronnie snatched the sheet from a bulge by the door and revealed a chintz-covered armchair. 'Voilà!' She made short work of the living room, unveiling ornate occasional tables, a burgundy brocade sofa and two matching settees, another settee, and a grouping of wood and upholstered chairs near the window, close to a glossy black spinet piano. It was a formal setting befitting finger sandwiches and tea. An old Victrola sat on top of a glass-doored bookcase. She opened it, pulled a black bound Bible from a shelf, read the front page. 'Odell Womack married Ethiopia Clayton,

July 5, 1933. Think they had a barbecue?'

Celeste didn't answer. She continued sweating and folding the sheets Ronnie had left in her wake into neat squares, careful not to shake loose much dust.

'Henry Leon Womack, born January 2, 1934.'

'Let me see that.' Celeste squinted at the names written in a halting, deliberate hand. 'Where's Mother's name?'

'Don't know.' Ronnie counted on her fingers. 'But I do know Henry was kinda early.' She grinned. 'So, Grandpa was a smooth operator.'

'Ronnie, grow up.' Celeste shoved the book in its place.

'Just gathering a little family history. And you're grown enough for the both of us, anyway.' Ronnie moved on to the dining room. 'Do you think some of this is antique? You know, the real kind, like worth something?' In under an hour, they had uncovered china and curio cabinets filled with knickknacks, pale green etched vases, and dishes decorated with delicate lilacs and ferns.

Celeste opened a cabinet and picked up a coffee cup. 'How beautiful.'

Ronnie held a gold-rimmed goblet up to the light and watched the cut glass prism dance a rainbow on the faded celery walls. 'I asked Doug if the buyer wanted the furniture and stuff too, but maybe we should get it appraised first.'

'*We* haven't decided to sell anything.' Celeste put the cup away then put hands on her hips.

'Well, *we* certainly haven't decided to keep it, either. I'm gonna open some windows.'

'They're probably stuck. Besides, maybe we shouldn't.'

235

'Why? It's ours. Anyway, these look new.' Ronnie turned the lock and the vinyl double-hung glided open without effort. 'Ta da! Wrong again!' Celeste stepped into the breeze and dabbed her forehead and neck with a wad of tissues that left white specks clinging to her damp skin.

Ronnie pushed open the swinging door and went into the kitchen. 'Whoa!' The room felt welcoming, from the wide-plank floors to the custard yellow cabinets with glass doors that lined the walls. Everyday utensils filled the shelves, and a blue Milk of Magnesia bottle was tucked in a corner, almost out of sight. It was like the prototype for a country kitchen from a decorating magazine. The deep double sink had enamel faucets and a view of the outdoors. A round, family-sized oak pedestal table sat in a windowed alcove, but stove, refrigerator, and dishwasher gleamed brand-new, energy-efficiency tags still in place. 'You gotta see this!' Ronnie wrote her initials in the dust that covered the round table.

'My goodness! It's as big as the living room.' Celeste opened the refrigerator door. The store's packing slip was still taped to the top shelf. 'Gaston Appliance . . . He brought all these last year.'

'He who?'

'Daddy. I found the receipts.'

'Why'd he do that? Maybe he and Ma were gonna move here. Lots of people do that. You know, retire to the Sun Belt.'

'Well, Mother certainly wasn't coming, so of course he couldn't. He must have planned to rent it out – or – I don't know – It would be a lot easier if he'd told me something. Anything is better than this.' Celeste sank into one of the ladder back chairs at the table.

Ronnie hiked herself up on the counter, determined not to let the fun of discovery sidetrack her from her goal. 'That's why we need to sell this place. Ma doesn't want anything to do with it. I don't want to be a long-distance landlord. Do you? I'm telling you, Pryce has a buyer. They're offering almost two hundred thousand dollars. We can split it and walk away with a nice piece of change!'

'We should go upstairs before it really gets hot in here.' Celeste pushed back from the table.

'Fine. Act like I'm not talkin' to you.' Ronnie jumped down, dusted her butt. 'Let's go!' She led the way through another swinging door into the hall and headed back to the front of the house. They poked their heads in the three doors they passed: a white-tiled bathroom; a small sitting room with a drop-leaf table, a wooden stool, and a black and gold pedal sewing machine on a wrought-iron stand. And finally they came full circle. Across the front hall from the living room double doors opened into a study about the same size as the sewing room next door. A roll-top desk and an oak swivel chair sat in front of the windows. The remains of an old calendar were tacked to the wall. It read 'Mid-State Brickworks' under a drawing of a brook cascading over smooth rocks in the forest.

'It looks like they walked away one day and never came back.' Ronnie saw that the pages at the bottom of the calendar had been ripped off until September 1957. 'This is kinda creepy when you think about it. Walking around in somebody's house like this. Except it's really Ma's house.'

'As you informed me a few minutes ago, it's *our* house, Ronnie.'

Ronnie stood at the bottom of the stairs looking up. 'You know what I mean. People lived here. This is their stuff. Yeah. I guess it's family, but we didn't *know* them. They didn't *know* us – except for Ma.'

This time, Celeste took the lead, avoiding the dusty bannister. The steps squeaked in complaint as they mounted, and busted spindles left snaggletoothed gaps along the railing. At the top, four bedrooms fanned out from the stairway, three furnished with suites of dark-stained furniture, one with white. An enormous four-poster rice bed with a two-tiered step beside it dominated the largest bedroom. A bathroom, with a huge porcelain claw-foot tub, also opened onto the center hall.

'You know we have to open every closet, go through every drawer, read every piece of paper.'

'That'll take forever.'

'You invited yourself, remember?'

'I can only stay a couple of days. I have to . . .'

'So you thought we'd just sell the whole shebang, take the money, and run? I told Everett you didn't have one ounce of business sense!' Celeste threw up both hands. 'We have to inventory all of this.'

'How come he didn't come too?'

'Who?'

'Everett. Your husband, remember him?'

Celeste rubbed the back of her neck. 'He, uh – couldn't get away right now. And before we can even think about selling, we have to find out what houses and land are going for around here.'

'Did you see any other houses? I didn't. Besides, I happen to think they're offering quite a bit of money. And if we throw in the furniture and stuff, we can probably get over two hundred for everything. Not even you could turn your nose up at that. I should go find a phone and call Doug, let him know we're out here.'

'Suit yourself, but I won't even discuss it with him, or *you*, until I know what's here.'

Ronnie huffed. 'Fine. You start up here. I'll go downstairs. Let's get this over with.'

Celeste thought about the afternoon heat rising. 'I'll take downstairs.'

'You have to be contrary, don't you!' Ronnie turned on her heels and disappeared into the nearest bedroom.

Even though Ronnie had opened all the windows, by three o'clock it was sweltering, even too hot to smoke. She had untucked her shirt, knotted it below her breasts, and pulled her ponytail up off her neck. She started in one of the smaller bedrooms, where she found men's clothes and shoes. Whoever he was, wasn't very big. His steel blue gabardine shirt fit Ronnie nicely. *What was the brother's name? Henry?* Judging by the styles, he'd stopped dressing there in the mid sixties. *Wonder what happened to him?*

In the bathroom there was a used block of Ivory in the daisy-shaped plastic soap dish on the sink, and she wondered who washed their hands last and how long ago it had been. Her mother had been so tight-lipped that Ronnie still wasn't sure how Della came to inherit the house. She tugged hard at the door to the medicine cabinet and almost fell when it finally opened. She'd never heard of half the stuff: Stanback Headache Powder, Lydia Pinkham's Tonic, a petrified jar of Tussy deodorant.

Across the hall in the big bedroom she thought the electric orange and green bedspread circa 1973 looked out of place surrounded by so much old, ornate furniture. On the bedside table she picked up a framed sepia portrait of a man wearing a fedora, tilted back too far on his head to be cool, and a double-breasted pin-striped suit that seemed a bit too skimpy for his robust frame. *My man knew he was clean.* He sat confidently on a bench, his ankle crossed over the other knee, in front of a backdrop bordered with tropical trees and flowers. *This has to be Ma's father. She looks just like him.* It was odd to see a face she knew so well on the person who obviously had it first. Ronnie studied the picture for a while, then laid it on the bed to take down to show Celeste and moved on to the drawer where she found an El Producto box that held stray buttons, safety pins, a triple-strand necklace of iridescent crystals and, folded carefully in a paper towel, a well-chewed set of false teeth. Judging by their size, they fit in a rather tiny mouth. *Musta belonged to Ma's mother – our grandmother – but nobody else in the family inherited that trait. All the folks I know about have big mouths.* She put the dentures back in a hurry but fastened on the beads. She fingered them around her neck as she moved to the closet.

The smell of flowery perfume and liniment met Ronnie as she opened the door. The outfits were so tightly packed there was no room to slide the hangers. The oldest clothes were medium sized; as they got more recent, they got smaller. After careful consideration she chose a navy and white polka dot shirtwaist that was big enough to pull on over her clothes, and she remembered how she loved to play in Della's closet. After she was all done up she'd poke out her little lips for Della to add the finishing touch. Lipstick.

Wonder if Ma used to play dress-up in here. Ronnie examined all the hats in a stack of boxes she took down from the shelf. A black straw number the size of a saucer struck her fancy, so she put it on and pulled the veil down to her chin. *All I need is some pumps with the toes peeking out and I'm ready for my closeup.* Ronnie squatted down and rummaged through the shoes, which were all too small, but she came across an Enna Jetticks box filled with report cards, two separate piles, each secured with a piece of twine, tied in a bow. Henry Womack's pile went from first through twelfth grade. Odella's started in the middle of the fourth grade and stopped at the end of the eleventh, but she got better marks in every subject. *Don't tell me she dropped out. Man, if I did that I'd still be hearin' about it! Wonder when Ma started calling herself Della? Not that I blame her. I haven't even been here a whole day, and I've got so much material to tease her about.* When Ronnie straightened up she noticed a black patent handbag with a brass clasp hanging from a hook. *I'd carry this now.* She put on one of the yellowed cotton gloves she found inside. There were two crumpled dollar bills and a brittle stick of Beechnut gum in the pocket, but it was the old church bulletin that caught her eye. ' "How Great Thou Art" Solo by Odella Womack' was underlined in pencil. *Ma? Singing in church?* Ronnie gathered the program and her other finds and went downstairs.

'Hey, look at this stuff.' Ronnie started over to where Celeste sat in a chair holding a piece of sheet music, piano bench propped open in front of her.

She looked up when she heard Ronnie. 'Do you remember— Is that all you've been doing, playing? You could have stayed home.'

'No, I've been busy. I just decided to dress for the occasion.' She curtsied.

Celeste didn't crack a smile. 'Do you remember when we got the piano?'

Celeste's voice had prongs so Ronnie knew her sister was worked up about something. 'Not exactly.' She barely remembered there was one in the house because no one had played it in years. For a while she and Celeste had gone to Mrs Horner's each Tuesday after school, where they were drilled on scales and contorted into proper hand position. Celeste had no ear for music, was terrified by Mrs Horner's gruff manner, and hated every minute of her half-hour session. And although Ronnie could carry a tune, she was completely inept at the piano. She got a kick out of serenading her parents with the few simple tunes she managed to memorize, but the novelty wore off quickly. When the Horners moved to Cleveland, Celeste thought her prayers had been answered, and Ronnie was ready to go back to singing or dance lessons, something she was good at. Their parents asked a couple of times if they wanted a new teacher, then the subject was dropped.

'It was that summer Mr Anderson was talking about this morning, the moon walk summer. When Daddy came back we got lots of new stuff.' Celeste stared out the window as she spoke. 'A stove, color TV, and that piano.'

'I remember the TV. I didn't want to go to day camp that August. I wanted to stay home and watch all the shows in color.'

'I heard Mother play it once,' Celeste continued.

'The piano?'

'It was before she was working at DMV, in the fall,

and I came home from school early one day. It was still warm, so the windows were open, and I heard this music. It was a pretty song, like a ballad I guess. Anyway, you know how the screen door always squeaked? When I opened it, the music stopped. By the time I got to the living room, the lid was down and she was dusting the piano, if you can believe that. I asked her to play some more and she said she didn't know what I was talking about. "I don't play no piano, Celeste. You know that." But I always believed it was her playing. Nobody else was home.'

'She sang too.' Ronnie leaned against the spinet and thrust the bulletin at Celeste.

'I found some more of those in the piano bench. And I found this.' Celeste handed Ronnie the blue book in her lap.

Ronnie opened it to the first page. Groups of neat, precisely drawn horizontal lines formed the staff, marked with curly treble and bass clefs, perfectly oval whole, half, and quarter notes. She flipped the pages. There were no lyrics and no titles, but the composer was the same. Inked in plump script on the upper right of each page was 'melody by Odella Womack.'

Ronnie held the book to her heart. 'This is pretty cool.'

'Why did she lie to me like that?!'

'Celeste, it wasn't . . .'

'Yes it was. She lied. She played the piano well enough to write music. Why wouldn't she tell me that?'

'Daddy must have known. He didn't say anything, either.' Ronnie cocked her right foot on its heel and looked down at the dust that had collected on her sandals. 'Who knows why they did anything. They sure as hell didn't discuss it with us.' Ronnie noticed that the circles under Celeste's eyes had deepened since morning, like she'd been crying. 'I think we've had enough for one day, and it would be better to find our way back before dark.' *Can't wait to see what'll turn up next.*

'Yeah. All right.' Celeste smoothed her linen skirt, but the wrinkles were set. 'We can start early tomorrow, ahead of the heat.' *God only knows what we'll find out then.*

'If Daddy was working on the place, I wish he had gotten to the air conditioning.' Ronnie trotted up the stairs to ditch her costume, except the crystals. Somehow she felt attached to them and she kept them on. When she locked the door behind them, she stopped on the porch and added the key to the others on her pink heart-shaped key ring. Aside from keys to her mother's house in Buffalo, it was the only one that still worked.

Celeste wanted to ask for the key back, for safe-keeping, but she kept quiet. She guided the car down the narrow road and squinted as the setting sun flickered through trees.

'I'm exhausted and I'm starving.' Ronnie turned around and watched the house disappear from view. 'If we don't go back to Pal's, where do you suggest we eat?'

'How am I supposed to know? I'm just not sure if I can take any more southern hospitality today.'

'What's wrong with it? I think they're nice. And I know the food will beat the hell out of anything else around here. It's like Mama's home cookin'! If Ma could cook!'

It was the magic word. 'Speaking of cooking—'

244

Celeste cleared her throat. 'I understand you encouraged my daughter to quit her job and pursue this insane notion she has of becoming a chef.'

Not this! Can't we be on the same side of somethin'? 'I didn't *encourage* her, as you put it. I told her it was her life, which it is. What did Ma say? "You can't cut your dresses by somebody else's pattern." '

'I don't want to hear that old-timey junk! And what do you know about raising a child?'

'Nothing. But Nik's not a child anymore.'

'She'll always be my child. But how could you have any idea what the responsibility of motherhood is like? You can't even take care of yourself!' Celeste checked both directions before getting on the highway that would again become Albermarle Avenue.

'She'll always be your daughter, but I got news for you. She's not your child. I bet you don't think of yourself as Della's child.'

'It's not the same! Mother wasn't very – motherly.'

'And you're the Queen Mum, is that it? Have you ever asked Niki how you score on the motherhood test?' Ronnie lowered the window.

'That's the stupidest thing I ever heard. And the air is on,' Celeste barked.

Ronnie ignored her and dangled her arm outside. 'Says you, but I personally don't think Ma did such a piss-poor job. She didn't make cookies for the bake sale, but she was always there when we needed her.'

'She was there when *you* needed her.'

'She came to all our stuff at school.'

'Wearing those hideous smocks she made. Maybe she should have used somebody else's pattern. I used to want to disappear through the floor.'

'So she wasn't a fashion plate.'

'I'm not discussing Mother! I'm talking about *you*, interfering in Niki's life, minding business that isn't yours.'

'Why are you so against her becoming a chef? I hear tell it might run in the family.'

'If it was true, don't you think we'd have heard it before now? And I sure haven't come across any evidence of a catering business today. Sounds like some crap Mother made up to make Nik feel better.'

'Maybe, maybe not. Damn, Celeste. She's been a great kid. No school trouble, no boy trouble, no drug trouble. Niki earned her degree, not you. Can't she do what she wants with it?' Ronnie looked up and saw the flag outside of the Elks Lodge approaching. 'You gonna stop at Pal's or you want to eat at the truck stop across from our five-star accommodations?'

'Fine. I don't care.' Celeste braked and pulled into a space in front of the restaurant behind a red Corvette convertible. 'Being a cook or chef or whatever you call it – it's not . . .'

'Not what?'

'– It's not professional!'

'Oh. You mean like a lawyer or like her father the doctor?' Ronnie scratched her head like she was thinking. 'Or a hooker? They say that's a profession too, right?' Ronnie knew she was pouring kerosene on hot coals. She could almost hear Celeste sizzle.

'Well now – that's pretty close to what you do isn't it?'

'What the hell are you saying?!' Whatever peace they had approached earlier in the afternoon was going up in flames.

'How do you manage to get favors from people like your realtor friend's friend? The banker, is it?'

'He made a phone call to a friend. It wasn't *even* more than that, so you can take your little sly implications . . .'

'And while we're at it, you don't expect me to believe you support yourself from acting. Or modeling either – certainly not at your age – not that you ever did.' She mumbled the last part but clearly enough for Ronnie to hear it.

'I'm gonna pretend you didn't say any of that, because it's the only way I know not to slap you.' Ronnie got out, slammed the door, and by the time Celeste unfastened her seat belt, was already in Pal's.

The fried chicken and pot roast greeted Ronnie before the hostess did, and she found herself really hungry for the first time in three days, in spite of her anger. Obviously Pal's Kitchen was the place to be on Thursday nights in Prosper. It was jammed, with nearly as many White diners as Black ones. There were no strained, hushed murmurs or delicate clinks of crystal. Forks clacked, plates rattled, and voices rose and fell in crescendos of words and laughter. A steely guitar blues from a forty-five record played on the flashy old jukebox across the room.

Celeste and Ronnie managed to get seated without drawing blood. They had barely settled themselves when Hambone burst through the kitchen doors, an enormous tray riding on his wide shoulder. He deposited two kiddie specials and a plate of smothered pork chops at the table where a plump blonde woman cooed to a baby in a high chair, held a pint-sized, towheaded boy in a lock between her knees, and carefully spooned the ice from the glass of a tearful, pigtailed little girl. Then he hustled to the counter, deposited the one plate left on his tray in front of a man reading a magazine, and exchanged a few lively words with him. Ronnie watched Hambone's belly bounce as he laughed and shook his head. Then he slipped the empty tray into a slot on the stand by the kitchen door, scurried to the register, and made change for two waitresses who stood there, dinner checks and money in hand. After he closed the cash drawer, he looked up and spotted Celeste and Ronnie. He spoke briefly to the man with the magazine before heading over.

'I'm so glad y'all decided to stop back!' Hambone hooked his thumbs under his suspenders. 'Can't go wrong with the fried chicken. It's the special on Thursday. It's on the menu every day, but folks seem to have got in the habit of comin' for it on Thursdays. If you ask me, it don't taste no different from the chicken we fix on Mondays. But if they wanna think it is, I ain't complainin'!'

Celeste gritted her teeth so she could bear his rambling chicken anecdote. Ronnie thought it was cute. His greeting took her mind off wanting to strangle Celeste.

Hambone surveyed the crowd and grinned. 'I hope it wasn't too bad out at the house. I don't get out that way much no more. You know, was a time I'd stop by pretty regular. Check on things and look in on Miz Ethiopia . . .'

'Now that's Ma's mother, right?' Ronnie was proud of herself for remembering what she'd read in the family Bible.

'Miz Ethiopia was her stepmama.' Hambone waved to a patron who entered the restaurant. 'We never did know her mama. She passed on, you know. That's when Odella first came to Prosper.'

'That's what Ronnie meant. Stepmother.' Celeste was quick to smooth over their ignorance. 'Mother always referred to her as Mama.'

'Well, a whole lot sure has changed. When Odella was growin' up she had no use for the lady, and she'd call her nothin' at all before she called her Mama.' Hambone looked down, remembering. 'Anyways, didn't nobody 'spect Miz Ethiopia'd live long after Odell passed on, but she was a darn sight stronger than she appeared to be. Proved us all wrong. Was pret' near a hundred when she died. So you two gon' have the chicken?'

'Sounds like it wouldn't be a trip to Prosper without it, isn't that right, sister dear?' Ronnie smiled innocently at Celeste.

'Uh-huh. Sure.' Celeste was too overloaded to care what she ate.

Across the room, the man Hambone had spoken to at the counter got up, dropped some bills on the counter, and tucked his magazine under his arm. He was a bit bowlegged and his walk had a little hitch to it, like the cowboys in black-and-white movies. He stopped by a table, chatted a moment, waved a friendly so-long, and continued in their direction. He was reed thin, which made him look much taller than he actually was, and he was dressed razor sharp. The cuffs of his smoothly pressed red and white striped shirt folded crisply over the elastic at the wrists of his scarlet silk bomber jacket. You could slice paper with the creases in his black trousers, and he wore black suede loafers, without socks. As he got closer, Ronnie could see that despite the wardrobe, the diamond in his left ear, and the copy of *Vibe* under his arm, he was older than he appeared from the other side of the

249

room. His dark, curly hair was gray at the temples, and the lines around his eyes mapped passages of time and experience.

He nodded at Celeste and Ronnie before he spoke to Hambone.

'See you tomorrow, man. And do yourself a favor. Don't go puttin' no money against the Panthers. They're gon' go all the way this year.' His voice was deep, rich, and sweet, like dessert. 'But if you insist I'll be happy to take you up on your bets.'

'Just make sure you left money to pay for your dinner!' Hambone teased.

Ronnie suspected that in his day, he'd been through all the skirts in town and then some. His eye lingered a moment at her necklace and she raised her hand to touch it.

'You ladies have a nice stay in Prosper.' He smiled. 'And when you see your mama, tell her Lester said hello.' He clapped Hambone on the shoulder. 'Later.' And he was out the door.

'I'll be right back with your dinner.' Hambone disappeared.

'We did not know Ma had a stepmother!' Ronnie leaned in toward Celeste.

'Well, you certainly don't think I'm going to let anybody else think we didn't!' Celeste hissed.

'And if she's not actually *from* here, where is she from?'

'How should I know? And right now, I don't even care! I meant to ask if they have wine.'

'All I know is the more we find out, the less we know.' Ronnie watched out the window as the man named Lester got in the red 'Vette and drove off. 'And how does she know this dude who wears an earring and drives a sports car?'

'Obviously that was a long time ago, and I'm sure he didn't do either back then. Besides he looks like – like . . .'

'Yes? Like what?'

Celeste sucked her teeth. 'You know exactly what I mean.'

'Celeste, you always mean the same damn thing.' Ronnie's eyes twinkled with mischief. 'I wanna know what Ma has to say about ol' Lester.'

13

'. . . waiting for the but.'

By the time the clock radio alarmed at six A.M., blaring a disco beat, Ronnie felt like she'd been run over by the Lexington Avenue Express. Her backache wrapped around to her belly like a girdle. This dawn patrol Celeste had them on was not Ronnie's cup of tea in the first place. Sunrise was closer to the time she would come dragging in from the night before, but this night had been anything but a party. Ronnie's worries had taken turns haunting the night, and sleep had been snatched in agitated naps between long bouts of wakefulness, all of it accompanied by the wheeze and snore of the air conditioner. She twisted the radio volume off, then dragged herself up on her elbow and reached for the phone to check her service. Usually she called in every hour, on the off chance someone meaningful was looking for her, like an agent or casting director. It dawned on her at 2:37 A.M. that she hadn't checked it in the three days she'd been in Prosper.

Ronnie needed her whole situation to be different in a hurry. Celeste seemed content to catalog every doodad and shoestring in the house like it would change the course of history. Ronnie had played along, figuring Celeste would get tired of this game and get down to business. Besides, as much as Ronnie grumbled, and she did make sure Celeste knew they were doing a whole lot of work for nothing, Ronnie enjoyed exploring the musty trunks and boxes, making up stories about the cotton slips, silk stockings, embroidered handkerchiefs, and other relics she found. Ronnie had cleared out a drawer in the big bedroom and started a collection of things she wanted to keep because they were pretty or odd, or she felt a strange connection to them, like the faded deck of playing cards she found stuffed in the foot of a white ankle sock. Blue ballpoint mustaches had been drawn on all the face cards that didn't already have them, queens included. Ronnie just knew they were Della's. Her mother taught her to play hearts and pinochle and rummy, and Ronnie loved to hang over her shoulder and help her play solitaire at the kitchen table. Sometimes Will played too, but Celeste rarely did. Said it was boring. Ronnie hadn't shown her stash to Celeste yet, but they still had a lot of business to discuss.

Ronnie let the phone ring a long time before the desk clerk grunted a sleepy greeting and gave her an outside line. She poked at the numbers, then entered her code and listened. *Kayla . . . Yeah, yeah. Same sad story. No love or fame connections in the Hamptons, but if there's a way, my girl will be out there trying again next weekend.* The whole jitney and party-hopping scene seemed a million miles away at this moment, like maybe on Pluto. Ronnie reached across the bed for her shoulder bag, which was under the clothes she'd dumped out of her carry-on last night to find her pajamas, an XXL T-shirt with a faded logo from some trade show she worked a long time ago. Despite the crappy room, she enjoyed the luxury of a queen-size bed with enough space for piles of magazines and clothes on the side where she wasn't sleeping. Ronnie dumped her last two pills in her hand and swallowed them with her own spit. *Gotta find a drugstore and get more of these bad girls.* She didn't bother to add up the hours since her last dose. If it hurt this bad, they had obviously stopped working.

Ronnie erased Kayla's message and went on to the next. *R. Philip – guess I should call to say I hooked up with his friend. As much good as it's done, it's not worth the quarter.* Last night she found a message from Doug slipped under the door and wondered what took him so long. *Some salesman. He needs to be about selling my sister so we can get this over with. Actin' like I got all year.* Ronnie shrugged her shoulder up to hold the phone, lit the half cigarette she had carefully tamped out the night before. It tasted nasty, but she smoked it anyway. *Haven't heard from him since he left me in this dump. You'd think he'd call at least to see if I'm still breathing.* Then she remembered him leaning up against the car that first morning, reading his paper, waiting for her. And she recalled Celeste's curt dismissal. *Guess I did say I'd call him – but still, this is business.* The fact that he was a man and some little part of her wanted him to call first, she swept that under the rug.

Ronnie blew smoke down over her bottom lip, made a mental note to call Doug at a slightly more reasonable hour and to decide whether to call R. Philip at all, then moved on to the next message. *Marilyn Ellis?!* Ronnie froze, as she listened to her supervisor, who sounded stiff, not chatty like usual.

254

Covering Ronnie's shifts wasn't working out. Marilyn wanted to confirm that Ronnie was on the schedule for Thursday evening and that it was imperative she be there. *No sweat. I'll be back by Tuesday and—* She dropped the receiver into the cradle. And as soon as she touched down she would be officially without a residence. She had been pushing all thoughts about her shaky situation to the back of her mind, but they always elbowed up front and center, bigger, uglier, and louder than before. The vise that squeezed her head and her guts felt another notch tighter, and it wasn't until the ash dropped off her cigarette and onto her knee that Ronnie realized her hands were shaking. She hurriedly crushed out the butt and turned up the radio to drown out the voice that kept screaming, *What the hell am I gonna do?*

'This is Johnny DuPree, your morning MC, and if your rooster don't crow, then let me cock-a-doodle-doo ya in the morning!' Ronnie let the patter of the smooth-voiced DJ distract her. 'You're listening to WDLA, and if you're old enough to remember when rock was somethin' you throw, then this record will bring back a whole lotta memories.' He played another cut with a heavy dose of rhythm, and Ronnie forced herself into the groove and up on her feet. She glanced in the skimpy bathroom mirror, stuck her tongue out at herself. It was going to take some serious effort to make herself presentable, because the act was wearing thin and right now she looked as whupped and scared as she felt. She hopped into the shower, making sure to wrap her hair carefully. She didn't have the patience to deal with two feet of wet, tangled weave.

The spray of warm water loosened up Ronnie's

brain, and her thoughts began to flow. By the time she dried off with the scratchy towel, she decided she needed to talk to Doug and see if his client would be interested in twenty-two and a half acres. That sounded like a whole lot of land to her, and that way Celeste could take her sweet time and Ronnie could pocket her sweet cash and be on her way.

Dressed in a short black skirt and a slightly damp, clammy cotton tank she'd hand washed last night, Ronnie was outside, perched on the fender of the rental, by ten minutes to eight. She wanted her sister in a good mood, and the best way to assure that was to keep things moving on schedule. When Celeste came out at eight, she was surprised that Ronnie had beaten her.

Celeste's lemon yellow shorts set stood out brightly against the hazy, humid day. She wore it to help her keep putting on a happy face. 'You're up early.'

So you can cross that off your list of things to bitch about. 'All this clean country air, it makes me feel so – alive.' Ronnie sounded like a stale air freshener ad, even to herself. She noticed that her sister looked a little wilted too. 'And how was your night?'

'Fine. Just fine.' But the load on Celeste's mind showed in the bags under her puffy eyes.

Ronnie saw the strain, but she also recognized the 'case closed' expression and didn't press the issue. She wasn't hankering for an argument before they left the parking lot.

'I made a grocery list. We can stop on the way.' Celeste started the car. She needed to get busy to keep her demons in check because she'd had close encounters with her real life last night too. She reached Lydia and managed to make the situation in Prosper sound

256

messy enough to require her attention for a few more days. Her friend sounded sympathetic, while also managing to rub in what an incredible time she and Everett were missing. 'Why doesn't he come on down?' Lydia said. 'You two are like family. You know we'll take good care of him, unless there's some *reason* he's not taking time off.' Celeste could tell Lydia was searching for the faintest whiff of turmoil, but Celeste was careful to keep all traces of concern out of her voice. Whatever it took to keep Lydia off the scent Celeste would do because she had no intention of showing up in Highland Beach without her husband.

And Celeste had been leaving messages for Everett, with only her own clipped voice on the answering machine as a reply. Finally, he had called last night. She was already in bed, filing her nails and working on her to-do list when she picked up the phone, expecting Ronnie with some nonsense. When she heard Everett say her name, Celeste got the high-voltage jolt that always thrilled her when they were dating and waiting for his calls had made her ache deep inside. He sounded so relaxed and matter-of-fact that she started asking him about regular things: the weather, the mail, watering the lawn. She had leaned back into her pillows, twirling and untwirling the phone cord around her index finger as she described her adventures since she left Buffalo. So at first, when he said he had been to a lawyer and filed a legal separation, she was sure she'd misheard him. He went on to explain that the papers would be waiting for her when she got back. And he was on his way to the jazz festival in Portugal day after tomorrow. Celeste's heart began to pound so loud and fast she could no longer hear him speak. She put the receiver down on the bedside table and sat, knees pulled up to her chest, arms wrapped around them, rocking. She didn't know how long she'd been sitting like that when the knock on the door interrupted her trance. Her phone had been off the hook so long that Everett phoned and asked the night clerk to check on her.

Celeste had paced the room, stoking her anger, rehearsing her harangue. It was 3:16 in the morning when she called her house to tell him off, but when she heard his sleepy hello, the steam seeped out of her. All she could do was hang up gently and cry.

'Hey, aren't you gonna stop?' Ronnie said just in time for Celeste to swerve into the Winn Dixie parking lot.

Ronnie tagged behind as Celeste maneuvered the cart to get more boxes of super-size, extra-thick trash bags, smaller resealable storage bags, tape, paper towels, a pound of sliced turkey from the deli, bread, an apple, and a pear. Ronnie tossed a box of tampons and a bottle of Advil into the cart and ignored the evil eye Celeste gave her when she slipped outside to the pay phones while Celeste waited on the checkout line.

Ronnie hated skirting the issue of her share of the bill; she knew Celeste kept a strict accounting. She'd never ask for the money outright. The debt would be transferred to Ronnie's already lengthy tab for use during some future fight. Ronnie's operating capital was dwindling, though. *If we can just unload this damn land.* She fished the card from her pocket and dialed.

'Mr Pryce, this is Ms Frazier. If you can find the time in your busy schedule, I would appreciate your stopping by my house in Prosper this afternoon. You know, the one on Little Pond you're supposed to be trying to sell. Would your buyer be interested in half the property? Let me know.' Ronnie hung up, hoping she sounded snippy enough to get a rise out of him, not desperate, which was the God's honest truth. Then she helped Celeste load the groceries into the car and followed her around back of the store, where a stock boy told them they'd find a stack of flattened cardboard boxes. They took as many as the compact car would hold, then they were off for another day of discovery, each working overtime to keep her own secrets in check.

As had become the routine, Celeste perked a pot of coffee in the white enamel stove-top percolator she found in one of the cupboards. Her liberal use of pine-scented disinfectant and her decorating touches had made the kitchen feel quite homey in the short time they had been in town. She had washed two place settings of the blue willow china she thought was so pretty, as well as bamboo-handled cutlery she'd found in the drawer next to the sink. A ruby glass vase filled with wild goldenrod, cosmos, and cornflowers she had picked from near the house, not too far into the woods, sat in the center of the table. She was so deep in thought that she didn't comment when Ronnie turned on the portable radio on the counter while she waited for her tea water to boil.

Ronnie searched the dial until she recognized the lively baritone of Johnny DuPree reading the community calendar, birthday greetings, and help wanted ads for the station. *How sweet. Do they read personal ads for cows and chickens too?* She kept surfing the dial and tried to gauge her sister's mood while Celeste got the remainder of a Danish ring out of the bread box, sized

259

it up, sliced it in two precise halves, and put them on two plates.

'Remember how we used to fight over who got the biggest half of anything when we were kids?' Ronnie pulled two paper towels from the roll and folded them into napkins.

'You started it, making a big deal if you didn't get exactly what I got.' Celeste sprinkled sugar out of a mason jar into her coffee cup, then handed the jar to Ronnie.

'Then Daddy'd get all serious.' Ronnie dropped her voice to her father's register. ' "Half is half. Ain't one bigger than the other." That's when you started bringing a ruler to the table till Ma threatened to spank you with it.'

Celeste had to choke down her coffee to keep from spitting it out with her laugh. She nibbled her breakfast a moment, mashed some crumbs off the counter with her finger and sprinkled them in the sink. 'I miss him all the time. He was so – I don't know, good, fair, easy to get along with.'

'Are you implying your mother is not easy to get along with?' Ronnie smirked.

'Don't just give her to me,' Celeste cracked. 'She's your mother too.' Celeste took a sip, thought a moment. 'You know, going through all this stuff – it seems so regular. What's the big deal about this place? Why does she hate it so much?'

'Who knows? And I don't see her playing true confessions anytime soon.' Ronnie broke off a small piece of coffee cake, crumbled it on her plate, took a deep breath. *And there's no time like the present.* 'Listen, I called Doug Pryce this morning – to ask if his buyer would settle for half the property.'

'Is that all you can think about, Ronnie? You're like a broken record!'

'And I'm gonna keep sayin' it until you hear me! You may have all summer to make this into some kinda archaeological dig, but I don't, and you're not gonna make me feel bad about wanting to sell this place and get out.' Hand on hip, foot tapping, Ronnie waited for the next volley.

But Celeste had no stomach for a battle; her wounds from last night were too fresh. She swallowed a sip of coffee, watched the scarlet blur of a cardinal dart past the window and out of sight. 'Is that really what you want to do?' she said quietly.

Ronnie was caught off guard by the sudden de-escalation. *I don't know – but I don't have a whole lotta choice!* 'Yes.'

Celeste poured more coffee. 'All right then. Let's see what he has to say.'

Hallelujah. 'Thank you.' The clock had stopped, with not much time to spare, and Ronnie felt like skipping upstairs, but she maintained her cool until she was discreetly out of sight. For the first time in a week she felt hopeful. She attacked Henry's room with plenty of hip in her hop, singing snatches of songs, wishing she had the radio to keep her company. And she checked her watch, wondering if Doug would show up. The odd assortment of items scattered among the run-of-the-mill clothes and underwear made her chuckle: a cocoa tin half filled with Indian-head nickels in the back of a dresser drawer, old razor blades impaled in a rusted bar of soap in the nightstand, a crowbar wrapped in a dingy pillowcase in the closet. Ronnie got a flash of someone trying to make sense of her remaining box of

261

possessions but she had to dump that thought in a hurry.

By one-thirty there was still no Doug. She and Celeste took a brief lunch, long enough to grab a sandwich and clear the dust from their nostrils. Celeste had her morning's finds displayed in the dining room: neat stacks of tablecloths and napkins with sticky notes on top indicating the count, a graceful cut-glass pitcher, a silver compote. She would have waxed poetic about each one, amazed that their mother had grown up with such nice things, but Ronnie cut her short so she could resume her own excavation.

By the time Ronnie folded the last pair of trousers and added them to the bulging black garbage bag on the floor, the sun had burned away the early haze. She unbent herself, braced her hands on her hips, and massaged her lower back. Then she heard the knock on the doorsill and Doug's 'Hello' through the screen door.

It's about damn time. Please let him have good news. Ronnie shuffled quickly to the bathroom, rinsed her hands, smoothed her wet palms over her hair, wiped at the sweat on her face with a paper towel, then trotted casually downstairs. 'At least you listen to your messages.' She could see him through the screen, palm pressed against the door frame.

'And I do my best to deliver – soon as people let me know what they want.' In the hand resting on his hip, Doug held a vinyl binder that was Pryce Real Estate green, the same color as today's tennis shirt. 'May I?' He watched her tuck in her T-shirt.

R. Philip had described Ronnie as a fox and provided a detailed summary of her attributes, at least the physical ones. When he first saw her come off the plane, Doug thought she looked okay, although she had enough hair for six people attached to her head, which didn't do anything for him. But right now she looked like a rumpled teenager. R. Philip also admitted, kind of sideways, that Ronnie had been more of a challenge than he anticipated. 'I mean, I took her out a bunch of times, off and on, and she never gave me a play,' he had said. 'Did it ever occur to you that she just doesn't dig your shit?' is what Doug told him, but frankly, he wasn't looking at her as a potential playmate. He had more female attention than he knew what to do with since he became a widower.

Doug had been unprepared when so many women he knew, including Janice's girlfriends, only gave him a two-week mourning period after she died. Then the phone calls started. Women asked him out, offered to come over and cook him dinner, left homemade meals in microwaveable containers on the porch. For a while he ignored them and focused on tasks with steps he could follow, like work, coaching softball, shooting hoops at the gym. When he was finally ready for some company, he kept running into women who wanted a lifetime commitment after brunch and a movie. There was no letup in Charlotte either, but he took it all like a nickel change; it was nice, but it didn't add up to much.

'Are you gonna tell me somethin' I wanna hear?' Ronnie crossed her arms and playfully blocked the doorway.

'If you're interested in what the buyer had to say.' He chewed on his mustache, tried to figure out why he was smiling to himself as he remembered the surprised look on her face when he first said hello at the airport.

With a sweeping gesture, Ronnie opened the door. 'By all means, come on.'

'Ronnie, who are you talking— Oh, uh, Doug is it?' Celeste dusted at a smudge on her shirt. 'I didn't realize . . .'

'He's got news.' Ronnie motioned toward the living room.

'Just a moment.' Celeste disappeared toward the kitchen while Doug took a spot on the sofa and Ronnie perched on a chintz chair arm, her fingers crossed in her pockets. She was glad Celeste returned quickly. Ronnie was suddenly too nervous to make small talk, and Doug didn't have many words to spare.

Celeste sat stiffly on the edge of another chair, crossed her legs at the ankles, and opened her agenda to the back where she kept her lists.

It figures! My sister would prepare a cross-examination. 'So, what's the scoop?' Ronnie clasped her hands, rubbed them together.

'First of all, who *is* this mystery buyer?' Celeste checked off question number one, leaving her pen poised to jot down the answer.

'What difference does that make?!' *And what are you up to?*

Doug consulted his binder. 'DW Enterprises.'

'What would a corporation want with this land?' Celeste asked.

'Why do you care, Celeste? It's their money.'

'I just want to know. Do you mind?' Celeste shot Ronnie a pointed glance. 'It might be worth more to them than they're offering, for one thing.'

Ronnie nearly strained an eye muscle to keep from rolling them.

'And what do they plan to do with the property?'

'I can't answer that.' Doug shifted back in his chair, crossed his leg. 'What I can tell you is they're willing to consider your offer.'

Time seemed to stop and Ronnie tensed, waiting for the but.

'They do have two stipulations.'

'Uh-huh.' She wanted to snatch the words out of his mouth.

'Their acreage needs to have access to the lake.'

'That's doable.' She balled her hands into fists.

'Their other requirement is they want the house.'

Celeste closed her book. 'I'm afraid that won't work. We are absolutely not ready to sell the house yet.'

Ronnie's face about fell into her lap. She struggled to keep the quiver out of her voice. 'Celeste, we need to discuss . . .'

'Not the house, Ronnie. Not yet.'

'Can we step outside for a second?'

'We can, but it won't make any difference.'

'If time in the house is an issue, I can see if they're willing to delay the closing.' Doug hoped to head off the collision.

'That sounds reasonable.' Ronnie followed Doug's change of direction.

'I'm sorry, but it puts us right back where we started. I am not willing to come to terms about this house until . . .'

'Why are you so determined to hold on to this place?!' Ronnie spoke through her teeth, because if she opened her mouth she'd holler.

'I don't owe you an explanation!' Celeste didn't exactly have one. *Selling this place is really the only reasonable thing to do.* But right now Prosper was her safe haven because those separation papers were waiting at home, and then Everett would be gone. 'And if you had an ounce of sense . . .'

'That's it!' Ronnie stood up. *She will not embarrass me again.* 'Listen, Doug, I'm sorry about all this. I'll be in touch.' She ducked out of the room and banged out of the screen door. She had no idea where she was heading, but she was not about to have another one of their little 'family discussions' in public. *What kind of lunatics must he think we are?* She took off, following the stepping-stones that curved through the yard from the stairs to the edge of the trees. When the path ended, her agitation propelled her down the hill, zigzagging to avoid prickly bushes and low-slung tree limbs, stumbling on loose rocks that rolled underfoot. She continued until the lake appeared before her, murky green at this narrow inlet. At waterside she plunked down on a stump. The sky was a dazzling blue that doesn't come in the box of Manhattan colors. Wispy clouds floated like vapor on the air. Ronnie dropped her head in her hands. A bullfrog grunt interrupted the uneven lapping of water on the shore. With her eyes closed, the wet musk of damp moss, dead trees, and pond scum sent Ronnie back to her first summer in sleep-away camp.

Celeste, a camp veteran, had worked her way up to junior counselor for her four-week session. Before the summer began she had regaled Ronnie with endless explanations of how things were done at camp and warned her it would be hard to fit in and make friends for a while. Ronnie took the first opportunity to prove

Celeste wrong. One of the older girls taunted her bunk about the legendary sea serpent that lived deep in the lake and dared one of them to go in. Without hesitation Ronnie jumped into the slick, still water that only looked like a real lake on the postcards they sent home. Now she rubbed her arm, expecting to feel the same thick slime that coated her skin and clung in green gooey clumps to her hair that day. Her bravado made the others cheer, and Ronnie became one of the camp ringleaders, the girl everyone wanted as a friend. 'Let's ask Ronnie!' 'Does Ronnie want to play?' 'Are you coming back next summer, Ronnie?' Celeste was outdone and Ronnie loved it. Her credo became take the dare. Do it *because* you're scared. Dance on the edge of the volcano. Whatever you do, just don't be ordinary.

Except I'm tired of being brave. Ronnie grabbed a stone and hurled it as hard as she could out over the water. *I'm tired, period. I want to sell this damn house so I can stop being terrified. Stop wondering if I can get by one more month.*

'That's pretty good.'

She whipped around to see Doug walking toward her.

Aw, damn, what am I gonna say to this man? 'It's the only camp skill I have left. That's also the last time I sat on a tree stump.' *Just act normal. You can do this.*

'No canoeing? No fire building?'

'You must be joking.'

Doug came up beside her. As tough as she liked to appear, he thought she looked as though she'd lost her last friend. He bent over and picked up a rock, then threw it side arm. It skipped three times across the water before it disappeared. 'I did some checking.' He

267

squatted down next to her and pointed. 'Hear the fishin's pretty good beyond that bend.'

'Darn. You know,' Ronnie looked over at him, 'I meant to pack my pole.'

'You may laugh, but I've done a lot of good thinking sitting in a rowboat with a line in the water.'

'The fishin' philosopher. You should have had a column.'

'There's a lot I should have written about.'

'You still got a pencil, don't you?' Ronnie cocked her head sideways. Somehow talking with Doug about ordinary nonsense helped her catch hold of herself for a second.

Doug smirked. 'I guess I've got a nub or two in my desk drawer.' He stood up. 'Anyway if you walk a little ways over, you can see houses across the way in Jessup. It's a relatively new community, but suburban Charlotte is creeping out here pretty fast. What I'm saying is, if this buyer doesn't work out for you, I'm sure I can find another one who will.' He knew Edna would be beside herself if she heard him, but his reporter's instincts said this story had as many sides as a prism, and each one shed a different color light on the situation. It was going to take these women a while to agree on the same shade.

'Not before Monday,' Ronnie mumbled, the truth oozing around the edges of her mask. The clock had started ticking again, loud, and she was running out of ways to stop it.

'Monday?'

'Nothing. Never mind.'

'We can't wrap this up by Monday, no matter what. Now, we can handle it all long distance, but I gotta tell you, you and your sister seem pretty far apart about what needs to happen here. It would help if you could stay in neutral corners long enough to decide what you want to do.'

'Excuse you!'

'Just an observation.'

'So now you feature editorials too. Only thing left is gossip and the funnies,' Ronnie snapped. 'You got a whole lot a nerve.'

'Tell you what, from now on I'll keep my comments to myself. I'm gonna go. I'll call Monday, find out where we are. Until then, you know how to find me.'

Ronnie tattooed the spongy ground with her heels, watched him stride up the hill. *Thinks he knows too damn much.* As Doug got farther away, though, Ronnie realized she had won that battle, but her prize was a trip back to the house to deal with Celeste. *Damn!* She got up and paced around the stump. Even the air felt unbearably heavy, like it would crush her to the ground. Another confrontation would be pointless at the moment. She just wanted to go back to her room and lie in the dark so she could figure out her next move. But if she was going to avoid Celeste that meant hitching a ride with Doug. *Damn!* He was disappearing into the trees. *How do I get myself in these—* 'Hey! Doug!' Her voice bounced off the silence. He stopped but didn't turn around. 'Can you give me a ride?'

He didn't answer but waited until she caught up. *Now he's gonna act like he's doin' me some big favor.* She followed him to the house, went inside long enough to grab her purse and tell Celeste she was leaving.

On the ride back she kept her mouth shut, looked at the scenery. She'd been in town less than a week, but she found herself looking for the curly faced calf grazing on a dandelion-dotted hillside just beyond the no-name gas station, the tufts of cotton clinging to a field of grass, and other sights that had become familiar in such a short time. They rode without speaking, Doug watching the road. Ronnie feeling a little guilty for leaving Celeste up at the house alone. *But that's how she wanted it from the beginning.* She managed a 'Thank you' when he stopped in front of the Tree Top. He stopped chewing the corner of his mustache long enough to manage a nod and a 'Yeah, sure.' Then he pulled off, leaving Ronnie alone with her misery.

After twelve hours of wrestling with the covers, Ronnie awoke feeling like bulldozed blacktop. Yesterday she'd had a half-day reprieve from her cramps, but they had returned and seemed to throb with every beat of her heart. She wanted to stay in bed, but she knew her sister would be all over her. So she pulled it together for another day at the Womack Museum.

She had debated her dilemma most of the night. She didn't know if she could face starting from scratch, clawing her way to bare bones survival so she could hang on to the edge by her fingernails a while longer, but the only solution she had hatched was to fess up, tell Celeste why she was in such a rush, how badly she needed the money, but as they passed Sunday morning not exchanging much more than terse 'excuse me's' and 'thank you's,' Ronnie couldn't fix her lips to lose that much face. The lectures alone would be endless, delivered in triumphant 'I told you so' glee that would confirm Ronnie had wasted the better part of two decades, and that was still too painful for her to admit.

Celeste engrossed herself in the details of other

people's lives. She found out the house was built in 1935 and that Odell and Ethiopia Womack were the first owners. Tucked in a tin box full of wooden thread spools she found papers for the sale of Mid-State Brickworks to a South Carolina company. Each new discovery gave her more ammunition for why it was so important that she stay and continue, more important than going home to face her own paperwork.

They stopped work early to freshen up for three o'clock, after-church supper at Lucille and Hambone's. Not that either Ronnie or Celeste was in the mood for a social call today, but these were old friends of their mother, and they *had* promised to come. That, and Hambone had reminded them every day, so there was no chance they could conveniently forget.

'That's the one.' Ronnie pointed at the single-story brick rectangle that looked to be modeled on a first grader's drawing of a house. 'It's so small. How in the world does he fit in there?'

'It's probably a tight squeeze,' Celeste said out of the corner of her mouth. As soon as the wheels hit the driveway, Hambone appeared on the steps. His red button-down shirt, matching suspenders, and white pants were a perfect complement to the tall red and white rosebushes, thick with flowers, that flanked the door.

'Y'all found us! See, I tol' you, Lucille!' He shouted and waved as he lumbered down the walk to greet them.

'Your directions were right on the money!' Ronnie waved the map he had drawn on the back of a restaurant place mat.

Lucille appeared at the door. 'I 'spec so. You 'bout worried 'em to death with instructions.' A ruffled pink apron protected her matching red and white ensemble. At Pal's, Hambone ruled the kitchen, but at chez Anderson, the cooking was Lucille's domain. It surprised most folks, but that's the way they'd done it for nearly fifty years. To look at her, skinny as she was, you wouldn't think she had an appetite at all, much less knew her way around a stove, but the truth was she loved to eat and could give Hambone a run for his money when it came to chowing down.

'Lord, Hambone, move outta the way and let 'em in the house!'

'I ain't stud'in' you.' But he moved aside and let Celeste walk past him. She was grateful to hear the drone of the air conditioning unit at the side of the house. Ronnie put her arm through his and they strolled up the path together.

'Come on in. I just made some sweet tea. 'Sides, it's much cooler in here.' She hugged them both and ushered them in where a grandfather clock that came within a hair's breadth of the ceiling filled the entryway. Around it family photos covered the wall: parents, kids, grands, and cousins, old black-and-whites and recent photo studio portraits smiled a warm reception that was continued by the sweet, buttery smells of scratch cake and homemade rolls, mingled with the scent of onion and savory spices.

'Is that Pal's famous fried chicken I smell?' Ronnie thought their invitation was sweet. There were people she'd known for years and they'd never had a meal together that didn't involve a waiter.

'Smothered chicken, but the buffalo fish is fried. And there's candied sweet potatoes, fresh tomatoes,

272

and okra, and snap beans from the garden, and . . .'

'She's makin' like she can cook.' Hambone winked conspiratorially.

'Proof is in the eatin'.' Lucille motioned them toward the living room. 'Make yourself to home. I'll be right back with the tea.'

And then they were engulfed by decor. Every inch of space in the room was accounted for. Celeste and Ronnie shuffled along the narrow aisle, past the large round glass and brass coffee table, and moved aside mounds of throw pillows, all in shades of green, to take seats on the ample leaf-patterned sofa.

Hambone plunked down in the big matching chair near the door. 'This is the first house we bought, and the last. We talked about movin' once upon a time, maybe someplace bigger, but no place else felt like home.'

'It's quite – impressive.' Celeste didn't know where to look first. Two end tables held cut crystal lamps and white china baskets full of nuts and candy. Brass etageres showcased porcelain figurines and hand-painted dishes. All sizes, shapes, and varieties of prints, from lounging tigers and still lifes with fruit and flowers, to frolicking brown cherubs and portraits of Dr King, J.F.K., and Jesus filled the walls so completely it was hard to tell what color the room was painted. And a riot of plants trailed, climbed, and flowered, covering the rows of glass shelves that stretched across the wide front window.

'Your mama was still here when we bought this place. Bet she wouldn't hardly recognize it now. Hmm. Seems to me I got a picture.' He raised himself up out of the chair and started searching a row of photo albums in a bookcase by the door. 'Her and

273

Will and Lester, out back – must be in one a these.'

'Goodness, let 'em get some refreshment 'fore you start draggin' out those old things.' Lucille appeared with a pitcher, an ice bucket, and four daisy-covered glasses on a tray. She sat on the love seat and poured while her husband kept searching. 'How're y'all makin' out at the house?'

'We were wondering about real estate prices in the area. I checked the *Observer*, but I didn't see any listings for Prosper.' Celeste sipped her tea and was surprised by the syrupy sweetness.

Come on. Not now. Ronnie knew she should be eager to hear the answer to this question, but she had so many other things to ask the Andersons. She settled into a corner of the sofa. 'Did you ever hear Ma sing?'

'Many a time. Couldn't nobody outsing Odella! Leastways not 'round here. And boy, she and Lester sure did sound good together.'

'Hambone!'

'I'm only tellin' her what she asked. Should I lie to the child?'

'No, but you could leave a few things for their mother to tell 'em.'

'I woulda thought they knew.'

'You mean the Lester we met in Pal's? He used to sing with Ma?' Ronnie leaned toward Hambone with anticipation.

'Yes indeedy.' He hooked a thumb in his suspenders, looking for a place to start. 'Truth is your mama and daddy and Lester were all friends.'

Celeste knitted her brows. He sounded like he was talking about some stranger, not her mother.

Lucille pursed her lips and looked over at Hambone.

274

'Henry too, for a time.' Hambone ignored Lucille's warning glance.

'And what happened to Uncle Henry?' Ronnie asked.

'I bet my macaroni and cheese is ready to come out the oven.' Odella and what she had and hadn't told her children was territory Lucille didn't want to get into over Sunday dinner. 'You two come on and help me put the food on the table. We'll sit down in a minute.'

Ronnie looked toward Celeste, but she looked away. 'Which way is the bathroom?' Ronnie asked.

'Come on, I'll show you.' Lucille led the way, her white vinyl bedroom slippers flapping against her heels. She pointed Ronnie down the hall.

Ronnie chuckled to herself when she eased open the door. The room, a riot of rain forest colors, was small and densely packed like the rest of the house. Nothing was left uncoordinated, uncovered, or unaccessorized. The purple toilet lid and tank covers matched the U-shaped rug in front of the bowl, which coordinated with the half circle in front of the sink, the bathmat on the floor, and the one draped over the side of the tub. A plastic peacock whose colorful plumage hid an extra roll of toilet paper sat on the counter next to a fuschia swan that held tiny soap eggs. Towel bars next to the vanity held guest towels, hand towels, and fingertip towels in alternating purpturq shades.

Ronnie tossed her purse on the counter, unbuckled her belt. *Hambone and Lucille are so nice – Ma must've missed—* Without warning, a white-hot pain, like a blowtorch flame, shot through her guts, doubled her in half, and dropped her to her knees in one fiery instant. *What the hell is happening?* She panted, quick and shallow, the air caught in a bubble between her throat and a scream she couldn't voice, then she rolled to her side. Ronnie'd had more pain than she cared to acknowledge for more than a year, but she never imagined it could turn into this.

The short fuzzy nap of the lavender rug tickled her nose, but she couldn't lift her head, couldn't move. Her agony pinned her in place. Curled in a fetal ball, fighting for the sliver of consciousness that remained, she prayed that someone would come or for the strength to make them.

The seconds felt endless as beads of sweat popped from her pores, evaporated on her fevered skin, leaving her shivering. *Celeste!* Her brain yelled. *Ma!* Ronnie's eyes darted, searching for a way to signal her distress. The door, with its crocheted knob cover, was little more than arm's length away, but Ronnie couldn't will her leg out straight to kick it. She held her breath and mustered enough energy to squirm and scoot, but she'd barely moved before she lost her breath to a gasp as the fire again seared her insides and brought with it a surge of nausea. She choked back the bitter liquid. *I won't lay here in my own puke.*

Then she spied the shelves above the toilet, crowded with jars of pastel powdered bubble bath, plastic tubs of multicolored, oil-filled beads, ceramic birds and flowers. *I can reach it if I just—* Clenching one fist tight to her belly and pressing her back against the tub for support, she strained to reach out an arm, hooked a finger around one of the support poles. She closed her eyes and pulled. The cabinet toppled into the tub.

276

In an instant Lucille burst into the bathroom. 'Oh, my Lord!' She knelt and dabbed at the sweat on Ronnie's face and neck with her apron. 'What happened? Where does it hurt you?' Jumbled fragrances perfumed the air with a sickening sweetness and a film of dusting powder blanketed the debris like early morning frost. Lucille swept away the rubble nearby until she could sit and put Ronnie's head in her lap.

Ronnie looked up at her and the tears seeped from the corners of her eyes. Help had arrived.

The crash brought Hambone right behind Lucille. 'What in the—' He stopped in the doorway, not sure if he should come in, or if this was one of those 'woman things' and they were going to chase him away.

'Grab one a them hand towels and run some cool water on it!' Lucille barked at her husband, then turned back to Ronnie. 'Are you pregnant?'

Ronnie's eyes widened. She gasped in another wave of pain and tried to grunt no. Hambone handed Lucille the wet towel and returned to the doorway.

'It's okay, honey. It's okay.' Lucille patted Ronnie's face with the damp terry cloth. 'Go get her sister. And call Doc Lomax. Don't stand there, George! Go!'

Celeste arranged the chicken on a platter in the kitchen. She heard the commotion but wasn't up for another of Ronnie's performances. She'd hear the story secondhand soon enough.

'Uh – It's Ronnie.' Hambone sounded shaken. 'She's sick or somethin'.'

'Sick?! Ronnie's not sick!' *What crap has she cooked up now?*

Hambone picked up the phone. 'I gotta call the doctor.'

'For goodness sake!' Celeste stomped toward the bathroom. *Still crying wolf.* Just like when they were kids, and she was convinced, even in the face of swollen glands or a fever, that Ronnie was faking some ailment so she could stay home from school and have Della fix her milk tea and raisin toast and make a big fuss. 'What is going on?' She reached the open door and saw Ronnie shivering on the floor, her skin ashen and gray, Lucille stroking her head, and she knew Ronnie wasn't faking.

Celeste felt faint and her heart started to pound. 'What—' She couldn't find enough words for a sentence. 'Ron—' She held on to the door. 'We have to . . .'

'Calm down. You can't help her like that,' Lucille warned. 'Is she allergic to anything?'

Celeste shook her head.

Lucille continued to dab Ronnie's forehead and neck with the damp towel. 'Did she eat something that could make her sick like this?'

Celeste shook her head again. 'I – I—' Then she shrugged her shoulders. 'I – uh – not that I . . .'

'Was she complainin' of anything?'

Celeste saw Ronnie at eight, trying her best to keep up with Celeste and her girlfriends who had decided to walk the six miles to All High Stadium and back one June Saturday, just because. Her parents made her take Ronnie, too. Rankled, Celeste just about wore everybody out, marching them double time. She left Main Street and paraded them the long way, up and down side streets, and while her friends complained, Ronnie never said a word in protest. She just did her little skip-hop-walk and tried to keep pace.

278

When they got back home, Ronnie's heels were blistered, her toes raw and bleeding.

She wouldn't tell me *if something was wrong.* 'No.' The sadness weighed heavy and the panic rose, just as Ronnie was engulfed by another wave of nausea, one she couldn't control. Celeste watched helplessly, able to respond only to Lucille's orders to moisten another towel while she rolled up the rug, dropped it in the tub, and began to peel Ronnie's soiled clothes off.

Hambone appeared in the doorway, then backed up, allowing Ronnie her modesty. 'Doc Lomax said take her to the hospital.' He spoke from the hall. 'I can do it fast as waitin' on the ambulance. She'll meet us there.'

'Get me one a your shirts, a robe, anythin' to put around her! We can't take her there half-nekked. And bring a blanket too.'

Ronnie's hair, wet from sweat, clung to her face. Lucille smoothed it back and cooed, 'There, there, child. It's gon' be fine. You hear me? You gon' be fine.' Hambone came back and thrust a red and blue striped bathrobe around the door. 'Celeste, help me get her into this.'

Lucille lifted Ronnie's torso and held her up long enough for Celeste to maneuver Ronnie's limp arms into the sleeves. She looked so small wrapped in Hambone's generous robe. Ronnie's eyes rolled, searching the room lethargically, until she focused on Celeste.

'Lessie, it hurts,' she whispered hoarsely, then her body went rigid, racked by another spike of pain.

Nobody had called her Lessie since she went on a tirade and refused to answer to it when she started high school. Celeste was lost and terrified, and she wanted Everett.

Anson County Hospital was twenty minutes away in Wadesboro. Hambone made it, door to door, in fourteen. Celeste sat beside Hambone, repeating, 'What am I gonna do?' over and over. Sitting in the backseat, Ronnie's head cradled in her lap, Lucille's soothing words were meant to calm everybody in the car. She was surprised by Celeste. She'd expected someone with that much gristle to be in complete control. Especially a doctor's wife.

Hambone carried Ronnie into the emergency entrance, where she was loaded onto a gurney and whisked away. Celeste searched Ronnie's purse for her insurance card and came up empty-handed.

She doesn't have any. To Celeste, not having health insurance was as inconceivable as going to the supermarket naked. The panic engulfed her again. 'She doesn't have insurance,' Celeste whispered to Lucille. 'I know she doesn't. What should I do?'

'You should call your mother.' Lucille sat next to Celeste in the nearly empty waiting room while Hambone paced. 'And *you* should sit 'fore you wear out these people's floor.'

'It's better if I keep movin'.' Hambone continued his journey to nowhere.

'I – I don't know. She didn't want us to come down here in the first place. It's not like she's going to die – you don't think she's going to die, do you?'

'No, child. She's not gonna die.' Lucille hoped. 'But she's real sick, and that's one a her babies. She wants to know. I'd want to know if it was one of mine. Wouldn't you?'

'She's not like that – you wouldn't understand . . .'

'Understand what? She's a mother whose child is in the hospital. None of the rest of it matters. She wants to know.'

Celeste sat bouncing her knees and wringing her hands. 'Maybe it's nothing serious. Why worry her if there's no reason?' She didn't look at Lucille, or at Hambone.

'Are you gon' call her, or am I?' Lucille asked.

14

'. . . a woman's rights and a daughter's guilt.'

'We'll be there directly.' Hambone sneaked a quick glance at Della, who nodded in response, then he returned his attention to the business of driving in the rain. After so many years, small talk felt awkward and shallow, the old banter and bicker out of place. So, unlike the road to the hospital in Wadesboro, which he knew in his sleep, the road to conversation was one he and Della hadn't traveled together for so long he didn't know the dips and curves, the yield signs and stop lights. The trip was a cautious, quiet hour.

Della stared out the window, impatient with the metronome beat, beat, beat of the wipers, anxious to be there. When she touched down in Charlotte, happy to be on the ground again, even if it *was* shaky, she expected it to look unfamiliar; she had never once been to this airport. But when they left the interstate, the old road she had traveled many times was unrecognizable too. It seemed smoother and wider, and where there had been a few barns and shanties and long stretches of nothing, now there were shopping centers, gas stations, fast-food franchises, a lot like Buffalo, really. Della knew the way, nonetheless. Just like she'd known Hambone as soon as she saw him. He recognized her immediately too. Waistlines had expanded, hair had grayed, time lines had etched their faces, and their shoulders stooped a bit from the weight of responsible lives, but the years hadn't physically changed either one enough to make them strangers. Each saw who the other had once been.

Last night, when the phone rang after midnight, Della put aside her game of solitaire and muted the TV. She had a gruff hello and some choice words on the tip of her tongue for whoever was so careless about dialing the phone so late at night, because this had to be a wrong number. No one in their right mind would call her at that hour.

'Odella?' Hearing that name, her name, it was like being grabbed by the scruff of her neck and snatched back forty years. Nobody, not even Will, had called her that since they left. 'Odella, this is—' Della recognized Lucille's chickadee squeak from the first three words because some things you don't forget, even when you close the door and think you've thrown away the key.

'Odella, ain't no good way to tell you,' Lucille began. 'We had to take your Ronnie to the hospital.' Right then it was like Della's world cleaved and she split in two; one Della dazed, in agonized disbelief, only able to watch as the other became hyperaware, decisive, methodically doing what needed to be done.

Ronnie's in the hospital.

The only other time Ronnie was in the hospital, Della had been right there too, and she had borne the brunt of the suffering. The first labor pain came while she was eating breakfast, a grilled cheese sandwich on raisin bread with a Kosher dill and orange juice. Della had been scared the first time, but now she knew what

283

it was, so she called Will at work and made arrangements for Celeste to be picked up after school. She finished her sandwich in the car with Will teasing her that this was gonna be one eating child because Della started eating the moment she found out she was pregnant and still hadn't stopped. Della looked up at the clock when she heard the first cry. It was 12:34 P.M. The doctor said it had been almost two days, and she'd lost track of how long she'd been trying to bring this baby into the world. But when her daughter, bald and squirming, grinned at her then nestled into her chest, Della forgot all the pain. She sang softly, just for the two of them, 'You are my sunshine, my only sunshine—'

Will wanted to name her Willa, or Willie Mae, since it didn't look like he was getting a son, but Della knew her name from that first meeting. Veronica. Veronica Lucille.

Della wrote the information Lucille gave her in the margins of a newspaper, struggling to keep her hand steady, to get it all down correctly. She asked if Celeste was all right and Lucille assured her she'd look after both her girls until Della could get there. A hazy fog crept in and cushioned the space around part of her, but the other part steered clear so she could think. This was a call she hadn't gotten before. For Della, it was always sudden, final. Her mother, her father, Will. No opportunity to comfort or be comforted. No farewells. This was different. Ronnie was in the hospital. The fog swirled around Della, made everything soft, but she wouldn't fall. This time it wouldn't hurt. And although she wasn't a religious woman, she knew God wouldn't offer her this chance, then wrench it away.

Ronnie will be all right.

But Della had to go. What else could she do?

Ronnie will be all right.

What else could she think? Not about her vow never to return. Not that her heart and her spirit were broken in Prosper. Not about how fervently she wished Will had dumped the place on Little Pond and saved her from this journey. And certainly not about the fact that from the moment Celeste stormed into her room waving that deed she knew no good would come from it.

So she made her first ever plane reservations. Climbed the attic stairs to get one of the brand-new suitcases Will ordered for their retirement. He had said, 'We gon' go *some*where, Della. Like you used to talk about.' Della was calm as she dug in the back of the closet to find the suits and dresses, tags still attached, that Celeste had bought her over the years. She remembered the suit with the fox fur collar she had on the day she left Prosper. How she thought she looked good and that gave her confidence. It didn't matter what she wore to the DMV or to CVS, but this was different. How she looked after a forty-year absence mattered. She didn't leave to do bad. Della packed and puttered until dawn. Then she called her job, notified her neighbors, stopped the paper, set the timer for the lights, and when the taxi came, she locked the door behind her.

'We're here.' Hambone slid the car between two others in the lot. The Anson County Hospital building was new, modern, and nothing like the place where they took her father, even though he was already dead. No 'colored' section. No separate door.

Della picked at a speck of lint on the sleeve of her

navy suit jacket. *Ronnie will be fine*. Hambone heaved himself out of the car, reached in the backseat, and grabbed an umbrella. *Open the door. Get out.* But she sat there gripping the handle. Hambone came around and opened it for her, stood a moment in the rain, not sure whether to extend his hand or wait, but Della couldn't make herself move. Then, clear as day, she felt a shove. She looked over her shoulder, but she knew no one was there. Hambone held the umbrella over her as she finally climbed out. Della looked back in the car, then up at the hospital. And just before the past and the present collided, the fog drifted in, offered its cushion once again, and she moved forward. Her steps were slow but sure. *Ronnie will be fine.* What else could she think?

'Mother.' Celeste looked rumpled. Tired. Her features even more pinched than usual. She met Della and Hambone at the elevator. Celeste grabbed both of her mother's hands, and Della was surprised by how cold they were. 'She's fine. They're bringing her back from recovery.' Her voice wavered a bit and she spoke more to herself than to her mother. The corridor bustled around them. Della, still in Celeste's icy grip, stepped aside to make way for a technician rolling a portable EKG machine. 'The operation was – it was only a cyst.'

'Let's go down the hall,' Hambone said, and they followed, still holding hands, to the waiting room where he, Lucille, and Celeste had camped all night.

Della eased herself into a chair. 'What kinda cyst?'

Celeste perched on the edge of the chair next to her. 'It had wrapped itself around her ovary. Seems it must've been there a while. But she's fine.'

'I been tellin' Odella, your mama, that she was gon' be fine the whole way here.' Hambone shoved his hands awkwardly in his pants pockets and looked around. 'Lucille? She go down for some coffee?' He took them out again and hooked his thumbs on his suspenders.

'Oh, I'm sorry, I forgot. No. She got a ride home to shower and change. She'll be back soon. And – uh – thanks for going to get Mother,' Celeste said.

'No trouble. No trouble at all.' Hambone busied himself at the window.

'I called Everett, and he talked to the doctors.' After they finished examining Ronnie, the doctors explained her condition and said surgery was the only option at this point. Lucille prompted Celeste to call Everett. She managed to pull herself together long enough to leave urgent, detailed messages on the machine at home and on his service, hoping he hadn't left for Portugal already. He called back within fifteen minutes, got as much information as she could offer before speaking with Dr Lomax and the surgeon who would perform the operation. Everett told her that any kind of surgery is a serious matter, but that Ronnie's procedure was not unusual and that it sounded like she was in capable hands. He didn't think it was necessary, but he offered to fly down, even if it meant postponing his vacation. She said she'd let him know. Everett was confident, reassuring. And although talking to him made her feel better, there was no reason for him to cancel his vacation. After their last conversation, Celeste wasn't up to facing him yet under the best of circumstances. Definitely not while handling her mother and Ronnie too. Not yet.

'Ma?' Ronnie blinked, trying to focus, trying to be awake. The urge to keep her eyes closed and drift back to sleep, to that dark, quiet cocoon she had just come from, was overwhelming.

'Shh.' Della kissed Ronnie's forehead and smoothed the tangled mess of hair. She could never explain how glad she was to see Ronnie, to talk to her, to feel her cool, dry skin beneath her lips, to smell her stale, sour breath. Celeste stood at the foot of the bed, holding on to Ronnie's feet through the sheet and watching a ritual she'd seen dozens of times. If she thought about it hard enough, Celeste could recall countless incidents of Della tending to Ronnie in the same exacting detail she cataloged them in. She expected the old familiar anger – and jealousy, that's what it was, but this time it wasn't there. This time Celeste was grateful as she slipped out of the room and left them alone.

'You didn't have to come.' Ronnie's voice was hoarse and scratchy, her lips chapped. *How can I be glad you did and wish you hadn't at the same time?* 'I know you didn't want . . .'

'Hush.' Della gently patted Ronnie's arm.

Never in her life had Ronnie felt so exhausted. Her arms were weary from holding up the walls. The roof had become too heavy to balance on her head. Her feet were bogged down in the muddy foundation. Ronnie's house of illusion had crumbled. She took a breath and forced her eyes to stay open. 'I'm so sorry – I didn't mean to . . .'

'You didn't get sick on purpose, did you?' Della teased and stroked her cheek.

Ronnie shook her head and started to speak. Her

288

mouth was so dry that her lips stuck to her teeth in a grimace. The words were stuck too, but she had to tell her mother. *I can't pretend anymore.*

'Does it hurt you?' Della watched the IV drip.

Yeah. It hurts. Ronnie could see the worry on her mother's face. She tried to lick her lips. 'I'm a little sore, but it's okay, they gave me a shot.' Della opened a glycerine swab and rubbed it across Ronnie's lips. 'Ma – I didn't mean for this to happen.' *I really didn't. This isn't the way any of it's supposed to turn out.* Ronnie felt a tiny swell of nausea, the truth bubbling in her throat, and she turned her head away.

'Of course you didn't.' Della cupped Ronnie's chin and turned her face back.

'But – you don't understand.' Ronnie swallowed hard. 'Ma – I – I can't pay for this – for anything—' *There. I said it.* 'I don't have any insurance. Haven't for – ever. It's been so hard. I – don't have anything.' She held her breath and waited. For so long Ronnie had believed this revelation would stop the world from spinning, but it didn't. That she would be hurled into space, alone and adrift, but she wasn't. Della was still beside her bed. Ronnie blinked again, this time she was awake, but she wanted to slow down the tears that welled up from deep inside.

'I know.'

'How? How did you . . .'

'I been guessing you had your struggles for years. Didn't know about the insurance. Celeste told me when I got here. That's plain foolishness, Ronnie. Pride is one thing, actin' stupid is another.'

Her mother was right. She had no defense for how stupid she'd been. 'I'm so sorry, Ma.'

'I'll take care of your bill, so don't lay there worryin'

about that now. Or maybe I should let them keep you behind this mess.'

'I'll pay you back. I promise I will.' And the tears came. 'I'm so sorry.'

'We'll figure all that out when you're better.'

In the flood, Ronnie couldn't distinguish the release from the relief. And while she cried until she couldn't anymore, Della fought back her own tears. *I knew she'd be all right. Thank you, Lord. Thank you.*

When Ronnie was asleep, Della, full of the anger she held onto until she knew Ronnie was safe, went down the hall to find Celeste. *If they had stayed where they belonged, none of this would be happenin'.* She'd give Celeste a piece of her mind first. *That girl never did understand leaving well enough alone.* Ronnie would get her piece when she was feeling better. But the same unseen hand that pushed Della out of Hambone's car, now snatched her, like a choke chain. She pulled up short next to the cart where an attendant stacked lunch trays. And before she turned the corner into the waiting room, she knew he was there. *I don't need this mess now.* She felt the deep, piercing vibration, like a tuning fork, like she hadn't felt in a long, long time. At the airport she had recognized Hambone at first glance, but she didn't have to see Lester to know he was there. She could feel him, just like she used to.

WEDNESDAY, APRIL 17, 1957
PROSPER, NORTH CAROLINA

Odella sat on the old hickory stump at the edge of the pond, hunched over her history book, deep in the

290

throes of the Industrial Revolution. There were six weeks left until the end of the term and then only one more year until graduation. 'Come on out, Lester, or whatever you're callin' yourself this week!' She never looked up from her book. Four years of singing with Lester taught her to tune in to him, where he wanted to take a song, where she should go in response. After a while, she discovered that she was pretty much always locked in to whatever frequency he was on whether she wanted to be or not. 'I know you're out there. You should quit tryin' to sneak up on me 'cause you ain't never gon' do it.'

Lester stepped through the bushes, one hand sagged in his pocket, the other holding a bottle of RC Cola. 'I been here at least five minutes, and you didn't know squat.' He'd been unable to slip through Odella's radar since the day she first honed in on him. Today was no different.

She slipped a Beechnut wrapper between the pages to mark her place, closed her book, and looked up at him. 'You a lie, Lester Wilson. You know well as I do you just got here.'

He couldn't figure out how she did it. This time he even took a different path down to the lake, careful not to step on a twig or snap any branches. He moved only when the breeze rustled through the trees. She couldn't have heard him.

''Sides, I thought you had somewheres to go.' She started to swing her long legs, then stopped and tugged the skirt of her plaid cotton dress over her knees. The impulse to show off waged its newly declared battle against her urge to cover herself up. Lately, Lester made her feel that way, and she didn't know why. She wished her mama was around so she could ask, because she could never fix her lips to ask Miz Ethiopia about stuff like that. *Maybe I can ask Lucille.*

'I do. Tonight. But Titus ain't that far.' Lester bent down, got himself a glimpse of leg, then picked up a handful of stones.

Since he finished high school, Lester had been looking for a way to get out of Prosper. He even moved back to Charlotte for a little while but reappeared after two months with no explanation. Odella had missed him, a lot, but she'd rather die than admit it. So she just shrugged her shoulders and met him as usual before choir practice and they picked up their rehearsals for the Easter Pageant exactly where they left off.

'Well, with that ol' piece a junk you drivin' it might be farther than you think. You best be startin' early.' Odella clasped her book to her chest, crossed her legs at the ankles.

Between Lester's odd jobs around town, helping out anybody who needed an extra hand, what he got from the churches where he sang for special programs and his 'gigs' as he called his performances at juke joints around south central North Carolina, he'd managed to buy an old Studebaker that looked like scrap metal, but it ran pretty good.

'Least it's mine.' He took a slug of RC, put the bottle on the ground.

'Nobody else fool enough to buy it.'

'I worked out my own arrangement of "Blueberry Hill".' He ignored her last comment and plunged into the reason he'd tracked her down, because as much as they sparred, he trusted Odella's opinion and her ear. They were used to reworking songs since most of the gospel songs and spirituals they sang were arranged for quartets like the Pilgrim Travelers or the Soul Stirrers, not for duets. 'I'm doin' it tonight, but I want you to hear it.' He tossed a rock into the pond and it made a soft *blop*. 'I'm gon' be outta here soon. Goin' all the way to the top.' He punctuated every sentence with a stone's throw. 'That's right. I'm gon' get me a record deal, be a star. See the places you been readin' about in them books, then come back and buy me a big piece a land, like the one your daddy got, for when I'm in between tours. You wait and see!'

'Uh-huh.' But Odella believed him, believed in him. She was sure that when he left for good he was gonna keep going, like the ripples in the pond, and she wanted to go too.

'You should come with me one a these times.' He sat next to her on the stump. 'Do some real singin'. With a real live audience.'

'I will – Soon.' She hated it when Lester was this close to her. It made her tingle, like when they sang harmony, except it wouldn't stop. When they were singing, she could control it better because she had something besides him to concentrate on. But this was like sitting next to him on the front seat of his raggedy car when he gave her a ride home from choir practice. She'd pretend they were boyfriend and girl-friend, like in the movies, or even married like Lucille and Hambone, until she'd remind herself that Lester and Will were like her brothers, the ones she wished she had instead of Henry. Besides, she'd watched the women in church watching Lester. They'd start to twitch in their seats, feeling spirit before he even opened his mouth. Young ones and old

293

alike were particularly fond of Lester's brand of cocoa. He'd gone with Eula Mae Dyson and Marvella Cox, the two prettiest girls at George Washington Carver High School, but he told Odella he wasn't looking to make some girl pregnant, ruin his big chance, and end up stuck in Prosper doing odd jobs for the rest of his life to support a bunch of snaggle-tooth kids. Said he wanted somebody smart, a girl who wanted more than a man to take care of her.

But Odella didn't fool herself. She had a good shape, all right. Even in her school clothes, she couldn't walk to town and back without commentary, but it wasn't enough. Pretty counted and she came up short. She knew she could make it better. Lucille had shown her how to put on lipstick and powder, but Odella stopped her when she wanted to pluck her eyebrows. She knew her stepmother wouldn't approve; she could feel Miz Ethiopia's withering gaze. She could wash her face before she went home, but she couldn't make the hair grow back, and pencil-drawn lines would only make it worse.

Odella clutched her book tighter. 'But right now you know I can't be goin' to no honky-tonks. I can't even go to Pal's no more.' This wasn't a new conversation, and it always turned out the same way. She wanted to see inside of one of those places with dim lights and hip-shaking music, to see if it was as exciting as Lester made it sound. Listening to him talk made her want to sing in front of an audience that wasn't filled with old ladies wearing ugly hats. She wanted to wear a pretty dress or maybe even an evening gown that Lester helped her pick out, to hear people clap for her, to leave Prosper and not look back. But she wished her mother was alive and they still lived in Cadysville, and she knew that couldn't happen either.

Not that she didn't have a voice. Folks raved about Odella Womack's singing. Her father even told her she sounded better than most of the singers he heard on the radio. She wanted to broach the subject of singing someplace other than church with him, but he stayed so busy at the brickyard, and when he came home he mostly ate dinner and went to bed, so she hadn't found the right time. As a matter of fact, Della never saw him look happy anymore, the way he used to when he was with Annie. He never sat on the porch with his wife on his knee or held her hand like Della used to sneak and watch him and Annie do. And the longer she'd been gone, the more distant he seemed from life on Little Pond Road.

Besides, she figured Henry had pretty much put the kibosh on her chances anyway. One Sunday morning, early, when she was coming downstairs with her white choir robe, she heard him telling his mother what a shame it was about the new jukebox in Pal's. Della knew he did it to spite her, probably for getting on so well with Hambone and Lucille, and with *his* friends Will and Lester. And right on cue Miz Ethiopia started her sermon. Said it was a sin and a shame they were playing that music at Pal's. They had been such nice young people, she said. Odell had walked by and said he thought they were smart. It would be good for business. 'Give colored folks in Prosper somethin' to do besides sit on the porch complainin',' he had said. But Henry reminded his mother how much time Odella spent with Lucille. Odella wanted to interrupt, but before she could, her stepmother told Odell that she thought it would be a good idea if Odella came straight home after she got her hair done from now on. No more hanging around the beauty parlor or the lunch counter because they would be attracting all kinds of lowlifes with that music. Odella could hear Miz Ethiopia giving her father one of her looks. She'd seen them often enough to know what they sounded like. Her father changed the subject, and that was that.

Odella was crushed. Lucille was only six years older than she was, but in many ways she reminded her of Annie. They didn't look alike unless you counted that neither one was bigger than a minute, but Lucille had the same way of making Odella want to be around her because that's where the fun was. Hambone obviously thought so too. He finished high school two years before Henry did and went into the army, which is where he learned to cook. Just before he was discharged, he wrote and asked her to marry him. Lucille still had the letter. Until Hambone and Lucille, Odella hadn't known any married people who were young and still had fun. And even though she argued with Hambone even more than Lester, Odella loved being around them and their new baby. But when Miz Ethiopia told her not to dawdle after she got her hair done, Odella obeyed even though she wanted to listen to Sonny Till and the Orioles and Johnny Ace on that big Wurlitzer more than anything. Lester and Will had told her that you put a nickel in the slot, and music filled up the whole restaurant and the beauty shop next door, like the Platters were actually there. But she never put herself between her father and his wife, ever. And since Henry cured her of playing the kind of music she wanted to on the piano, she'd lock her door, turn on the radio in her room real low so nobody else could hear, and dream about her and Lester having a hit record.

'Ask Mr Womack. He knows I'll look out for you.' Lester offered Odella his bottle of soda.

She took a drink and handed it back to him. 'When I'm ready. And *you* can't hardly look after yourself.'

'You ready now, and you know you wanna come with me. All the time talkin' 'bout gettin' outta here. Where you gon' go by yourself? You and me, we could make it big.' Lester ran his index finger down the length of her forearm and stopped at her wrist.

'Am I gon' hear this song or just hear *about* it?' Odella pushed him off the tree stump and hoped he didn't feel her tremble at his smooth touch.

'Hey.' Will ducked under a low hickory branch and stepped into the clearing. 'Sorry I ain't had a chance to get cleaned up, Odella, but I jus' now left the job.' Will took off his cap, nodded, and brushed red dust from his overalls. He and Henry worked at the brick-yard, although Odella suspected Will did most of the working and Henry just tried to boss people around.

'You through slavin' for today?' Lester took another swig of soda.

'Hell yeah. Shoot. I gotta get outta here. My cousin Melvin moved to Buffalo, New York. Got him a good-payin' job at the steel plant. If I'm gon' sweat, might as well be for good money.' Will reached in his bib pocket and handed Odella a five-cent Butterfinger. 'Here, I brought you this.'

'Mmm.' Odella zipped off the paper, started to take a bite, then looked up at Will. 'You want some?'

'No. If I did, I'd a got me one.' Will jammed his

hands in his overall pockets and shifted his weight from one foot to the other.

'You didn't offer me.' Lester folded his arms across his chest.

'You right, I didn't.' Odella took a big bite and licked her lips in his direction.

'Ain't stud'n' you.' Lester sucked his teeth.

'If you still goin' to Titus, I'll go with you, Lester.'

'Cool,' Lester said. 'See! Ol' Will here wasn't goin' tonight, but looks like he changed his mind. Maybe you'll change yours. I been tryin' to get Odella to do one a these gigs with me, but she won't even ask her daddy can she.'

'Odella don't need to be doin' no gig. Them kinda joints ain't no place she should be singin', and if you had any sense you'd know that.'

'Man, you don't get it. We could be big time, me and Odella.'

'She doin' jus' fine like she is. Odella don't . . .'

'When y'all finished decidin' what I need to do with my life –' Odella stood and put her hands on her hips. '– Maybe you'll sing the song!' She spoke to Lester, 'I ain't got all night.'

Lester cleared his throat, and Will sat on the stump Odella vacated.

'Ladies and gentlemen, pre-senting Johnny DuPree!!'

'Who?' Odella started to giggle. This was at least the fourth stage name he'd come up with in the last year, but he knew for sure Lester Wilson had to go. 'Move.' She bonked Will over with her hip and sat beside him on the stump. He reached his arm around her. His hands felt rough and scratchy. 'Move your ol' heavy arm, Will.' She shrugged it off.

'You heard me,' he said defiantly. 'I like it. Johnny DuPree. It's the best one yet. It sounds like a star, don't it, Will?'

'It just sound made-up to me, Lester.' Will scraped mud off his boots with a stick.

'Well, I like it,' Odella decided. And so it stayed.

The lunch cart was nowhere in sight when Della finally gathered herself. She stood up tall and rounded the corner. Celeste stood at the far end of the waiting room, talking to him. His back was to the door. He was still long and lean, like a lickin' stick, Hambone used to say, like the last time she saw him. He'd let his hair go back to natural. Della had never liked it conked.

'Mother. I don't know if –'

Lester turned around.

He told me the truth and I didn't believe him. Della continued walking, trying to keep her steps in a straight line.

'– You know Mr Wilson. Ronnie and I met him at Pal's. He came to see if there was anything he could do.'

I can do this. 'Lester.' Della adjusted her purse on her shoulder then held out her hand.

'Odella.' He clasped her hand but didn't shake it. 'It's been a long while.' Then he let go.

'Yes. It has.' Della jammed the hand he released into her jacket pocket and hoped he didn't feel her tremble. His hands were still soft, like they used to be. And he still had that kinda bowlegged stance, with his shoulders leaned back just a touch so you were drawn into him. She thought he'd come pretty close to fitting in one of those narrow, royal blue suits he used to favor, back in the day, with the black shirt and skinny tie and 'JD' in rhinestones on the tie tack. Della wasn't surprised by the earring in his ear. Somehow, it suited him.

'I'm glad your daughter will be all right. I was telling Celeste here that if you-all needed anything, to just call. I saw Lucille this morning. She told me what happened – she didn't say you were coming, though.'

Oh, she didn't, did she? 'Must have slipped her mind.'

'That would be a first.' Lester flashed her a smile. They both knew Lucille's forgetfulness was no accident, but both Della and Lester let the oversight pass. The situation was strained enough. 'You look good, Odella. The years must have been kind to you.'

'Umph.' Della looked down at her hands. She knew what was in the mirror. There had been a change of seasons since she saw him thirty years ago. She was in her summer then. Ripe, bold, confident, but *wrong*, so very wrong about him. These were the short, cold days of winter. The ones that made summer a haunting memory. But she *was* glad she had worn one of those suits Celeste paid too much money for.

He looked down at his shoes then back at her. 'Uh – sorry to hear about Will.'

Will. She wanted to blame him for their standing here like strangers, but that train left the station too many years ago to try and catch it now. She fidgeted with the zipper pull on her bag. 'Yes. It was mighty sudden.' *I can do this.* 'Lester, last time we spoke I said some things . . .'

'No need, Della.' He waved her off quietly. 'You

300

didn't know.' He looked at her for an instant, then looked off.

Celeste scrutinized their faces, hoping for a clue to the meaning of their coded conversation, but she didn't find one.

Lester cleared his throat. He didn't know what else to say. 'I better get going. And remember, if y'all need help with anything—' He nodded and left.

Della sank into a chair, tried not to watch him walk away. She'd been up all night, been on an airplane for the first time in her life, her daughter, who had no health insurance, just had an emergency operation. Talking to Lester used up what little juice Della had left.

'What was that about?' Celeste took the seat across from her mother.

'Huh?' Della said, distracted.

'You and Mr Wilson. It looked to me like . . .'

'And give me one reason I should care what it looks like to you.' Della glared at Celeste, then picked up a *Reader's Digest* from the end table next to her.

Celeste looked surprised. 'That's a hideous thing to say.'

Della flipped through a few pages until she found the middle was stuck together with a wad of gum. 'If you hadn't started this – You just had to come down here meddlin' in stuff you don't know nothin' about.' She threw the magazine back on the table.

'That's it exactly. There's a whole part of your life I don't know anything about. That you've been keeping some deep dark secret. But whatever it is, that makes it a part of my life! Ronnie's too,' she added as an afterthought.

'Look what it got you!' Della knew it wasn't Celeste's fault Ronnie got sick and that it would have happened whether she was in Prosper or New York City. But Celeste, already treading on territory where she had no business, was now in knee-deep and Della had no intention of being pulled into the mire with her. 'Ever since you were a little girl, you've been tryin' to fix stuff that wasn't broken. Trying to make everything better. Neater. Prettier. Straighter. And that includes me.'

'Mother, your voice.' Celeste didn't see this one coming, so she wasn't prepared to duck.

Della got louder. 'Well I got news for you, Celeste Anne English, some things are fine the way they are. They don't need no help from you.' Della paused to take a breath. 'If you wanna fix somethin', try fixin' the mess you made of your marriage.'

Celeste was stunned. 'You have no idea what you're talking about.' How could her mother know her secret? She had no right.

'Don't sit up in my face and lie to me, Celeste. Everett took me out to dinner, to make sure I knew that even if you two divorce I can always count on him like a son. Do you have any idea how I felt, sittin' up there like a simpleton? You'd think my own child would tell me . . .'

'I am not your *child*, Mother!' The words exploded out of Celeste's mouth. 'I am a grown woman, and what goes on in my house is my business!' And just like a boomerang, those words came back and dropped in her ear in Ronnie's voice. She had argued with her sister then, told her she had never been a mother and that she was wrong. Of course your child is always your child, she had said, but she was reacting

302

like a mother that day. Right now she was feeling like a daughter.

Della's expression shifted in a rainbow of emotion from outrage to hurt. Without another word, she pushed herself out of the chair, turned her back and walked away, leaving Celeste stranded, between a woman's rights and a daughter's guilt.

15

'. . . the fan was on, they just weren't
sure when the shit would hit.'

On the ride back to the Tree Top after visiting hours,
Celeste and Della chitchatted with Hambone as
necessary but didn't say a word to each other. He had
arranged for one of his kitchen crew to deliver
Celeste's rental car back to the motel. When he asked
if they wanted to stop at Pal's for dinner, Celeste said
they were too tired.

'Y'all must be hungry.' Hambone patted his
belly in sympathy. 'Least we can stop for some
takeout.'

'Ah – Sure. Thanks.' It suited Celeste fine because
her jaw was too set to actually chew in public.

'Uh-huh. That's fine.' Della had had enough of
everybody for one day.

As they entered Prosper proper, the rain that had
welcomed Della home earlier in the day started up
again, and she dropped out of the conversation.
Through the misty drizzle, she eyed the town she
hadn't seen in a lifetime. Some that was old remained,
like the town hall and the square, but she found

herself superimposing the old upon the new. She didn't realize how jarring it all was until Hambone parked and she looked out at the cool blue neon Pal's sign.

'You used to be . . .'

'Yep. Cross, over there.' He pointed. 'Lucille still is. The whole street got renovated in the seventies. They built this side new, so we took advantage and did some expandin'. Whatchu want?'

'Somethin' good, Hambone. Somethin' good.' Della gazed across the street. All the storefronts were modern, with plate-glass windows and professional signs. 'You still make barbecue sandwiches?'

'With my sweet and sassy sauce that's so good it makes you lick your fingers and shiver?' Hambone did a little shimmy behind the wheel. 'It's one of our specialties. Still make the sauce myself. Should I make that two?'

Celeste nodded.

Della hadn't thought about those sandwiches, piled high with tender shreds of pork shoulder, since she stopped thinking about Prosper. While Hambone went inside, Della looked across shiny wet asphalt at the storefront where the restaurant used to be. Above the new facade was a black awning that read 'Lucille's Beauty Studio' in gold script. But what she recalled was the big board that Lucille had carefully lettered PAL'S in green paint with black trim around it that used to decorate the old window. And in the bottom left-hand corner of that window had been a little sign: 'Shampoo, Press & Curl, $2.00.' The patter of rain on the car even sounded the way it used to on Pal's corrugated tin roof.

305

'So where you say you singin' tomorrow afternoon?'
Lucille dabbed at the yellow grease on the back of her
hand, smoothed a fingerful onto a section of Odella's
hair.

'Mount Calvary. Over in Titus. You and Hambone
should come. It ain't but about an hour away.'

'I just might do that, but you know I have a hard
enough time gettin' that man to one church service,
much less two!' Lucille pulled the curling iron from
the stove, clanked it open and closed a few times, then
tested the temperature on the burn-stained white
towel folded on the counter.

'Why they like that? Even Papa's that way. Miz
Ethiopia makes him go to church. She don't never say
nothin' about it in front of me. Well, she don't have
much to say to me no way 'less it's to bawl me out,
but I know she's the only reason he goes. I mean he
likes my singin' and all, but most Sundays I watch him
with his head down, sound asleep when Reverend
Garland's preachin'.' Odella twisted her head slightly
and tried to sneak a peek at what Lucille was doing.

'Hold still 'fore I burn you. I'm almos' finished.
Then you can look all you want.'

'Okay.' Odella slumped back in her chair. The
cloudy, secondhand glass propped up on the counter
didn't offer a clear image under the best conditions.
On a rainy, dreary afternoon like this one, the most
she would get was an idea of what she looked like.

Lucille clamped the hot iron onto a hunk of
Odella's hair. The grease sizzled and tendrils of smoke
drifted toward the ceiling. 'You'd probably sleep

durin' them sermons too, exceptin' you're sittin' up there in the choir where everybody can see you!' She set the iron back beside the burner. 'That should do it. I can comb you out, but with all this rain, you might wanna do it yourself tomorrow.'

'You can go ahead and style it.' Lester was comin' by this evenin' so they could rehearse one more time. 'It'll be all right.'

Lucille pulled a rat-tailed comb through Odella's hair and began to arrange the curls. 'You got a rain scarf?'

'No. I got a new umbrella, though. One of them fancy ones with the ruffles around the outside.'

'That's mighty nice, but ain't nothin' like a good rain scarf. Wind'll blow water right under that umbrella.' Lucille unfastened the plastic cape around Odella's shoulders, and her tone became very professional. 'I always recommend them to my customers.'

'That's 'cause you sellin' 'em.' Odella couldn't miss the cardboard display leaning against the mirror with the small plastic envelopes stapled to it. 'Lucille, you ain't even slick.' Odella examined her hairdo. The way Lucille styled it, with a wave in the front that kind of dipped down over one eye, it looked grown up. Just like she wanted it to. She reached in her pocketbook for her change purse and the three dollar bills her father had given her. 'But I will take one, just in case.'

'Always better to be safe than sorry.' Lucille tugged one of the packets free, handed it to Odella, then counted out eighty-five cents change from the metal box on the counter.

'See you tomorrow.' Odella thought about putting the scarf on, but she decided it wasn't raining *that* hard and she didn't want to mash her hair down, so she tucked it and her change into her purse, grabbed her umbrella from the corner by the door, and left.

Strolling up Albermarle Avenue, Odella twirled her umbrella like a parasol and wondered if Lester would say her hair looked nice. Lost in a daydream about the two of them singing on a gospel radio show some day, she sailed along toward home.

'Wait up!'

Odella heard him, but she didn't turn around.

'Hey! You hear me! Wait up!'

Henry was the only person in all of Prosper who never, ever called her by name. He just said what he had to *at* her.

Odella quickened her pace. She didn't want any trouble with Henry. She just wanted to get to the house. She took a deep breath when she heard his heavy footfalls splash behind her.

'You can't be hoggin' that whole umbrella for yourself.' He poked his head under the rim. 'I'll be soaked through 'fore I get home.'

Jammed up next to her in his dungaree jacket and overalls, Henry smelled musty, like old cigarettes and not enough soap. She knew he'd been at the brickyard for at least half the day. Where he was coming from now she couldn't say. He didn't hang with Will and Lester much anymore, so they weren't likely to be around to bail her out. 'There ain't room under here for two people, Henry!' Odella protested.

'Then it won't be me gettin' wet.' Henry grabbed the handle and pulled the umbrella in his direction.

'Stop!' She jerked it back. 'I just got my hair done!'

'Like that's gon' make you pretty?' He snatched the umbrella and ran ahead.

308

'Gimme that back!' Odella caught up and lunged for him, but he danced out of reach. 'Come on, Henry!' She held her purse over her head as she chased him, but she could feel her hair starting to melt, her wave drooping down over her eye.

'You want it so bad—' He skipped backward, holding the umbrella out then yanking it away when she reached for it. 'Beg me.'

Mad tears washed Odella's face. She was just glad he couldn't see them in the rain. 'Hell with you!' She stopped running and hunted in her purse for the rain scarf.

'Then I guess you'll be a nappy-headed jigaboo singin' in church tomorrow! Let's see how Lester likes that.' Henry laughed as he trotted ahead, tossing the umbrella in the air and catching it.

Odella fumbled with the accordion pleats of the plastic scarf, feeling like it was already too late. She covered her head but pulled the ties so tight that one popped off, so she walked the rest of the way home holding it together under her chin, the rain dripping down her sleeve and blowing around her.

When she got to Little Pond she saw that Henry had abandoned the umbrella, opened upside down, under the azalea bush. One of the spokes poked through the fabric. She grabbed it and shuffled up the porch steps, trying to smooth it closed, trying not to make any noise. As mad as she was she just wanted to get upstairs to her room and assess the damage before crossing Miz Ethiopia's path.

Odella eased open the hall door. The house smelled like burnt fish. Her father's wife never seasoned anything enough and she cooked it to death. Two steps in Odella squeezed the door shut.

'Is that you, Odella?' Miz Ethiopia called from the kitchen in her prickly voice. 'It's about time you got home.'

Odella could hear her approaching. She wanted to hide, but the floor didn't open up and swallow her in time.

'It doesn't take that long to get – What in the world?!' Miz Ethiopia's withering look cut Odella to the quick.

Water trickled from Odella's hair and ran down her neck and her temples. Her clothes were wet down to her bra and panties. She knew it was pointless to mount a defense. It was Saturday evening, which meant her father had already been home, cleaned up, had supper, and was on his way. He wouldn't be back until well past her bedtime, and he was her only prayer of being heard. Henry could do no wrong as far as his mother was concerned. Now, it was simpler to keep quiet and hope this was over soon.

'I don't know why your father wastes his money trying to make you look like something.' Miz Ethiopia took Odella by the chin, swiveled her head from side to side, examining her hair. 'You had precious little to start with, and you don't have sense enough not to call attention to yourself.' She never raised her voice, but her words sliced clean and deep as a switchblade. 'And what happened to your umbrella?'

Odella saw Henry sniggling over the upstairs railing, and she knew there was no point broaching that subject. 'It got broke.'

'It got broke? All by itself? Jumped up and got broke?' Everything about Miz Ethiopia was just so: her shiny black hair cascading over her shoulders, her clothes tailored to fit her trim figure precisely, her

310

wide dark eyes framed by thick lashes and arched brows, her modulated voice and exactly chosen words. Odella would have thought she was pretty if she had been somebody else and always wondered how her father could have loved a woman as full of life as Annie but stayed with someone as cold and spiteful as his wife. 'First of all, the word is *broken*, and secondly *it* didn't break anything, but you obviously did. I guess it was too much to expect you to take care of something nice . . .'

'All righty. We're ready to roll.'

Della was startled when Hambone opened the back door and deposited a small brown shopping bag on the seat, but in the dark she could hide her distress. And right now she could do without any more random recollections, intrusions from the past. On the way to the motel Celeste asked him to stop at the package store too, because she definitely needed some wine. Before Hambone carried Della's suitcase up to Ronnie's room, Celeste handed her mother the key and snorted 'Night.' And while she should have been sleeping, Celeste fumed at Everett for daring to think she'd confide their problems to her mother, of all people. She sipped wine from the plastic-wrapped plastic cup in the bathroom and licked her wounds, because she felt like all of them, her mother, her husband, her sister, and her daughter, all of them were in cahoots, determined to chip away at her armor until she sent up the white flag. She just didn't understand what she'd done to deserve this, and it made her resentful and just plain mad. So most of the night the screws continued to turn. By dawn, she had lockjaw.

*   *   *

'What's the matter with you two?' Ronnie was sitting up in bed, a vision in blue striped front and back hospital gowns, when Celeste and Della dragged in the next morning. She'd done her best to smooth her hair with her IV-free hand, but it still looked like week-old roadkill. 'Have you been up all night sucking lemons, or am I actually dying and they didn't tell me yet?' She half smiled, hoping she really was only making a joke.

'You're going to be fine. Not that you have sense enough to take care of yourself anyway. Isn't that why you're here?'

'That's enough,' Della interrupted. She passed a rugged night as well. Oh, she wasn't bothered about upsetting Celeste. That was routine even when she wasn't trying, but this time Della knew exactly what she was doing. She wanted to rattle Celeste, make her look at herself and what she was about to lose. What kept Della tossing and turning was how the past she had fought so long to keep at bay just jumped up, sank its teeth into her, and apparently had no intentions of letting go. She wasn't a person to go digging up what was done. Della had no interest in history, hers or anybody else's. She buried it and moved on. She thought she had put the last of her yesterdays in the ground last October when Will died. It wasn't that she had the rest of her tomorrows laid out all bright and shiny, but she stopped counting on blue skies a long, long time ago. Truth was, last night, as tired as she was, Della found it hard to sleep in a room full of ghosts, even though she'd brought them along on the trip herself.

'You know, maybe I'll stay over here in the neutral corner. Let you two heavyweights duke it out.' Ronnie dropped her head back on the pillow, feeling tired and bruised, as much from the collapse of her world around her ears as from the physical breakdown. It had taken a lot of energy to keep pretending to herself there was nothing wrong when she'd been living on painkillers like they were a food group. She hadn't had time to process the doctor's explanation yet; it involved an ovary, a blocked fallopian tube, and something called a torqued chocolate cyst. Ronnie was just relieved it wasn't as life-threatening as it was painful.

'No. I believe you are the main event, as usual.' Celeste retucked the hospital corners at the foot of the bed. 'And if your mouth is any indication, you must be feeling better.'

Ronnie actually looked better too, thanks to some pain-free sleep. Neither Della nor Celeste had seen a scrub-faced Ronnie in recent memory, but without her paint and the 'seen it all–done it all' attitude that went with it, she looked surprisingly young. She made Della think of the days before Ronnie started taking her allowance downtown to the cosmetics aisles of W. T. Grant's. Celeste was just plain envious of Ronnie's smooth, unlined skin.

'Since you mentioned it, I'm not exactly ready to run a marathon.' Ronnie scooted her hips forward, trying to find a comfortable position in the rigid hospital bed. 'But I'll take the way I feel this morning over the last two days anytime. The doctor said I might get out of here tomorrow. I can't do much of anything for a couple of weeks, but at least . . .' Then Ronnie's eyes clouded over and her lip began to quiver. She grabbed a handful of sheet in her fist. This was good news. It was supposed to make her happy.

313

What a joke. She looked from her mother to her sister and knew she had no choice but to tell them all of it. That she had nowhere to go when they let her out. And when she didn't show up at the Sable Shades counter Thursday, she most likely wouldn't have a job either. Maybe it would make Celeste see why it was so important to go through with selling the place, even if it was only her half. Ronnie took a deep breath and decided that if the world didn't end yesterday, it probably wouldn't today either.

'I – I have to tell you the rest.'

'Rest of what?' Della asked.

Ronnie laid out the unadulterated truth, no filler, no by-products. She told them about Rake, about her series of slapdash living arrangements, about how little work she had had over the last several years. On one side of the bed, Celeste listened with a smug 'I knew it' expression. On the other, Della's concern changed to a frown, and by the time Ronnie delivered an accounting of the now defunct $10,000 rainy-day fund, Della wore a full-fledged scowl.

'It's a good thing you're layin' in that bed 'cause it's the only thing that keeps me from smackin' you right into tomorrow!' Now Della was mad. 'How long have you been livin' like this?' She moved the hospital gown Ronnie used as a robe when the aide got her up to walk this morning and plopped down in the chair next to her bed. Since the other bed in the room was still empty, Celeste hopped up there, primed to watch the fireworks. She knew her dollars and cents were ticking away too but wasn't about to say so.

Ronnie felt like she did when she was ten and got caught trying to change a C to a B on her report card, only a whole lot worse. She cast her eyes down and played with the edge of the waffly yellow blanket. 'A while,' she said softly.

'Well, that's just plain stupid. I told your father it wasn't as easy or as good as you made it out, but I had no idea you were livin' hand-to-mouth! Why didn't you say somethin' before now!?'

'Ma, it wasn't exactly hand-to-mouth. You make it sound like I was livin' on the street.' Ronnie still averted her eyes. She knew she was cornered.

'Close to it,' Celeste interjected.

For once Ronnie didn't have a defense or an act prepared. She knew all along her parents would have helped her, if they knew she needed it. She just never wanted them to know, always planned to pull it off in the final reel, make them proud as the credits rolled.

'Well, you can come on back home with me. When you're feelin' better you can find somethin' to do. At least you'll have a decent roof over your head.' Della was so upset she could hardly talk. She rubbed two tears back up into her temples with her middle fingers. 'They're hiring folks out at UB, all kinds of jobs. My new neighbor –' now she turned to Celeste, '– the one your sister thinks is raising hoodlums –' she turned back to Ronnie and continued, ' – works on the Amherst Campus. We can talk to her.'

'I don't . . .'

'Sittin' up, are we?' Lucille's squeak interrupted them. 'Mornin' everybody!' She stood in the doorway holding a bunch of daisies.

I can't go home. But Ronnie smiled at Lucille. 'Hi!' *Shit.* Ronnie knew this conversation with her mother wasn't over, and she wanted to finish it. She was certainly happy to see Lucille, and grateful to her. Ronnie didn't know how she would have survived her attack without Lucille's calm, reassuring presence. But this was family business, as Della would say, and you don't put family business in the street. All his life, Will had tried to impress upon Ronnie that dreading a thing was worse than doing it. Of course, it wasn't a philosophy Ronnie embraced. Procrastination was her MO. 'Never do today what you can put off until it goes away.' But she had found the fatal flaw in that logic. And it was actually feeling good to tell the truth.

'You look a darn sight better than you did when I saw you last, Miss Ronnie!' Lucille chirped from where she stood and looked at Della like she was waiting to be invited in.

'Lucille.' It was a statement of identification and recognition more than a greeting. Della's gesture, not quite a smile, not quite a nod, was slight enough to be missed if, like Ronnie and Celeste, you weren't paying attention.

Lucille walked into the room and stood near the foot of Ronnie's bed. Celeste took the flowers and went to the nurses' station to get something to put them in.

Della got up. 'Thank you for . . .'

'Don't be thankin' me for nothin'. You'd a done the same thing if need be. I'm glad we could help, such as it was.' Lucille turned to Della. Her eyes spoke a million things she'd wanted to say through the years. 'Umph. Umph. Umph. It's been a long time.'

'Yes. I has.' Della moved a little closer to Lucille.

Just as she recognized Hambone, and knew Lucille's voice over the phone, Della would have known Lucille anywhere, white hair and all. With Hambone, Della saw who they had been. But now she saw very clearly who she and Lucille had become. If looking at Hambone was a flashback, being face to face with Lucille was like looking in the mirror, and Della knew Lucille saw it too. The years were there. Every one of them, and the problems, joys, fears, solutions, disappointments, questions, triumphs, and answers lined up and marched through the split second that passed between them. They didn't know each other well anymore, but womanhood was a common denominator. What was above the line might be different, but you could always reduce what was below the line to the same number.

'I'm just so sorry it took this to bring you back.'

Della didn't know what to say because she was sorry to be back at all, so she just nodded.

They were stuck for words, so they stood awkwardly next to each other, Della's gray head towering above Lucille's white one.

'This is all they had.' Celeste returned holding a blue plastic pitcher. She disappeared into the bathroom to fill her makeshift vase.

Lucille took the opportunity to move on. 'Now, Miss Ronnie, that hair of yours looks like it's been through the spin cycle.' Ronnie had to crack a smile. 'Why don't you let me take that mess out.'

'You don't have to do that,' Ronnie said.

'Don't you have customers waitin' on you?' Della asked.

'I've come a long way since the old days. I got three other girls in the shop. Course most of the steady clients are mine. And most of 'em want their hair just like they been wearin' it for the last hundred years.' Lucille winked at Della. 'Ain't them the same tight curls I put in your head the last time I saw you?' Della humphed and patted her neat, boring gray spirals.

Then Lucille turned back to Ronnie. 'I guarantee you'll feel a whole lot better.' She opened the tote bag she had with her. Lucille had come prepared.

'Uh,' Ronnie hesitated. Even when it was looking rough because she couldn't afford to have it done, she hadn't been without a weave or a wig since disco was in diapers. But she had found the mirror under the lid of her tray table this morning. There was no use holding on since the rest of the charade was over. She sighed, 'Okay.'

Celeste emerged from the bathroom and put the flowers on the windowsill. 'Won't that take hours?'

'Maybe a couple,' Lucille said. 'Why don't y'all go get a bite to eat or do some shoppin'. There's a mall not too far from here. I bet Miss Ronnie would like a real nightgown, wouldn't you? And she won't be wearin' them tight jeans when they let her outta here. Pick her up a few things that are loose – and cool,' she added as an afterthought. 'And think about what you'll need in the house for a week or so.'

'The house?' Celeste realized Lucille was talking about Little Pond. 'Oh, no. We're not planning to stay there.' She watched her mother to gauge her reaction, but Della's expression didn't change. They had been too busy feuding to discuss what they would do after Ronnie's release from the hospital. Della had been so enraged about Prosper and the house that Celeste wasn't sure she'd come, even if Ronnie *was* sick. It never occurred to Celeste to suggest they stay there, even for a little while.

Ronnie wanted to tell them not to go through all this trouble. She could take care of herself, but nobody was buying that story anymore, not even her. So she counted ceiling tiles above her bed, wishing one of them would open and she could float out of the room.

'Well, she surely don't want to be gettin' on no airplane right away. She's gon' need a few days to recuperate, at least. Y'all are perfectly welcome to stay with Hambone and me if there's somethin' wrong with the place out there. It'll be tight, but we can manage.'

'We can stay right at the Tree Top.' But even as Celeste spoke, she realized how difficult it would be caring for Ronnie in that place. And Celeste was fed up with the lumpy bed, the paper thin walls, the antiseptic smell. She had already made Little Pond feel homey. There were sheets, towels, and new appliances waiting to be used. It wouldn't take much to get the place ready for houseguests, but still—

Lucille shrugged and turned her attention to raising the head of Ronnie's bed to a sitting position. By the time Della and Celeste left, she'd already covered Ronnie and her bed in black plastic capes and laid out her combs and scissors. She unraveled the loose braid Celeste had made in an attempt to control the thicket of hair. 'Any longer and somethin' would be burrowin' in here.' She opened a plastic garbage bag for the discards.

'That bad, huh?' *Even a ten-year-old can take care of her hair, but I screwed that up too.* She clasped her hands tightly in her lap and held her breath to keep from crying. She had done quite enough of that in the last two days, and she decided it was time to suck it up and move on.

'It's gon' be all right. When I'm finished you'll be lookin' so smart you won't know why you didn't do this a long time ago.'

Lucille's touch was gentle as she made sections and

secured them with pink clips. Even when she pulled no punches, Ronnie found talking to her comforting too. 'Did you used to do Ma's hair?'

'Yeah. I worked on that hard head many a day.'

Ronnie snickered. 'It was already hard, huh?'

'Yes ma'am. But I suspect more times than not, she was the one hurt by it. Seems to kinda run in the family.' Lucille winked.

'Lucille's right, you know. It would be easier and more pleasant to stay at the house.' Celeste tested the waters as they wandered around the lingerie department at Belks. 'I've been straightening up some since we've been here. It wouldn't take much more . . .'

'Medium should fit her all right, don't you think?' Della kept sifting through a mound of nighties, purposely sidestepping Celeste's remark.

'That's what I buy for Niki.' Celeste held up a white eyelet gown. 'How about this?'

'Ronnie is recuperatin', not gettin' married.' Della headed off toward three racks marked 'Take 40% off.' 'That's what we should get.' She pointed to a display of jelly bean colored jumbo cotton T-shirts.

'But they're so loud.'

'They're bright and cheery.'

It was the usual point, counterpoint.

'You know she won't be in any shape to buckle a seat belt around her belly for at least a week.' Celeste decided to try another approach. 'And as you know, that motel is dismal.'

Della knew she was going to have to address the issue sooner or later, but her plate was brimming, her mouth was full, and going to the house was more than she could swallow at the moment. She watched

Celeste run her hand over a lacy black number with spaghetti straps. 'Are you seein' another man?'

'What!?'

'Well that's sure not for your sister, and if Everett is leavin' you, why else would you want a fancy nightgown?'

'For goodness sakes!' Celeste dropped the nightgown.

'You wouldn't be the first woman who thought the grass was greener . . .'

'I was just *looking*, Mother.'

Della wanted to ask more questions, to understand what was going on. She was truly shocked when Everett told her about the breakup. Celeste wasn't the easiest person to get on with, but they seemed to have had that figured out. Except Celeste was acting like it wasn't a big deal. Della had seen her child more upset about picking up the wrong brand of detergent than she appeared to be about the demise of her marriage, but there wasn't anything more to say about it. Della knew Celeste was as stubborn as they come, and she was likely to cut her tongue out before she admitted there was something wrong that she couldn't handle. So Della sucked her teeth and went in search of cotton drawers, because she had seen those silly thong things Ronnie wore, and for the life of her she didn't know how they could be comfortable any time. She knew they wouldn't be now. She glanced up from the display, caught Celeste's reflection in the mirror on the other side of the department. *She looks more like her now than she ever did.* But Celeste was nothing like Annie, not the way Della remembered her. Since she'd come back to Prosper, some old memory or 'what if?' seemed to leap out at every corner she turned. She watched Celeste, unnoticed, a little while longer and thought about the women on her job who sounded devastated when they talked about getting older and finding they looked like their mothers, frown lines and all. It seemed like a privilege to Della. She could still see her father in her face, especially when she was tired, but she could never mistake herself for Annie, not even in a fun house mirror. Annie hadn't lived long enough to look old, to be a yardstick for Della to measure herself by, but here was Celeste, looking like her grandmother might have looked if – like someone Della never brought herself to mention to her. She knew it was wrong, but she held those memories close, afraid there wasn't enough to share.

Finally Celeste felt Della's stare. 'You can ignore me if you want to,' she said when she joined her mother. 'You can change the subject. You can walk away. But it doesn't change the fact we have to go somewhere when Ronnie gets out of the hospital.'

'Yes, I guess we do,' Della replied. She carried her armful of panties and nightshirts to the cash register and didn't say any more about it.

They picked up some baggy shorts and two cotton sundresses in sportswear, and grabbed canvas sneakers from the shoe department on their way out. When they arrived back at the hospital, shopping bags in hand, Ronnie was sitting up in bed, dozing. Her store-bought mane was gone. Her own, close-cropped hair, au naturel, remained. The after was so different from the before that Celeste gasped.

Ronnie's eyes fluttered open. She reached her hand up to her head, and although she didn't say a word, her tentative expression said, 'What do you think?'

'This sure is a lot better than that other.' Della dropped her packages on the empty bed. 'All that hair hanging down to your behind . . .'

'Which nobody thought was yours, anyway. And I know it cost a fortune.' Celeste added her load to her mother's.

'Will somebody tell me if I need to put a bag over my head?!'

Della leaned back and gave Ronnie a good once-over. *Looks like my bald-headed baby.* She brushed hair clippings off her cheek. 'You look right cute. Lucille did a real nice job, but she always did have the gift.'

Celeste turned her attention to the cut glass vase of freesia and irises on Ronnie's bedside table. 'Where did all these flowers come from?' She lightly lifted the fall of one of the deep purple irises.

'Not bad, huh?' Ronnie smiled coyly.

Celeste parked her hand on her hip and waited for an answer.

'They're from Everett.'

'And those?' Celeste pointed to the wicker basket of miniature roses on the windowsill next to Lucille's daisies.

'From Doug Pryce.'

'He must really want to make this sale.' Celeste went over to the window and tapped the rim of the wicker basket that held the roses. 'How in the world did he find out?'

Ronnie shrugged.

'A bed full of shoppin' bags and a room full of flowers.' Della paused a second. 'Not bad at all, for a girl with dust in her pockets, and no pot to . . .'

'Thank you, Ma.' Ronnie knew she wasn't just teasing. 'So what's in the bags?'

Della only half watched the fashion show. Her mind was on Little Pond.

'I didn't know they still made bloomers.' Ronnie held up a pair of sensible panties.

'Did the nurse say for sure you'd be released tomorrow?'

Ronnie sobered up before the next exhale. She knew they hadn't finished their conversation about her unsettled future. 'As long as my incision passes inspection and I don't have a fever.'

'Celeste, what do we need to do so we can stay out at the house?' You could tell by the gruff edge in Della's voice that this was a bitter pill, but she was choking it down.

What brought this on? 'Not much. There are sheets and towels there. I'd run them through the wash, just to freshen them up, but I can do that tonight – or tomorrow.' Celeste said it as matter-of-factly as she could.

'Then that's where we'll stay.'

Ronnie and Celeste exchanged a glance that said the fan was on, they just weren't sure when the shit would hit.

16

'There were no good old days, only now.'

'You're drivin' too fast,' Della complained as Celeste passed one slow-moving car, then another.

Celeste checked the speedometer. 'I'm actually five miles below the speed limit, Mother.'

'Well, you're goin' faster than those cars back there.' And Della was in no hurry to arrive.

'They obviously have nothing but time, but we need to get there before the phone company or we'll have to reschedule.' Hambone had taken care of having the phone service connected on a temporary basis.

'It doesn't feel too fast to me.' Ronnie pressed a pillow against her belly to keep it steady from the road dips and bumps. She didn't usually feel compelled to stick up for Celeste, but Della had been steady on both of their cases all morning. At the hospital she groused at Ronnie for not being packed when they got there. Ronnie had had a rough night. Her incision throbbed, she didn't sleep because she couldn't find a comfortable position, but she wouldn't complain or ask for medication, afraid that if she did, they might keep her another day, which would only add to her bill, which she couldn't pay anyway. Fighting back tears as Della lit into her, she tried to explain that it had taken her two hours to get showered and dressed and that she couldn't move any faster, but it didn't get her any slack.

'Was I talkin' to you?' Della barked.

No, you were biting my head off. Ronnie flipped the radio on to distract her from the barrage.

'And I'm not payin' for no speedin' ticket.' Della paused a moment, and Ronnie and Celeste both prayed they had heard the end of her diatribe. 'Used to put you in jail for that down here, if you were colored.'

'I've been driving since I was sixteen and I've never had a ticket.'

'There's always a first.' Della hugged herself and exaggerated a shiver. 'Are you trying to freeze us to death?' It was only middling cold in the car, and she knew she was being impossible, but she couldn't help it and she didn't care. This was the last place on earth she wanted to be, and the closer they got to Little Pond, the more she felt trapped and lashed out. It was their fault she was here, and they were getting Will's share too. This wasn't easy for her, and it wasn't going to be for them, either. 'The rest of us don't wanna have icicles just 'cause you're havin' hot flashes.'

'I'm having no such thing.'

'Don't you think I've seen you sweatin' like a steelworker when it's two degrees outside? If I had a nickel for every time in the last year I heard you say, "Is it hot in here?" I'd be a rich woman. I went through the change too, you know.'

'That's ridiculous.' They hadn't had one of these talks since the day Celeste's sixth-grade class witnessed the arrival of her womanhood. Della was called

326

to pick Celeste up from the nurse's office where she had cried until she made herself sick because she had no idea what was going on. By the time Della stumbled through her rendition of the facts of life, Celeste was mortified. She felt just about that embarrassed now. 'I'm not old enough.'

'I was there when you were born. I know how old you are,' Della jabbed from the backseat.

I cannot be old enough . . . This was not a topic Celeste cared to debate, so she turned the AC down and kept her eyes on the road.

'This is Johnny DuPree, and even when ya don't know I'm lookin', I got my eye on ya.' The DJ's rap filled the moment of silence.

'Turn that mess off! I can't hear myself think!' *And I can't listen to no Johnny DuPree right now!*

Celeste beat Ronnie to the off button. Right now her mother was more annoying than fingernails on a chalkboard.

'Aren't you gonna stop for groceries?' Della asked.

'We have some. I'll go out later for more. We can't afford to miss the phone company.'

'You act like you're expectin' a call,' Della said pointedly. 'Who would that be from?'

'I won't discuss this, Mother,' Celeste hissed.

'Don't forget the drugstore. We have those prescriptions to fill,' Della snapped.

Great. Something else I can't pay for. Ronnie squirmed in her seat, screwed up her mouth, but she stayed quiet, grateful that, for the moment, nobody was picking on her.

'I haven't forgotten. There's a pharmacy in Prosper. I'll go after we get her settled.'

And mercifully, as the highway turned into

Albermarle Road, Della settled down too. Or at least she got quiet. She closed her eyes and swallowed hard to keep down the memories of her first reluctant car ride to Prosper. She wasn't prepared yet to see anybody else she might know or who might remember her. There was no point in wasting energy on minor haints when she knew the big ones were waiting.

The slow crunch of gravel signaled their arrival, but Della's eyes stayed closed. She'd spent a good part of the time since Lucille's phone call trying to knit herself back together, but once again she was on the verge of splitting in two. The sad little girl who arrived at this house so long ago joined with the scared, confused young woman who left and swore she'd never come back, both begging Della to stay in the car. But the mother of two grown women, grandmother of another, that side pushed her to do what had to be done.

'I think she's asleep,' Celeste whispered.

'I'm not sleepin'.' *One, two* . . . Della opened her eyes. She'd seen the house many times in her mind's eye, but in the dappled sunlight it wasn't nearly as oppressive as she recalled. The house looked older, a little run-down, not as imposing as it used to be. *Like me, I guess.*

Della pushed open the car door. *Smells the same.* The twang of the red earth beneath her feet, the dank, mossy musk of the lake on the other side of the woods, they were still familiar perfume. *Just keep it together.* She heard a low grunt overhead, looked up and saw the big dark bird circling way above them. 'Snakebirds,' she muttered to herself. '*They got long, skinny necks and they look like snakes when they in the*

328

water, but they ain't no such a thing as a bird that turn into snakes,' Will had told her.

'You smart and Henry's a liar,' Lester had added. 'He's jus' sayin' that to scare you.' That was the day they became her friends, and Henry never forgave her for that.

'You say something, Mother?' Celeste asked.

'Never mind.' Della shook free of the memory. 'Come on, Ron. If you scoot over you can grab onto our arms and pull yourself up when you're ready,' Della instructed.

'I can't wait to get this over with.' Ronnie held her pillow tight as Celeste helped ease her legs out of the car. She took a breath and slowly inched over until her butt was perched on the edge of the seat. *If it hurt this bad gettin' out of the car, I'll be wrecked by the time I get upstairs.* But she managed to pull onto her feet.

'Does it hurt?' Della asked. She'd never had an operation. Only been in the hospital when Celeste and Ronnie were born, and that hurt, but when it was over it was gone. She didn't know what a six-inch slice across the bottom of your belly felt like.

'You can do it. Just take one step at a time,' Celeste encouraged.

One step at a time. It's just a house. Della held her arm straight and strong for Ronnie. Her upper lip she kept stiff for herself. Before they got to the steps, Hambone's big, blue Caddy pulled up the drive, kicking up a rusty dusty cloud.

Celeste, Ronnie, and Della's one, two, three stair-step heads turned when they heard the car. Hambone hustled over to them.

'Lucille was out here earlier and left y'all some food. But I thought you could use a hand gettin'

Ronnie in the house. She ain't supposed to be takin' no stairs for a while. I had my gallbladder out, couple a years back,' Hambone said, verifying his knowledge of approved postsurgical activities. 'I'll have her upstairs in no time flat.' Before anybody could object, he scooped Ronnie into his arms and carried her up the walk to the front door. Celeste scurried to open it for them, then headed back to the car.

'I'd like a minute down here before we go up, if that's okay.'

'Whatever you want, little lady.' He deposited her on the settee by the window. 'This good?'

Ronnie nodded.

Hambone found Della outside on a wicker porch chair. 'Looks pretty near the same, don't it?'

'I guess it does. It's been an awful long time, Hambone.' Although Della could still picture every nook of that house.

'I know what you mean. The phone people been here?' he asked.

'You got here same time we did, so how would I know?' Della rolled her eyes at him.

'Now that sounds like the Odella Womack I used to know.' Hambone grinned and hooked his thumbs around his suspenders.

Celeste stumbled up the steps, three purses on her shoulder and lugging Ronnie's duffel bag. 'If it wasn't so damn hot—' She caught herself before she finished, but not before Della looked at her and nodded.

'You shouldn't be totin' that.' He grabbed the suitcase from her. 'Let me get the rest of 'em, while your sister's taking a rest.'

'You an old man, Hambone. How you gon' manage

330

the suitcases *and* have the strength to carry Ronnie?'

'Yep. Soundin' more and more like ol' Odella every minute.' Hambone laughed. 'And for your information, I carry fifty-pound sacks of potatoes and flour better than them young boys who work for me, so my mind tells me I can carry Ronnie just fine.'

'And if you were half as smart as you are fat, your mind would tell you somethin' worth knowin'.'

'Didn't I always say you should never trust a skinny cook?' Hambone stood in profile, showing off his girth.

'All right. Be my guest. Carry all you want. Just don't be complainin' to Lucille about your aches and pains tomorrow.'

Hambone waved away her warning and helped Celeste unload the car, then followed her inside for iced tea.

Della knew she couldn't stay on the porch forever. She braced her hands on the chair arms. *One, two, three* . . . stood and walked inside.

It really did look like her father would stride out of his study any minute. Like Miz Ethiopia would call out from the kitchen, 'Odella? That you?' Like Henry would come sneaking up on her from some unsuspected corner. But they were all dead now. And never in a million years did Della think Miz Ethiopia would leave this house to her. Della ran her hand over the mahogany hall table, listened to Hambone joshing with Celeste and Ronnie in the living room.

Della walked to the back of the house, into the kitchen. The appliances were new, but the cabinets were the ones she remembered. She stood at the window, her eyes locked on what was left of the chicken coop.

'Don't you peck me, you mean ol'biddy,' Odella warned as she sidled up to the brooding pen, her water bucket still in hand. She'd already seen to the other chickens outside, so the frenetic chatter and wing flapping had simmered down. Only thing left was to check on this hen who'd been sitting inside on her clutch of eggs for weeks. Then she could head down to the pond to study. And to see if Lester or Will showed up.

'Let me see if you got any peeps yet and I'll leave you alone.' Cautiously she slid her hand along the side of the nest. 'Just let me— Ow!!' The hen squawked and went for her arm. 'Stupid bird! Look what you did!' She examined the damage.

'Whatchu doin' in there?!' Henry straddled the doorway, a silhouette against the bright sun at his back.

Odella jumped and overturned the bucket, splashing water on her legs and feet. 'See what you made me do!' She wiped at her legs with the tail of her dress. 'Don't sneak up on me that way!' The henhouse was a place she didn't expect to run into Henry. The only point Odella had in her favor with him was that since her arrival in Prosper, he didn't have to tend the chickens anymore. Only thing he still did was wring their necks when his mother needed one for dinner. It had taken Odella a long time to get used to the ornery birds and their stinky droppings, but once she got the hang of it she could finish her job by rote. So she'd scatter feed and replay her old *Life* magazine daydreams of beautiful, far-off places. Or conjure up something about Lester, like how giddy she felt the day he let her take the first sip out of his bottle of RC. 'And any fool can see what I'm doin'!'

'Who you callin' fool?'

'It's just a sayin'.' Odella was sure Henry was the most annoying person who ever drew breath. 'Why are you here?'

'This is my house. I can be any damn where I want!' Henry was moody in general, and the worse his grades got the harder his father rode him. Last night Odell reamed him out all through dinner, called him a dunce. Odella was certain she had turned her head before she smirked.

'You must be talkin' about this chicken coop 'cause everythin' else is Papa's.' Normally she avoided confrontations with Henry. She didn't even like him to look at her because she never knew which of his two faces would be showing, and any little thing could set him off, but right now her feet were squishing in her shoes, her arm was bleeding, and she was going to have to clean up the wet straw and put down fresh before she headed for the pond.

'You shut up! Ain't none of it yours and it never will be!' Henry bellowed.

'I don't want it no way!' Odella bent down to pick up her bucket, and Henry was on her before she could straighten up.

'Think you better than me, don't you?!' He grabbed her arm and flung her into the back wall. 'Callin' me a fool!'

The impact shook the narrow shed and knocked the breath out of her. 'Stop it . . .'

Before she could move he grabbed her shoulders and slammed her into the wall again. 'You thought it was funny last night, what Pa said!' Henry hurled himself against her, full force. He was smaller than Odella, but rage amplified his power.

'No!' Too terrified to feel the pain, Odella pushed and squirmed, trying to get free. He'd shoved her around before, but never like this.

'I saw you grinnin'!' Sweat ran down his temples. 'Like I'm some kinda joke!' He snatched her wrists, crushed them against her chest. 'I'll tell you what's funny! Him sayin' I should be more like you! I should be like his damn bastard!'

'Let go a me, Henry! That's not what he meant!' She wriggled against him, stomping, kicking.

'Didn't give me his name, but you got it!'

'Mama named me! I swear!'

Then Henry got still and his eyes flashed cold. 'Your mama?! You stand here and talk to me about your mama?! I'm a show you what he did to your mama!' He grasped both her wrists in one hand and started pawing at her skirt.

'Stop it!' Odella exploded in a panicked fury. She slid herself down the wall, felt splinters in her back from the rough wood. When she got near his shoulder she bit down as hard as she could, but her mouth flew open when he punched her in the gut.

'Bite me, you bitch!' Henry hurled her facedown in the wet hay and chicken shit, twisted her arms behind her back, straddled her legs.

'Don't, Henry! Please!' Odella screamed as he pulled her white cotton panties down to her knees and stretched out on her back, fumbling with his pants, grunting and wheezing.

Odella bucked and rolled to throw him off her, but she couldn't. 'Henry, no!' The scream scraped her throat.

He planted his knee between her thighs to pry them apart.

'Nigga, I'll kill you!' In one motion Will lifted Henry and heaved him through the doorway. The chickens fluttered and cackled wildly. Henry tried to scramble to his feet and run, but Will tackled him and started to pound him with leaden fists.

Odella got to her feet, fixed her clothes as best she could, and ran outside. Henry was limp, unable to fight back. She could see blood running from his nose and mouth. Will's face was like stone as he whaled away on him. 'Don't kill him, Will!' She grabbed at his arms. 'Please don't kill him!'

'Look what he did to you!' Will's voice cracked.

Odella stood before him, trembling, coated in filth. 'I'm all right! He didn't do nothin'! You stopped him, Will!' She started to cry. Please, Will! I don't want you to get in trouble.'

'Awright, Odella.' Will stood, dug in his pocket for his handkerchief, and handed it to her, keeping his eyes averted. He couldn't look at her that way. 'Awright.'

Henry got up off the ground, staggered toward the house.

Odella wiped at her tears. 'And please don't tell Papa! I gotta live here. It'll only make things worse.' She looked in his eyes. 'Promise.'

'Awright,' Will sighed.

Della hurried out of the kitchen, toward the voices in the living room, but she hung back in the hall a moment to collect herself. She didn't notice Ronnie stretched out on a settee by the window.

Ronnie watched as Della folded her arms across her

335

chest, rubbed her shoulders as if to give herself a hug. She tried to place the look on her mother's face. Ronnie had seen anger before, and she was familiar with that sadness that shaded Della's face without warning or explanation, but this was different. Della looked shaken.

What's it like for Ma, being here? Ronnie never knew her mother to relive the past. Della's philosophy had always been there were no good old days, only now. She'd been so angry about the house, but here she was walking around in it, in her past. All of a sudden Ronnie found herself trying to imagine Della sitting on the bench with her blue composition book, writing her music, and she wondered what on earth had made her leave it all behind. Ronnie liked the feeling of singing, whether it was to herself under the covers or to a crowd. The thought of walking away from something you love made her sad for her mother, and for herself because that looked exactly like the corner she'd painted herself into.

'You 'bout ready to head upstairs, Missy?'

Hambone snatched Della out of her reverie. She felt flustered when she caught Ronnie's eye and realized she'd been watching, but Hambone was there to defuse the moment. 'Look a here, George Anderson . . .'

'Ooohwee, using my whole name, like I'm in trouble or somethin'.'

'I'm tryin' to keep your sorry self outta trouble. You don't have to carry her . . .'

'Woman, hush and move out my way.'

Hambone lifted Ronnie and walked toward the stairs. Celeste was two steps ahead, leading the way. 'We can put her in the master bedroom. It's the biggest one,' Celeste said over her shoulder.

Della looked up the stairs after them, her eyes purposefully avoiding the railing and the missing spindles.

'I told them if y'all need anythin' to call me.' Hambone, wiping his brow with a big white handkerchief, trudged back down the steps. 'You awright?'

Della leaned against the front door, looking out into the yard, still catching her breath. 'Yeah – I'm fine. I should be askin' you that.' Della jugged with Hambone awhile, and before he left he promised to stop by to check on them.

Finally Della stoked up a head of steam big enough to carry her upstairs and into the bedroom that Odell and his wife had shared. This room had no strong memories. She was rarely in it. When she got there, Ronnie was propped against the pillows in the fourposter while Celeste busied herself unpacking. Della thought Ronnie still looked slightly gray against her fuschia sleep shirt and the white sheets.

'Celeste, you need to go fill those prescriptions now, 'cause it'll be time for Ronnie to take 'em. And if you wait much longer you'll be complainin' about how hot it is.'

'I'll go in a minute. I want to get these things organized.' Celeste hung a sundress in the closet.

'Well then, gimme the keys and I'll go!' Della paced at the foot of the bed.

'I said I'd go as soon as I'm finished, Mother! Will you give me a chance to breathe?!'

They picked at each other, back and forth, every subject a cause for disagreement. Ronnie tried to ignore them, but she felt their bickering land like body blows, wearing her down, punishing her for causing this mess in the first place. Finally she couldn't take another word.

'I'm sorry, okay!' Celeste and Della whirled around to face her. The yelling hurt, so Ronnie pressed down with her pillow, but she had to say this. 'You're both mad. I know it's my fault! But believe me, I wish this never happened!' Tears streamed down her cheeks. 'Ma, I'm sorry you had to come back to Prosper. I know you don't want to be here. I don't know why, and you won't tell anybody, but I'm grateful you came. I said I'm gonna pay you back, and it may take a while, but I swear I will!' She swallowed some air, wiped her nose with the back of her hand. Celeste handed her a tissue. 'And I know that as far as you're concerned, sister dear, I've always been a pain in the behind, and you're just dying to say, "See! I told you she wasn't ever going to be an actress." So say it!' Ronnie blew her nose and looked at Celeste for a comment.

Celeste gave her another tissue. 'Ronnie, I never . . .'

'Yes you did. And I know you're enjoying this! And yes, as you've already figured out, I've been hassling you to sell this place because I need the money – again. Man, have I done some stupid stuff in my life! Big time! So I can't say jack. I'm probably getting more than I deserve, but I screwed up enough to know I have to do better.' She flopped her head back on the pillow and closed her eyes. 'I wish we could be in the same room together for more than two minutes without somebody fighting. You do the same thing with Niki, Celeste. You never give anybody a break!' Ronnie gulped for a breath. 'When we were little, I used to try so hard to be good enough to be your little sister. You did everything right – you were so neat and tiny – and perfect. I wanted to be like you, but I couldn't ever be that – together, no matter how hard I tried. I couldn't even get you to like me.' Ronnie talked and cried. Della and Celeste stood there not knowing what to say. 'And I always wished I could make you happy, Ma.' Ronnie's voice got quieter. 'At least get you to say you were proud of me. Daddy did, but I couldn't get it out of you, not even when I had that stupid billboard and everybody you knew talked about it. I heard you brag to other people, but you never said a word to me.' By now she was talking mostly to herself. 'Guess proud is not gonna happen right now.' She trailed off. Limp. Spent.

In a few minutes Ronnie was asleep, leaving Celeste and Della wounded and on their own.

17

'The footprints are always behind you.'

'You want some lemonade?' Celeste called from the bottom of the stairs.

'Yeah. Thanks. That would be great.' Ronnie sat in the rocking chair by the window, still hugging her pillow and gazing out over the backyard to where she knew the lake was. *Wish I could see past the trees.* She'd only been up an hour, but already she wanted to get back in bed. *Is this ever gonna stop?* Sitting, standing, walking to the bathroom, all things she had taken for granted a week ago, now involved planning, and once she executed them her energy was sapped.

Two days after the Event, as Ronnie called it, mother and daughters spoke only to exchange necessary pleasantries. It was like she'd tossed a rotten egg into the room. The odor was rank and thick, and it lingered, but they cleaned it up quickly and went out of their way to act like they didn't smell it. They tiptoed around the remaining eggshells scattered throughout the house, afraid to shatter the fragile peace. She wondered if they actually thought she was a little wacko after her outburst, but she didn't care. For a little while Ronnie had enjoyed the dubious truce.

Celeste stayed busy, somehow managing to fill her to-do list. She ran errands, like getting oscillating fans for the bedrooms and a box window fan for the kitchen. She washed and ironed all the table-cloths and napkins from her neat piles, polished furniture and washed floors, like she was planning to take up residence, and she prepared meals, such as they were, mostly sandwiches, broiled chicken, salads, and vats of lemonade, something she rarely made at home. At scheduled intervals she'd peek in Ronnie's room from the hallway to ask, in an un-naturally cheerful voice, if she was hungry or needed anything.

Della was in charge of dispensing pills and reban-daging Ronnie's incision. Ronnie felt kind of strange, lifting up her dress, rolling down her panties, and letting her mother tend to her wound. It was harder than letting a complete stranger mess around down there. She had grilled the nurse about how prominent her scar would be and whether she'd always have the belly pooch that hung over it now, but the hands-on intimacy with her mother made her squeamish. Never mind they were both women with the same equip-ment package. Della certainly hadn't been in that region since Ronnie had grown short and curlies, so they carefully avoided each other's eyes and got through it as quickly as possible. And aside from her nursing duties Della mostly stayed in the kitchen, a room where she hadn't spent much time back then. She had asked Miz Ethiopia a few times if she needed help with the cooking, but the answer was always no. After a while Della didn't bring it up anymore; she stayed out of her father's wife's kitchen. Now it was her sanctuary, the place where she drank her coffee, worked her puzzles, played solitaire, and watched her TV shows right on schedule. If she didn't look too far to the left or right, she could pretend she was still at home in Buffalo, and maybe she could get away before the place had a chance to settle on her clothes, seep into her pores.

Ronnie rocked forward, rested her hands on the windowsill, and pushed herself out of the chair. She reached behind her, grabbed the pillow, and clutched it to her abdomen as she shuffled across the room. She knew the cease-fire couldn't last, but for the first time since she was a teenager they were stuck at close range, under the same roof. They'd be there at least another week, and Will wasn't around to keep them civil. Right now the most important thing to Ronnie was that the fussing was on hiatus, because she had finally lost the game of procrastination she'd been playing, big time, and she had to get her head together. For once in her life she wasn't looking for distractions.

When Celeste had asked, ever so nicely, if Ronnie would like the one TV in the house brought up to her room, she surprised herself by saying no. TV was in your face, and after seventeen years in New York, she'd had quite enough daily assaults. She was surprised by how soothing she found the birdsong that wakened her before first light. This was definitely a calmer start to her day than the growl and grind of the 4:00 A.M. garbage trucks that had become her routine. Instead of the constant thunder of traffic, howling horns, wailing sirens, and exhaust fumes with taste and texture, now trees rustled outside her window and softly scented the room with pine. There was no urgency to these sounds and smells. They played backup to her thoughts, although at a much slower tempo than the driving beat she'd gotten used to. When she wanted entertainment, she played the radio, alternating between an oldies station out of Charlotte and WDLA. They provided a rhythm for the blues that came and went as she dealt endless hands of solitaire and pondered her future.

It wasn't that she was that sad. In fact, physically Ronnie felt better than she had in a long time. Fear had kept her from checking out the nagging, intermittent pain in her belly for more than a year. Fear that it was something terrible. Fear that even if it wasn't fatal, she didn't have insurance and couldn't pay for whatever it was.

This morning she'd been thinking about patching things up with her mother and Celeste. She'd had no idea she was about to burst at the emotional seams until the tirade started and she couldn't stop. Living on a financial precipice had kept the pressure on, but she was used to that. The first thread had popped with the Rake episode. The house in Prosper seemed to be the stitch in time, but Celeste's refusal to sell started the seam splitting again. Ronnie barely managed to hold on, hoping her sister was just being difficult and would eventually change her mind. By the time she found herself writhing on Lucille and Hambone's bathroom floor, it had all started to unravel, and listening to her mother and sister fight had finally torn her to shreds. The Event provided a release she didn't know she needed, but at this point, she didn't have the strength to keep up appearances. *My stuff is pretty much out there any ol' way, so 'let's pretend' is over.* She needed it real if she was ever going to find her way out of the mess she'd made. *And I guess the first step is getting them to speak to me again.*

Ronnie heard Celeste rattling ice trays in the kitchen. She raised her foot to the first step of the little stool beside the bed and rested. *That's after I get myself in this bed so my sister doesn't think I'm completely— Listen to me. 'Let's pretend' is over except I'm scared to let my own sister see that I might need help – again.* She held the pillow more tightly as she took step two. *Ain't that nothin'.* Ronnie turned around and sat on the thick, soft mattress.

'Here you go.' When Celeste bustled into the room and handed her a frosty glass, Ronnie was sitting up in bed like she'd been there all along. 'Would you like anything else?' She had already turned to go.

'Some company.' Somebody had to go first, so Ronnie took the chance.

'Pardon?' Celeste didn't know what to say.

'Don't go.' Ronnie took a sip. 'Listen, I'm sorry about the other day – I was kinda – rough.'

'Kinda?' Celeste had the whole speech committed to memory.

'I didn't mean for it to come out like that.'

Celeste brushed her hair away from her face. 'But did you mean it?'

Damn. Here we go. 'Well – uh—' *Keep it real.* 'Yeah.'

Celeste leaned against a bedpost. 'I've called you some choice names in the last few days too.'

'I bet. You can run 'em past me if you want. I deserve it.' Ronnie laughed, hoping Celeste would too. 'That hurts.' She grabbed her pillow.

Celeste cracked a grin. 'I know. They told you to hold on when you cough or sneeze, but nobody mentioned laughing.' She looked down at her hands, rolled her wedding band around her finger. 'And

344

yeah, you do deserve it. You haven't exactly made any of this easy.'

Ronnie felt a comeback land on her tongue, but she kept her lips sealed and braced for whatever Celeste had to dish out.

Celeste wandered over to the dresser and straightened the tray that held a matching tortoiseshell dresser set. She had replayed a lot of conversations in the last few days, with Niki, with Everett, with her mother. Somehow she always came off as the villain. 'Am I really that bad?' She looked at Ronnie.

Ronnie sipped her lemonade. 'What do you mean bad?'

'Don't tell me you're hedging. There's no point getting shy now.' She picked up the hairbrush, rubbed her thumb across the boar bristles. 'Come on. Give it to me straight.'

Ronnie looked at her big sister over the rim of her glass, trying to figure out what was on her mind. 'Okay.' She took a gulp, then smiled. 'Yeah. You can be a pill. You never give anybody any slack and . . .'

'Okay. I haven't forgotten. You made yourself very clear already.' Celeste sat on the foot of the bed, still playing with the brush. 'I get it. I just don't know what to do about it.'

'I hear that.' Ronnie rubbed the back of her hand, which was still tender from the IV. 'We're not in such different places, you and me – I take that back. At least you have a job and an address. Oh yeah, and let's not forget you're married to the greatest guy in the world. A true prince among men.' She bowed her head and held up the sheet beside her as if to curtsy.

'I guess.' Celeste wasn't expecting Everett to come up. *I should tell her.* But it was hard to admit being

345

left by the prince. She wasn't prepared to trade confidences, especially when she ran the risk of being the heavy again. Celeste stood up. She needed a break from this topic. 'I really like your hair. I know I didn't say it before, but it's pretty hot.'

'Hot? My sister using the word *hot* to describe something other than coffee?'

'I work in a high school, you know. I can only be so lame. Want me to brush it for you?'

Do what? 'Uh – I – sure.' Ronnie sat up and edged to the side of the bed. 'If you can find enough to brush.'

Celeste climbed up and kneeled beside her. Ronnie hadn't used much more than a washcloth on her hair since Lucille cut it, but the bristles felt good against her scalp, and Celeste's touch was surprisingly gentle.

'I used to do this when you were a baby. You were too little to remember.'

'I guess I was.' Ronnie closed her eyes to enjoy the feeling.

'When they brought you home you were bald as a cue ball and I was afraid you were going to stay that way. I asked Mother and Daddy to take you back and get one with hair.'

'So you thought I was defective from the beginning.'

Celeste ignored the comment. 'They assured me your hair was coming, and after a while the fuzz appeared. As soon as there was enough to do anything with, Mother handed me this tiny brush with bristles soft as cotton.' Celeste's voice floated with the memory. 'And it was my job to brush your hair. It was so soft – and I'd make this one big fat curl on the top of your head.'

'You had me lookin' like a cartoon, didn't you?'

Celeste smirked. 'A little.'

'Uh-huh. See, I knew you never liked me.'

Celeste stopped brushing and sat next to Ronnie. 'You really think that, don't you?'

They were sitting so close it was hard for her to say yes. 'The thought crossed my mind once or twice.'

'I do like you, Ronnie. I may not always understand you –' She tapped Ronnie's leg with the brush. 'And I'm *not* glad things haven't worked out the way you wanted. Really I'm not.'

'For real?' Unbelieving and hopeful, for a moment Ronnie sounded like a kid.

'Cross my heart.' And Celeste did.

'You know, we've never done this.'

'What?'

'Sit on the bed and talk, like sisters.' Ronnie elbowed Celeste in the side. 'It's not too painful, huh?'

'Ask me tomorrow. It always hurts worse the next day.'

'If there are no side effects, you think maybe we could do this again? Sometime?' Ronnie asked.

'– Sure – I guess so.' Celeste needed to find a place for all this sisterly affection. 'But if I don't get downstairs, Mother will think you chewed me up and swallowed me instead of spitting me out, like you did last time.' She got up and put the brush back on the dresser. 'And Ron, we'll work this house thing out. I promise.'

'Speaking of the house, did Ma give up any information about livin' here? Playin' the piano? Somethin'?'

'If I heard it, you did.'

They both stopped at the sound of Della's footsteps on the stairs. She poked her head in Ronnie's room. 'There's a man downstairs named Doug Pryce . . .'

'Doug? Here?' Automatically Ronnie reached up and smoothed her head, where there used to be hair.

'I didn't know you were here long enough to be keepin' company . . .'

'He's a real estate agent, Ma.'

'Whoever he is, he wants to know if he can come up.' Della spoke from the safety of the doorway.

'I don't know. What does he want?'

'Said he stopped by to see how you're feelin'. People down here are either neighborly or nosy, but I don't know him so I don't know which he is.'

'He's not from here. Well I guess he is, but he moved to L.A. years ago. They don't drop in on people out there.'

'He surely isn't here to pressure us about this sale?' Celeste put her hands on her hips. 'That's not even decent.'

'No, but he used to be a reporter and now he sells real estate. Could anybody be pushier?' Ronnie and Celeste laughed. Della didn't seem to think it was funny.

'Gimme a couple of minutes, then you can send him up.'

'What am I supposed to do with him until you're ready?'

'Talk to him, Ma. This'll only take a minute.'

Della grumbled and disappeared back down the stairs.

'Celeste, would you get me one of those dresses?' Ronnie eased over to the side of the bed. 'Whatever he wants, I cannot have a conversation with this man in my pajamas.' She pulled her lime green sleep shirt over her head.

'This one?' Celeste held a black and white polka dot sundress out of the closet.

'Uh. No.' *Why does it matter?* 'Give me the other one.'

'Really? When I picked it out, Mother told me you'd never wear it.' While Ronnie sat on the side of the bed, Celeste helped her slip the pink sundress over her head.

'I don't know. It's somethin' different from my usual black, brown, or navy. Does it look okay with my new hot hair?'

'Yeah. Want your makeup?'

Ronnie thought about it, but she wasn't even in the mood to paint on her five-minute quickie face. 'Just hand me a lipstick.' In two swipes and a blot her lips were coppery red. 'Should I stay here or move over there?'

Celeste looked from bed to chair. 'I'll help you.' She eased Ronnie down and got her settled in the bedside chair. Then Celeste smirked. 'I think you were wearing more clothes before.'

Ronnie looked down at the neckline and the glimpse of cleavage it revealed. She tugged the bodice up, but it slipped back down. 'You picked this?' Not that Ronnie was modest, but she wasn't trying to get Doug's attention, at least not that way. She was already feeling exposed, vulnerable, and the dress only added to it. She tugged at the front again, then with a shrug gave up and hid behind her hugging pillow. 'Ready.'

'You want me to stay?'

'Nah. Send him up.' She crossed her legs primly at the ankles. *Let her rip.*

Doug tapped on the wall by the door before stepping into view. 'Hey.'

'Welcome to the recovery room,' Ronnie said. *Why is this making me nervous?*

Doug came in. 'Wow. That's some surgery they did. What do they call it, a hairodectomy?'

'Radical hairodectomy. It was the only way.' The twinkle in his eyes was like sunlight, warm and welcoming, and Ronnie's face brightened with a smile.

'You look—'

'Shorn?' Her hand shot to her head.

'No. No. No. Nothing sheepish about it.' He stroked the corners of his mustache with his thumb and forefinger. 'It's pretty bold.' He tilted his head to the side for another angle. 'Very becoming.'

'Becoming what is the question.' She rubbed her bare neck. 'Kidding. I think it's okay too, but it'll take me a while to get used to it – Glad it's not winter. I'd freeze to death.'

'Yep. It's definitely all right.' He nodded his approval.

'Thanks,' Ronnie said shyly. She didn't know why she was self-conscious. *Not sheepish, remember!* 'Speakin' of lookin' different—' Doug appeared cool and crisp in his tan suit, pale blue shirt, and tie. She looked at his loafers and was surprised at the multi-hued blue swirls on his socks. *Pretty sharp! The boy cleans up good.* 'You get dressed to visit me?'

'This?' He smoothed his tie down into his jacket. 'No.'

Guess he pricked my bubble.

'I've got a bank meeting later. And look at you. I

350

didn't think pink was an approved New York color.'

'When in Prosper . . .' *Did I just say that?*

'In any case I'm happy you're doing better. It must be rough getting sick away from home, without your own doctor.'

'I'm not sure it would have been easier in New York. I'm just glad it's over.' She had no intention of giving Doug the scoop on her dicey circumstances. 'And maybe one day I'll even let this out of my sight.' She patted the pillow. 'But right now, I don't make a move without it!'

'I remember that from when Janice had surgery.'

Ronnie didn't know what to say on the subject of his late wife's operation. *Either their thing was really deep, or he's a little weird.* 'Have a seat.' So she plowed past it.

'No. This is just a quick stop. I brought you something.'

'I haven't thanked you for the flowers yet. They're beautiful.' Ronnie pointed to the basket of roses on the windowsill, feeling stupid again. *Bold!* 'How'd you find out I was in the hospital, anyway?'

'A man has his methods.'

What conversation are we having? 'So I've heard.' If there was flirting involved, Ronnie was usually three steps ahead, but she was never completely sure if the entendre was really double with Doug or if he was just being straightforward.

'You're asking me to reveal my sources. That's serious business.'

'Just this once.'

Doug folded his arms, arched an eyebrow. 'Prosper's still small enough that word of most things gets around.'

351

'That's unique.' Ronnie figured she could walk down Broadway wearing peacock feathers and singing hip-hop and nobody she knew would have heard about it. She thought out loud a second. 'Must be somebody Hambone told . . .'

'Hambone?'

'Old family friend I just met. But first things first, what did you bring? If it's the contract, we're . . .'

'No, but I do have some news on that front. But before we get to that.' He reached back into the hall and produced a fishing rod and reel.

'You are outta your mind!' Ronnie held herself and laughed. 'A gen-u-wine fishin' pole?'

'You bet. Worms not included.'

'You know, I was sittin' by the window a little while ago, wishin' I could see the water. But somehow fishin' never came up!'

'I'm telling you, it's good for what ails you. I don't know if you'll get to use it before you leave, but it'll be a souvenir. Put it in a corner in your apartment. Hang your hat on it. It's sure to be a conversation piece in your part of the world.' Doug leaned the pole against the wall. 'But I guess you won't need a reminder of this trip.'

'Hardly. But I can definitely tell you no one's ever given me one of those before.'

'Are you guys all right up there?'

'Fine, Celeste!' Ronnie dropped her voice. 'My sister is dying to know what's goin' on.'

'I'm sure. She gave me a pretty strange look when she saw me with the pole. Anyway, the official reason I came out was to let you know the buyer understands that things this trip haven't gone exactly the way you anticipated.'

'You mean you don't think I had all this planned when I called you? What was it?' Ronnie puzzled a second. 'Was it really only two weeks ago?'

'Time flies . . .'

'I'm not having fun yet, Doug.'

'Well, my client said you and your sister can take your time. The offer stands, and when you're ready, I hope we can find a solution that'll make everybody happy.'

'Why are they being so nice? They don't know us.'

'Gotta have a reason to be nice, huh?'

'You know what I mean.'

'Nice, patient, whatever you call it, it's for real. You can trust me on that, even if I can't convince you about fishing.' He saluted. 'I'm outta here. Gotta see a man about a house.' He chuckled. 'Real estate humor's pretty lame, isn't it?'

Ronnie smiled and nodded.

'Call me when you guys figure out what you want to do, or before you head home. Whichever comes first.'

The word *home* made her queasy. 'Will do. And thanks for everything. I guess we've been a real pain in the . . .'

'Assets are our business, our only business – I warned you about the jokes.' Doug headed for the door but turned around just before he walked out. 'Let me know if you ever use it.' He tapped the rod and disappeared. Ronnie listened to his footfalls double time down the stairs, quickly followed by Celeste's dainty shuffle coming up.

'Why in the world did he bring you that thing?'

'Wouldn't you like to know!'

The rest of the day and the next passed uneventfully, with Ronnie upstairs, Della downstairs, and

353

Celeste shuttling between. Sunday's adventure was Ronnie's first trip downstairs, which was slow but uneventful. Celeste had fixed her a spot in the living room, but although she was more mobile, she wasn't any more energetic and napped intermittently. Lucille stopped by late in the afternoon with a pecan pie. Friday and Saturday were her busiest days in the shop, so this was her first trip out to the house since the Frazier family had set up temporary residence. But Della had been expecting the visit and she knew Lucille had more on her mind than how Ronnie was doing.

'She looks good, Odella.'

Della looked up from her word puzzle when Lucille walked out to the porch. Unread sections of the Sunday paper lay in a pile at Della's feet. 'Pays to be young.' She leaned to the side to get a paper towel out of her pants pocket, lifted her sweating glass of ice water, and mopped up the ring on the rusting wrought-iron table between the two chairs. Della had hoped to avoid this conversation, but deep down she knew that wouldn't happen, couldn't happen. After all, she'd tried to get away without coming back to Prosper too, hadn't she?

'I can't hardly believe it was just a week ago.' Lucille eased into the other wicker chair. Her denim shirt-dress fell open around her legs, and she massaged her knees like she was used to them aching. 'Umph, umph.' She shook her head in disbelief. 'It was just about this time too. We were gettin' ready to eat.'

Della folded the damp towel into quarters and put it away. 'I'm sorry they came down here with this mess, disruptin' your life. You and Hambone are too busy for all this foolishness.'

'Never too busy for family.' Lucille paused to let her words settle over Della. 'Odella – I mean Della. That's how you call it now.'

'Call me what you want, Lucille.'

'Awright then, Odella, you know you became family to us not long after you got to Prosper. So your children – well, they're family too.' She sat on the edge of the big chair because if she slid all the way back, her feet wouldn't touch the floor. 'I'm gon' say this 'cause I promised myself I would – if I ever got the chance.' She waited for Della to look her in the eye. 'It was wrong what you did. Not one word in forty-some years. Not one. You don't treat folks like that.' Della looked down at her sneakers. She would rather have had a toothache; it would have been less painful than hearing this. Lucille was the last person she intended to hurt, but this talk was about the effect of her disappearance, not the cause. 'Not folks that care about you.' Lucille's normally chirpy voice was sad and solemn. 'I understand why you left. Nobody would fault you for that. But you never answered one letter. Not even a Christmas card. Hambone told me it was the best way you knew to carry your load. Took me a long time, but I finally made my peace with it.' Della pried her eyes off the ground and peeped at Lucille again. 'And with you, in case you're interested. I ain't mad. I know you been dreadin' my comin' out here. 'Fraid I was gon' plow up a perfectly nice field. When I saw you at the hospital it was written 'cross your face, plain as day.'

Della cleared her throat. She wanted to explain herself, but the time for that had passed. She averted her eyes from Lucille's X-ray gaze and paused at the azalea bush beside the house. *I wonder what it looks like*

355

when it's in bloom. It was almost as tall as the porch roof now. *I wish this was over.* Della had given many a lecture, but she hadn't been on the receiving end in years. Neither Celeste nor Ronnie would have believed their mother could listen this long without comment. In a few seconds she faced back around to finish taking her licking because she knew Lucille had no intention of stopping until she had said her piece. She also knew Lucille was right.

'Everybody got pain. Some worse than others, but it's a part of life. I know what you wanted and I know you didn't get it, except that don't excuse you from considerin' anybody but yourself. You not the girl who came here with her heart in a sling, or the young woman who left with it that way, but she's still in you. We are our past, Odella. You can't get away from it no matter how long and hard you try. Actin' like a part of your life didn't happen don't wash it away!' Lucille tapped her long, narrow feet against the floorboards. 'Miz Ethiopia had a long life to think about what she done. She knew Henry wasn't no good, but she didn't do nothin' about it. I guess she tried to make amends for what he did and what she didn't do by leavin' you this place. In the end both she and Henry had a whole lot to answer for.' Lucille paused.

Della nodded her head. She didn't know if Lucille was taking a breath or giving her a chance to ask about Henry, but mending this old friendship was more important. *I just hope Henry got whatever he deserved. No more, no less.* Right now, she didn't need to know. 'You want some ice water or some lemonade?'

'Thank you, no. I got to get goin' in a minute.' Lucille looked at Della another few seconds. 'It looks to me like you been stumblin' around, trippin' over your own big feet, tryin' to walk away from here, 'cept I got news for you, Odella. The footprints are always behind you.'

Eyes filled, Della bobbed her head slowly and swallowed back her tears. 'Lucille – I didn't mean to . . .'

'Don't.' Lucille held up her hand. 'I don't need no "I'm sorry." I tol' you, I'm through with all that old stuff. I still care about you, always have, guess I always will.' She stood to go. 'But Celeste and Ronnie, they need to know a whole lot more'n they do.' She smoothed the front of her dress. 'Come on, walk with me. I got something for you in my car.'

The wicker creaked as Della got up and followed Lucille off the porch.

She pushed a button on her key ring, and the trunk of her car popped open before they got there. 'I done had this a whole lot longer than I expected.' Lucille nodded at the inside of her trunk. 'Just like you left it.'

Della stared at the butterscotch leather valise. She used to think about this bag all the time at the beginning, but as time passed, she stopped wondering. It never occurred to her that Lucille still had it. *Why'd she keep it?* 'Why'd you keep it?'

'You asked me to.' She patted Della's arm. 'Go on, take it.'

Della reached out tentatively, the way you approach an unknown dog, even when you've been assured he won't bite. She hesitated, her hand hovering above the leather handle, but finally, she fastened her fingers around it and hauled the suitcase out into the afternoon sunshine.

'How much longer y'all gon' be here?' Lucille got behind the wheel.

357

'Mostly depends on Ronnie. And Celeste ain't in no hurry to get back either.' Della's thoughts drifted off. When she saw Lucille's quizzical look, she added, 'It's a long story.'

'Uh-huh, always is. Especially with our children.' Lucille started the engine. 'And I thought it was hard when they were little, but it got worse when they called themselves grown.'

'Yes, indeedy!' Della said.

'Worse on us and on them too I 'spect. Umph. You should see Jessie, Dianne, and George Jr. And we got four grands! Can you believe it? I don't feel old enough to be this old!' Lucille recognized the troubled look on Della's face. It wasn't much different now than it was then. 'You know, me and my kids, we had us some battles, 'specially Dianne. Lord, my girl enlisted in the army, and first I knew she had bags packed and was walkin' out the door. Umph. This took me a while, but I figured out that the more I let my kids see who I was when I was young, mistakes and all, the more they let me see who they were grown. Now, I'm still Mama, and we don't have to share *everythin'*, but it's kinda comfortable now.'

Lucille patted the steering wheel, then reached for the gearshift. 'Come on by one morning and we'll swap stories. You don't need an invitation.' She put the car in drive, then stopped again. 'Ronnie told me her middle name. Thanks.' And she drove off, leaving Della to ponder in her wake.

'What's that suitcase doing on the porch?' Celeste asked when she got back from Winn Dixie with a car full of groceries.

'Is it botherin' you?' Della snapped as she helped Celeste carry the bulging paper bags into the kitchen.

358

'No. It's just that—'

'Is it bothering anybody else?' Della grumbled as she started unpacking food. 'You plannin' on stayin' through the winter?'

'Forget I asked, Mother. However long we're here, we needed some things. There was no sense in making a thousand little trips to the store when I could make one.'

But Della had walked out of the kitchen by then, and Celeste left the suitcase alone. Just another straw on the camel's back.

18

'. . . we could be so good together.'

Maybe it's time. Della sat on the side of the white iron bed, listening for sounds of nocturnal wakefulness. All she heard was the beating of her own heart and the insistent cricket chorus. That twittering accompanied Buffalo nights too, but it didn't fill the house, echo off the ceiling, dance through the halls like it did here. Like she remembered from her nights in this room. It was twice the size of her room at home in Cadysville, and she recalled her first nights in it when she would lie awake counting the nosegays on the wallpaper or the slats in the wainscoting. The nights she pretended it was Annie down the hall sleeping in the room with her father. The nights she prayed to wake up in the morning and be in her old bed in her old room. As weeks turned into months, and she resigned herself to her new life, sleep claimed her nights again.

And when she went up to bed her first night back in this house, Della walked into her old room and wondered what the nights would have in store for her now. The furniture was the same, and when she removed the lowest drawer of the painted white dresser, the OW she had carved on the bottom with a penny nail was still there too. Nothing here had changed, but maybe she had. It was only a room in the same way she was discovering Little Pond was only a house. So she counted slats, thirteen until the one that was cracked, twenty-six more to the window, just like always. After that, the nights were hers, and Della played solitaire, read magazines, and worked her puzzles like always, then drifted off for her usual four or five hours of shut-eye. But tonight she couldn't get that bag waiting for her on the porch out of her mind. When she crept downstairs, careful to avoid the squeaky one, she was sure Ronnie and Celeste were fast asleep. They had walked around the suitcase for two days, acting like it wasn't there, and Della hadn't missed the looks her daughters threw in her direction every time they passed it, but they gave it and her a wide berth. She wasn't ready to address it until now.

Bag in hand, she returned upstairs with the same stealth as she had descended. Della padded silently down the hall and closed her door. She placed it on her bed and unfastened the straps that held it closed. It had never been locked. Slowly she raised the lid. Before it was open all the way, she reached in and pulled out the blue taffeta dress.

FRIDAY, AUGUST 23, 1957
TITUS, NORTH CAROLINA

'Come on outta there, Odee. We on in five minutes.' Lester whispered loud so she could hear him through the bathroom door, above the raucous music in Tremayne's Klub Kozy. 'O-dee?!'

Odella stared in the motley, cracked mirror in the

ladies' room, a lean-to beside the club. It looked more like an outhouse, but at least it had four walls and a lightbulb jury-rigged from the main power line. The men had to take care of their business in the narrow strip of woods out back. *I can't do this.* School had just started, and Odella hadn't heard a word her teachers said all day. Her liver quivered imagining tonight, her real, professional singing debut. She and Lester had been sneaking to practice for weeks, down by the pond, blending songs he already used with new duets and solos for her. They picked big hits from the radio, and he talked about the rhythm of a set, how you had to arrange the music from fast to slow, from ballads to blues to guide the audience along with you. During rehearsals Will was their only audience and critic, although his main comment was, 'Odella don't need to be doin' this.' He even tried to talk her out of it, but she wouldn't listen. 'I gotta get out of Prosper, Will,' she'd told him. In secret, Odella had worked out the piano arrangements, and now she rolled the sheets of music like a funnel in her hands. *I can't do this.* Tonight she and Lester would split twenty dollars plus tips and two shots of booze apiece if they wanted it. She took a final look in the mirror and hardly recognized the person looking back. It certainly wasn't Odella Womack from Cadysville, North Carolina. Before Lester had picked her up, Lucille had greased and pressed her hair till it looked like a patent leather bouffant. Her eyebrows were drawn in a dramatic arch, and Odella didn't know whose Orange Flip lips those were on her face, but her mouth was dry as old shoe leather. Lucille had made her buff the dry patches on her heels with a pumice stone and slather Vaseline on her arms and legs so her skin gleamed.

Odella's toe knuckles were jammed so tight into Lucille's clear plastic ankle-strap heels that her feet were already numb, but when she complained about the rigors of her wardrobe, Lucille pooh-poohed and assured her, 'Glamour is painful but worth it.' Odella pressed on the spit curls Lucille had glued to her temples. *It's just singin'. I can do it!* She pushed the weathered boards nailed together and attached to the wall with a rusty spring hinge, and the door creaked open. She looked at Lester with a dazed expression. 'I can't do this.' Odella's arms crossed high on her chest, covering the décolletage of her dress. There was nothing she could do to hide the way the taffeta outlined her hips, tapered down past her knees so she had to walk in mincing steps. She looked down into her very voluptuous cleavage, which was highlighted by a triple strand of crystal beads she'd managed to sneak out of Miz Ethiopia's drawer. 'It wasn't supposed to be so – so—'

'Ain't nothin' wrong with that dress. You look exactly like you supposed to. Like a singer!'

The makeshift walls of the Kozy, red and gold Moroccan patterned linoleum tacked directly to furring strips, vibrated with the rhythm of the wailing jukebox and barely contained the Friday night crowd, primed with mean payday green and ready to shake off the workweek blues. The music clung to the thick August night and battled with laughter, sweet talk, and cussing to be heard. Tremayne's was on Lester's regular circuit, and after more than a year he had finally convinced Odella to work it with him.

Odella jumped when she heard a woman's squeal, followed by raunchy laughter. 'Lester Malachi Wilson, this was a mistake.'

'You gon' be smokin', Odee. Trust me.' The head-lights of a wheezing pickup truck pulling onto the crunchy brown grass cast them in long shadows. Lester gently pried her arms down, and she let them hang at her sides. 'How else we gon' make it to the top?' He raised her chin with his forefinger, looked in her eyes, and she could feel his raw energy shoot through her and give her a boost.

'What if somebody knows me?' Odella didn't really suspect that would happen. They were far from Prosper, and nobody she knew went to places like this, but right now she was looking for any excuse not to go through with it. Her father and Miz Ethiopia thought she was babysitting little Jessie while Hambone and Lucille were in Rocky Mount overnight. That in itself had been a hard sell. Miz Ethiopia started her harangue about the jukebox, but this time her father held his ground, stilled her comments, and said he thought it would be fine. Odella would be at the house, not at Pal's after all. And that was that.

Of course her father's trust only made Odella feel more guilty about lying. But she was seventeen and dying to do something grown up, something that would get her away from that house and from Henry. Lester's plan was the best she'd heard, and she loved to sing, so she had put her guilt in her pocket and stuffed the dress she had made in secret on Wednesday afternoons in a paper sack under some magazines and a change of underwear and headed to Lucille's after school for her rendezvous with Johnny Du Pree. She was put out with Will for not coming, but he was acting kind of funny anyway, so she decided it was best he stayed home.

364

'Ain't nobody from Prosper even heard a this place. I been here five or six times already. Ain't no reason for folks to come way over here when they got perfectly good juke joints close by.' Odella knew he was right. 'They're gon' love us, Odee. I'm tellin' you, baby, tonight is just the beginning.' He grabbed both her hands in one and pulled her toward the door. 'You wait and see.' With his free hand, he straightened his skinny tie, patted his hair, and adjusted the pocket square she made him to match her dress. His narrow blue suit emphasized his wide shoulders and his trim, muscled build. They waited outside, holding hands, until the music stopped and they heard Tremayne's honking voice, then Lester guided her just inside. Sultry air greeted them at the door. He buffed the toes of his pointy shoes on the backs of his trouser legs.

'Hey! Lissen up!' Tremayne, who was four foot and change with sandy yellow hair, skin to match, and a patch over his left eye, stepped onto the stage, an old hay wagon turned upside down. The crowd continued to rumble and roar so he banged on a dented soup pot with a big metal ladle for order. 'Was y'all raised in a barn?!' Three young men at a three-legged table down front answered with farmyard noises. 'Hit the nail on the head huh!' Tremayne spanked his pot until the crowd settled down enough to hear him. 'We got a real treat for y'all.'

Odella squeezed Lester's hand tight as a vise. Christmas lights in red, green, blue, and gold outlined the room, and silvery tinsel hung shaggy from the ceiling. She'd never seen so many people jammed this tight together. She took a deep breath to steady herself, and her lungs filled with a heady mix of Chesterfields, Old Spice, Pabst Blue Ribbon, Dixie

365

Peach, Wild Turkey, My Sin, fried catfish, barbecue, and sweat.

'Now, y'all open yo' ears, shut yo' moufs. Put yo' hands together and give a warm Klub Kozy welcome to one a yo' favorites. Mr Smooth – Mr Cool – Mr Johnny DuPree! And tonight, as a extra added attraction, he's brung with him the lovely and talented Miss Della Lester!'

Odella about yanked his arm out of the socket. 'Della Lester?!'

'Odella Womack is just plain country.'

Whoops, whistles, and hollers rose from the audience. Johnny DuPree headed through the maze of mismatched tables and chairs, dragging the new Della Lester behind him. He jumped up on the stage, spun around on one foot to face the audience, did a split, and sprang back up like his legs were rubber with a spring attached, then he reached down and lifted Odella up next to him. She didn't know he could do splits or that he was so strong. Her eyes darted around, scanning the crowd. All the faces looking back, none of them wearing ugly hats, made her giddy. A little voice in her head told her to smile, so she locked her lips in a frozen grin. Johnny yanked the sheet music from her hand and gave it to the old man at the ancient upright. Odella felt like she barely knew how to talk, let alone sing. *I can't do this!*

As the piano man pounded out the intro, Lester winked, grabbed her around the waist, and squeezed the music out of her like an accordion.

'Hey everybody, let's have some fun. You only live once and when you're dead you're done, so let the good times roll . . .'

The crowd was with them from the git go and

swayed, clapped, and sang along. They were at the center of a sho 'nuff party, and by the second verse the rhythm took over and Odella forgot to be scared. It was just like always when they sang, in church or down by the lake. The song, and their blended voices, his deep and tangy, hers sharp and sassy, carried then along. Johnny preened and strutted, and Odella matched him step for step in a way she didn't know she could.

Johnny jumped down and stood by the piano when it was time for Odella's first solo. She almost panicked, standing up there alone, but she sang directly to Johnny for the first few bars, then she was strong enough to look into the audience, at least long enough to hook them. After that she closed her eyes to conjure up the emotion of the lyrics. Emotions she hadn't yet felt. *'If you don't think, you'll be home soon, I guess I'll drown in my own tears.'* Her voice swooped and soared, touching her and everybody else in the room deep down at the root.

It felt to Odella like they had just begun when the set was over. She looked at Johnny, who beamed back at her, then grabbed her hand. They took their bows, dashed off stage, and made their way out the way they'd come in, but this time there was applause, enthusiastic shouts, and hand grabs to escort them.

'See, I *told* you there wasn't nothin' to be scared of! Didn't I!?' Once they got out beside the building, Johnny did his spin then grabbed Odella by the shoulders and shook her playfully. 'You did it, baby! Tomorrow them folks will be tellin' their friends, "Whoo, now that Della Lester, she can *sang!*"' Sweat ran down both sides of his face, met at the point of his chin, and dripped to the ground.

'Della Lester, huh! And did you *ask* me if you could change my name?!' Odella fanned herself with her hands, trying to cool down, but it felt like she was trying to stir a vat of thick, hot soup.

'No, but it sounds good, don't it?!'

She tried to make like she was mad, but she couldn't stifle the grin. 'Yeah!' *Della Lester*. It sounded high-class. Della Lester could go places and do things Odella Womack only dreamed about. *And* it was part of his name. She wiped the sweat off her brow and flung the pellets off her hand.

'See, I told you I'd look out for you.' Lester took a fresh handkerchief from his inside pocket and gently dabbed the water from Odella's forehead. She stood stock-still, but inside it was like she stuck her toe in an electric socket, except it was kind of good. When he was done, he dried off his face and neck.

'Della Lester sounds like somebody who wears diamonds and furs, drives a Cadillac, and has a fancy apartment in New York City.' Hot rivulets trickled down her back and her belly. Their time on stage had gone by in a blur, and she was still not sure it wasn't a dream, but she was intoxicated with the night and the possibilities.

'Now you're talkin'! We can do this all over the state, and then—' He churned his arms like the axles on a locomotive and chugged around her, building up speed. 'Next stop – Memphis – Chicago – Cleveland – Baltimore – and New York City! All aboard!' He blew the train whistle and Odella laughed. 'All it takes is for the right person to hear us, and bam! We'll be whipping out hit records, and the folks back in Prosper will be listenin' to us on the radio and talkin' about "Remember them when!" I'm tellin' you, Odee, this is just the beginning. I can feel it!' He stopped, and the look in his eyes was one Odella had never seen before. At first she looked away, but slowly, drawn by a force she couldn't resist, she answered his gaze. Johnny moved closer, and before she knew what happened she was in his arms.

The air that moments ago had been too thick was suddenly too thin for Odella to breathe. *This is Lester!* They were pressed body to body, so close she couldn't tell if it was her heart pounding or his. Somehow her arms found a place wrapped around his neck, and then she was squeezing him too. *This is crazy.* She tried to pull away, but he wasn't letting her go. Hands flat against her back, he drew her closer, his cheek prickly next to hers, and she felt a slow tingle way down low in a spot that hadn't awakened until now. Odella closed her eyes. Just to think. Just for a second, but then she was surrounded by the smell of him, crisp and fresh like soap, spicy like the lavender and licorice of Sen-Sen. And when he nestled his face in the crook of her neck, kneaded her back, the blood rushed to Odella's head and she felt like it would explode.

'Odee, we could be so good together.'

The tickle of his lips, his breath, soft against her ear made Odella shiver. She could always feel his presence, but this close was overwhelming. She always told herself she was foolish to daydream about Lester Wilson. Now here she was in his arms, and she wanted to believe him, but daydreams don't come true. *Do they?*

Lester took her face in his hands. 'You're somethin' else, you know that,' he said hoarsely. Lester had been drawn to her from the first time he saw her, in that muddy white dress, standing by her father's car.

Crazy as that was. He couldn't explain it then, and he wasn't sure he could explain it now. Odella wasn't exactly beautiful, but the prettiest girls didn't have what she had, a presence he couldn't call by name, but he felt it strong and knew she did too.

Odella's knees turned to mush, and she thought she would faint dead away, so she just held on. And not a moment too soon. He felt her weight shift, sink into him. The velvety softness of his lips brushed her own, and she didn't know what to do in response so she stopped breathing through her mouth. Odella pushed back with her lips and held the air in her lungs until she got dizzy, then panted in short, staccato wheezes through her nose. When she felt his tongue pry her mouth open, she panicked and clenched her teeth against the invasion. But that didn't last long. Lester's hands slipped down to her waist, made their way around to her back again, and when they came to rest in the curve above her butt, she relaxed her jaw and let him in. Lester was a flavor she'd not tasted before, salty and mysterious. He tantalized her appetite, and suddenly Odella was hungry and she knew what to do. She let her tongue wander, exploring his mouth like his hands explored her body. She rubbed the back of his neck, felt the bristly hairs left by the razor the barber used to neaten up his hairline.

Arms locked around each other, they swayed to a song they wrote as they went along. Then sweaty and hearts racing, they heard voices, opened their eyes, and saw they had company. He took her hand and led her to the car.

'I should change my dress before we go. I don't want to get caught.'

'Keep it on. I like it. I like the way it sounds.' He

ran the tip of his fingernail down her side, and the shiny fabric hummed. 'Won't nobody see you before I take you by Lucille's.'

'But—'

'I promised nobody you know would be here, didn't I?' He smiled, reached past her to open the car door but stopped for a kiss on the way.

Odella brushed him away. 'So you did!' She got in the car, thinking about how many times she sat right there, next to Lester, wishing what happened tonight would happen, and she wondered if he knew.

He climbed in and started the engine. 'What you doin' way over there?' Lester stretched his arm across the back of the seat and waited. She slid into place, happy in a way she never knew existed.

They had been driving about an hour when he pulled off the road onto the edge of a tobacco field, cut the engine, and turned off the headlights. He pulled her closer and traced the low neckline of her dress with his finger. His touch was light and sure, and Odella felt the panic and the hunger rise again. She knew that kissing wasn't all there was to it, but she didn't exactly know how everything else happened. Logically and physically it didn't make sense, but she had heard that it was supposed to be magic. She just didn't know if she was ready.

Lester kissed her neck, the swell of her breasts. 'Odee?'

She heard the rustle of the taffeta, felt his hand work its way under her skirt, and her insides liquified. 'Huh?' she managed.

He massaged her knee, and his hand moved slowly up her thigh. When he reached the top of her stocking and slipped his finger under her garter, he felt her

371

resist, stiffen. He took his hand away. 'We ain't gon'
do nothin' you don't wanna do.' He lifted her chin. 'I
want you to be my girl.'

'Its not that – I—' She had a flash of lying facedown on the floor in the chicken coop, Henry pressed
against her back. She hadn't told Lester about that
day, didn't want him to know. And as much as she
didn't want to be thinking about that now, it hung
over her.

'It's okay. You and me, we gon' make it, Odee.' He
kissed her gently. 'You'll tell me when you're ready.
You won't have to say a word. 'Cause even when you
don't know I'm lookin', I got my eye on you. Always
have.'

Della clutched the dress tight. It was musty, but the
icy hot blue never faded. *And I made you promise not
to tell anybody we were going together. We fooled most
folks, at least for a while, but Will knew. I think he knew
from the beginning.*

19

'Ain't nothin' hurts worse than a lie.'

Ronnie shuffled into the kitchen, her hugging pillow tucked under her arm. She poked her head out the back door to get her lungs full of early morning air, feeling pretty chipper and pleased with herself for getting showered, dressed, and downstairs before nine with no help. And when she dug around in her purse looking for her wallet and checkbook to talley up the actual sad state of her finances, she came across a pack of cigarettes and realized she hadn't touched one since before the surgery. Ronnie had made a career of quitting, but right now she just didn't have the urge, and that felt good. She spied Della at the table in her housecoat and spongy pink curlers, finishing a toaster waffle. The slack nonexpression on her face, the slump to her shoulders struck Ronnie. *Ma's not that old. Why does she look like that?* 'Hey, Mamacita.'

'We should be plannin' to go home soon.' Della had been up all night with nothing to chew on but her own thoughts and memories. She was sick of that taste and ready to sink her teeth into something else. 'I know you don't *want* to move back to Buffalo, but I can't see much else for you to do.' She folded her hands in front of her, like it was a done deal.

Ronnie recognized the no-nonsense voice and realized she'd walked smack into an ambush. *Oh, shit. Ma's on a mission.* She still hadn't come up with a concrete bail-out plan, but she knew it had to be radical; there wasn't much left of her old life to salvage. And the game clock was ticking down to double zero. The one thing she was sure about was that moving home now would make her feel like a total failure. 'I can't have a life there.'

'Looks to me like you ain't had much a one in New York neither.' Della swallowed some coffee. 'You want eggs for breakfast?'

Food wasn't a priority, but it would give Ronnie a moment to collect her thoughts. 'I can't keep eating like that. I'll be big as a house!'

'You have to get your strength back.' Della got up and turned the heat on under the iron skillet and the kettle.

'Isn't there any yogurt or fruit?' Ronnie examined her choices in the refrigerator.

Della came up behind her, reached in, and took two eggs from the door. 'You eat that when you're sick, not when you're tryin' to get well.' She broke them over a bowl and whipped them into a frenzied froth.

'Fine! I think I'll have eggs.' *I can't live like this.* Ronnie plunked down on a kitchen chair, and in no time Della set a plate of pebbly scrambled eggs and slightly burned toast slathered in butter in front of her. 'Ma, it's been a long time since we lived under the same roof. We're . . .'

'You won't have to live with me after you're on your feet.' Della sat down with a cup of tea for Ronnie and more coffee for herself. 'Lord knows I ain't lookin' for a roommate. When you're up and around, you could move into one of the houses if you want to. There's plenty of addresses to choose from. You might even want to help Shorty manage the rentals. Maybe that way I wouldn't sell all of 'em. Keep it a family business.' She heaped sugar in her cup and stirred. 'Although I do have to sell another one since your hospital stay used up the money I was gon' give Niki for school.' Della sipped again to give her pointed reminder of how little choice Ronnie really had a chance to sink in. 'I don't know what you gon' do, but I know you got to do somethin'.' It didn't look to Della like either of her children was in any hurry to leave Prosper, so she decided it was time to move things along. 'We can't stay here forever. Your sister's layin' in supplies like she's expectin' a blizzard and . . .'

'I wasn't plannin' to stay forever!' Ronnie pushed her plate away. 'Ma, give me *some* credit. Until now I've always taken care of myself. And it may look to you like I loafed around wastin' time, but I hustled every day, tryin' to get the next gig, tryin' to get noticed by the right people. And let me tell you, there are worse actors than me makin' a livin' at it. I just couldn't seem to catch a break.' Ronnie crumbled the crust off her toast. 'All I'm askin' is for a little more time to figure some things out.'

'You had seventeen years. How much more time do you need?' Della was unmoved.

'That's not fair!' Ronnie knew it sounded juvenile, but she was scrambling.

'Did somebody finally steal that suitcase off the porch?' Celeste, brow furrowed, headed for the coffeepot.

'No,' Della snapped.

'Well, what happened to it?'

'It's *my* business what happened to it. Just like it's *your* business why Everett is divorcin' you.'

'What?!' Ronnie jerked around so fast she almost toppled her teacup. She was feeling good because she thought the wall between her and Celeste had come down some in the last few days, but there were obviously still enough bricks left to block the way. 'You didn't say one word.'

'Now, I don't see you bendin' over backward explainin' to nobody what happened to your marriage.' Della plowed over Ronnie's comment and headed straight for Celeste. 'So don't you keep worryin' me about my bag.'

The unexpected blow dazed Celeste, but she still had enough wits about her to duck out of the way. 'I don't have to take this!' She hurried from the room, snatched her purse from the chair in the hall.

Della was hot on her tail. 'You need to go home and tend to your own mess instead of hiding out down . . .'

Celeste slammed the door so hard the house shook and windowpanes rattled. Della was rattled too, down to the bone. But it wasn't Celeste that got to her; it was the violent crash, still echoing in her ears. She grabbed hold of the bannister and sank to the steps.

TUESDAY, SEPTEMBER 10, 1957
PROSPER, NORTH CAROLINA

'I knew it soon as she set foot in this house!'

The front door slammed like a gunshot and rattled the house to its foundation. Odella jumped in her

376

bedroom chair. She knew Henry meant her, and she knew he meant to stir up trouble.

'She ain't nothin' but a ho. Just like her mama!'

Odella's hands sank to her lap, and the sweat on her skin turned icy. She'd been sitting by the window, mending a nylon slip, trying to get some air on this muggy evening and repeating every word Lester said when he called her, long-distance, from Cleveland. Then all hell broke loose.

'You must be drunk, boy! And you better get out my house till you're sober!' Odell, still wearing a T-shirt and blue work pants, bellowed from the landing.

'Ain't hardly drunk!' Henry stomped up the steps, and when Odella peeked out of her door he and Odell were standing toe to toe in the hall. Father was still a head taller and half again wider than son, but Henry was swelled with defiance. 'I was by the barbershop today. Man in the next chair tol' me my sister sure could sing, and I know he ain't been to nobody's church. Said he saw her in some gin shack over in Titus. Seems she and Lester been gallivantin' 'round, call themselves singin'. And who knows what else they do.' Henry's hollering rang through the house. 'She ain't been baby-sittin' on the weekends for Lucille and Hambone no more than I have!'

Odella had hoped she and Lester would be bags packed, headed out of town with no looking back by the time anybody found out. Will and Lucille were the only ones who knew she was planning to go, and she made them swear not to tell. Will looked hangdog, but he knew why she had to get away. What could he say? Lucille didn't know what Henry had tried to do to her and did her best to convince Odella to wait, at least till she finished high school. But when Lucille realized there was no changing her friend's mind, she slipped Odella advice on taking care of herself and an old tan leather suitcase that looked better than the ratty blue one she had brought with her from Cadysville. Odella had already stashed some of her best clothes in it because the time was coming. Lester was already out on the road, setting things up. He had begged her to come with him, even surprised her with a tweed suit with a real silver fox collar that he bought in Charlotte. Said it would be her traveling clothes, ''Cause homemade won't make it for you no more.' The suit was the most beautiful thing she'd ever seen, and at night she'd pull it out from the back of the closet, rub her face in the smooth, soft fur, and dream about being famous and making records. Della Lester and Johnny DuPree. It sounded so far-fetched, but Lester believed, and that was enough for her. Being with Lester was all she really needed. She had planned to tell her father, right as they were leaving Prosper, thought maybe he'd understand. Odella decided she owed him at least that. She hadn't figured out how to put it yet, but it looked like time had run out. She was going to have to say something right now.

'If you believe everythin' you hear in a barbershop, then I raised a fool.' Odell poked his son's shoulder with a corner of the newspaper in his hand.

Henry smacked the paper aside, and the pages skittered across the floor. 'You quick to make me the fool! You do it at the brickyard. You do it here!'

'You don't like the way I run my business or my house, you know what you can do.' Odell's low rumble threatened, like he was on the verge of erupting.

'You would throw *me* out and have *her* sittin' up in

here like – like she somethin' special!' Henry hollered. 'The garbage goes outside!'

Odell snatched Henry by the front of his shirt. 'Don't you ever talk to me like that, boy . . .'

'Ain't none a your damn boy!' Henry squirmed out of his father's grasp. 'And what you gonna do about her and her damn lies?! You brought her up in here like you proud of her. Even gave her your damn name! And what am I supposed to do? Huh? What about your wife?!' He jabbed an irate finger in the air.

Odella knew this pot had been bubbling for years and now it had boiled over. She felt like she had to go out there. She was scared, but this was her battle, and she had to fight it. She just wished Lester was in town.

'Papa?' Odella opened the door before she chickened out and walked to the head of the stairs where her father and Henry had squared off. 'Me and Lester – we *have* been singin' around some.' Eyes cast down, she caught sight of Miz Ethiopia's sour face peering up from the dining room. 'But I swear that's all we . . .'

'Now you see!' Henry poked her. 'She the one been lyin'.'

'Watch yo'self, boy!' Odell warned.

When Odella got up the nerve to look at her father, his disappointed expression made her feel two feet tall. 'I – I wanted to tell you—' She stumbled over her own guilt. 'I was gonna, but . . .'

'*Now* who you gon' put outta your house?' Henry glared at Odella. 'You can look all innocent here in your proper little high-collar dress, but that's not what you wear to them joints, is it?! Way I heard it, your singing wasn't the only thing you was featurin'.' Henry yanked at her skirt.

'Don't!' Odella pulled away.

'Leave her be!' In one motion Odell spun Henry by the arm and slammed him up against the wall. 'This ain't your concern.' Odell's wide hands covered most of Henry's chest as he pinned him against the delicate floral patterned wallpaper.

'I'm sick a you tellin' me what to do!' Henry ranted in an uncontrollable squeal. His eyes burned with hate as he swung his fists wildly, his arms too short to reach their target.

'Stop it y'all!' Odella tugged on her father's arm, stumbled on the newspaper underfoot. 'Please stop!' She despised Henry, but she didn't want her father to beat him. At least not for this. It would give her brother another reason to make her life miserable.

Odell shook off his daughter's grasp, then grabbed the front of Henry's shirt again and hoisted him off his feet.

'Papa, please – This is my fault.' One of Henry's fists bashed her temple, and she clutched at the railing to keep from going down.

Odell dangled Henry until all the struggle went out of him. 'Now, go on 'bout your business.' He abruptly let go, and Henry landed in a heap on the floor and scrambled to his room. Then Odell turned heavy eyes on Odella. 'Ain't nothin' hurts worse than a lie.' His gaze left her nowhere to hide.

Odella shriveled with shame. 'Papa – I—' She couldn't find any cooling words to soothe his wound. 'I – I didn't mean—' Then, out of the corner of her eye, she saw Henry charge, quick as a mad dog, toward Odell, wielding a crowbar high over his head. 'Papa! Look out!' Odella's yell scraped her throat, but to her ears it was like a distant, fading echo. The action played out in front of her faster than the sound could catch. Faster than she could stop.

Odell pivoted just in time to intercept the iron bar midswing. He and Henry scuffled on the landing, like mortal enemies until Odell slid on the fallen newspaper, and the force of Henry's fury sent him tumbling.

'Papa!' Odella lunged, grabbed the tail of her father's shirt. The momentum of his fall ripped it from her hand, tore loose two of her fingernails, but she never felt her own pain. 'No-o-o!' Odella's thick, hoarse scream saturated the air, but she never heard it. She felt the house quake, watched helplessly as he rolled head over heels over head down the stairs, his head bouncing on the steps, his arm crashing through a section of spindles. There was deathly silence when he came to rest at the bottom. When she saw him splayed out on the floor, Odella felt a massive hand crush her heart and squeeze the air from her lungs.

'Papa—' She felt her lips move, but her whisper was thin and parched. Slowly she edged down the steps, her back pressed to the wall. 'Papa.' Odella held back a sickening wave as she stepped over the bulk of his torso and dropped to her knees beside her father. His head arched back at an impossible angle, his mouth agape, his stare empty.

Before she could reach out her hand to touch him, Henry pounced and pinned her to the floor the crowbar pressed across her throat. Her tongue waved, but she couldn't swallow her own spit.

'It's a damned shame he fell. Ain't no more to it. Ain't that right?' Henry's face was contorted into a grotesque mask, and his hot spit showered her with every word he spoke. The veins in Odella's head felt like they would burst, and the room grew dim, but she could see Miz Ethiopia looking on, not moving a muscle to help her. But she hadn't moved a muscle to help her husband, either.

'If you ever breathe a word about this – or what happened in the chicken coop, I'll get you, gal. You won't know when, but I'll kill you, and Will too if I have to.' Henry squeezed harder. 'You understand me?'

Before she passed out, Odella nodded yes.

'Ma? Are you all right?' Ronnie was unnerved to find her mother slumped on the steps, head in hand.

Still dazed, Della looked up at Ronnie, trying to shift her focus from the past back to the present.

'Should I call for help?'

'I don't need help! I need for the two of you to start acting like you got some sense so we can get on outta here!'

20

'. . . it's okay to say "when."'

Gravel sprayed from beneath Celeste's tires like buck-shot as she sped away from the house. It didn't matter where she went as long as it was away from her mother. *I hate her! I just hate her!* Celeste stopped in the middle of the road, no longer able to see through her tears. *Nothing I do is right, not for her, or Niki, or Everett, or my sister. None of them!* Her hands trembled on the steering wheel. She leaned back against the headrest and bawled like a child. Right then, the thing she wanted most in the world she couldn't have. She wanted her daddy. She wanted to confide in him, like she always had, since she was a little girl and she'd come home with her feelings hurt, boohooing. She could see him standing in the basement, wearing faded khaki work pants and dusty shoes, holding a hammer or a wrench. He'd stop whatever he was doing, get his hankie out of his hip pocket, squat down, and wipe her eyes. Her daddy would talk to her. And he'd listen as she told him how she'd done everything exactly right, tried to show the other kids how to do it right, and it still hadn't worked out. She wanted to tell him now.

Celeste fished a tissue out of her purse, dabbed at

her eyes, blew her nose. And what would he say? As soon as she asked the question, she heard Will. 'It did work out, sugar. Just not the way you planned it, that's all.' She could feel the calluses on his hand as he cupped her chin. 'Sometimes you got to be willin' to change up your direction, Lessie, or whatever it is will sideswipe you and leave you layin' by the side of the road wonderin' what hit you.' *Wonderin' what hit you.* Celeste had composed herself enough to ease up to the road.

Without knowing exactly how she got there, Celeste parked in front of Pal's. She was too upset to eat, but she had to be somewhere, so she checked the mirror on the sun visor, put on shades to cover her red, froggy eyes, and went inside. The restaurant bustled like a beehive and smelled like bacon and good coffee.

'Morning! You by yourself?' Hambone had flounced out of the kitchen with half a cantaloupe and cottage cheese with a cherry on top. 'Come for a little carryout to take on back?'

'Uh – No. Breakfast for one.'

'Well, happy to see ya. It'll be a minute 'fore we have a table.'

'I can sit right there.' She moved toward an empty stool at the counter.

'How's Miss Ronnie doin'?' Hambone moved along with her.

'Fine,' Celeste said curtly, then caught herself. 'Well, not fine exactly, but she's doing really well. Improving every day!' It sounded phony even to her, but she couldn't find middle ground this morning.

'And your mama?'

'Couldn't be better. I'd like some coffee, Hambone. If it isn't too much trouble?'

Hambone felt the shift in gears. 'Comin' right up.' Still carrying the melon, he spoke to the girl behind the counter, who immediately picked up the carafe and headed in her direction.

After making a lengthy show of examining the menu, Celeste finally ordered a stack of buttermilk pancakes with eggs over easy, bacon, orange juice, and coffee. She knew she'd never eat it all, but it was a lot of food, which gave her a lot of time.

Celeste cut tiny wedges from the big golden circles on her plate, chipped away at the ends of the extra crispy bacon until it looked like the pseudobits you shake from a jar. When she pierced the egg yolk with her fork and watched the gooey liquid run into the rim of her plate, she felt inexplicably sad and had to fight to keep the tears at bay. She'd played with her food for half an hour when Lucille, dressed in her turquoise smock, popped through the door. Celeste managed to give the same answers to the questions Hambone had asked. She felt self-conscious with her shades on inside, like Lucille knew she was hiding something.

'Well, you tell 'em both I said hey!' Lucille's hand rested on Celeste's shoulder, and the warm touch felt comforting. Without warning a tear slipped from the corner of Celeste's eye and splashed on her cheek before she had a chance to catch it. *What is the matter with me?!*

Lucille smoothed it away with her thumb and kept talking. 'And soon as Ronnie's able, we'll have that dinner that never happened 'fore y'all go back.' She started away, then turned back around. 'When you're done here, stop on over. Let me work you in for a shampoo. I bet that'll feel good.'

'You know, I haven't gone this long without getting

my hair done in twenty-five years.' Celeste smiled. 'Thanks.'

'All right, then. See you when you finish up.' She patted Celeste, then headed toward Hambone at the cash register.

With her shades for cover, Celeste watched Hambone and Lucille reenact the loving morning ritual she'd seen on her first day in Prosper. Her small hand on his meaty arm. His big, round head bobbed and nodded as they laughed. Opposite in every way but so in sync, an easy give-and-take passed between them like current.

And like a shot Celeste felt the ache in her heart, the hole in her life. *I miss Everett so much!* She gasped aloud, then cleared her throat and drank some juice as explanation to the young man to her right, with a sun tattoo on his forearm, who turned to see if anything was wrong.

Hambone rested his pudgy paw on Lucille's narrow waist and leaned over. She stood on tiptoes, kissed him bye, and this time when he squeezed her butt, she pinched him. Celeste thought about the time she pushed Everett away because he was sticky or wet, or somehow it didn't seem proper. *Proper to who?*

Panic propelled Celeste out of her seat. *What the hell have I done?* She fumbled for her wallet, left money by her place, and headed toward the phone in the back. It was still in a wood and glass booth, and she sat on the perch, left the accordion door ajar so the light wouldn't come on. She dialed her home phone number, prayed for Everett to pick up. *One ring. Two rings –* '*You've reached the residence of—*' She hung up slowly, remembering he wasn't due back from

386

Portugal for another few days. Then she heard his words, the finality in his voice. *'Always is over.' And what could I say on the phone to make that any different?* She stared at the keypad, adding the numbers in horizontal rows. *Six, fifteen, twenty-four.* Feeling all the time she'd let slide by and all the distance she'd put between them. Celeste added the numbers in columns. *Twelve, fifteen . . .* A tap on the glass brought her around.

'Ma'am? Are you okay?' Mary the hostess stood outside.

'Yes – Fine – The number was busy – I guess I can try again.' Celeste waved and began pressing keys. Her fingers found another familiar pattern.

'This is me. You know what to do.'

Not again. She wanted to scream but steadied her voice enough to leave a message. 'This is your – This is Mom. I haven't spoken to you since – Uh – In a while—'

'Just a second.'

The male voice was unfamiliar, but Celeste knew who it was. She could still see his picture. And she winced as she heard Niki's loud whisper. 'Don't pick it – Aw shit—'

'Hello – Uh-oh – Hold on—'

Celeste shielded her ear from the shrill whistle of feedback. It stopped when he turned off the machine. 'Hello, Brian – This is Brian, isn't it?'

'Yes, ma'am. Brian Cadieux.'

Celeste could also see that box of condoms. 'I'd like to speak to my daughter.'

'Sure. Hold on.'

'Brian? I look forward to meeting you,' Celeste added quickly, hoping that when the time came she'd have found a way to mean it, since he meant so much to Niki.

'Thanks. I look forward to that too.'

Somehow Celeste was surprised by how manly he sounded. How confident. *Nicole's ol' man.* It almost made her laugh. *I wonder if Mother went through that with me and Everett.*

'What a surprise, Ma. It's not Tuesday.'

Celeste ignored the sarcasm. 'I don't really want anything.' *Except that you not completely despise me.* 'I was just checking on you . . . to see how you're doing.'

'You just caught me. I'm unplugging the phone in a minute. The car's packed. We're on our way outta here.'

'You're leaving? Atlanta? Already?' *How could she be prepared for a move? Without any help.*

'I told you we were going in early July. Or did you forget?'

She's got help. It's just not from me. 'The time got away from me.' Celeste could feel Niki's force field, hear her impatience to be done with this call. 'I'm still in Prosper. Your aunt is too. She's been in the hospital . . .'

'What happened?!'

'She'll be fine.' Celeste filled Niki in on the recent events. 'How long are you planning to take for the drive?'

'Couple a days. No big rush.'

'I know it might be out of your way—' Celeste took a deep breath. 'I'd really love to see you, Niki – You and Brian.' For once an idea went from her head to her lips and she said it before she had the chance to reason her way out of it.

'I don't know.'

388

'No lectures, no advice, I promise. I just want to see you before you start your – before you start school. Besides, it'll lighten things up around here. And I know it would make Ronnie feel better.'

'Any blood yet?'

'No more than usual—' *Who am I kidding?* 'Maybe a little more. We've had our moments.' Celeste felt like she could hear Niki thinking.

'I won't promise, but give me the address and stuff and I'll see.'

As soon as she hung up, Celeste got out her agenda book and dialed before she lost the momentum. 'Doug Pryce, please.'

After Celeste's escape, Ronnie retreated to the living room and spent the rest of the morning agonizing over the pieces to her puzzle, moving them around in hopes of finding a solution that didn't involve a complete loss of face and loss of faith in herself. And unilateral surrender to her mother. *I'm not that out of it.* So, for the first time in years, Ronnie attempted to write a résumé. Not the kind that accompanied her head shot and listed her acting credits; she updated that regularly. The balled-up pages at her feet were her attempts to arrange her patchwork of temp jobs and part-time work to showcase her marketable skills.

What is anybody gonna hire me to do? Ronnie scratched jagged lines through her latest effort, ripped the page off the pad, and folded it into a paper airplane. After launch it took a nosedive and disappeared under the table. *Crash and burn, the story of my life.* She looked at the next blank page. *All right. Cut the drama and think.* Trying to put down in black and white what she knew how to do made her edgy.

389

A little of this and a little of that is how she generally thought about it, but that was too vague. Ronnie could do basic word processing. She could talk to anybody, although she couldn't figure out a category for that. *Gets along with people? Sounds like a beagle.* She could do makeup, and she'd been pretty successful at selling Sable Shades, which should have been the highlight of her career to date. Ronnie figured Marilyn Ellis would have given her a good recommendation if she hadn't fired her first. None of it looked substantial enough to account for so many years of her life. *Did I accomplish anything?*

By the time Della called her for lunch, Ronnie felt the net tightening around her. She picked the bologna out of her sandwich, rolled it up, and popped it into her mouth, glad Della didn't seem ready to pick up where they had left off. Ronnie downed her iced tea and wished she felt strong enough to walk down to the pond. Maybe she could think clearer sitting on the stump, tossing stones in the water.

'Ma, you ever go fishin' in the lake?'

'Not much. I used to like goin' there 'cause couldn't nobody see you unless they knew you were there. Your daddy used to fish sometimes. He and – a friend. They'd catch a few sunnies, but nothin' you could make a steady diet on.' Della rinsed a plate and placed it in the drainboard. 'Why? You plannin' on a new hobby since that young man brought you that fishin' pole?'

'Nooo! I was just askin'.' She felt silly. Ronnie wasn't expecting to get snagged. 'I like it there too. It's peaceful.'

'Is that so? Humph.' She dried her hands on a dish towel. 'You know he's sweet on you, that Doug.'

'Ma, please. He's a real estate agent who happens to be a nice guy.' Nice had always meant boring as soggy cornflakes in Ronnie's lexicon, but that's not how she meant it this time. *Everett's a nice guy . . .*

'I know. You sent me to talk to him the other day.'

'What did you say to him?'

'Wasn't your conversation.' Della dried her hands on a paper towel. 'And I don't know when your sister is planning to show herself around here. She can't keep runnin'.'

Ronnie had been so busy in her own problems she hadn't thought about how upset she was with Celeste. *I open up like a can of soup, spill my guts. But she didn't think enough of me to say boo about her and Everett splitting up. Like I'm the only one whose life is a wreck.* Everett was good people. Ronnie used to think if she could find a guy like that she'd really have something. *If they can't keep it together, I don't have a prayer.*

Ronnie left Della in front of the TV and, glass of iced tea in hand, went to sit on the porch, hoping the small change of scenery would stimulate her thoughts. She tried to go back to her résumé writing but ended up with a page full of doodled curlicues. Based on her steady improvement she estimated she'd be able to start her job search in another week, and she braced herself to look for a full-time, for-real job, one with medical coverage. Then there was the matter of what she was going to be, now that she had to grow up, or at least stop chasing a dream she couldn't quite catch, and concentrate on building a more stable foundation. Ronnie had gone through the classifieds to see what jobs she might qualify for. She had circled ads for administrative assistants, airlines, banks, customer service reps, sales, discouraged by the number of places that listed a college degree as a minimum requirement. Then she got a lump in her throat when she thought about doing the same thing five days, forty hours a week, month after year, ad infinitum.

But all the 'what if's' Ronnie explored fell apart when she had to explain where she was going to live and what she was going to live on to start out. In desperation she even considered taking Kayla up on her offer to stay in Brooklyn with the witches, at least long enough to convince her friend it was time to leave the coven so they could get a place together. Then Ronnie went back inside to the living room and called Kayla, who had a week's worth of stories about getting over, getting by, getting seen, getting laid, and getting paid in the city. Midway through the conversation, Ronnie felt like she'd heard this tune too many times, like a song that repeats and repeats in your head until you're sick of it and you don't want to hear it again for a long time. When Kayla asked when she was coming back, Ronnie said, 'I don't know if I even *wanna* come back.' It was the truth, and it surprised her as much as it did Kayla. Ronnie hung up, more confused than before. *What the hell am I gonna do?*

When she heard car tires, she figured it was Celeste. *'Bout time.* Ronnie had plenty to say to her, like how trust works both ways, but she was surprised to hear men's voices drifting in through the open windows.

'You seem pretty familiar with the property. Any thoughts on how you'd like your acreage to run?'

Ronnie tucked her tank top in her shorts. *What is Doug doin' here?!*

'Nothin' hard-and-fast. If we start at the northern

boundary of the land and go twenty acres in, that would encompass the house. And both parcels would have lakefront.'

She smoothed a hand over her head. *Who's that with him? His voice sounds so familiar.*

'You expectin' somebody?' Della appeared at the living room door, looking perturbed, but she already knew who it was.

'Sounds like Doug brought the buyer here, but I don't know what for. Celeste hasn't agreed to anything.' Ronnie heard their footsteps approaching.

'Yes, sir, this place brings back a whole lotta memories.'

A whole lotta memories?! That's him! Ronnie finally placed the silky baritone as she headed to the door. 'Ma, I think he's a local DJ named Johnny DuPree.'

But Della, hands on hips, was already standing in the doorway. 'What in the devil are you doin' here?'

'I wasn't sure you were still in Prosper, Della.' Lester smiled sheepishly at her. 'I'm lookin' to buy me a piece of this place since your girls wanna sell it.'

'Wait a minute. I'm confused.' Ronnie saw the man she had met as Lester. He looked long and cool in royal blue linen pants, the matching shirt worn loosely over them. His red Corvette was parked by the road in front of Doug's car. 'You sound just like this radio guy – Johnny DuPree, your morning MC.' Ronnie mimicked his delivery.

'Guilty as charged.' Lester answered Ronnie, but he looked at Della, who looked away.

That explains the earring. 'If you and Ma are old friends, how come you didn't tell us you wanted to buy this place?' Ronnie put her hands on her hips until she realized her mother was doing the

393

same thing. Then she dropped her arms to her sides.

'I've had the word out for years that I was interested in this property. Edna, Doug here's mama, is an old friend from my Charlotte days. I asked her to keep an eye open and if it ever came on the market to let me know. When I found out y'all were comin' down, I said make the offer, but use DW Enterprises, one of my company names. I didn't want to put pressure on anybody, and I didn't want to be in the middle of your family business.'

Della avoided Lester's glance and edged toward the steps.

Doug spoke up. 'I just found out myself. Mother never mentioned the buyer by name, and we've communicated mostly through an assistant in his office. Can we come inside and continue this?'

'This isn't my business – If you'll excuse me.' Della headed down the stairs.

'You can stay, Ma.' Ronnie wanted company for whatever talk they were about to have, but Della headed for the path and never looked back.

Ronnie showed the two men inside. Lester peered in the rooms off the hall. 'It was the biggest house in town, back then. When I was growing up, I always wanted a place like this.'

'It's still pretty big, but don't go by me. I've been livin' in apartments with rooms the size of closets for too long. And you're certainly welcome, Lester, but I'm not sure why Doug brought you out. Celeste hasn't budged, and since we own it fifty-fifty—'

'You don't know she called me?' Doug asked.

'When?'

'This morning – said you-all were prepared to sell the house and we should move forward.'

'She did?' Ronnie's heart skipped a beat, but it wasn't from joy. This was the news she'd been waiting for, but she had the same sick feeling that came over her when she stepped in her ransacked apartment, like she'd lost something she couldn't replace.

'In fact I spoke with her a few times. She suggested we come out today if we could swing it, so we can talk about how the land would be divided while you're both here. She said she'd be back this afternoon. Is something wrong?'

'No. I – uh – haven't heard from her – I'm not even sure where she is.' There was so much noise in Ronnie's head she struggled to string the words together. 'Uh, let's sit in here.' She led the way to the living room.

Doug and Lester took turns discussing surveyors, boundary lines, and lake access. They drew maps on the pad in Doug's folder, and Ronnie nodded, but all she heard was the voice that started small and grew steadily louder. *I want to stay here!* Definitely not the words she was expecting, but they were the only ones she could hear. *This doesn't make sense.* But Ronnie felt right in this house, which she couldn't admit even to herself until now. She hadn't felt right in so long it was hard to recognize.

'So what do you think? – Ronnie?'

It took a moment before she realized Doug had said her name. 'I'm sorry. You're both gonna think I'm crazy.' Ronnie took a deep breath, huffed it out. 'I can't do this.'

'Okay. What's your suggestion?' Doug scooted up to the edge of the chintz armchair. 'There are lots of possible ways to divide the acreage.'

'The house – I mean, I can't sell the house.' *I*

can't believe that just came out of my mouth.

Lester looked confounded. 'I thought we were all in agreement here.'

'So did I.' Doug looked pissed.

'This is my fault.' Ronnie moved next to Lester on the sofa. 'My whole reason for coming here was to hound my sister into selling this place. But in the time we've been staying here I've kinda gotten to like it. And I'm at this point in my life where I need to switch up. Do something completely different, and Prosper is about as different from Manhattan as it gets.'

'Can't argue with that.' Lester cracked a wry smile.

'I apologize for this misunderstanding.' Doug glanced over at Ronnie like he was waiting for an explanation.

'Ain't nothin' but a thang.' Lester unfolded his long legs and stood up. 'So you're gonna stay with us awhile.'

'If I can work it out.'

'Let me get this straight. Are you keeping all the acreage, or can we do some business here?' Doug clasped his hands together and leaned forward.

At first Ronnie thought she should leave well enough alone, but she knew that to stay she'd need some money, at least to get a car. She got a gleam in her eye, stood up next to Lester. 'Can I interest you in some lovely lakefront property that's ripe for development? It would make an excellent site for a home. A compound, really. I mean, main house, guest house, garage, stables.' She made a wide sweep with her hand to encompass the grand estate she described. 'Something befitting a radio personality like yourself.'

'You're a handful, aren't you?' Lester grinned.

'At least. Sometimes two.'

'Why don't you and Doug here have a talk about it and let me know what you come up with. I'm gonna take a little walk, if that's all right with you.'

'Of course. I don't know where Ma went.'

'I bet I can find her. And Doug, my man, I'll talk to you before I leave.'

'Sure thing.' Doug gathered his papers, shoved them in his folio, and he and Ronnie accompanied Lester to the porch and watched him walk toward the path to the lake.

Doug sat on the top step. 'So, have you developed a sudden attachment to the family estate, or is this some kind of twisted way to get back at your sister? Or to make me look bad?'

'Look, I'm sorry. I didn't know I was gonna say that before it came out of my mouth. I swear.' She eased down next to him, looked around her. Everything, the trees, the grass, the air, buzzed and hummed with life. This place had survived neglect, maybe it needed the same second chance she did. 'I also didn't expect Celeste to do a flip-flop like that. She can be like a pit bull with a pork chop.' She started laughing. 'The one time I get her to come around, I go and change my mind. Oh, man, is she gonna give me mucho hell. Ma too.' She held her stomach, but was pleasantly surprised to find it didn't hurt to laugh anymore. 'I'm not a nut job, Doug. Honest.' She rested a hand on his knee for a hot second and was startled by the tingle. *What's that about?* 'You ever do something that seemed crazy, but it turned out to be right?'

'I'd say quitting my job and moving back to

Charlotte falls in that category.' He shrugged. 'Sometimes you gotta do what you gotta do, even if nobody understands but you.'

'It needs to make *some* sense. Ma and Celeste had to kinda bail me out, and I need to show 'em I can take it from here.' Ronnie looked over at Doug. 'At this point I need to prove it to myself. I got diddly to go back to in the Apple.' *Why am I telling him this?* 'It's a long story, but selling this place meant I could afford another go-round in New York, or L.A. for that matter, except I'm not up for any more of the city shuffle. At least not now. I guess I had to fall on my butt to realize it's okay to say "when."' Ronnie held her head in her hands for a moment, and Doug waited until she looked up again. 'I didn't mean to start rambling.'

Doug had been a reporter long enough to know when somebody needed to tell a story, but he wasn't obliging her for professional reasons. 'You'll know if I'm bored. I snore.'

Ronnie grinned. 'Fair enough.' And as she told her story, Doug did one of the things he did best: listen.

Before long they were interrupted by the chirping of Doug's cell phone. 'Celeste? Yes, we're both here – It's not a problem, really – I've heard it always takes longer than you expect at the hairdresser.' He grinned and raised an eyebrow at Ronnie. 'No need to rush. Uh – no – not exactly – I think you should talk with your sister.' He handed the phone to Ronnie.

21

'. . . what could have been, what would have been, and what was.'

'What are you doin' down here?' Della groused. 'Your business is up at that house.' *Cause I got enough mess stirred up without addin' you to it.* She sat on the old hickory stump, half looking at the murky water, not daring to turn around and look at him. Whatever wrangling Ronnie and Lester had to do about Little Pond was between them. Della wanted no part in it.

'My business, huh? If I didn't know better, I'd swear you were tryin' to run me off.' Lester strolled into the clearing from the woods. 'You still knew I was here. Always wondered how you did that.'

A tingle traced the back of Della's neck when he stopped behind her. *Same as I knew you were at the hospital before I saw you.* Only now the vibration was stronger because they were alone. 'I don't know, Lester!' She shrugged. 'I could always tell, that's all.'

He bent down, scooped up a handful of pebbles. 'It's pretty overgrown down here.'

'What in the world do you want with it, then?! Of all the places you have been in your life, why would you come back to Prosper?' Della asked her questions to the lake because she didn't dare face him yet.

'You really wanna know?' Lester selected a flat, gray stone from the cluster in his hand. 'It's home.' He rubbed the rock between his thumb and forefinger. 'If you wanna be technical, I was born in Charlotte, but Prosper's true home for me. And I've dragged my rusty dusty within fifty miles of anywhere you point to on a map, pitched my tent in a few of 'em, at least long enough to keep my son from feeling like a gypsy.'

He has a son? In all these years she'd never imagined Lester with a family. Not one that didn't include her. A sigh slipped through Della's lips.

'Truth is, I had a good life here, once. I do again. And as for this particular place –' He hurled the stone so far over the water that they barely heard it splash. '– When we were kids, back before I had two quarters to rub together, I wanted to own all this land. It was the biggest spread around, but nobody in it was happy. I was fool enough to think that if it was mine – ours – we'da been happy here.'

'Why are you tellin' me this?'

''Cause you asked – 'Cause I shoulda said it a long time ago when it counted.'

The velvet of Lester's voice wrapped itself around Della the way it used to when they were young and she used to feel like her heart wouldn't beat without him. *This don't make no kinda sense.* 'That was two lifetimes ago, yours and mine.'

'Doesn't mean it's not worth sayin'. I was always sorry I wasn't here when Henry killed your father. Maybe I could have . . .'

'Wasn't nothin' you coulda done. Nobody could. Took me a while to believe that myself, but it's true.

Henry was one a them people that got evil where the good should be.'

'He didn't start out that way, but the older he got, the more rotten he got. Me and Will, we knew it. It got him killed in the end.' Lester spoke over the top of Della's head.

A breeze rustled the leaves and blew ripples across the water. 'I guess Will heard he was dead when he was down here in 'sixty-nine, but I wouldn't let him tell me nothin' about it.' Henry had been her personal boogeyman for so long that it was almost comforting to have him around to hate. But everybody she ever knew seemed determined to jump up in her face and make her take a second look, and it looked like Henry was no exception. 'What happened to him?'

Lester shook the stones in his hands like dice. 'Was in 'sixty-seven I was in New Orleans. Heard he was missing more'n a week before they found him in the woods, just south of here, near where the church picnics used to be.'

Della nodded. She hadn't thought about the place in years, but she knew exactly where he meant.

'Somebody stabbed him. Never found out who, or why, but I bet he finally mouthed off to the wrong person.'

'Humph.' Della stared at the pond. 'I used to think hearin' he got his would make me feel good. I guess bad don't make you feel better.'

'It was bound to happen. I used to think he'd out-grow the nasty streak.'

'No. That works for some. But bad like that? It grows with you – and if the world is lucky it kills you before you kill somebody else.' Della kicked the heel of her sneaker against the tree. They stayed that way for a while, both thinking, neither speaking.

Lester cleared his throat. 'Della, whatever made you think I wasn't comin' back for you?' He looked at the pebbles in his hand, then lifted his gaze to her.

Della finally turned and looked at him, but the hurt in his eyes, the pain in his voice made her quickly turn away. *I shoulda trusted you, but I was so scared.*

TUESDAY, SEPTEMBER 17, 1957
PROSPER, NORTH CAROLINA

'Whatchu gon' do, Odella?' Will reared back on a Coca-Cola crate, his back propped against the wood plank walls of Pal's storeroom. 'You can't stay here but so long.' His hat was cocked down over his eyes, but its stingy brim didn't offer much shade from the glare of the naked lightbulb hanging from the ceiling.

'I don't know yet, Will. I still can't think straight.' Odella stood next to the shelves lined with cans of shortening, sacks of beans, and other restaurant supplies. There had been too much crazy stuff this past week. She was numb, had been since she came to at the foot of the stairs, her father's body still splayed on the floor next to her. When Will found her the next day, sitting by the lake, at first she wouldn't talk to him. She stared straight ahead, but Will knew something was wrong, something big. She looked disheveled, hair standing all over her head, but more than that, her eyes looked stone-cold.

'You sure you got all your stuff?' Will looked at the suitcase in the corner. 'We can go to the house. Henry ain't gon' try nothin' while I'm watchin' him. He knows I'll whup his ass. He'd wait till my back was turned, and I ain't about to do that.'

Odella remembered her composition books in the piano bench. 'Everythin' I need. I ain't never goin' in that place again. Not while I'm livin'.' She cupped her left hand around her right. The bandages were gone, but her bare fingertips were still tender where she'd torn off the nails, trying to hold on to her father.

'I know you upset 'cause a your daddy, but that's still your house.'

'I don't want nothin' else from there!'

'Aw right. Don't get upset.' Will stuffed his hands in the pockets of his plaid sport jacket. He pulled out a sheet of white tablet paper, folded it into smaller and smaller squares.

It felt strange to Odella, being in Pal's after midnight, without plates clattering or Hambone mouthing off. But the air still smelled like onions and grease. She didn't know what she would have done if they hadn't let her stay, because after the funeral she couldn't bear to be in that house. Before the burial she'd lie awake at night, a chair barricading her door. Once the show was over, she had to get out. 'I wish I'd gone with Lester. He begged me to come. Maybe none a this woulda happened.' Lester had been gone three weeks now, scouting new places for them to sing, making connections, he called it. He wanted to take her, but she said she needed more time to get ready. Last time he called he was in Baltimore, on his way to Cleveland. It was the first long-distance call she ever got. They only spoke a minute. Long enough for him to tell her he might go as far as Chicago or even New York because they cut records there. And to say he missed her.

Will refolded his paper. 'I talked to Lester last night—'

'When were you gon' tell me!?' Odella put her hands on her hips.

Will shoved his hat back on his head. 'I didn't know how to put it.'

'Put what?' She held her breath.

'He called your house. Henry started blessin' him out, so he hung up and called me – I told him what happened.'

'What did he say? When is he comin' back?'

Will jammed the paper in his pocket. 'He ain't.'

'What?!' Odella's pulse throbbed in her neck.

'He's goin' to Chicago. Said there's a record company there wants to sign him.'

'When's he comin' for me?' She barely had breath to speak.

'He ain't comin', Odella. Said he had to strike while the iron was hot – I'm sorry.'

It was like somebody threw all the pieces of her life in the air, and none of them had landed in the same place. 'What do you mean he ain't?' She sank to the cot, too dizzy to stand.

Will came and sat beside her. 'I can't make this no better than it is, or you know I would.'

'You told him everythin' that happened? About Henry, what he did to Papa – about me livin' here?'

'Yep.'

Right then Odella felt alone and as hollow and abandoned as a dry well.

Will moved closer, put his arm around her. 'Odella – I'm leavin' Prosper too.'

'What?'

'I can't stay here no more. Ain't no reason.' He took

off his hat, sat it on his knee. 'I been sayin' I was goin' to Buffalo to get me a job at the steel plant. My cousin says they're hirin' now, so I gotta make a move.' Will took her hand. Odella looked startled. 'Come with me.'

'What?'

'I know Lester had you all goosed up about this singin' thing, but that wasn't gon' be no kinda life for you. Hangin' 'round honky-tonks. Wishin' on stars.' He squeezed her tighter. 'Marry me, Odella. I'll take care a you, like a man's supposed to.'

Odella stared in Will's direction. She knew his lips were moving, but she couldn't hear him because she was still trying to make sense of what had been said. She pressed her hand to her chest, trying to keep her heart from pounding through her skin. Lester had dropped her the first chance he got. She wouldn't believe it if anybody but Will had told her. And now he was talking about getting married. *Will Frazier?*

'Are you all right?'

Odella returned to the room when she felt him shake her. 'I don't know, Will.'

'You don't have to promise nothin' now. Come with me to Buffalo. You'll be gone from here.' Will squeezed her hand. 'I sure hope you give me a chance.'

Odella looked at him, mouth open, not knowing what to say.

'Think on it. I'm leavin' in a couple of weeks. I know that means you'll be missin' out on your last year of school.'

'I ain't hardly thinkin' about that right now.'

'Well, let me know whatchu wanna do.'

Odella looked over at him. She trusted Will

405

more than blood. He looked out for her like a real brother would. *I just never thought about marryin' him.* She was so confused. 'I don't know, Will. Give me some time.'

'Sure thing.' He kissed her hand, put on his hat, and left.

Odella turned out the light and lay on her cot. She could see the crescent moon through the small window in the back door. And she didn't know what in the world she was gonna do.

'Odee?' Lester walked around and stood next to her.

She lifted her head, looked up at him, and her heart skipped a beat. *After all this time? I'm too old for this foolishness.* It took a few seconds to compose herself enough to answer. 'Long story. It doesn't even matter anymore. I know Will lied on you, and I guess part of me knows why.' She turned back to the pond. 'I let it go long time ago.'

'Forgiveness is a mighty big thing, Odee.'

'Oh, it ain't up to me to forgive. That work's a little too important for us down here.' She raised her eyes skyward a moment.

'Never thought about it like that.' Lester opened his palm flat and examined the stones. 'Will was always sweet on you, Odee. I knew that too. When he saw his chance, he took it. I blamed him for a long time. Blamed you awhile too. But none of it did any good.' Lester looked out over the lake. 'He treated you good?'

Della looked back at him, puzzled by the question. 'Will? Of course. Couldn't have asked for a better father or husband.' She saw Lester bow his head, then look off into the woods. 'I mean—'

'No need to explain.' Lester hurled another stone into the pond. 'Will Frazier was a good man. And you deserved that.'

'What about you?' It was time for her to turn the tide of this conversation.

'Let's see. Been married. Been divorced. Been around.' He punctuated each phrase with the toss of a pebble, then chuckled. 'More of the last than anything else. Truth is, I'm not sure how good I woulda been to you back then. I got a little full of myself. And I'm back to drinkin' RC again.'

'Does flingin' them stones make it easier for you to speak your mind?'

'What?'

'You used to do that whenever you had somethin' big to say.' The banter felt familiar to Della. All that was missing was her history book.

'I did? Guess some things don't change – and some things do.' He bent down for another handful and would have stolen a look at her legs except she was wearing pants. So he squatted, resting his butt on his heels. 'My son runs my station in Wilmington.'

'Wilmington? I heard you once or twice since I been down here. Made Ronnie turn that mess off.' Della smirked. 'How many do you have?'

'Six. Four in North Cakalackee. Two in South. My first one and my favorite is the one here, though. WDLA.'

'WDLA?' At first she didn't get it, then the light-bulb came on. 'You don't mean?'

He nodded. 'Seemed right I name it after you.'

She looked at him and shook her head. 'Still makin' up names, huh?' Despite the white fuzz at the temples and the furrows in his brow, he looked good, still full of energy. And he was still a snazzy dresser. She felt frumpy by comparison.

'I think I'm still pretty good at it too.' He reached for a twig. 'Anyways, I been thinking about buyin' another group that just came up for sale, but at my age, I don't know if I still want to work that hard.'

'Seems like a long way from that summer I saw you in Buffalo to owning a bunch of radio stations.'

'Not so long. Matter of fact, it was pretty direct. The sixties and rock and roll, it changed the music business.' Lester drew circles in the dirt. 'I was old-timey and work dried up faster than a Texas creek bed. Couldn't get more'n a few gigs here and there, couldn't get air play on the radio no more. I was mad at the whole world, but after I figured out nobody cared, I looked for some other way to use my voice.'

'I still got your records. Ain't played 'em in years.' Della peeked at him out of the corner of her eye.

'Well, do tell.' He stopped drawing and cocked his head to look at her sideways. 'You still sing, Odee? Church and stuff like that?'

'No.' She crossed and uncrossed her feet at the ankles. 'I stopped long time ago. Didn't feel it anymore.'

'That's a shame. I still ain't heard nobody could match you.' His voice trailed off for a moment. He scuffed out the circles he had made with the toe of his shoe. 'Anyway, about three years after I started DJing, there was a government program around to give minority folks a shot at owning and operating radio stations, and I got the chance to buy into one. Later, my partner sold out to me, and the rest is, as they say, history.'

'So you did become a rich man.' Della stood up.

'And now you want to buy this place.' She brushed dust and bits of dead leaves from the seat of her trousers. She stopped when she realized he was watching.

Caught, he grinned, shoved his hands in his pockets, and looked at her face. 'I wouldn't exactly say rich, but I've done all right. I think I could have enjoyed it more, though. Which is kinda how I feel about Little Pond. It's about time somebody enjoyed it. I'd like to clean up the sludge here around the shore, clear out some of this old dead wood. You should see what they've done with the waterfront over in Jessup.'

'You're crazy as you always were, Lester Wilson!' She turned to go.

'Odee?' He reached out and touched her arm as she passed him.

Della stopped. The same electricity that had always passed between them coursed through her when his fingers touched her skin.

'I don't know what your girls are gon' do about this place, since they can't seem to make up their minds.' Lester glanced down at his shoes, then back at Della. He didn't expect her to still shake him up, but he felt it when he first saw her at the hospital. When his parents shipped him out to the country after an 'almost' brush with the law, Lester developed a swagger and bravado meant to let everybody know he was a little bit ahead of their game. After all, he was from Charlotte. Henry Womack was the first boy he met, followed by Will and then nearly everyone else in Prosper, and they were duly impressed with his shiny, city ways. Then Odella showed up, and he knew from the beginning he wasn't fooling her. Most people he came in contact

409

with were still impressed, but right now that didn't matter. 'I know you got to be gettin' back – but – I—'

'Spit it out, Lester. I hope you don't fumble around like that on the radio!' She laughed. 'If you wanna know what my daughters are gonna do, I'm out of it. Woulda let the land and everything on it rot 'cause I wasn't ever comin' back. Except Will talked me into signin' it over to him. They got it when he passed. I never could get Celeste and Ronnie to agree on anythin', so if that's what you're askin'—'

'Uh – No – It's not that.' He knew Della didn't buy his hotshot act then, and he liked that about her. And he could not believe, standing here forty-odd years later, that she still made him feel like a bumbling schoolboy. 'I – Can I take you to dinner?'

Her arm still felt hot where his hand had been, and she fought the urge to rub the spot. This felt so strange. 'Lester, you don't have to do that. I'm sure you got plenty of company.'

'Do you see my arm twisted behind my back? Huh?' He took both of her hands.

'Uh – Well – No.'

'Then let me take you out. I believe in taking second chances.'

Della thought for a moment, about what could have been, what would have been, and what was. And for the first time in years, she didn't know what was to come. 'I'd like that, Lester.' She shocked herself. 'Tomorrow?'

He crooked his arm, she slipped hers through it, and they headed back to the house.

'I think you're grabbing at straws.' Celeste, who had finally shown up after her unintended full day of beauty, sat next to her sister on the step. 'It seems like a good idea now, but that's because you haven't tried it. What on earth would you do here?'

'I can start a whole new life down here. Doug was telling me how good the job market is.' Ronnie felt more hopeful after their talk.

Doug stood by the porch railing, observing the back-and-forth volleys. The tone seemed less hostile than the earlier encounters he'd seen. Celeste wasn't even too upset about Ronnie's change of heart. The employment issue seemed to be the sticking point. 'If it doesn't work out, she can always leave.'

'Yes, I've read there's a lot going on in the corporate sector of Charlotte, but you—'

'I'm sure I can find something. I even thought of talking to Lucille about offering makeup lessons and applications at the salon, kinda my own little freelance business. And I won't have to worry about a place to live. I've got one.' Ronnie looked back at the house. 'I know it sounds nuts, but I kinda like it.'

'You don't even have a – what in the name of—' Celeste elbowed Ronnie in the side.

'Ouch!' A little too hard. Ronnie winced.

'Psst!' Celeste hissed in Ronnie's ear and nodded toward the path.

'That hurt.' Ronnie frowned at Celeste. 'Did you forget I just had an operation?!'

'Be quiet and look!' Celeste's eyes had locked on a target.

Ronnie followed Celeste's pointed gaze and saw her mother coming through the trees, having a spirited talk with Lester. But Ronnie knew Celeste was fixated on Della's arm looped through his. 'Who'd a thunk it?' Ronnie grinned.

'Is that all you have to say?!' Celeste stood up and threw her hand in the air. 'Fine! Everybody *has* taken leave of their senses! What does she think she's doing?' Celeste demanded.

'Looks to me like she's taken a walk with an old friend. And from where I sit, looks like a pretty good one!' Ronnie was still smiling when Della, suddenly aware of the viewers, withdrew her arm from Lester's as they neared the house.

'So,' Lester spoke before he reached them. 'Have we come to an agreement yet?'

'Lester?' Ronnie felt the now or never moment and jumped in. 'If you're still interested in buying twenty acres from the south boundary, with lakefront, no house, we have a deal.' She turned to Celeste. 'Okay?'

Celeste hesitated.

'Trust me this once, Celeste.'

Celeste looked at her sister, then at Lester. 'Deal.'

'What are you gon' do with the house?' Della interrupted.

'Live in it.' Ronnie smiled at her mother.

'Have you even thought about a job, Ronnie?' Della persisted. 'And you can't live out here without a car! Do you even still have a driver's license?' Della launched her questions.

'You work for the DMV, Ma! Last time I checked, New York City was still part of New York State! Of course I have a license! And since we're obviously going to talk about this now –' Ronnie looked at her family then at Doug and Lester – 'I'll get a job. Doing something. It can't be any harder than where I've been! At least I'll have a roof over my head.'

Doug interjected. 'I don't think she'll have a big problem finding work.'

'Who asked you!?' Della snapped.

'I did,' Ronnie said defiantly. 'And I'll ask everybody I know, everybody I meet. Isn't that what you always say?' She turned to Celeste, who sank back down on the step. 'It's not what you know, it's who you know? Well for once I'm gonna take your advice! Speaking of who you know – Lester? I've heard the announcements for jobs at the station almost every day on the radio. You work there. Who should I see about putting in an application?'

'What in the world do you know about a radio station?' Celeste couldn't believe what she was hearing.

'Don't need to know much about radio for some of them,' Lester said. 'If you're really interested we can talk about it. I know someone who has an in with the boss!' He winked at Della.

'Thank you.' Ronnie bowed her head. 'See!' she said to her mother and sister.

'Good. I'll have Doug here draw up the new paperwork, and we'll be cookin' with gas!'

Ronnie shook Lester's hand, then gave Della and Celeste a big, silly grin.

'Just like your mama.' Lester smiled at Della. 'When she thought she'd said somethin' smart. Isn't that right, Odee?'

'I did no such thing, Lester Wilson!' Della almost giggled.

'Odee?' Ronnie looked at them over imaginary glasses.

'I'll pick you up tomorrow about six?' Lester pecked Della on the cheek.

'Fine.'

'I'm outta here too.' Doug got out his car keys. 'I'll

get the ball rolling and be in touch with everybody ASAP. Ronnie, any questions about Charlotte, give me a ring. I'll be happy to give you a tour if you like.'

'Sounds like a plan.' Ronnie smiled.

Lester nodded to Celeste and Ronnie, then he and Doug headed toward their cars. Before Lester got in his, he turned and waved. Della grinned and waved back.

Ronnie smirked, watching her mother act like a schoolgirl.

And Celeste simmered. 'What was all that about?'

'Wasn't about nothin'.' Della's eyes followed Lester's car as he drove off.

'That's not how it looked to me-ee,' Ronnie sang and sidled up next to Della.

'And do you think he offers that tour to *all* his clients?' Della joked.

'How can you carry on like that?!' Celeste's face had clouded. 'Daddy's been gone less than a year and I . . .'

'Celeste, it's not what you . . .'

'I don't understand you, Mother! I just don't!' Celeste trotted into the house.

22

'. . . just let it all hang out.'

The next morning Della was the first one stirring. She shuffled through the rooms downstairs in the half light, letting her hands glide over lampshades and books, rest on chairbacks and desktops, finally embracing how familiar she felt here in spite of decades spent denying the memory. Walking the hall toward the front of the house she traced her finger along the oak wainscoting the way she used to when she was a girl and nobody was looking. A tragedy had first brought her to Prosper, and another one chased her away. This trip could have been tragic too, but mercifully it wasn't. Ronnie was fine, Della was grateful, and now she was ready to make her peace with this house, this town. *It wasn't all good, but it wasn't all bad, either.*

Della stood for a long time at the living room doorway in her yellow nightgown, envisioning the room the way it used to be, full of sober furniture, covered with knickknacks and antimacassars. She remembered how stuffy it seemed, how gingerly she used to walk through the room so she wouldn't break anything. Then her father bought the piano, and it was the only thing in there that mattered to her.

Cautiously, Della approached the piano, sat on the bench. Her piano. She reached out her hand, lightly touching the shiny black surface. When she got to the safety latch, her hand froze, anticipating Henry's oppressive presence hovering over her, still sworn to keep her from playing what her heart called for. But in that instant she realized there was nothing left of Henry but dust and a ghost she'd been dragging around too long. A breath of relief replaced the too familiar dread as she lifted the lid, positioned her hands over the keys. She didn't know what she was going to play, but her fingers would know.

So she began, softly at first, with a melody she hadn't even hummed to herself in years, one that first came to her on an evening full of june bugs, down by the pond, and she'd later written it in her blue composition book. It felt good as the notes swirled around her, traveled through her. Last night all she heard was static between herself and her daughters, over secrets kept and misunderstandings. If anything was going to change, she knew it had to start with her. Maybe it was time for music. Music and the truth.

After a while Della had heard Ronnie's footsteps upstairs, then water running in the bathroom, heard Ronnie pause, trying to make out the sounds from downstairs. She heard Celeste's door open and their whispers. Just as she had heard them cough in their sleep when they were little, or toss and turn, fitful and restless on a hot night. She would go into their rooms, give them a sip of water or turn their pillow to the cool side, and they never knew she'd been there, because they never really woke up. They weren't supposed to know. She was. She was the mother.

So Della played louder as they tiptoed downstairs, like kids on Christmas Eve trying to catch Santa leaving goodies under the tree. And now she heard their breath as they stood in the doorway behind her.

But she kept playing, because yesterday, after Lester had gone, she realized Lucille was right. She was a mystery to her daughters. She had eased her own mind by locking away the pieces of her life she couldn't make fit, but she finally saw that it had left Celeste and Ronnie with an incomplete picture of who their mother was and how she got that way. Della went to sleep thinking about Lucille's advice and knowing it was time to add color and shading to her self-portrait.

Celeste and Ronnie stood on the threshold, wondering what this change was all about, waiting to see who would make the first move.

Roots was on Ronnie's tenth-grade reading list the last time she'd questioned Della about what it was like when she was a girl. 'All that old-timey stuff don't matter. What happens now is what counts.' Later Celeste, pregnant with Niki, broached the subject and inquired about the family medical history, reasoning that since her grandparents hadn't made it to old age, there might be some things she needed to know. Della shot down Celeste's questions as she had Ronnie's. 'Ain't no point worryin' 'bout what you can't change no way.'

When Della started to hum, resonant and rich, Ronnie could no longer resist. She entered the room, sat on the couch. Celeste looked on from the doorway.

Della finished her song and stared at her hands. The hands that used to play this piano didn't have ridges in the fingernails, slack skin, or knobby joints. She finally looked up at Ronnie. 'I gave this up an awful long time ago.'

Celeste, who had been braced for the worst, relaxed her stance, let herself be drawn closer.

'But why, Ma?' Ronnie asked. 'You sound so good.'

'Oh, it's all rusty now. I *used* to be good. Least that's what folks said. And I guess I was.' Della looked from one daughter to the other. 'But it caused way more trouble than it was worth.' She saw the questions written on their faces and knew the answers were written on her heart. 'Lord—' She let her fingers walk a C scale. CDEFGABC. 'There's just so much y'all don't know.' She shook her head. 'I guess this is as good a place as any to start.'

Celeste eased down on the piano bench next to her mother. Both she and Ronnie, still not sure they weren't dreaming, tried not to look too eager, for fear it might stop Della. They needn't have worried. She had held it all long enough. There wasn't any more room. There wasn't any more strength. She was tired.

'Me, your father, and Lester were all friends,' Della began, but then stopped. She looked off, beyond Ronnie and Celeste and into a past that was so full of shadow even she wasn't sure she knew her way around. Finally she gathered herself, at least enough to spare the bits and pieces she needed to leave a trail behind her. She would have to find her way back. 'It didn't start out that way, and it didn't end up that way either, thanks to Henry. But for a while . . .'

Della began in the middle, her arrival at Little Pond, alone, afraid with her whole world turned inside out. By the time she paused for a breath on her way back to Cadysville and Annie, Celeste was hard at work trying to find a place for the notion of her mother as – *illegitimate?* Ronnie, on the other hand, was drawn into the unfolding tale, captivated by the depth of love Della described between Odell and Annie and sorry they didn't get to live it together. *Ma was a love child?*

Della had become Scheherazade, and there were a thousand more stories to go, so she zigzagged through time and place, letting it come out as it came up. She knew if she stopped to organize it, like Celeste would prefer, she might not make it all the way through. Her story kept getting blown off course by questions and comments, and Della had to struggle to get back on track, to keep her train of thought.

When she finally arrived at that afternoon in the chicken coop when Henry tried to rape her and Will saved her, Della's tale stalled. She looked at Celeste and Ronnie a long moment, grateful they never had to go through what she did.

Della built up enough steam and lurched forward again. In halting words, she minced through her recollection, searching for a way to tell what she had never spoken before.

Celeste felt the floor drop out from under her. She had barely thought of her mother as a *woman*, certainly not as a vulnerable teenage girl. For once in her life she didn't know what to say so she scooted closer to her mother. Close enough for their shoulders to touch. Close enough to feel the weight that had been there so long.

Ronnie got up and dragged one of the straight-backed chairs up to the piano. She gripped the seat to control her trembling hands, and her breath came in short, shallow wisps. Light-headed and nauseated, she forced herself to swallow hard against the bile rising in her throat. She knew how terrified, trapped, and violated she had felt in that photographer's studio. She never dreamed of telling her mother or anyone what happened to her; it would be too embarrassing. Besides, Della would have no way to understand. Now Ronnie realized she had never given her mother credit for having lived a life that wasn't totally safe and predictable.

Della's voice still quivered as she moved on to why she and Will left Prosper for Buffalo and recounted the night Henry killed her father. As she spoke, she could feel him plunging too hard and fast for her to catch him, see the rail posts splinter as they broke his fall. She picked up the composition book from the music stand, rolled it into a tube. 'It was the awfulest thing I ever saw.' Della rocked side to side to keep herself together.

Celeste rocked with her, put an arm around her, tried to help her carry the load. Celeste felt awkward at first, cradling her mother, but soon settled into the rhythm of the embrace.

Ronnie was outraged. 'Your stepmother watched and didn't try to help you?!' As far as she knew her grandparents were dead. Had been since their mother was little. That was the party line. She always thought of her mother as a loner, without people. That's how Della came, relatives not included. She'd never given Ronnie any reason to think about the void those losses left or the sadness that remained. 'Why didn't they put him in jail!? Under the jail!? Even if you didn't tell, how come they didn't find out during the investigation?'

'What investigation?' Della chuckled. 'Way out here in the woods didn't nobody see or hear nothin' but us. So a Black man who owned his own business, drove new cars, and had more money than half the White folks fell down the stairs and broke his neck in his own house. Didn't nobody *investigate* things like that.' Della rolled the music book into a slender tube. 'Accident or on purpose, some thought it was good riddance to – anyway, that's why Will wanted to get away from down here. At least one of the reasons.'

Ronnie reached over and rubbed her mother's soft fleshy arm. 'Ma, I'm so sorry I made you come back here.'

'I was too, at first.' Della eyed them both, patted Celeste's knee. 'I'm not anymore.'

They each let her words sink in for a moment, but not too long. There was more to talk about.

'So what happened to him? Henry?' Ronnie asked.

'I just found out myself. I always expected this place would be his.' Della shook her head. 'Lester told me somebody stabbed him to death. Years ago.'

'Good for him!' Ronnie had to restrain herself from clapping. If she despised this man so intensely just from hearing about him, she couldn't imagine what her mother must have felt.

'I spent too many years hatin' him for what he did – and myself for lettin' him threaten me into not doin' anything about it – I gotta let it go now. Took a while for me to learn that punishment and forgiveness don't always seem equal, but it works out, if you give it time.'

Della uncurled the book and smoothed it out across her lap while she told them how she thought Lester had dropped her as soon as he got a whiff of success, and then how Will finally stepped forward to let her know how he felt and asked her to marry him. It was hard talking to them about Will. What they knew about him as their father was a little different from things she knew about him as a man. 'If I don't move now, my knees won't never work again.' Della stood up and peeled her damp nightgown from the backs of her thighs. She needed a break.

It was afternoon and the air in the living room had grown close. The three of them, in their nightgowns, were unaware that they had too.

Della fanned herself as she headed toward the kitchen. 'And I don't know about y'all, but I'm hot and my stomach thinks my throat is cut.'

Ronnie got up, stretched, and followed after her. 'Why didn't you keep singing, or at least playing? We had a piano sitting in the living room all those years and you never used it.'

Celeste, dabbing sweat from her neck with a tissue, joined the procession. 'Well –' She almost didn't bring it up, but it had always bothered her. '– Never, except for that time I caught you and you told me . . .'

'I know what I told you that day –' Della took three glasses from the cabinet, then an ice tray from the freezer '– and I'm sorry. I just couldn't explain it then. I couldn't.' She spoke to Celeste while she popped a handful of cubes into each glass. 'Besides, things aren't always what they seem.' She turned on the tap, pulled back the curtain, and looked out the window while she let the water run cool. 'I found that out the summer your father bought that piano.' Distracted by what she knew was to come, Della filled her own glass, took a long drink over the sink, refilled it, and went to the table.

Celeste watched her mother sit, then went over to the sink, filled the other two glasses, and handed one to Ronnie. 'That was the summer of the first moon walk.'

'That was the summer we got the color TV,' Ronnie said.

'It was the year before that summer that I saw Lester again. Hadn't seen him since we left here and didn't expect I ever would, but I guess I'd been mad all that time. One day the three of us were out – Where had I taken you critters? I don't remember where we'd – yes I do – We all went to the dentist. Y'all remember Dr Howard? Boy, you hated that trip.' Della smiled faintly at the memory.

'It was hot that day, hot for Buffalo. But after that first winter when we moved up there and it was cold as the devil, I swore I'd never complain about hot again.' Della took a sip and wiped her cool, damp hand over the back of her neck.

'Doc had an office full, as usual, so it was late afternoon when we got out. You didn't have no cavities, Ronnie, so you went skippin' ahead down Jefferson, playin' hopscotch with the street cracks. Celeste, you walked with your hand covering your mouth where it was still crooked from the Novocaine. I tried to tell you it didn't look that bad, and if you'd put your hand down nobody would notice, but as usual, you didn't listen.'

Ronnie elbowed Celeste. 'Some people never change.'

'Look who's talking.' Celeste swatted Ronnie.

'Anyway, we passed in front of the Pine Grill, and who did I see on a poster but Mr Johnny DuPree.'

'The Pine Grill?' Celeste had a hard time visualizing her mother jammed in the crowded, noisy club. She could almost smell the Hai Karate, taste the Harvey Wallbangers, hear the Ohio Players. *The Pine Grill?* She and her friends had used fake IDs to get in when she was a teenager. Imagining her mother hanging out in the same place was a challenge.

'Hasn't that been closed about a million years?' Ronnie asked.

Della nodded. 'But it used to be the place to go, at least one of 'em. There were quite a few spots around town. And Will and I used to go out from time to time.' She looked at Celeste. 'Didn't see no need to tell you where we were goin', Miss Busybody.' Della picked up her deck of cards and turned the box around and around in her hand. 'For the rest of the walk home I told myself I should let bygones be bygones. Lester had once been a real good friend.' She opened the flap and ran her thumbnail along the top of the deck. 'I was kinda surprised he was still singin' in clubs since he hadn't had a hit in a few years, but he'd done all right for himself. Me and your father were doin' okay.' She shook the cards into her left hand. 'But I guess what I really wanted was to cuss him out. So I went.'

Celeste's jaw dropped. 'You sneaked off to see this man without telling Daddy!?' She sputtered, appalled that her mother could have done such a thing. 'How could you?' Before the question was out of her mouth, she saw herself sneaking around on Everett. *Is that what this is all about!? She had an affair with this man?* 'Are you trying to tell us that . . .'

424

'Maybe if you shut up long enough you'll find out what she's trying to tell us!' Ronnie interrupted.

'Both of you can hush.' Della started shuffling the deck in a slow-motion cascade. 'Anyhow, I remembered Lester liked to feel a place out before a performance, so I went early, way before show time. When I got there, he was right where I thought he'd be. Walkin' back and forth across the stage, blocking out his moves. I got a little dressed up that day. Went to the Sample Shop and bought a new dress – pale blue with a white portrait collar.' She didn't tell them that Will had been trying to get her to do some shopping for herself for a while and that this finally seemed like a good enough reason. 'Got shoes too. Navy leather with a strap across the arch that fastened with a white button.'

'I remember those,' Celeste said.

'Thought I looked pretty good, if I do say so myself. He recognized me the second I walked in the door.'

'You got done up to go see this man?! An old boyfriend?' Celeste interrupted again. The notion of her mother primping for any reason was foreign enough, but to go see another man?

Della looked from one daughter to the other. 'I know neither one of you thinks I ever cared about that kind of stuff – I used to – but that was before . . .' Then she resumed her tale. 'Anyway, he hopped right off the stage. He always liked to do that.' She paused, remembered the heat of his hands around her waist when he used to help her down.

'And?' Ronnie snatched Della back to the story. 'Did you cuss him out?'

'Oh, yes I did. Laid him low.' Della shook her head. 'He tried telling me that Will had promised to bring

425

me to meet him in Cleveland on his way to Buffalo. He swore he waited two weeks. Even told me the name of the place where Will was supposed to be bringin' me. He said after we didn't show up that he went back to Prosper lookin' for me, and folks told him I'd gone off to marry Will. Had the nerve to stand up there with his conked hair and say he thought I was comin' to tell him what happened and apologize. I called him a liar and everything but his name. I didn't even know I could say all that.' Della smiled, tickled by the memory of her vitriol. 'It made me feel good to see him squirming and still tryin' to lie. I finished my say-so and walked out. Left him and his shiny shoes sittin' at the bar holding a can of Carling Black Label.'

'So why would you even speak to him now, much less walk arm in arm?' Celeste waved away the offending image of Della strolling up the hill with Lester. 'Maybe we shouldn't even sell this place to him.'

'Hold on a minute, now.' Ronnie jumped in before Celeste got carried away. 'What does all that have to do with the piano, Ma?'

Della's ice had melted, and her glass of water sat in a puddle of sweat. She picked it up, drained the last swallow. 'Wish I never saw that blasted piano.'

'I know Daddy bought it and a bunch of other stuff after he took a trip down here.'

'So I wouldn't kill him.' She put the cards down, avoiding the wet spot on the table. 'This may be the hardest part for me to tell you, and it won't be easy for you to hear neither. And you need to know that we got past all that more'n twenty years ago.'

'What?!' Ronnie fidgeted in her seat. It was getting

harder for her to be comfortable on the hard chair, but she was too curious about her mother's story to move.

Celeste was growing more uncomfortable too, but it had nothing to do with her seat. She was afraid to know where Della's tale was leading. Afraid it would reveal more than she could handle.

'Lester was tellin' the truth.'

'He couldn't have been!' Celeste jumped to her father's defense. 'Daddy said . . .'

'I was there. You weren't. I know what your father said.' Della got up and went to the refrigerator. She needed some help to get through this part of her story, and making sandwiches was about the only distraction she could think of on such short notice. 'Will was workin', and you two were helpin' me clean out the closets and pack up old clothes to send to the Salvation Army. It was July, and I was already thinkin' about back to school, but I knew not to say that to the two of you or there'd a been nothin' but long faces.' Della took out a package of deli ham and the jar of mustard. 'We spent the mornin' fillin' up big green garbage bags with stuff y'all had outgrown or wouldn't wear 'cause it wasn't in style. Your job was to check the pockets before I folded them up.' Della opened the breadbox. 'Make sure we weren't givin' away more'n we thought we were.' She spread mustard on six slices of whole wheat bread. 'We had the bags sittin' by the back door waitin' for the truck to come pick 'em up.' She turned to Celeste. 'Then you dragged out a box of stuff that we must've put in the basement when we first moved from Chester Street and just forgot about. You found this old red and green plaid sport jacket of your father's. Humph. He had that coat on when he asked me to marry him.'

'The one still hangin' in the hall closet?' Celeste asked.

'Yep. I left it there so he wouldn't ever forget.' Della laid slices of ham on the bread, then nodded toward Ronnie. 'And you just about fell out laughing. That jacket *was* pretty ugly.' Della got a flash of Will sitting on that crate in Pal's storeroom. *Lester called it back-woods country.* 'But you put it on and started actin' real silly, talkin' funny like one of your cartoon characters or somethin'. The sleeves were practically down to your ankles, and you were flappin' your arms. We were all crackin' up then.' Della grabbed three plates from the cabinet and put a sandwich on each one. 'When you finally took it off, Celeste went diggin' in the pockets.' *And I wished you hadn't been so determined at your job.* 'I don't know how you managed to fish that little folded up scrap of paper out through the hole in the pocket where it fell down in the linin'. And then you asked if we knew anybody in Cleveland.'

Ronnie's hand shot up over her gaping mouth.

Della got a knife out of the cutlery drawer and sliced the sandwiches in half the square way. 'It was the address where he was supposed to bring me to meet Lester.'

Celeste looked like her world had crashed down around her ears. 'How could Daddy lie to you like that?'

'I know he didn't do it to hurt me. If anythin', he was tryin' to protect me. I guess he was doin' what he thought was best. But right then, it was all I could do not to throw somethin' before I could send you all out to play.' Della leaned against the counter, bracing the weight of the memory. 'Anyway, the night you found that paper, your daddy called to tell me he'd be late.

Some tenants he had to evict had helped themselves to the bathroom sink and toilet and left a mess that he and Shorty had to clean up. I said fine. Never let on. I put y'all to bed early, and you pitched a fit 'cause it was still light out and there was no school to get up for. But there were some things your little ears didn't need to hear.'

That night, when Will walked in the back door and sat down on the steps to take off his work boots, he didn't know what she knew. Unaware of what awaited him, he climbed the stairs, footsteps tired and heavy, his sweaty, smelly socks sticking slightly to the linoleum. He grabbed his favorite glass, a quart mason jar, filled it to the top with ice cubes and grape soda. Then he joined Della who sat in front of a game of solitaire at the kitchen table. But when she looked up from her cards and into his face, he saw a Della he'd never seen before. She reached in the pocket of her housecoat and put the note, still folded, in front of him.

'He knew what it was without openin' it. Before I could say two words he started talkin' real fast. He admitted what he did, told me Lester had called my house lookin' for me. It was after Papa's funeral, but Lester didn't know what had happened. By then I was stayin' at the back room at Pal's with Lucille and Hambone 'cause I couldn't sleep here. When Henry cussed him and hung up, he called Will to find out what the hell was goin' on. Lester was all excited 'cause some producer, or whatever you call it, from a record company wanted him to come to Chicago and make a record. He was plannin' to drive home to get me, 'cause he was sure they'd want me too as soon as they heard me. When Will told him what had

429

happened, Lester was gonna leave right then for me. That's when I guess your daddy's feelin' got the best of him. He told Lester he had me stayin' with his sister and she didn't have no phone. Then he said he was leavin' for Buffalo, and Cleveland was right on the way, so he'd drop me off. Maybe he really intended to right then. I don't know, but by the time I heard it, Will told me Lester was through with me. Asked me to marry him. And from that day to this, I ain't never been to Cleveland.'

The hum of the refrigerator was the only sound while Celeste and Ronnie absorbed the meaning of the story.

'Why did he keep the note all those years?' Ronnie asked.

Even now, Della didn't know why he hadn't thrown it away. It would have been so easy. A toss in the trash, a flutter out the window of the car as they snaked along the Scajaquada Expressway.

'That I'll never know. After a while I guess he just forgot it.' Della, still holding the knife, shrugged her shoulders as she answered. 'We tried to keep it away from you two, but it was a bad summer after that. Boy, every time I laid eyes on your father I'd get mad all over again, and Will couldn't say nothin' 'cause – he couldn't. Anyway, he decided to go away for a while. Give me a chance to cool down.'

'That's why he came here.' Celeste didn't mean to say it out loud. 'Hambone told us he was in Prosper that summer.'

Della nodded and continued her purge. 'When he got back, I was still hot. Next thing I knew he'd gone out and bought that piano. He was tryin' to make it up to me. I know he was. But I just couldn't play.

430

Even when I got around to not bein' mad anymore, I didn't want anythin' to do with that piano. Seemed everywhere I turned, no good never came from it.' She put the knife in the sink. 'I know he lied because he loved me. Your father was a good man. From day one I knew that. And after a while I realized that it took a powerful lot of love to make a man honest as him live with a lie that big for so long. I believe he thought if I went to Cleveland I'd be followin' Lester's dream, not mine. And of course he thought he would do better by me than Lester. And maybe he was right – about both things.' She carried the sandwiches to the table. 'Anyhow, I'll never know.'

'Did you love Daddy? At all?' Celeste asked. And she realized that as much as she didn't want to know what was behind that door, she had to. Maybe there were some answers for the questions she hadn't dared to ask herself. *Do I love Everett? Did I?*

Della sat down and took a deep breath. 'I did. Still do and always will. Forty-five years is a long time to stay with one man just 'cause you promised you would.' Della pushed her sandwich aside and picked up the cards again. 'What we had was good – strong – comfortable. With your father, I felt safe and at home for the first time since my mother died. He protected me against Henry. Maybe that's why it was so hard when I found out he'd lied to me. I trusted him so much.' She shuffled. 'It just wasn't the same as – I never felt that—'

'Mother!?' Celeste never thought of Della having feelings like that. She was the mother.

'Spark? Fire? Passion?' Ronnie, on the other hand, had no doubts about wanting to know what was on the other side of the door. She wanted to yank it open

431

and rummage around, find stuff to try on, see how it fit, like she'd done in the closets upstairs. 'Come on, Ma?! Don't stop there,' she teased.

'Well – I guess. All of that. It's a special feelin' – there's somethin' about the way it gets you all stirred up, hatchin' crazy plans. It warms you up, cools you down, makes you dizzy. Once you know that, you always know what it is – and *isn't*.'

Celeste played with the crust on her sandwich, pinching it off in tiny bits.

'So it wasn't that I didn't love your father. It just wasn't – like that.'

Ronnie lifted the bread off her sandwich, picked out a slice of ham, started to take a bite, then put it back on the plate.

'I know this has been more than a mouthful to swallow. But it took me too long to get started, and now I need to finish. This won't take but another minute or so.' Della paused, collected herself. 'You're more like me than you'd like to admit, both of you. I used to pretend it wasn't so, but ain't no point to it.' She turned to Ronnie. 'Missy, you need to hold on to somethin', make it yours. I guess I pushed what you thought were your dreams, because they once were the same ones I thought I had. Problem is I can't live mine through you. Your father might have been right, and I didn't even know if I really wanted all that, but you have to find out for yourself what *you* really want. Maybe your decidin' to stay down here a while is for the best. You been chasin' your tail too long, and at least you finally figured out you'll never catch it.'

Now she spoke to Celeste. 'And you got to let go of

all that petty, picayune stuff you hold onto like it's so important. One day, I hope before it's too late, you'll find out it ain't worth squat. You're all closed up, shut off from the people who care about you, Everett and Niki. Shut off from yourself even. And I know exactly where you got it from. I didn't mean to put that on you, but you picked it up anyway. Let that mess go before that's all that you have left. Don't waste your todays.'

'I didn't mean for it to be like this.' Celeste wasn't paying attention when she reached for her glass. She tipped it over and water spilled onto the table and into her lap. She covered her face but couldn't hold back the tears. 'I'm sorry.'

'I know this ain't about that spilt water.' Della got up and grabbed a dish towel. 'And it probably wouldn't hurt you to get yourself some hormones. They sure did me a world of good when I was your age. But if these tears are for Everett, shouldn't he see 'em?' Della mopped up the water on the table and the floor.

'I loved him like that – like you were talking about – I really did. I don't know what happened,' Celeste blubbered.

'You do so know what happened! You kept workin' on it, pickin' at it, tryin' to fix it, till you finally broke it. I don't know if you can do anythin' about it now, but try. Don't let this be like that speakin' contest you entered in eighth grade. You didn't win. You wouldn't talk about it and you never tried again.' Della tossed the wet towel in the sink.

'You remember that?' Celeste blew her nose on the napkin Ronnie handed her.

'Of course I remember. You were so grown up that day, up on that stage soundin' so intelligent. I was proud of you.'

'You were?'

'I never told you. I know.' Della looked at Ronnie now. 'And I never told you, either. Your daddy wasn't the only one braggin' about what you were doin'. I was always proud of both of you. I shoulda told you that – I thought you knew.' Della picked up her glass and uneaten sandwich from the table and put them on the counter. 'Call him. Go home. Hidin' down here won't solve nothin' back there. I gotta go to the bathroom.'

The segue was abrupt, direct, welcome, and so like Della. It was the first thing Celeste and Ronnie had heard in hours that actually sounded like the mother they knew.

Having dug her way from beneath the load she had buried herself under years ago, Della left the kitchen feeling years lighter. But Celeste and Ronnie sat, poised on the edge of the excavation, surrounded by all that had been unearthed and afraid that any sudden movement might damage the artifacts that had been discovered or, worse, cause the hole to cave in on itself.

'Wow.' Ronnie fiddled with the abandoned deck of cards.

'Yeah, I know,' Celeste replied, staring off into space.

They stayed that way awhile, looking stunned. Their mother had excused herself from the awkward nakedness of the morning's revelations and left them trying to figure out whether to avert their eyes, cover up, or just let it all hang out.

'Let's go for a walk,' Ronnie said after a while.

'You feel up to it?' With her middle finger Celeste mashed the sandwich crumbs that had fallen on the table and sprinkled them on her plate.

'Today I need it.'

'We can go up and change . . .'

'How many acres we got here? Forty-five? I think this great big nightshirt will do just fine. Already got my sneaks on.' Ronnie wiggled her feet.

Celeste started to object, then laughed and hitched up her blue and white striped pajama bottoms. 'Ready when you are.'

Outside the sun hung directly overhead. Ronnie's steps were slow and deliberate. Celeste fanned her PJ top to create a breeze and shortened her stride to stay by her sister's side.

'I've been itchin' to go to the pond for a week. You haven't been yet, have you?'

Celeste shook her head.

'Not scared, are you?' Ronnie remembered Celeste's hesitation the day they arrived. 'I can hold your hand.'

Celeste swatted at Ronnie. 'I'm ignoring you.' As they marched around the side of the house, her eyes were drawn to the chicken coop. 'Ma went through so much – I mean her mother dying so suddenly – Coming here to live, basically with strangers, even if they were family – And Henry – What he tried to do to her—' She shuddered, then looked at Ronnie. 'How could she keep *that* to herself?'

Ronnie walked on a few yards, looking at the ground in front of her, hands clenched at her sides before she answered. 'She was hurt and ashamed, afraid people would blame her. At least Daddy knew, so she wasn't totally alone – Like I was.'

'Huh?' Celeste couldn't imagine Ronnie meant what she thought she heard.

'It was right after I moved to New York.' Her tongue primed by her mother's candor, Ronnie struggled to give voice to a memory that had lived its whole life as a whisper. 'The photographer who shot that cigarette ad – It was a nightmare.'

Celeste took hold of one of Ronnie's balled-up fists, smoothed it open, and gripped her sweaty hand.

'Those damn billboards were everywhere. And I hated every one of them. But Ma, Daddy, everybody was so proud. Even you were – a little bit. I couldn't screw all that up, so I kept my mouth shut.'

'I am so sorry.' Celeste pulled her closer, slid her arm around Ronnie's waist.

'You didn't know.' Ronnie draped an arm over Celeste's shoulder.

'That's not the point. You should have been able to tell me, but I never gave you a reason to think you should confide in me.' She tilted her head, rested it on Ronnie's shoulder. 'I'm sorry for that too.'

Ronnie squeezed Celeste's shoulder. 'It's okay. We'll make up for it now.'

They continued in silence until they reached the clearing. 'This is it. The pond in Little Pond. Doesn't look like paradise, but I like it here, looking at the water, listening to the birds.' Ronnie took a seat on the hickory stump. 'Doug says we can clear up the crap, maybe have a place for a rowboat or somethin'. That would be kinda hip.' She positioned her oars in the air. 'Row, row, row your boat, gently down the . . .'

'Do you really want to do this? Stay here by yourself?' Celeste stood in a patch of dappled sun at the

436

water's edge. 'You don't have to, you know. We can work something else out.'

'It's what I want. Honest. I'm really gonna find a job and make this fly. At least for now.' Ronnie peeled a strip of bark off the stump. 'And I don't know how long she's gonna stay, but looks like Ma has some unfinished business here too.'

'Mother with some man who's not Daddy is still too weird for me to process right now.' Celeste pulled up a blade of grass and twirled it between her fingers.

'Guess you have homework to do.'

'It's not my biggest assignment, though.' Celeste walked over and sat next to Ronnie. 'What am I gonna do about me and Everett? I don't want to lose him.'

'Humph! I'm probably the last one on the planet you wanna ask for advice.' Ronnie looked Celeste in the eye. 'But just be straight with him and see how it goes. If you want an ear, you know my digits.'

'Thanks.' One fat teardrop fell from Celeste's eye, landed on Ronnie's knee. 'And in case you haven't been too sure lately, I love you.'

'Back atcha, sis.' Ronnie smiled. 'I just wish I had a picture of you out here in your jammies. I bet there are people who'd pay good money for it!'

23

'. . . steps in a new direction.'

Celeste had been in the shower more than half an hour, ever since she forced herself to come in from the pond and get moving. She felt too raw and exposed for her usual steaming water, and now she was having a hard time bringing herself to get out of the soothing, tepid spray. *I can't stay in here forever.* There were new players in her family drama, and the old ones, including herself, had new wrinkles; the heroes were tarnished, the villains not so guilty, and her own lofty place above it all cut down to size.

Reluctantly she turned off the water, stepped onto the bathmat, and snatched her towel from the rack next to the tub. *All of this came out of nowhere. What am I supposed to do now?* Celeste patted dry, trying to figure out her next move. She was used to discounting her mother's advice, but it was time to listen. *Because she's right.*

I love Everett. Always have. Always will. There was nothing Celeste could do to change the past, but seconds of the present were ticking away, and she knew she didn't have any to waste.

Still wrapped in her towel, Celeste grabbed her robe off the hook behind the door, but before she put it on she caught her reflection in the full-length mirror, square in the eyes. *You're all closed up . . . Shut off from yourself even.* Her mother's words came back to her as she pulled off the shower cap and continued the exploration. *What am I hiding?* She let the robe drop to the floor, then abandoned the towel beside it and forced her eyes to drop down and examine her body. She acknowledged the dark rings around her neck that didn't used to be there when she was younger. They reminded her of the rings inside a tree trunk that told its age. For years she'd been covering them with necklaces and high-necked shirts and not admitting how much they bugged her.

Celeste moved on to her breasts, which didn't point front and center anymore without Lycra and underwires. *These definitely don't belong to a young chippy – but they're healthy, and they look pretty good for a chippy in her middle years.* Her belly, stretch marks and all, had a little pooch to it, right below the navel. She turned to the side and considered her butt, which was wider than it used to be but still round and firm. She wasn't young and high and tight all over anymore. *But this is me and I look all right.* Celeste touched her arms, chest, rubbed the flat of her hand against her stomach. Her skin was still soft and smooth. *Why haven't I been able to—?* She shook her head. *If I haven't even seen myself, then I sure haven't seen Everett or Niki either. Not the way they are.* Celeste thought of the 'just so' polish she'd smeared on the people and things in her life of her 'just so' friend Lydia and what a phony she really was. *I've wasted so much time trying to be what I'm not.* She swung open the door and marched down the hall to her room, naked as the day she came into the world.

And without stopping to cover up, she hopped up on her bed, ripped the to-do list off her pad, and tossed it in the wastebasket. She stared at the blank page, searching for a place to begin.

Dear Everett,
   I can only hope you'll read this, because if I were you, I'm not sure I would. I've been stubborn and stupid and just plain wrong . . .

Celeste went on for twelve pages, no holding back. She apologized for being rigid and insensitive, pleaded for the chance to make a change, told Everett how much she admired him, loved him, didn't want to lose him. The words came in a rush, almost faster than she could write them down. And before she could reread, edit, or correct, Celeste jumped into the first thing she pulled from the closet, ran a comb through her hair, and dashed downstairs.

'Hey! Where are you goin'?' Ronnie called from over the upstairs railing.

'To the post office. I'll be right back!'

'I'll ride with . . .' But Celeste was already gone, so Ronnie, who was washed, brushed, and dressed, made her way downstairs, wondering what prompted the postal emergency since there was no hint of it when they came in from the pond.

Ronnie found Della in the kitchen playing solitaire. 'You're mighty dressed up for a kitchen table card game, Queen Bee!' She eyed Della's short-sleeved yellow suit, black scoop-neck shell, and black patent pumps. Ronnie even detected a smidgen of lipstick. 'Oh – that's right. Somebody's got a hot date tonight,' she teased.

'I've got no such thing!' Della snatched up the cards and shuffled again.

'Dinner? A man? No. Not just a man. An old boyfriend. Spells D-A-T-E to me.'

Della rolled her eyes. 'You never did good in spellin'. And before I forget, Doug Pryce called. Said he'd be out this evenin' with papers for y'all to sign.'

'So soon? I'm surprised.'

'Humph! Seems to me that man is either desperate to make this sale or he has an interest in all this that's not just about real estate.'

'If you think that I – that he – That's crazy, Ma.'

'So you're sayin' it only *looks* like somethin' it's not? Now where have I heard that?' Della cocked her head at Ronnie and waited.

'You win, but you look kinda cute for your – appointment.'

'Never mind all that.' Della smirked, and even though she wasn't about to admit it, she was glad to hear she looked nice. She arched the two piles of cards into a bridge and they fell neatly into a single stack.

'Remember how I used to try to do that?'

'And have cards flyin' all over the room?!' Della shuffled the deck again.

'Wanna play rummy?'

'Humph. Haven't played that since – Humph.' Five hundred rummy used to be a game for a snowy Saturday, a rainy summer Tuesday, or to take Ronnie's mind off a scraped knee. Della taught Celeste first, but she didn't have much interest in card games. When Ronnie was old enough to learn, Della thought Celeste might enjoy it more, since three players made the game more interesting, but Celeste still didn't see the point. So it became Ronnie and

441

Della's game. When Della won, Ronnie would complain that she could catch up if they played another hand, then another. After a while, they upped the winning score to a thousand, then two, until it finally became ten thousand rummy. Della was sure there was still the score sheet for an unfinished game, wrapped around a deck of cards in the back of a kitchen drawer at home.

Della looked at the woman across from her and still saw her baby girl. She smiled to herself and dealt two hands, seven cards each.

'What?' Ronnie caught the smile.

'Nothin'.' Della put the remaining stack in the center of the table, turned the top card faceup. 'Nothin' at all. It's your turn, or have you forgotten how to play?'

'I'll keep score.' Ronnie grabbed one of Celeste's notepads, drew a T down the middle of a blank page, and printed 'MA' on the left and 'ME' on the right.

'Your addin' wasn't much better than your spellin'. Hope you've improved with age.'

'I can manage.' Ronnie fanned her cards, arranged them according to suit, then scrutinized her hand.

Della watched her, amused. She used to be able to finish cooking dinner during Ronnie's turns. She would consider all her options and the possible results of every move before she made it. Somewhere along the line, all that deliberation gave way to whim and desperation in the potluck that had become Ronnie's life. *Yes. Maybe this'll be good for her. She can take her time down here. Examine her hand.*

In the middle of their third hand Ronnie laid down three eights, threw away the deuce of hearts. 'As soon as I get some money from selling the land, I'll pay you back for the hospital and all.'

Della retrieved the deuce. 'Don't worry about that right now. I'm thankful I got it to spare.' She laid down the ace and the three to go with it. 'Now don't think I won't take your money, 'cause I sho 'nuff will. But you concentrate on straightenin' yourself out. There's time later.' Della winked. 'You add on my score?'

'What else am I doin' with this pen?' After she reached the new total she looked up. 'Thanks, Ma.' Ronnie winked too. 'I'm a little scared.'

'Anybody with good sense would be.' She patted Ronnie's hand.

Ronnie smiled. 'Are you plannin' to discard any-time soon?'

'Don't rush me!'

It was 647 to 514 in Della's favor when Celeste came into the kitchen. 'Who's winning?' She pulled up a chair and slipped off her shoes.

'Ma. But I'm about to catch up. You went out in that?' Ronnie pointed to Celeste's blouse. 'You're missing a button.'

'I was in a hurry. Had to send a letter overnight mail. Even us mules get the point if you hit us hard enough.' She grinned and gave Della a knowing glance. 'When can you deal me in?'

'You?' Ronnie sputtered.

Celeste crossed her arms and leaned towards Ronnie. 'Afraid I'll kick your butt?'

'Hardly! And to show you what kind of a sister I am, I'll concede to Ma in this first game, so I can get right to whippin' you!' Ronnie gathered the cards, shuffled them badly.

'Humph. If Celeste's gon' play, maybe we should

make it a penny a point. You could get started on a down payment for that car you gon' be needin'!'

'Very funny, Mother.'

They had played three trash-talking hands and were in the middle of the fourth when they heard the knock on the front door.

Della looked at the clock on the stove. 'It's too early to be Lester.'

'Doug's bringing the new contracts,' Ronnie said to Celeste. 'Must be him.'

'Anbody here? Ma? Grandma?' Niki called through the screen.

Celeste dropped her cards and jumped up. 'I asked her, but I didn't say anything because I didn't think she'd come.'

'Somebody must be home. The door's open.'

'This is the country, Brian. People leave their doors open.'

'She brought a man with her? Brave!' Ronnie whispered to Della as Celeste trotted out of the room.

Brian leaned his long, wiry body against the door jamb. 'And when did you get to be an expert on country ways? After you had me carry you across that stream because you were afraid of snakes?' He stood a head taller than Niki.

'I just wanted you to carry me!' Niki tilted her head up to kiss him.

Just as Celeste threw open the screen door. 'I can't believe you came!'

'Ma!' Niki quickly retracted her lips. 'Don't worry, we're not gonna stay, I . . .'

'You just got here! You can't start talking about leaving!' Celeste hugged Niki tight and kissed her on the cheek, leaving Niki puzzled by the joyous

444

reception. 'And you must be Brian.' Celeste took his hand in both of hers. 'Come in! And welcome to Little Pond! Mother! Ronnie!'

'I'm right here.' Della came into the hall and threw her arms open wide when she saw Niki. 'You're not too grown to gimme some sugar, are you?'

'Nope!' Niki folded herself into her grandmother. 'How's Aunt Ronnie? Ma said . . .'

'Aunt Ronnie's doin' fine.' Ronnie joined them. 'What did she tell you? I was on my last legs?'

'No.' Niki laughed, extricated herself from her grandmother, and hugged Ronnie. 'Just that you'd had a pretty rough time, and if I was a good and dutiful niece, I'd stop and see you on the way to Hyde Park.' She saluted. 'Good and dutiful reporting.'

'So are you gon' let your young man just stand there?' Della prompted.

'Oh! Yeah.' She pulled him in the door. 'Everybody, this is Brian Cadieux.'

'Nice to meet you, Brian.' Ronnie stepped forward and offered her hand. 'She did warn you about us?'

'Well, we can't keep standing here in the hall. The living room is right – or maybe it's cooler on the porch?' Della suggested.

'First I have to check out this place!' Niki craned her neck to look into the living room. 'Wow! It really looks like somebody lives here.'

'Seems somebody's going to do just that.' Celeste eyed Ronnie, then followed Niki who was headed for the dining room. 'Are you going to tell her, or shall I?'

'Tell me what?' Niki ran her hand over the maple sideboard, her finger along the embroidered hem of a napkin. 'Nice,' she said, almost to herself.

'I'm sure your version will be much more

445

interesting than mine, so be my guest.' Ronnie bowed slightly and joined the tour.

'You're welcome to join them,' Della said to Brian.

'We've been in the car for hours. I'd really like the bathroom and a glass of water. In that order.'

Della showed him the way and continued to the kitchen where she met up with the chatter and laughter of mother, daughter, and auntie.

'Wow! That's kinda cool!' Niki said when Celeste finished filling her in on Ronnie's decision to stay in Prosper. 'It'll be an adventure! I'm just finding out that I like being able to start new, in a different place. I mean, I loved Atlanta, and after Ithaca it was just what I needed. But I'm ready to move on. I'm looking forward to the next stop!'

'Cooking is a very portable career!' Brian added as he joined them. 'I've lived all over the world since I left New Orleans. And I expect this opportunity to teach at the CIA will open even more doors.' He accepted the glass Della handed him. 'Thanks.' He brushed his locks behind his ears, tilted his head back, and took a long swallow.

'Yep. This is just the next stop. Who knows where we'll go after I finish my training?'

Who knows where we'll *go?* It was a mouthful, but Celeste kept it down. 'I guess change keeps you fresh.' *What did Everett say? You need to shake up your life or the good stuff settles on the bottom.*

'And I've learned goo gobs about people and food from moving around,' Brian added. 'Niki, I've gotta run out to the car. Be right back.' He squeezed her shoulders.

'Not bad, Niki girl. Not bad at all!' Ronnie watched Brian stride down the walk.

Niki grinned. 'I think he's pretty special!'

Celeste watched Niki watch Brian and fought to control a wave of sadness. *Just like I used to think your father was special.*

'Speaking of change – What's up with y'all?' Niki folded her arms across her chest and looked at her family. 'Ronnie's got a buzz cut, Ma's barefoot, and Grandma, I haven't seen you so dressed up since my graduation. Is it something in the water? Should we go buy some bottled?' Niki dropped her voice and did her best horror movie announcer imitation. 'Or will the strange force lurking in the old family manse overtake the unsuspecting newcomers?'

'Not much to tell about my hair. The weave got raggedy. Lucille took it out for me,' Ronnie said.

'Who's Lucille?'

'That's a whole 'nother story. Let's save it for later. When we can really dish!' Ronnie laughed.

'And you, Ma. No slippers? Shoes thrown under the kitchen table. I don't know.'

Celeste sucked her teeth. 'I was just sitting around . . .'

'Since when does that matter?' Niki asked.

Celeste smiled. 'Since now.'

'The real news here is Miss Della!' Ronnie teased. 'Isn't that right, Ma?'

'Hush up that foolishness. Ain't no news. I was plannin' to go out, that's all.'

'With?' Ronnie prompted.

'With an old friend,' Della answered.

'He's not just an old . . .'

'He?!' Niki sputtered. 'You have a date?!'

'I don't have no such thing! Don't get Niki started on this mess too. Besides, now that you're here, I

447

think I'll see if we can do it another time. How long you gon' stay?'

'We're heading out this evening. We can get a couple of hours up the road before we stop. My first class starts in four days. All I really wanted to do was check on Aunt Ronnie and make sure there was no mayhem going on here. You know how the three of you can be!'

'Well, I've told you I'm fine, and as you can see there are no serious wounds,' Ronnie said. 'But why don't you stay the night? Get a fresh start tomorrow? While your grandma is out carousing, maybe we can all go to Pal's. That'll be a hoot! And I'm dying to have something besides sandwiches and broiled chicken. No offense,' she said to Della and Celeste, 'but that stuff's starting to make hospital food a fond memory!'

'Humph!' Della said and went to call Lester.

'What's Pal's?' Niki asked.

'Boy do we have an earful for you,' Ronnie said.

'I don't know if we should put all that on her.' Celeste gathered up the three ghost hands of rummy from the kitchen table.

'Well, wasn't that the point? This is stuff we all need to know, Niki included.' Ronnie settled in the chair and put her hand on her belly. 'Whew! I really needed to do that.'

Della came back from the phone. 'They said he's gone already. I hate for him to drive out here for nothin'.'

'I wouldn't call it nothing! I've seen him lookin' at you, and I think he'll take a look-see if that's all he can get. For now.' Ronnie grinned at her mother.

Della looked as close to a blush as any of them had

448

ever seen. They burst out laughing just as Brian and Lester walked in.

'Did we miss something?' Lester asked.

'No!' The four women shouted all at once.

'Of course, you're Odee's granddaughter!' Lester smiled at Niki. 'Lester Wilson. You remind me of her.' He looked at Della. 'It doesn't even seem that long ago.'

'I do?' Niki, tall and strong, always thought she got that from her father. No one had ever compared her to her grandmother. But she could see that Lester was genuinely taken with the resemblance and realized she liked the comparison, the connection. 'Thanks.'

'You're crazy, Lester. But then you always were.' Della smiled at him. 'Listen, I'm sorry to do this, but could we go to dinner another night? Niki and her friend are leavin' tomorrow and I . . .'

'Not a problem. I'm disappointed, but I understand.'

Brian whispered to Niki, and she nodded. 'What if we cook?' She looked at Ronnie. 'You'll get a meal that's a whole lot better than hospital food.' Then turned to Lester and Della, who stood side by side. 'You two can still have dinner and –' She winked at Lester. '– No one will go home disappointed.'

'And I'll get to ask all the questions I want about that car of yours,' Brian added.

Lester turned to Della. 'As long as I can get a rain check on our date.'

Della smirked and looked beyond Ronnie, who had definitely made note of the *d* word. 'I think that might work out. If you play your cards right.' She turned to Brian. 'But makin' dinner is too much trouble.'

'I know how you feel about a stove, Grandma, but we like to cook!'

'Then it sounds like a plan to me!' Ronnie said.

'There's not much to choose from here.' Celeste opened the refrigerator.

'Celeste, you know you about bought out the store,' Della reminded her.

'Well, you couldn't prove it by the way we've been eatin' around here.' Ronnie laughed.

'I'm sure we'll be okay with whatever we find.' Niki moved her mother aside and rummaged through the shelves.

'You sure you're a chef?' Della looked Brian up and down. 'Friend of mine's had a restaurant more than forty years and he says, "Never trust a skinny cook."'

'Yes, ma'am. Not only do I cook, I love to eat too.'

'Puh-lease! Spare me the "I'm naturally skinny" routine!' Ronnie joked. 'It's too painful.'

'Thank you.' Niki popped up from her exploration of the fridge with a handful of tomatoes and a plastic bag of string beans. 'I run six or seven miles a day and still have to watch what I eat. But this one. Eats seconds and dessert and looks like this.' She patted his flat belly.

Celeste was taken by how radiant Niki looked. *She's really happy.* 'Nik? Could I talk to you? Alone?'

Niki looked up warily. 'Uh – sure.'

'It'll only take a minute.' Celeste walked out the back door.

'Fine.' Niki braced herself for whatever tidal wave of complaints her mother had built up. 'Here. See what else you can scare up.' Niki handed Brian the vegetables and followed her mother out the door and down the steps.

Celeste hadn't gone far down the path that led to the woods. She heard Niki, stopped, and waited for her to catch up. When Niki was at her side, Celeste took her hand, and they walked down the path Ronnie had shown her. Down by the pond. She perched on the edge of the hickory stump and patted it for Niki to take a seat too.

'As you have probably gathered, this trip has turned out to be quite different from what I expected. And today I can say I'm glad. If you'd asked me yesterday or the day before, I'm not sure my answer would have been the same.' Celeste stopped and took a good look at Niki. 'What I'm trying to say is I'm sorry. I've been wrong about so many things, but one of the worst has been that I was wrong about you – thinking I knew what you should be doing with your life. I'm your mother, and sometimes I still think of you as my little girl. It's hard for me to accept you're a grown woman and that you have the right to make your own choices, good ones and bad ones, and I have to respect them. I don't have to agree with you or even be consulted.' She smiled. 'Unless *you* want to, of course.' Celeste laughed, wrapped an arm around Niki's shoulder. 'You're bright, Nicole. And kind and beautiful and responsible. Everything a mother could want for her child. Any woman would be proud to have you as her daughter – and I'm no exception.' Now she cradled Niki's face. 'I love you. I want you to be happy.'

Niki was all prepared to do battle again, so she was caught off guard. 'Ma – I mean Mother – I don't know what . . .'

'Shh.' Celeste held her index finger up to her lips. 'Ma is fine. And you don't have to say anything. This was my little speech, and you were my intended

451

audience. All you have to do is go on being who you are, doing what you've been doing.' Celeste saw the tears pooling in Niki's eyes. 'This isn't about tears. This is about laughing at what an idiot I've been. Come on. Let's go back before they send a search party!' She got up and tugged Niki in the direction of the house. 'There's so much more I want to tell you. Things I just found out myself, but now isn't the time. After you get settled maybe we'll do a girls' weekend in the city and I'll fill you in.' Niki fell in step beside her mother. 'And I like Brian, at least from what I've seen. I don't know him, mind you, but I can tell he really cares about you. You two remind me of your father and me – a long time ago – I've written him – said some of the things I just said to you and then some more. He's due back from Portugal today. My letter should arrive tomorrow. I'll go home and face the music, whatever it is, the day after that. I may be too late, but I want you to know I'm going to try. We're a family. I really want it to stay that way.'

'Me too, Ma.' Niki's voice cracked unexpectedly, so she cleared her throat in a feeble attempt to mask the emotion trapped there. Then, almost as an after-thought, she quickly pecked her mother on the cheek and pulled open the kitchen door.

While Niki and Brian worked their magic with the loot from their refrigerator raid, Ronnie took a much-needed nap, and out on the porch Della and Lester talked and laughed about whatever subject blew their way. Lester did his best smooth talking, trying to convince Della that Ronnie could probably use help a little while longer and maybe Della shouldn't plan on going back yet. She pooh-poohed him, but she'd already decided on staying a few weeks more to see after Ronnie. And to get reacquainted with old friends like Lucille and Hambone – and Lester.

Celeste decided this was the perfect occasion to christen the dining room. She hummed and smiled to herself as she set the table with the china from the breakfront and folded each napkin into a perfect triangle, not because it was proper, but purely because right now she was happy and she wanted to celebrate with her family. She didn't try, even once, to supervise the cooking. It was actually a relief not to have to play overseer. She felt it as clearly as Ronnie had felt her lungs fill with air she could breathe when the smoke machine she'd been running overtime finally self-destructed, as distinctly as Della had felt the dead weight of her secrets lifted from her soul. Celeste knew she still had a long way to go, but like her mother and her sister, she'd taken enough steps in a new direction to believe she was on the right path.

When the savory smells emanating from the kitchen made it obvious there was a feast simmering, Della called Hambone and Lucille, who said they'd make it for dessert.

'If I had known there was a party going on, I'd have come another time,' Doug said when he arrived and saw all the activity. Celeste had just finished with the table and offered to set another place, but he begged off until Ronnie came down. She got herself together in a hurry when she heard his voice and jokingly threatened not to sign the contracts if he didn't stay for dinner. Doug laughed and quickly gave up trying to make an exit.

'After all the trouble we've been, it's the least we can do!' Ronnie was glad to see him, and she really wanted a chance to talk to him when there was no crisis and she wasn't performing, just being herself.

The meal started with a salmon mousse that they all thought was out of this world. Then came a huge salad with freshly made croutons, and the tomatoes, onions, garlic, and Celeste's leftover wine became a sauce for the sautéed chicken Niki and Brian served over linguine Celeste had picked up by mistake, thinking it was a box of spaghetti.

'It's hard to believe this came from the same groceries we been eatin' all along!' Della announced. And just as amazing, they got through an entire family meal without a cross word from anyone. She wasn't sure that had happened in the history of the Frazier family, but it felt good. *I could get used to this.*

'Nothin' beats a little know-how,' Lester said as he pushed back from the table. 'Especially in the kitchen.'

'You haven't eaten Della's cooking, have you?' Ronnie teased, then turned to Brian. 'Are there any more at home like you? A brother, maybe?'

'He didn't do it by himself!' Niki elbowed Brian.

Brian put his arm around Niki's shoulders. 'Sorry, no brothers. I do have two sisters!'

'Thanks anyway! The one I have is more than enough,' Ronnie cracked. She wasn't fooling herself. She didn't expect they would ever become a warm, fuzzy, huggy, kissy kind of family, but the gap had narrowed considerably.

Just as the last forkful was eaten and they all swore they were about to burst, Lucille and Hambone arrived with a huge peach cobbler.

'It's my specialty,' Hambone said as he put it down on the table.

Lucille took a seat next to Della. 'Everythin' is your specialty, let you tell it.'

After dessert, coffee, and conversation, Niki and Brian started gathering the dishes.

'Cooks don't do KP!' Lester said. 'Your grandmother and I will take care of cleanup. You-all officially have the rest of the night off. You've earned it.'

'I'll help you,' Celeste chimed in, but Ronnie kicked her under the table before Celeste could get up.

'Go enjoy your daughter's company. We can handle it, can't we, Odee?' Lester took the plates from Niki.

'I expect we'll do just fine,' Della replied and reached for the empty pasta platter.

It was Lucille's turn to nudge Della under the table.

'I don't think I'm gonna be much company, Ma. I'm beat and we need to get on the road early.' Niki plopped back down.

'Why don't you take the bedroom upstairs that nobody's using? Brian can sleep down here in the study,' Celeste suggested.

'Are they plannin' on separate rooms when they get where they're goin'?' Della stood up, hands on her hips and waited, but no one ventured an answer. 'Just what I thought.' She picked up her stack of dishes. 'Then why don't they just go on upstairs and go to bed?'

'Mother!' Celeste looked at Ronnie, who shrugged.

'Listen.' Della grabbed two glasses with her empty hand. 'Haven't we all had enough pretendin'? I know I have. That's how we got in this mess in the first

455

place.' She headed to the kitchen but stopped in the doorway. 'Sleep tight. Both of you.'

'Thanks, Grandma.' Niki smiled and hugged Della, whose hands were too full to hug Niki back.

'It's about time for me to get going. I've got a long one tomorrow.' Doug got up.

'I'll walk you out.' Ronnie couldn't keep a straight face, and Doug's departure was a great cue for an escape.

'I can't believe my mother said that,' Ronnie announced to Doug when they got outside.

Doug chuckled. 'My theory is this "understanding" thing skips a generation. My mother was a one-woman hit squad with me, but she's Granny Sweetness with my kids. I kinda like it, though. Helps make 'em closer.'

'Hmmm, the Pryce theory of family relations. You got any other theories in your pocket?' Ronnie brushed against his arm and felt the jitters all of a sudden, as she finally let it sink in that she'd like to get to know this man as more than her broker.

'Nothing but these babies.' He patted the contracts in the jacket pocket of his khaki suit. 'I don't see any reason why we can't close pretty soon.'

'Sounds good to me.' Ronnie clasped her hands behind her back, searching for something to say, but her tongue was tied. 'Nice night. It's good the nights are cool. Good for sleeping.' *Is that the best I can do?*

'Yep. I'd say so.' He smoothed his mustache with his fingertips. 'Hey look, I enjoyed the company. I'll ah – give a call.'

'Bet.' Ronnie watched him start down the steps, not wanting him to go yet.

Three steps down the path he turned around.

'Ronnie – I've got a proposition for you that has nothing to do with property.'

'Yeah?' She leaned against the porch rail.

'Since I'm not on the meter right now – And you'll let me know if I'm outta line—'

'Yeah?'

'How 'bout I take you out next week. Show you 'round since you're planning to stay.

A big grin came over Ronnie's face. 'How 'bout let's go fishin'?' *Did I just say that?* 'I could try out that pole you gave me.' Her smile felt lopsided, a little goofy, like she hadn't flirted with a man in a hundred years. *Maybe I haven't meant it in a while.*

'Well – uh—'

'My father would say, "Don't dig it here!" ' Ronnie laughed. 'The well, I mean.'

'That's almost as bad as my real estate jokes.' He cocked his foot up on the bottom step, his eyes shining a warm smile. 'But it would be my pleasure. One morning next week.'

'I figure I should start learning the local customs if I'm gonna become a Prosperite. Prosperian? Prosperer?!' Ronnie laughed. 'I've got a lot to learn.'

'I bet you're a quick study.' Doug swatted at a moth flying around him. 'But we gotta start early. Are you a morning person?' he asked.

'Crack a dawn these days.'

'Great! I'll call you.' Doug smiled at her. 'From my home phone.' He headed toward his car, then turned to look at her. 'And whether we catch anything or not, I'm a pretty good cook.'

Ronnie smiled back and waved. *I guess I'm goin' fishin'.* She watched until his taillights disappeared.

The next morning Celeste got up at first light to see

Niki and Brian off. At the car she threw her arms around Brian. 'Take care of her.'

'You know it,' he replied and loaded their bags into the trunk.

Celeste wasn't sure what to say to Niki, but her daughter cut through the words and swooped in for a hug. 'Love you, Ma.'

Celeste barely got out, 'Me too,' then hustled them on their way.

She put on a pot of coffee, carried a cup upstairs, and sipped while she started to gather her things to go home tomorrow and worried what Everett would do after he read his letter. When she heard signs of life from her mother's room, she went down the hall.

Della sat at the foot of her bed, still waking up. 'Niki and Brian get off okay?'

'Uh-huh.' Celeste sat down next to her.

'Humph. They look right cute together.' Della smiled to herself then looked over at Celeste's long face. 'Ain't no point in my tellin' you not to worry, Mother. You're gon' do it anyhow, but I think Niki will do just fine – with Brian or with whichever somebody she chooses. I think the girl's got more sense than any of us.'

'Y'all didn't start the party without me, did you?' Ronnie came in and took her place in the bedside lineup. 'Who's this?' She picked up the brown-skinned rag doll with the black woolly hair that lay near Della's pillow. 'I didn't see her when I cleaned up this room.' She laid the doll across her lap.

'That's Susie. She's the very first doll my mama gave me.' Della smoothed the doll's lacy white dress.

'You mean Miz Ethiopia?' Celeste asked.

458

'No. No. My mama – Her name was Annie.' Della looked at Celeste. 'And the older you get, the more you favor her.'

'I do?' Celeste never thought she looked like any-body in her family, so this was a surprise.

'Do you have any pictures?' Ronnie asked.

'Not a one. Only what I remember – I sure do miss her.'

It was the first time Celeste or Ronnie had heard Della talk about her mother.

'Anyhow, let me get this old body cranked up before I want to get back in the bed.' Della stood up.

'Mom, I called the airline yesterday. I'm going home tomorrow.'

Celeste hadn't called her Mom since she got too grown to be that familiar. 'Well – that's good.' Della nodded her head, propped her hand on the doorknob. *I guess there's one more thing we got left to do.* 'Then there's someplace we need to go today,' she said.

Della hurried them through breakfast, showers, and dressing without telling them the destination. They were in the car, ready to pull off, when Celeste heard the phone ring. She yanked off her seat belt and raced inside like her life depended on it, leaving Della and Ronnie scratching their heads.

A few minutes later Celeste returned. She'd obvi-ously been crying, but she smiled wide when she slid behind the driver's seat. 'That was Everett. He's picking me up at the airport.' Celeste cleared her throat, grabbed the wheel with both hands. 'So? Where I am heading?'

'Go left on Albermarle.' Della folded her hands in her lap and looked straight ahead. She took a deep breath before she spoke again. 'It wouldn't be right if y'all didn't see Cadysville, where I was born – Visit my mama's grave.'

'Ma?' Ronnie was hesitant. 'When's the last time you went there?'

'Come Christmastime it'll be fifty-one years.'

'Do you still remember the way?' Celeste asked as they passed Pal's on their way through Prosper.

'It's all comin' back to me.' Della leaned forward in the backseat, a hand resting on each daughter's shoulder and gazed through the windshield.

They didn't go far before they saw the bright green sign. 'Cadysville 102 miles,' Ronnie read aloud.

Della relaxed back into her seat. 'Humph. It always seemed further away than that.'

THE END

Authors' Note to the Readers

Dear Reader,

When we were tossing ideas around for this book, we weren't sure what road we were taking, or where it would end up. It's tempting to walk a familiar path – it's safe, and you know where it goes. But we wanted more of an adventure, so after several months of discussion we decided to take off in a different direction.

Some journeys, like the one we took you on in *Tryin' to Sleep in the Bed You Made*, span decades. With *Far from the Tree* we were looking for one of those unexpected trips that turns your life upside down in an instant and barely leaves you time to pack. And whatever the circumstances that caused you to leave so suddenly – hopefully you return home with a new experience, a new friend, a new vision, a new you.

As we talked, we kept coming back to the strained relationship between Patricia Reid and her mother, Verna, two of the characters we wrote about in *Tryin'*. Despite the years of hurt and misunderstanding between them, most folks who wrote us wanted them to work it out.

Mothers and daughters – is there a more basic,

and more complicated relationship on the planet? Especially once everybody is grown. The idea of venturing into this territory was both scary and exciting.

So, through Della, Celeste, Ronnie, and Niki, we decided to explore what would happen if mothers and daughters were forced to rediscover one another outside of their accustomed roles. What's it like for the daughters to realize that before she was your mother, she was a woman, just like you? How do the mothers feel when they finally recognize the women their daughters have become? So often we forget that we walk on common ground.

And the truth is that whether we like it or not, whether it skips a generation or even two, none of us ever truly falls *Far from the Tree*.

We welcome hearing from you, so if you'd like to let us know how you feel about *Tree*, please drop us a line or an e-mail, or visit our new Web site. We have to say that we were blown away by your response to *Tryin'*. We had no idea whether we'd hear from a soul, but now, more than 15,000 letters later, we're still amazed and honored by the time so many folks took to write us back. You shared not only your reactions to the book, but you told us how *Tryin'* related to your own personal experiences, some of them funny, some difficult and painful. And we were particularly happy to hear that so many people read the book and were moved to try to mend friendships that had unraveled, to reach out to find friends who have slipped out of touch, or to make the time to tell a friend how much they really mean.

Although it may have taken us a while, we tried to

answer every letter we received. If somehow we neglected to respond to you, please accept our apologies and know that we'll try to do better this time!

Don't let the good stuff settle on the bottom,

Virginia DeBerry   Donna Grant

DeBerry Grant
P.O. Box 5224
Kendall Park, NJ 08824
E-mail: *Farfromthetree@aol.com*
Web site: *www.deberryandgrant.com*